PENGUIN (Ŏ) CLASSICS

SHIVA PURANA: VOLUME 1

Bibek Debroy is a renowned economist, scholar and translator. He has worked in universities, research institutes, the industry and for the government. He has widely published books, papers and articles on economics. As a translator, he is best known for his magnificent rendition of the Mahabharata in ten volumes, the three-volume translation of the Valmiki Ramayana, the *Harivamsha*, *Bhagavata Purana*, *Markandeya Purana*, *Brahma Purana* and additionally *Vishnu Purana*, published to wide acclaim by Penguin Classics. He is also the author of *Sarama and Her Children*, which splices his interest in Hinduism with his love for dogs.

PRAISE FOR THE *BHAGAVATA PURANA*

'An exhaustive but accessible translation of a crucial mythological text'—*Indian Express*

'The beauty of recounting these stories lies in the manner in which the cosmic significance and the temporal implications are intermingled. Debroy's easy translation makes that experience even more sublime' —*Business Standard*

'The Puranas are 18 volumes with more than four lakh *shloka*s, and all in Sanskrit—the language of our ancestors and the sages, which only a few can speak and read today and only a handful have the mastery to translate. Bibek Debroy is one such master translator, who wears the twin title of economist and Sanskrit scholar, doing equal justice to both'—*Outlook*

PRAISE FOR THE *MARKANDEYA PURANA*

'[The] *Markandeya Purana* is a marvelous amalgam of mythology and metaphysics that unfolds a series of conversations in which sage Markandeya is asked to answer some deeper questions raised by the events in the Mahabharata'—*Indian Express*

'Bibek Debroy's translation of the *Markandeya Purana* presents the English reader with an opportunity to read the unabridged version in English. As he writes in the Introduction, "*But all said and done, there is no substitute to reading these texts in the original Sanskrit.*" If you cannot read the original in Sanskrit, this is perhaps the next best thing'—Abhinav Agarwal

PRAISE FOR THE *VISHNU PURANA*

'Bibek Debroy's unabridged translation brings his trademark felicity of prose. Copious footnotes, numbering over a thousand, and a scrupulous attention to keeping this a translation and not an interpretation make this a much-needed and valuable text'—Firstpost

'Like the others, this Purana captures ancient and medieval stories and concepts of Hinduism in a range and complexity that no other Sanskrit texts offer . . . The *Vishnu Purana* ends on a sombre note, but not without offering the hope that those who chant Vishnu's name can still reclaim dharma'—*Business Standard*

'Immense credit to the translator for keeping the flow as light and engaging as the original may allow and for capturing and conveying intact the soul of the *Vishnu Purana* . . . In essence, this text functions as a concise encyclopaedia of perhaps the most evolved research and thought of the time and a 360-degree portrayal of Lord Vishnu in myriad forms aggregated from various oral or lost sources and tales . . . A treasure trove; a slow-paced perusal of the text is an eye-opener, an education in itself'—*New Indian Express*

PRAISE FOR THE *BRAHMA PURANA*

'In two volumes and over 1,000 pages, Mr Debroy's translation of what is called the *Adi Purana* (or the original Purana) brings alive the many myths and legends surrounding Hindu gods, traditions, customs and ways of living'—*Business Standard*

SHIVA PURANA

Volume 1

Translated by

BIBEK DEBROY

PENGUIN BOOKS

An imprint of Penguin Random House

PENGUIN BOOKS

USA | Canada | UK | Ireland | Australia
New Zealand | India | South Africa | China

Penguin Books is part of the Penguin Random House group of companies
whose addresses can be found at global.penguinrandomhouse.com

Published by Penguin Random House India Pvt. Ltd
4th Floor, Capital Tower 1, MG Road,
Gurugram 122 002, Haryana, India

First published in Penguin Books by Penguin Random House India 2023

Translation copyright © Bibek Debroy 2023

All rights reserved

10 9 8 7 6 5 4 3 2 1

The views and opinions expressed in this book are the author's own and the
facts are as reported by him which have been verified to the extent possible,
and the publishers are not in any way liable for the same.

ISBN 9780143459699

Typeset in Sabon by Manipal Technologies Limited, Manipal

www.penguinbooksindia.com

For Sadguru, Jaggi Vasudev

Contents

Introduction

The word 'Purana' means old, ancient. The Puranas are old texts, usually referred to in conjunction with Itihasa (the Ramayana and the Mahabharata).[1] Whether Itihasa originally meant only the Mahabharata, with the Ramayana being added to that expression later, is a proposition on which there has been some discussion. But that's not relevant for our purposes. In the Chandogya Upanishad, there is an instance of the sage Narada approaching the sage Sanatkumara for instruction. Asked about what he already knows, Narada says he knows Itihasa and Purana, the Fifth Veda.[2] In other words, Itihasa-Purana possessed an elevated status. This by no means implies that the word 'Purana', as used in these two Upanishads and other texts too, is to be understood in the sense of the word being applied to a set of texts known as the Puranas today. The Valmiki Ramayana is believed to have been composed by Valmiki and the Mahabharata by Krishna Dvaipayana Vedavyasa. After composing the Mahabharata, Krishna Dvaipayana Vedavyasa is believed to have composed the Puranas. The use of the word 'composed' immediately indicates that Itihasa-Purana are *smriti* texts, with a human origin. They are not *shruti* texts,

---

[1] For example, *shloka*s 2.4.10, 4.1.2 and 4.5.11 of the Brihadaranyaka Upanishad use the two expressions together.
[2] Chandogya Upanishad, 7.1.2.

ix

which have a divine origin. Composition does not mean these texts were rendered into writing. Instead, there was a process of oral transmission, with inevitable noise in the transmission and distribution process. Writing came much later.

Pargiter's book on the Puranas is still one of the best introductions to this corpus.[3] To explain the composition and transmission process, one can do no better than to quote him.

> The Vayu and Padma Puranas tell us how ancient genealogies, tales and ballads were preserved, namely, by the *sutas*,[4] and they describe the *suta*'s duty . . . The Vayu, Brahmanda and Visnu give an account, how the original Purana came into existence . . . Those three Puranas say—Krsna Dvaipayana divided the single Veda into four and arranged them, and so was called Vyasa. He entrusted them to his four disciples, one to each, namely Paila, Vaisampayana, Jaimini and Sumantu. Then with tales, anecdotes, songs and lore that had come down from the ages he compiled a Purana, and taught it and the Itihasa to his fifth disciple, the *suta* Romaharsana or Lomaharsana . . . After that he composed the Mahabharata. The epic itself implies that the Purana preceded it . . . As explained above, the *suta*s had from remote times preserved the genealogies of gods, rishis and kings, and traditions and ballads about celebrated men, that is, exactly the material— tales, songs and ancient lore—out of which the Purana was constructed. Whether or not Vyasa composed the original Purana or superintended its compilation, is immaterial for the present purpose . . . After the original Purana was composed, by Vyasa as is said, his disciple Romaharsana taught it to his son Ugrasravas, and Ugrasravas the sauti

---

[3] F.E. Pargiter, *Ancient Indian Historical Tradition*, Oxford University Press, London, 1922.

[4] *Suta*s were bards, minstrels and raconteurs.

appears as the reciter in some of the present Puranas; and the *sutas* still retained the right to recite it for their livelihood. But, as stated above, Romaharsana taught it to his six disciples, at least five of whom were brahmans. It thus passed into the hands of brahmans, and their appropriation and development of it increased in the course of time, as the Purana grew into many Puranas, as Sanskrit learning became peculiarly the province of the brahmans, and as new and frankly sectarian Puranas were composed.

Pargiter cited reasons for his belief that the Mahabharata was composed after the original Purana, though that runs contrary to the popular perception about the Mahabharata having been composed before the Puranas. That popular and linear perception is too simplistic, since texts evolved in parallel, not necessarily sequentially.

In popular perception, Krishna Dvaipayana Vedavyasa composed the Mahabharata. He then composed the Puranas. Alternatively, he composed an original core Purana text, which has been lost, and others embellished it through additions. The adjective 'Purana', meaning old account or old text, became a proper noun, signifying a specific text. To be classified as a Purana, a Purana has to possess five attributes—*pancha lakshmana*. That is, five topics must be discussed—*sarga, pratisarga, vamsha, manvantara* and *vamshanucharita*. The clearest statement of this is in the Matsya Purana. Unlike the Ramayana and the Mahabharata, there is no Critical Edition of the Puranas.[5] Therefore, citing chapter and verse from a Purana text is somewhat more difficult, since verse, if not chapter, may

---

[5] The Critical Edition of the Valmiki Ramayana was brought out by the Baroda Oriental Institute, now part of the Maharaja Sayajirao University of Baroda. The Critical Edition of the Mahabharata was brought out by the Bhandarkar Oriental Research Institute, Pune.

vary from text to text. With that caveat, the relevant *shloka* (verse) should be in the 53rd chapter of the Matysa Purana. *Sarga* means the original or primary creation. The converse of *sarga* is universal destruction and dissolution, or *pralaya*. That period of *sarga* lasts for one of Brahma's days, known as *kalpa*. When Brahma sleeps, during his night, there is universal destruction.

In measuring time, there is the notion of a *yuga* (era) and there are four *yugas*—*satya yuga* (also known as *krita yuga*), *treta yuga*, *dvapara yuga* and *kali yuga*. *Satya yuga* lasts for 4,000 years, *treta yuga* for 3,000 years, *dvapara yuga* for 2,000 years and *kali yuga* for 1,000 years. However, these are not human years. The gods have a different timescale and these are the years of the gods. As one progressively moves from *satya yuga* to *kali yuga*, virtue (*dharma*) declines. But at the end of *kali yuga*, the cycle begins afresh, with *satya yuga*. An entire cycle, from *satya yuga* to *kali yuga*, is known as a *mahayuga* (great era). However, a *mahayuga* is not just 10,000 years. There is a further complication. At the beginning and the end of every *yuga*, there are some additional years. These additional years are 400 for *satya yuga*, 300 for *treta yuga*, 200 for *dvapara yuga* and 100 for *kali yuga*. A *mahayuga* thus has 12,000 years, adding years both at the beginning and at the end. 1,000 *mahayuga*s make up one *kalpa* (eon), a single day for Brahma. A *kalpa* is also divided into fourteen *manvantara*s, a *manvantara* being a period during which a Manu presides and rules over creation. Therefore, there are 71.4 *mahayuga*s in a *manvantara*. Our present *kalpa* is known as the Shveta Varaha *kalpa*. Within that, six Manus have come and gone. Their names are (1) Svayambhuva Manu, (2) Svarochisha Manu, (3) Uttama Manu, (4) Tapasa Manu, (5) Raivata Manu and (6) Chakshusha Manu. The present Manu is known as Vaivasvata Manu. Vivasvat, also written as Vivasvan, is the name of Surya, the Sun God. Vaivasvata

Manu has that name because he is Surya's son. Not only do Manus change from one *manvantara* to another. So do the gods, the ruler of the gods and the seven great sages, known as the *saptarshi*s (seven *rishi*s). Indra is a title of the ruler of the gods. It is not a proper name. The present Indra is Purandara. However, in a different *manvantara*, someone else will hold the title. In the present seventh *manvantara*, known as Vaivasvata *manvantara*, there will also be 71.4 *mahayuga*s. We are in the 28th of these. Since a different Vedavyasa performs that task of classifying and collating the Vedas in every *mahayuga*, Krishna Dvaipayana Vedavyasa is the 28th in that series. Just so that it is clear, Vedavyasa isn't a proper name. It is a title conferred on someone who collates and classifies the Vedas. There have been twenty-seven who have held the title of Vedavyasa before him and he is the 28th. His proper name is Krishna Dvaipayana, Krishna because he was dark and Dvaipayana because he was born on an island (*dvipa*). This gives us an idea of what the topic of *manvantara* is about. This still leaves *pratisarga*, *vamsha* and *vamshanucharita*. The two famous dynasties/lineages were the solar dynasty (*surya vamsha*) and lunar dynasty (*chandra vamsha*) and all the famous kings belonged to one or other of these two dynasties. *Vamshanucharita* is about these lineages and the conduct of these kings. There were the gods and sages (*rishi*s) too, not always born through a process of physical procreation. Their lineages are described under the heading of *vamsha*. Finally, within that cycle of primary creation and destruction, there are smaller and secondary cycles of creation and destruction. That's the domain of *pratisarga*. In greater or lesser degree, all the Puranas cover these five topics, some more than the others. The Purana which strictly adheres to this five-topic classification is the Vishnu Purana.

There are Puranas and Puranas. Some are known as Sthala Puranas, describing the greatness and sanctity of a specific

geographical place. Some are known as Upa-Puranas, minor
Puranas. The listing of Upa-Puranas has regional variations
and there is no country-wide consensus about the list of Upa-
Puranas, though it is often accepted that there are eighteen.
The Puranas we have in mind are known as Maha-Puranas,
major Puranas. Henceforth, when we use the word Puranas,
we mean Maha-Puranas. There is consensus that there are
eighteen Maha-Puranas, though it is not obvious that this
number of eighteen existed right from the beginning. The
names are mentioned in several of these texts, including a
shloka that follows the *shloka* cited from the Matsya Purana.
Thus, the eighteen Puranas are (1) Agni (15,400); (2) Bhagavata
(18,000); (3) Brahma (10,000); (4) Brahmanda (12,000);
(5) Brahmavaivarta (18,000); (6) Garuda (19,000); (7) Kurma
(17,000); (8) Linga (11,000); (9) Markandeya (9,000);
(10) Matsya (14,000); (11) Narada (25,000); (12) Padma
(55,000); (13) Shiva (24,000); (14) Skanda (81,100); (15)
Vamana (10,000); (16) Varaha (24,000); (17) Vayu (24,000)
and (18) Vishnu (23,000).

A few additional points about this list. First, the
Harivamsha is sometimes loosely described as a Purana, but
strictly speaking, it is not a Purana. It is more like an addendum
to the Mahabharata. Second, Bhavishya (14,500) is sometimes
mentioned, with Vayu excised from the list. However, the Vayu
Purana exhibits many more Purana characteristics than the
Bhavishya Purana. There are references to a Bhavishyat Purana
that existed, but that may not necessarily be the Bhavishya
Purana as we know it today. That's true of some other Puranas
too. Texts have been completely restructured hundreds of years
later. Third, it is not just a question of Bhavishya Purana and
Vayu Purana. In the lists given in some Puranas, Vayu is part of
the 18, but Agni is knocked out. In some others, Narasimha and
Vayu are included, but Brahmanda and Garuda are knocked
out. Fourth, when a list is given, the order also indicates some

notion of priority or importance. Since that varies from text to text, our listing is simply alphabetical, according to the English alphabet. Fifth, when one uses the term Bhagavata, does one mean Bhagavata Purana or Devi Bhagavata Purana? The numbers within brackets indicate the number of *shloka*s each of these Puranas has or is believed to have. The range is from 9,000 in Markandeya to a mammoth 81,100 in Skanda. The aggregate is a colossal 409,500 *shloka*s. To convey a rough idea of the orders of magnitude, the Mahabharata has, or is believed to have, 100,000 *shloka*s. It's a bit difficult to convert a *shloka* into word counts in English, especially because Sanskrit words have a slightly different structure. However, as a very crude approximation, one *shloka* is roughly twenty words. Thus, 100,000 *shloka*s become 2 million words and 400,000 *shloka*s, four times the size of the Mahabharata, amounts to 8 million words. There is a reason for using the expression 'is believed to have', as opposed to 'has'. Rendering into writing is of later vintage, the initial process was one of oral transmission. In the process, many texts have been lost, or are retained in imperfect condition. This is true of texts in general and is also specifically true of Itihasa and Puranas. The Critical Edition of the Mahabharata, mentioned earlier, no longer possesses 100,000 *shloka*s. Including the *Harivamsha*, there are around 80,000 *shloka*s. The Critical Edition of the Mahabharata has, of course, deliberately excised some *shloka*s. For the Puranas, there is no counterpart of Critical Editions. However, whichever edition of the Puranas one chooses, the number of *shloka*s in that specific Purana will generally be fewer than the numbers mentioned here earlier. Either those many *shloka*s did not originally exist, or they have been lost. This is the right place to mention that a reading of the Puranas assumes a basic degree of familiarity with the Valmiki Ramayana and the Mahabharata, more the latter than the former. Without that familiarity, one will often fail to appreciate the context completely. More than passing familiarity with the Bhagavat Gita, strictly speaking a part of the Mahabharata, helps.[6]

Other than the five attributes, the Puranas have a considerable amount of information on geography and even geological changes (changes in courses of river) and astronomy. Therefore, those five attributes shouldn't suggest the Puranas have nothing more. They do, and they have, therefore, been described as encyclopedias. Bharatavarsha is vast and heterogeneous and each Purana may very well have originated in one particular part of the country. Accordingly, within that broad compass of an overall geographical description, the extent of geographical information varies from Purana to Purana. Some are more familiar with one part of the country than with another. Though not explicitly mentioned in the five attributes, the Puranas are also about pursuing *dharma, artha, kama* and *moksha,* the four objectives of human existence, and about the four *varna*s and the four *ashrama*s. The general understanding and practice of *dharma* is based much more on the Puranas than on the *Veda*s. Culture, notions of law, rituals, architecture and iconography are based on the Puranas. There is beautiful poetry too.

Perhaps one should mention that there are two ways these 18 Puranas are classified. The trinity has Brahma as the creator, Vishnu as the preserver and Shiva as the destroyer. Therefore, Puranas where creation themes feature prominently are identified with Brahma (Brahma, Brahmanda, Brahmavaivarta, Markandeya). Puranas where Vishnu features prominently are

---

[6] The Bhagavat Gita translation was published in 2006 and reprinted in 2019, the translation of the Critical Edition of the Mahabharata in 10 volumes between 2010 and 2014 (with a box set in 2015) and the translation of the Critical Edition of the Valmiki Ramayana in 2017. The translations are by Bibek Debroy, and in each case, the publisher is Penguin.

identified as Vaishnava Puranas (Bhagavata, Garuda, Kurma, Matysa, Narada, Padma, Vamana, Varaha, Vishnu). Puranas where Shiva features prominently are identified as Shaiva Puranas (Agni, Linga, Shiva, Skanda, Vayu). While there is a grain of truth in this, Brahma, Vishnu and Shiva are all important and all three feature in every Purana. Therefore, beyond the relative superiority of Vishnu vis-à-vis Shiva, the taxonomy probably doesn't serve much purpose. The second classification is even more tenuous and is based on the three *gunas* of *sattva* (purity), *rajas* (passion) and *tamas* (ignorance). For example, the Uttara Khanda of the Padma Purana has a few *shlokas* along these lines, recited by Shiva to Parvati. With a caveat similar to the one mentioned earlier, this should be in the 236th chapter of Uttara Khanda. According to this, the Puranas characterized by *sattva* are Bhagavata, Garuda, Narada, Padma, Varaha and Vishnu. Those characterized by *rajas* are Bhavishya, Brahma, Brahmanda, Brahmavaivarta, Markandeya and Vamana. Those characterized by *tamas* are Agni, Kurma, Linga, Matysa, Skanda and Shiva.

Within a specific Purana text, there are earlier sections, as well as later ones. That makes it difficult to date a Purana, except as a range. Across Purana texts, there are older Puranas, as well as later ones. Extremely speculatively, the dating will be something like the following. (1) Agni (800–1100 CE); (2) Bhagavata (500–1000 CE); (3) Brahma (700–1500 CE); (4) Brahmanda (400–600 CE); (5) Brahmavaivarta (700–1500 CE); (6) Garuda (800–1100 CE); (7) Kurma (600–900 CE); (8) Linga (500–1000 CE); (9) Markandeya (250–700 CE); (10) Matsya (200–500 CE); (11) Narada (900–1600 CE); (12) Padma (400–1600 CE); (13) Shiva (1000–1400 CE); (14) Skanda (600–1200 CE); (15) Vamana (450–900 CE); (16) Varaha (1000–1200 CE); (17) Vayu (350–550 CE); (18) Vishnu (300 CE–450 CE) and (19) Bhavishya (500–1900 CE). Reiterating once again that there is no great precision in these ranges, by this reckoning, the

Vishnu Purana is the oldest and some parts of the Bhavishya Purana are as recent as the 19th century.

As mentioned earlier, there is no Critical Edition for the Puranas. Therefore, one has to choose a Sanskrit text one is going to translate from. If one is going to translate all the Puranas, it is preferable, though not essential, that one opts for a common source for all the Purana texts. In all the Purana translations, as a common source, I have used, and will use, the ones brought out by Nag Publishers, with funding from the Ministry of Human Resource Development. It is no different for the Shiva Purana.[7] To the best of my knowledge, other than this translation, there are only two other unabridged translations of the Shiva Purana in English. J.L. Shastri was the editor of the first and a board of scholars undertook the translation, published under the title 'Ancient Indian Tradition and Mythology in English Translation'.[8] In the course of this translation, extensive comparisons have been made with the Shastri translation. The Sanskrit texts used for the two translations are similar, but not always identical. However, differences are minor. More importantly, the discerning reader, who compares the two, will find that we have differed in interpreting words and sentences. The second unabridged translation is by Shanti Lal Nagar.[9]

In the second half of the 19th century, the contribution of Calcutta and Bengal towards preserving the Itihasa-Purana legacy was remarkable. Consider the following. (1) Kaliprasanna Singha's unabridged translation of the Mahabharata in

[7] *The Sivamahapuranam*, Nag Publishers, Delhi, 1986.

[8] *The Siva-Purana*, translated and annotated by a Board of Scholars, edited by J. L. Shastri, 4 volumes, Motilal Banarsidass Publishers, Delhi, 1970.

[9] Shanti Lal Nagar, *Siva Mahapurana, An Exhaustive Introduction, Sanskrit Text, English Translation with Photographs of Archaeological Evidence*, 3 volumes, Parimal Publications, 2007.

Bengali; (2) The Sanskrit and unabridged Bengali translation of the Burdwan edition of the Mahabharata; (3) The unabridged Bengali translation of the Mahabharata, published by Pratap Chandra Roy; (4) The unabridged English translation of the Valmiki Ramayana by William Carey and Joshua Marshman; (5) Hemachandra Bhattacharya's unabridged translation of the Valmiki Ramayana in Bengali; (6) Ganga Prasad Mukhopadhyaya's verse translation of the Valmiki Ramayana; (7) Panchanan Tarkaratna's Sanskrit editions and Bengali translations of Valmiki Ramayana, Adhyatma Ramayana and several Puranas; (8) Unabridged translations of the Mahabharata in English by Kisari Mohan Ganguli and Manmatha Nath Dutt; (9) Asiatic Society's[10] Bibliotheca Indica Sanskrit editions of Agni Purana, Brihad Dharma Purana, Brihad Naradiya Purana, Kurma Purana, Varaha Purana and Vayu Purana; and (10) F. E. Pargiter's unabridged English translation of Markandeya Purana. (11) And most important of all, Horace Hayman's Wilson translation of the Vishnu Purana, in five volumes, between 1864 and 1870.[11] Though Wilson's translation wasn't part of the Bibliotheca Indica corpus, it was part of the same broad tradition. Wilson's work was almost certainly the first unabridged translation of any Purana into English and the scholarship was remarkable. An act of research and scholarship still needs to be undertaken, cross-referencing names, genealogies and incidents across Itihasa and Purana texts. Often, when the same incident is narrated in different Purana texts, there are differences in nuances and details. Since ours is a translation, we have

---

[10] Asiatic Society went through several name changes, but it can simply be called the Asiatic Society.

[11] Horace Hayman Wilson, *The Vishnu Purana, A System of Hindu Mythology and Tradition*, Trubner & Company, London, 1864–1870.

deliberately refrained from undertaking such an exercise. But the Horace Hayman Wilson translation did seek to do that. Before that work can be undertaken, the Purana corpus has to be translated, meaning translation into English. More often than not, practices of *dharma* are based on the Itihasa-Purana corpus. The Purana project, published by Penguin, is part of that translation endeavour. Translations of Bhagavata Purana, Markandeya Purana, Brahma Purana and Vishnu Purana have already been published and Shiva Purana is the fifth.

As has been mentioned earlier, the composition of Shiva Purana is dated to between 1000 and 1400 CE. It is a relatively later Purana. The Shiva Purana has a considerable degree of overlap with the Vayu Purana, dated to between 350 and 550 CE. It is the consensus that the Vayu Purana evolved earlier. R. C. Hazra's dissertation is still one of the best introductions to the Purana corpus, for all the Puranas.[12] Because of that later date of composition, Hazra paid short shrift to the Shiva Purana, not even mentioning it as a separate Purana. He focused instead on Vayu Purana.

> The Vayu is perhaps the oldest of the extant Puranas. The Mahabharata speaks of a 'Purana proclaimed by Vayu;' the Harivamsa refers to 'Vayu' as an authority; Banabhatta says in his Harsa-carita that he attended the reading of the Vayu Purana in his native village; and Alberuni repeatedly quotes and names a Vayu Purana in his account of India. The character of the Vayu as a Mahapurana has sometimes been called into question. The cause of this doubt is the use of the title 'Siva' or 'Saivya' for 'Vayaviya' in the majority of the lists of the 'eighteen Mahapuranas'. But this substitution,

---

[12] *Studies in the Puranic Records on Hindu Rites and Customs*, R. C. Hazra, University of Dacca, 1940. This has since been reprinted several times, by different publishers.

which has been taken wrongly in favour of the comparatively late sectarian Upapurana called 'Siva-purana', is based on the Saiva character of the Vayu . . . Hence it seems that the attempt to raise the Siva-purana to the status of a Mahapurana was due to a comparatively late sectarian zeal.

A quote from Wilson's Preface[13] will add to what has already been said and Wilson was less dismissive of the Shiva Purana.

The Siva or Saiva Purana is, as above remarked, omitted in some of the lists; and, in general, when that is the case, it is replaced by the Vayu or Vayaviya. When the Siva is specified, as in the Bhagavata, then the Vayu is omitted; intimating the possible identity of these two works.

In all Puranas, there are chapters that are almost verbatim reproductions of sections from the Mahabharata, Harivamsha and other Puranas. One should not deduce that a specific Purana text has copied from another, since these various texts might have had a common origin. That apart, even when the *shloka*s seem to be virtually identical, there are interesting changes in words and nuances. This has a bearing on the Hazra and Wilson arguments. Today, given the texts we possess, it is impossible to unambiguously establish the original text. There may very well have been an original proto-Vayu Purana and an original proto-Shiva Purana. Who can determine which preceded which? Suffice to say, there was a consolidation of the present Shiva Purana, perhaps even as late as between 1000 and 1400 CE, though something like 1000 CE to 1100 CE seems more reasonable. After all, each Purana evolved and was added to. In terms of its present structure and attributes, the Shiva Purana displays all the characteristics of a Maha-Purana. One

[13] Op. cit.

shouldn't be dismissive. The Shiva Purana is an important text in the corpus of texts that forms the edifice of Shaiva *dharma*. There are Shaiva *agama* texts that are part of this corpus too, 28 to be precise. There are Upa-Puranas as part the corpus, for instance, Shivadharma Purana, Shivadharmapurva Purana, Shivarahasya Purana and Maheshvara Purana. Whether it is Puranas or other texts, the Shiva Purana exhibits the influence of texts on Shakti and *tantra*.

We are told in the text [Chapter 9-2(2)] that the Shiva Purana originally consisted of 100,000 *shloka*s and was divided into 12 Samhitas or sections—Vidyeshvara, Rudra, Vainayaka, Uma, Matri, Rudraikadasha, Kailasa, Shatadrudra, Kotirudra, Sahasrakotirudra, Vayaviya and Dharmasamja. These aggregated to 100,000 *shloka*s. However, we are also told that Vedavyasa abridged the original Shiva Purana and compressed it into 24,000 shlokas, retaining seven Samhitas and eliminating five (Vainayaka, Matri, Rudraikadasha, Sahasrakotirudra and Dharmasamja). In the Sanskrit text of the Shiva Purana used by us, seven chapters and 373 *shloka*s from the Skanda Purana have also been included, since they concern the Shiva Purana. Accordingly, we have also translated these and our translation has 464 chapters and 24,646 *shloka*s (as shown in the table that follows). With the Skanda Purana segment deducted, there are 457 chapters and 24,273 *shloka*s (reasonably close to the stated 24,000). The seven Samhitas that remain are Vidyeshvara (25 chapters, 1,540 *shloka*s), Rudra (197 chapters, 10,268 *shloka*s), Shata Rudra (42 chapters, 2,188 *shloka*s), Koti Rudra (43 chapters, 2,187 *shloka*s), Uma (51 chapters, 2,679 *shloka*s), Kailasa (23 chapters, 1,285 *shloka*s) and Vayaviya (76 chapters, 4,126 *shloka*s). Rudra Samhita is long and is subdivided into five subsections or *khanda*s (Srishti, Sati, Parvati, Kumara and Yuddha). The longish Vayaviya Samhita also has two subsections or *bhaga*s (Purva and Uttara). A word about the numbering we have followed for the chapters, such as Chapter 423-8.2(1). The first number is a consecutive numbering of chapters of the entire Shiva Purana, while the second number indicates the number of the Samhita. (With the Skanda Purana segment included, this numbering extends to eight, not seven.) If there is a decimal point after the number given to the Samhita, this indicates the part of the Samhita. For instance, 8.2 indicates the second part of Vayaviya Samhita. Finally, the number within brackets indicates a consecutive numbering of chapters within that Samhita.

As with every Purana, there are layers within layers and the account is not recited by a single person. The basic template is, of course, the standard one of Suta reciting the Purana to sages who have assembled for a sacrifice in Naimisha forest. But there are also sub-strands of Vyasa recounting parts to sages, Brahma relating it to Narada, Nandi relating it to Sanatkumara, Upamanyu relating it to Krishna, Vayu relating it to the sages and even Shiva reciting parts to Parvati.

In the translations of the Bhagavat Gita, the Mahabharata, the *Harivamsha*, the Valmiki Ramayana, the Bhagavata Purana, the Markandeya Purana, the Brahma Purana and the Vishnu Purana,[14] we followed the principle of not using diacritical marks. The use of diacritical marks (effectively the international alphabet of Sanskrit transliteration) makes the pronunciation and rendering more accurate, but also tends to put off readers who are less academically inclined. Since diacritical marks are not being used, there is a challenge of rendering Sanskrit names in English. Sanskrit is a phonetic language and we have used that principle as a basis. Applied consistently, this means that words are rendered in ways that

---

[14] *The Bhagavata Purana,* Volumes 1–3, Penguin Books, 2018. *The Markandeya Purana*, Penguin Books, 2019. *The Brahma Purana*, Volumes 1–2, Penguin Books, 2021. The *Vishnu Purana*, Penguin Books, 2022.

may seem unfamiliar. Hence, Gautama will appear as Goutama
here. This is true of proper names, and, in a few rare cases, of
geographical names. The absence of diacritical marks causes
some minor problems. How does one distinguish Mahadeva
Shiva from Parvati Shivaa? Often, the context will make the
difference clear. If not, we have written Mahadeva as Shiva
and Parvati as Shivaa. In translating, the attempt has been to
provide a word-for-word translation, so that if one were to
hold up the Sanskrit text, there would be a perfect match. In
the process, the English is not as smooth as it might have been,
deliberately so. In this particular translation, we have also been
pedantic, perhaps unnecessarily so. For example, the text refers
to Krishna as both Shri Krishna and Krishna. We have strictly
adhered to whatever the text says, word for word. There was
another minor issue one should flag. In most texts, chapters
have headings. If chapters don't have headings, the colophon
at the end of the chapter indicates what the heading or title
of the chapter should be. The Shiva Purana text has no such
chapter headings before the chapter, and sometimes, does
not even have them in the colophon. Therefore, the chapter
headings we have given are subjective, based on the contents of
that particular chapter, unless of course the colophon suggests
a chapter heading.

The intention is to offer a translation, not an interpretation.
That sounds like a simple principle to adopt, and for the most
part, is easy to follow. However, there is a thin dividing line
between translation and interpretation. In some instances,
it is impossible to translate without bringing in a little bit of
interpretation. Inevitably, interpretation is subjective. We have
tried to minimize the problem by (a) reducing interpretation;
(b) relegating interpretation to footnotes; and (c) when there
are alternative interpretations, pointing this out to the reader
through those footnotes. But all said and done, there is no
substitute to reading these texts in the original Sanskrit.

Finally, the Shiva Purana is not an easy Purana to translate, read and understand. That's often because the average reader is relatively unfamiliar with *mantra*, *mandala*, *tantra*, *yantra*, *chakra*, Shakti concepts (*iccha*, *jnana*, *kriya*), rituals and the theology (for want of a better word) of Shaiva *dharma*. Shiva's 36 *tattva*s are different from the *tattva*s of *samkhya*, with many people being somewhat familiar with the latter. Shiva is in the centre of a *mandala*, surrounded by the five *kalaa*s (Nivritti, Pratishtha, Vidya, Shanta and Shantyatita). Depending on time and space, there are six paths to reach the supreme consciousness (*varna*, *mantra*, *pada*, *kaala*, *tattva*, *bhuvana*) and there are five sheaths (time, limited knowledge, attachment, destiny and limitation) that constrain one from reaching that supreme consciousness. As for Shiva himself, there are the five aspects of Sadyojata, Vamadeva, Aghora, Tatpurusha and Ishana. If this sounds esoteric, it is undoubtedly so. But a reading of Shiva Purana is also a convenient means of becoming exposed to these topics.

Shiva Purana

	Chapter		Number of *shloka*s
The Skanda Purana segment	1-1(1)	Greatness of Shiva Purana	51
	2-1(2)	Devaraja's story	40
	3-1(3)	Chanchula's story	57
	4-1(4)	Chanchula's emancipation	50
	5-1(5)	Binduga's emancipation	60
	6-1(6)	Rules for listening	65
	7-1(7)	Rules and restraints	50
Total in the Skanda Purana segment	7		373
Vidyeshvara Samhita	8-2(1)	The sages describe *kali yuga*	38
	9-2(2)	Greatness of Shiva Purana and its components	67
	10-2(3)	The objective and the means	27
	11-2(4)	More on the means	23
	12-2(5)	Greatness of *lingam*	31

1

	13-2(6)	Rivalry between Brahma and Vishnu	28
	14-2(7)	The column of fire	33
	15-2(8)	The humbling of Brahma	21
	16-2(9)	The *lingam* and Ishatva	46
	17-2(10)	Aumkara *mantra*	39
	18-2(11)	Worshipping the *lingam*	69
	19-2(12)	Shiva temples	43
	20-2(13)	Good behaviour	85
	21-2(14)	*Agni yajna*	46
	22-2(15)	*Deva yajna*	61
	23-2(16)	Worship of deities	117
	24-2(17)	AUM and *panchakshara mantra*	153
	25-2(18)	Bondage and liberation	162
	26-2(19)	Parthiva *lingam*	37
	27-2(20)	Worship of Parthiva *lingam*	66
	28-2(21)	More on *lingam*s	56
	29-2(22)	*Naivedya* and *bilva*	36
	30-2(23)	*Rudraksha* and Shiva's names	45
	31-2(24)	*Bhasma* and its greatness	116
	32-2(25)	Greatness of *rudraksha*	95
Total in Vidyeshvara Samhita	25		1,540

	52-3.1(20)	Shiva's departure for Kailasa	62
Total in Srishti Khanda	20		1,222
Sati Khanda	The section on Sati		
	53-3.2(1)	Sati's conduct in brief	46
	54-3.2(2)	Kama's origin	43
	55-3.2(3)	Kama's curse	78
	56-3.2(4)	Kama's marriage	34
	57-3.2(5)	Sandhya's story	68
	58-3.2(6)	Sandhya's austerities	62
	59-3.2(7)	Arundhati marries Vasishtha	27
	60-3.2(8)	Description of Vasanta	53
	61-3.2(9)	Kama's powers and his aides	63
	62-3.2(10)	Conversation between Brahma and Vishnu	61
	63-3.2(11)	Durga's praise and Brahma's boon	51
	64-3.2(12)	Daksha's boon	37
	65-3.2(13)	Daksha curses Narada	40
	66-3.2(14)	Sati's birth and childhood	59
	67-3.2(15)	Nanda vows and Shiva's praise	67
	68-3.2(16)	Brahma and Vishnu pray to Shiva	58
	69-3.2(17)	Sati gets the boon	73
	70-3.2(18)	Bestowing of the daughter	37
	71-3.2(19)	Shiva's pastimes	76

	95-3.2(43)	Arranging Daksha's sacrifice	44
Total in Sati Khanda	43		2,313
Parvati Khanda	The section on Parvati		
	96-3.3(1)	Himachala's marriage	32
	97-3.3(2)	An earlier account	42
	98-3.3(3)	Prayer to Devi	39
	99-3.3(4)	Comforting the gods	50
	100-3.3(5)	Mena's boon	50
	101-3.3(6)	Parvati's birth	54
	102-3.3(7)	Parvati's childhood pastimes	25
	103-3.3(8)	Conversation between Narada and Himalaya	56
	104-3.3(9)	The dream	36
	105-3.3(10)	Bhouma's origin	28
	106-3.3(11)	Shiva and the mountain meet	42
	107-3.3(12)	Shiva and the mountain converse	36
	108-3.3(13)	Conversation between Parvati and Parameshvara	60
	109-3.3(14)	Taraka and Vajranga's origin	43
	110-3.3(15)	Tarakasura's austerities and kingdom	56
	111-3.3(16)	Assuring the devas	46
	112-3.3(17)	Conversation between Indra and Kama	43
	113-3.3(18)	Kama's disturbances	45
	114-3.3(19)	Kama's destruction	52

	137-3.3(42)	Meeting between the divinity and the mountain	31
	138-3.3(43)	Shiva's wonderful pastimes	65
	139-3.3(44)	Mena gains her senses	102
	140-3.3(45)	Shiva's beautiful form	46
	141-3.3(46)	Arrival of the groom	36
	142-3.3(47)	Festivities inside Himalaya's house	55
	143-3.3(48)	Bestowing the bride	56
	144-3.3(49)	Vidhatri's delusion	47
	145-3.3(50)	Amusements	45
	146-3.3(51)	Kama comes back to life	43
	147-3.3(52)	Feeding the groom's party	40
	148-3.3(53)	Preparations for Shiva's return	37
	149-3.3(54)	*Dharma* of a virtuous wife	83
	150-3.3(55)	Shiva's return to Kailasa	38
Total in Parvati Khanda	55		2,699
Kumara Khanda	The section on Kumara		
	151-3.4(1)	Shiva's amusement	63
	152-3.4(2)	Birth of Shiva's son	73
	153-3.4(3)	Kartikeya's pastimes	40
	154-3.4(4)	Search for Kartikeya	67
	155-3.4(5)	Kumara's *abhisheka*	67
	156-3.4(6)	Kumara's extraordinary conduct	33

	157-3.4(7)	Start of the war	41
	158-3.4(8)	The battle in general	52
	159-3.4(9)	Taraka fights against Shakra, Vishnu and Virabhadra	54
	160-3.4(10)	Taraka's death	52
	161-3.4(11)	Bana and Pralamba are killed	33
	162-3.4(12)	Kartika, Shiva and Shivaa	56
	163-3.4(13)	Ganesha's origin	39
	164-3.4(14)	Quarrel with the *gana*s	63
	165-3.4(15)	Description of Ganesha's battle	72
	166-3.4(16)	Severing of Ganesha's head	37
	167-3.4(17)	Ganesha gets his life back	59
	168-3.4(18)	Ganesha obtains the title of Ganadhipa	79
	169-3.4(19)	Prelude to Ganesha's marriage	55
	170-3.4(20)	Ganesha's marriage	45
Total in Kumara Khanda	20		1,080
Yuddha Khanda	The section about the war		
	171-3.5(1)	Description of Tripura	78
	172-3.5(2)	Praise by *deva*s	63
	173-3.5(3)	*Dharma* of Tripura	54
	174-3.5(4)	Initiation of residents of Tripura	64
	175-3.5(5)	Delusion of Tripura	63

	176-3.5(6)	Praise of Shiva	55
	177-3.5(7)	Praise by *deva*s	44
	178-3.5(8)	Description of the chariot	30
	179-3.5(9)	Shiva's advance	44
	180-3.5(10)	Burning of Tripura	44
	181-3.5(11)	Praise by *deva*s	41
	182-3.5(12)	*Deva*s return	41
	183-3.5(13)	Shakra gets his life back	52
	184-3.5(14)	Jalandhara's birth and marriage	40
	185-3.5(15)	Battle between *deva*s and Jalandhara	66
	186-3.5(16)	*Deva*s fight back	44
	187-3.5(17)	Vishnu and Jalandhara fight	50
	188-3.5(18)	Conversation between Narada and Jalandhara	51
	189-3.5(19)	Jalandhara sends a messenger	51
	190-3.5(20)	Ordinary *gana*s and *asura*s fight	62
	191-3.5(21)	Special fights	55
	192-3.5(22)	Description of Jalandhara's fighting	52
	193-3.5(23)	Violation of Vrinda's faithfulness	51
	194-3.5(24)	Description of Jalandhara	58
	195-3.5(25)	Praise by *deva*s	37
	196-3.5(26)	Dispelling of Vishnu's delusion	61

197-3.5(27)	Shankhachuda's origin	36
198-3.5(28)	Shankhachuda's austerities and marriage	41
199-3.5(29)	Shankhachuda's rule and earlier birth	59
200-3.5(30)	Prayer to the lord of *deva*s	40
201-3.5(31)	Shiva's advice	55
202-3.5(32)	The messenger is sent	35
203-3.5(33)	Mahadeva's advance	49
204-3.5(34)	Shankhachuda's advance	25
205-3.5(35)	Conversation between Shiva and the messenger	50
206-3.5(36)	The mutual fight	36
207-3.5(37)	Shankhachuda fights	45
208-3.5(38)	Kali fights	37
209-3.5(39)	Shankhachuda's soldiers are killed	45
210-3.5(40)	Shankhachuda is killed	43
211-3.5(41)	Tulasi's curse	64
212-3.5(42)	Killing of Hiranyaksha	49
213-3.5(43)	Killing of Hiranyakashipu	43
214-3.5(44)	Andhaka's austerities	71
215-3.5(45)	The battle commences	54
216-3.5(46)	Andhaka's fight	41
217-3.5(47)	Swallowing of Shukra	53

	218-3.5(48)	Swallowing of Shukra continued	48
	219-3.5(49)	Andhaka becomes a *gana*	42
	220-3.5(50)	Shukra obtains knowledge about *mritasanjivani*	53
	221-3.5(51)	Usha's story	62
	222-3.5(52)	Usha's story continued	63
	223-3.5(53)	Aniruddha and Usha amuse themselves	54
	224-3.5(54)	Banasura, Rudra, Krishna and others fight	63
	225-3.5(55)	Slicing of Bana's hands	48
	226-3.5(56)	Banasura becomes a *ganapati*	34
	227-3.5(57)	Slaying of Gajasura	73
	228-3.5(58)	Slaying of Dundubhi-nirhrada	50
	229-3.5(59)	Slaying of Vidala and Utpala	42
Total in Yuddha Khanda	59		2,954
Total in Rudra Samhita	197		10,268
Shata Rudra Samhita			
	230-4(1)	Shiva's five *avataras*	50
	231-4(2)	Shiva's eight forms	17
	232-4(3)	*Arddha-nar-nara avatara*	31
	233-4(4)	Story of Rishabha	48

	257-4(28)	Yatinatha Brahma-hamsa *avatara*	41
	258-4(29)	Krishna-darshana *avatara*	59
	259-4(30)	Avadhutehsvara *avatara*	44
	260-4(31)	Bhikshuvarya *avatara*	78
	261-4(32)	Sureshvara *avatara*	78
	262-4(33)	Brahmachari *avatara*	65
	263-4(34)	Sunartaka-nata *avatara*	39
	264-4(35)	*Avatara* as a virtuous *brahmana*	37
	265-4(36)	*Avatara* as Ashvatthama	44
	266-4(37)	Prelude to Kirata *avatara*	68
	267-4(38)	Arjuna's austerities	65
	268-4(39)	Slaying of Muka *daitya*	53
	269-4(40)	Conversation between the *bhilla* and Arjuna	49
	270-4(41)	Kirateshvara *avatara*	67
	271-4(42)	Twelve *jyotirlingam*s	60
Total in Shata Rudra Samhita	42		2,188
Koti Rudra Samhita			
	272-5(1)	Greatness of *jyotirlingam*s and *upalingam*s	44
	273-5(2)	Greatness of Shiva's *lingam*s	31
	274-5(3)	Anasuya and Atri's austerities	39

	275-5(4)	The greatness of Atrishvara	61
	276-5(5)	Death of the *brahmani* and Nandikeshvara	39
	277-5(6)	The *brahmani* goes to heaven	66
	278-5(7)	Greatness of Nandikeshvara	35
	279-5(8)	Greatness of Mahabala	28
	280-5(9)	The *chandali*'s good destination	39
	281-5(10)	The greatness of Mahabala Shiva *lingam*	51
	282-5(11)	The greatness of Pashupatinatha Shiva *lingam*	21
	283-5(12)	The nature of the *lingam*	54
	284-5(13)	Origin of Vatuka	77
	285-5(14)	Origin of Somanatha *jyotirlingam*	62
	286-5(15)	Description of Mallikarjuna *jyotirlingam*	23
	287-5(16)	Greatness of Mahakala *jyotirlingam*	52
	288-5(17)	Greatness of Mahakala *jyotirlingam* continued	78
	289-5(18)	Greatness of Omkareshvara *jyotirlingam*	27

290-5(19)	Greatness of Kedareshvara *jyotirlingam*	26
291-5(20)	Greatness of Bhimeshvara *jyotirlingam*	67,920
292-5(21)	Origin and greatness of Bhimeshvara *jyotirlingam*	54
293-5(22)	Rudra's arrival in Kashi	40
294-5(23)	Greatness of Kashi-Vishveshvara *jyotirlingam*	57
295-5(24)	Greatness of Tryambakeshvara and Goutama	33
296-5(25)	Goutama's arrangements	58
297-5(26)	Greatness of Tryambakeshvara	57
298-5(27)	Greatness of Tryambakeshvara continued	50
299-5(28)	Greatness of Vaidyanatheshvara *jyotirlingam*	76
300-5(29)	Depredations of *rakshasa*s in Darukavana	53
301-5(30)	Greatness of Nageshvara *jyotirlingam*	44
302-5(31)	Greatness of Rameshvara	45
303-5(32)	Sudeha and Sudharma	52
304-5(33)	Origin and greatness of Ghushmesha *jyotirlingam*	56

	305-5(34)	Vishnu obtains Sudarshana chakra	35
	306-5(35)	Shiva's one thousand names	133
	307-5(36)	The fruits of the one thousand names	38
	308-5(37)	Shiva's devotees	55
	309-5(38)	Greatness of Shiva Ratri	88
	310-5(39)	Shiva Ratri's *udyapana*	23
	311-5(40)	Greatness of Vyadheshvara and Shiva Ratri	102
	312-5(41)	Nature of emancipation	27
	313-5(42)	Difference between *saguna* and *nirguna*	32
	314-5(43)	Nature of *jnana*	59
Total in Koti Rudra Samhita	43		2,187
Uma Samhita			
	315-6(1)	Conversation between Krishna and Upamanyu	71
	316-6(2)	Upamanyu's instructions	52
	317-6(3)	Shiva's greatness	78
	318-6(4)	The power of Shiva's *maya*	39
	319-6(5)	Major sins	40
	320-6(6)	Different types of sins	58
	321-6(7)	Yama's messengers and the path to hell	59
	322-6(8)	Description of hell	45
	323-6(9)	Description of consequences in hell	46

	346-6(32)	Kashyapa's lineage	52
	347-6(33)	Description of creation continued	31
	348-6(34)	The manvantaras	78
	349-6(35)	Description of Vaivasvata manvantara	42
	350-6(36)	Manu's lineage and nine sons	61
	351-6(37)	Manu's lineage continued	59
	352-6(38)	Satyavrata to Sagara	57
	353-6(39)	Kings of surya vamsha	46
	354-6(40)	The power of ancestors	60
	355-6(41)	The seven hunters	53
	356-6(42)	The power of ancestors continued	23
	357-6(43)	Worship of Vyasa	8
	358-6(44)	Vyasa's origin	140
	359-6(45)	The avatara of Mahakalika	78
	360-6(46)	Mahishasura's death and Mahalakshmi's origin	63
	361-6(47)	Deaths of Dhumralochana, Chanda, Munda and Raktabija	66
	362-6(48)	Manifestation of Sarasvati	50
	363-6(49)	Uma's manifestation	43
	364-6(50)	Shatakshi avatara	52
	365-6(51)	Nature of kriya yoga	88
Total in Uma Samhita	51		2,679

	387-7(23)	Rites on the twelfth day, after a mendicant's death	45
Total in Kailasa Samhita	23		1,285
Vayaviya Samhita			
Purva Bhaga (first part)			
	388-8.1(1)	Origin of *vidya*	68
	389-8.1(2)	Sages present their case	31
	390-8.1(3)	The Naimisha account	63
	391-8.1(4)	Vayu's arrival	24
	392-8.1(5)	*Jnana* about Shiva's *tattva*	64
	393-8.1(6)	*Jnana* about Shiva's *tattva* continued	76
	394-8.1(7)	Greatness of Kala	26
	395-8.1(8)	Lifespans of the three divinities	31
	396-8.1(9)	Creation, preservation and dissolution	24
	397-8.1(10)	Description of Brahmanda	48
	398-8.1(11)	Description of creation	36
	399-8.1(12)	Description of creation continued	77
	400-8.1(13)	Creation of Brahma and Vishnu	47
	401-8.1(14)	Manifestation of Rudras	21
	402-8.1(15)	Praise of Shiva and Shivaa	35

	403-8.1(16)	Manifestation of Devi Shakti	28
	404-8.1(17)	Account of creation	65
	405-8.1(18)	Sati gives up her body	62
	406-8.1(19)	Virabhadra's origin	67
	407-8.1(20)	Destruction of the sacrifice	43
	408-8.1(21)	Punishment of *devas*	41
	409-8.1(22)	Destruction of Daksha's sacrifice	72
	410-8.1(23)	Prayer to Girisha	56
	411-8.1(24)	Shiva's residence and sports on Mount Mandara	58
	412-8.1(25)	Devi becomes Gouri	48
	413-8.1(26)	The tiger's destination	29
	414-8.1(27)	Gouri's return	37
	415-8.1(28)	Nature of *bhasma*	20
	416-8.1(29)	*Vagartha*	36
	417-8.1(30)	Questions about Shiva's *tattva*	53
	418-8.1(31)	Instructions about *jnana*	100
	419-8.1(32)	Best practices	56
	420-8.1(33)	Rules of Pashupata *vrata*	98
	421-8.1(34)	Upamanyu's austerities	59
	422-8.1(35)	Upamanyu's conduct	65
Total in Purva Bhaga	35		1,764
Uttara Bhaga (second part)			
	423-8.2(1)	Krishna obtains a son	27

Total in Uttara Bhaga	41		2,362
Total in Vayaviya Samhita	76		4,126
Total in Shiva Purana	464		24,646

The Skanda Purana Segment

Chapter 1-1(1)¹ (Greatness of Shiva Purana)

Shri Shounaka said, 'O Suta!² O immensely wise one!
O lord! O one who knows the outcomes of all the various
determinations. In particular, please tell me about the essence
of all the Puranas. How are good behaviour, devotion and a
sense of discrimination enhanced in one's own self and in one's
sons? How do virtuous people act so as to dispel their own
deviations? In this terrible *kali yuga*, all beings generally obtain
asura traits. What is the supreme path that can cure them of
this? What is that supreme object which ensures the best of
the best? At present, what is the means that is the purest of the
pure? In particular, what means can be used to swiftly purify
one's *atman*? O father!³ With a sparkling mind, how can one
always obtain Shiva?'

¹ Though included in Shiva Purana texts, Chapters 1.1 to 1.7 are
not really from Shiva Purana. They are actually from Skanda Purana.
But since they are about the greatness of Shiva Purana, they are often
included in Shiva Purana texts.
² Suta narrated the Puranas to the sages, led by Shounaka,
assembled in the forest of Naimisha (Naimisharanya).
³ The word used is *tata*. While this means father, it is respectfully
used to address anyone who is senior.

27

Suta replied, 'O tiger among sages! Since you are eager and lovingly wish to hear about this, you are blessed. Hence, I will use my intelligence to reflect on the great and excellent sacred texts and tell you. This is the outcome of all the various determinations and enhances devotion. O child! It is divine and satisfies Shiva. Listen to this medication. It is excellent and destroys the great fear arising from the predatory serpent known as Kala.[4] O sage! This is the supreme Shiva Purana, stated by Shiva himself. The sage Sanatkumara instructed Vyasa and out of respect for him[5] and for the welfare of those born in *kali yuga*, Vyasa abridged them. O sage! Especially for the purification of the minds of those born in *kali yuga*, there is nothing other than Shiva Purana. O sage! After accumulating great merits in an earlier birth, an immensely fortunate and intelligent person will develop affection for it. This Shiva Purana is a supreme and excellent sacred text. On earth, it should always be served and known as Shiva's form. If an excellent man devotedly reads it or listens to it, he instantly obtains Shiva, something that can only be attained by using every possible means. Therefore, men must make every kind of effort to read this sacred text. If one listens to it lovingly, everything desired is obtained as a fruit. When a man listens to Shambhu's[6] Purana, a man is cleansed of sins. After enjoying extensive objects of pleasure, he obtains Shiva's world. As soon as one hears about Shambhu's account, one obtains the good merits obtained from performing a *rajasuya* sacrifice or one hundred *agnishtoma* sacrifices.[7]

---

[4] Time, destiny, death.

[5] Sanatkumara. Originally, the Puranas were composed by Brahma, who taught them to Sanatkumara, one of the four sons born through Brahma's mental powers. Sanatkumara instructed Vedavyasa about the Puranas. In turn, he abridged them and classified them into eighteen. So runs the tradition.

[6] Shambhu is Shiva's name.

[7] *Rajasuya* is a royal sacrifice, *agnishtoma* is a fire sacrifice.

O sage! Those who hear the excellent sacred text of Shiva Purana should not be thought of as mere mortals. There is no doubt that they are like forms of Rudra.[8] Sages know that the dust from the lotus feet of those who hear this Purana and chant it are like the dust from *tirthas*.[9] Embodied beings who desire to go to the supreme region should always devotedly listen to the unblemished Shiva Purana. O supreme among sages! If a person is unable to listen to it constantly, let him control his *atman* and listen to it for one *muhurta*[10] every day. O sage! If a man is unable to listen to it every day, let him listen to the Shiva Purana on auspicious months. If people listen to the Purana for one *muhurta*, for half a *muhurta*, for a quarter of a *muhurta* or for a *kshana*,[11] they do not suffer from any hardships. O lord of sages! A man who listens to this Purana burns down the great forest of *karma* and crosses *samsara*.[12] O sage! Good merits are obtained from all donations and all sacrifices. Those stable fruits are obtained from listening to Shambhu's Purana. O sage! Especially during *kali yuga*, there is no greater *dharma* for men than listening to Shiva Purana. This is the means for achieving emancipation. There is no doubt that through properly hearing and reciting Shambhu's Purana, men obtain the fruits obtained from *kalpadruma*.[13] In *kali yuga*, there are evil-minded people who are deceitful in their *atmans*. They do not follow *dharma*. The nectar known as Shambhu Purana is

[8] Rudra is Shiva's name.
[9] A *tirtha* is a sacred place of pilgrimage with water. A *kshetra* is a sacred place of pilgrimage without water. But the words are sometimes used synonymously.
[10] A *muhurta* is a period of 48 minutes.
[11] *Kshana* is a small measure of time, with differing interpretations. A second or an instant is accurate enough.
[12] The cycle of birth, death and rebirth, the image being of crossing over to the other shore.
[13] The tree (*druma*) that yields all the wishes thought of (*kalpa*).

for their benefit. A man who drinks this *amrita* does not suffer from old age and becomes immortal. The *amrita* of Shambhu's account also ensures that no one in the entire family suffers from old age. They become immortal. It must always be served. It must always be served.[14] In particular, it must always be served. This account of Shiva Purana becomes supremely purifying as soon as one hears the narration of Shiva Purana. What can I say about the fruits obtained by those who hold Shiva in their hearts?'

'The text has 24,000 *shloka*s, divided into seven *samhitas*.[15] Full of the three kinds of *bhakti*,[16] one must lovingly listen to it. The first *samhita* is Vidhyeshvara Samhita, the second is Rudra Samhita. The third is known as Shata Rudra, while the fourth is Koti Rudra. The fifth is known as Uma Samhita, while the sixth is Kailasa Samhita. The seventh is known as Vayaviya. There are thus seven *samhita*s. With these seven *samhita*s, this divine text is known as Shiva Purana. It is equal to Brahma.[17] It is supreme and yields every kind of objective. If a person lovingly reads the entire Shiva Purana, with its seven *samhita*s, he is spoken of as *jivanmukta*.[18] Until the excellent Shiva Purana reaches his ears, a man is ignorant and whirled around on earth. What is the point of listening to many sacred texts and Puranas? They only lead to confusion. The Shiva Purana announces that it alone can bestow emancipation. If the account of the Shiva Purana is heard in any house, that house becomes a *tirtha* and the sins of all those who reside in that house are destroyed. Indeed, one

---

[14] To ensure emphasis, the text has this repetition.

[15] A *samhita* is a collation of verses.

[16] The first kind of *bhakti* is pure *bhakti*, without any desire for fruits. A second kind of *bhakti* desires fruits. A third kind of bhakti is mixed *bhakti*, where both objectives exist.

[17] Interpreted as the *brahman*. However, a straightforward interpretation is that it is equal to the Brahma Purana, the first Purana.

[18] A person emancipated (*mukta*) while he still retains life (*jivan*).

thousand *ashvamedha* sacrifices and one hundred *vajapeya* sacrifices[19] do not amount to one sixteenth of what is obtained from Shiva Purana. O supreme among sages! A person who has committed a sin is known as a sinner only as long as he has not heard the Shiva Purana, full of great devotion. There are sacred rivers, Ganga and the others. There are seven cities, Gaya and the others. None of them is equal to this Shiva Purana. If one desires the supreme objective, every day, one should devotedly read, with one's own mouth, one *shloka*, or half a *shloka*, from Shiva Purana. If one understands the meaning and speaks about Shiva Purana, or if one constantly reads it devotedly, there is no doubt that the person's *atman* is auspicious. If an intelligent person devotedly listens to it at the time of death, Mahesha[20] is extremely pleased with him and grants him a place in his own abode. If a person lovingly worships Shiva Purana every day, he enjoys every object that he desires. After this, he obtains a destination with Shiva. Attentively, the Shiva Purana must always be wrapped in a piece of linen garment. A person who honours it in this way will always be happy. The unblemished Shiva Purana is everything for a person who is devoted to Shiva. If he desires happiness in this world and in the next one, he must make every effort to lovingly serve it. The supreme and unblemished Shiva Purana bestows the four objectives of human existence.[21] It must always be heard. In particular, it must always be lovingly read. It is supreme among the *Veda*s, Itihasa and sacred texts and ensures great benefit. The Shiva Purana must always be understood by those who desire emancipation. For those who seek to know about the *atman*, this Shiva Purana is supreme. Among all supreme objects, it must always

---

[19] *Ashvamedha* is a horse sacrifice, *vajapeya* is a type of sacrifice at which *soma* is offered.

[20] The great lord, Shiva.

[21] The four *purushartha*s of *dharma*, *artha*, *kama* and *moksha*.

be served and worshipped by the virtuous. It pacifies the three kinds of hardship.[22] It bestows happiness and must always be loved more than one's own life. It pleases Brahma, Hari, Isha and the immortals.[23] With every kind of happiness in my mind, I worship Shiva Purana. May Shiva be pleased with me and bestow on me devotion at his own feet.'

Chapter 2-1(2) (Devaraja's story)

Shounaka said, 'O Suta! O immensely fortunate one! O Suta! You know the supreme meaning and are blessed. Out of your compassion, you have made us hear this divine and extraordinary account. It purifies the mind and destroys a torrent of sins. We have heard this wonderful account that generates satisfaction in Shiva. There is nothing on earth that is equal to this account. There is nothing else that is superior. Because of your compassion, we have certainly got to know about this. In *kali yuga*, who are the sinners who get purified by this account? O Suta! Out of your compassion, please tell us, for the sake of gratifying the world.'

Suta replied, 'There are men who commit sins. They are deceitful and wicked in their conduct. They are constantly devoted to desire and other vices. They too are purified by this. This is an excellent *jnana-yajna*.[24] It always bestows objects of pleasure and emancipation. It cleanses all sins and brings satisfaction to Shiva. There are those who are overwhelmed by thirst.[25] They are bereft of the truth and censure their fathers

---

[22] Relating to *adhidaivika* (destiny), *adhibhoutika* (nature) and *adhyatmika* (one's own nature).
[23] Hari is Vishnu and Isha is Shiva.
[24] A sacrifice in pursuit of *jnana* (knowledge).
[25] That is, desire.

and mothers. They are insolent and cause violence. Even such
people are purified by this. There are those who abandon the
dharma of their own *varna* and *ashrama*.[26] They are full of
envy. In *kali yuga*, even they are purified by this *jnana-yajna*.
There are deceitful ones who indulge in fraud. They are cruel
and heartless. In *kali yuga*, even they are purified by this *jnana-
yajna*. There are those who sustain themselves by appropriating
the property of *brahmana*s and are addicted to being deviant.[27]
In *kali yuga*, even they are purified by this *jnana-yajna*. There
are those who constantly indulge in sin. They practice fraud
and are extremely wicked. In *kali yuga*, even they are purified
by this *jnana-yajna*. There are those who are filthy and evil in
intelligence. They survive on the possessions of serene *devas*.[28]
In *kali yuga*, even they are purified by this *jnana-yajna*. This is
the most sacred of Puranas. It destroys major sins. It bestows
objects of pleasure and emancipation and ensures satisfaction
to Shiva.'

'In this connection, an ancient history is recounted. As soon
as one hears it, sins no longer remain. In the city of Kiratas,[29]
there was a *brahmana* whose learning was deficient. He turned
away from the *dharma* of *devas* and sold juices to the poor.[30]
He deviated from the practice of bathing at the time of *sandhya*
and followed the means of subsistence meant for *vaishyas*.[31]

[26] As in the four *varna*s, *brahmana, kshatriya, vaishya* and *shudra*
and the four *ashrama*s, *brahmacharya, grahasthya, vanaprastha* and
sannyasa.
[27] *Vyabhichara*, usually deviant in sexual matters.
[28] Implying that they steal from temples.
[29] *Kirata*s were hunters.
[30] Since they are poor, they shouldn't have been asked to pay.
Alternatively, *daridrorasa* may mean that he sold liquor.
[31] *Sandhya* is the period between day and night and means dawn
or dusk. Sometimes, midday is also referred to as *sandhya*. At these
times, one should bathe. Trade, buying and selling, is for *vaishyas*, not
*brahmana*s.

He was known as Devaraja, and he deceived people who trusted him. He deprived *brahmanas*, *kshatriyas*, *vaishyas* and *shudras* of their possessions. Through such fraudulent means, he accumulated wealth. Through many such acts of *adharma*, he gathered wealth for himself. But since he was a sinner, he did not spend the slightest bit of this on acts of *dharma*. On one occasion, the *brahmana* went to a lake to have his bath. A courtesan named Shobhavati arrived there. On seeing her, he was agitated. Realizing that the wealthy *brahmana* had come under her subjugation, the beautiful lady was delighted. As a result of their conversation, love was generated in his mind. He wanted to make her his wife. She also consented that he would become her husband. In this way, they came under the subjugation of desire and sported for a very long time. When seated, lying down, drinking, eating and playing, they behaved towards each other as couples do and resided accordingly. His mother, father and wife[32] repeatedly tried to restrain him. But he did not pay heed to their words and continued to indulge in this wicked conduct. On one occasion, he succumbed to his intolerance. While they were asleep in the night, the wicked person killed his parents and wife and stole their wealth. His mind was full of desire for the courtesan. He handed over his wealth and the wealth he obtained from his father and others to her. The sinner ate what should not be eaten. He wished to drink liquor. That worst of *brahmanas* always ate from the same vessel as the courtesan.'

'On one occasion, urged by destiny, he arrived in the city of Pratishthana.[33] He saw a Shiva temple there, surrounded by virtuous people. While the *brahmana* was there, he suffered from a terrible fever and constantly heard Shiva's account, uttered from the mouth of another *brahmana*. Suffering

---

[32] There was an earlier wife.
[33] Usually, but not invariably, identified as Paithan in Maharashtra.

)

from the fever, at the end of a month, Devaraja died. Yama's servants bound him up in nooses and forcibly conveyed him to Yama's city. However, Shiva's attendants were there, dressed in white and wielding tridents in their hands. All their limbs were smeared with ashes, and they wore *rudraksha* beads.[34] They arrived from Shiva's world and angrily went to Yama's city. They reprimanded his messengers and repeatedly struck them. They released Devaraja and placed him on a wonderful *vimana*.[35] Making him sit there, the messengers eagerly started to leave for Kailasa. At this, there was a great tumult in Yama's city. Hearing this, Dharmaraja[36] emerged from his own residence. He saw those four messengers, who seemed to be like Rudra himself. Dharmaraja, who knew about *dharma*, followed the norms and worshipped them. Using the insight of knowledge, Yama got to know about the entire incident. Scared, he did not ask the great-souled Shambhu's messengers anything. Having been worshipped, they sought his leave. They went to Kailasa and handed him over to Shiva and Amba,[37] who are oceans of compassion. The accounts of Shiva Purana are blessed and supremely purifying. As soon as he hears it, a sinner is emancipated. Sadashiva's excellent abode is a great and supreme region. Those who know the *Veda*s say that it is located above all the worlds. The *brahmana* Devaraja was a sinner. Because of his greed, he caused violence to *brahmana*s, *kshatriya*s, *vaishya*s, *shudra*s and many other beings, robbing them of their lives. He killed his mother, his father and his wife. He was a drunkard and had intercourse with a courtesan. However, as soon as he arrived there, he was instantly emancipated.'

[34] Beads loved by Shiva, seeds of the *Elaeocarpus*. Literally meaning Rudra's eye.
[35] Celestial and divine vehicle.
[36] Yama.
[37] Parvati, meaning mother.

Chapter 3-1(3) (Chanchula's story)

Shounaka said, 'O Suta! O immensely fortunate one! O Suta! O immensely intelligent one! You know everything. Through your favours, I have repeatedly become successful in my objective. On hearing this Itihasa , my mind is greatly delighted. Please narrate another account about Shambhu, so that our love for him is increased even more. In this world, even those who drink *amrita* are not honoured with emancipation. But drinking in the nectar of Shambhu's account immediately bestows emancipation. You are blessed. You are blessed.[38] Shambhu's account is blessed. You are blessed. As soon as a man hears it, he goes to Shiva's world.'

Suta replied, 'O Shounaka! Listen. I will tell you about a great secret since you know the *Veda*s and are foremost among Shiva's devotees. In the region near the ocean, there was a village known as Bashkala. The people who lived there were wicked. They deceived and did not follow the *dharma* of the *Veda*s. They were evil and dwelt in an evil region. They were insolent, did not follow *deva*s and used deception for subsistence. Though they practiced agriculture, they used force and wielded weapons. They indulged in fraud and were greatly addicted to intercourse with women. They did not possess *jnana* or non-attachment. They did not know about true *dharma* and about ensuring the welfare of others. They were firm in their addiction to hearing about wicked accounts. Their intelligence was like that of animals. The minds of those deceivers were such that they turned away from their own *dharma*s and followed that of other *varna*s. They always indulged in wicked deeds and were constantly interested in material objects. All the women were wicked

---

[38] The repetition is for the sake of emphasis.

svairinis,[39] addicted to sin. They were wicked in intelligence, practicing *vyabhichara*. They were devoid of all good conduct. Such wicked people lived in the village known as Bashkala.'

'There was a *brahmana* named Binduga there and he was a great wretch. He was extremely evil in his *atman* and a great sinner. He always followed extremely wicked paths. He had a wife named Chanchula. But his mind was so overcome by desire that he became the husband of a courtesan. Though his own wife always followed *dharma*, he abandoned her. Suffering from the arrows of love, the evil one amused himself with the courtesan. In this way, a long period of time elapsed and he continued to indulge in his wicked acts. However, Chanchula still suffered on account of love. Scared of giving up her own *dharma*,[40] she bore that hardship. Her beauty faded and she was no longer in the bloom of youth. She was overwhelmed by desire and gave up her own *dharma*. In secret and in the night, when her husband could not see, she started to have intercourse with her paramour. She deceived him. Deviating from virtue, she followed a wicked path. O sage! On one occasion, he saw his wife, Chanchula, engage in this wicked conduct. In the night, he saw her, overwhelmed by desire, having intercourse with her lover. Witnessing his wife's wickedness, his mind turned towards an evil course of action. While his wife was engaged in intercourse with her paramour at night, he angrily rushed towards them. The deceitful and evil paramour saw that Binduga had returned home. The deceiver swiftly fled from that house. At this, Binduga caught hold of

---

[39] A *svairini* is a loose and wanton woman. There were different types though. *Svairinis* are loose women who have sex with anyone they want, but only with those from the same *varna*. *Kaminis* are loose women who have sex with anyone they want, irrespective of *varna*. *Pumshchalis* have no sense of discrimination and are almost like harlots.

[40] Of devotion towards her husband.

his wife. He repeatedly abused her and struck her with his fists. The woman was beaten by her husband. The deceitful *svairini*, Chanchula, became angry. She spoke to her deceitful husband, Binduga. Chanchula said, "Full of evil intelligence, every day, you succumb to desire and pleasure yourself with a courtesan. You abandon your own youthful wife, who is devoted to serving her husband. I am beautiful. I am young. My mind is also overwhelmed by desire. Please tell me. When I am deprived of pleasuring myself with my husband, what course of action do I have? I am extremely beautiful. I am young. I am agitated. How will I withstand the pangs of desire? Deprived of your companionship, my mind is suffering." The foolish person, evil in intelligence and worst among *brahmana*s, was addressed by her in this way. The deceitful sinner, Binduga, who had turned away from his own *dharma*, replied to her in this way. Binduga said, "What you have said is indeed true. Your mind is agitated by desire. O beloved! I will tell you what is beneficial for you. Listen. Give up this fear. Without any fear in your mind, dally with a new paramour every day. Give them their pleasure and take from them whatever riches you can. Hand over all that wealth to me. My mind is attached to that courtesan. This will indeed bring great benefit to us, to you, as well as to me." His wife, Chanchula, heard her husband's words. Evil in her intelligence, she accepted her husband's words. With wicked minds, the couple entered into this agreement. Without any fear, evil in intelligence, they indulged in this wicked course of action. In this way, the couple practiced this wicked conduct. A long period of time elapsed. Foolish in intelligence, they followed this futile pursuit.'

'In the course of time, Binduga, the evil-minded *brahmana* who was the husband of a *vrishali*,[41] died. The deceiver went

---

[41] While *vrishala* means *shudra*, it also means outcast. *Vrishali* is the feminine. This probably refers to Binduga being the husband of a courtesan, not to his being Chanchula's husband.

to hell. Foolish in intelligence, he went through many kinds of hardship in hell. He then became a terrible *pishacha*[42] in the Vindhya mountains. When her husband, Binduga, died, she continued to reside in her own house, indulging in wicked conduct. Extremely foolish in intelligence, she spent a long period of time with her sons. The woman, Chanchula, continued to amuse herself with her paramours. Overwhelmed by desire, she found her pleasures. After some time, her youth passed. On one occasion, through the urging of destiny, an auspicious occasion arrived.[43] Along with her relatives, the woman went to the *kshetra* of Gokarna.[44] Along with her relatives, she roamed around, here and there. In that connection, she went to that *tirtha* and bathed there. In a temple, there was a *daivajna*,[45] who was speaking about Shambhu's sacred account from the Puranas. From his mouth, she heard a bit of this auspicious account. Women who are attached to paramours go to hell. There, Yama's servants insert hot iron rods inside their vaginas. The person expounding from the Puranas spoke about this, so as to develop non-attachment among those who heard. Hearing this, she became anxious and trembled. When the narration was over and the people had left, the scared woman approached the *brahmana* in private. She addressed the one who had spoken about Shiva. Chanchula said, "O *brahmana*! Listen. Without knowing my own *dharma*, I indulged in wicked conduct. O lord! On hearing about this, please show me your unlimited compassion and save me. O lord! Foolish in intelligence, I have committed an extremely

[42] Demon, flesh-eater.

[43] A *parva*, a special day earmarked for sacred activities.

[44] Literally, Gokarna means cow's ear. Located near Mangalore in Karnataka, Gokarna has a Shiva temple (Mahabaleshwara). Gokarna is at the estuary of the Aghanashini (destroyer of sins) river. Adjacent to the temple is a pond known as *koti tirtha*.

[45] *Daivajna* means astrologer, one who knows the future.

grave sin. Blinded by desire, I spent my entire youth in fickle behaviour. Hearing your words about the development of non-attachment, a great fear has been generated in me, combined with trembling. Shame on my foolish intelligence. Shame on the sin I have committed as a result of being overwhelmed by desire. I have turned away from my own *dharma* and have committed the reprehensible act of being addicted to material objects. In pursuit of a little bit of happiness, I have destroyed my own tasks. I have committed a grave and terrible sin and have unwittingly cause hardship. What calamities am I headed towards? Alas! What terrible miseries will this lead to? Who can tell? My mind has turned towards excessively wicked paths. When the time for death arrives, I will see Yama's fearful messengers. When they strike me and bind nooses around my neck, how will I maintain my patience? In hell, when my body is sliced into fragments, how will I tolerate it? The great pains there lead to special miseries. During the day, I will not be able to move my organs of sense. How will I not be able to grieve? In the night, how will I be able to obtain the desired sleep? I will be overwhelmed with grief. Alas! I have been burnt down. Alas! My heart is being shattered. I have destroyed myself in every possible way. I have been a sinner in every possible way. Alas! O destiny! You have bestowed this great sin and great hardship on me. You have deceived me. My own *dharma* would have given me every kind of happiness. But I was made to deviate from it. O *brahmana*! There are miseries when an embodied being is impaled on a stake or is flung down from the top of a mountain. But this misery is one crore times that. A sin like mine is great. Generally, it cannot be purified by performing one hundred horse sacrifices or bathing in Ganga for one hundred years. What will I do? Where will I go? Who will I seek refuge with? Who in this world will save me? I am descending into an ocean that is hell. O *brahmana*! You are my *guru*. You are my mother. You are my father. Save me.

Please save one who is distressed. I seek refuge with you." With non-attachment generated in her, she fell down at his two feet. Full of compassion, the intelligent *brahmana* raised her up and spoke to her.'

Chapter 4-1(4) (Chanchula's Emancipation)

The *brahmana* said, 'Hearing accounts from the Shiva Purana leads to non-attachment. It is good fortune that through Shiva's great favours, your understanding has been awakened at the right time. O wife of a *brahmana*! Do not be afraid. Go and seek refuge with Shiva. Through Shiva's favours, all your sins will instantly be destroyed. I will tell you something else that is full of Shiva's deeds. That will lead you to a destination that brings every kind of happiness. Such intelligence only develops from listening to virtuous accounts. You are full of repentance. Thus purified, you are no longer attached towards material objects. The greatest atonement for sinners is repentance for the sins they have committed. All virtuous people have described this as the means for cleansing all sins. As instructed by virtuous people, if a person performs *prayashchitta*,[46] purified by repentance, all sins are purified. If a man makes up his mind to perform *prayashchitta*, he longer has any fear. There is no doubt that repentance generally conveys a person towards a desirable destination. Hearing the account of the Shiva Purana leads to a purification of the mind that cannot be obtained through anything else. This is like a mirror being cleaned, so that it becomes sparkling. There is no doubt that this account purifies the mind like that. Shiva and Amba remain in the minds of men who have purified themselves.

---

[46] Atonement for sins.

With *atman*s thus purified, they attain a supreme destination with Shiva and Amba. Therefore, for every category, it is held that this account is the best mode. It is for this reason that Mahadeva himself devised this account. This account leads to the mind being immersed in *dhyana* on Girija's husband.[47] *Jnana* is generated from *dhyana* and thereafter, there is certain *kaivalya*.[48] If a person listens to this account, but is unsuccessful in performing *dhyana* on Shankara,[49] he accomplishes that *dhyana* in a subsequent birth and goes to a supreme destination with Shambhu. There are many sinners who have heard this account and have performed *dhyana* on Uma's husband.[50] Having tormented themselves, they have obtained success. Hearing this account is the most beneficial *bija* for men.[51] If one follows this path in the proper way, the bonds of worldly existence are destroyed. Hearing the account, fixing Shambhu in the mind and in the seat of the heart, and purification of the consciousness are enough. That devotion towards Mahesha and his two sons certainly leads to divine favours.[52] Therefore, there is no doubt about emancipation. In its absence, a person's intelligence is bound to *maya*.[53] He should be known as an animal. There is no doubt that he can never be freed from the bondage of *samsara*. O wife of a *brahmana*! Therefore, withdraw your mind from material objects. With your mind full of devotion, listen to Shambhu's account. This is supremely

---

[47] Girija means daughter of the mountain, that is, Parvati. Therefore, Girija's husband is Shiva. *Dhyana* is meditation/contemplation.

[48] Emancipation.

[49] Shiva.

[50] Uma is Parvati.

[51] *Bija* means seed and is a mystic *akshara* (syllable) from a *mantra*, known as *bija mantra*.

[52] Mahesha is Shiva, the two sons are Ganesha and Kartikeya.

[53] Illusion. In the absence of devotion.

purifying. Listen to this virtuous account about Shankara, the *paramatman*. With your consciousness thus purified, you will obtain emancipation. Meditate on Shiva's lotus feet and your mind will become sparkling. I am telling you the truth. You will obtain emancipation in a single birth. This is the truth.'

Suta continued, 'Having spoken to her in this way, the excellent *brahmana* turned his mind towards obtaining Shiva's favours. He was silent and, with a purified *atman*, became engaged in performing *dhyana* on Shiva. Binduga's wife, Chanchula, was pleased in her mind. Addressed in this way by the *brahmana*, her eyes filled with tears. With a delighted mind, she fell down at the feet of that Indra among *brahmana*s. She joined her hands in salutation and said, "I have obtained my objective." Rising up, she joined her hands in salutation and spoke, the *aksharas*[54] faltering. With her mind full of non-attachment, she addressed the *brahmana* who was Shiva's great devotee. Chanchula said, "O *brahmana*! O Shiva's great devotee! O lord! You are blessed. You are the one who has seen the supreme destination. You are engaged in ensuring the welfare of others. You are described as an extremely virtuous person. Please save me. O virtuous one! I am descending into an ocean that is hell. I wish to hear you speak about Shiva Purana. In my mind, there is non-attachment about all material objects. Now, there is great devotion in my mind for listening to this Purana." Saying this, she joined her hands in salutation and obtained his favours. Desiring to hear about the Purana, she remained there, serving him. In that spot, the extremely intelligent *brahmana*, who was supreme among Shiva's devotees, made the woman listen to the virtuous account of the Purana. In that great *kshetra*, she heard the excellent account of the Shiva Purana from the excellent *brahmana*. The account enhances devotion, *jnana* and non-attachment and bestows

---

[54] An *akshara* has a single vowel sound, a syllable.

emancipation. Hearing this virtuous and supreme account, she accomplished an excellent objective. Favoured by the compassion shown by a good *guru*, she swiftly obtained purity of consciousness. Through Shiva's favours, she performed *dhyana* on Shambhu's form. In this way, seeking refuge with a good *guru*, her mind turned towards Shiva. She repeatedly meditated on Shambu's form, who is *sacchidananda*.[55] She always bathed in the water of the *tirtha*. She had matted hair and attired herself in bark. She smeared her limbs with ashes and wore a garland of *rudraksha* beads. She performed *japa*[56] on Shiva's name and controlled excessive speech and food. Following the path indicated by the *guru*, she satisfied Shiva. O Shounaka! In this way, Chanchula performed excellent *dhyana* on Shambhu and a long period of time elapsed. She did this, full of the three kinds of devotion.[57] When the designated period was over, Chanchula voluntarily gave up her body. Sent by Tripurari,[58] a *vimana* swiftly arrived. It was adorned in many kinds of ways and was full of his many divine *ganas*.[59] Accompanied by Mahesha's excellent attendants, she ascended it. Sparkling and with all the dirt removed, she was instantly conveyed to Shiva's city. She assumed a divine form and her limbs were divine. She was resplendent, with celestial ornaments. She wore the half-moon on her crest and her complexion was fair.[60] Having gone there, she saw the three-eyed Mahadeva. He is the eternal one

[55] The supreme *brahman* or *paramatman*, truth (alternatively existence), consciousness and bliss.

[56] Meditation, with silent chanting of the name.

[57] Hearing, chanting the name and meditating.

[58] Shiva's name, literally, the enemy of Tripura. Shiva destroyed Tripura, three cities of the demons.

[59] *Gana*s are Shiva's companions.

[60] Gouri means fair and is Parvati's name. Chandrashekhara (the moon on the crest) is Shiva's name. There is thus an allusion to a form that half-resembled Shiva and half-resembled Parvati.

and he was being served by Vishnu, Brahma and other *devas*.
Full of devotion, Ganesha, Bhringi, Nandishvara, Virabhadra
and others worshipped him. His radiance was like that of one
crore suns. His throat was blue. He had five faces and three
eyes. The moon was on his crest. Gouri, with a dazzle like that
of lightning, was resplendent on his left side. He was as fair
as camphor. Gouri's lord wore every kind of ornament. His
body was smeared with white ashes. Extremely resplendent, he
was attired in a white garment. Seeing Shankara, the woman,
Chanchula, was filled with delight. Filled with supreme joy,
she repeatedly prostrated herself before him respectfully.
Delighted, she joined her hands in salutation. She was humble,
content and full of love. Her body-hair stood up in delight and
tears of joy flowed from her eyes. Full of compassion, Parvati
and Shankara allowed her to approach. Because of her good
fortune, she was able to see them. Parvati lovingly made her
a divine companion. Chanchula, Binduga's beloved, thus
obtained celestial happiness. That eternal world is dazzling and
is full of supreme bliss. She obtained a permanent residence
there and her mind was filled with joy.'

Chapter 5-1(5) (Binduga's Emancipation)

Shounaka said, 'O Suta! O immensely fortunate one! O Suta!
Since your mind is immersed in Shiva, you are blessed.
Having heard this wonderful account, our devotion has
increased. Having gone there and having obtained an excellent
destination, what did Chanchula do? Please tell us that. O
immensely wise one! In particular, what about her husband?'

Suta replied, 'On one occasion, she approached Devi
Parvati and prostrated herself before her. Overwhelmed with
great bliss, she joined her hands together and praised her.

Chanchula said, "O Girija! O Skanda's mother! Men always worship you. You are the one who always bestows happiness. You are Shambhu's beloved. You are the form of the *brahman*. Vishnu, Brahma and others serve you. You possess *gunas*.[61] You are also *nirguna*. You are the subtle and original Prakriti. Your form is *sachhidananda*. You are the one who causes creation, preservation and dissolution. You possess the three *gunas*. You are the abode of the three divinities.[62] You are the supreme one who establishes Brahma, Vishnu and Mahesha." Chanchula, who had already obtained a virtuous end, addressed Maheshi[63] in this way and stopped. Her shoulders were bent down. Her eyes were full of tears of love. Parvati, loved by Shankara, was filled with compassion for her. Full of great love, the one who loved her devotees, spoke to Chanchula. Parvati said, "O Chanchula! O friend! O beautiful one! I am extremely pleased with this praise. Please ask for the boon you desire. There is nothing that cannot be given to you." Thus addressed by Girija, Chanchula prostrated herself before her. Asked in this way, she was filled with great love. She joined her hands in salutation and bent her head down. Chanchula said, "I do not know where my husband is now. Nor do I know the destination he will go to. O Girija! O unblemished one! Please act so that I can be with him. O fortunate one! O one who shows compassion towards those who are distressed! O Mahadevi! O Maheshani! My husband is the husband of a *vrishali*. He died before me. I do not know what has happened to that sinner." Hearing Chanchula's words, Parvati spoke to her. The affectionate Girija addressed her in extremely loving words. Girija said, "O daughter! Your husband, Binduga, is

---

[61] The *gunas* are *sattva* (purity), *rajas* (passion) and *tamas* (darkness). *Nirguna* is a form without these *gunas*.

[62] Brahma, Vishnu and Shiva.

[63] Feminine of Mahesha.

foolish and a great sinner. The foolish one became attached to a courtesan. After death, he went to hell. For a large number of years, he underwent many kinds of hardships in hell. The one with evil in his *atman* still needed to exhaust his sins. Therefore, he has been born as a *pishacha* in the Vindhyas. Right now, he is a *pishacha*, suffering from many kinds of miseries. He suffers from miseries caused by *vata*[64] and always must bear hardships." Hearing Gouri's words, Chanchula was moved to tears. Because her husband was going through these sorrows, she too was extremely miserable. She steadied her mind and prostrated herself before Maheshvari again. With an anxious heart, the lady asked again. Chanchula said, "O Maheshvari! O Mahadevi! Please show me your compassion. Though my husband is a deceiver and has committed wicked deeds, please save him. My husband is wicked, evil in intelligence. O Devi! I bow down before you. Please tell me how he can swiftly attain a virtuous end." Parvati is affectionate towards her devotees. Hearing her words, with a pleased mind, she spoke to her friend, Chanchula. Parvati said, "If your husband hears Shiva's supreme and sacred account, he will overcome this hardship and attain a virtuous end." She lovingly heard these words of Gouri, with *akshara*s like *amrita*.'

'She repeatedly joined her hands in salutation and bent her shoulders down. On hearing about his account, her husband would be cleansed of all sins. Therefore, she prayed that he might obtain a virtuous end. She repeatedly beseeched Shiva's beloved to ensure this. Maheshi Gouri is affectionate towards her devotees and took pity on her. Hence, she summoned Tumburu, the one who sang about Shiva's account. The

---

[64] In *Ayurveda*, the three *dosha*s or humours in the body are *vata*, *pitta* and *kapha* and they are always striving against each other. These can be loosely translated as wind, bile and phlegm. Stated simply, Binduga was suffering from indigestion.

daughter of the mountain affectionately addressed the king of the gandharvas.[65] Girija said, "O Tumburu! O one loved by Shiva! O fortunate one! Do what is in my mind. With her, quickly go to Mount Vindhya. There is an extremely terrible and extremely fearful pishacha there. With a great deal of affection, listen to his account. I will tell you everything. In a former life, this pishacha used to be a brahmana named Binduga. That wicked person used to be the husband of this lady, my friend. He was the husband of a vrishali. At the time of sandhya, he did not bathe and perform the other rites of purification. He was angry and foolish in intelligence. He ate what should not be eaten. He hated virtuous people. He took what should not be taken. He was violent and wielded weapons. He ate with his left hand. He oppressed those who were afflicted. He was cruel and set fire to the homes of others. He always associated with chandalas.[66] He was a great deceiver and enjoyed courtesans. The sinner abandoned his own wife and associated with those who were wicked. As a result of that association with a courtesan, he completely destroyed all his good merits. Desiring wealth, without any fear, he made his wife accept paramours. He indulged in this wicked conduct until he died. In the course of time, he died. He went to Yama's city, the terrible place enjoyed by those who are sinners. The evil-souled one went through many kinds of hell there. Right now, that deceiver has become a pishacha in Mount Vindhya, enjoying wicked things. In front of him, attentively narrate the extremely sacred and divine Shiva Purana, which destroys every

[65] Gandharvas are semi-divine species, celestial singers and musicians.

[66] One usually equates chandala with shudra, but there were eight different types of shudras, though the listing varies. For instance, vyadha (hunter), vyalagrahi (those who eat snakes), vagatita (one with whom one does not speak), chandala (brahmana mother, shudra father) and so on.

kind of sin. As soon as he hears the account of Shiva Purana, his *atman* will be purified, and he will be cleansed of all sins. He will no longer be a *preta*.[67] Binduga will be freed from his present hardships as a *pishacha*. After this, follow my command and bring him before Shiva." Thus addressed by Maheshani, Tumburu, Indra among the *gandharvas*, was delighted. He told himself that he was extremely fortunate. Following the command, Tumburu, loved by Narada, ascended an excellent *vimana*, along with the beloved.[68] He went to Mount Vindhya and saw the *pishacha* there, with a gigantic body and large jaws. He was malformed. Sometimes, he laughed. Sometimes, he wept. Sometimes, he spoke excessively. Tumburu, who sang about Ishana's excellent account, was extremely strong. He forcibly seized that extremely fearful *pishacha* and bound him up in nooses.'

'Tumburu did this so that he could narrate the Shiva Purana. Having decided this, he made arrangements for great festivities. There was a great uproar in all the worlds. "Having been commanded by Devi, Tumburu has gone to Mount Vindhya, so as to make the *pishacha* listen to Shiva Purana." So as to hear this account, all *devas* and *rishis* hastened and assembled there. All of them went there to lovingly hear about Shiva Purana and it was a wonderful assembly. Bound in

---

[67] A *preta* is a ghost, the spirit of a dead person, or simply something evil. A *bhuta* has the same meaning. Strictly speaking, there are differences between *preta*, *bhuta* and *pishacha* (one who lives on flesh). A *preta* is the spirit (not necessarily evil) of a dead person before the funeral rites have been performed. A *bhuta* (not necessarily evil again) is the spirit of a dead person who has had a violent death and for whom, proper funeral rites have not been performed, and may not even be performed. A *pishacha* (necessarily evil) is often created deliberately through evil powers. But the three terms are often used synonymously.

[68] That is, Chanchula.

nooses, the *pishacha* was made to sit down. With a lute[69] in his hand, Tumburu started to sing the account of Gouri's husband. He started with the first *samhita* and ended with the seventh *samhita*. He clearly described the entire Shiva Purana, along with its greatness. Listening lovingly to the Shiva Purana, with its seven *samhita*s, all the listeners felt that they had accomplished their objectives. Hearing the extremely sacred account of Shiva Purana, the *pishacha* was cleansed of all his sins and gave up his form as a *pishacha*. He swiftly assumed a divine form, fair in complexion and attired in white garments. All his limbs were adorned with dazzling ornaments. He resembled the three-eyed Chandrashekhara. Assuming a divine form, along with his own beloved, who already possessed a divine form, he himself sang about the illustrious conduct of Parvati's husband. All *deva*s and *rishi*s saw him, along with his wife. They were amazed and were filled with great happiness. Hearing about Mahesha's extraordinary account, they achieved their objective and were pleased. Praising Shankara's fame, they returned to their own respective abodes. Binduga, divine in his *atman*, ascended an excellent *vimana*. With his beloved by his side, he was stationed in the sky and looked extremely radiant. Singing about Mahesha's excellent and agreeable qualities, along with his beloved and accompanied by Tumburu, he reached Shankara's abode. Mahesha and Parvati welcomed Binduga. He was lovingly made a *gana* and she became Girija's friend. That world is full of supreme bliss. It is full of radiance and is eternal. He obtained a sparkling residence there and became full of supreme happiness. I have thus narrated this sacred Itihasa, which destroys sins. It is unblemished and enhances devotion. Shiva and Shivaa[70] take great delight in it. If a person

---

[69] *Vallaki.*

[70] Parvati. To distinguish between the two, Parvati's name will be written as Shivaa, while Shiva is Mahesha.

controls himself, listens to this with devotion and chants it, he enjoys extensive objects of pleasure and at the end, he obtains emancipation.'

Chapter 6-1(6) (Rules for Listening)

Shounaka said, 'O Suta! O immensely wise one! O Suta! You are Vyasa's disciple. I bow down before you. You are blessed. Your great qualities are such that you are described as Shiva's great devotee. Please tell me about the rules for listening to the illustrious Shiva Purana, whereby the listener can completely obtain all the excellent fruits.'

Suta replied, 'O sage Shounaka! I will tell you about the rules for listening to Shiva Purana, so that the complete fruits are obtained. The person must first invite a *daivajna* and satisfy him. A pure and sanctified *muhurta* must be chosen for commencement, so that it is completed without any impediments. News about this auspicious event's occurrence must be attentively sent to different regions, so that Shiva's devotees, who desire an auspicious objective, can arrive. Women, *shudra*s and some others are often kept at a distance from hearing about Hari's account or the chanting of Shankara's account. They should also arrive, so that their understanding is kindled. In different regions, there are Shambhu's devotees who are eager to listen to his account being recited. They must be welcomed and lovingly invited to this event. "There will be thus be an assembly of virtuous people and great festivities.[71] There will be an extremely wonderful occasion, with Shiva Purana being recited. Full of love, come and drink the nectar of the illustrious Shiva Purana. Full of love, please show us your

---

[71] This is the message being sent.

compassion and come. If you do not have the time, full of love, come for at least a single day. This is a rare occasion. Under all circumstances, please do come, even if it is for a short while." In this way, full of humility and joy, they must be invited. Those who arrive must be affectionately welcomed, in every possible way. Excellent places for listening to Shiva Purana are Shiva's temple, a *tirtha*,[72] a grove or a house. The ground must be purified, smeared and decorated with minerals. On the occasion of the great festivity, there must be divine and wonderful decorations. The house must be cleaned. Everything not worthy must be kept in one corner of the house, so that it cannot be seen. A raised platform must be constructed, adorned with pillars made out of plantain trees. There must be fruits and flowers in abundance, and everything must be covered with a canopy. The four directions must be decorated with flags and banners. Every task must be undertaken with a great deal of affection, so that there is delight in everyone. One must think of a divine seat for Shankara, the *paramatman*. The narrator must also be given a divine seat, one that is pleasant to sit on. As each one deserves, there must be agreeable spots for the listeners.[73] O sage! For ordinary people, there must be other spots. Everything must bring pleasure to the mind, as is the case at the time of a marriage. O Shounaka! All other daily thoughts and worries must be set aside. The narrator will face the north and the listeners will face the east. Know that the feet must never be placed in a contrary direction.[74] Alternatively, the narrator can face the east, seated between the worshipper

---

[72] A *tirtha* is a sacred place of pilgrimage with water. A *kshetra* is a sacred place of pilgrimage without water. But the words are often used synonymously.

[73] These are special seats for special people.

[74] This probably means that the feet must never be stretched out towards the narrator.

and the worshipped.[75] Honoured by the listeners, the narrator can also be seated so that he faces them. As long as he is seated in Vyasa's seat, narrating the Purana, the *brahmana*[76] must never bow down to anyone else until the narration is complete. Whether he is a child, a youth, an old man, a poor person or an excessively weak person, a person who knows the Purana must always be worshipped by anyone who desires to earn good merits. For embodied beings, the words that flow from his mouth are like a *kamadhenu*.[77] Therefore, a person who is inferior in intelligence must never become someone who knows the Purana. After many births, one obtains the qualities required to become a *guru*. Among all *gurus*, a person who knows the Purana is supreme and special. There are those who are suffering as a result of thousands of crores of births. If a person bestows emancipation on them, there can be no greater *guru* than him. A person who desires to recite Shiva Purana must be extremely intelligent. He must know the Purana. He must be pure and accomplished. He must be serene and must have conquered malice. He must be virtuous, full of compassion and eloquent. It is only then that he can speak about this sacred account. The narration must begin at sunrise and continue for three and a half *praharas*.[78] This narration must not take place before those who are cunning, evil doers, those who have crooked professions or those who are contemptible in any other way. It must not be narrated in a place that is full of wicked people or infested with bandits. This sacred account must not be narrated in the house of a cunning person. Men who are reciting this account must stop the account for one *muhurta*

---

[75] The narrator is seated between the listener and Shiva's image.

[76] The narrator.

[77] A cow (*dhenu*) that yields all the desired (*kama*) fruits.

[78] A *prahara* is a period of three hours. So it continues for ten and a half hours.

at midway, for performing ablutions and releasing urine and excrement. On the day before the discourse, the narrator must shave himself. As long as the discourse is going one, he must make efforts to undertake his *nitya karma*[79] briefly. Following the prescribed norms, by the side of the narrator, there must be another person who will help him. This other person must be learned and must be capable of dispelling the doubts of people. So as to remove impediments to the narration, Gananatha must be worshipped first.[80] The lord of the narration, Shiva, and specifically, the text,[81] must also be worshipped.'

'The account of Shiva Purana must be listened to, full of love and attentiveness. The listener must follow the norms and be pure. He must be pure in mind and pleasant in heart. If the narrator or the listener is distracted by many other things, succumbs to *kama* and the six vices,[82] is addicted to women or is a heretic,[83] there will be no good merits. If one listens to the account with a pure mind and heart, casting aside ordinary thoughts of wealth, homes and sons, one will obtain excellent fruits. Listeners who are full of faith and devotion, not desiring many other tasks and those who are pure and restrained in speech, obtain good merits. The worst among men listen to this account without devotion. Such listeners do not obtain any fruits. Instead, birth after birth, they suffer hardships. Those who listen to the account without worshipping the Purana, according to the means they can afford, are fools. They remain

---

[79] *Nitya karma* consists of rites performed every day. *Naimittika karma* consists of rites performed on a special occasion and *kamya karma* consists of rites undertaken for desired fruits.

[80] The lord of the *gana*s. In this context, meaning Ganesha.

[81] That is, the book. We have not used the word book, since book suggests a printed text.

[82] The six vices of *kama* (desire), *krodha* (anger), *lobha* (avarice), *moha* (delusion), *mada* (arrogance) and *matsarya* (jealousy).

[83] *Pakhanda.*

poor and are not purified. When the narration is going on, men who show disrespect to the narration and go elsewhere are men whose wealth and wives are destroyed even as they are enjoying them. Men who listen to this account with their head-dresses on their heads are men who give birth to evil sons who defile their lineage. In the case of men who chew on betel leaves while the narration is going on, when they die, Yama's servants make them eat their own excrement in hell. In the case of men who listen to this narration while seated on a lofty seat, after suffering in hell, they are born as crows. In the case of men who listen to this narration while seated in *virasana*[84] and other similar postures, after all the suffering in hell, they are born as poisonous trees. In the case of men who listen to this narration without honouring the narrator first, after all the suffering in hell, they are born as *arjuna* trees.[85] In the case of men who listen to this account while lying down, even if they are not sick, after all the suffering in hell, they are born as *ajagaras*[86] and similar species. In the case of men who listen to this account while seated at the same level as the narrator, they commit a sin equal to that of a person who violates his *guru*'s bed. Such people always go to hell. Those who criticize the narrator in the course of this extremely purifying account are born as dogs. They suffer miseries in hundreds of inauspicious births. Those who engage in futile debating while the narration is going on, suffer terrible hardships in hell and are born as donkeys. Those who rarely listen to this purifying narration while it is going on, suffer terrible hardships in hell and are born as pigs.[87] Wicked people who cause obstructions while this narration is going on, enjoy terrible hardships in hell

---

[84] Literally, posture of a hero. A seated position used by ascetics.
[85] Tall tree, *Terminalia arjuna*.
[86] The python/boa constrictor.
[87] These are wild pigs, the next sentence mentions domestic pigs.

for one crore years and are born as village pigs. Reflecting on this, a listener must be pure in his *atman* and show great reverence towards the narrator. Because of these reasons, he must be intelligent enough to lovingly listen to the narration. To remove all impediments, Ganesha must be worshipped at the start. Every day, at the end, there must be a brief rite of *prayashchitta*.[88] *Navagraha*s and *bhadradeva*s must always be worshipped.[89] Following the norms used for worshipping Shiva, the text must be worshipped. The text is like the form of Shiva himself. At the end of the worship, humbly joining one's hands in salutation, the text must be praised. "The illustrious Shiva Purana is like Maheshvara himself. For the sake of hearing, I accepted you. Please be satisfied with me. Your task is to bring my wishes to fruition. Let my hearing of this account be completed without any impediments. I am immersed in this world, which is like an ocean, and am distressed. Please save me from the world that is an ocean. In the form of crocodiles, my limbs have been seized by *karma*. O Shankara! I am your servant." The Shiva Purana is like Shiva's form himself. In this way, with pitiful words, he must praise it. He must then worship the narrator. Following the norms for worshipping Shiva, he must worship the narrator, with flowers, garments, ornaments, incense, lamps and other things. In front of him, with a pure mind, he should observe all the rituals and until the end of the narration, he must attentively follow them, to the best of his capacity. "Your form is like that of Vyasa. You are foremost among those who enlighten. You are accomplished

---

[88] In case there have been any deviations in the course of the narration. The ensuing sentences are also meant for the end of the narration.

[89] *Navagraha*s (nine planets) are Surya (Sun), Chandra (Moon), Mangala (Mars), Budha (Mercury), Brihaspati (Jupiter), Shukra (Venus), Shani (Saturn), Rahu and Ketu. *Bhadradeva*s are a class of *deva*s who bring good fortune.

in texts about Shiva. Through the light from this narration, please destroy my lack of *jnana*." To perform *japa* of the Shiva *pancharna mantra*, he must always devotedly invite five excellent *brahmana*s, or at least one *brahmana*.[90] O sage! I have thus described the rules for listening to the narration with devotion, for listeners, as well as for devotees. What else do you wish to hear?'

Chapter 7-1(7) (Rules and Restraints)

Shounaka said, 'O Suta! O immensely wise one! O Suta! O bull among those who are Shiva's devotees! You are blessed. You have made us listen to this wonderful account, which brings everything that is auspicious. O sage! For the welfare of all the worlds, please tell us about the *niyamas*[91] a man who intends to listen to the Shiva Purana must observe.'

Suta replied, 'O Shounaka! Listen faithfully to the *niyamas* for such men. If a person follows the *niyamas* and listens to this virtuous account, there are no impediments and excellent fruits are obtained. Men who have not had *diksha*[92] are not entitled to hear this narration. O sage! Therefore, the listeners must accept *diksha* from the narrator. A person who is devoted to listening to the account must practice *brahmacharya* and sleep on the ground as long as the narration is going on. Every day, he must eat only when the narration is over and out of a

---

[90] If he lacks the means to invite five *brahmana*s, one will do. The *pancharna mantra*, with five (*pancha*) *akshara*s, is *Namo Shivaya* (*na-mo-shi-va-ya*). The word *arna* means a letter of the alphabet, or *akshara*. Hence, *pancharna*.

[91] *Niyama* means the rules and restraints.

[92] A process of consecration/initiation for a ceremony, or for a process of instruction.

plate made out of leaves.[93] If he has the capacity, is pure and
is Shiva's excellent devotee, he must fast and listen devotedly
until the narration of the Purana is over. Drinking only ghee[94]
and drinking only milk, he must listen cheerfully. He can listen
while subsisting on fruits, or eating once a day, or avoiding even
that. Devoted to the narration, he can eat only havishyanna[95]
once a day. The listening is important, the food depends on
what can be done easily. If the listener thinks that it will be
easier for him to listen if he eats, that should be done. Fasting
is not superior when it causes an obstruction to listening to the
account. However, a person who is intent on listening to the
account must always avoid heavy food, dvidala,[96] burnt food,
nishpava,[97] mashur dal, defiled food, leftover food, brinjal,
watermelon,[98] gourd,[99] radish, pumpkin, coconut, anything
that is a root, onion, garlic, asafoetida, turnips[100] and anything
else that causes intoxication. A person intent on listening to the
account must avoid anything described as meat. He must avoid
kama and the other vices and he must not criticize brahmanas.
A person intent on listening to the account must not criticize
a woman who has sons and is devoted to her husband. A
person intent on listening to the account must not look at a
woman who is going through her period, speak to an outcast

[93] Patravalli, plate made out of leaves strung together.

[94] Clarified butter.

[95] Havishya/havishyanna is food that can be offered as oblations.
It is simple and has no seasoning. It is only eaten on special occasions,
such as when a vow is being observed.

[96] Dvidala is grain with two opposite faces, like gram.

[97] Corn.

[98] Kalinda has been translated as watermelon, though it can also
be a type of myrobalan.

[99] The word used is pichanda, meaning belly. So, it probably
means a pot-bellied gourd.

[100] The word grinjana means turnip but is also a kind of garlic.

or have a conversation with those who hate *brahmana*s and the *Veda*s. A person intent on listening to the account must always be truthful, pure, compassionate, restrained in speech, upright, humble and generous in mind. One may listen to the account with a specific desire or without any desire. If there is a specific desire, that desire will be fulfilled. If there is no desire, the person will obtain *moksha*. A poor person, a person suffering from the disease of consumption, a sinner, an unfortunate person and a man without children should listen to this virtuous account. Women who suffer from the seven types of ailments, *kakavandhya* and others, and those who have miscarriages should listen to this account.[101] O sage! Everyone, man or woman, must listen to the account of Shiva Purana, following the prescribed rules. The days when Shiva Purana is recited should be understood as extremely pure, equal to the performance of one crore sacrifices. Donations made on these days, even if they are limited, are superior and instantly deliver fruits. Following these rules and vows, one should listen to this excellent account. If one acts in this way, one will be filled with prosperity and supreme bliss. The rules of *udyapana* are the same as those observed on a *chaturdashi* day.[102] A wealthy person who desires fruits must always follow these. Devotees who possess nothing need not practice *udyapana*. They are purified from the act of listening alone. It is held that those

[101] Different kinds of infertility in women are listed in texts on Ayurveda, the number isn't always seven. For example, *kakavandhya* (the womb drying up after delivering one child), *anapatya* (primary infertility), *garbhasravi* (repeated abortions), *mritavatsa* (repeated still-births), *balakshaya* (when the woman lacks the strength to conceive), *nalaparavartini* (a woman who only delivers daughters) and *janmavandhya* (barren since birth).

[102] *Chaturdashi* is the fourteenth lunar day and the text means rites observed on such a day. *Udyapana*, for any ceremony, means the concluding rites.

without desires are Shambhu's true devotees. In this way, when the festivities and sacrifice connected with listening to Shiva Purana are over, the listeners must devotedly make efforts to undertake worship. O sage! Shiva's worship must be properly performed in front of the text. Following the norms, proper worship must then be done of the narrator. An auspicious piece of new cloth must be given to cover the text and a piece of cord to tie it up. Those who donate a piece of cloth and a cord for the Purana, obtain objects of pleasure and *jnana* in every birth that they go through. Following the norms, the narrator must be praised and given extremely expensive gifts, garments, ornaments and in particular, divine vessels. Men who give a seat for the text to be placed on, blankets, deerskin, garments and couches and slabs[103] obtain desired objects of pleasure and enjoy residence in the world of heaven. They remain in Brahma's abode for the duration of a *kalpa*[104] and go to Shiva's abode thereafter. O tiger among *brahmana*s! After the great festivities, these are the rules for worshipping the text and the narrator. The learned person who has helped the narrator must also be worshipped, but with a lesser quantity of riches. The assembled *brahmana*s must be given food, riches and other things. At the time of the great festivities, there must be singing, dancing and the playing of musical instruments. O sage! From the day following the discourse, the listener will become especially non-attached and must read the Gita spoken by Shiva to Ramachandra.[105] For the sake of peace, an intelligent householder who is a listener must purify himself

---

[103] To place the text on.

[104] *Kalpa* is the duration of Brahma's day. At the end of Brahma's day, when it is Brahma's night, there is a secondary cycle of dissolution/destruction. When night is over, the secondary cycle of creation begins afresh.

[105] The Shiva Gita (Ishvara Gita) from the Kurma Purana.

by offering oblations of *ghee*. O sage! These oblations must be rendered for every *shloka* of Rudra Samhita, or with every *shloka* of *gayatri mantra*, since in truth, the Purana is identical with it.[106] Alternatively, the fundamental *pancharna mantra* for Shiva can be used. A learned person with the capability must offer oblations and give the oblations of *ghee* to *brahmanas*. So as to counter any transgressions that may have been committed in the course of the narration, he must devotedly read, or hear, Shiva's one thousand names. There is no doubt that this will lead to success, with all the fruits being obtained, since there is nothing in the three worlds that is superior to this. Eleven *brahmanas* must be fed honey and *payasam*.[107] For the successful completion of the vow, they must be given *dakshina*.[108] O sage! If he possesses the capacity, he must make a beautiful image, using three *palas* of gold.[109] This can be in the form of a lion and can be engraved with the auspicious *aksharas* of the name of the Purana. Following the norms, a man can write this himself or get it written. Controlling himself, an intelligent person must worship his preceptor with mounts, horses, other objects, *dakshina*, garments, ornaments and fragrances. This brings satisfaction to Shiva. O Shounaka! Through the powers of these donations and the powers of the Purana, he will obtain Shiva's favours and will also be freed from the bonds of a worldly existence. These are the rules for the auspicious Shiva Purana. If these are completed, objects of pleasure and emancipation are bestowed. I have thus told you everything about the illustrious Shiva Purana and its greatness.

[106] That is, *gayatri mantra*. *Gayatri* is a metre, as well as a *mantra*. The first line of *gayatri mantra* is *bhur bhuvah svah*.

[107] A dish made out sweetened milk and rice.

[108] A sacrificial fee. Also the fee rendered to a *guru* after the successful completion of studies.

[109] *Pala* is a measure of weight.

What else do you wish to hear? It bestows everything that is
desired. Among all the Puranas, the illustrious Shiva Purana is
held to be the foremost. It pleases Shiva greatly and counters
the disease of a worldly existence. Indeed, having been born
in this world of the living, if a person performs *dhyana*
on Vishvanatha[110] and listens to his account, extolling his
qualities, such a person crosses this worldly existence. "He is
not affected by any differences on account of the *gunas*. He
manifests himself inside and outside this universe. He is radiant
in his own greatness. He is inside and outside the mind. His
form exists in all words, thoughts and conduct. Shiva is infinite
bliss. I seek refuge with him.'"

This ends the Skanda Purana segment.

---

[110] The lord of the universe, Shiva's name.

Vidyeshvara Samhita

Chapter 8-2(1) (The Sages Describe *Kali Yuga*)

He is auspicious from the beginning to the end. He has no origin. There is no one who is his equal in sentiments. He is the noble one. He is the immortal Isha, without old age. He is the divinity of the *atman*. He possesses five faces. The powerful one brings delight and good conduct to the five elements. Let the inclinations of my mind be immersed in Shankara Ambikesha.[111]

Vyasa said, 'There is a great *kshetra*, a *dharmakshetra*, at the confluence of Ganga and Kalindi.[112] This is the supremely sacred Prayaga, the path to Brahma's world. There were sages who had controlled their *atman*s. They were devoted to the *dharma* of truth. Those immensely fortunate and immensely energetic ones performed a sacrifice there. Hearing that a sacrifice was being held there, Vyasa's disciple, the great sage, Suta, who was supreme among those who recounted the Puranas, went there and saw those Indras among the sages. On seeing that Suta had come, the sages were delighted. Following

[111] Ambikesha (Ambika's lord) is Shiva's name. This is a benedictory *shloka*, not part of the main text.
[112] Kalindi is another name for Yamuna. All the Puranas were originally recounted by Vedavyasa.

the norms, with cheerful minds, they honoured him. Full of humility, they joined their hands in salutation and spoke to him, after having followed the norms and cheerfully praised the great-souled one.'

"O Romaharshana! O omniscient one! Because of your good fortune and the honour shown to you, you know all the Puranas, having received their complete meaning from Vyasa. Thus, you are the receptacle of accounts beings find to be wonderful. Their substance is like jewels, and you are like an ocean, the store of jewels. There is nothing in the past, the present or the future and nothing in the three worlds that is not known to you. It is our good fortune that you have come here to meet us. Your arrival should not be in vain, and you should not leave without doing us a favour. It is true that we have already heard everything, about the auspicious and the inauspicious. Nevertheless, we are not content, and we wish to hear again and again. O Suta! O one with a virtuous inclination! There is one thing that remains to be heard. If you are favourably disposed towards us, please tell us this secret. The terrible *kali yuga* has arrived and men are devoid of everything auspicious. All of them are attracted towards wicked conduct and have turned their faces away from true modes. They are engaged in criticizing others. They desire the possessions of others. Their minds are attracted towards the wives of others. They are engaged in causing violence to others. Their insight is such that those foolish non-believers think that the body is the *atman*. Their intelligence is like that of animals. They hate their mothers and fathers. Wives become their divinities and they are the servants of desire. *Brahmana*s are overtaken by avarice and to earn a living, sell the *Veda*s. All their learning is for the sake of earning wealth and they are deluded and insolent. They have abandoned the tasks of their own *jati*s.[113]

---

[113] A *jati* is the class one has been born into and is different from a *varna*.

They generally deceive others. At the three times of the day, they do not observe *sandhya*. They are devoid of any understanding about the *brahman*. They do not possess compassion. They take themselves to be learned. In their conduct, they have abandoned the vows. They are engaged in agriculture.[114] They are cruel in nature. Their minds are filthy. In that way, all the *kshatriyas* are engaged in giving up their own *dharma*. They associate with the wicked and are engaged in sin. They are addicted to *vyabhichara*. They are not brave and do not like fighting, more interested in running away. They practice the wicked means of subsistence of *shudras*, like resorting to theft. Their minds are the servants of desire. They do not possess knowledge about *shastras* and *astras*.[115] They do not protect cattle and *brahmanas*. They do not protect those who seek refuge. They always seek out opportunities for dalliances with women. They do not follow the virtuous *dharma* of protecting the subjects. They are devoted to objects of pleasure. They are wicked and destroy the subjects. They find delight in causing violence to beings. The *vaishyas* do not follow the *samskaras*.[116] They are engaged in giving up their own *dharma*. They have resorted to evil means so as to earn for themselves and are engaged in malpractices with balances.[117]

[114] As will become clear, everything said here is about *brahmanas* and *brahmanas* are not supposed to engage in agriculture.

[115] The text uses both *astra* and *shastra*. These are both weapons and the words are often used synonymously. However, an *astra* is a weapon that is hurled or released, while a *shastra* is held in the hand.

[116] There are thirteen *samskaras* or sacraments. The list varies a bit. But one list is *vivaha* (marriage), *garbhalambhana* (conception), *pumsavana* (engendering a male child), *simantonnayana* (parting the hair, performed in the 4th month of pregnancy), *jatakarma* (birth rites), *namakarana* (naming), *chudakarma* (tonsure), *annaprashana* (first solid food), *keshanta* (first shaving of the head), *upanayana* (sacred thread), *vidyarambha* (commencement of studies), *samavartana* (graduation) and *antyeshti* (funeral rites).

[117] That is, scales used for weighing.

They are wicked in intelligence and have no devotion towards
gurus, *devas* and *brahmanas*. They do not feed *brahmanas*. In
general, they are misers, with tight fists. Their inclinations are
towards becoming the paramours of women. Addicted to desire,
their minds are filthy. Their minds are overwhelmed by avarice
and delusion, and they are no longer interested in *purta*[118] and
other good deeds. While the *shudras* are also like that, there are
some *shudras* who act like *brahmanas*, assuming radiant forms.
Those foolish ones are interested in giving up their own *dharma*.
To become lords and take away the energy of *brahmanas*, they
practice a lot of austerities. Engaged in pronouncing *mantras*,
they cause the deaths of infants. They worship the *shalagrama*
stone[119] and other objects and are also engaged in offering
oblations. However, their thoughts are contrary. They are
crooked and hate *brahmanas*. Those who are wealthy engage in
wicked deeds. Those who are learned engage in debating. Those
who speak about worship and expound about *dharma* are
themselves the ones who cause subversion of *dharma*. Those who
are insolent seek to become excellent kings. Those who donate
a lot, do this with a great deal of insolence. Taking themselves
to be their own masters, they regard *brahmanas* and others as
servants. Those foolish ones give up their own *dharma*. Wicked
in intelligence, they cause a confusion of *varnas*. They are always
full of great pride and destroy the four *varnas*. Thinking that
they have been born in an extremely good lineage, they bring
about a transformation in the four *varnas*. They are foolish
and indulging in wicked deeds, they destroy all the *varnas*. The
women are generally deviant and disrespectful towards their
husbands. They oppose their fathers-in-law and fearlessly eat
filth. They are addicted to wicked coquettish gestures. They

[118] Civic works, like constructing roads, digging wells and
planting trees.
[119] Stone sacred to Vishnu.

are evil in conduct and overwhelmed by desire. They always indulge in intercourse with their paramours, turning their faces away from their own husbands. The sons are evil and have no devotion towards their mothers and fathers. They always read what should not be read and their bodies are grasped by disease. In this way, the intelligence is destroyed, and they give up their own *dharma*. O Suta! How can they obtain a proper destination in this world or in the next one? This is a thought that always agitates our minds. Indeed, there is no *dharma* that is equal to that of doing a good turn to others. You know about all the means for obtaining success. Therefore, out of your compassion, please tell us what the easiest method is now to destroy this torrent of sins."

Vyasa continued, 'Suta heard these words spoken by the sages who had cleansed their *atman*s. He remembered Shankara in his mind and replied to the sages.'

Chapter 9-2(2) (Greatness of Shiva Purana and Its Components)

Suta said, 'O virtuous ones! You have asked a virtuous question, one that will bring welfare to the three worlds. Out of affection towards you, I will remember my *guru* and answer you. Please listen attentively. The entire essence of Vedanta exists in the excellent Shiva Purana.[120] This saves one from a torrent of sins and yields the supreme objective in the world hereafter. Shiva's supreme fame destroys the sins of *kali*

---

[120] The six schools of *darshana* or philosophy are *nyaya, vaisheshika, samkhya, yoga, mimamsa* and Vedanta. Vedanta means the end of the *Vedas* and refers to the Brahmana, Aranyaka and Upanishad texts.

yuga. O *brahmana*s! It arises and always ensures the obtaining of the four kinds of objectives[121] as fruits. O supreme among *brahmana*s! As soon as one studies the supremely excellent Shiva Purana, one proceeds towards a desirable end. Sins, with the killing of a *brahmana* as the foremost, last only for as long as the Shiva Purana does not arise in this world. The great portents of *kali yuga* fearlessly wander around only as long as the Shiva Purana has not arisen in this world. All the various sacred texts contest each other only as long as the Shiva Purana has not arisen in this world. Shiva's own nature and greatness are difficult to understand only as long as the Shiva Purana has not arisen in this world. Yama's cruel messengers fearlessly wander around only as long as the Shiva Purana has not arisen in this world. All the other Puranas roar in this world only as long as the Shiva Purana has not arisen in this world. All the various *tirtha*s contest each other on earth only as long as the Shiva Purana has not arisen in this world. All the various *mantra*s contest each other on earth only as long as the Shiva Purana has not arisen in this world. All the various *kshetra*s contest each other on earth only as long as the Shiva Purana has not arisen in this world. All the various *pitha*s[122] contest each other on earth only as long as the Shiva Purana has not arisen in this world. All the various kinds of donations contest each other on earth only as long as the Shiva Purana has not arisen in this world. All the various *deva*s contest each other on earth only as long as the Shiva Purana has not arisen in this world. All the various determinations contest each other on earth only as long as the Shiva Purana has not arisen in this world. O *brahmana*s! O excellent sages! I am incapable of describing the fruits of listening to a recital of this Shiva Purana. O unblemished ones!

---

[121] The *purushartha*s.

[122] Literally a seat or pedestal. After Daksha's sacrifice, Sati's various limbs fell down at these *pitha*s and there are temples there.

Nevertheless, I will describe to you a little bit of its greatness, as spoken to me by Vyasa earlier. Focus your minds and listen attentively. Full of devotion, if a person reads a *shloka*, or half a *shloka*, of this Shiva Purana, he is instantly freed from sins. According to capacity, if a person devotedly and attentively reads this Shiva Purana every day, he is spoken of as *jivanmukta*. If a person devotedly worships this Shiva Purana from one day to another day, there is no doubt that he reaps the fruits of undertaking a horse sacrifice. Driven by an ordinary desire, if a person listens to this Shiva Purana from someone other than me, he is freed from sins. If a person bows down to this Shiva Purana from a distance, there is no doubt that he obtains the fruits of worshipping all *devas*. If a person copies down the text of this Shiva Purana himself and gives it to Shiva's devotees, listen to the sacred fruits that he obtains. There are rare fruits obtained by those who study the sacred texts, the *Vedas* and their commentaries. All those fruits are obtained by him. If a person fasts on the day of *chaturdashi* and explains this Shiva Purana in an assembly of Shiva's devotees, he is excellent. He obtains the wonderful fruits obtained from chanting the *gayatri mantra akshara* by *akshara*. He obtains everything desired in this world and progresses towards *nirvana*.[123] Let me tell you about the good merits obtained by a person who fasts and stays awake on the night of *chaturdashi*, reading or hearing it. This is true. At the time of a complete solar eclipse, there are many good merits obtained by a person who donates, wealth equal to his own weight, to *brahmanas*, with Vyasa as the foremost, in all the sacred *tirthas*, Kurukshetra and the others. It is no doubt true that this person[124] reaps all those fruits. *Devas*, with Indra at the forefront, wait to carry out the commands of a person who chants Shiva Purana day and night. If a person

---

[123] The stage of emancipation when everything is extinguished.
[124] The one who reads or hears Shiva Purana.

who performs good deeds constantly reads and hears this Shiva Purana, his good merits are multiplied one crore times. If a person controls himself and reads the illustrious Rudra Samhita, within three days, his *atman* is purified, even if he has killed a *brahmana*. If a person is silent and reads Rudra Samhita thrice every day near Bhairava's image, he obtains everything that he desires. If a person does *pradakshina* of a *vata* or *bilva* tree and reads Rudra Samhita, the sin of killing a *brahmana* is dispelled.[125] Kailasa Samhita is said to be even greater. Its form is that of the *brahman* and it manifests the meaning of *pranava*.[126] O *brahmana*s! Shankara himself knows the entire greatness of Kailasa Samhita. Vyasa knows half and I know half of that. I will tell you a little bit about it. I am incapable of telling you in entirety. When they know it, the minds of people are instantly purified. O *brahmana*s! In this world, I do not see any sin that is not destroyed by Rudra Samhita. It always provides a path. Having churned the ocean of the Upanishads, Shiva happily produced it for Kumara.[127] A person who drinks this nectar becomes immortal. If a person wishes to save himself from the sin of killing a *brahmana* and other sins, he should prepare himself to read this Samhita for a month. He will thus be freed. If a person recites this Samhita, the sins of accepting what should not be accepted, eating what should not be eaten and indulging in prohibited conversation are destroyed. If a person reads this Samhita in Shiva's temple or in a grove of *bilva* trees, the good merits obtained cannot be described in words or even comprehended. If a person devotedly reads this Samhita while

---

[125] *Pradakshina* is more specific than a mere act of circumambulation. This circling or circumambulation has to be done in a specific way, so that the right side (*dakshina*) always faces what is being circled. *Vata* is the fig tree. The *bilva* tree is sacred to Shiva.

[126] AUM.

[127] Skanda, Kartikeya.

feeding *brahmanas* at a *shraddha* ceremony,[128] all his ancestors go to Shambhu's abode. If a person fasts on *chaturdashi* and reads this Samhita under a *bilva* tree, he becomes like Shiva himself and is worshipped by *devas*. The other Samhitas yield everything that is desired. But these two[129] are special because they are full of *vijnana*[130] and his pastimes.'

'Such is the text known as Shiva Purana, as revered as the *Vedas*. It is as revered as the *brahman* and was composed by Shiva. It is said that this Purana originally had twelve extremely sacred Samhitas as its divisions—Vidyeshvara, Rudra, Vainayaka, Uma, Matri, Rudraikadasha, Kailasa, Shatadrudra, Kotirudra, Sahasrakotirudra, Vayaviya and Dharmasamja. O *brahmanas*! I will tell you about the entire enumeration. Listen attentively. Vidyeshvara had 10,000 *shlokas*. Rudra, Vainayaka, Uma and Matri sections of the Purana had 8,000 *shlokas* each. O *brahmanas*! Rudraikadasha had 13,000 *shlokas*. Kailasa had 3,000 *shlokas* and Shatarudra half that number. Kotirudra had 9,000 *shlokas* and the part of the text known as Sahasrakotirudra 11,000 *shlokas*. Vayavaiya had 4,000 and Dharmasamja 12,000. All these divisions aggregate to 100,000 *shlokas* for Shiva Purana. Vyasa abridged this to 24,000 *shlokas*, around one-fourth of the original Shiva Purana, and retained seven Samhitas. At the beginning, the Purana text composed by Shiva had a size that amounted to a hundred crore *shlokas*. However, composed in ancient times, that has long been forgotten. In *dvapara yuga*, Krishna Dvaipayana and other Vedavyases abridged this to 400,000 *shlokas*, segregated

---

[128] Funeral ceremony.

[129] Kailasa Samhita and Rudra Samhita.

[130] The words *jnana* and *vijnana* are often used synonymously and both words mean knowledge. When distinct meanings are intended, *jnana* signifies knowledge obtained from texts and *gurus*, while *vijnana* signifies knowledge obtained through inward contemplation and self-realization.

into eighteen Puranas. Shiva Purana is said to have 24,000
shlokas. These *shlokas*, with the seven Samhitas, are as revered
as the *brahman*. The first Samhita is Vidyeshvara, the second
is known as Rudra. The third is known as Shatarudra and the
fourth is Kotirudra. The fifth is known as Uma and the sixth
is known as Kailasa. The seventh is known as Vayaviya. These
are held to be the seven Samhitas. With these seven Samhitas,
this divine text is known as Shiva Purana. This is equal to the
brahman. It is supreme and bestows the greatest destination. If
a person lovingly reads this entire Shiva Purana, he is spoken of
as *jivanmukta*. Hundreds of other texts, *shruti, smriti,* Puranas,
Itihasa and *agama*,[131] do not deserve to be regarded as even
one sixteenth of Shiva Purana. This unblemished Shiva Purana
was recited by Shiva and later collated and abridged by Vyasa,
Shiva's devotee. It brings benefit to all living beings. It destroys
the three kinds of hardships completely. It bestows everything
auspicious on those who are virtuous. It sings about the *dharma*
that is without any deceit. It expounds the foremost *vijnana*
of Vedanta. The learned, devoid of jealousy, get to know
about the three objectives of human existence.[132] Indeed, Shiva
Purana is the crest of all the virtuous Puranas. It sings about the
supreme, described in the *Veda*s and Vedanta. A person who
lovingly reads it, or hears it, is loved by Shambhu and attains
the supreme destination.'

Chapter 10-2(3) (The Objective and the Means)

Vyasa said, 'Hearing Suta's words, the supreme *rishi*s
replied, "Please make us hear the wonderful Purana,

---

[131] *Agama*s are texts other than the *Veda*s, such as the *tantra* texts.
[132] *Dharma, artha* and *kama*.

which represents the essence of Vedanta." Hearing the words of the sages, Suta was extremely delighted. He remembered Shankara and replied to the excellent sages.'

'Suta said, "O *rishi*s! All of you remember the unblemished Shiva and listen. Shiva Purana, foremost among the Puranas, represents the essence of the *Veda*s. If one sings it lovingly, one obtains the three objectives of devotion, *jnana* and non-attachment. The virtuous have described it as special, constituting what is to be known in the *Veda*s. O *rishi*s! All of you hear this Purana, which has the essence of the *Veda*s. A long time ago, after many *kalpa*s had repeatedly passed and the task of creation in the present *kalpa* presented itself, there was a great dispute among sages from six different lineages. Some said, 'This is superior.' Others held, 'No. That is superior.' When there was this great dispute among them, they went to Brahma, the Dhatri,[133] and asked him about the one without decay. All those eloquent ones humbly joined their hands in salutation and spoke to him. 'You are the Dhatri of the entire universe. You are the cause behind all kinds of causes. Who is the entity who is the most ancient? Who is supreme among the supreme?' Brahma replied, 'He is the one speech withdraws from.[134] He cannot be approached through the mind. He is the one from whom everything, beginning with Brahma, Vishnu and Rudra and including all the elements and the senses, first originated. He is the divinity Mahadeva. He is omniscient and is the lord of the universe. He can only be seen through supreme devotion, not through any other means. Full of great devotion, Rudra, Hari, Hara and the other lords among the gods always wish to see him. What is the need to speak a lot about this? One is emancipated through devotion to Shiva. Devotion to

---

[133] Both Dhatri and Vidhatri are words for the Creator. Dhatri is the one who nurses, while Vidhatri is the one who arranges.

[134] Speech cannot approach (describe) him.

the divinity is because of his favours. It is from his favours that
devotion results. This is like a seed resulting from a shoot and
a shoot resulting from a seed. O *brahmanas*! Therefore, all of
you come to earth to obtain Isha's favours. You must perform
a long sacrifice that lasts for one thousand years. He will be
the divinity who presides over the sacrifice. He is the essence
of the learning in the *Vedas*. It is through Shiva's favours that
the objective and the means can be known.' The sages asked,
'What is the supreme objective? What constitutes the supreme
means? What should a *sadhaka* be like?[135] Please tell us the truth
about this.' Brahma replied, 'Obtaining Shiva as a destination
is the *sadhya*. Serving him is *sadhana*. *Sadhaka* is the person
who obtains his favours so as to be indifferent towards fruits
that are not permanent. The *karma* spoken about in the *Vedas*
must be performed without any pride. The great objective is
obtaining the supreme Isha as a destination, through *salokya*
and all the others, in due order.[136] According to the degree of
devotion, everyone obtains a supreme fruit. There are many
kinds of *sadhana*. Isha has himself spoken about them. I will
briefly tell you about the substance of *sadhana*. Using the ears
to hear about him, using the tongue to chant about him and
using the mind to think about him—these are said to be the
greatest *sadhana*. Maheshvara must be heard about, spoken
about and thought about. The *shruti* texts are proof that this
is the *sadhana* that enables one to proceed towards the *sadhya*.
Resort to this *sadhana* alone and accomplish all objectives.
In this world, anything that is manifest can be seen with the

[135] *Sadhya* is the attainable objective, *sadhana* is the means.
Sadhaka is the person who is using the means to attain the objective.
[136] *Salokya* is the ability to reside with the Lord, *samipya* is
proximity to the Lord, *sarupya* is to be like the Lord in form and
sayujya is identification with the Lord. These are different grades of
emancipation.

eyes. The unmanifest is everywhere. Knowing this, one must strive with the ears. Therefore, one must start with hearing. A learned person hears what emerges from the *guru*'s mouth. After that, an intelligent person strives for the others, chanting and thinking. When all the means are properly perfected, right up to thinking, there is union with Shiva and *salokya* and the others gradually occur, in due order. All ailments are destroyed. After this, one attains supreme bliss. Indeed, the practice is difficult. But subsequently, everything becomes auspicious, right from the beginning.'"'

Chapter 11-2(4) (More on the Means)

' " The sages asked, 'O Brahma! What is the nature of *manana*?[137] What is the nature of *shravana*? How is *kirtana* done? Please describe these accurately.'"'

'"Brahma replied, 'The mind loves reasoning. Worship, *japa*, thinking about Isha's form, sports and names purifies the mind. *Manana* is always obtained through Ishvara's favourable glance. Therefore, among all the *sadhana*s, this is regarded as the most important. Singing what has been heard about his *atman*, using well-articulated lines to speak about Shambhu's qualities, form, pastimes and names, and using even unpolished speech constitute *kirtana*. This is a medium type of *sadhana*. Among the learned, *shravana* is famous in the world, when it is done with a steadfastness that is greater than the attentiveness with which one dallies with women. When one uses every opportunity possible to listen to words that worship the supreme Shiva, this is *shravana*. *Shravana*

[137] *Manana* is thinking, *shravana* is hearing and *kirtana* is chanting.

occurs first, when one associates with virtuous people. After this, *kirtana* of Pashupati becomes firm. But the best of the lot is *manana*. However, all these result through Shankara's benevolent glance.'"'

'Suta said, "O lords among sages! There is an ancient occurrence about the greatness of *sadhana*. For your sake, I will tell you about it. Please listen attentively. In ancient times, my *guru* Vyasa, the son of the sage Parashara, performed austerities on the auspicious banks of Sarasvati. But he was anxious. As he willed, the illustrious Sanatkumara arrived there, astride a radiant *vimana*, and saw my preceptor there. He arose from his *dhyana* and saw Aja's son.[138] Full of great curiosity and agitation, the sage prostrated himself before him. He offered him *arghya*[139] and a seat that was worthy of someone who was the equal of a *deva*. Pleased, the lord spoke to my humble preceptor in words that were deep in meaning. Sanatkumara said, 'O sage! You must meditate on a true object. Shiva can himself be realized and perceived. Without any aides, why are you performing these austerities here, and for what purpose?' Thus addressed by Kumara,[140] the sage stated his wish. 'Through the favours of many like you who have established the path of the *Veda*s for this world, I have lovingly pursued *dharma*, *artha*, *kama* and *moksha*. Thus, I have become a *guru* to everyone. But it is extremely extraordinary that I have still not achieved the *jnana* necessary to strive for emancipation. I am performing austerities for the sake of emancipation, but do not know how that can be brought about.' The illustrious Kumara was thus requested by the sage. O Indras among *brahmana*s! Since he was competent, he told him about the certain means

---

[138] Aja is one without birth and means Brahma.

[139] A guest is offered *arghya* (a gift), *padya* (water to wash the feet), *achamaniya* (water to rinse the mouth) and a seat.

[140] Sanatkumara.

for achieving emancipation. 'Shravana, kirtana and manana of Shambhu are said to be the three best types of sadhana. This is in conformity with the knowledge of the Vedas. Earlier, I too was confused because other methods agitated me. I practiced unwavering austerities on Mount Mandara. As a result of Shiva's command, the illustrious Nandikeshvara[141] arrived there. The illustrious one is full of compassion and is himself the lord of all Ganeshvaras.[142] Out of affection towards me, he told me about the excellent sadhana for achieving emancipation—shravana, kirtana and manana of Shambhu. This is in conformity with the Vedas. Shiva himself told me that these are the three means for emancipation. O brahmana! Therefore, repeatedly perform these three, shravana and the others.' After telling Vyasa this, along with his followers, Vidhatri's son ascended a vimana and returned to his supreme and auspicious abode. I have thus briefly told you and about this supreme and ancient account. The sages asked, 'O Suta! You have spoken about the three means of achieving emancipation, shravana and the others. If a person cannot undertake these three, shravana and the others, what else can free him? Is there any karma that leads to emancipation, even if not undertaken carefully?'"

Chapter 12-2(5) (Greatness of Lingam)

'Suta said, "To cross over the ocean that is samsara, a person who is incapable of following the three means, shravana and the others, should establish Shankara's sign of lingam and worship it every day. For the sake of unlimited wealth, he must always worship the lingam. According to his

---

[141] Nandi, Shiva's companion and attendant.
[142] Ganeshvara is a lord of ganas.

capacity, he must offer objects to it, but without deceiving others. He must serve devotedly, by constructing pavilions, gates, *tirtha*s, *matha*s[143] and *kshetra*s and undertaking festivities. He must devotedly worship garments, fragrances, garlands, incense and lamps. He must offer many kinds of food as *naivedya*, *apupa*s and dishes, with umbrellas, standards, whisks, *chamara*s and other accompaniments.[144] All this royal worship must be offered to the sign of the *lingam*. According to capacity, one must prostrate oneself and perform *pradakshina* and *japa*. Devotedly, one must always perform *avahana* and other virtuous rites.[145] One must worship Shankara's sign of the *lingam* in this way. Even if one gives up *shravana* and the others, one can thus please Shiva and obtain success. Earlier, great people have been emancipated only through worshipping the sign of the *lingam*."'

'The sages asked, "All the large number of *devata*s are worshipped everywhere only in the forms of their images. How is it that Shiva is worshipped everywhere both in his image and as a *lingam*?"'

'Suta replied, "O lords among sages! This is an extremely wonderful and sacred question. About this, the speaker is Mahadeva himself and no other being. I will progressively tell you what Shiva said. I have heard this from the mouth of my *guru*. Shiva alone is described as *nishkala*.[146] He is the form of the *brahman*. Since he also has a *sakala* form, he is both *sakala* and *nishkala*. As *nishkala*, without form, he can be approached as *lingam*. When he is *sakala*, with form, he can be approached in the form of his image. Other divinities are not spoken of as

---

[143] Monastery, place of learning or temple.

[144] *Naivedya* is offering of food, *apupa* is a sweet cake, *chamara* is a whisk made out of yak hair.

[145] *Avahana* means invoking the deity's presence.

[146] Without form. *Sakala* means with a form.

the *brahman*. Therefore, they have *sakala* forms and are not *nishkala*. That is the reason people always worship him in his sign of the *lingam*. The others are not the form of the *brahman* and are never *nishkala*. That is the reason other lords among gods are never worshipped through *nishkala* signs. The other large number of *devata*s are not the forms of the *brahman* and possess *jivatman*s. They are silently worshipped only in *sakala* forms, through their images. Apart from Shankara, the others possess *jivatman*s. Shankara is the *brahman*. In explaining the meaning of *pranava*, it has been established that he is the essence of Vedanta. Earlier, on the slopes of Mount Mandara, Nandikeshvara was asked this by the intelligent sage Sanatkumara, Brahma's son."'

"'Sanatkumara said, 'Other than Shiva, all the other *deva*s are seen to be severally worshipped everywhere in the forms of their images. Shiva alone is seen to be worshipped both as *lingam* and as an image. O fortunate one! Please tell me the virtuous truth about this and awaken my understanding.'"'

"'Nandikeshvara replied, 'It is impossible to answer this question without revealing the truth about the sign of the *brahman*. O unblemished one! Since you are full of devotion, I will tell you what Shiva himself said. Since Shiva's form is that of the *brahman*, he is *nishkala*. Therefore, he is always worshipped as *nishkala lingam*, and this is in conformity with the *Veda*s. Since he possesses both *sakala* and *nishkala* forms, he is also worshipped as *sakala*. The worship of a *sakala* form is also revered in this world. Other than Shiva, all the others possess *jivatman*s. Therefore, they are only worshipped as images, and this is in conformity with the determination of the *Veda*s. Since the others possess their own manifestations, they must only be worshipped in *sakala* forms. Indeed, in the texts, it has been said that Shiva can be seen both as *lingam* and image.'"'

"'Sanatkumara said, 'O immensely fortunate one! You have spoken about the practice of both the *lingam* and the image for Shiva, so as to achieve the supreme objective, and about the worship of images for others. Thus, the supreme sign for this divinity is the manifestation of the *lingam*. O Indra among *yogis*! I wish to hear about the manifestation of the *lingam*.'"

'"Nandikeshvara replied, 'O child! Listen. Out of affection towards you, I will tell you about this supreme objective. In an earlier *kalpa*, it has been heard that the worlds were distressed because of the advent of Mahakala.[147] The great-souled Brahma and Vishnu fought with each other. To destroy their arrogance, Parameshvara displayed himself between them, in the form of a *nishkala* column. He showed them his own form. He showed them his own *lingam* as a sign, with *nishkala* Shiva in that column. For the welfare of the universe, he showed them his own *lingam*. Since then, Ishvara's form as *nishkala lingam* and Shiva's *sakala* image became accepted in the worlds. Other than Shiva, all the other *devas* are only thought of in the forms of their images. The images of *devas* only bestow auspicious objects of pleasure. Shiva's *lingam* and image bestow auspicious objects of pleasure and emancipation.'"

Chapter 13-2(6) (Rivalry between Brahma and Vishnu)

' "Nandikeshvara said, 'O Indra among *yogis*! On one occasion in ancient times, Vishnu was lying down, asleep, with a serpent as a couch. He was surrounded by supreme prosperity and his attendants. At that time, travelling as he willed, Brahma, supreme among those who know about

---

[147] Mahakala is the great Destroyer (Time).

the *brahman*, arrived there. He asked Pundarikaksha,[148] beautiful in all his limbs, who was lying down. "What kind of man are you? Despite seeing me, you are lying down, like an insolent person. O child! Get up and look at me. Your lord has come here. When a person sees that a *guru* who deserves to be worshipped has arrived, if he is so foolish as to act in such an insolent way, *prayashchitta*[149] is recommended for such a hater." Hearing these words, he[150] was filled with rage, but behaved calmly externally. "O child! May all be well with you. Enter and be seated on this seat. Why does your face seem anxious? Why are your eyes agitated?" Brahma replied, "O Vishnu! O child! With the speed of time, an extremely important person like me has arrived. I am the grandfather of the universe. O child! I am your protector." Vishnu said, "O child! Since the entire universe is located inside me, your thoughts are like those of a thief. You originated from a lotus in my navel. You are my son and are speaking in vain." Confused, they argued with each other and sought to establish superiority over the other. "I am the lord. I am superior, not you. I am the lord." Wishing to kill each other, they got ready to fight. As those two immortal and brave ones fought, so did their mounts, the swan and the bird.[151] The followers of Virinchi[152] and Vishnu also fought on either side. Desiring to witness this extraordinary battle, all the different kinds of *deva*s arrived there on their own respective *vimana*s. As they watched, they showered down flowers from the sky. The one with Suparna as his mount angrily released arrows and many kinds of weapons, impossible to withstand,

[148] The lotus-eyed one, Vishnu's name.
[149] Rite of atonement.
[150] Vishnu.
[151] The respective mounts of Brahma and Vishnu (the bird means Garuda). Suparna is Garuda's name.
[152] Brahma.

and struck Brahma on his chest. Angry, Vidhatri also released
them, impossible to withstand, towards Vishnu's chest. There
were arrows that were like the fire and many kinds of weapons.
It was evident that this clash between them was wonderful,
unclear and difficult to grasp. The large number of *deva*s
witnessed and praised it but were also greatly agitated. As
Vishnu suffered, he became extremely enraged. The intelligent
one affixed the Maheshvara weapon and directed it towards
Brahma. Brahma also became extremely angry. He made the
universe tremble, affixed the terrible Pashupata weapon and
directed it towards Vishnu's chest.[153] As these rose into the sky,
it was as if ten thousand suns had arisen. There were thousands
of fierce mouths, and a fearful storm arose. In that terrible clash
between Brahma and Vishnu, these two weapons faced each
other. Such was the battle between Brahma and Vishnu. All the
different types of *deva*s were distressed and greatly agitated. O
son! They spoke to each other, just as agitated *brahmana*s do
when kings fight.'"

'"Creation, preservation and destruction occur through
Bhava's[154] favours. They flow from him, and the wielder of the
trident is the *brahman*. Without his favours and without his
wishes, no one, anywhere, can even split a blade of grass. As a
result of their fear, *deva*s thought that they should go to Shiva's
eternal abode on Mount Kailasa, where Chandrashekhara
resides. They saw Parameshvara's abode, which is in the
shape of Pranava. They prostrated themselves and entered his
residence. They saw the bull among *deva*s seated there, in an
assembly hall and on a pavilion that was inlaid with jewels.
He was resplendent and Uma was with him. His folded right
leg was placed atop his left and his lotus hands were placed on

[153] The Maheshvara weapon and the Pashupata weapon are both
named after Shiva.
[154] Bhava is Shiva's name.

his legs. His large number of *ganas* were all around him and he possessed all the auspicious signs. Fixed in their attention, accomplished women fanned him with whisks. He is praised in the *Vedas* and Ishvara always shows his favours. On seeing Isha, the immortals were content, and their eyes filled with tears. O child! From a distance, those large numbers prostrated themselves like staffs.[155] On seeing them, the lord of *devas* asked his *ganas* to bring them closer. Delighting the *devas*, the divinity who was like a crest jewel among the *devas*, spoke to them. His deep words were full of meaning and were sweet and auspicious.'"'

Chapter 14-2(7) (The Column of Fire)

' ''Ishvara said, 'O children! May all be well with you. Following my commands, I hope that the entire universe is under the subjugation of *devatas* and that everyone is engaged in his own *karma*. O gods! I already knew about the battle between Brahma and Vishnu. Your evident torment is like a speech that has already been made.'"'

'"In this way, Amba's husband, smilingly comforted the gods who had arrived, using words that one would use for children.[156] Ishvara told the assembly of gods that he would go to the place where Hari and Dhatri were fighting. In that

---

[155] *Dandavat*, like a staff (*danda*). This means lying completely prostrate on the ground and is also known as *sashtanga pranama*, *ashta* meaning eight and *anga* meaning limb. Eight of one's limbs must touch the ground. Though the number eight is sometimes interpreted metaphorically, literally, it means two feet, two knees, two hands, the chest and the forehead. These must touch the ground.

[156] This is Nandikeshvara continuing his narration.

assembly, he accordingly instructed hundreds of Ganeshas.[157]
As the supreme Isha prepared to leave, hundreds of musical
instruments were sounded. Ganeshvaras clad themselves in
armour, with many kinds of ornaments and mounts. Ishvara,
Ambika's husband, ascended an auspicious chariot that was in
the shape of Pranava and was marked with the auspicious signs
of five rings. His sons, the ganas and Indra and all the other
gods followed him. There were colourful standards, fans and
whisks made out of yak hair. Flowers were showered down
on the assembly. There was singing and dancing. Honoured
by everyone and accompanied by the supreme goddess,[158]
Pashupati went to the battlefield, along with all the soldiers.
When he saw the two of them fighting, he hid himself inside the
clouds. The sound of the musical instruments stopped and the
voices of the ganas also quietened down. The brave Brahma and
Achyuta[159] wished to kill each other and the Maheshvara and
Pashupata weapons had been released. The blazing weapons
released by Brahma and Vishnu were burning down the three
worlds. Isha saw that it was as if the terrible time of dissolution
had arrived. In their midst, the one who is *nishkala* assumed
the form of an extremely terrible column of fire. Those blazing
weapons were capable of destroying the worlds. However,
in an instant, they fell into the great column of fire that had
manifested itself. This was extraordinary. Those wonderful
weapons were pacified and turned auspicious. They[160] spoke
to each other. 'What is this extraordinary form? This is beyond
all senses. What is this column of fire that has arisen? We must
ascertain its top and bottom.' Those two brave ones were

---

[157] Here, Ganesha or Ganeshvara means lords of *ganas* and not
Vinayaka specifically.
[158] Parvati.
[159] The one without decay, Vishnu's name.
[160] Brahma and Vishnu.

proud of their prowess. Eager to test it out, they decided to leave quickly. 'Let us attempt this together. Neither one of us is capable of finding this out alone.' Saying this, Vishnu assumed the form of a boar and set out to explore the bottom. Brahma assumed the form of a swan and set out to explore the top. Hari penetrated Patala and went even further down.[161] However, he could not find the foundation of the column that was as radiant as the fire. Exhausted in the form of a boar, Hari returned to the former battlefield. O child! Your father, Vidhatri, went up into the sky. He saw a wonderful *ketaki* flower[162] dislodged from above. It was full of great fragrance and had not faded, even though it had been dislodged many years ago. On witnessing what those two were going through, the illustrious Parameshvara had laughed and when he had shaken his head, because of his favours, the excellent *ketaki* flower had been dislodged. 'O lord of flowers![163] Why are you falling? O king of flowers? Who wore you?' 'The top of this column is immeasurable.[164] I have been falling down for a long time and I have now reached the middle. Therefore, I do not see how you can wish to see the top.' 'In the form of a swan, I have reached up to this point and you must do something to serve me.[165] O great friend! For my sake, you must now do what I wish for. With me, you must go to Vishnu's presence. Having gone there, you must tell Achyuta that Dhatri has seen the end of the column.' Saying this, he repeatedly prostrated himself before the *ketaki* blossom. 'The instruction of the

---

[161] Patala is a generic term for the nether regions. But seven separate nether regions are also mentioned—Atala, Vitala, Nitala, Sutala, Talatala, Rasatala and Patala.

[162] Until cursed, the *ketaki* (*pandarnus odoratissimus*) flower used to be on Shiva's head.

[163] Brahma addressed the *ketaki* flower in this way.

[164] The flower is replying.

[165] This is Brahma speaking.

sacred texts is that in a time of calamity, the utterance of a falsehood is praised.'[166] When they reached there, Dhatri saw that Achutya had returned exhausted, his happiness destroyed. Therefore, he danced with joy. Like a eunuch who lies,[167] he spoke words full of deep meaning to Achyuta. 'O Hari! I have seen the top of the column and this *ketaki* flower is a witness. Tell him.' Following Dhatri's words, in his presence, the *ketaki* flower endorsed the false words. Thinking these words to be true, Hari bowed down before Vidhatri. Using the prescribed sixteen forms of *upachara*, he worshipped him.[168] Thereafter, so as to chastise Vidhatri, who had practiced deceit, Ishvara himself assumed a form and emerged from that *lingam* made out of fire. Seeing the lord arise, he trembled again and clasped his feet with his hands.[169] 'Your form has no beginning and no end. It is because of our deluded intelligence and our desires that we thought otherwise. You are *sattva* and you are the source of compassion. Please show us your favours and pardon us our sin. Indeed, this must have been caused by your pastimes.' Ishvara replied, 'O child! O Hari! I am pleased with you. Despite hankering after lordship, you have not deviated from true words. Therefore, I am telling you that among people, you will be treated on an equal footing as me and will receive the

[166] This need not be within quotes. But it is natural to presume this is what Brahma said.

[167] Presumably to a woman.

[168] It is recommended that sixteen objects (*shodasha upachara*) should be used for worship. The list varies but will typically include some combination of five *amritas* (ghee, milk, curd, molasses honey), five objects from a cow, five jewels, five kinds of leaves, seven kinds of clay, seven kinds of grain, seven types of minerals, eight types of gifts (*padya, achamaniya*, seat, garments, flowers and so on), five *upacharas* (fragrances, flowers, incense, lamp, *naivedya*) and so on. In some specific instances, sixty-four kinds of *upachara* are mentioned.

[169] As the next sentence will make clear, this is a reference to Vishnu.

same kind of worship. From now on, you will have your own separate *kshetra*, the establishment of your own image, your own festivities and your own worship.' Thus, in ancient times, the divinity was pleased at Hari's adherence to the truth and while the large number of *deva*s looked on, granted him an equal status."'

Chapter 15-2(8) (The Humbling of Brahma)

❝❝Nandikeshvara said, 'Mahadeva then created an extraordinary being from the middle of his own eyebrows. This was Bhairava, designed to destroy Brahma's pride. In that arena, he prostrated himself before his lord, Shiva, and asked, "O lord! What should I do? Please command me quickly." "O child! This Vidhatri is himself the first divinity in this universe. There is no doubt that you should worship him with your swift and sharp sword." With one hand, he[170] seized the tuft of hair on the fifth head[171] that had insolently uttered those false words. As he got ready to sever this head, the sparkling sword shook in his hands. Your father trembled like the leaf of a plantain tree or a creeper in the wind. His excellent garments and ornaments were scattered. His upper garment was loosened. His hair was dishevelled. He fell down at Bhairava's lotus feet. O son! Achyuta saw the state Vidhatri was in. Full of compassion, he fell down at the lotus feet of our master and sprinkled them with his tears. Like a child addressing his own father in faltering words, he joined his hands in salutation and spoke. Achyuta said, "O Isha! A long time ago, it is through your efforts that he got these five heads as a symbol. Therefore,

---

[170] Bhairava.
[171] Originally, Brahma possessed five heads.

you should pardon him now. Please show him your favours
and restrain your rage towards Vidhatri." Thus entreated by
Achyuta, in the presence of the large number of gods, Isha was
pacified. He asked Bhairava to refrain from punishing Brahma.
After this, the divinity addressed the deceitful Vidhatri, who
had bent down his shoulder. "O Brahma! Desiring worship
and lordship, you resorted to deceit. From now on, you will
not be worshipped in the worlds. Nor will you have your own
place, your own festivals and other things." Brahma replied, "O
lord! O great power! Please show me your favours. O one who
bestows boons! I think that this saving of my head is a boon. O
illustrious one! O friend! O origin of the universe! I prostrate
myself before you. You are the one who tolerates all kinds of
sins. O Shambhu! O one who wields the mountain as a bow!"
Ishvara said, "If there is no king, there will be fear and this entire
universe will be destroyed. O Aja! O child! Therefore, you will
bear the burden of chastising the worlds with your staff. I will
also bestow another boon on you, one that is extremely difficult
to obtain. Accept it. In all sacred ceremonies, homes and
sacrifices, you will be the *guru*. Even if a sacrifice is completed
with all the complements and *dakshina*, without you, it will be
futile." After this, the divinity addressed the deceitful *ketaki*,
guilty of bearing false witness. "O *ketaki*! You are deceitful.
Go far away. From now on, I will no longer regard you as a
beloved flower with which I can be worshipped." When the
divinity said this, all the different *deva*s repulsed it and banished
it from their presence. *Ketaki* replied, "O protector! I prostrate
myself before you. Because of your command, my birth will be
rendered futile. O father! You should pardon me my sin and
make my existence successful. When one remembers you, sins
committed knowingly or unknowingly are destroyed. Now that
I have seen you, how can the sin of uttering a falsehood remain
with me?" In the midst of the assembly, the illustrious one was
praised in this way by the *ketaki* flower, which prostrated itself.

Ishvara said, "Since I speak the truth, it is not appropriate that I should wear you. However, my followers will wear you and therefore, your birth will not be unsuccessful. You can also be placed in any canopies that are raised above me." In this way, the illustrious one showed his favours to the *ketaki* flower, Vidhatri and Madhava.[172] Praised by all the *devas*, he was radiant in the midst of that assemblyhall.'"

Chapter 16-2(9) (The *Lingam* and Ishatva)

" "Nandikeshvara said, 'Meanwhile, Vidhatri and Madhava still stood there, prostrating themselves before the lord. Joining their hands in salutation, they stood there silently, on the left and on the right. They instated the divinity, along with his family, on an excellent seat. They worshipped him with sacred and auspicious personal objects. Personal objects should be known as those that last for a short or long while—necklaces, anklets, bracelets, diadems, jewels, earrings, sacrificial threads, upper garments, garlands, silken garlands, rings for the fingers, flowers, betel leaves, camphor, sandalwood, unguents made of aloe, incense, lamps, white parasols, fans, standards, whisks made out of yak hair and other divine objects whose greatness cannot be thought of or spoken about. All of those are appropriate for the lord. Pashupati must be worshipped with these, and ordinary animals cannot obtain them.[173] O *brahmana*! Everything excellent is worthy of being

---

[172] Vishnu.

[173] Since Shiva is Pashupati (lord of animals), there is a play on words, using the word *pashu*. While we have translated this as ordinary animal, in this context, it means all ordinary beings, human or animal.

offered to the lord. Isha wished to establish an order in which
all these objects should be offered. Therefore, following his
desired order, he separately handed them over to those present
in that assembly. When these objects were accepted, there was
a great tumult there. In ancient times, Brahma and Vishnu were
the ones who worshipped Shankara first. While they stood
there and bowed there, the one who enhances devotion was
pleased and spoke to them, smilingly.'"'

"'Ishvara said, 'O children! I am pleased with the way you
have worshipped me today, on this great day. From now on, this
day will become even more sacred. This *tithi* will be famous as
Shiva Ratri and will be loved by me.[174] If a person worships the
sign of my *lingam* on this day, he effectively worships the being
who is responsible for the creation, preservation and destruction
of the universe. Without any deception, to the best of his strength,
a person must properly worship me, conquering his senses and
fasting through day and night on Shiva Ratri. The fruits that are
obtained by constantly worshipping me for an entire year are
instantly obtained as fruits by worshipping me on Shiva Ratri.
This is the period when my *dharma* is increased, just as the tide
in the ocean when the moon rises. This is the day on which my
sacred temple should be established, and festivities undertaken.
O children! In ancient times, the day when I manifested myself
in *sakala* form as a column of fire was the day on which Ardra

---

[174] Every *chaturdashi tithi* of *krishna paksha* (the dark lunar
fortnight) is Shiva Ratri (the night of Shiva). Out of these twelve
Shiva Ratris, the one in the month of Phalguna (February/March) is
special and is known as Maha Shiva Ratri (the great Shiva Ratri).
The twelve months are Vaishakha (April/May), Jyeshtha (May/
June), Ashadha (June/July), Shravana (July/August), Bhadrapada/
Bhadra (August/September), Ashvina (September/October), Kartika
(October/November), Margashirsha (November/December), Pousha
(December/January), Magha (January/February), Phalguna and
Chaitra (March/April).

nakshatra was in the ascendant in the month of Margashirsha.[175] If a person sees me and Uma when Ardra is in the ascendant in Margashirsha, he becomes my friend. If he worships my sign of the *lingam*, I love him more than Guha.[176] On that auspicious day, the mere act of seeing me brings sufficient fruits. Through worshipping me, the fruits obtained cannot be adequately expressed in words. That apart, in the field of battle, I showed myself in the form of a *lingam*. Since I stretched myself out in the form of a *lingam*, that place will be known as Lingasthana.[177] This column is without a beginning and without an end. O sons! However, so that the universe can see it and worship it, it will become minute.[178] This *lingam* will bestow objects of pleasure. It is the means for enjoying objects of pleasure and emancipation. Seeing or touching it, or meditating on it, will free beings from the cycle of birth. The *lingam* that arose resembled a mountain of fire. From now on, it will be known as Arunachala.[179] There will be many other greater *tirtha*s there. Residing or dying there will ensure emancipation for beings. Chariot festivals and other auspicious activities by all the people who dwell there, donations, oblations and *japa*, will lead to fruits that become one crore times more. Among all my *kshetra*s, this will be the greatest *kshetra*. As soon as embodied beings remember me here, they will be emancipated. This extremely beautiful *kshetra* will therefore be the greatest. This will be full of everything

[175] The *nakshatra*s aren't quite stars. They can be constellations too. There are twenty-seven *nakshatra*s.
[176] That is, Kartikeya.
[177] Place of the *lingam*.
[178] *Anu* has been translated as minute.
[179] There is a temple to Shiva (Annamalaiyar) in Tiruvannamalai district, Tamil Nadu. This is on Mount Arunachala. Arunachala means red mountain, and this (in Tamil Nadu) is referred to as the Kailasa of the south. But there is also a Mount Aruna (Arunachala) to the west of Kailasa.

fortunate. This auspicious place will bestow every kind of emancipation. Worshipping me, Ishvara, there in my sign of the *lingam* will bring the fruits of five kinds of emancipation— *salokya, samipya, sarupya, sarshti* and *sayujya*.[180] May all of you quickly accomplish your desires."'"

'"Nandikeshvara continued, 'Thus, the illustrious one showed his favours to the humble Vidhatri and Madhava. When they had fought against each other earlier, their respective soldiers had died. He used his own powers and revived them through showers of *amrita*. So as to dispel their foolish enmity, he spoke to them again. "My own form is of two types, *sakala* and *nishkala*. Since no one else possesses these two forms, no one else is Ishvara. O sons! I first showed myself as a column that has no form and later, in this form. I have spoken about my *nishkala* form as the *brahman* and my *sakala* form as Isha. These two forms exist only in me and not in anyone else. Therefore, no one else, not even you two, can ever claim to be Isha. Though this is extremely surprising, it is because you were enveloped in ignorance that you took yourselves to be Isha. I arose from the ground there so that I could destroy your sense of ego. Hence, cast aside your pride and fix your mind on me, as Isha. It is through my favours that everything in the worlds is manifest. What has been stated by a *guru* has repeatedly been cited as proof. It is out of my affection towards you that I am revealing this mystery about the *brahman*. I am the supreme *brahman*. My own nature is both *sakala* and *nishkala*. It is to show my favours that I assume the forms of the *brahman* and Isha. O Brahma! O Keshava![181] O sons! When I am great and cause greatness, I am the *brahman*. My *atman* is impartial and pervasive. There is no doubt that all other beings do not possess

---

[180] *Sarshti* has not been mentioned before. It means prosperity that is equal to that of the Lord's.
[181] Vishnu.

this *atman*.[182] It is out of my favours that, at the beginning, I created the universe out of the lotus. Since I am Isha, all these activities flow out from me and not from anyone else. To make my nature as the *nishkala brahman* understood, I presented myself in the form of the *lingam*. After that, to make my form as Isha known, I manifested myself in this form. This was the result of my form as Isha and should immediately be recognized as my being Isha.[183] This *sakala* form, which instantly materialized, should be known as me being Isha. The *nishkala* column signifies me being the *brahman*. My *lingam* is my symbol and sign. O sons! The two of you will worship it every day. This represents my *atman* and will always ensure that people are brought to my presence. This *lingam* is no different from me and must always be greatly worshipped. O sons! Wherever a *lingam* like this is established, I am present there. If a *lingam* is established, the fruit is one of similarity with me.[184] If a second *lingam* is established there, the fruit is one of union with me.[185] The establishment of the *lingam* is important, its nature is of minor importance.[186] It becomes a *kshetra* when one thinks of the *lingam* and the signs are present everywhere.""'"

Chapter 17-2(10) (Aumkara *Mantra*)

'Brahma and Vishnu said, "O lord! Beginning with creation, please tell us about the signs of the five things that have to be done."'

[182] They possess *jivatmans*, but they are not the *paramatman*.
[183] The column was the *nishkala* form and the *lingam* was the *sakala* form.
[184] That is, *sarupya*.
[185] That is, *sayujya*.
[186] Probably meaning the material with which the *lingam* is made.

'Shiva replied, "Out of compassion towards you, I will tell you and make you understand about the five secret things that I do. O ones without decay! Creation, preservation, destruction, disappearance and showing favours—these are the five things that I always accomplish. Creation of the world is *sarga*. Its establishment is known as *stithi*. *Samhara* is annihilation. *Tirobhava* is concealment. Through *anugraha* or favours, I bestow emancipation. These five are my tasks. But like a shadow that silently stands near a gate, they are carried out through others. Creation and the others are carried out for the sake of expansion and contraction of the world, while the fifth ensures emancipation. But they are all firmly established in me as a cause. Those who are my people can see these five in the elements— creation in the earth, preservation in the water, destruction in the fire, concealment in the wind and the showing of favours in the firmament. Everything originates in the earth. Because of water, everything flourishes. Everything is afflicted by the fire. Everything is carried away by the wind. Every kind of favour is shown by the firmament. Those who are learned should know this. To carry out these five tasks, I possess five faces. Four faces are in four directions and the fifth is in their middle. O sons! Because of your austerities, you have received two of the tasks— creation and preservation. Since you approached me and since I love you greatly, out of affection, I have granted these to you. In that way, Rudra and Mahesha performed the two subsequent tasks.[187] No one else is capable of taking up what is known as *anugraha*. Through the passage of time, the two of you have forgotten about the pre-assigned tasks decided earlier. Unlike that, Rudra and Mahesha have not forgotten their tasks. I have granted them a position that is equal to mine in form, attire, tasks, mount, seat, weapons and everything else. They undertake those tasks for me. O children! Your foolishness arose because you stopped

---

[187] Destruction and concealment respectively.

meditating on me. If you had retained the knowledge, you would not have the pride that you yourselves were Mahesha. From now on, to obtain the *jnana*, you will perform *japa* of the *mantra* known as Aumkara. For those who are my own, it also destroys pride. I have instructed you about my *mantra* of Aumkara, which is pervasive in its auspiciousness. Aumkara first originated from my mouth and develops understanding about me. It is the speech, and I am the one spoken about. This *mantra* is like my *atman*. By remembering it, one always remembers me. 'A' emerged first from the mouth towards the north, 'U' from the mouth towards the west, 'M' from the mouth towards the south and the *bindu* from the mouth towards the east. The *nada* emerged from the mouth in the middle and all five combined to become one.[188] Let me say it again. They combined to become a single *akshara*. It should be known that everything that originates has a *nama* and a *rupa*.[189] They are pervaded by this *mantra*, which also signifies Shiva and Shakti. To make one understand about the *sakala* form, the five *akshara*s were born after that, with 'NA' and others following 'AA' and others in due order.[190] From these five *akshara*s, the five types of Matrikas originated.[191] Gayatri *mantra*, with the three lines, also emerged from the head and the four faces.[192] All the *Veda*s and crores of *mantra*s originated from

[188] A + U + M = AUM or Aumkara. *Bindu* (dot) is the nasal sound and *nada* is the overall sound.

[189] Respectively name and form.

[190] This means AUM NAMAH SHIVAAYA, with the five *akshara*s of NA + MAH + SHI + VAA + YA. Given the way the text states it, SHIVAAYA NAMAH AUM is probably meant.

[191] Matrikas are divine mothers. The usual list of Matrikas has eight: Brahmi, Maheshvari, Chandi, Varahi, Vaishnavi, Koumari, Chamunda and Roudri. But this list is not standardized.

[192] Gayatri/Savitri *mantra*, from the *Rig Veda*, has three lines (*pada*). *Gayatri mantra* is usually written as *bhur bhuvah svah, tat savitur vareniyam, bhargodevasya dhimahi, dhiyo yo nah prachodayat*. But the *mantra* actually starts with *tat savitur vareniyam*. Hence, three lines.

this. These *mantras* lead to various kinds of success. But every kind of success is obtained through the single *mantra*.[193] Objects of pleasure and emancipation are obtained. All these *mantras* are royal and auspicious and directly yield objects of pleasure."

'Nandikeshvara continued, "Along with Ambika, he again assumed the role of their *guru*. As they faced the north, he gently placed his lotus hands on their heads and taught them the supreme *mantra*. They uttered it thrice and in due order, received the *mantra*, *yantra* and *tantra*.[194] The two disciples offered themselves up as *dakshina*.[195] They clasped their hands together. Standing near the preceptor of the universe, they spoke to him. Brahma and Achyuta said, 'We prostrate ourselves before the one who is *nishkala* and without form. We prostrate ourselves before the one whose energy is *nishkala*. We prostrate ourselves before the lord of everything. We prostrate ourselves before the one who is in all *atmans*. We prostrate ourselves before the one who is spoken of as Pranava. We prostrate ourselves before the one whose symbol is Pranava. We prostrate ourselves before the one who undertakes creation and the other activities. We prostrate ourselves before the one who has five faces. We prostrate ourselves before the one whose five forms are the *brahman*. We prostrate ourselves before the one who undertakes the five kinds of activities. Your *atman* is the *brahman*. You are infinite in your qualities and potencies. You possess *sakala* and *nishkala* forms. We prostrate ourselves before Shambhu, the *guru*.' In this way, Brahma and Vishnu bowed down before the *guru*. Ishvara replied, 'O children! You have been shown and told everything. As instructed by the goddess, you will perform

---

[193] This could mean Aumkara, but probably means Namah Shivaaya.

[194] *Yantra* is a mystical diagram, *tantra* is a secret ritual.

[195] While *dakshina* is a sacrificial fee, it is also the fee given by a *shishya* to a *guru* after the successful completion of studies.

japa with the Pranava *mantra*. It is identical with me. Your *jnana* will be extremely stable. All your fortune will be eternal. When *japa* is performed on *chaturdashi*, with Ardra in the ascendant, nothing will be destroyed. If this is done when Surya transits Ardra, the good merits will be one crore times more. In so far as worship and the offering of oblations are concerned, the last quarter of Mrigashirsha *nakshatra* and the first quarter of Punarvasu *nakshatra* should be known to be the same as Ardra *nakshatra*.[196] The *nakshatra* must be seen at dawn and within a period of three *muhurtas*[197] after dawn. It should be accepted that *chaturdashi* continues up to midnight. The first part of the night and its opposite are praised.[198] Worship of the sign of the *lingam* and worship without a *lingam* are both excellent. However, for those who desire emancipation, worship without the sign of the *lingam* is superior. Others will use and themselves establish the sign of the *lingam*, using Aumkara *mantra* and the *mantra* with five *akshara*s, offering excellent articles of worship. If they worship with *upachara*,[199] they will easily obtain excellent destinations.' Having instructed the two disciples in this way, Shiva vanished from the spot."'

Chapter 18-2(11) (Worshipping the *Lingam*)

'The sages asked, "How must the *lingam* be established and what are its indications? What is the right method of worshipping it, the time and the place?"'

---

[196] Mrigashira *nakshatra* immediately precedes Ardra and Punarvasu *nakshatra* immediately follows Ardra.

[197] A *muhurta* is equal to 48 minutes.

[198] That is, dusk and dawn.

[199] Offering.

'Suta replied, "To make you understand, I will tell you everything. Please listen attentively. The time must be auspicious and favourable, and the place must be a sacred *tirtha* or the bank of a river, as desired. But wherever the *lingam* is established, it must be worshipped every day. As one wishes, it can be made out of earth, water or fire. If the *lingam* possesses the auspicious signs mentioned, then the worship leads to fruits. If it possesses all the auspicious signs, then the worship leads to instant fruits. If the *lingam* is moved around, it should be subtle. If it is stationary, it can be large. Possessing the signs, it must be placed on an auspicious seat that has been devised. The seat can be circular, with four faces, or in the form of a triangle. With such a base for the *lingam*, great fruits are obtained. If the seat is shaped like a couch in the middle, few fruits are obtained. At first, the *lingam*s were made out of clay or rock. Later, they were made of iron and other materials. If the *lingam* is stationary, a seat made out of the same material is praised. Even if the *lingam* is moved around, this is the case, with the exception of the one created by Bana.[200] An excellent *lingam* is one which measures a span that equals twelve fingers of the devotee. If it is shorter, the fruits are less. If it is longer, no harm is done. If a moveable *lingam* is shorter than twelve fingers of the devotee by the length of one finger, there is no harm either. In the beginning, a *vimana*[201] shall be constructed, with *deva*s and *gana*s represented. This should be placed in a firm *garbha-griha*,[202] which is as beautiful as a mirror. This will be adorned with jewels, the most important of which are the

---

[200] Banasura (the *asura* Bana) was Shiva's devotee. He worshipped a *rasa-lingam/parada-lingam* (made out of mercury), constructed for him by Vishvakarma, the architect of the gods.

[201] In this context, meaning a housing for the *lingam*. For large *lingam*s, this will naturally be a temple.

[202] The sanctum sanctorum of the housing.

nine jewels—blue sapphire, ruby, cat's eye, yellow sapphire,²⁰³ emerald, pearl, coral, hessonite and diamond. These are the nine jewels and with the seat, the *lingam* must be placed in the midst of these great objects. Starting with Sadyojata, in due order, the *lingam* must be worshipped in five different places.²⁰⁴ Many kinds of oblations must be offered into the fire, also for Uma and other members of his family. The *guru* and the *acharya* must be worshipped with wealth. Relatives must be given whatever they wish for. Those who seek wealth must be given whatever mobile or immobile objects they desire. All sentient and insentient beings must be attentively satisfied. The place must be filled with gold and sparkling jewels. Pronouncing mantras for Sadyojata and the *brahman*, one must perform *dhyana* on the supreme and auspicious divinity. The great *mantra* of Aumkara, along with its *nada*, must be uttered. The *lingam* will then be placed on the seat for the *lingam* and the two joined together. When the *lingam* and the seat are brought

---

²⁰³ Yellow sapphire is mentioned in usual lists of nine jewels (*navagraha*). But while the text mentions the names of the other eight jewels, it does not mention yellow sapphire. Instead, it uses the word *shyamam*, which means dark or blue-black. There is no jewel with this name. But Shyama was also the name for Thailand. So, this might have been a term for yellow sapphires that came from Thailand. It is also possible that *shyamam* means onyx, though this is not normally listed as one of the nine jewels.

²⁰⁴ Shiva has had several manifestations. Five of these are Sadyojata (linked with earth), Vamadeva (linked with water), Tatpurusha (linked with wind), Aghora (linked with intellect) and Ishana (linked with the *jivatman*). One must start with Sadyojata and worship all five. This must be done in five places—fire (as oblations to *deva*s), the *guru* (representing *rishi*s), relatives (representing ancestors), guests (representing humans) and other beings. A householder must perform five great sacrifices (*pancha mahayajna*) every day—honouring *deva*s, honouring *rishi*s, honouring ancestors, honouring humans and honouring animals/birds. In the hierarchy of teachers, *guru* is inferior to *acharya*.

together, they must be joined with material that makes the union permanent. When the sign of the *lingam* is established in this way, it is extremely auspicious. For the sake of a festival, the sign of the *lingam* can be taken outside, uttering the *mantra* with five *akshara*s. The *lingam* must be accepted from *guru*s, or it must be one that has been worshipped by virtuous people. When the sign of the *lingam* that is worshipped is like that, it bestows a destination with Shiva. Then again, the *lingam* is said to be of two types—mobile and stationary.[205] Trees and creepers are spoken of as stationary *lingam*s. Worms, insects and other things are spoken of as mobile *lingam*s. The stationary must be served, and the mobile must be offered oblations. The learned say that cheerfully tending to these with love is like worshipping Shiva. Amba is everywhere in the seat and the eternal Shiva is everywhere in the *lingam*. Just as Shankara is established with the goddess Uma on his lap, in that way, the seat is established, always holding up the *lingam*. Thus established, with *upachara*, the great *lingam* must be worshipped. The daily worship and use of standards and other things will depend on one's capacity. Thus established, the *lingam* directly bestows a destination with Shiva. Or the *lingam* can also be worshipped with the sixteen kinds of *upachara*. If one worships it in the proper way, one gradually moves towards a destination with Shiva. These are—*avahana, asana, arghya, padya, anga-achamana, abhyanga-snana, vastra, gandha, pushpa, dhupa, dipa, nivedana, niranjana, tambula, namaskara* and *visarjana*.[206] Alternatively, one can follow the

[205] Meaning, Shiva is everywhere.

[206] This is one possible listing of the sixteen kinds of *upachara*. They respectively mean invocation, seat, gift, water for washing the feet, bathing the limbs, smearing the limbs with oil, garments, fragrances, flowers, incense, lamps, offerings of food (the food is known as *naivedya*, *nivedana* is the act of offering), offering lamps (*niranjana* means spotless), betel leaves, prostrating oneself and releasing the deity.

norms and offer *arghya* and *naivedya*.[207] If *abhisheka*,[208] *naivedya*, *namaskara* and offering of oblations is always done, according to one's capacity, this gradually bestows a destination with Shiva. Depending on where, one can offer the *upachara* to a *lingam* established earlier by a human, a *rishi* or a *deva*, or to one that is Svayambhu.[209] With worship and offerings, some fruits will be obtained. After *pradakshina* and *namaskara*, one gradually proceeds to a destination with Shiva. Shiva is obtained as soon as one sees the *lingam* and follows the rituals. There are fruits if the devotee makes a *lingam* out of clay, cow dung, flowers, *karavira*,[210] fruits, molasses, butter, ashes or cooked food—as one desires, and worships it according to the rules. Some have said that Shiva can be worshipped on one's thumb. In such kinds of tasks connected with a *lingam*, there are no prohibitions. According to the qualities of the effort made, Shiva bestows fruits everywhere. Alternatively, one can donate a *lingam* or give the money required to make a *lingam*. Anything devotedly given to a devotee of Shiva's bestows a destination with Shiva."'

'"Alternatively, every day, one can perform *japa* with the Pranava *mantra* ten thousand times. It should be known that chanting Pranava *mantra* one thousand times, at the time of the two *sandhyas*, takes one to Shiva's abode. When one performs *japa*, if one ends with Aumkara, this purifies the mind. When one is in *samadhi*,[211] the chanting must only be done in one's mind. At all other times, it can be pronounced. *Bindu* and

---

[207] One need not offer all sixteen.

[208] Sprinkling the deity with water, a ceremonial bath.

[209] A Svayambhu *lingam* manifests itself on its own, without anyone having established it.

[210] *Karavira* is oleander (*nerium odorum*). This probably means the fruit, not the flower.

[211] *Yoga* has eight elements—*yama* (restraint), *niyama* (rituals), *asana* (posture), *pranayama* (breathing), *pratyahara* (withdrawal), *dharana* (retention), *dhyana* (meditation) and *samadhi* (liberation or deep meditation). That's the reason the expression *ashtanga* (eight-formed) *yoga* is used.

nada are known to be as effective as Pranava. Therefore, one must always lovingly perform *japa*, using the *mantra* with five *aksharas*. During the two *sandhyas*, if this is done one thousand times, this bestows Shiva's region. When this is done by a *brahmana* and starts with Pranava, it is special. If one receives the *mantra* from a *guru*, with the proper *diksha*, one obtains fruits. Bathing at the time of Kumbha,[212] receiving a *mantra* through *diksha*, performing *nyasa* of the Matrikas,[213] a *brahmana* who is pure in his *atman* and a *guru* who possesses knowledge—these are special. *Brahmanas* should start[214] with '*namah*'. Others should end with '*namah*'. Following the norms, some women can end with '*namah*'. Some say that *brahmana* women should start with '*namah*'. Performing *japa* five crore times makes one Sadashiva's equal. If one utters it one crore, two crore, three crore or four crore times, one reaches the abode of Brahma and the others. *Japa* can be performed with the entire *akshara* one hundred thousand times or with the separate *aksharas* one hundred thousand times.[215] If one pronounces the *akshara* one hundred thousand times, it should be known that this yields Shiva's abode. If a person performs *japa* with the *mantra* one thousand times every day and continues with this one thousand for one thousand days,

---

[212] Kumbha *rashi* is the zodiac sign of Aquarius. Traditionally, bathing at a *tirtha* is auspicious when Jupiter (Brihaspati), the Sun (Surya) and the Moon (Chandra) transit through specific signs of the Zodiac. The text probably means that the Sun should transit through Kumbha.

[213] *Nyasa* means to place. *Anga-nyasa* is the mental appropriation (*nyasa*) of different limbs of the body (*anga*) to different divinities. *Kara-nyasa* is similarly done to different parts of the hand (*kara*). This is an act of purification. *Nyasa* can also mean the placement of Matrikas in different parts of a mystical diagram (*yantra*).

[214] Pronouncement of a *mantra*.

[215] Probably meaning AUM Namah Shivaaya as a whole, or AUM, Namah and Shivaaya separately.

he obtains success in whatever he wishes. He must always feed *brahmanas*. In the morning, a *brahmana* must always perform *japa* with the Gayatri *mantra* one thousand and eight times. He will then gradually attain Shiva's abode. Observing the rules, he must perform *japa* with the *mantras* and *suktas*[216] of the *Vedas*. The *dasharna mantra*[217] must be chanted ninety-nine times, nine hundred times, or nine thousand and nine hundred times. It should be known that following the *Vedas* takes one to Shiva's abode. There are many other *mantras*, with other *aksharas*. One should perform *japa* with these one hundred thousand times. If a *mantra* consists only of a single *akshara*, one should perform *japa* with that *akshara* one crore times. After this, one must devotedly perform *japa* one thousand times. If one does this, according to one's capacity, one gradually obtains a destination with Shiva. Until death approaches, one must always chant a *mantra* that brings him pleasure. If one performs *japa* with 'AUM' one thousand times, because of Shiva's command, one obtains everything one wishes for. If he constructs a garden full of flowers or a tank for Shiva, if he does some cleaning for Shiva, if he does anything for Shiva, he obtains a destination with Shiva. One must always devotedly reside in Shiva's *kshetra*. This bestows emancipation on everyone, sentient or insentient. It confers liberation. Therefore, until he dies, a learned person must reside in Shiva's *kshetra*. If the *lingam* has been constructed by a human, it should be known that the region up to a distance of one hundred *hastas* from it is sacred.[218] Like that, if the *lingam*

---

[216] *Sukta* is a hymn.

[217] A *mantra* with ten *aksharas*. This probably means AUM Namah Bhagavate Rudraaya.

[218] Measures of distance are not standardized. *Hasta* is the length of a hand, *aratni* is the length of an elbow, that is, a cubit. *Dhanus* is the length of a bow, usually given as four *hastas*.

has been constructed by a *rishi*, the region up to a distance of
one thousand *aratni*s from it is sacred. If the *lingam* has been
constructed by a *deva*, it should be known that the region up
to one thousand *aratni*s from it is sacred. If it is a Svayambhu
lingam, the region up to one thousand *dhanuse*s is sacred.
Following Shiva's words, tanks, wells and ponds located in this
sacred *tirtha* should be known to be equal to Shiva Ganga.[219] By
bathing, donating or performing *japa* there, one goes to Shiva's
abode. Until one dies, one must seek refuge in Shiva's *kshetra*.
The offering of *pinda*[220] on the tenth day after cremation, the
monthly offering of *pinda* and the annual offering of *pinda*
should be done in a *kshetra* that is Shiva's *kshetra*. One is
then freed from all sins and instantly obtains Shiva's abode. If
one resides in such a place for seven nights, five nights, three
nights or even one night, one gradually obtains Shiva's abode.
Depending on one's own *varna*, qualities and conduct, a man
obtains worlds. However, devotion enables a man to rise above
his *varna* and obtain fruits that are disproportionately more.
Anything done with a particular desire in mind, instantly
bears fruits. Anything done without any desire in the mind,
yields a destination with Shiva himself. At the three times of
a day, morning, midday and evening, the rites must duly be
performed. One should know that rites in the morning are
ordained, those at midday are for the attainment of desires
and those done in the evening are for the sake of pacification.
This is also true of rites undertaken at night. The period of
night is divided into *yama*s and the two *yama*s in the middle
are known as *nishitha*.[221] In particular, the worship of Shiva at

---

[219] Ganga that flows through Shiva's matted hair.

[220] Funeral oblation offered to a deceased ancestor or relative.
This is done immediately after death, once every month for a year
after death, and then at the end of a year, or every year.

[221] *Yama* is a period of three hours and night lasts for twelve
hours. *Nishitha* is the six hours centred around midnight.

that time yields everything that one wishes for. Knowing this,
a man should act accordingly and obtain the mentioned fruits.
Especially in *kali yuga*, success in obtaining the fruits depends
on performing this *karma*. If a man's mind turns towards these
rites, irrespective of what rights he is entitled to, if he follows
good conduct and is scared of sin, he will obtain the fruits."'

'The *rishi*s said, "O Suta! O supreme among *yogi*s! Please
tell us briefly about the sacred *kshetra*s, resorting to which,
men, women and others attain the objective. Please also tell us
about the practices in Shiva's *kshetra*s."'

'Suta replied, "Listen attentively to all the *kshetra*s and the
practices there."'

Chapter 19-2(12) (Shiva Temples)

'Suta said, "O wise *rishi*s! Hear about the Shiva *kshetra*s
that bestow emancipation. For the sake of the welfare
of the worlds, I will also tell you about the practices there.
Following Shiva's command, the earth extends for fifty crores
of *yojana*s,[222] is covered with mountains, forests and groves
and holds up the world. There are Shiva's *kshetra*s wherever
there are habitations. Out of compassion and with a desire to
bestow emancipation, the lord has himself thought of these
divine *kshetra*s. There are those established by *rishi*s, others
established by *deva*s. There are others that are Svayambhu.
All these are for the protection of the worlds. In these *tirtha*s
and *kshetra*s, one must always undertake the tasks of bathing,
donations and performing *japa*. Otherwise, men will suffer
from disease, poverty, dumbness and various other things. In

---

[222] A *yojana* is a measure of distance, between eight and nine
miles.

Bharata Varsha, if a man has resided and died in a place where there is a Svayambhu *lingam*, he will again be born as human. O learned ones! If a sin is committed in a *kshetra*, it cannot be dislodged. Therefore, if one resides in a sacred *kshetra*, one must never commit a sin. A man must make every effort to reside in such a sacred *kshetra*."

'"There are many *kshetras* along the shores of the ocean, at the confluences of hundreds of rivers. The sacred River Sarasvati is said to have sixty such confluences. Hence, if a wise person resides along its banks, he gradually attains Brahma's world. The sacred Ganga flows from the Himalaya mountain and has hundreds of mouths. There are many sacred *tirthas* along its banks too, Kashi and others. Its banks are particularly praised when Brihaspati is in Capricorn in the month of Margashirsha.[223] The river Shonabhadra[224] has ten auspicious mouths that yield all the fruits that one desires. Through fasting and bathing there, a person obtains Vinayaka's abode.[225] The great river, Narmada, has twenty-four mouths. Through fasting and bathing there, a person obtains Vishnu's abode. Tamasa has twelve mouths and River Reva has ten mouths.[226] The extremely sacred Godavari destroys the sins of killing a *brahmana* or a cow. It is said to have twenty-one mouths and bestows Rudra's world. The sacred river, Krishnaveni,[227] destroys all sins. It is said to have eighteen mouths and bestows Vishnu's world. Tungabhadra has ten mouths and bestows Brahma's world. Suvarnamukhari[228] is said to be sacred and has nine mouths. Those dislodged from

---

[223] The text uses the word Mriga to mean Capricorn.

[224] The river Sona/Sone.

[225] Vinayaka is Ganesha.

[226] Tamasa (Tons) is a tributary of Ganga and Reva (often equated with Narmada) is a tributary of Narmada.

[227] Krishna and Venna.

[228] Suvarnamukhi, in the Rayalaseema region.

Brahma's world are born there. If one resides along the banks of the auspicious Sarasvati, Pampa, Kanya and Shvetanadi, one obtains Indra's world.[229] The extremely sacred and great river, Kaveri, flows from Mount Sahya. It is said to have twenty-seven mouths that yield everything that is desired. Its banks bestow heaven and the worlds of Brahma and Vishnu. In that way, the river Shaivya,[230] bestows all the desired fruits and Shiva's world."'

'"When Brihaspati and Surya are in Mesha, one should bathe and worship in Naimisha and Badari.[231] This bestows Brahma's world. When Surya is in Simha or Karkataka, one should bathe in Sindhu.[232] A learned person will drink and bathe in the waters of Kedara[233] and obtain *jnana*. When Brihaspati is in Simha in the month of Simha,[234] one should bathe in Godavari. In ancient times, Shiva himself has said that this bestows Shiva's world. When Surya and Brihaspati

---

[229] Pampa, often identified with Tungabhadra, is a tributary of Tungabhadra. Shvetanadi is probably Sitanadi, which joins Mahanadi. Kanya is difficult to identify.

[230] Although by no means certain, this could be the Shivakashi river in Karnataka.

[231] Mesha is the sign of Aries. Naimisha is the forest of Naimisharanya and Badari is Badarikashrama (Badrinath).

[232] Simha and Karkataka are respectively Leo and Cancer. Sindhu is Indus.

[233] Mandakini river in Kedarnath.

[234] The names of lunar months are different from those of solar months. Simha is a solar month, corresponding to the *rashi* of Simha and is in August/September. It roughly corresponds to the lunar month of Bhadrapada. The solar months are Mina (lunar Chaitra), Mesha (lunar Vaishakha), Vrisha (lunar Jyestha), Mithuna (lunar Ashada), Karkataka (lunar Shravana), Simha (lunar Bhadrapada), Kanya (lunar Ashvina), Tula (lunar Kartika), Vrishchika (lunar Margashirsha), Dhanus (lunar Pousha), Makara (lunar Magha) and Kumbha (lunar Phalguna).

are in Kanya,[235] one should bathe in Yamuna and Shona.
The learned know that this yields great objects of pleasure in
the worlds of Dharma and Dantin.[236] Like that, when Surya
and Brihaspati are in Tula,[237] one should bathe in Kaveri.
The learned know that Vishnu himself said that this yields
everything one wishes for. In the month of Vrishchika, when
Surya and Brihaspati are in Vrishchika,[238] one should bathe
in River Narmada and obtain Vishnu's world. If one bathes
in River Suvarnamukhari when Brihaspati and Surya are in
Dhanus, one obtains Shiva's world. Brahma has said this. In
that way, in the month of Margashirsha, when Brihaspati
is in Mriga,[239] one should bathe in Jahnavi.[240] Brahma said
that this bestows Shiva's world. After enjoying oneself in
the worlds of Brahma and Vishnu, one obtains *jnana*. In the
month of Magha, when Surya is in Kumbha,[241] *shraddha*
ceremonies, the offering of *pinda* and donating water mixed
with sesamum saves crores of ancestors from both the father's
and the mother's lineages. The learned know this. When
Surya and Brihaspati are in Mina, bathing in Krishnaveni is
praised. Bathing in that *tirtha* in that month bestows Indra's
world. A learned person will seek refuge in, and dwell near,
the rivers Ganga and the one that flows from Sahya.[242] If he
does this, it is certain that his sins will be instantly cleaned.
There are many other *kshetras* that bestow Rudra's world.
Tamraparni and Vegavati yield the fruits of Brahma's

---

[235] Virgo.
[236] Dantin is the one with tusks, Ganesha.
[237] Libra.
[238] Scorpio.
[239] Capricorn.
[240] Ganga.
[241] Aquarius.
[242] That is, Kaveri.

world.[243] The *tirthas* that exist along the banks of these two bestow heaven. There are many other sacred *tirthas* that exist in between these two. The wise ones who reside there reap the corresponding fruits. However, wise people who reside there obtain these fruits only through good behaviour, good action and good sentiments. Auspicious deeds performed in a sacred *kshetra* yield many kinds of prosperity. But wicked deeds performed in a sacred *kshetra* also become much greater. While residing in such a place, if one performs a wicked deed only for the sake of subsistence, the consequences are not permanent. Good deeds, in thoughts, words and action are said to bestow prosperity. O *brahmanas*! The consequences of committing a sin in one's mind are also like that. It is possible for a mental sin to smear a person from one *kalpa* to another *kalpa*. Such a sin can only be destroyed through *dhyana*. There is no other way one can wish to destroy it. O *brahmanas*! A sin committed in words is destroyed through *japa*, drying up the body[244] and donating wealth. Otherwise, it cannot be destroyed in crores of *kalpas*. In cases, an increase in wicked deeds destroys the good merits earned earlier. Both good deeds and wicked ones have three stages—the part that is the seed, the part that is the increase and the part where they are enjoyed. As long as they are in the form of seed, they can be destroyed through *jnana*. In the stage of increase, they can be destroyed through the steps mentioned. But in the stage of enjoyment, they have to be enjoyed. Even crores of good deeds will not suffice then. When seeds or sprouts are destroyed, only what remains needs to be enjoyed. Worshipping *devas*, donating to *brahmanas* and performing austerities makes it easier for men to tolerate the period of

---

[243] Tamraparni is Thamirabarani (Tamil Nadu) and Vegavati is Vaigai (Tamil Nadu).
[244] Through austerities.

enjoyment. Therefore, a person who desires happiness must refrain from committing wicked deeds.'"

Chapter 20-2(13) (Good Behaviour)

'The sages asked, "We wish to hear about *sadachara*,[245] practicing which, a learned person can conquer the worlds. Please tell us about *dharma* and *adharma*, respectively leading to heaven and hell."'

'Suta replied, "A *brahmana* with *sadachara* is known as *vidvan*. A *brahmana* who possesses *sadachara* and practices the conduct of the *Veda*s is known as a *vipra*. A *brahmana* who possesses only one of these two is a *dvija*. A *brahmana* who possesses a little bit of good conduct and a little bit of the *Veda*s is known as a *kshatriya brahmana*. He becomes a servant of the king. With a small bit of good conduct, if a *brahmana* practices agriculture and trade, he is a *vaishya brahmana*. One who ploughs the field himself is known as a *shudra brahmana*. A *brahmana* who is jealous and causes harms to others is spoken of as a *chandala brahmana*. A *kshatriya* who rules over the earth is *rajan*, the others are held to be ordinary *kshatriya*s. Those who buy and sell grain are *vaishya*s, the others are spoken of as *vanijaka*s. A person who serves *brahmana*s, *kshatriya*s and *vaishya*s is referred to as *shudra*. A *shudra* who tills the land is *vrishala*, the others are *dasyu*s."'

'"Everyone must get up in the morning and facing the east, think of *deva*s. He will next think of *dharma*, *artha*, difficulties, receipts and expenditure. The direction in which one gets up in the morning determines the fruits for the day—lifespan, hatred, death, sin, fortune, ailments, nourishment and strength. The

[245] Good behaviour.

last part of the night is known as Usha and the last half of this is known as Sandhi.[246] A *brahmana* should get up at that time and release urine and excrement. He must do this outside the house and in a place that is far away from it. He must sit facing the north. If there are obstructions in doing this, he can face any of the other directions. He should not sit facing water, a fire, a *brahmana* or the image of a deity. He must cover his penis with his left hand and his mouth with the other hand. When he gets up after releasing excrement, he must not look at the stool. He must clean himself with water that has been collected and not with external water.[247] This should be done without descending into a *tirtha* of *deva*s, ancestors or *rishi*s. Using mud, the anus must be cleaned seven times, five times or three times. The penis can be cleaned with mud that is the size of a cucumber, but the anus must be cleaned with mud that amounts to a *prasriti*.[248] When he gets up, he must wash his hands and feet and rinse the mouth eight times. But the water should not be spat out into an external body of water. After this, the teeth must be cleaned, with leaves or with a twig. However, while doing this, one must avoid the use of the index finger. Next, worshipping *deva*s of the water, he will pronounce the *mantra*s and have his bath. Those who are incapacitated will immerse themselves up to the neck or up to the waist. Otherwise, he will immerse himself in water up to the knees and pronouncing the *mantra*s, have his bath. A learned person will take water from a *tirtha* and offer oblations of water to *deva*s and others. He must take

---

[246] Usha is sometimes translated as dawn. The day is divided into eight *yama*s, each *yama* lasting for three hours. Four *yama*s are day and four *yama*s are night. Usha is the last *yama* of night and the final one and a half hours of night represents Sandhi, the period of conjunction between night and day.

[247] That is, he must not clean himself inside a waterbody.

[248] *Prasriti* is the length of the palm when the hand is stretched out and the palm is open.

a *dhoutavastram* and wear it in *panchakaccha* fashion.[249] In all rites, an *uttariyam*[250] must also be used. When having a bath in a river or a *tirtha*, the garment must not be washed at the time of having a bath. After the bath, a learned person will take it to a tank or well, or inside the house. Using water from the tank or well, he will clean the garment by pounding it on a rock or plank of wood. O *brahmana*s! When the garment is cleaned through such pounding, the ancestors are pleased."

"'Using the *mantra* uttered by Jabalaka, Tripundraka ash must be smeared on the forehead.[251] If a person enters the water without doing this, he desires to go to hell. For the pacification of sins, water must be sprinkled on the head, uttering the *mantra*, '*Apo hi stha*'.[252] For freedom from sins, water must be sprinkled on the joints of the legs, uttering the *mantra*, '*yasya kshayaya*'. The learned know that bathing using *mantra*s involves sprinkling water on the feet, the head, the

---

[249] A washed piece (*dhouta*) piece of cloth (*vastram*), worn as a lower garment, is *dhoutavastram*, usually known as *dhoti*. *Pancha* is five and *kaccha* is the act of tucking the garment into the waist. The lower garment is worn with five such tucks.

[250] Upper garment.

[251] This is a reference to the Bhasmajabala Upanishad, where Jabala, Shiva's devotee is told by Shiva about the smearing of ash (*bhasma*) on the body, in particular, the Tripundraka/Tripundra, the three horizontal lines that are smeared on the forehead using the three middle fingers. Sometimes, this is also done with sandalwood paste.

[252] This is the *apah suktam* from *Rig Veda* 10.9. What's been cited in the text is only the first three words of a complete *mantra* consisting of nine verses. Those three words translate as, 'O Water! Because of your presence.' This sounds incomplete and the complete first line is, 'O Water! Because of your presence, the atmosphere is pleasant and imparts us with vigour.' A subsequent verse has the two words *yasya kshayaya*, meaning 'whose decay'. Addressed to water again, the complete line is 'Thus, you going to one who is suffering is sufficient to revive him.'

chest; then the head, the chest, the feet; and finally, the chest, the feet and the head, in that order. When there is a physical ailment, when there is fear from the king or the kingdom and when there is a great calamity, it is sufficient that this bathing with *mantra*s is done with a slight touch of water. In the morning, one should sip water and rinse the mouth, uttering *mantra*s to Surya. In the evening, this must be done while uttering *mantra*s to Agni. At midday, water must be sprinkled on the head. O *brahmanas*! After performing *japa* with *gayatri mantra*,[253] *arghya* must be offered to the sun in the eastern direction. Along with the *mantra*, *arghya* must also be offered at midday and in the evening. In the morning, the *arghya* will be offered by raising up both the hands. At midday, the *arghya* will be released through the fingers. In the evening, the water will be released on the ground, facing the western direction. At midday, the sun must always be viewed through the gaps between the fingers. One must perform *atma-pradakshina*,[254] rinse the mouth with water and purify oneself. Performing the *sandhya* rites before the right *muhurta* in the evening is futile. If *sandhya* has been performed at the wrong time, or if *sandhya* has been omitted for a day, depending on the number of days, one must perform *japa* with *gayatri* one hundred times more every day.[255] If the omission happens for more than ten days, one must recite the *gayatri* one hundred thousand times. If the omission has occurred for more than a month, one must go through the *upanayana* ceremony once again. To obtain success, Isha, Gouri, Guha, Vishnu, Brahma, Indra, the two

---

[253] In the morning.

[254] *Pradakshina* of one's own self. This is figurative, contemplating that one is identical with the *paramatman* and realizing that everything is therefore going around one's own self.

[255] If the omission has been for one day, the *gayatri japa* will be one hundred times more. If the omission has been for two days, the *gayatri japa* will be two hundred times more and so on.

Ashvins, Yama and other *deva*s must be propitiated. One must offer oblations to Brahma. Sprinkling the mouth with water, one will then be purified. A learned person must control himself and be seated to the right of a *tirtha*, in a revered *matha*, in the temple of a *deva*, or in his own house. The seat must be stable, and his mind must be fixed. He will prostrate himself before all *deva*s and first recite Pranava *mantra*, followed by *gayatri mantra*. While reciting Pranava, he must realize the union between the *jivatman* and the *brahman*. 'We worship the creator of the three worlds, Achyuta, the one who ensures preservation, and Rudra, the Destroyer. We worship the self-illuminating one, who is behind our organs of perception and action, our minds, our inclinations and our intellects. He is the one who constantly urges us towards knowledge about *dharma* and bestows objects of pleasure and emancipation.' A person who uses his intelligence to perform *dhyana* in this way will certainly obtain the *brahman*. Unable to accomplish this, since he is a *brahmana*, let him perform *japa* every day. Every day in the morning, a bull among *brahmana*s must recite this one thousand times. The others will recite this according to capacity. At midday, the *japa* must be performed one hundred times. One should know that it must be done twenty times in the evening, with Shivashtaka.[256] Beginning with *muladhara*, he must meditate on the twelve *chakra*s,[257] focusing on Vidyesha,

[256] The text says Shikhashtaka. *Shikha* is the tuft of hair and with *ashtaka* (eight) we have eight tufts of hair. This makes no sense and we have changed it to Shivashtaka, the eight verses that are a prayer to Shiva—*prabhum prananatham vibhum vishvanatham* and so on.

[257] A *chakra* is the focal point in a body, used for meditation. The usual list has twelve *chakra*s—*muladhara, svadhishthana, manipura, anahata, vishuddha, ajna* and *sahasrara*. In the twelve *chakra* system, there are six within the body and six that are outside the body, higher and universal. The six within the body are *muladhara, svadhishthana, manipura, anahata, vishuddha* and *ajna*. The higher six are *sahasrara, narayanana, brahmanana, trikuthi, svaminana* and *muktanana*.

Brahma, Vishnu, Isha, the *jivatman* and Parameshvara. Taking himself to be one with the *brahman*, he must perform *japa* with 'Soham'.[258] Starting with *brahmarandhra*,[259] he will meditate on the ones outside the body. Starting with the principle of Mahat, there are thousands of bodies.[260] Gradually, he must perform *japa* on each of these, one at a time, and progress. Thus, the *jivatman* uses *japa* to unite with the other one, the supreme. It is said that this is accomplished with two hundred Shivashtakas. The learned say that is the progression in *japa*, using *mantras* for *japa*. The learned also say that one thousand such *japas* bestow the status of Brahma and two thousand bestow the status of Indra. One can protect oneself by doing this for a fewer number of times and ensure that one is born as a *brahmana*. After worshipping the sun, a person must do this every day. It is said that a complete *brahmana* is one who has done this one million and two hundred thousand times. A person who has recited the *gayatri* fewer than one hundred thousand times is not fit to perform any rite connected with the *Vedas*."'

'"When a person has attained seventy years of age, he must leave for the forest. A person who has left for the forest must perform *japa* with the Pranava *mantra* twelve thousand times every morning. If there is omission of this daily act of *japa* on any day, it must be made up the next day. If this omission continues for more than a month, *japa* must be performed one hundred and fifty thousand times. If the omission is for more than this, he must formally take to the forest once again. Having

---

[258] 'I am he.'

[259] *Brahmarandhra* is the centre of the brain and *sahasrara* is located inside *brahmarandhra*.

[260] *Tattvas* are principles and *Mahat tattva* is the primordial principle from which creation takes place. The bodies stand for different universes.

done this, the sin can be pacified. Otherwise, one goes to the hell named Rourava. A person who wishes for something must strive for *dharma* and *artha* and not anything else. A *brahmana* must wish for emancipation and always pursue *jnana* about the *brahman*. *Artha* results from *dharma*. Objects of pleasure result from *artha*. Non-attachment is generated from objects of pleasure. That is, *artha* earned through *dharma* must be spent on objects of pleasure and this results in non-attachment. If *artha* is earned through contrary methods, attachment results. The pursuit of *dharma* is said to be twofold—through objects and through the body. Objects can be offered in the form of oblations and other things. The body can bathe in *tirthas* and do other things. A wealthy person can become poor. But austerities enable a person to obtain a divine form. The lack of desire makes a person pure and there is no doubt that purity leads to *jnana*. In *krita* and the other *yugas*,[261] austerities were praised. However, in *kali yuga*, the pursuit of *dharma* is through objects. In *krita*, *jnana* was obtained through *dhyana*. In *treta*, success came through austerities. In *dvapara*, success was obtained through sacrifices. In *kali yuga*, *jnana* is obtained through the worship of images. Fruits are in exact proportion to the good or bad deeds that have been performed. However, differences in the body and in the quality of objects can lead to an increase or decrease. *Adharma* is violent in nature, whereas *dharma*'s nature is that of happiness. Unhappiness results from *adharma* and *dharma* makes a person happy. It should be known that wicked conduct leads to misery. It should also be known that good conduct leads to joy. Therefore, for success in obtaining both objects of pleasure and emancipation, people should follow *dharma*. If a person provides means of subsistence to a *brahmana* and four of his family members, he resides in Brahma's world for one hundred years. It is known that one

---

[261] *Krita, treta* and *dvapara*.

thousand *chandrayana* vows²⁶² lead to Brahma's world. A *kshatriya* must act so as to provide means of subsistence to one thousand families. It is known that this bestows Brahma's world. If he does this for ten thousand families, it bestows Indra's world. Those who know the *Veda*s know that a man obtains the world of the *deva* who he placed at the forefront when he performed the act of donations. A person devoid of wealth must always seek to accumulate austerities. He should go to *tirtha*s and practice austerities there. He will then enjoy eternal happiness."'

"'I will now speak about the earning of wealth. Listen attentively. A pure *brahmana* must receive after officiating at sacrifices. But he must earn this wealth without any distress and without any hardship. A *kshatriya* earns through the strength of his arms and a *vaishya* through agriculture and animal husbandry. If the wealth earned through proper means is donated, this ensures success. Through the favours of a *guru*, everyone obtains success in the pursuit of *jnana* and success in the pursuit of *moksha*. The nature of success in the pursuit of *moksha* is obtaining supreme bliss. O *brahmana*s! Among all men, this is generated only if they associate with virtuous people. When the time arises, a householder who desires his own welfare must donate everything to *brahmana*s—wealth, grain, fruits and food that is not grain. Water must be given to those who are thirsty. Food must be given to pacify ailments that result from hunger. Donations of food are of four types— from the field, unhusked grain, uncooked food and cooked

²⁶² *Chandrayana* is a kind of fasting that follows the progress (*ayana*) of the moon (Chandra). On the full moon night, one only eats fifteen mouthfuls of food. For the fifteen lunar days following the full moon, this is decreased by one mouthful per day. For the fifteen lunar days following the new moon, this is increased by one mouthful per day.

food. Until one has not heard about Shiva, or until the food
has not been digested, there is no doubt that a person who
performs the good deed of donating food earns half the good
merits the receiver possesses. Therefore, a receiver of donations
must cleanse this sin through austerities. Otherwise, he will go
to Rourava hell. One's own wealth should be expended in three
ways—for *dharma*, for enhancing the wealth and for objects
of pleasure. For *dharma*, one should perform *nitya karma*,
naimittika karma and *kamya karma*. The second part must
be spent in the beneficial act of enhancement of wealth. The
final part can be spent on the enjoyment of objects of pleasure.
One tenth of what has been earned through agriculture must
be spent on cleansing the sin.[263] The remnant can be spent on
dharma and the other things. Otherwise, a person will go to
Rourava. If he does not do this, he is evil-minded, and it is true
that he will bring about his own destruction. A discriminating
person who earns his subsistence through usury must set aside
one-sixth for donations. Pure and excellent *brahmana*s who
receive, must give away one-fourth as donations. If wealth
is received unexpectedly, an excellent *brahmana* will gave
away half. Everything received from a wicked person must
be flung away into the ocean of charity. Before giving away,
the recipient should be invited. This enhances the donor's
enjoyment of objects of pleasure. According to capacity, a
person must always give everything that he is asked for. If an
object asked for is not given, that debt will be carried forward
into the next life. A discriminating person will never talk about
another person's faults. In particular, a *brahmana* will never
speak about such things that he may have seen or heard about.
A learned person will never speak things that cause rage in
the hearts of beings. To attain prosperity, at the time of the

---

[263] Presumably because agriculture has caused violence to living
beings.

two *sandhya*s, he should observe the fire rites. A person who is unable to do it on both occasions shall do it once, following the norms and worshipping the sun and the fire with oblations of paddy, grain, *ghee*, fruits and roots. Following the norms, food that has been properly cooked in an earthen vessel must be offered in the vessel itself. If no food is available, the main oblation of *ghee* will suffice. Learned ones who know have spoken about many such acts of *nitya karma*. Alternatively, looking towards the face of the sun, one can only perform *japa*. In this way, those who wish to ensure their own welfare should act accordingly. They must always practice *brahma yajna*[264] and be devoted to worshipping *deva*s. They must always worship the fire. They must be devoted to worshipping the *guru*. They must satisfy *brahmana*s. All of them will then enjoy themselves in heaven."'

Chapter 21-2(14) (*Agni Yajna*)

'The *rishi*s said, "O lord! Please tell us progressively abut *agni yajna*, *deva yajna*, *brahma yajna*, worshipping the guru and satisfying *brahmana*s."'

'Suta said, "The offering of oblations into the fire is known as *agni yajna*. For those who are in the *ashrama* of *brahmacharya*, it is also known as *samidhadana*.[265] O *brahmana*s! Until *oupasana*,[266] for people who are in the first *ashrama*, the specific vow to the fire is through kindling. O *brahmana*s! Those who have retired to the forest and those

---

[264] That is, *pancha mahayajna*, the duty of every householder.
[265] The collection of kindling.
[266] The sacrifice into the fire, as performed by a householder.

who are mendicants have consigned the fire[267] into their
*atman*s. Their welfare lies in eating limited quantities. That
act of eating is itself an oblation.[268] Those who have embarked
on *oupasana*, must carefully protect the sacrificial fire in a
pit or a vessel and guard it against the wind. In the case of
intervention by the king or by destiny,[269] the fire must certainly
be preserved inside the *atman* or in the *arani*.[270] When the usual
fire has to be abandoned out of fear, this is said to be a means
of depositing the fire. O *brahmanas*! The offering of oblations
to the fire in the evening is known to ensure prosperity. The
offering of oblations to the sun in the morning is known to
bestow a long lifespan. During the day, the fire enters the sun.
Therefore, this is also known as *agni yajna*. The offering of
oblations to Indra and all *deva*s through the fire is known as
deva yajna. This is beneficial and can be in the form of rites
like offering cooked food in the earthen vessel in which it has
been cooked. It is known that acts like the first tonsure of the
head are performed with an ordinary fire. When a *brahmana*
practices *brahma yajna*, he satisfies *deva*s. Studying the *Veda*s
is said to be *brahma yajna*.[271] It is recommended that everyone
must always practice this, without any specific rules. However,
there is also *deva yajna* without the fire. Faithfully and lovingly,
hear about this.'"

[267] The fire maintained by householders.

[268] Offered to the digestive fire.

[269] Unforeseen situations that do not allow for the usual household
fire to be preserved.

[270] *Arani* stands for the two churning sticks used to kindle a fire,
by rubbing them against each other.

[271] Studying the *Veda*s honours the *rishi*s. This is one of the five
components of *pancha mahayajna*. *Brahma yajna* has two definitions,
the broader one equates it with all of the five components of *pancha
mahayajna*, the narrower one with only one of these.

'"Mahadeva is omniscient and is an ocean of compassion. At the beginning of creation, for the welfare of all the worlds, the lord thought of different days of the week. The omniscient one is a physician for *samsara*. He is the supreme medication among all medications. For the sake of good health, the lord made the first day his own day. After this, he used his own *maya* to bestow a boon on his son. There were hardships when he was born and to tide over this, the next day was for Kumara. The lord thought of this day so that one can overcome laziness. For the sake of preserving the worlds, Vishnu became the protector. For the sake of protection and nourishment, the lord thought of the next day for him. The next day enhances the lifespan and was for the one who grants a long lifespan, Parameshthi Brahma, the creator of the three worlds. The lord thought of this day so that the lifespan of the world can be increased. In the beginning, so that the three worlds might flourish, he thought of virtue and sin. Accordingly, the divinities of the next two days became Indra and Yama. He next thought of bestowing objects of pleasure on the worlds and taking away death. The natures of Aditya and the others are such that they signify happiness and unhappiness.[272] At the beginning, these divinities of the days were thought to be established in the circle of luminary bodies established in the sky. Worshipped on their respective days, they bestow their respective fruits—in the due order, good health, prosperity, destruction of ailments, nourishment, long lifespans, enjoyment of objects of pleasure

---

[272] There were difficulties connected with Kumara's (Skanda's) birth. He was deposited in a clump of reeds and reared by Krittikas, thus becoming Kartikeya. Different divinities are associated with different days of the week. In the listing given here, and there are alternative listings. Shiva's day is Monday, Kumara's day is Tuesday, Vishnu's day is Wednesday, Brahma's day is Thursday, Indra's day is Friday, Yama's day is Saturday and Aditya's (Surya's day) is Sunday.

and prevention of death.[273] It is said that if the respective *deva*s are worshipped on different days of the week, one obtains the respective fruits. However, even if other *deva*s are worshipped, it is really Shiva who bestows the fruits. To please *deva*s, five kinds of worship have been thought of—*japa* of a *mantra*, offering of oblations, donations, austerities and worship of the image on an altar, in front of the fire or in front of a *brahmana*. The worship should be undertaken with the sixteen kinds of *upachara*. Out of the five kinds of worship, the succeeding one is superior to the preceding one.[274] If a preceding one cannot be undertaken, a succeeding one should be followed. To pacify ailments of the eyes or the heads or to cure leprosy, Aditya must be worshipped and *brahmana*s must be fed, for a day, for a month, for a year or for a period of three years. If a person's *prarabdha karma*[275] is strong enough, this destroys disease, old age and similar things. It should be known that performing *japa* for a *deva* bestows the fruits that correspond to that particular day. The first day of the week is special for pacifying sin and offerings should be made on that day. For *deva*s and *brahmana*s, Aditya's day is special."'

"'For the sake of prosperity, a learned person will worship Lakshmi[276] and others on Somavara,[277] using rice mixed with *ghee*. Alternatively, *brahmana*s can be fed, along with their wives. To pacify ailments, Kali and others must be worshipped

---

[273] Corresponding to the seven days of the week.

[274] That is, oblations are superior to *japa*, donations are superior to oblations and so on.

[275] That bit of accumulated *karma* that has come to fruition in the present life.

[276] The goddess of wealth and prosperity.

[277] Somavara is Monday, Bhoumavara is Tuesday, Soumyavara is Wednesday, Guruvara is Thursday, Bhriguvara is Friday and Mandavara is Saturday.

on Bhoumavara. Using gram, *mudga*[278] and an *adhaka*[279] of rice, *brahmana*s can be fed. A learned person will worship Vishnu on Soumyavara, with curds and rice. If this is done, sons, friends and wives will always be nourished. To obtain nourishment and ensure a long lifespan, a learned person will worship *deva*s on Guruvara, using a sacred thread, garments and milk and *ghee*. To obtain objects of pleasure, a person must control himself and worship *deva*s on Bhriguvara. *Brahmana*s must be satisfied with cooked food that has the six kinds of flavours.[280] Their wives must be satisfied by donating garments and other auspicious things. To ward off untimely death, a learned person will worship Rudra and others on Mandavara, offering oblations of sesamum. He will donate and use cooked food mixed with sesamum to feed. Having worshipped in this way, a learned person will obtain the benefits of good health and other things. In daily worship of *deva*s, special worship, bathing, donations, *japa*, oblations, satisfying *brahmana*s, worshipping *deva*s when there is a conjunction of *nakshatra*s on specific *tithi*s, or on the first day or other days, it is the omniscient lord of the universe who assumes all those specific forms and bestows good health and other fruits. This depends on the time, the place and the recipient. The objects used depend on the extent of devotion and the local customs. Gradually, the divinity enables one to cross over and bestows good health and other things. For good health and prosperity, a householder should worship Aditya and the planets when an auspicious period starts, when an inauspicious period ends and when his birth *nakshatra* is in the ascendant. This worship of *deva*s yields all the desired fruits one wishes for.

---

[278] *Moong* dal.

[279] *Adhaka* is a measure used for grain, equal to one-fourth of a *drona*.

[280] Astringent, sweet, bitter, pungent, salt and sour.

*Brahmana*s should use *mantra*s, others should not use *mantra*s. According to his capacity, a man must always do this. A man who desires auspicious fruits must do this on the seven days. The poor worship *deva*s through austerities. The rich use wealth to worship. Full of devotion, they repeatedly undertake these acts of *dharma*. Having enjoyed all kinds of objects of pleasure, they are born on earth again. To always enjoy objects of pleasure and extend them, all those who are rich should accumulate *dharma* by planting trees for shade, digging tanks and establishing the *brahman*.[281] After some time, when these auspicious acts mature, he obtains success in the acquisition of *jnana*. O *brahmana*s! If a man reads this chapter, hears it or makes it heard, he obtains the fruits of a *deva yajna*."'

Chapter 22-2(15) (*Deva Yajna*)

'The *rishi*s said, "O Suta! O one who knows the meaning of everything! O excellent one! Please tell us about the place and other things."'

'Suta replied, "A pure house bestows the same fruits as a *deva yajna* and related rites. A cow-pen yields fruits that are ten times as much. The banks of a waterbody yield fruits that are ten times as much. The root of a *bilva* tree, the root of an *ashvattha* tree or the base of a *tulasi* plant yield fruits that are ten times as much.[282] It should be known that an abode of *deva*s or the banks of a river yield fruits that are ten times as much. A *tirtha* on a river yields fruits that are ten times as much as those of an ordinary river. The banks of the seven Gangas yield fruits that are ten times as much. The seven Gangas are described as

---

[281] This possibly means establishing temples.
[282] *Asvattha* is the holy fig tree, *tulasi* is the holy basil.

Ganga, Godavari, Kaveri, Tampraparni, Sindhu, Sarayu and Reva. The shores of the ocean yield fruits that are ten times as much. Ten times more than these are the fruits obtained on the summits of mountains. Out of all these, it should be known that the place where the mind is at peace is the best."

"In *krita yuga*, the fruits of sacrifices and donations are known to have been complete. In *treta yuga*, the benefits became three-fourths. In *dvapara yuga*, it is known that one always obtains half the complete fruits. In *kali yuga*, the fruits obtained are only one-fourth. When only one quarter of *kali yuga* is left, the fruits obtained are only half of this.[283] It should be known that a pure *atman* and an auspicious day yield the complete auspicious fruits. However, the learned know that the fruits become ten times more at the time of *sankranti*.[284] At the time of *vishuva sankranti*, it becomes ten times more. At the time of transition from one *ayana* to another, it is said to become ten times more. Like that, it becomes ten times more at the time of *mriga sankranti*. It becomes ten times that at the time of a lunar eclipse. At the time of a complete solar eclipse, it is known to become ten times that. Surya is the form of the universe and at that time, it is united with poison. Therefore, ailments spread. So as to pacify the poison, one should bathe,

---

[283] The meaning of this *shloka* is not clear, and we have taken some liberties. It seems to suggest that the fruits decrease as a specific *yuga* progresses.

[284] *Sankranti* is the movement of the sun from one sign of the zodiac (*rashi*) to another. Thus, there are twelve of these. The entry of Surya into Capricorn, with the movement from *dakshinayana* to *uttarayana*, is known as *makara sankranti* or *mriga sankranti*, while its entry into Cancer, with the movement from *uttarayana* to *dakshinayana*, is known as *karka sankranti*. The entry into Gemini, Virgo, Sagittarius and Pisces are known as *shadashiti*. The entry into Taurus, Leo, Scorpio and Aquarius are known as *vishnupada*. The entry into Aries and Libra is known as *vishuva sankranti*.

donate and perform *japa*. The time when the poison is pacified is said to become a time that is auspicious. When one's natal *nakshatra* is in the ascendant, and when a vow has been completed, are times known to have the same efficacy as the period of a solar eclipse. The time one spends associating with great and virtuous people is said to bestow fruits that are ten times those of a solar eclipse. Those devoted to austerities, those devoted to *jnana*, *yogi*s and mendicants are those who deserve to be worshipped. They are *patras*[285] who are responsible for the destruction of sins. A *brahmana* who has performed *japa* with *gayatri mantra* two million and four hundred thousand times is also such a *patra* and enjoys the complete fruits. The sacred texts say that a person who saves from downfall is a *patra*.[286] He is known as *patra* because he saves a donor from sin. In that way, *gayatri* is said to be that which saves the reciter from downfall.[287] A person devoid of riches cannot donate riches to another person. In this world, only a wealthy person can donate riches to others. Similarly, only those who are purified and are pure themselves are worthy of saving men. A *brahmana* who has purified himself by performing *japa* with *gayatri* is spoken of as a pure *brahmana*. Hence, in donations, *japa*, oblations, worship and in all other rites, it is such a *brahmana* who is worthy of being given donations. He is a *patra* who saves others. For giving cooked food, a hungry man or woman is a deserving *patra*. At that time, one must control oneself and invite an excellent *brahmana*, using words full of meaning and donating riches to him. Such a person is capable of bestowing the desired fruits. It should be known that voluntary donations to a person confer the complete fruits. When donations are given after one is asked, it should

---

[285] In this context, *patra* means a worthy recipient.
[286] Etymologically, saves (*trayate*) from downfall (*patana*).
[287] Etymologically, saves (*trayate*) the reciter (*gayaka*).

be known that only half the fruits are obtained. It should be known that donations to servants only yield one quarter of the fruits. O bulls among *brahmana*s! When one donates riches to a person who is distressed and lacks means of subsistence, only because he happens to be a *brahmana*, this act bestows objects of pleasure in this world for ten years. If this happens to be a *brahmana* who knows the *Vedas*, this bestows heaven for ten years. If this happens to be a *brahmana* who does *japa* with *gayatri mantra*, this ensures Satyaloka for ten years.[288] It is known that if this *brahmana* happens to be Vishnu's devotee, this ensures Vaikuntha.[289] If this *brahmana* happens to be Shiva's devotee, it is known that Kailasa is ensured. Different kinds of donations ensure all the desired objects of pleasure in different worlds. If a man gives a *brahmana* cooked food, along with ten accompaniments, on a Sunday, in his next birth, he enjoys freedom from disease for ten years. Along with cooked food, these ten kinds of accompaniments are: displaying a lot of honour while inviting; smearing the body with oil; tending to the feet; offering a garment; worshipping with fragrances; serving cakes made in *ghee*; offering food with the six kinds of taste; offering betel leaves; offering *dakshina*; and prostrating and following him for a while when he departs. This is known as offering cooked food with the ten kinds of accompaniments. If a person does this on a Sunday, he does not suffer from ill health for one hundred years. On Monday or the other days, he obtains the fruits that are associated with that particular day. It should be known that the fruits of donating food are enjoyed in this world and in the next birth. If he gives food to ten *brahmana*s on each of the seven days, he enjoys good

---

[288] The seven upper regions are Bhuloka, Bhuvarloka, Svarloka, Maharloka, Satyaloka, Tapoloka and Janaloka. The seven nether regions are Atala, Vitala, Nitala, Sutala, Talatala, Rasatala and Patala.
[289] Vishnu's world.

health and other benefits for one hundred years. In this way, if
a man gives to one hundred *brahmana*s on Sunday, he enjoys
good health in Sharva's[290] world for one thousand years. If he
gives to one thousand *brahmana*s, he enjoys the benefits for ten
thousand years. In this way, a learned man can understand the
benefits on Monday and the other days. On Sunday, if a person
gives cooked food to one thousand *brahmana*s, whose minds
have been purified by chanting *gayatri*, he enjoys good health
and other benefits in Satyaloka. If he gives to ten thousand,
he enjoys Vishnu's world. If he gives cooked food to one
hundred thousand, he enjoys Rudra's world. Men who seek
learning must give to children, taking them to be the equal of
the *brahman*. Men who desire sons must give to young men,
taking them to be the equal of Vishnu. Men who seek *jnana*
must give to the aged, taking them to be Rudra's equal. Men
who desire intelligence must give to young girls, taking them
to be Bharati's[291] equal. Excellent men who desire objects of
pleasure must give to young women, taking them to be the
equal of Lakshmi. Those who seek the *atman* must give to old
women, taking them to be Parvati's equal."'

'"Pure objects are said to be those earned through *shilavritti*,
unchavritti and *dakshina* due to a *guru*.[292] These are known to
yield complete fruits. Gifts offered by pure people are spoken
of as medium objects. Those obtained through agriculture and
trade are spoken of as inferior objects. *Kshatriya*s and *vaishya*s
should respectively earn through valour and trade. For *shudra*s,
superior objects are said to be those earned through acting as

---

[290] Sharva is one of Shiva's names.

[291] Sarasvati's.

[292] There are grains left after a crop has been harvested, or after
grain has been milled. If one subsists on these left-overs, that is known
as *unchavritti*. *Shilavritti* means gathering the stalks and surviving on
those. These clauses are meant for *brahmana*s.

servants. For women who seek *dharma*, objects are obtained from the father or from the husband. If one desires prosperity, cattle and other objects must be given in the twelve months, Chaitra and the others, when an auspicious occasion presents itself. These twelve are a cow, a plot of land, sesamum, gold, *ghee*, garments, grain, molasses, silver, salt, a pumpkin and a maiden. Donations of cows, milk products and cow dung counter any taints resulting from wealth or grains. Cow's urine counters any taints resulting from water and oil. Physical taints are countered through three objects—milk, curd and *ghee*. Those who are learned know about the nourishment these bring about. O *brahmanas*! Gifts of land ensure the donor's establishment in this world and in the world hereafter. The learned know that gifts of sesamum always provide strength and help to ward off death. Gift of gold nourishes the digestive fire and increases vigour. The gift of *ghee* nourishes and that of learning is known to bestow a long lifespan. The gift of grain ensures prosperity in obtaining food. Gift of molasses ensures sweet food. Gift of silver increases semen, while gift of salt ensures that the six flavours are obtained. It is known that the gift of a pumpkin ensures nourishment. O *brahmanas*! All these increase all kinds of prosperity. All the objects of pleasure are obtained in this world and in the next world. The gift of a maiden ensures objects of pleasure and makes a person a *jivanmukta*. Learned people who desire success make gifts of fruits like jackfruit, mango, wood-apple, fruits of other trees, plantain, herbs, fruits from creepers, gram, *mudga*, other fruits, vegetables, chillies, mustard and other vegetable products. To provide satisfaction to sense organs like the ears, learned people donate sounds that are pleasant to hear. These also make the four directions content. *Vedas* and sacred texts must be understood from the mouth of the *guru* himself. A believer's intelligence is said to be that which accepts that *karma* leads to fruits. Devotion that is a result of fear in the mind, because of relatives or the king, is inferior. A poor person must worship through every possible means, words and deeds. Worship through words consists of pursuit of learning, *mantra*s and *japa*. Physical worship consists of visiting *tirtha*s, observing vows and other daily rites. Whatever method is used, whether it is little or a lot, as long as the mind is such that this is offered to a *deva*, this is thought to lead to objects of pleasure. One must always follow the two tasks of austerities and donations. Depending on the seeker's *varna* and qualities, refuge must be offered. The learned know that satisfaction of *deva*s leads to every kind of object of pleasure. A learned person always obtains an excellent birth in this world and objects of pleasure in this world and the next one. If the inclination is such that everything is offered to Ishvara, one obtains *moksha*. If a man constantly reads this chapter, or listens to it, his intelligence turns towards *dharma*, and he obtains success in acquiring *jnana*."'

Chapter 23-2(16) (Worship of Deities)

'The *rishi*s said, "O excellent one! Please tell us about the rules for worshipping earthen images. What rules must be followed in the worship so that everything desired is obtained?"'

'Suta replied, "You have asked an extremely virtuous question, about what always confers everything desired. It instantly pacifies miseries. I will tell you. Listen. It wards off death at the wrong time. It even wards off death itself. O *brahmana*s! It immediately bestows wives, sons, wealth and grain. This leads to everything that is wished for, cooked food, other edible objects and garments. The worship of an earthen image yields everything desired on earth. In this connection, it has been determined that both men and women have rights. The clay required must be collected from the water of a river, pond or well. It must be crushed and purified with fragrances. It must be cleaned properly with milk. On an excellent platform, using the hands, one must knead the clay and make an image. The body and the limbs must be shaped properly and adorned with the respective weapons. The image must be seated in *padmasana*[293] and must be lovingly worshipped. The images worshipped can be of Vignesha,[294] Aditya, Vishnu, Amba and Shiva. However, a *brahmana* must always worship Shiva in the form of Shiva's *lingam*. To be successful in obtaining the fruits, the sixteen kinds of *upachara* must be used. With *mantras*, a flower must be used to sprinkle water over the image. The *naivedya*, consisting of *shali* rice, must always be measured out in *kudavas*.[295] For worship in a house, it should amount to one *kudava*. For worship in a temple constructed by humans, one *prastha* should be used. For worship in temple constructed by *devas*, three *prasthas* must be used. For a Svayambhu image, five *prasthas* are appropriate. This is known to yield complete fruits. If double or thrice the amount is used, the fruits are known to be greater. It is true that if this worship is performed one thousand times, a *brahmana* goes to Satyaloka. The learned know that a vessel made out of iron or wood, twelve *angulas*[296] in width, twenty-four *angulas* in length and sixteen *angulas* in height is known as a *shiva*. One-eighth of this measure is a *prastha*, held to be equal to four *kudavas*. When ten *prasthas*, one hundred *prasthas* or one thousand *prasthas* of water, oil, fragrances and other things are used to measure out for worshipping a human,

---

[293] The lotus position.

[294] Ganesha, the destroyer of impediments.

[295] *Shali* is a fine variety of rice. *Kudava* is a measure used for grain, equal to twelve handfuls. Four *kudavas* amount to one *prastha*.

[296] The width of a finger.

rishi or Svayambhu *lingam*, this is known as *mahapuja*.[297]
The *abhisheka* of the image is for purifying one's *atman*. The
offering of fragrances is for auspiciousness. *Naivedya* ensures
a long lifespan, while incense is for the sake of prosperity. The
lamp is for acquisition of *jnana*, the betel leaf is for objects
of pleasure. Therefore, in every worship, these six things must
be carefully undertaken. *Namaskara* and *japa* yield everything
that is desired. For men who desire objects of pleasure and
liberation, these must always be done at the end of a *puja*.
A man must always worship every object in his mind before
going through the rite. If *deva*s are worshipped, various worlds
are obtained. Desired objects of pleasure are also obtained in
the inferior worlds. O *brahmana*s! I will now describe special
forms of *puja*. Please listen devotedly."'

'"By worshipping Vignesha, one obtains everything one
desires in this world. The special days for worshipping him are
Friday, *chaturthi*[298] in *shukla paksha* in the months of Shravana
and Bhadra and in the month of Dhanus, when Shatabhisha
nakshatra is in the ascendant. In the proper way, Vignesha must
be worshipped at these times. Alternatively, one can worship
every day, for a period of one hundred or one thousand days.
Because of the divinity, the fire and the devotion, constant
worship bestows sons and everything desired on men. Every
sin is pacified, and impediments are destroyed. It is known
that worshipping Shiva and the others on their respective days
purifies the *atman*. All kinds of *kamya* worship[299] depend on
the *tithi* and the conjunction of *nakshatra*s. It is known that
the day represents the *brahman* and depending on the *tithi* or
the *nakshatra*, there is no increase or decrease in the length of
the day. The day is from sunrise to sunset and rites for Brahma

---

[297] Great *puja*.
[298] Fourth lunar *tithi*.
[299] Undertaken with a specific desire in mind.

and the others must be undertaken during their respective days. Worship of *devas* on *tithi*s bestows complete objects of pleasure on men. The first part of the night is praised for worshipping the ancestors. The second part of the day is praised for worshipping *devas*. If the *tithi* is such that it extends over more than one day,[300] for rites connected with *devas*, that part of the *tithi* that extends from sunrise to midday must be accepted. This is also the case for determining auspicious *nakshatras*. Through *puja*, *japa* and other things, the proper rites must be undertaken on the respective days. All the complete objects of enjoyment are successfully obtained through this rite. One is filled up through this rite. That is how the word *puja* should be understood, *puh* and *jayate*.[301] Depending on one's mental state, desired *jnana* is also included as an object of enjoyment. That is how the meaning of the word *puja* is understood among ordinary people and is also understood in this way by people who know the *Veda*s. *Nitya* and *naimittika* rites yield benefits over a period of time. But the fruits of *kamya* rites are instantaneous. *Nitya* rites are performed every day. *Naimittika* rites are performed every month, every fortnight or every year. Therefore, the fruits of such *karma* occur respectively, after a period of a fortnight and so on. The great *puja* of Ganapati is performed on *chaturthi* in *krishna paksha*. This destroys sins for a fortnight and yields fruits for a fortnight. If the *puja* is performed on *chaturthi* in Chaitra, it yields fruits for a month. If it is performed in the months of Simha or Bhadra, it is known to bestow fruits for a year. Aditya must be worshipped on Sunday, on *saptami*, when the *nakshatra* Hasta is in the ascendant and on *saptami* in *shukla paksha*, in the month of Magha. It is known that the worship of Vishnu yields expected desires and prosperity, if performed

---

[300] A *tithi* can extend over two solar days.
[301] *Jayate* means generated. *Puh* means purification. *Puja* is something that generates purification.

on Wednesday, on *dvadashi*[302] in the months of Jyeshtha or
Bhadrapada, or on *dvadashi*, when Shravana *nakshatra* is
in the ascendant. The worship of Vishnu on *dvadashi* yields
good health. If one donates the twelve kinds of gifts, cattle
and the others, along with the accompaniments, one obtains
the fruits. Such fruits are obtained through satisfying Vishnu.
On *dvadashi*, twelve *brahmanas* must be assigned twelve of
Vishnu's names. Lovingly, they must be honoured with the
sixteen kinds of *upachara*. In this way, twelve *brahmanas* can
be assigned twelve names of any *deva*. When they are honoured,
this causes delight to the *deva*. Amba should be worshipped
on Monday and on *navami*[303] in the month of Karkataka or
Margashirsha. When a person who desires prosperity worships
Amba, he obtains all the objects of pleasure as fruits. *Navami*
in *shukla paksha* in the month of Ashvina yields everything
desired as fruit. Monday and *chaturdashi* in *krishna paksha* are
special for the worship of Shiva. When Ardra *nakshatra* is in
the ascendant and Maha-Ardra[304] are special for worshipping
Shiva. *Chaturdashi* in *krishna paksha* in the month of Magha
yields everything that is desired. It ensures a long lifespan,
dispels sins and gives men everything desired. Chaturdashi in
the month of Jyeshtha is also like Maha-Ardra. Shiva's image
must be worshipped with sixteen *upacharas*, and his feet seen,
also when Ardra is in the ascendant in Margashirsha. It should
be known that the worship of Shiva confers objects of pleasure
and emancipation on men.'"

'"The worship of *devas* on their respective days is special
in Kartika. When Kartika month arrives, a learned person will
worship all the *devas*, using donations, austerities, oblations,
japa and *niyama*. The image will be worshipped with the

[302] Twelfth lunar *tithi*.
[303] Ninth lunar *tithi*.
[304] That is, Maha Shiva Ratri.

sixteen kinds of *upachara* and a *brahmana* will pronounce
the *mantras*. When *brahmana*s are fed, a person is freed from
desires and afflictions. Worshipping *devas* in Kartika yields
all the objects of pleasure. Ailments are dispelled and demons
and evil planets are destroyed. If oil and cotton seeds are
used to worship Aditya on Sundays in Kartika, leprosy and
similar ailments are countered. If *haritaka*,[305] chillies, garments
and milk are donated and Brahma instated, the disease of
consumption is countered. If lamps and mustard are donated,
epilepsy is countered. On Mondays in Kartika, men should
worship Shiva. This pacifies great penury and increases every
kind of prosperity. Houses, fields and household implements
must be donated. On Tuesdays in Kartika, men should worship
Skanda. By donating lamps and bells, one soon becomes
eloquent in speech. On Wednesdays in Kartika, men should
worship Vishnu. By donating curd and cooked rice, one obtains
good offspring. On Thursdays in Kartika, men should worship
Brahma. The donation of honey, gold and *ghee* increases
objects of pleasure for men. On Fridays in Kartika, the one
who has a face like an elephant[306] should be worshipped.
Donations of fragrances, flowers and cooked food increase
objects of pleasure for men. If gold and silver are donated,
barren women obtain excellent sons. On Saturdays in Kartika,
the guardians of the worlds should be worshipped. *Diggajas*,[307]
serpents, those who protect bridges, Tryambaka[308] Rudra and
Vishnu, the dispeller of sin, should be worshipped. Brahma
must be worshipped for *jnana*. The worship of Dhanvantari[309]

[305] Yellow myrobalan.

[306] Ganesha.

[307] There are four elephants that dwell in the four directions.
These are known as *diggajas*, an elephant (*gaja*) for each direction
(*dik*).

[308] Three-eyed.

[309] The physician of the gods.

and the two Ashvins removes diseases and accidental death
and instantly pacifies ailments. Gifts of salt, iron, oil, beans,
trikatuka,[310] fruits, fragrances, water and liquids and solids
measured out in *prastha*s and *pala*s lead to heaven. At dawn
in the month of Dhanus, Shiva and all the others must be
worshipped. This progressively leads to the achievement of
success. For *naivedya*, *shali* rice and *havishya* are especially
praised. Especially in the month of Dhanus, *naivedya* must
be in the form of various kinds of cooked rice. A person who
donates cooked food in Margashirsha obtains everything he
desires as fruits. His sins are destroyed. He accomplishes his
desires and has good health. He follows *dharma* and obtains
proper knowledge of the *Veda*s. He follows good practices. He
obtains great objects of pleasure in this world and in the next
one. At the end, he obtains eternal union. Success in obtaining
knowledge of Vedanta is accomplished in Margashirsha. At
dawn, for the duration of three days in Margashirsha, a person
must worship *deva*s. Desired objects of pleasure are obtained
in the month of Dhanus. In the month of Dhanus, the rites
can be undertaken until the time of *sangava*.[311] A *brahmana*
must conquer his senses and fast in the month of Dhanus. Until
midday, he must perform *japa* with *gayatri mantra*, the mother
of the *Veda*s. After this, until he goes to bed, he must perform
japa with *panchakshara*[312] and other *mantra*s. Having obtained
jnana, when he gives up his body, such a *brahmana* will obtain
emancipation. Other men and women will bathe thrice a day
and always perform *japa* with *panchakshara mantra*. They will
obtain pure *jnana*. If one constantly performs *japa* with the
desired *mantra*, all the great sins are destroyed."'

---

[310] *Trikatuka/trikatu* is a mix of three ingredients—black pepper,
long pepper and ginger.
[311] The second *yama*, after dawn.
[312] *Pancharna mantra*.

"'Particularly in the month of Dhanus, a great *naivedya* should be offered. This must have *shali* rice measured out in weight; peppers amounting to one *prastha*; twelve articles counted out; one *kudava* each of honey and *ghee*; one *drona*[313] of *mudga*; twelve kinds of dishes; sweet cakes made in *ghee*; sweetmeats made out of *shali* rice; twelve *prastha*s each of curds and milk; twelve coconuts and other fruits that are counted out; twelve betel nuts; thirty-six leaves; camphor powder; five kinds of fragrances;[314] and betel leaves. These are the characteristics of a great *naivedya*. This great *naivedya* must be offered to the divinity. According to *varna*, this must then be progressively distributed to the devotees. Having offered *naivedya* in this fashion, a person becomes the lord of a kingdom in this world. Having offered a great *naivedya*, a man goes to heaven. O bulls among *brahmana*s! If a person offers this great *naivedya* one thousand times, he goes to Satyaloka and spends an entire lifespan in that world. If a person offers this great *naivedya* thirty thousand times, he goes to worlds that are higher still and is not reborn again. It is said that thirty-six thousand offerings of a great *naivedya* constitute the *naivedya* of a lifetime. Donation of such an offering is said to make a person completely full. Since this offering makes a person completely full, it is known as the *naivedya* of a lifetime. If a person offers the *naivedya* of a lifetime, there is no rebirth for him. The *naivedya* of a lifetime must be offered on an auspicious day in the month of Kartika. The excellent *naivedya* of a lifetime should be offered at the time of *sankranti*, when the natal *nakshatra* is in the ascendant, on the day of the full moon and on the annual birthday. This can also be offered in other months when there is a conjunction of one's natal *nakshatra*. It can also be offered when there is a

---

[313] A measure of capacity.
[314] Cloves, nutmeg, camphor, aloe and *kakkola* berry, all in a mixture.

conjunction of Saturn with the natal *nakshatra*. The offering of
the *naivedya* of a lifetime is like offering up one's own life and
one obtains the corresponding fruits. Shiva is delighted when
one offers up one's own life and grants *sayujya* with him. This
offering of the *naivedya* of a lifetime should only be made to
Shiva."'

'"The *yoni* and the *lingam* are Shiva's own forms. and he
is the one who determines birth. Therefore, to prevent births,
this worship of a lifetime must be made to Shiva. The entire
universe, mobile and immobile, has *bindu* and *nada* inside it.
Bindu is Shakti and *nada* is Shiva. The universe has Shiva and
Shakti inside it. *Bindu* holds up *nada*.[315] *Bindu* holds up the
entire universe. *Bindu* and *nada* are established, providing a
foundation for the entire universe. When *bindu* and *nada* are
united, everything becomes complete. There is no doubt that
the universe is born as a result of this completion. The *lingam*
represents the union of *bindu* and *nada* and is said to be the
cause of the universe. *Bindu* is the goddess and Shiva is *nada*.
Shiva's *lingam* represents their union. Therefore, to prevent
birth, one should worship Shiva's *lingam*. The goddess is the
mother of the universe. Shiva is the father of the universe.
When the parents are constantly worshipped, there is an
increase in great compassion. Out of this compassion,
prosperity is bestowed on the worshipper. O bulls among
sages! Thus, hidden gains are also obtained. Shiva's *lingam* is
worshipped in the form of the mother and the father. Bharga
is said to be in the form of Purusha and Bhargaa is said to
be in the form of Prakriti.[316] Purusha is said to be unmanifest
and is the form of a hidden conception, inside. Prakriti is
said to be a conception that is extremely well manifest, but
inside. Purusha is the first conception. Therefore, Purusha is

---

[315] In the sign (ं), the dot is *bindu* and the semi-circle is *nada*.
[316] Bharga is Shiva and Bhargaa is Parvati.

spoken of as the father. The union of Purusha and Prakriti is spoken of as the first birth. When Prakriti becomes manifest outside, it is spoken of as the second birth. Though born, a being is as good as dead. It obtains proper birth only through Purusha. There are certainly others who think and say that birth is the result of *maya*. The word *jiva* is said to be that which decays from the time of birth.[317] Another meaning of the word *jiva* is that it is bound from the time of birth.[318] Therefore, from the time of birth, a person should worship the *lingam*, so as to be freed from the noose of birth. Prakriti is spoken of as Bhaga because it enhances the progress towards prosperity.[319] The ordinary senses enjoy sound and the other objects of the senses that result from Prakriti. It is mostly heard that the word *bhoga*[320] means that which has been given by Bhaga. Bhaga is primarily Prakriti, but Shiva is spoken of as Bhagavan. Bhagavan is the one who bestows *bhoga*. There is no one else who can confer *bhoga*. Bhagavan is the lord of *bhoga*. Therefore, learned ones speak of him as Bharga. When Bhaga is combined with *lingam*, there is union between Bhaga and *lingam*. For objects of pleasure in this world and in the next one and for constant enjoyment of objects of pleasure, one should worship Shiva's *lingam*, Bhagavan Mahadeva. In the form of Surya, he gives birth to the worlds and his symbol indicates that birth. One should worship Purusha in the form of the *lingam*. The *lingam* indicates the cause behind birth. The meaning of *lingam* is that it is a sign of existence. Therefore, one should meditate on the *lingam*. The *lingam* signifies Purusha and takes one to Shiva. The *lingam* is spoken of as the sign of union

---

[317] *Jiva* is living being. It decays (*jiryate*) from the time of birth.
[318] Bound in the noose of *karma*.
[319] *Bham* (splendor) and *gacchati* (to go), combining to get Bhaga.
[320] Meaning enjoyment.

between Shiva and Shakti. He is delighted at his sign being worshipped and the signs of what that symbol does become unimportant. The signs of what that symbol does are birth and death. One thus withdraws from birth and death. Using the sixteen kinds of *upachara* and means that are internal or external, one should therefore worship Shiva's *lingam*, standing for Purusha and Prakriti. Worshipping in this way on Sunday wards off birth. Using Pranava, the great *lingam* should be worshipped on Monday. On Monday, *abhisheka* with *pancha gavya*[321] is particularly efficacious—cow dung, cow's urine, milk, curd and *ghee*. These constitute *pancha gavya*. Milk, honey and molasses can also be separately used. The *naivedya* of rice cooked in cow's milk must be offered with the chanting of Pranava. Pranava is *dhvani lingam*; *nada* is Svayambhu *lingam*; the *yantra* is *bindu lingam*; 'M' is *pratishthita lingam*; 'U' is *chara lingam*; and 'A' is *guru lingam*. There is no doubt that a *jiva* who worships the six *lingam*s is liberated.[322] The devoted worship of Shiva frees men from the cycle of birth. One-fourth of this benefit is obtained by wearing *rudraksha* and one-eighth by smearing *vibhuti*.[323] Three-fourths are obtained by performing *japa* with *mantra*s and worshipping with complete devotion. A man who is devoted to Shiva's *lingam* and worships it, is liberated. O *brahmana*s! If a person controls himself and reads or hears this chapter, his devotion towards Shiva increases and becomes steady."'

---

[321] Five products that come from a cow.

[322] *Dhvani* is sound, *nada* is a loud roar. *Yantra* is a mystical diagram used for worship. Reference is to AUM. *Pratishthita* is one that is established and does not move, while *chara* is one that is mobile. *Guru* means large. AUM can be written as OUM or AUM. The text uses AUM.

[323] Ashes, smeared on the forehead.

Chapter 24-2(17) (AUM and *Panchakshara Mantra*)[324]

'The *rishis* said, "O great sage! Please tell us about the greatness of Pranava and the six *lingams*. O lord! Please tell us how, in due order, Shiva's devotee should undertake the worship."'

'Suta replied, "O stores of austerities! You have asked the right question. Only Mahadeva knows the answer to this question. No one else knows. However, because of Shiva's favours, I will tell you about it. May Shiva grant you, and us, a great deal of protection. *Samsara*, this ocean of worldly existence, has evolved out of Prakriti. The learned know that Pranava is a new and excellent boat used to cross it. Pranava is known to mean, 'There is no *prapancha* for you.'[325] Pranava is known to mean, 'That which leads to liberation.' There are *yogis* who use this to perform their own *japa*. There are worshippers who use it as their own *mantra*. This bestows new and divine *jnana* and destroys all *karma*. It is said to be devoid of *maya* and is described as new. It is new and pure in nature and conveys towards the great-souled one. The learned know that this is new in what Pranava does. Pranava is said to be of two types, with a difference between gross and subtle. The subtle is known to consist of a single *akshara*, while the gross is known to consist of five *aksharas*. The subtle is not manifest. But the letters of *pancharna*[326] are extremely clearly manifest. The subtle represents the entire essence and is meant for a *jivanmukta*. As one searches for the meaning of the

---

[324] There are sections in this chapter that are difficult to understand and translate. Several meanings are esoteric in nature. Hence, it does not follow that the translation is exactly right.

[325] *Prapancha* is the visible universe.

[326] *Pancharna* and *panchakshara* are the same.

mantra, one's own body is dissolved. When one's own body is dissolved, one certainly merges completely into Shiva. Through only performing *japa* with this *mantra,* one certainly achieves that union. If one performs this *japa* thirty-six crore times, one certainly achieves that union. The subtle is known to be of two types, with differences of short and long. There is 'A', 'U' and 'M' in that order, along with *bindu* and *nada.* Time and place are built into it. The long Pranava is known to exist only in the hearts of *yogis.* The short Pranava is known to have the three— 'A', 'U' and 'M'.[327] These three represent Shiva, Shakti and their union. Those who desire that all their sins are destroyed, should perform *japa* with this short version. There are five elements, earth and the others. There are the five objects of the senses, sound and others. Together, these amount to ten. The desires that pursue these ten are spoken of as *pravritti.*[328] The short version is for those who follow *pravritti,* while the long version is for those who follow *nivritti.* The sound of Aumkara is uttered before *vyahriti*[329] and other *mantras.* It is used before the *Vedas* and also at the time of the two *sandhyas.* If a man performs *japa* with this nine crore times, he is purified. If he again performs *japa* with this nine crore times, he conquers the element of earth. If he again performs *japa* with this nine crore times, he conquers the element of water. If he again performs *japa* with this nine crore times, he conquers the element of fire. If he again performs *japa* with this nine crore times, he conquers the element of wind. If he again performs *japa* with this nine crore times, he conquers

---

[327] The implication seems to be that *bindu* and *nada* are only known to *yogis.*

[328] *Nivritti* is detachment from fruits and renunciation of action. *Pravritti* is action with a desire for the fruits.

[329] *Vyahriti* means the words *bhuh, bhuvah* and *svah,* uttered after AUM.

the element of space. If he again performs *japa* with this nine crore times each, he conquers the objects of the senses, smell and the others. If he again performs *japa* with this nine crore times, he conquers *ahamkara*. Every day, if a man performs *japa* with this one thousand times, the person becomes pure. O *brahmana*s! Therefore, *japa* with this ensures success. If a person uses Pranava to perform *japa* one hundred and eight crore times, his understanding is awakened, and he achieves pure *yoga*. There is no doubt that a person who has achieved pure *yoga* is *jivanmukta*. One must always perform *japa*. One must always perform *dhyana* on Shiva. Pranava is his form. There is no doubt that a great *yogi* in *samadhi* is like Shiva himself. One must again perform *japa*, using *nyasa* of *rishi*s, *chhanda*s[330] and *deva*s on one's own body. Indeed, a person who uses Pranava to perform *nyasa* of the Matrikas on his body, becomes a *rishi*. When *nyasa* is done with the ten Matrikas in this way, one obtains success in the six paths.[331] Those who pursue *pravritti* should resort to the gross Pranava."'

'"*Shivayogi*s are of three types—those who follow *kriya*, those who follow *tapas* and those who follow *japa*. There are those who worship with wealth and other things, performing *kriya*[332] with limbs of the body and doing *namaskara*. They are spoken of as *kriyayogi*s. There are those who worship after controlling their external sense organs. They eat little and do not harm or cause injury to others. They are spoken of as *tapoyogi*s.[333] There are those who possess all these. But

---

[330] Metres.

[331] The 'six' could apply to many things. But it may also mean *anga-nyasa*, with the heart, the forehead, the crown of the head, the part from the ears to the waist, the eyes and around the head, the standard six parts of the body for such *nyasa*.

[332] The word *kriya* has multiple meanings. Here, it means rites.

[333] The word *tapas* can only be imperfectly translated as austerities since it has a nuance of scorching and purifying oneself.

in addition, they are never angry and are devoid of all desires. They are serene and are always engaged in *japa*. Such people are known as *japayogis*. *Shivayogis* are those who use the sixteen kinds of *upachara* to undertake worship. Such a man gradually achieves *salokya* and pure emancipation."'

"'O *brahmanas*! I will now tell you about *japayoga*. Listen attentively. It is said that a person who observes austerities must also undertake *japa*, so as to cleanse himself. O *brahmanas*! The gross form of Pranava is Shiva's *panchakshara*. This represents five principles and has Shiva's name, preceded by *namah*.[334] If a man performs *japa* with *panchakshara*, he obtains every kind of success. *Japa* with *panchakshara* must be performed with Pranava preceding it. O *brahmanas*! A person must approach a *guru* and take instructions from him. Following this, he must be seated comfortably on the ground. The *japa* must start in *shukla paksha* and end in *krishna paksha*.[335] The months of Magha and Bhadra are special and the best of times for this. As long as this is going one, he must eat only once a day and in limited quantities. He must control his speech and restrain his senses. He must always render service to his master, his king and his parents. As soon as he performs this *japa* one thousand times, he will become pure and be freed from all debts. *Japa* with *panchakshara* must be undertaken five hundred thousand times. While doing this, one should remember Shiva. Shiva is seated in *padmasana*. He is adorned with Ganga and the crescent moon. Shakti is seated on his left thigh. Surrounded by large numbers of *gana*s, he is radiant. He is clad in the skin of an animal. His hands are in the form of *varada* and

---

[334] *Namah Shivaaya.*
[335] From *chaturdashi* in *shukla paksha* to *chaturdashi* in *krishna paksha.*

abhaya.[336] He is the one who always bestows compassion. One must remember Sadashiva. He must first be worshipped in one's mind, placing him in one's heart or in the solar disc. After that, having performed the rites of purification, a learned person will seat himself, facing the east. He will then perform *japa* with the *panchakshara mantra*. On the morning of *chaturdashi* in *krishna paksha*, he must first complete his *nitya karma*. He must then be seated in a pure and agreeable spot. He must control himself and purify his mind. Using the *panchakshara mantra*, he must perform *japa* twelve thousand times. He must invite five excellent *brahmanas* who are Shiva's devotees, along with their wives. Among these, the one who is distinguished as a *guru* will represent the embodied form of Shiva, the Samba form.[337] A second will represent the Ishana form, a third will represent the Aghora form, a fourth will represent the Vama form and the fifth will represent the Sadyojata form. These excellent *brahmana* devotees will represent these five forms of Shiva.[338] After objects required for the worship have been collected, the worship can start. Following the norms of worshipping Shiva, oblations will be offered into the fire. Before oblations are offered into the

[336] *Mudra*s are positions of the hand. One hand is in *varada mudra*, the position of granting boons. This has the hand pointing downwards, palm uppermost and fingers pointing downwards. The second hand is in *abhaya mudra*, the position that signifies freedom from fear. The hand is held up, the palm facing outwards.

[337] That is, along with Amba.

[338] Shiva has multiple forms. These five forms correspond to the directions. Stated very simply, Sadyojata is the form that bestows happiness and unhappiness and faces the west. Vama/Vamadeva is the form that represents the *turiya* state of consciousness and faces the north. Aghora is the form that represents *jnana* and faces the south. Tatpurusha (referred to in the text as Samba, or the one with Amba) stands for bliss and faces the east. Ishana represents space and faces upwards.

fire, he should place his sacred thread below his mouth.[339]
The oblations must be offered ten times, one hundred times
or one thousand times and the *ghee* must be from the milk
of a *kapila* cow.[340] A learned person can offer the oblations
himself, or get it done by Shiva's devotees one hundred and
eight times. When the oblations are over, *dakshina* must be
offered. The *guru* must be given a bull and a cow. Ishana
and the others must also be honoured and the *guru*, Samba
in form, is honoured. He will bathe his own body with
water obtained from washing their feet. This immediately
yields the fruits of bathing in thirty-six crore *tirtha*s. Full of
devotion, he must offer them cooked food, along with the
ten accompaniments. The *guru*'s wife must be thought of as
Paraa.[341] She and the wives of Ishana and the others must be
worshipped. They must be offered *rudraksha*s and garments.
According to wealth, they must be fed supreme food, along
with cakes and sweet cakes.[342] Once the offerings and the
donations have been made, they must be fed sumptuously.
The *japa* ceremony is then concluded with prayers to the lord
of the *deva*s. When a man accomplishes *purashcharana*[343]
in this manner, it is as if he now possesses a *mantra*. If he
again performs *japa* five hundred thousand times, he is freed
from all sins. For every set of five hundred thousand *japa*s, he
obtains the prosperity of all the worlds, Atala and the others

---

[339] *Homa* is the offering of *ghee* into the fire. For different rites,
the sacred thread (*upavita*) is worn in different ways. Before *homa*,
there is a practice of winding the *upavita* around the neck. Below the
mouth probably refers to this.

[340] *Kapila* means tawny, but often means an excellent cow.

[341] The supreme and great goddess, Adi Paraashakti or Mahadevi.

[342] Respectively, *vataka*s and *apupa*s.

[343] A term particularly used in *tantra*. This means to accomplish
a task, with a specific objective in mind, within a stipulated period of
time.

and progressively increasing to Satyaloka. If he dies in the middle, after enjoying objects of pleasure, he will return to earth and continue to perform *japa*. If he again performs five hundred thousand *japa*s, he obtains *samipya* with Brahma. If he again performs *japa* five hundred thousand times, he obtains the fortune of *sarupya*. If he completes ten million *japa*s, he becomes Brahma's equal. He obtains *sayujya* and his tasks are like those of Brahma. He enjoys objects of pleasure until Brahma brings about dissolution. In the next *kalpa*, he is born as Brahma's son. He again blazes in austerities and is progressively liberated."'

'"Earth and the other worlds were progressively fashioned out of the elements. Starting with Patala and ending with Satyaloka, there are fourteen of Brahma's worlds. Above Satyaloka, there are fourteen of Vishnu's worlds, ending with Kshama. In the world of Kshama, Vishnu is engaged in his tasks, basing himself in the supreme habitation of Vaikuntha. Lakshmi is also established there, with him, engaged in the task of protecting those who enjoy great objects of pleasure. Above this too, there are twenty-eight words, ending with Shuchi. Rudra, the destroyer of beings, is established in Kailasa, in Shuchiloka. Above this, there are fifty-six worlds, ending with Ahimsa. The city of Jnana-Kailasa is in Ahimsa-loka. Having done everything, Karyeshvara[344] is established there, in his form of disappearance. Kalachakra[345] is established at the end of this. The region beyond this is Kalatita.[346] Shiva, the lord of Kalachakra, is established there. He assumes the form of a buffalo as Dharma and unites everyone with Kala.[347] The four legs of the buffalo are falsehood, impurity, violence and lack

---

[344] The lord of all action.
[345] The wheel of time.
[346] Beyond time.
[347] Destiny or time.

of compassion. He can assume any form he wills, and he is these four feet, falsehood and the others. In the form of that dark-complexioned and large buffalo, he is also other things— lack of belief, lack of prosperity, wicked association, constant utterance of words which are outside the pale of the *Veda*s and addiction to anger. That is the reason he is spoken of as Maheshvara. The region of disappearance is up to this spot. Below this spot are those who enjoy *karma*. Above this spot are those who enjoy *jnana*. Below is the *maya* of *karma*. Above it is the *maya* of *jnana*. The word *maya* is explained in the following way. '*Ma*' stands for Lakshmi and '*ya*' makes one proceed towards enjoyment of *karma*.[348] Similarly, the word *maya* is also explained in the following way. '*Ma*' stands for Lakshmi and '*ya*' makes one proceed towards enjoyment of *jnana*. Above all this, is the region of perpetual enjoyment. Below all this, is the region known as that of temporary enjoyment. Disappearance is below this. There is no disappearance above this. The bondage of nooses exists below this. There is no bondage above this. Those who follow *kamya karma* circle around below this region. Those who pursue *karma* without desire are described as those who enjoy above this region. Those who are devoted to worshipping *bindu* circle around below this. Those who worship the *lingam* without desire are those who advance above this region. Those who worship gods other than Shiva circle around below this. Those who are devoted to Shiva alone, advance above. There are one crore *jiva*s below and another one crore exist above. Those who are in *samsara* are below. Those who have been emancipated are indeed above. Those who worship natural objects circle around below. Those who worship objects connected with Purusha are the ones who advance upwards. Shakti-*lingam* is below, and Shiva-*lingam* is above. The *lingam* that is shrouded is below, while the *lingam*

---

[348] *Maya = Ma + ya. Ya* means to proceed towards.

that is uncovered is above. The *lingam* that has been thought of is below, but the *lingam* that has not been thought of is above. The external *lingam* is below, but the internal one is above. There are one hundred and twelve Shaktilokas below. The *bindu* form is below, but the *nada* form is above. The world of *karma* is below, the world of *jnana* is above. *Namaskara* is above and it destroys *ahamkara*. The meaning of the word *jnana* is the following. Anything that is the result of birth is *janija* and the word '*na*' is a negative.[349] Whatever counters the temporary is *jnana*. Those who worship elements circle around below this. Those who worship the *adhyatmika*[350] proceed above. In that great world, the *vedi*[351] part only extends up to the *atma-lingam*. The eight bonds of Prakriti[352] only extend up to this *vedi*. In the *Veda*s, and in popular beliefs, this is the way it is."'

'"There are those who are engaged in the worship of Shiva. He is astride the buffalo that is *adharma*. Such people are devoted to the *dharma* of the truth. Hence, they cross Kalachakra and go beyond. Above this, is the bull of *dharma*, in its form of *brahmacharya*. Truth and the others constitute its legs, and it stands in front of Shivaloka. Its horns are forgiveness, its ears are peace, its eyes are belief and its heavy breathing stands for the intellect and the mind. This bull is adorned with chants from the *Veda*s. This bull should always be known as the cause behind the various rites. This bull of *dharma* and rites is stationed beyond Kalatita. It is said that the lifespans of Brahma, Vishnu and Mahesha are a day each.

---

[349] This is a very contrived derivation of *jnana*. *Janih* is birth/creation, *janija* is something that is the result of creation and is therefore temporary. *Na* (not) + *janija* (temporary) = *jnana*.

[350] Concerning the *jivatman*, knowledge about the *jivatman*.

[351] *Vedi* means altar. But here, it seems to apply to the base of the *lingam*.

[352] Earth, water, fire, air, space, mind, intellect and *ahamkara*.

But above this, there is no night or day. Nor is there birth or death. There is only the truth that is the cause. There is only the *brahman* that is the cause. Smell and the subtle objects of the senses, devised out of the subtle elements, are always above. The nature of subtle smell is such that it exists in the fourteen worlds. The fourteen worlds where Vishnu is the cause are also there. It is also held that there are twenty-eight worlds where Rudra is the cause. Above this, there are fifty-six worlds where Isha is the cause. Beyond this, is the world known as *brahmacharya*, revered by Shiva. Jnana-Kailasa is there, and it is covered in five sheaths. It has five circles and five components of the *brahman*. With Adi-Shakti, Adi-lingam is there. Shiva is the *paramatman* and this is spoken of as Shiva's abode. With Para-Shakti, Parameshvara is there. He is accomplished in the five tasks of creation, preservation, destruction, disappearance and showing favours. His body is *sacchidananda*. He is always engaged in the *dharma* of *dhyana*. He is always engaged in showing favours. He is seated in *samadhi*. He is radiant in his own *atman*. One can see him gradually, by performing the rites of *sandhya* and engaging in *dhyana*. One should regard *nitya karma* and worship as Shiva's tasks. All rites are Shiva's tasks. This extends *jnana* about Shiva. There is no doubt that all those who come within his range of vision are liberated. Understanding the nature of one's *atman* and finding happiness within one's own *atman* are liberation. This is based on rites, austerities, *japa*, *jnana*, *dhyana* and *dharma*. When one sees Shiva, one finds happiness within one's own *atman*. Just as the sun spreads its own rays, one is swiftly purified. Shambhu is accomplished in bestowing compassion, and one obtains *jnana*. Ignorance is dispelled and one obtains *jnana* about Shiva. The nature of *jnana* about Shiva is such that one finds happiness within one's own *atman*. When a man finds happiness within his own *atman*, he becomes successful in all his objectives.'"

'"Through again performing ten million *japa*s, he obtains Brahma's world. Thereafter, through again performing ten million *japa*s, he obtains Vishnu's world. Thereafter, through again performing ten million *japa*s, he obtains Rudra's world. Thereafter, through again performing ten million *japa*s, he obtains Ishvara's world. Thereafter, if he controls himself and performs many kinds of *japa*s, he reaches Kalachakra, the start of Shivaloka. Kalachakra has five wheels, each encasing the preceding one. Delusion about creation is Brahma's wheel. Delusion about objects of enjoyment is Vishnu's wheel. Delusion about anger is Rudra's wheel. Circling around is known as Ishvara's wheel. Delusion about *jnana* is Shiva's wheel. The learned have spoken about the five wheels in this way. If he again performs ten crore *japa*s, he reaches the abode of Brahma, who is the cause. If he again performs ten crore *japa*s, he obtains prosperity there. In this way, an immensely energetic one gradually obtains Vishnu's region. Progressively, such a great-souled one obtains prosperity. Fixed in attention, if a person performs one hundred and five crore *japa*s, he obtains Shivaloka, which is outside the fifth sheath. There is a silver pavilion there and an excellent riverbed. In the form of austerities, a bull can be seen there. This is the place of Sadyojata, the supreme fifth sheath. There is the place of Vamadeva, the fourth sheath. After this, there is the abode of Aghora, the third sheath. There is the auspicious second sheath, that of Samba Purusha. Beyond this is Ishana, the first sheath. There are five pavilions there, the abode of *dhyana dharma*. The fifth pavilion is of Balinatha, who bestows a full complement of *amrita*. Beyond this, the fourth pavilion has an image of Chandrashekhara. The third pavilion is the abode of Somaskanda. Those who believe say that the second pavilion is Nritya Mandapa. The extremely beautiful first pavilion is the abode of Mulamaya.[353] Beyond this is *garbha*

---

[353] Primary illusion.

griha,[354] the supreme and auspicious place for the *lingam*. Shiva's glory is known to exist beyond Nandi's region. Nandishvara is situated outside, worshipping the *panchakshara*. This knowledge has been passed down through a succession of *gurus*. I obtained it from Nandishvara. What exists beyond this is only known to Shiva and cannot be experienced. It is only through Shiva's favours that one can experience the glory of Shivaloka. Those who believe say that no one is capable of knowing it otherwise. In this way, *brahmana*s who are in control of their senses are gradually liberated."'

"'I will progressively tell you about the others. Listen lovingly. *Brahmana* women must take instruction from *gurus* and perform *japa*, using the word *namah* at the end. For long lifespans, they must perform *japa* with *panchakshara* five hundred thousand times. To counter the state of being women, they must again perform *japa* five hundred thousand times. Having become a man, a learned person will gradually be liberated. To counter the status of being a *kshatriya*, a person must perform *japa* five hundred thousand times. After having again performed *japa* five hundred thousand times, he will become a *brahmana*. When this man becomes a *brahmana* who possesses the *mantra*, he will be gradually liberated. A *vaishya* will perform *japa* five hundred thousand times to remove the status of being a *vaishya*. When he again performs *japa* five hundred thousand times, it is said that he becomes a *kshatriya* who possesses the *mantra*. When he again performs *japa* five hundred thousand times, he removes the status of being a *kshatriya*. When he again performs *japa* five hundred thousand times, he is said to become a *brahmana* who possesses the *mantra*. When a *shudra* performs *japa* two million and five hundred thousand times, using the word *namah* at the end, he becomes a *brahmana* who possesses the *mantra*. It is after this

---

[354] Inner apartment, sanctum sanctorum.

that he becomes a pure *brahmana*. Whether one is a woman, a man, a *brahmana* or some other *varna*, whether one is already afflicted or whether one is afflicted in any kind of way, one must always perform *japa*, using the word *namah* at the beginning, or at the end. For women, it is said that the *guru* will instruct properly."'

'"After completing five hundred thousand *japas*, a *sadhaka* will perform a great *abhisheka* and offer a great *naivedya*. To give Shiva pleasure, he will honour Shiva's devotees. When Shiva's devotees are worshipped, Shiva is greatly pleased. There is no difference between Shiva and Shiva's devotee. He is Shiva. The *mantra* is the form of Shiva himself. This is the conception of Shiva. When he uses this, Shiva's devotee becomes like the supreme Shiva in his own body. It is known that the rites followed by Shiva's devotees represent all the rites of the *Veda*s. The more a devotee performs *japa* with Shiva's *mantra*, the greater is Shiva's presence in his own body. There is no doubt about this. For women who are Shiva's devotees, Devi is the form of the *lingam*. As long as *japa* with the *mantra* is performed, there is Devi's presence. An intelligent person who worships Shiva assumes his name and form. However, even when he has become Shiva, he should worship Para Shakti. He can worship Shakti in the symbol of the *lingam*, or he can worship her *maya* in the form of a painting. Taking Shiva's *lingam* to be a form of Shiva, he can think of himself in the form of Shakti. Alternatively, he can take the *lingam* to be a form of Devi Shakti and think of himself as Shiva. Shiva's *lingam* is the form of *nada* and Shakti is the form of *bindu*. Either one can be regarded as more important, or both can be thought of in united form in the *lingam*. When Shiva and Shakti are worshipped, the fundamental conception is that of Shiva. Shiva's devotee takes the *mantra* to be a form of Shiva and himself to be a form of Shiva. He will worship with the sixteen kinds of *upachara* and accomplish his desires. This service to the *lingam* by Shiva's devotee generates happiness in Shiva and delights him even more. Therefore, along with his wife, Shiva's devotee should worship the divinity, along with his wife. After this, without any deception, he should worship five, ten or one hundred of Shiva's devotees, along with their wives, feeding them and giving them wealth, with or without *mantra*s. He and his wife will then assume the form of Shiva and Shakti and not be born on earth again."'

'"The part below the navel is Brahma's region. The part up to the throat is Vishnu's region. For Shiva's devotee, in the body, the face is spoken of as the *lingam*. When someone dies, a cremation ceremony is performed. After the cremation of the dead person is over, one should worship Shiva, the primordial father. After this, he should worship the primordial mother and honour Shiva's devotees. If this is done, the dead person goes to the world of the ancestors and is gradually liberated. A person with *tapas* is superior to ten people with *kriya*s. A person with *japa* is superior to one hundred people with *tapas*. A person who possesses *jnana* about Shiva is superior to one thousand people with *japa*. A person with *dhyana* is superior to one hundred thousand people who possess *jnana* about Shiva. A person in *samadhi* is superior to one crore people who are in *dhyana*. Since the succeeding ones are superior to the preceding ones, it is they who should be chosen for showing honours. The specific nature of the fruits that result is difficult for even learned persons to comprehend. Hence, an ordinary person is incapable of understanding the greatness of Shiva's devotee. The worship of Shiva's devotee is equal to worshipping Shiva and Shakti together. Hence, a person who devotedly performs this worship attains Shiva and becomes like Shiva. If a *brahmana* reads this chapter, which is in conformity with the Atharva Veda, he obtains *jnana* about Shiva and rejoices with Shiva. O lords among sages! If a person possesses specific knowledge about this, he must make Shiva's devotees hear it.

O learned ones! Through Shiva's favours, he will obtain success and Shiva will show him compassion."'

Chapter 25-2(18) (Bondage and Liberation)

'The *rishi*s asked, "What is the nature of bondage and what is the nature of liberation? O one who knows about everything! Please tell us."'

'Suta replied, "I will tell you about bondage and the means for obtaining liberation. Listen lovingly. It is said that a *jiva* is bound if he is tied down by the eight bonds of Prakriti. A person who has been freed from the eight bonds of Prakriti is said to be liberated. Therefore, being freed from the subjugation of Prakriti is liberation. When a *jiva* who is bound has been freed, he is spoken of as a liberated *jiva*. The eight bonds of Prakriti are known to be intellect, *ahamkara*, the one that possesses the *guna*s and the five *tanmatra*s.[355] These are Prakriti's attributes. A body originates from these eight attributes of Prakriti, and it is said that *karma* originates from the body. Another body results from *karma* and as a result of *karma*, there is birth. This occurs repeatedly. It should be known that the body is of three types—the gross, the subtle and the causal. It is said that the gross engages in activities, the subtle enjoys the objects of the senses. The causal enjoys the nature of the *karma* the *jiva* undertakes. As fruits of that *karma*, it enjoys joy and misery, the consequence of good and bad deeds. Therefore, a *jiva* is repeatedly bound in the ropes of *karma*. Bound to *karma*, the three types of body are constantly whirled around, like a wheel. To counter the circling around of the wheel, the creator

---

[355] The mind possesses the *guna*s and the five *tanmatra*s are the five subtle elements.

of the wheel must be worshipped. Prakriti and its attributes
are the giant wheel. Shiva is beyond Prakriti. Mahesha, who is
beyond Prakriti, is the creator of the wheel. Like a child drinks
or spits out water as he pleases, Shiva is established, with the
jiva and Prakriti and its attributes under his subjugation. Since
he keeps everything under his subjugation, he is spoken of as
Shiva.[356] Shiva alone is omniscient, complete and free from
desire. Maheshvara's mental powers are known as omniscience,
contentment, understanding that is without any beginning,
independence, a power that is constant and never goes away and
infinite capacity. Therefore, it is because of Shiva's powers that
Prakriti and its attributes are under his subjugation. To obtain
Shiva's favours, it is Shiva alone who must be worshipped. He
is complete and without desires. How can he be worshipped?
Any task that is the outcome of his instructions leads to him
being pleased. Hence, following Shiva's instructions, people
worship his sign of the *lingam*, or his devotees. He must be
worshipped using deeds, thoughts, words and wealth. The
supreme Shiva Mahesha is beyond Prakriti. As a result of this
worship, he is truly pleased and shows specific favours to the
worshipper. As a result of Shiva's favours, *karma* and the
other things gradually come under one's control. Starting with
karma and ending with Prakriti, everything comes under one's
control. Such a person is spoken of as liberated. He is radiant,
happy within his own *atman*. This body is the consequence of
karma. As a result of Parameshvara's favours, this too comes
under control. Therefore, the person resides in Shivaloka and
is spoken of as having obtained *salokya*. When the *tanmatras*
come under control, *samipya* with Samba is achieved. In
weapons and in action, he achieves *sayujya* with Shiva. When
he obtains his great favours, the intellect also comes under

[356] Here, the word Shiva is being derived from *vasha*, to keep
under control or subjugation. The one who does this is Shiva.

control. The intellect represents the working of Prakriti. Hence, this is known as *sarshti*. Thereafter, through his great favours, Prakriti itself comes under control. Without any effort, he then obtains Shiva's mental powers. He obtains Shiva's omniscience and capacity and is resplendent in his own *atman*. Those who are accomplished in the *Veda*s and the *agama* texts speak of this as *sayujya*. In this way, by first worshipping the *lingam*, one gradually becomes liberated. Therefore, to obtain Shiva's favours, one must undertake the rites connected with Shiva's worship. One must always undertake rites for Shiva, austerities for Shiva and perform *japa* with Shiva's *mantra*. One must increasingly strive for *jnana* about Shiva and perform *dhyana* on Shiva. Until one goes to sleep and until the time of death, one must think about Shiva. If he desires what is auspicious, he must worship him with fresh flowers and other things."'

'The *rishi*s said, "Please tell us everything about the rules for worshipping Shiva, using the *lingam* and other things."'

'Suta replied, "O *brahmana*s! I will accurately tell you about the worship of the *lingam*. Listen. The first *lingam* is Pranava, and it bestows everything one wishes for. If it is subtle and *nishkala* in form, it is spoken of as subtle Pranava. The *sakala* form is spoken of as the gross *lingam* and is represented in *panchakshara*. The worship of these two is described as austerities and both directly yield emancipation. There are many kinds of Purusha *lingam*s that are formed out of the elements of Prakriti. Shiva himself can speak about them in detail. No one else knows. I know about the *lingam*s that are formed out of materials from the earth and I will tell you about these. The first is Svayambhu *lingam*, while the second is Bindu *lingam*. The third is Pratishthita *lingam*, while the fourth is Chara *lingam*. The fifth is Guru *lingam*. When he is satisfied with the austerities of *deva*s and *rishi*s and wishes to show his presence, in his *nada* form, Sharva assumes the form of a seed inside the earth. Having assumed this stable form, he sprouts

through the ground and manifests himself. Since this originates
through an act of self-creation, this is known as Svayambhu
lingam. If a devotee worships this *lingam*, his *jnana* increases
on its own. On a silver or golden vessel, or on the ground or an
altar, the devotee can draw a *lingam* with his own hand. Using
the pure Pranava *mantra*, he can draw the *lingam* in the form
of a *yantra* and undertake its *pratishthana* and *avahana*. This
lingam has *bindu* and *nada* and can be stationary or mobile.
Though this is only formed conceptually, there is no doubt that
this also follows Shiva's instruction.[357] Shambu exists wherever
one believes he does and yields fruits. The devotee can draw
the *yantra* with his own hand on anything that is natural and
stationary. After performing *avahana*, he can worship with the
sixteen kinds of *upachara*. He can then obtain the prosperity
himself and through practice, obtain *jnana*. To accomplish
success in their *atmans*, *devas* or *rishis* use their own hands to
set up, using *mantras*, a *lingam* in a pure circle. Pure in their
thoughts, they establish an excellent *lingam*. This Purusha
lingam is spoken of as a Pratishthita *lingam*. If one constantly
worships this *lingam*, one obtains Purusha's prosperity. Great
brahmanas and extremely rich kings use artisans to devise and
establish *lingams*, with the use of *mantras*. Such a Pratishthita
lingam can be made of natural or artificial objects and yields
prosperity and objects of pleasure. One which is full of energy
and permanent is known as a Purusha *lingam*. One which is
weak and temporary is spoken of as a Prakrita *lingam*. In the
three worlds, an *adhyatmika* or Chara *lingam* is one that is
progressively conceptualized in different parts of the body—
the penis, the navel, the tongue, the tip of the nose, the tuft of
hair and the waist. A mountain is spoken of as Purusha, while
the earth is spoken of as Prakriti. Trees are known as Purusha,

---

[357] This is Bindu *lingam*.

while creepers are spoken of as Prakriti. *Shashtika* rice[358] is known as Prakriti, while *shali* rice and wheat are Purusha. Prosperity is Purusha and is known to bestow the eight kinds of *siddhi*s, *anima* and the others.[359] Those who believe say that *stridhana*[360] and such objects are Prakriti."

"'Among Chara *lingam*s, Rasa *lingam* is spoken of as the foremost.[361] Rasa *lingam*s bestow *brahmana*s with every kind of wish. Auspicious Bana *lingam*s bestow large kingdoms on *kshatriya*s. Svarna *lingam*s make *vaishya*s the masters of a great deal of wealth. Auspicious Shila *lingam*s are extremely purifying for *shudra*s. A Sphatika *lingam* or a Bana *lingam* bestow everything desired on everyone. If one does not possess the *lingam* that is appropriate to one's own self, there is no harm in worshipping a *lingam* that is meant for another. For women, especially those who have husbands, a Parthiva *lingam* should be used. For widows who still possesses *pravritti*, a Sphatika *lingam* is praised. Widows who are on the path of *nivritti* and follow excellent vows should worship Rasa *lingam*, whether they are children, young or aged. Pure Sphatika *lingam*s give women every object of pleasure. For those on the path of *pravritti*, worship of *pitha*s yields everything desired

---

[358] A type of fast-growing rice.

[359] *Siddhi*s mean powers. Specifically, *yoga* leads to eight major *siddhi*s or powers. These are *anima* (becoming as small as one desires), *mahima* (as large as one desires), *laghima* (as light as one wants), *garima* (as heavy as one wants), *prapti* (obtaining what one wants), *prakamya* (travelling where one wants), *vashitva* (powers to control creatures) and *ishitva* (obtaining divine powers).

[360] A woman's private property, over which, she alone has independent control.

[361] Rasa *lingam*s are made out of mercury, Bana *lingam*s are natural stones found in riverbeds, Svarna *lingam*s are made out of gold and Shila *lingam*s are made out of rock. Sphatika *lingam*s are made out of crystal, while Parthiva *lingam*s are made out of earth.

on earth. Every kind of worship should be undertaken in a vessel. When *abhisheka* is over, *naivedya* made out of *shali* rice must be offered. When the worship is over, the *lingam* must be covered and kept in a separate part of the house. When the worship is over, everyone should be fed the food they are naturally used to eating."

'"For those who follow the path of *nivritti*, the worship of a subtle *lingam* is recommended. Worship is undertaken of the *vibhuti* and it is *vibhuti* that is offered. After having performed the worship, the *lingam* must always be borne on the head.³⁶² *Vibhuti* is said to be of three types—from an ordinary fire, from the fire of rites connected with the *Veda*s and from Shiva's fire. The ash produced from an ordinary fire will be used to purify objects made out of clay, iron, silver and even grain. Articles used for worship, sesamum and other things, garments and other things, must also be purified with ashes. Articles polluted by dogs must also be purified with ashes. As is appropriate, ashes must be mixed with water or need not be mixed with water. When rites connected with the *Veda*s are over, the ash must be worn on the forehead. Since the rites have been undertaken with *mantra*s and the fire, the ash takes the form of the rites. Therefore, wearing the ash is like internalizing the rite in one's *atman*. After chanting the Aghora *mantra*, *bilva* wood must be burnt.³⁶³ This is described as Shiva's fire and the ashes resulting from this are ashes obtained from Shiva's fire. Cow dung and bovine products from a *kapila* cow must be burnt first. After this, wood from *shami*, *ashvattha*, *palasha*, *vata*, *aragvadha* or *bilva* will be

³⁶² The *lingam* is in the form of *vibhuti* and the ashes are worn on the forehead.
³⁶³ The Aghora *mantra* runs *Aum aghorebhya atha ghorebhya ghora ghoratarebhya* and so on. It can be found in the twenty-first *anuvaka* of *Mahanarayana Upanishad*.

burnt.[364] When these are burnt, that is also Shiva's fire, and the resultant ash is that obtained from Shiva's fire. Pronouncing Shiva's *mantras*, the wood must be burnt in a bed of *darbha* grass. After properly straining with a piece of cloth, the ashes will be placed in a new pot. For one's own resplendence, the ashes must be collected. The meaning of the word *bhasma* is something that must be honoured and worshipped.[365] Hence, earlier, Shiva also acted accordingly. A king collects taxes from his kingdom. In that way, men burn crops and survive on their essence. The digestive fire burns many kinds of food that are ingested. Having burnt them, the essence nourishes the body. Parameshvara Shiva is the lord of *prapanchaka*.[366] In his own dominion, he burns *prapanchaka* and accepts the essence. Having burnt *prapanchaka*, Shiva smears the ashes on his own body. Through that guise of burning, he accepts the essence from the universe. That jewel is his own and Isha himself applies it to his own body. The essence of space is in his hair. The essence of wind is in the breath that flows from his mouth. The essence of fire in his heart. The essence of water is in his waist. The essence of water is in his knees and in all his other limbs. Tripundraka represents the essence of Brahma, Vishnu and Rudra. Therefore, Maheshvara wears it in the form of a *tilaka*[367] on the lower part of his forehead. *Bha-vriddhi-sarvam-iti-manyate-svayam*[368]—in this way, he himself brings the essence of everything in *prapancha* under

---

[364] *Shami* is the name of a tree believed to contain fire, *palasha* is a tree (*butea monosperma*) and *aragvadha* is the Amaltas.

[365] The word *bhasma* (*bhasman*) or ash is derived from the root of something that shines.

[366] The same as *prapancha*.

[367] Mark made on the forehead.

[368] Literally meaning, 'He himself thinks that let everything flourish because of this'. This is a derivation for the word *bhasma*— *bha+s+ma*.

this control. Since he is the one who brings everything under
this subjugation, he is spoken of as Shiva.[369] The word *simha*
is used for someone who causes violence to all animals. But it
is also someone to whom no animals can cause violence. The
word *simha* is derived in that way.[370] Similarly, the word Shiva
also has a derivation. '*Sh*' stands for permanent happiness and
bliss, '*i*' is spoken of as Purusha and '*va*' stands for Shakti.
When the sweet union of the three takes place, one speaks of
it as Shiva. Therefore, a devotee must make his own *atman*
identical with Shiva and worship Shiva. The ash must first
be powdered and then applied as Triupundraka. At the time
of worship, it is mixed with water. However, for the sake
of purification, it can be used without water. Whether it is
night or day, whether it is a man or a woman, the devotee
must sip the water used for worship and wear the ash as
Tripundraka. If a person mixes ashes with water and wears it
as Tripundraka while worshipping, it is certain that he obtains
the complete fruits of worshipping Shiva. With *mantra*s to
Shiva, if one wears the *bhasma*, one moves outside the pale
of the *ashrama*s. Such a person is only devoted to Shiva and
the devotee is spoken of as one who follows Shiva's *ashrama*.
Being devoted to Shiva's vow, he does not observe any of the
rites of purification connected with birth or death. He wears
bhasma on his forehead, or a *tilaka* made out of mud. He can
apply this with his own hand, or it can be applied by the hand
of the *guru*. But this is the sign of being Shiva's devotee."'

'"The image of a *guru* is that of one who obstructs all the
*guna*s and the word *guru* is derived accordingly.[371] He is the
one who obstructs deviations caused by *rajas* and the other
*guna*s. The supreme Shiva is beyond the *guna*s and he assumes

[369] A derivation given earlier.
[370] *Simha* is lion and the word is derived from *himsa* (violence).
[371] From *guru* = *guna* + *ruddha* (obstruct).

the form of the *guru*. He takes away transgressions caused by the *guna*s and makes one understand about Shiva. That is the reason disciples speak of a *guru* as trustworthy. Hence, a learned person knows that the *guru*'s body is Guru *lingam*. Service to the *guru* amounts to worshipping Guru *lingam*. It has been heard that service is through deeds, thoughts and words. Anything the *guru* has instructed must be carried out, whether one is capable or incapable, even if this means the loss of life or wealth. Doing this purifies the *atman*. Hence, a *shishya* is spoken of as someone who is worthy of being ordered.[372] An excellent *shishya* offers everything to the *guru*, starting with his body. He must first offer food to the *guru* and eat only after he has been commanded to do so. Because he is worthy of being constantly instructed, a *shishya* is spoken of as a son. The tongue is like a penis, the *mantra* is like semen and the ears are like a vagina that has been sprinkled. Like a son, he is a son born through the *mantra*. Therefore, he must worship the *guru*, like a father. The biological father immerses the son in *samsara*. But the *guru* is a father who kindles understanding and makes him cross over *samsara*. Knowing the difference between the two fathers, he must worship the *guru*. He must tend to his limbs and give the *guru* the wealth and other things he has earned. He must massage his feet. Every limb belonging to the *guru* is like a *lingam*. He must give him riches and footwear. He must wash his feet and bathe him. He must worship him with *abhisheka*, *naivedya* and food. The worship of the *guru* is like the worship of Shiva, the *paramatman*. He must eat what is left after the *guru* has eaten. All of this purifies his own *atman*. The *guru*'s leftover food should be thought of as water and cooked food, left after being offered to Shiva. O *brahmanas*! Just as these are accepted by Shiva's devotee, that leftover food must also be accepted. If anything is taken without the *guru*'s

---

[372] *Shishya* (disciple) is derived from the root for ordering.

permission, all of it will considered theft. One must be careful in accepting a *guru*. A *guru* must possess special knowledge. One must try to free oneself from ignorance. Only a person who possesses special knowledge is capable of doing that."'

'"For success in completing a task, one must first pacify all impediments. When impediments are removed, it is only then that all elements of a task are successfully completed. Hence, in all rites, a learned person must first worship Vighnesha.[373] To counter all impediments, a learned person must worship all *deva*s. The first kind of impediments are *adhyatmika*— fever, problems with the joints and disease. The second kind of impediments are held to be *adhibhoutika*—*pishacha*s and jackals; infestations of termite hills; lizards and other beings falling down suddenly; seeing tortoises, snakes and wicked women inside the house; untimely delivery by trees, women and cows; and other such untimely occurrences of hardships. *Adhidaivika* impediments are said to be—omens like a bolt of lightning; epidemics; smallpox; cholera; plague; typhus; an evil planet traversing the natal *nakshatra*; an evil conjunction of a planet in its own *rashi*; and seeing nightmares. There can also be incidents where one touches a dog, a *chandala* or an outcast who has come to the house. When any of these occurs, it signifies hardships. Therefore, to pacify these kinds of taints, an intelligent person will perform a *yajna* for peace. For this, a spot must be chosen in a temple, in a settlement of cows, in a *chaitya*[374] or in the courtyard of one's own house. The place must be elevated and must be two *hasta*s high. It must be ornamented with one's own hand. One *bhara*[375] of paddy must

---

[373] Vighnesha, lord (*Isha*) of impediments (*vighna*), is Ganesha, the remover of impediments.

[374] The word *chaitya* has several meanings—sacrificial shed, temple, altar, sanctuary and a tree that grows along the road.

[375] Unit of weight.

be spread out there. A lotus must be drawn in the middle and others drawn in all the directions. A new and giant pot, with a thread tied around it, must be purified with *guggula dhupa*[376] and placed in the centre and similar such purified pots must be laid out in the eight directions. Bunches of mango leaves with stems and *kusha* grass must be placed in the eight pots. They must be purified with *mantras* and five different objects placed inside them. An excellent jewel, like blue sapphire, will be placed in each of the pots, one by one.[377] Along with his wife, a learned person will next invite his *acharya*, who knows about the rites. A golden image of Vishnu, Indra and the others will be placed in each of the pots, so that the heads, up to the chests, emerge from the tops of the pots. Vishnu will be invoked and worshipped in the pot that is in the middle. Beginning with the eastern direction, using the *mantras*, Indra and the others will be invoked and worshipped, one by one.[378] They will be addressed by name, in the dative case,[379] in the due order and ending with *namah*. The *acharya* will be used to perform *avahana* for each of them. Along with the *acharya*, the assistant priests will use the *mantras* to perform *japa* one hundred times. When the *japa* is over, to the west of the pot, oblations will be offered into the fire. Learned people will do this one crore times, one hundred thousand times, one thousand times or one hundred and eight times. This can be done for one day, nine days or for as long as the sun completes its circle.[380] Depending on the time and the

[376] A fragrant gum resin used as incense.
[377] That is, nine jewels all together.
[378] The eight guardians of the directions are Indra (east), Agni (south-east), Yama (south), Nirriti (south-west), Varuna (west), Vayu (north-west), Kubera (north) and Ishana (north-east). Vishnu is for the nadir and Brahma for the zenith.
[379] Used when one gives something to someone, *chaturthi* or the fourth case in grammar.
[380] We have interpreted the word *mandala* in this way.

place, this must be done as is appropriate. If the oblations are
for peace, the kindling used must be from the *shami* tree. If it
for making a living, the *palasha* tree can be used. Other than
kindling, objects like cooked food and *ghee* will be used, using a
mantra to address a divinity by name and offering the oblation.
Any article used at the beginning of the rite must continue to
be used until the rite has been completed. At the end of the rite,
there must be pronouncements of benediction.[381] The sanctified
water must be sprinkled on everyone. After this, *brahmana*s
must be fed, the number fed being the same as the number of
oblations that have been offered. O learned ones! The *acharya*
and the assistant priests will be fed *havishya*. At the end of the
oblations, so that everything remains beneficial, Aditya and the
planets must be worshipped. In due order, each of the assistant
priests will give be given *dakshina* and an excellent gem. After
having performed ten kinds of donations,[382] there must be large
quantities of donations to others—boys invested with sacred
threads, householders, forest-dwellers lacking wealth, maidens,
women with husbands and widows. All the articles used in the
rite must be offered to the *acharya*.'"

'"Yama is said to be the lord of omens, epidemics and
miseries. Therefore, to please him, Kaladana[383] must be
performed. An image of Kala must be made in the form of a
man, using one hundred gold coins or ten gold coins.[384] This
will hold a noose and a goad. Along with *dakshina*, this
golden image will be given as donation. For a long lifespan,
the donation of sesamum is praised. To counter disease, *ghee*

---

[381] Known as *punyahavachanam*, pronouncements of benedictions
and peace.
[382] Known as *dasha* (ten) *danam* (donations), where ten kinds of
objects are given to *brahmana*s.
[383] Donation of Kala.
[384] The word used for a gold coin is *nishka*.

or a mirror should be given. One thousand *brahmanas* must be fed. Those who are poor can feed one hundred. Those who are extremely poor and lack riches, will do this according to capacity. To pacify *bhutas*, a great worship of Bhairava must be undertaken. At the end of the rite, a great *abhisheka* and *naivedya* will be offered to Shiva. After this, there must be the feeding of *brahmanas*, on a large scale. Through the performance of such a sacrifice, there will be the pacification of all taints. Every year, in the month of Phalguna, such a rite of pacification must be performed. When there is an immediate calamity, this must be performed instantly or within a month. A person who has committed a major sin must worship Bhairava. If there is a great epidemic, the *sankalpa*[385] must be taken first. If a person is poor in every possible way, he will donate a lamp. If he is incapable of undertaking even that, he will bathe and not donate anything. A devotee must prostrate himself before the sun and pronounce the *mantra* one hundred and eight times. A learned person will pronounce it one thousand times, ten thousand times, one hundred thousand times and one crore times. *Namaskara* is a form of sacrificing oneself that satisfies all *devas*. 'I offer my intellect to your form and prostrate myself. Anything empty does not appeal to you. Without your glance being directed towards it, this body is nothing. Since I have prostrated myself, my body is like empty space, without any *ahamkara*. You are the lord. I am your servant. Therefore, I am no longer empty now.'[386] As is appropriate, one must think of doing *namaskara* to sacrifice oneself. In this connection, *naivedya* and betel leaves must be offered to Shiva. *Pradakshina* of Shiva must be done one hundred and eight times. One should make others do it one thousand times, ten thousand times, one hundred thousand times and one crore times. *Pradakshina*

---

[385] The resolution, the reason for undertaking the *puja*.
[386] This is the prayer used when sacrificing oneself.

of Shiva instantly destroys every kind of sin. Ailment is the
root cause of misery and sin is the root cause of ailment. It
is said that *dharma* alone dispels all sins. Any act of *dharma*
performed with Shiva in mind removes all sins. Among all acts
of *dharma* performed for Shiva, *pradakshina* leads the others.
Japa is a form of a rite where Pranava assumes the form of
pradakshina. The pair of birth and death is spoken of as a wheel
of *maya*. The pedestal where offerings are made[387] is spoken
of as Shiva's cycle of *maya*. Beginning with the Balipitha, one
must perform the *pradakshina* step by step until one reaches
the Balipitha again. Doing *namaskara* is said to complete the
process of *pradakshina*. Birth and death originate with him and
prostrating oneself is a form of surrender. The pair of birth and
death is thus offered up to Shiva's *maya*. When one offers this
pair up to Shiva, one is not born again. As long as one is under
the control of bodily functions, a *jiva* is spoken of as bound.
When one is no longer under the control of the body, the learned
speak of this as emancipation. The supreme cause, Shiva, is the
one who gets the wheel of *maya* going. When the pair is offered
up to Shiva, Shiva himself wipes it clean. Shiva is the one who
conceived the pair, and it is offered up to him. O learned ones!
It should be known that Shiva loves *pradakshina*. *Pradakshina*
and *namaskara* done to Shiva, the *paramatman*, and worship
with the sixteen kinds of *upachara*, yield fruits. There is no sin
on the surface of the earth that cannot be destroyed through
pradakshina. Therefore, all sins should be destroyed with
pradakshina. A person worshipping Shiva should also be silent
and possess truthfulness and other qualities. He must follow
each one of the rites, austerities, *japa*, *dhyana* and *jnana*. As a
result of rites and the others, prosperity, a divine body, *jnana*, the
dispelling of ignorance and proximity to Shiva are obtained as
fruits. The fruits are obtained through the act and the darkness

---

[387] Known as Balipitha—*bali* (offerings) and *pitha* (pedestal).

of ignorance is removed. As a result of this understanding, birth itself is cleansed. Shiva's devotee will undertake the rites as is appropriate, depending on the time and the place and on the state of his body and wealth. With wealth earned in a proper way, a wise person will reside in Shiva's region. He will refrain from causing injury to beings and his mind will be free of worries. When food is cooked while chanting the *panchakshara mantra*, it is known to yield happiness. When food is obtained by a poor person through seeking alms, this too yields *jnana*. Food obtained through seeking alms by a poor person who is Shiva's devotee increases devotion towards Shiva. *Yogis* devoted to Shiva say that such food obtained through seeking alms is like a sacrifice to Shambhu. Through any means, wherever on earth, a devotee must always eat pure food. He will be silent and not reveal the secret. He will not reveal Shiva's greatness to a person who is not a devotee. He will not reveal the secret of Shiva's *mantra*. No one other than Shiva knows it. Shiva's devotee will always reside near Shiva's *lingam*. O learned ones! By resorting to a stationary *lingam*, a person himself becomes stable. If one worships a mobile *lingam*, it is certain that one will gradually be liberated. Briefly, these are the excellent means that can be used to obtain every kind of emancipation. Vyasa spoke about this in earlier times and in those ancient times, I heard it from him. May all of us be fortunate. May our devotion towards Shiva be steadfast. O learned ones! A man who constantly reads or hears this chapter, obtains *jnana* about Shiva and obtains Shiva's compassion."'

Chapter 26-2(19) (Parthiva *Lingam*)

'The *rishis* said, "O Suta! You are blessed. May you live for a long time. O Suta! You are blessed. You are Shiva's

devotee. You have spoken well about the greatness of the
lingam and the fruits it bestows. Vyasa spoke about Mahesha's
Parthiva *lingam*, which is the best. Please again tell us now
about its greatness."'

'Suta replied, "O *rishi*s! All of you listen to everything
with devotion. I will speak about the greatness of Shiva's
Parthiva *lingam*. Parthiva *lingam* is described as the best
among all *lingam*s. Many *brahmana*s have obtained success
by worshipping it. O *brahmana*s! Having worshipped Parthiva
lingam, Hari, Brahma, *rishi*s and Prajapatis obtained everything
that they wished for. There are many others who have obtained
supreme success by worshipping it—*deva*s, *asura*s, humans,
*gandharva*s, *uraga*s and *rakshasa*s.[388] In *krita yuga*, *lingam*s
were made out of jewels. In *treta yuga*, they were made out
of gold. In *dvapara*, they were made out of mercury. In *kali
yuga*, Parthiva *lingam*s are regarded as the best. Among all
his eight images, the earthen image is regarded as the best.[389]
O *brahmana*s! Since the austerities and worship of this are
unique, it yields great fruits. Among all *deva*s, Maheshvara is
the oldest and the best. In that way, among all *lingam*s, the
Parthiva is spoken of as the best. Among all rivers, the river
of the gods[390] is the oldest and the best. In that way, among
all *lingam*s, the Parthiva is spoken of as the best. Among all

---

[388] *Uraga*s are the same as *nagas/pannagas*. They are not quite the
same as snakes (*sarpa*s), since they can assume any form at will and
have semi-divine traits. We will translate *sarpa*s as snakes and *uraga*s
as serpents.

[389] The eight forms of Shiva can be interpreted in different ways.
He often has eight names—Bhava, Sharva, Rudra, Pashupati, Ugra,
Mahadeva, Bhima and Ishana. (The list of eight names does vary
though.) His eight forms are also identified with the five elements,
the sun, the moon and the sacrifice. There is thus no unique way to
interpret the number eight.

[390] Ganga.

*mantra*s, Pranava is remembered as the greatest. In that way, Parthiva *lingam* is most fit to be worshipped and its worship is the best. Among all *varna*s, the *brahmana* is spoken of as the best. In that way, among all *lingam*s, Parthiva *lingam* is spoken of as the best. Among all cities, Kashi is spoken of as the best. In that way, among all *lingam*s, Parthiva *lingam* is spoken of as the best. Among all vows, the vow on Shiva Ratri is supreme. In that way, among all *lingam*s, Parthiva *lingam* is spoken of as the best. Among all *devi*s, Shiva Shakti is spoken of as supreme. In that way, among all *lingam*s, Parthiva *lingam* is spoken of as the best. Instead of Parthiva *lingam*, if one worships any other *deva*, that worship is futile. Bathing and donations are fruitless. A worshipper of Parthiva *lingam* is purified and blessed. He has a long lifespan. He obtains contentment, nourishment and prosperity. All supreme *sadhaka*s must do this. For success in obtaining everything that is desired, one should worship Parthiva *lingam*, full of faith and devotion and using whatever *upachara* is available. If a person worships Parthiva *lingam* on an auspicious altar, such a person obtains beauty and prosperity in this world. At the end, he is born as Rudra. Listen. A person who uses *bilva* leaves to worship Parthiva *lingam* at the time of the three *sandhya*s every day, obtains auspicious fruits for twenty-one births. In his own body, he obtains greatness in Rudra's world. If he is seen or touched, the sins of all mortals are dispelled. There is no doubt that he is *jivanmukta*, possessing *jnana*. He is Shiva. As soon as one sees or touches him, one obtains objects of pleasure and emancipation. Having created a Parthiva *lingam*, if a person worships Shiva every day, or if he visits Shiva's temple for as long as he lives, he remains in Shiva's world for many years, in Shiva's presence. If he has worshipped with desire in his mind, he is reborn and becomes an Indra among kings in Bharata. If a person has always worshipped the excellent Parthiva *lingam* without any desires, he always remains in Shiva's world and obtains *sayujya*. If a *brahmana* does not worship Parthiva *lingam* every day, he goes to a terrible hell and is impaled with an extremely terrible trident. One should use any means possible to try and devise a *lingam*. One should check whether the Parthiva lingam satisfies the *panchasutri* norms.[391] The *lingam* must consist of a single piece. Separate pieces must not be joined together to make it. For example, if two pieces are joined together, one will not obtain the fruits of the *puja*. Whether it is made out of a jewel, gold, mercury, crystal or yellow sapphire, the Parthiva *lingam* must be made out of a single piece. All Chara *lingam*s must be made out of a single piece. It is said that stationary *lingam*s can be made out of two pieces. Depending on whether it is a Chara *lingam* or a stationary *lingam*, one must think about a single piece or more than one piece. The base is Mahavidya,[392] the *lingam* proper is the divinity Maheshvara. That is the reason stationary *lingam*s are said to be the best when they consist of two pieces. Following the rules, a stationary *lingam* must be made out of two pieces. Those who know the determinations of the Shaiva texts say that a mobile *lingam* must consist of a single piece. Those who say that a Chara *lingam* can be made out of two different pieces are deluded in their knowledge. Sages who know about the sacred texts do not agree with this conclusion. There are foolish men who make a stationary *lingam* out of a single piece and a mobile *lingam* out of two pieces. They do not obtain fruits from the *puja*. Thus, the rules of the sacred texts are that anything known as a Chara *lingam* must be made out of a single piece and a stationary *lingam* should be made out of two pieces. It is then that one obtains supreme happiness. If

---

[391] Literally, five threads. While this has been interpreted metaphorically, one measures the *lingam*'s height, circumference and width. This must be in exact proportion to the base and the *pitha*'s circumference, the latter being double that of the *lingam*.

[392] Great knowledge.

one worships a Chara *lingam* that is made out of a single piece, this bestows complete fruits. If one worships a Chara *lingam* that is made out of two pieces, this is said to lead to great harm. If one worships a stationary *lingam* that is made out of single piece, this does not yield the fruits one desires. One must never act against what the sacred texts have said."'

Chapter 27-2(20) (Worship of Parthiva *Lingam*)

'Suta continued, "Hear about the way devotees should follow the *Veda*s and worship a Parthiva *lingam*. It is only the path indicated by the *Veda*s that bestows objects of pleasure and emancipation. A person must bathe according to the norms given in the codes. Following the norms, he must observe the *sandhya* rites. He must undertake *brahma yajna* and follow the water rites for the ancestors. A man must follow the norms and undertake all the *nitya karma*. Remembering Shiva, he must adorn himself with *bhasma* and wear *rudraksha*. If one follows the norms of the *Veda*s properly, then he is successful in obtaining the complete fruits. Full of supreme devotion, the excellent Parthiva *lingam* must next be worshipped. It is recommended that the worship of Parthiva *lingam* must be carried out along the bank of a river or pond, in a mountain or a forest, in Shiva's temple or in a pure spot. O *brahmana*s! One must carefully collect clay from a pure spot and attentively fashion Shiva's *lingam*. It is said that *brahmana*s must use white clay, those who live through their arms[393] must use red clay, *vaishya*s must use clay that is yellow in complexion and

---

[393] *Kshatriya*s.

*shudra*s must use black clay. If this is not available, anything available can be used. However, with the collected clay, the *lingam* must be fashioned with great care. The auspicious clay must be placed in an extremely auspicious region. It must be purified with water and kneaded gently. Following the path indicated in the *Veda*s, the auspicious Parthiva *lingam* must be fashioned."'

"'If it is worshipped with devotion, objects of pleasure and emancipation are obtained as fruits. I will describe the recommended method. Listen. Using the *mantra* 'Namah Shivaya',[394] objects used for the worship will be washed. Using the *bhurasi mantra*,[395] the ground will be purified. This ensures success. The water will be purified with the *aposman mantra*.[396] The entry of depredations will be barred with the 'Namaste Rudra' *mantra*.[397] With the 'Namah Shambhavya'[398] *mantra*, the spot will be purified. Affixing the word 'Namah', the *panchamrita*[399] will be sprinkled. Shankara's excellent Chara *lingam* will be faithfully instated, using the *mantra*

---

[394] *Mantra*s in this chapter cause a problem because the *mantra* is not intended to be the familiar *Namah Shivaya* alone. There is a complete *mantra*, of which, what is mentioned is a part. These *mantra*s are typically from Chapter 16 of the Vajasaneyi Samhita, associated with the *Yajur Veda*. For example, this *mantra* not only mentions obeisance to Shiva, but also to Shiva under his names of Sambhava, Bhava, Shankara, Mayaskara and Shivatara. This one is from 16.41 of Vajasaneyi Samhita.

[395] *Bhurasi bhumirasi aditirasi* etc., used for purifying the ground. This is 13.18 of Vajasaneyi Samhita. 'You are the earth. You are the ground. You are Aditi, who holds up the world.' Words to that effect.

[396] 4.2 of Vajasaneyi Samhita. 'May the water, who is our mother, purify us.' Words to that effect.

[397] 16.1 of Vajasaneyi Samhita. 'O Rudra! I bow down to your rage. I bow down to your arrows.' Words to that effect.

[398] *Shambhavaya* is the dative of Shambhu. This is the 16.41 mentioned earlier.

[399] Five kinds of *amrita*—milk, curd, *ghee*, honey and sugar.

'*Namah Nilagrivaya*'.[400] Devotedly, one must use the *mantra*, '*Etatte Rudravasam*'[401] and following the path of the *Veda*s, offer an excellent seat. The *avahana* must be performed with the *mantra* '*ma no mahantam*'.[402] With the *mantra*, '*ya te Rudra*',[403] the Chara *lingam* must be seated. With the *mantra* '*yamishum*',[404] the *nyasa* of Shiva must be performed on different parts of the body. Fragrances must be offered with the *mantra* '*adhyavochat*'.[405] With the *mantra* '*asou jiva*',[406] *nyasa* must be performed of other *deva*s. One must approach the divinity with the *mantra* '*asou yovasarpati*'.[407] The *padya* must be offered with the words '*Namah Nilagrivaya*'.[408] The *arghya* must be offered with the Rudra-Gayatri *mantra*.[409]

[400] Nilagriva, blue-throated, is one of Shiva's names. Nilagrivaya is the dative. This is 16.28 of Vajasaneyi Samhita. In this, other names of Shiva are mentioned—Bhava, Rudra, Sharva, Pashupati, Nilagriva and Sitikantha.

[401] 3.61 of Vajasaneyi Samhita. 'O Rudra! This is your seat' and so on.

[402] 16.15 of Vajasaneyi Samhita. 'Do not harm us, old or young' and so on.

[403] 16.2 of Vajasaneyi Samhita. 'O Rudra! With your auspicious form . . .' and so on.

[404] 16.3 of Vajasaneyi Samhita. 'With the arrow you hold in your hand . . .' and so on.

[405] 16.5 of Vajasaneyi Samhita. 'O eloquent one! O foremost among divine physicians . . .' and so on.

[406] Literally, 'this being'.

[407] 16.7 of Vajasaneyi Samhita. 'May the one who moves . . .' and so on.

[408] Nilagrivaya is the dative of Nilagriva. 16.8 of Vajasaneyi Samhita. 'I prostrate myself before Nilagriva Sahasraksha . . .' and so on.

[409] There are variations of the *gayatri mantra*, addressed to specific *deva*s. The one mentioned here is Rudra-Mahadeva *gayatri*. As cited in *Mahanaryana Upanishad*, it is '*tatpurushaya vidmahe mahadevaya dhimahi tanno rudra prachodoyat*'. 'May we comprehend that Purusha. For that, we meditate on Mahadeva. May Rudra urge us towards that objective.'

The *achamaniya* must be offered with the *mantra* addressed
to Tryambaka.⁴¹⁰ The bathing with milk will be done with the
mantra '*payah prithivyam*'.⁴¹¹ The bathing with curd will be
done with the *mantra* '*dadhikravnah*'.⁴¹² The bathing with *ghee*
will be done with the *mantra* for *ghee*. It is said that the bathing
with honey and sugar must be done with the three hymns,
'*madhu vata*', '*madhu naktam*' and '*madhuman nah*'.⁴¹³ This
is the way bathing is done with *panchamrita*. Alternatively,
the bathing with *panchamrita* can be done with the *mantra*
used for *padya*.⁴¹⁴ The tying of the waistband must lovingly be
done with the *mantra* '*ma nastoke*'.⁴¹⁵ The upper garment will
be offered with '*namo dhrishnave*'.⁴¹⁶ Following the norms, a
devotee will offer the garment to Shiva, with the four hymns
from the *Veda*s, '*ya te heti*.'⁴¹⁷ An intelligent person will lovingly
offer fragrances with the hymn '*namah shabhyah*'.⁴¹⁸ *Akshata*

⁴¹⁰ This is the famous *Mahamritunjaya mantra*. 3.60 of Vajasaneyi
Samhita. '*Tryambakam yajamahe sugandhim pushtivardhanam.*' 'We
worship the fragrant Tryambaka, who enhances our nourishment.'
⁴¹¹ 18.36 of Vajasaneyi Samhita. 'May you store milk in the
earth . . .' and so on.
⁴¹² 23.32 of Vajasaneyi Samhita. The address is to a divine horse,
Dadhikravan.
⁴¹³ These are famous hymns, especially the first, which runs,
madhu vata ritayate madhu ksharanti sindhavah. They are 13.27-29
of Vajasaneyi Samhita. 'May the winds be sweet. May the rivers be
sweet. May the night be sweet. May the dawn be sweet. May the tree
be sweet. May the sun be sweet.' Words to that effect.
⁴¹⁴ *Namah Nilagrivaya*, mentioned earlier.
⁴¹⁵ 16.16 of Vajasaneyi Samhita. 'Harm not our offspring' and so
on.
⁴¹⁶ 16.36 of Vajasanayi Samhita. 'I prostrate myself before
Dhrishnu', Dhrishnu meaning the bold and confident one.
⁴¹⁷ These four hymns, 16.11-14 of Vajasaneyi Samhita, are about
Shiva's bow and arrows, which should protect and not harm.
⁴¹⁸ 16.28 of Vajasaneyi Samhita. 'I prostrate myself before dogs
and before those who own dogs.'

will be offered with the *mantra* '*namastakshabhyah*'.[419] Flowers will be offered with the *mantra* '*namah paryaya*.'[420] *Bilva* leaves will be offered with the *mantra* '*namah parnaya*'.[421] Following the norms, incense will be offered with '*namah kapardine*'.[422] In that way, the lamp will be offered with the hymn '*namah ashave*'.[423] The excellent *naivedya* will be offered with the *mantra* '*namah jyeshthaya*'.[424] *Achamaniya* will again be offered with the *mantra* to Tryambaka.[425] The fruit will be offered with the hymn '*ima rudraya*'.[426] With the hymn '*namo vrajyaya*' everything will be offered to Shambhu.[427] The eleven Rudras will be worshipped with eleven offerings of *akshata*, using the two *mantra*s, '*ma no mahantam*' and '*ma nastoke*'.[428] *Dakshina* will be offered with the three hymns that begin with the word 'Hiranyagarbhah'.[429] A learned person

---

[419] *Akshata* is unhusked grain. The *mantra* is 16.27 of Vajasaneyi Samhita, mentioning homage to artisans and chariot-makers.

[420] 16.42 of Vajasaneyi Samhita. 'I prostrate myself before the one who enables the crossing over of *samsara*' and so on.

[421] 16.46 of Vajasaneyi Samhita. 'I prostrate myself before the one who exists in leaves' and so on.

[422] 16.29 of Vajasaneyi Samhita. 'I prostrate myself before the one who has matted hair' and so on.

[423] 16.31 of Vajasaneyi Samhita. 'I prostrate myself before the one who moves swiftly' and so on.

[424] 16.32 of Vajasaneyi Samhita. 'I prostrate myself before the one who is the eldest and the youngest' and so on.

[425] *Mahamritunjaya mantra*, mentioned earlier.

[426] 16.48 of Vajasaneyi Samhita. 'To the Rudra who hears words of praise' and so on.

[427] 16.44 of Vajasaneyi Samhita. 'I prostrate myself before the one who exists in settlements of cows.' Words to that effect.

[428] There are eleven Rudras, but the listing of the names differs. These two *mantra*s have been mentioned earlier.

[429] 13.4–13.6 of Vajasaneyi Samhita. 'Hiranyagarbha was the one who arose first' and so on.

will perform *abhisheka* with the *mantra* '*devasya tva*'.[430]
Following the norms, the lamps will be waved before Shambhu
with the *mantra* '*namah ashave*'. The offering of flowers will
be rendered with the hymn '*ima rudraya*'. Chanting '*ma no
mahantam*', a wise person will perform the *pradakshina*. An
intelligent person will do *sashtanga pranama* with the *mantra*
'*ma nastoke*'. He will show Shiva *mudra* with the *mantra* '*esha
te*', Abhaya *mudra* with the *mantra* '*yato yatah*' and Jnana
mudra with the Tryambaka *mantra*.[431] Maha *mudra* will be
shown with the *mantra* '*namah senabhyah*'.[432] Dhenu *mudra*
will be shown with the hymn '*namah gobhyah*'.[433] After
showing these five *mudra*s, he will perform *japa* with Shiva's
mantra.[434] A discriminating person will perform *japa* with the
Shatarudriya *mantra*.[435] A discriminating person must then
undertake *panchanga patha*.[436] Visarjana must be performed

[430] 11.28 of Vajasaneyi Samhita. This is an invocation to Agni,
who is dug out from the earth.

[431] *Esha te* is 9.35 of Vajasaneyi Samhita, whereby offerings are
made to various *deva*s. *Yato yatoh* is 36.22 of Vajasaneyi Samhita,
whereby protection is sought from all quarters. Tryambaka *mantra*
is *Mahamritunjaya mantra*. As stated earlier, *mudra*s are positions
for the hands. There are several *mudra*s. The five mentioned here are
Shiva *mudra* (in the form of the *lingam*), Abhaya *mudra*, Jnana *mudra*
(for knowledge), Dhenu *mudra* (resembling a cow) and Maha *mudra*
(more a position of *dhyana*, rather than a hand position). But in this
context, Maha *mudra* probably refers to a hand position.

[432] 16.26 of Vajasaneyi Samhita. 'I prostrate myself before
armies.' Words to that effect.

[433] 'I prostrate myself before cows.'

[434] *Namah Shivaya*.

[435] Literally, *Shatarudriya* means one hundred Rudras and is a
mantra to Rudra, from the *Yajur Veda*.

[436] *Panchanga* patha may mean a rite whose meaning has now
been lost. Otherwise, *panchanga* (five limbs) *patha* (reading) refers to
jyotisha (astronomy/astrology). *Panchanga* of *jyotisha* refers to *tithi*,
nakshatra, *rashi*, yoga (conjunction) and *karana* (the end of half a *tithi*).

with a *mantra* announcing the *deva*'s departure. The details of following the norms of the Vedas and worshipping Shiva have thus been described. Briefly listen to the excellent norms given in the Vedas. The clay must be collected with the *Sadyojata* hymn.[437] The water must be sprinkled with a *mantra* to Vamadeva. The Aghora *mantra* must be used to fashion the *lingam*. Following the norms, the Tatpurusha *mantra*[438] must be used to perform the *avahana*. The *mantra* to Ishana must be used to affix the *lingam* to the pedestal.[439] An intelligent devotee will briefly follow all the other norms. An intelligent devotee will follow the norms and undertake the worship with sixteen *upacharas*, using the *panchakshara mantra* or any other *mantra* that has been given by the *guru*. 'We meditate on Bhava, Bhavanasha, Mahadeva, Ugra, Ugranasha, Sharva and Shashimouli.'[440] With great devotion, an intelligent person will worship Shankara in the manner indicated, carefully avoiding any transgressions. If Shiva is devotedly worshipped in this way, he bestows fruits."'

'"If one follows the order indicated in the Vedas, this is said to be the method. O *brahmanas*! However, other than this, I will mention the other ordinary methods to undertake the worship properly. The means of worshipping Parthiva *lingam* is said to be recital of Shiva's names. Hear about this. O best among sages! This yields everything that one desires. For collecting the clay, kneading it, establishing it, invocation, bathing, worship, seeking

---

[437] This has not been mentioned earlier and is 29.36 of Vajasaneyi Samhita. It is an invocation to Agni.

[438] The *mantra*, '*ya te Rudra*'.

[439] 27.35 of Vajasaneyi Samhita, stating that Ishana pervades the universe.

[440] These are Shiva's names. Bhavanasha is the one who destroys worldly existence, Ugra is the fierce one, Ugranasha is the one who destroys terrible things and Shashimouli is the one who wears the crescent moon on his head.

forgiveness and *visarjana*, the respective names used are Hara, Maheshvara, Shambhu, Shulapani, Pinakadhrik, Shiva, Pashupati and Mahadeva. One must prefix AUM. The names must be used in the dative case and must end with '*Namah*.' This is the order. The rites must be undertaken with great devotion and supreme joy. *Nyasa* must be properly performed and there must be *anganyasa* on both the hands. Using the *mantra* with six *aksharas*,[441] one must perform *dhyana*. Devotees must meditate on Shiva seated on his seat in Kailasa, being worshipped by Sananda and others.[442] Shiva is like a forest blaze, the afflictions of the devotees are the kindling. He is immeasurable. He is the ornament of the universe, embraced by Uma. One must always meditate on Mahesha in the following way. 'He is like a mountain made of silver. He wears the beautiful crescent moon on his forehead. His limbs blaze with resplendent jewels. The supreme hunter wields an axe. His pleasant face grants freedom from fear. He is seated in the lotus posture. He is worshipped by large numbers of immortals who surround him. He is attired in the skin of a tiger. He is the primordial being in the universe. He is the seed of the universe. He dispels all fears. He has five faces and three eyes.' Meditating in this way, one must worship Parthiva *lingam*. Following the norms, he must perform *japa* with the *panchakshara mantra* taught by the *guru*. O Indras among *brahmanas*! An intelligent devotee must praise the lord of *devas* in many kinds of ways and prostrate himself. He must read the Shatarudriya *mantra*. He must happily collect *akshata* and flowers, with his hands held in *anjali*.[443] Full of great devotion, he must faithfully pray to Shankara, using the following *mantra*. 'I belong to you. My breath

[441] *AUM Namah Shivaya.*

[442] Sanaka, Sananda, Sanatana and Sanatkumara are four sages, born through Brahma's mental powers.

[443] The palms joined and held together in the form of a cup, a gesture of offering.

of life is your *gunas*. O lord! My consciousness is always fixed in you. You are on ocean of compassion. O Bhutanatha! Knowing this, show me your favours. Inadvertently and knowingly, I have done various things in the course of *japa* and worship. O Shankara! Through your favours, may all those yield excellent fruits. I am a great sinner, and you are the great one who instantly purifies. O Gouri's refuge! Knowing this, do whatever you wish. O Mahadeva! The *Vedas*, the Puranas and the determinations of many kinds of *rishis* have been unable to comprehend you. O Sadashiva! How can I possibly know about you? O Maheshvara! In every possible way, I belong to you. You should save me. O Parameshvara! Please show me your favours.' Having said this, the devotee will place the *akshata* and the flowers over Shiva's *lingam*. O sages! Following the norms, in a *shastanga* way, he will prostrate himself before Shambhu. Following the norms, an intelligent person will then perform *pradakshina*. He will then again praise the lord of *devas*, devotedly using words of praise. Having uttered these words through his throat, a pure and humble devotee will then prostrate himself. Having taken the permission, he will then perform the act of *visarjana*. O tigers among sages! I have thus described the rules for worshipping Parthiva *lingam*. This bestows objects of pleasure and emancipation and increases devotion towards Shiva. If a person reads this chapter with a pure mind, or listens to it, he is freed from all sins and obtains everything that he desires. He obtains a long lifespan and freedom from disease. He obtains fame and heaven. This excellent account bestows sons, grandsons and happiness.'

Chapter 28-2(21) (More on *Lingams*)

'The *rishis* said, "O Suta! O immensely fortunate one! O Suta! O Vyasa's disciple! We bow down to you. You have properly explained the modes of worshipping Parthiva *lingam*. Depending on differences in desires, please tell us about the rules for resorting to a different number of Shiva's Parthiva *lingam*s. You are devoted to those who are distressed and show them your compassion."'

'Suta replied, "O *rishi*s! Listen to all the rules for worshipping Parthiva *lingam*s. Through only following these, a man becomes successful in all his tasks. Without fashioning a Parthiva *lingam*, if a person worships any other *deva*, that worship is futile. Self-control and devotions are in vain. In accordance with the desire, I will describe the number of Parthiva *lingam*s. O best among sages! These numbers instantly bestow the fruits. The first *avahana*, *pratishthana* and *puja* are separate. The shape of the *lingam* is known to remain the same everywhere. Everything else is distinct. A man in search of learning must cheerfully worship one thousand Parthiva *lingam*s. This will certainly yield the fruits. A man in search of wealth must fashion five hundred Parthiva *lingam*s. A person seeking sons must use one thousand and five hundred, while one desiring garments must use five hundred. A person desiring emancipation must use one crore, while a person desiring land must use one thousand. A person desiring compassion must use three thousand, while a person in search of a *tirtha* must use two thousand. A person desiring well-wishers must use three thousand, while a person seeking control must use eight hundred. A person desiring to kill someone must use seven hundred, while a person desiring to confound someone must use eight hundred. It is said that a person intent on expulsion[444] must use one thousand. A person seeking to stupefy must use one thousand, while a person desiring to kindle hatred must use five hundred. A person seeking to free himself from bondage must use one thousand and five hundred excellent

---

[444] To ward off harmful omens, objects or people.

*lingam*s. A discriminating person who seeks to save himself from fear caused by a great king will use five hundred. It is known that two hundred Parthiva *lingam*s must be used if there is fear from thieves and similar things. It is said that five hundred Parthiva *lingam*s must be used if there is fear from *dakini*s.[445] In the case of poverty, five thousand must be used. Ten thousand yield every object of desire. O excellent sages! I will now speak about the daily norms. One is said to dispel sins, while two *lingam*s bring success in the pursuit of wealth. It is said that three *lingam*s are sufficient to accomplish every wish. It progressively gets better and better as more than the preceding number is used. However, there are differences in views among sages and I will tell you about that. If an intelligent person fashions ten thousand Parthiva *lingam*s, he has no reason for any fear. This certainly takes away the fear on account of a great king. To be freed from prison, an intelligent person will fashion ten thousand. To be freed from fear on account of *dakini*s and similar things, he should fashion seven thousand. A person who has no sons will devise fifty-five thousand. If a person uses ten thousand *lingam*s, he will get daughters. Through ten thousand *lingam*s, a person obtains Vishnu's prosperity. Through a million *lingam*s, one obtains unmatched prosperity. If a man fashions one crore *lingam*s, he becomes like Shiva on earth. There is no need to think about this. The worship of Parthiva *lingam*s yields the fruits of one crore sacrifices. This always bestows objects of pleasure and emancipation on men who desire them. If a person constantly spends his time without worshipping a *lingam*, he suffers from great harm. He becomes evil-souled and wicked in conduct. If one places all donations, many kinds of vows, *tirtha*s, *niyama*s and *yajna*s together on one

---

[445] A *dakini* is a demoness, usually feeding on flesh and blood.

side[446] and the worship of *lingam* alone on the other, the two
will be equal. In *kali yuga*, it is evident in the world that the
worship of *lingam* is the best. There is nothing else. That is the
determination of the sacred texts. The *lingam* bestows objects
of pleasure and emancipation. Many kinds of hardships are
countered. If a man undertakes this worship constantly, he
attains *sayujya* with Shiva. Since Shiva's unblemished *lingam*
is constantly worshipped even by *maharshi*s, there are rules on
worshipping all these *lingam*s."'

'"It is said that there are three types of *lingam*s—superior,
middling and inferior. O tigers among sages! I will tell you about
their measurements. Listen. Sages who are accomplished in the
sacred texts say that a superior *lingam* must be four *angula*s
in height and must have a beautiful pedestal. One that is half
this size is said to be middling. One that is quarter this size is
said to be inferior. I have thus described the three types, one
after another. Full of faith and devotion, if a person worships
many *lingam*s every day, he obtains everything, irrespective of
whether he has, or does not have, desires in his mind. In the
four *Veda*s, there is nothing described that is as sacred as the
worship of a *lingam*. This is also known to be the determination
of all the sacred texts. Therefore, discarding everything else, in
particular the net of *karma*, a learned person worships only
the *lingam*, full of great devotion. If the *lingam* is worshipped,
the entire universe, with all its mobile and immobile objects, is
worshipped. When one is submerged in the ocean of *samsara*,
there is no other means of saving oneself. This happens even if
the worship is done unknowingly and even if it is done because
one is addicted to material objects. Other than worshipping the
lingam, there is no other raft in this universe. To accomplish all
their objectives, Hari, Brahma and other *deva*s, sages, *yaksha*s,

---

[446] Of a pair of scales.

rakshasas, *gandharvas*, *charanas*,[447] *daityas*, *danavas*,[448] Shesha
and other *nagas*, Garuda and other birds, Prajapatis, *kinnaras*[449]
and men worship the *lingam* with great devotion. All of them
achieve the desired wishes that are there in their hearts. Using
the respective *mantra*, *brahmanas*, *kshatriyas*, *vaishyas*,
shudras and those born from a *pratiloma* marriage[450] always
lovingly worship the *lingam*. O sages! What is the need to speak
a lot? O *brahmanas*! Everyone, women and others, have a right
to worship the *lingam*. For *brahmanas*, it is best to worship
according to the rules laid down in the *Vedas*. Others should
not undertake the worship indicated in the *Vedas*. *Brahmanas*
must follow the *Vedas* and worship in accordance with the rites
of the *Vedas*. They should not follow any other path. Bhagavan
Shiva has himself said that. There are *brahmanas* like Dadhichi,
Goutama and others. Because of curses, their intelligence has
been scorched. They no longer have faith in the rites of the
Vedas. A mortal who rejects the *Vedas* and follows the rites
indicated in *smriti* texts is a person whose *sankalpa* will not
lead to any fruits. It should be known that Shambhu himself
has said that the worship must be conducted in this fashion.
He pervades the three worlds, and he must be worshipped in
his eight forms. The eight forms that are described are earth,
water, fire, wind, space, the sun, the moon and the person who
is undertaking the sacrifice. The eight forms that are to be
worshipped are Sharva, Bhava, Rudra, Ugra, Bhima, Ishvara,
Mahadeva and Pashupati. Along with his family, Shambhu

[447] Celestial singers and bards.
[448] The words *daitya* and *danava* are sometimes used as synonyms.
Daityas are the sons of Diti, through the sage Kashyapa. *Danavas* are
the sons of Danu, through the sage Kashyapa. *Daityas* and *danavas*
are thus kin. The word *asura* (counterpoint of *sura* or god) is also used
as a synonym.
[449] Equivalently, *kimpurusha*, a semi-divine species.
[450] Where the mother's *varna* is superior to that of the father's.

must be worshipped with great devotion. Beginning with the
north-east direction, they must be worshipped in the due order,
with sandalwood paste, *akshata* and leaves. In due order,
they are Ishana, Nandi, Chanda, Mahakala, Bhringi, Vrisha,
Skanda, Kapardisha, Soma and Shukra. Virbhadra is in front
and Kirtimukha is at the rear. After this, following the norms,
the eleven Rudras must be worshipped. After this, he should do
japa with the *panchakshara mantra* or with the Shatarudriya
mantra. Having uttered many kinds of praises, there must be
panchanga patha. Then, after having done *pradakshina*, he will
prostrate himself and there will be *visarjana* of the *lingam*. I
have thus described the way one must lovingly worship Shiva.
In the night, the tasks for the divinity must always be performed
while facing the north. Purified, one must always worship Shiva
while facing the north, not while facing the east. The reading of
Shiva's and Shakti's *Samhita* must not be done while facing the
north or the west. These must always be to the rear. A learned
person will not worship Shankara without Tripundraka from
bhasma, a string of *rudraksha* and *bilva* leaves. O best among
sages! When one sets out to worship Shiva and ashes are not
available, Tripundraka must be drawn on the forehead with
clay.'"

Chapter 29-2(22) (*Naivedya* and *Bilva*)

'The *rishi*s said, "We have earlier heard words to the effect
that Shiva's *naivedya* should not be taken away.[451] O
sage! Please tell us the determination about this and please also
tell us about the greatness of *bilva*.'"

[451] By others.

'Suta replied, "O sages! All of you please listen to this attentively now. I will happily tell you everything. Since you follow Shiva's vows, you are blessed. Shiva's *naivedya* can be partaken of by Shiva's devotee, one who is clean and pure, firm in his decision about the vows and one who has banished unacceptable thoughts. Even if one sees Shiva's *naivedya*, sins go far away. When one partakes of Shiva's *naivedya*, crores of good merits arrive. One thousand sacrifices are of no avail. Hundreds of millions of sacrifices are futile. When one partakes of Shiva's *naivedya*, one attains *sayujya* with Shiva. If there is the spread of Shiva's *naivedya* in a house, everything in that house becomes pure and it is a source of purification of others. When Shiva's *naivedya* is offered, it should be happily accepted on one's head. After having remembered Shiva, it should be eaten carefully. When Shiva's *naivedya* is offered, if a man accepts something else instead, or eats it later, he is associated with sin. If a person is not interested in eating Shiva's *naivedya*, he becomes the worst of sinners and is certain to go to hell. When one offers it to Shiva in one's heart, or to an image made out of moonstone, silver or gold, and then eats it, after having been initiated into becoming Shiva's devotee, one can cross over. For a person who has been initiated into becoming Shiva's devotee, this bears the trait of great *prasada*.[452] The partaking of *naivedya* from all *lingam*s is auspicious. This is also true of men who have been initiated into worshipping others but possess devotion towards Shiva in their *atman*s. Listen cheerfully to the determination about partaking of Shiva's *naivedya*. O *brahmana*s! It is said that partaking of Shiva's *naivedya* when it has been offered to a *shalagrama lingam*, a Rasa *lingam*, a *lingam* made out of rock, silver or gold, a *lingam* established by gods and *siddha*s, a *lingam* in Kashmira, a *lingam* made

---

[452] Food after an offering is made to a divinity.

out of crystal or jewels and all the *Jyotirlingams*[453] is equal
to the completion of a *chandrayana* vow. It is extraordinary
that even the slayer of a *brahmana* is cleansed as soon as
he partakes of this. All sins are destroyed. Men cannot
eat it when Chanda has a right to it.[454] However, when
Chanda does not have a right to it, men can devotedly eat it.
Chanda does not have a right to Bana *lingam*s, iron *lingam*s,
Svayambhu *lingam*s and other extremely radiant images. If
one follows the norms, and after bathing the *lingam*, sips the
water thrice, the three kinds of sins[455] are swiftly destroyed.
The leaves, flowers, fruits and water offered as part of Shiva's
naivedya must not be accepted. Everything that has come into
contact with a *shalagrama lingam* is pure. O lords among
sages! Therefore, anything that has been placed on top of the
lingam must not be accepted. Anything that has not touched
the *lingam*, but is outside, is known to be extremely pure.
That has therefore been determined as *naivedya* which can
be taken."'

'"Attentively and lovingly, hear about the greatness of
bilva. *Bilva* is Mahadeva's form and is therefore praised
even by *deva*s. One cannot comprehend its greatness but is
only capable of knowing a little bit. There are famous and
sacred *tirtha*s in the worlds. All those *tirtha*s are present at
the root of a *bilva* tree. The root of a *bilva* tree has the form
of Mahadeva's undecaying *lingam*. Anyone who worships it

---

[453] A *Jyotirlingam* is a natural *lingam* that blazes in energy
and radiance. Every *Jyotirlingam* is a Svayambhu *lingam*, but
every Svayambhu *lingam* is not a *Jyotirlingam*. There are twelve
*Jyotirlingam*s and the standard list is Somanatha, Mallikarjuna,
Mahakaleshvara, Omkareshvara, Kedaranatha, Bhimshankara,
Vishveshvara, Vaidyanatha, Rameshvara, Tryambakeshvara,
Nageshvara and Ghrishneshvara.

[454] Chanda is one of Shiva's attendants.

[455] In thoughts, words and deeds.

is pure in his *atman* and certainly obtains Shiva. If a person sprinkles water on his head at the root of a *bilva* tree, it is as if he has bathed in all the *tirtha*s on earth. He is purified. When he sees that the excellent region around the root of a *bilva* tree is full of water, Mahadeva obtains unmatched delight. If a man worships the root of a *bilva* tree with fragrances, flowers and other objects, he obtains Shiva's world. His happiness and offspring increase. If a person lovingly devises a garland of lamps at the root of a *bilva* tree, he becomes full of true *jnana* and merges into Mahesha. If a person gathers sprouts and branches from a *bilva* tree with his hand and then worships the *bilva* tree, he is freed from sins. If a person faithfully feeds Shiva's devotee at the root of a *bilva* tree once, his good merits become one crore times what they usually are. At the root of a *bilva* tree, if a person donates food cooked in milk and *ghee* to Shiva's devotee, he is never born poor. I have spoken to you about the divisions and sub-divisions of worshipping Shiva's *lingam*. O *brahmana*s! Depending on whether one follows *pravritti* or *nivritti*, there are two kinds of differences. For those who follow *pravritti*, all the worship must be in the form of *puja* done on the pedestal. At the end of *abhisheka*, the *naivedya* of cooked food must be of *shali* rice. At the end of the worship, the *lingam* must be kept away in a pure casket in a separate part of the house. A person who follows *nivritti* must perform the worship in the palm of his hand[456] and offer his own food as *naivedya*. For those who follow *nivritti*, the supreme and subtle *lingam* is recommended. He will worship the *vibhuti* and also offer the *vibhuti*. Having performed the worship, he must always hold the *lingam* on his head."'[457]

---

[456] With the *lingam* in the palm of the hand.
[457] In the form of the ashes.

Chapter 30-2(23) (*Rudraksha* and Shiva's Names)

'The *rishi*s said, "O Suta! O immensely fortunate one! O Suta! O Vyasa's disciple! We bow down to you. Please tell us about the greatness of *bhasma*, the greatness of *rudraksha* and the greatness of his excellent names. Please tell us about these three, so that our minds are pleased and delighted."'

'Suta replied, "You have asked me a virtuous question. This brings benefit to the world. You are extremely blessed and sacred, the ornaments of your lineages, since the extremely auspicious Shiva is himself your divinity. The accounts of Sadashiva are always loved in this world and are dear to you. Such blessed people have accomplished their objectives. Their taking birth in physical bodies is successful. Those who worship Shiva uplift their lineages. When names of Shiva, Shivaa and Sadashiva, emerge from the mouths of people, sins do not touch them. It is as if they are burning coal made of *khadira*[458] wood. When a mouth utters the words, 'O Shri Shiva! I prostrate myself before you', that mouth becomes a sacred *tirtha* that destroys all sins. If a man looks at such a mouth lovingly, it is quite certain that he reaps the fruits of visiting a *tirtha*. O *brahmana*s! A place where all three exist together is auspicious. The mere sight of such a place is like reaping the fruits of bathing in Triveni.[459] Shiva's name, *vibhuti* and *rudraksha*—these three are extremely sacred and are said to be like Triveni. The sight of a person who possesses all three in his body is extremely rare in this world and destroys sins. There is no difference between the sight of such a person and

---

[458] A type of tree.

[459] Triveni is the confluence of Ganga, Yamuna and Sarasvati, in Prayaga.

Triveni. There is no doubt that a person who does not know this is a sinner. If a man does not wear *rudraksha* on his body, if he does not have *vibhuti* on his forehead and if he does not utter Shiva's names, he is the worst among men and should be shunned. Shiva's name is like Ganga. *Vibhuti* is like Yamuna. *Rudraksha* is like Vidhatri's daughter.[460] They destroy all sins. Brahma, the beneficial one, formerly placed the fruits of all three present together on the body on one side and bathing in Triveni on the other side[461] and found that they were equal. Learned men obtain these fruits. Since these were found to be equal, learned men must always wear them. Since that day, Brahma, Vishnu and the other gods wear these three since their sight destroys sins."'

'The *rishi*s said, "You have spoken about the fruits obtained from these three. O one excellent in vows! But you should specifically tell us about the greatness of Bhava's names."'

'Suta replied, "O *rishi*s! O immensely wise ones! The immortals possess this *jnana* about Shiva. O *brahmana*s! Listen lovingly and attentively to this greatness. This is a great secret, even in the sacred texts, the Puranas and the *shruti* texts. O *brahmana*s! However, out of affection towards you, I will reveal it to you now. O supreme among *brahmana*s! With the exception of Maheshvara, who is beyond everything in this cosmic egg and beyond cause and effect, who knows about the greatness of these three? But briefly, I will tell you about this greatness. O *brahmana*s! Listen cheerfully. This destroys all sins. Like a great forest conflagration, Shiva's names burn down a mountain of sins. They are easily reduced to ashes. This is true. This is undoubtedly true. O Shounaka! With sins as roots, there are many kinds of miseries. Shiva's names destroy these. Nothing else destroys them completely. A man on earth

---

[460] That is, Brahma's daughter, Sarasvati.
[461] Of a pair of scales.

who devotedly performs *japa* with Shiva's names is one who
follows the *Veda*s, is auspicious in his *atman*, is blessed and
is held to be learned. O sage![462] Many kinds of *dharma* exist,
followed by those who desire fruits. The foremost among these
is faith in performing *japa* with Shiva's names. O sage! Men
perpetrate many kinds of sins on earth. Shiva's names destroy
all of these. O sage! Men commit many sins, the killing of a
brahmana and other things. Shiva's names are spoken of as
wonderful and unmatched, since they destroy all these. Shiva's
names are like a boat obtained by those who wish to cross
over the ocean that is *samsara*. There is no doubt that they
destroy the sins that are the root cause of *samsara*. O great
sage! For beings, the root cause behind *samsara* is sins. Shiva's
names are like an axe that certainly destroys these. For those
who are afflicted by the blazing fire of sins, Shiva's names are
like *amrita* that should be drunk. As long as one is scorched
by the blazing fire of sins, one can never obtain peace. Shiva's
names are like nectar that showers down and floods. Thus, in
the midst of this blazing *samsara*, there is nothing to grieve
about. There are great-souled ones who have developed great
devotion towards Shiva's names. Because of this, they instantly
obtain emancipation, in every possible way. O lord among
sages! It destroys all sins. However, one obtains devotion
towards Shiva's names only after scorching oneself through
austerities across many births. In general, emancipation can
be easily obtained by those who have unwavering devotion
towards Shiva's names and not by anyone else. That is my
view. If a person commits many sins, but lovingly performs
japa with Shiva's names, there is no doubt that he is freed from
all these sins. This is like a tree being reduced to ashes in a
forest blaze. In that way, Shiva's names burn down those sins.
O Shounaka! If a person wears the sacred *bhasma* on his limbs,

---

[462] Singular, because only Shounaka is being addressed now.

if he lovingly performs *japa* with Shiva's names, there is no doubt that he crosses over this terrible *samsara*. If a man steals the property of *brahmana*s and kills many *brahmana*s, when he lovingly performs *japa* with Shiva's names, he is not touched by these sins. Having considered all the *Vedas*, it has formerly been determined that the best mode for crossing over *samsara* is performing *japa* with Shiva's names. O best among sages! What is the point of speaking a lot? I will only mention one *shloka* about the greatness of Shiva's names, which destroy all sins. 'Shambhu's names have the purifying power of destroying all sins, more than a man's power to commit those sins.'[463] O sage! Earlier, King Indradyumna committed a great sin.[464] But through the power of Shiva's names, he obtained an excellent destination. O sage! In that way, there was a *brahmani*[465] who committed many sins. Through the power of Shiva's names, she obtained an excellent destination. O best among *brahmana*s! I have thus told about the greatness of these excellent names. Now hear about the greatness of *bhasma*, which destroys all sins and is purifying.'"

Chapter 31-2(24) (*Bhasma* and Its Greatness)

'Suta said, "There are said to be two kinds of *bhasma*. They are supreme and bestow all that is auspicious. I will tell you about their traits. Listen carefully. One is known as *maha-*

---

[463] Though not clearly stated, this seems to be the *shloka* cited.

[464] King Indradyumna's story is identified more with Vishnu. While constructing a temple to Vishnu, along the shore of an ocean, he cut down a tree.

[465] Feminine of *brahmana*.

bhasma, the second is spoken of as *svalpa-bhasma*.[466] The ashes known as *maha-bhasma* have many different kinds of forms. This kind of *bhasma* is said to be of three types—*shrouta*, *smarta* and *loukika*.[467] The one known as *svalpa-bhasma* is said to be of many different types. It is said that *shrouta bhasma* and *smarta bhasma* must only be used by *brahmana*s. All the others can use the supreme *loukika bhasma*. Bulls among sages have said that *brahmana*s must wear *bhasma* only after pronouncing *mantra*s. It is known that others will wear it without using *mantra*s. When the ashes are obtained after burning cow dung, this is known as *agneya bhasma*. O great sage! It is this object that should be used for Tripundraka. Learned ones should use *bhasma* that is collected from *agnihotra*. Ashes that result from other sacrifices can also be used to wear Tripundraka. When the *bhasma* is worn, being mixed with water or without water, the seven *mantra*s from Jabala Upanishad to Agni and others, must be used.[468] Depending on the *varna* and the *ashrama*, a *mantra* should be used or should not be used. If Tripundraka is worn with water, one must lovingly do it with *mantra*s from Jabala Upanishad. When the *bhasma* is not mixed with water, Tripundraka must be in the form of three horizontal lines. Those who desire emancipation must not be distracted and give it up. It is said that it must always be worn. Shiva and Vishnu wear the horizontal Tripundraka constantly. So do *Devi* Uma, Lakshmi, *brahmana*s, *kshatriya*s, *vaishya*s, *shudra*s,

---

[466] Respectively, great *bhasma* and little *bhasma*.

[467] *Shrouta bhasma* is obtained from rites described in *shruti* texts, *smarta bhasma* from rites described in *smriti* texts. *Loukika bhasma* is ordinary *bhasma*, obtained from fires in general.

[468] The *Jabala Upanishad* was spoken by Yajnavalkya. It doesn't have such *mantra*s. What is meant is *Bhasma Jabala Upanishad*. That has seven *mantra*s—Agni is this *bhasma*, Vayu is this *bhasma*, water is this *bhasma*, earth is this *bhasma*, space is this *bhasma*, *deva*s are this *bhasma* and *rishi*s are this *bhasma*.

those of mixed *varna*s and those who have fallen down. They perform *uddhulana*[469] and wear Tripundraka *bhasma*. Those who do not perform *uddhulana*, and lacking devotion, do not wear Tripundraka, lack the good conduct prescribed for their *varna*s and *ashrama*s. Those who lack devotion and do not perform *uddhulana* and Tripundraka cannot be liberated from *samsara*, not even after crores of births. Even after one hundred thousand *kalpa*s, if a person lacks the devotion and does not perform *uddhulana* or wear Tripundraka, he lacks *jnana* about Shiva. If a person lacks the faith to perform *uddhulana* and wear Tripundraka, he is tainted with great sins. This is the determination of the sacred texts. If a person lacks the faith and does not perform *uddhulana* or wear Tripundraka, every rite performed by him leads to contrary fruits. These beings hate Sharva and are tainted with great sins. O sage! They develop an extremely firm hatred towards *uddhulana* and Tripundraka."'

'"For Shiva, a man must undertake the fire-rites. He must then touch the ashes with the *mantra* '*tryayusham*'.[470] He is freed from all sins. At the time of the three *sandhya*s, a person who makes the mark of Tripundraka with white ash is freed from all sins and rejoices with Shiva. At the time of *savana*,[471] if a person marks Tripundraka on the forehead, when he dies, he obtains the original worlds enjoyed by beings. Without bathing with *bhasma*, no one will recite the *mantra* with six *akshara*s. The *japa* will be performed in the proper way, only after ashes have been used to make the Tripundraka mark. Even he is without compassion, a worst among men, even if has

---

[469] Sprinkling the ashes.

[470] 3.62 of Vajasaneyi Samhita. This has a reference to the three lives of Jamadagni, Kashyapa and *deva*s, with the desire that the worshipper should also have similar three lives (*tri ayusham*).

[471] *Savana* is the three times a day (morning, noon and evening), when an offering of *soma* is made.

committed all the sins, even if he is a sinner, foolish or fallen, as long as he has used ashes to make the mark, all the *tirtha*s assemble in his presence, in whichever region he resides. A being with Tripundraka is worthy of worship by all gods and *asura*s, even if he is a sinner. What need be said about a person who is devoted, pure in his *atman*? A person who possesses *jnana* about Shiva, a person who makes the mark with ashes, can go to whichever region he wishes. But all the *tirtha*s assemble there. What is the need to speak a lot? Learned people must always wear the ash. They must always worship the *lingam* and perform *japa*, using the *mantra* with six *askhara*s. Brahma, Vishnu, Rudra, sages and gods are incapable of speaking about the greatness of wearing *bhasma*. Even if a person has given up the conduct of *varna*s and *ashrama*s, even if he has given up the rites of the *varna*s and even if he has committed sins, as soon as he wears Tripundraka, he is freed. Having discarded the wearing of *bhasma*, men who undertake rites are not liberated from *samsara*, not even after crores of births. A *brahmana* who uses ashes to mark Tripundraka on his head is like a person who has studied everything from his *guru*, a person who has performed every rite. Men who strike when they see those who wear *bhasma*, are born as *chandala*s in their next births. The learned understand this. It is said that *brahmana*s and *kshatriya*s must devotedly apply ashes to their limbs, using the '*ma nastoke*' *mantra*.[472] A *vaishya* or a woman will use the Tryambaka *mantra*. A *shudra* will use the *panchakshara* *mantra*. Others, widowed women and the like, will use the rule decreed for *shudra*s. The *panchabrahma mantra*[473] is recommended for householders. The Tryambaka *mantra* is the rule for those who are in *brahmacharya*. For those who are in the forest, it is said that the rule is to use the Aghora *mantra*.

[472] Mentioned earlier.
[473] 29.16 of Vajasaneyi Samhita, a *mantra* addressed to Agni.

Mendicants will use Pranava to wear Tripundraka. Those who are beyond the pale of *varna*s and *ashrama*s are full of the conception 'I am Shiva'.[474] They are restrained *Shivayogis* and always hold Ishana. No *varna* should give up the excellent practice of wearing *bhasma*. Nor should any other being. This is Shiva's instruction. If a person has bathed himself in *bhasma* and particles of ash cling to his limbs, it is as if he wears that many Shiva *lingam*s on his body. There is no doubt that Tripundraka *bhasma* emancipates *brahmana*s, *kshatriya*s, *vaishya*s, *shudra*s, those from mixed *varna*s, women, widows, girls, heretics, those in *brahmacharya*, householders, those in the forest, those in *sannyasa* and those who follow other vows. When fire is touched, voluntarily or involuntarily, it burns. Similarly, whether it is worn voluntarily or involuntarily, *bhasma* purifies all men."'

'"No man should eat a little bit of food, or drink a little bit of water, without applying *bhasma* or wearing *rudraksha*. Whether he is a householder, a forest-dweller, a mendicant, belonging to a *varna* or an outcaste, if he does this, he goes to hell. In this event, a person from the *varna* system will be liberated when he performs *japa* with *gayatri mantra*. A mendicant is freed with Pranava. A person who criticizes Tripundraka, actually criticizes Shiva. Those who faithfully wear it, actually wear him. Shame on the forehead that is devoid of *bhasma*. Shame on the village that is devoid of a Shiva temple. Shame on a birth that does not worship Isha. Shame on accounts that do not seek refuge with Shiva. Maheshvara Hara is the support of the three worlds. It is a sin to see a person who criticizes him. It is a sin to see a person who criticizes the wearing of Tripundraka. Such people are sinners and are only destined for hell. They are born as those of mixed *varna*s, pigs, *asura*s, donkeys, jackals

[474] *Shivoham* (I am Shiva).

and insects. They do not see the sun or the moon during the
day or night. They only see nightmares. Unless they perform
japa with Shatarudriya, they cannot be liberated. If a foolish
man criticizes the wearing of *bhasma*, it is a true statement
that such a person is destined for hell and has no salvation. O
sage! A *tantrika*[475] has no rights in a *yajna* meant for Shiva.
A person who wears the Urddhva Tripundraka[476] also has no
rights. A person who wears the symbol of a blazing *chakra*[477]
is also similarly barred. The Brihad Jabala Upanishad[478] has
said that there are many worlds to be obtained. Taking that
into consideration, efforts must be made to wear *bhasma*. Just
as sandalwood paste can be applied on top of sandalwood
paste, more *bhasma* can be applied on top of Tripundraka
ash. However, an intelligent person will not wear anything
else over the *vibhuti* applied on the forehead. Women will
wear the ashes on the forelocks of their hair, and this is also
true of *brahmani* widows. Those in the *ashrama*s must always
wear the *vibhuti*. It destroys all sins and bestows the fruit of
final emancipation. Following the norms, the ashes must be
used to make a Tripundraka mark. A person who does this
is freed from a multitude of major and minor sins. A person
in *brahmacharya*, a householder, a person in *vanaprastha*,
a mendicant, a *brahmana*, a *kshatriya*, a *vaishya*, a *shudra*,
a worst among men and a person who has been cast out—
when they perform *uddhulana* and wear Tripundraka, all
these are purified. When *bhasma* is applied in the proper
manner, heaps of sins are taken away. In particular, a person

[475] Practitioner of *tantra*.
[476] When three vertical, instead of horizontal, lines are used, the
mark of a Vishnu devotee.
[477] The mark of Vishnu's devotee again.
[478] A text devoted to *bhasma* and Tripundraka. It is spoken by a
descendant of sage Jabali.

who wears *bhasma* is freed of the following sins: killing a woman or a cow; killing a hero; killing a horse; stealing the possessions of others; outraging another person's wife; criticizing others; stealing another person's field; oppressing another; stealing crops and pleasure grounds; arson of a house; accepting gifts of cattle, gold, buffaloes, sesamum, blankets, garments, cooked food, grain and water from those who are inferior; having intercourse with public courtesans, intoxicated women, *vrishalis* and dancers; having intercourse with women who are going through their season, maidens and widows; the sale of flesh, hides, juices and salt; calumny, false arguments and perjury and love of falsehood. There are many such innumerable sins. As soon as Tripundraka is worn, these are instantly destroyed. If one steals Shiva's objects, criticizes Shiva anywhere or criticizes Shiva's devotee, *prayashchitta* can never purify such a person. However, if a person wears *rudraksha* on his body or Tripundraka on his forehead, even if he is a *chandala*, he is worshipped. He is supreme among all the *varna*s. There are *tirtha*s in this world, Ganga and other rivers. If a person wears Tripundraka on his forehead, he obtains the good merits of bathing in all of these. Among seven crore great *mantra*s, the *panchakshara mantra* is the foremost. In that way, there are crores of other *mantra*s. But Shiva alone is the reason behind all of them. O sage! As a result of these *mantra*s, all *deva*s become friendly. But if a person is radiant in the wearing of Tripundraka, all of them become accessible to him. A person who wears Tripundraka saves one thousand predecessors and one thousand successors in his own lineage. He enjoys all the objects of pleasure in this world. He has a long lifespan and does not suffer from ill health. When his life is over and he dies, he enjoys happiness. He obtains the eight kinds of *siddhi* as attributes. He assumes a divine and auspicious form. He ascends a divine *vimana*, served by celestial beings from heaven. In due order, he enjoys extensive objects of pleasure in the worlds of *vidyadharas*,[479] extremely energetic *gandharvas* and Indra and the other guardians of the worlds. He obtains the status of a lord of subjects. He reaches Brahma's abode and sports with one hundred maidens. He enjoys many kinds of objects of pleasure, for as long as Brahma's lifespan lasts. He then enjoys objects of pleasure in Vishnu's world, for a duration that spans ten Brahmas.[480] After this, he reaches Shiva's world, where all his desires are met forever. There is no doubt that he finally obtains *sayujya* with Shiva there. After considering the essence of all the Upanishads repeatedly, this is the determination that has been arrived at. Tripundraka is the best. A *brahmana* who criticizes *vibhuti* will be born as a lower *varna*. He will go to terrible hells and endure hardships for the duration of a four-faced Brahma. A man who wears Tripundraka at the time of *shraddha, yajna, japa*, offering of oblations to Vishvadevas and worshipping gods is pure in his *atman* and conquers death. To get rid of filth, one bathes with water. A bath with *bhasma* always purifies. Bathing with *mantras* takes away sin. Bathing with *jnana* takes a person to the supreme destination. *Bhasma* is the most sacred of *tirthas* and if a man bathes with it, he obtains fruits that are equal to fruits obtained by bathing in all the *tirthas*. Bathing with *bhasma* is a supreme *tirtha*, as if one is bathing in Ganga every day. *Bhasma* is directly Shiva's form. *Bhasma* purifies the three worlds. If a *brahmana* undertakes donations, *jnana, dhyana* and *japa* without wearing Tripundraka, these become futile. Men who are in *vanaprastha*, maidens and men who have not had *diksha*, must mix it with water and wear it up to midday. After that, water should not be used. In this way, if a man controls his mind and always wears Tripundraka, he

---

[479] Semi-divine species.
[480] For the duration of Brahma's lifespan.

is known as Shiva's devotee. He obtains objects of pleasure and emancipation. *Rudraksha* bestows many things that are auspicious. If a man does not have *rudraksha* on his limbs and does not wear Tripundraka either, his birth is futile. I have thus briefly spoken to you about the greatness of Tripundraka. This is a mystery to all living beings. You must keep it a secret."'

'"O bulls among sages! There are three lines that are made. All those who are learned have spoken about what it must be like on the forehead. It should start from the middle of the eyebrows and extend to the end of the eyebrows on either side. To make the Tripundraka, another line of the same dimension is drawn on the forehead. In between, using the middle and the ring finger, a line is drawn in the opposite direction. A line drawn with the thumb is also known as Tripundraka. Alternatively, the three middle fingers can be used to carefully take the ashes and draw three lines. If one wears Tripundraka faithfully, one obtains objects of pleasure and emancipation. There are nine *deva*s associated with each of the three lines and they are located on different limbs. I will speak about them. Listen attentively. Mahadeva is the divinity for the first line, which stands for 'A', the *garhapatya* fire,[481] the earth, *dharma*, the *guna* of *rajas*, the *Rig Veda*, the power of *kriya* and the morning *savana*. O tigers among sages! Those who are devoted to taking *diksha* about Shiva should know this. Maheshvara is the divinity for the second line, which stands for 'U', *dakshinagni*,[482] space, the *Yajur Veda*, the power of *iccha*,[483] the *jivatman* inside and the *savana* at midday. O tigers among sages! Those who are devoted to taking *diksha* about Shiva should know this.

---

[481] The fire that burns in every household.
[482] The fire that burns in the southern direction.
[483] Will power.

Shiva is the divinity for the third line, which stands for 'M', the *ahavaniya* fire,[484] the *paramatman*, the *guna* of *tamas*, the firmament, power of *jnana*, the *Sama Veda* and the third *savana*. Those who are devoted to taking *diksha* about Shiva should know this. In this way, full of devotion, one must always do *namaskara* to the divinities of the locations and then wear Tripundraka. One will then be purified and obtain objects of pleasure and emancipation. O lord among sages! I have thus spoken to you about the divinities located in the different limbs. In that connection, now listen devotedly to these locations. The *nyasa* must be done in thirty-two places, sixteen places, eight places or five places. The thirty-two excellent places are the head, the forehead, the two ears, the two eyes, the two nostrils, the mouth, the neck, the two arms, the two elbows, the two wrists, the chest, the two flanks, the navel, the two testicles, the two thighs, the two knees, the two calves, the two heels and the two feet. In these places, when wearing Tripundraka, the learned will mention the names of fire, water, earth, wind, the directions, the lords of the directions and the Vasus.[485] The eight Vasus are said to be Dhara, Dhruva, Soma, Apa, Anala, Anila, Pratyusha and Prabhasa. One can also control oneself and apply Tripundraka in sixteen places—the head, the forehead, the neck, the two shoulders, the two arms, the two elbows, the two wrists, the chest, the navel, the two flanks and the back. The names of the divinities to be established there are the two Ashvins, Shiva, Shakti, Rudra, Isha, Narada and nine Shaktis, Vaamaa and others.[486] These are the sixteen divinities. The

---

[484] The fire used for sacrifices.

[485] Ten directions, ten lords of these directions and eight Vasus.

[486] Usually, the nine Shaktis are listed as Kushmanda, Mahagouri, Kalaratri, Siddhidatri, Katyayani, Brahmacharini, Shailaputri, Skandamata and Chandraghanta.

names of the two Ashvins are said to be Nasatya and Dasra. Alternatively, the sixteen places are the head, the hair, the two ears, the mouth, the two arms, the chest, the navel, the two thighs, the two knees, the two feet and the back. The sixteen divinities are said to be Shiva, Chandra, Rudra, Brahma, Vighnesha, Vishnu, Shri in the heart, Shambhu, Prajapati in the navel, Naga, the two Nagakanyas, the two Rishikanyas in the two feet and the *tirtha*s and the ocean on the extensive back. These are the sixteen *tirtha*s. The eight places are said to be the private parts, the forehead, the excellent two ears,[487] the two shoulders, the chest and the navel. The divinities are said to be Brahma and the seven *rishi*s.[488] O lords among sages! I have thus told you about the rules for using *bhasma*. Alternatively, knowledgeable people wear the *bhasma* in five places—the head, the two arms, the chest and the navel. Considering the time and the place, one should do whatever is possible about *uddhulana* and wearing of Tripundraka. Remembering Shiva, Tripundraka can be applied on the forehead alone, chanting '*Namah Shivaya*'. He is the three-eyed one. He is the foundation of the three *guna*s. He is the origin of the three divinities.[489] Tripundraka can be applied to the sides, chanting '*Ishabhyam Namah*'.[490] It can be applied on the forearms, chanting '*Bijabhyam Namah*'.[491] If it is below, the obeisance will be to the ancestors. If it is

[487] The ears are probably counted as one. Otherwise, there would be nine places.

[488] The *saptarshi*s. The *saptarshi*s are the seven great sages. The list varies, but the standard one is Marichi, Atri, Angira, Pulastya, Pulaha, Kratu and Vasishtha. In the sky, the *saptarshi*s are identified with the constellation of Ursa Major (Great Bear).

[489] Brahma, Vishnu and Rudra.

[490] With Isha in the dual, this means both Shiva and Shakti.

[491] I prostrate myself before the two seeds.

above, the obeisance will be to Umesha.[492] On the back, or
on the back of the head, the obeisance will be to Bhima."[493]

Chapter 32-2(25) (Greatness of *Rudraksha*)

'Suta said, "O *rishi* Shounaka! O immensely wise one! O
great lord who is Shiva's form! Listen to the greatness of
rudraksha. I will tell you about it briefly. *Rudraksha* is loved
by Shiva and is supremely purifying. It is said that the sight,
the touch and *japa* with it removes all sins. O sage! Shiva is
the *paramatman*. To do a good turn to the worlds, earlier, he
spoke about the greatness of *rudraksha* in front of Devi."'

'"Shiva said, 'O Devi! O Maheshani! O Shivaa! Listen to
the greatness of *rudraksha*. Out of my love for you and desiring
the welfare of devotees, I am telling you about it. O Maheshani!
In earlier times, I observed austerities for thousands of divine
years. Though I controlled myself, my mind was agitated. O
Parameshani! As Paresha, in my self-possessed form, I desired to
benefit the worlds. Hence, in my sport, I opened my eyes. From
my beautiful half-open eyes, drops of tears fell down. From
those drops of tears was born the tree known as *rudraksha*.[494]
To show favour to my devotees, they became stationary.
They were given to Vishnu's devotees and to the four *varnas*.
*Rudraksha*s grown from the ground in Gouda[495] are loved
by Shiva. They are also grown in Mathura, Ayodhya, Lanka,

---

[492] Umesha means Uma and Isha, together. Above and below is
with reference to the waist.

[493] Bhima means the terrible one. Shiva's name.

[494] Literally, Rudra's eyes. *Rudraksha*s are seeds of the tree
Elaeocarpus ganitrus.

[495] The region around Bengal. The capital of Gouda is now in
Malda district.

Malaya, Mount Sahya, Kashi and other places. The *shruti* texts have said that they can shatter heaps of sins that are intolerable to others. *Rudrakshas* are auspicious. Following my command, *rudrakshas* from earth have been classified into the categories of *brahmanas*, *kshatriyas*, *vaishyas* and *shudras*. The learned know that the respective colours for these are white, red, yellow and black. Men should respectively wear the *rudraksha* that corresponds to their own *varnas*. Those who desire fruits will obtain the fruits of objects of pleasure and emancipation if they wear *rudrakshas* according to *varna*. Since Shiva is always pleased with them, this is particularly true of Shiva's devotees. One that is of the size of a Dhatriphala[496] is said to the best. The one that is of the size of Badariphala[497] is spoken of as medium. One that is inferior is the size of *chanaka*.[498] I will next speak about the method. O Parvati! Listen. This is with a desire to ensure the welfare of devotees. O Maheshvari! Even if it is the size of a Badariphala, it yields fruits in the world, ensuring happiness and the enhancement of good fortune. The one that is the size of a Dhatriphala destroys every kind of harm. That which is like *gunja*[499] achieves fruits in every kind of attempt. The lighter it is, the greater the fruits bestowed by it. The learned say that a fruit which is one-tenth in weight is the best.[500] The wearing of *rudraksha* is said to lead to the destruction of sins. Since it certainly ensures success in every endeavour, it must certainly be worn. O Parameshvari! Nothing else is seen in the world that is as auspicious in bestowing fruits as *rudraksha*. There is nothing as effective as such a *mala*.[501]

---

[496] The myrobalan *amalaka*.
[497] Fruit of the jujube tree.
[498] Chickpea.
[499] A shrub that has a red-black berry.
[500] One-tenth of what is not clear.
[501] String, rosary, necklace.

O Devi! *Rudraksha*s are auspicious if they are even, glossy, firm, large, without spikes and well-formed. Then they always yield desired objects of pleasure and emancipation. There are six kinds of *rudraksha* that must always be avoided—defiled by worms, cut, broken, without protrusions, with sores and ones that are not circular. That which has a natural hole from one end to the other is excellent. When the hole has been carefully bored by humans, it is middling. As a consequence of wearing *rudraksha*, great sins are destroyed. If a man wears eleven hundred *rudraksha*s, his form becomes like that of Rudra. If eleven hundred *rudraksha*s are worn, the fruits are such that it is impossible to describe those fruits even in one hundred years. It is held that a coronet shall be made out five hundred and fifty. A virtuous, devoted and excellent man will make three strings with *rudraksha*s, each string consisting of three hundred and sixty beads. Full of devotion, such a supreme *upavita* will be made out of *rudraksha*s. O Maheshvari! It is said that three *rudraksha*s must be worn on the tuft of hair and on the left and right ear, six each. One hundred and one must be worn around the neck and eleven must be worn on each arm, elbow and wrist. Men who are devoted to Shiva wear three on the *upavita*. Finally, it is held that five must be worn around the waist. O Parameshvari! If a person wears that many *rudraksha*s, his form is like that of Mahesha, and everyone prostrates before him. When such a person is seated in *dhyana*, people say, "He is Shiva" or "He is Hara". When they see him, they are freed from all their sins. This is said to be the norm when there are eleven hundred *rudraksha*s. If that many are not available, there is another auspicious procedure. I will speak about that.[502] One *rudraksha* must be worn on the tuft of

---

[502] This must be an independent statement. Even if one assumes there are three strings in an *upavita*, the number just described falls slightly short of one thousand.

hair, thirty on the head, fifty around the neck, sixteen on each of the arms, twelve on each of the wrists and five hundred on the shoulders. A *mala* or *upavita* will be fashioned out of one hundred and eight. In this way, a person who is firm in his vows will wear one thousand *rudraksha*s. When his mind is like that, he is like Rudra himself and all the gods bow down before him. O lord of sages![503] One *rudraksha* on the tuft of hair, forty on the head, thirty-two around the neck, one hundred and eight on the chest, six in each of the ears and sixteen on each of the arms. Depending on the size of the wrist, double that number[504] can be worn on the wrist. When a person happily wears this number, he becomes Shiva's great devotee. He becomes like Shiva and is worthy of worship. All the others look at him and worship him.'"'

""'It must be worn on the head with a *mantra* to Ishana. It must be worn on the ears with the *mantra* to Tatpurusha.[505] It must be worn around the neck and also on the chest with the *mantra* to Aghora. An intelligent person will wear it on the wrist with the *bija mantra* to Aghora. A string fashioned out of fifteen *rudraksha*s will be worn around the stomach, with a *mantra* to Vamadeva. Three, five or seven *mala*s can be worn with the *panchabrahma mantra*. Alternatively, all the *rudraksha*s can be worn with the *mula mantra*.[506] Liquor, flesh, garlic, onion, the *shigrum* horseradish, *shleshmataka*[507] and *vit-varaha*[508] must be avoided. O Uma! It is recommended that a *brahmana* should wear a white *rudraksha*, a *kshatriya* should happily wear a red *rudraksha*, a *vaishya* should wear a yellow *rudraksha* every

---

[503] Since Shiva is speaking to Devi, this is an inconsistency.
[504] Thirty-two.
[505] Rudra-Mahadeva *gayatri*.
[506] The basic *mantra* of *AUM Namah Shivaya*.
[507] Fruit of *Cordia latifolia*, a medicinal plant.
[508] The village pig. However, this has already been covered in the prohibition on meat.

day and a *shudra* must necessarily wear a black *rudraksha*. This is the path indicated in the *shruti* texts. Irrespective of *varna* and irrespective of whether one is a householder, resides in the forest or is a mendicant, this secret and supreme rule must be followed and must not be violated. Everything can be obtained if one wears *rudraksha* in the proper way. Otherwise, one goes to hell. If one desires the auspicious, one should not wear one that is smaller than an *amalaka* in weight, is broken, has protrusions, has been bitten by worms, has undesirable holes or is inferior in any way. A *rudraksha* that is the size of a chickpea must be avoided. O Uma! *Rudraksha* is a subtle form of my *lingam* and is always praised. Following Shiva's command, all the *ashrama*s and *varna*s, women and *shudra*s, should wear it. Those who are mendicants must always use Pranava to wear *rudraksha*. If he wears it in the morning, he is freed from all sins committed during the night. If he wears it at night, he is freed from all sins committed during the day. This is also true of morning, midday and evening. In this world, those who wear Tripundraka, matted hair and *rudraksha*, do not go to Yama's world. "Those who are radiant with a single rudraksha on their head, wear a Tripundraka in the middle of the forehead and those who perform *japa* with the *panchakshara mantra*, must be worshipped by you.[509] They are indeed virtuous people. Bring to Yama's abode a person who does not have *rudraksha* on his limbs, Tripundraka on his forehead and the *panchakshara mantra* in his mouth. Those who wear *bhasma* and *rudraksha* possess powers, known and unknown. They must be worshipped by all of us and must never be brought here." In this way, Kala[510] instructed his servants. All of them were silent and extremely surprised and agreed. O Mahadevi! Thus, *rudraksha* destroys all sins. Those

---

[509] Yama's command to his servants.
[510] Yama.

who wear it are loved by me and are pure. O Parvati! Even if such a person has committed sins, he is purified. A person who wears *rudraksha* on his hands, arms and heads cannot be killed by any being and roams around the earth in Rudra's form. He must always be worshipped by all the gods and *asura*s. Since he destroys the sins of anyone who sees him, he is worshipped like Shiva. If a person is not liberated through *dhyana* and *jnana*, he must wear *rudraksha*. He is freed from all sins and attains the supreme destination. When a person performs *japa* with a *mantra*, the auspicious qualities become one crore times more if he wears a *rudraksha*. If a man wears it, he obtains good merits that are ten crore times more. O Devi! As long as a living being wears it on his body, till such time he is protected against untimely death. When one sees a person with Tripundraka and *rudraksha* on his limbs, a person who is performing *japa* with *Mahamritunjaya mantra*, one obtains the fruits of seeing Rudra himself. He is loved by the five divinities.[511] He is loved by all *deva*s. O beloved! Wearing a *mala* of *rudraksha*, a devotee should perform *japa* with all the *mantra*s. Devotees of Vishnu and other *deva*s also wear *rudraksha* without any hesitation. In particular, devotees of Rudra always wear *rudraksha*.'"'

'"'There are said to be different kinds of *rudraksha*s. I will speak about their differences. O Parvati! Listen faithfully. They bestow objects of pleasure and emancipation. A *rudraksha* with a single face is Shiva himself and bestows the fruits of objects of pleasure and emancipation. As soon as one sees it, sins like the killing of a *brahmana* are dispelled. Where it is worshipped, Lakshmi cannot be far away. All kinds of calamities are destroyed and everything desired is obtained. One with two faces is Isha, lord of *deva*s. It bestows as fruit everything that is desired. In particular, this *rudraksha* swiftly destroys the sin

---

[511] Interpreted in this context as Ganesha, Devi, Surya, Rudra and Vishnu.

of killing a cow. A *rudraksha* with three faces is always a direct means of attaining the objective. Through its powers, all kinds of learning become firmly established. One with four faces is Brahma himself. It destroys the sin of killing a man. If one sees it, or touches it, the fruits of the four *purushartha*s are obtained. One with five faces is the Lord Rudra himself and is named Kalagni. It bestows every kind of emancipation and everything that is wished for. One with five faces destroys all sins, such as having intercourse with someone one shouldn't have intercourse with or eating something one shouldn't eat. One with six faces is Kartikeya and should be worn on the right arm. There is no doubt that one is freed from sins like the killing of a *brahmana*. O Maheshani! One with seven faces is named Ananga. O Devi! If one wears it, a poor person becomes a lord. A *rudraksha* with eight faces is known as Vasumurti and Bhairava. If a person wears it, he lives for the complete lifespan. After death, he becomes a wielder of the trident. One with nine faces is known as Bhairava or the sage Kapila. O Maheshvari! Durga, with her nine forms,[512] is established in it. With supreme devotion, such a *rudraksha* should be worn on the left hand. There is no doubt that such a person becomes a lord of everything, like me. O Maheshani! One with ten faces is the divinity Janardana himself. O Devi! O Ishi! If one wears it, one obtains everything that is desired. O Parameshvari! A *rudraksha* with eleven faces is Rudra. If one wears it, one becomes victorious everywhere. A *rudraksha* with twelve faces should be worn on the hair of the head. All the twelve Adityas are present in it.[513] One with thirteen faces is known as Vishvadeva. A man who wears it obtains everything that he wishes for. He has good fortune and everything auspicious. One with fourteen faces is the supreme Shiva. If one devotedly wears it on the head, all sins are destroyed. O daughter of the lord of the mountains! I have thus spoken about differences among *rudraksha*s, differences based on the number of faces they possess. I will now tell you about the respective *mantras*. Listen lovingly. For one face, *AUM Hrim Namah*. For two faces, *AUM Namah*. For three faces, *AUM Klim Namah*. For four faces, *AUM Hrim Namah*. For five faces, *AUM Hrim Namah*. For six faces, *AUM Hrim Hum Namah*. For seven faces, *AUM Hrum Namah*. For eight faces, *AUM Hum Namah*. For nine faces, *AUM Hrim Hum Namah*. For ten faces, *AUM Hrim Namah Namah*. For eleven faces, *AUM Hrim Hum Namah*. For twelve faces, *AUM Krim Kshoum Roum Namah*. For thirteen faces, *AUM Hrim Namah*. For fourteen faces, *AUM Namah*. For success in achieving everything one wishes for, full of faith and devotion, one should wear a *rudraksha* with the respective *mantra*. One will then be freed of laziness. If any man on earth wears a *rudraksha* without the *mantra*, he goes to a terrible hell for the duration of fourteen Indras.[514] On seeing a *mala* of *rudraksha*s, *bhuta*s, *preta*s, *pishacha*s, *dakini*s, *shakini*s, others who cause harm and any other artificial creations due to *abhichara* maintain a distance.[515] They are scared of this image. O Devi! O Parvati! On seeing a *mala* of *rudraksha*s, Shiva, Vishnu, Ganapati, Surya and other gods are pleased. O Maheshvari! On knowing about this greatness of

[514] Since every *manvantara* has a different Indra, for fourteen *manvantara*s or one *kalpa*.

[515] *Abhichara* is a magical *mantra* used for malevolent purposes. *Shakini*s and *dakini*s are evil and destructive demonesses, the words are often used synonymously.

rudraksha, it must be properly worn, along with *mantra*s, so that devotion and *dharma* are enhanced.'"'

'Suta concluded, "Shiva, the *paramatman*, spoke in this way to the daughter of the mountain, about the greatness of *bhasma* and *rudraksha* and about how they yield objects of pleasure and emancipation. It should be known that a person who wears *bhasma* and *rudraksha* is loved by Shiva. There is no doubt that wearing them increases powers and confers objects of pleasure and emancipation. A person who wears *bhasma* and *rudraksha* is spoken of as Shiva's devotee. A person who is devoted to performing *japa* with the *panchakshara mantra* is inclined to be complete. If one worships Mahadeva without *bhasma*, Tripundraka and a *mala* of *rudraksha*s, this does not yield the desired fruits. O lord among sages! I have told you everything that I have been asked about earlier—the greatness of *bhasma* and *rudraksha* and about how they ensure prosperity and everything wished for. If one constantly listens to this greatness of *bhasma* and *rudraksha*, with devotion in one's mind, one obtains everything one desires. This is a supreme and auspicious account. In this world, such a person enjoys every kind of happiness and has sons and grandsons. In the world hereafter, he is exceedingly loved by Shiva and obtains emancipation. O lords among sages! I have narrated Vidyeshvara Samhita to you. This yields every kind of success. Because of Shiva's command, it always bestows emancipation."'

This ends Vidhyeshvara Samhita.

Rudra Samhita

Srishti Khanda

Chapter 33-3.1(1) (The Sages Ask)

'I prostrate myself before Shri Ganesha. I prostrate myself before Gouri and Shankara. This begins the second Samhita, Rudra Samhita. Gouri's husband is the cause behind the creation, preservation and dissolution of the universe. He is the one who knows the truth. He is infinite in his deeds. He resorts to *maya* but is himself beyond *maya*. His form cannot be thought of. His unblemished form is pure understanding. I prostrate myself before that Shiva. I prostrate myself before the infinite Shiva, who exists before Prakriti. He is the tranquil Purushottama. Using his own *maya*, he has created everything. Like space, he is inside it and outside it. I prostrate myself before Shiva, whose own secret form is not manifest. He himself acted so as to create this universe. The universe constantly revolves around him, just as pieces of iron do around a magnet.'

Vyasa said, 'Shambhu is the father of the universe. Shivaa is the mother of the universe. Ganadhisha[516] is their son. I will describe after seeking refuge with them. On one occasion, the sages who were residents of Naimisharanya,

---

[516] Ganesha.

Shounaka and others, were filled with supreme devotion and asked Suta.'

'The *rishi*s said, "We have heard the virtuous and auspicious account of Videyshvara Samhita. This beautiful account speaks of the objective and the means and is loved by devotees. O Suta! O immensely fortunate one! O Suta! May you be happy and live forever. O father!⁵¹⁷ Please make us hear Shankara's supreme account. This undecaying *jnana* is like *amrita*. We have drunk this account from your mouth, which is like a lotus. However, we are still not content. O unblemished one! Therefore, we wish to ask you something again. Through Vyasa's favours, you know everything and have accomplished your objective. There is nothing that is unknown to you, the past, the present and the future. Because of your devotion, you obtained the supreme compassion of your *guru*, Vyasa. In particular, you have got to know everything. You have made your life meaningful and successful. O wise one! Please tell us now about Shiva's supreme form. Especially tell us about the divine conduct of Shiva and Shivaa. Maheshvara is *nirguna*. In this world, how does he assume a *saguna* form? Despite reflecting on it, we do not know Shiva's true nature. Before creation, in what manner is Shambhu's own form established? In the midst of creation, how does the Lord continue to engage in his pastimes? When it is the end, how is the divinity Maheshvara established? How is Shankara, who brings auspiciousness to the world, pleased?⁵¹⁸ When Mahesha is pleased, what auspicious fruits does he bestow on his own devotees and on others? Please tell us all this. We have heard that Bhagavan is instantly pleased.

⁵¹⁷ The word used is *tata*, translated as 'father' because Suta is doing the narration.

⁵¹⁸ The word Shankara means someone who bestows auspiciousness and prosperity.

Full of compassion, he is unable to witness great exertions made by his devotees. Brahma, Vishnu and Mahesha—these three have originated from the divinity Shiva's body. When Mahesha is complete, he is himself like another Shiva. Please tell us about his manifestations, and especially about his conduct. O lord! Please also tell us about Uma's origin and her marriage, about their domestic life and their supreme pastimes. O unblemished one! You should tell us all this and anything else worth narrating."'

Vyasa said, 'Thus asked, Suta was filled with joy. He remembered Shambhu's lotus feet and replied to the lords among sages.'

'Suta said, "O lords among sages! You have asked a proper question. You are blessed. Your intelligence is such that faith has been generated towards Sadashiva's account. Questions about Sadashiva's account purify three kinds of men and women, those who ask, those who narrate and those who hear. It is like the waters of Jahnavi. O *brahmana*s! Except for those who kill animals, which man will not be delighted at a recital of Shambhu's qualities? It always delights three kinds of people. When it is recited by a person who has extinguished thirst, it is like medication for this disease of worldly existence. It delights the mind and the ears and bestows every objective. According to my intelligence, I will tell you about the substance of your questions and about Shiva's pastimes. O *brahmana*s! Please listen lovingly. What you have asked me is exactly what Narada asked his father,[519] when he was sent by Hari, who is nothing other than a form of Shiva. Brahma is Shiva's devotee. Therefore, on hearing his son's words, his mind was pleased. Full of delight and joy, he spoke about Shiva's fame to that excellent sage."'

---

[519] Narada was born through Brahma's mental powers.

Vyasa continued, 'Hearing the words spoken by Suta, the excellent *brahmanas* were filled with curiosity and asked about that excellent conversation.'

'The *rishis* said, "O Suta! O immensely fortunate one! O Suta! O immensely intelligent one! O Shiva's supreme devotee! Hearing your enchanting words, our minds have been filled with curiosity. When did this great conversation, which generates happiness, between Vidhatri and Narada occur? That conversation was about Girisha's supreme pastimes, and it frees one from worldly existence. O father! Please tell us about the conversation that occurred earlier between Vidhatri and Narada about Shankara's fame. Tell us about the substance of the questions."'

Vyasa continued, 'Hearing the words of the sages, who had cleansed their *atmans*, Suta was greatly delighted and replied, detailing that conversation.'

Chapter 34-3.1(2) (Narada's Austerities and Pride)

'Suta said, "Narada, supreme among sages and Brahma's son, was humble in his *atman*. On one occasion, he made up his mind to engage in austerities. There is an extremely beautiful cave in the Himalaya mountains. With great force, the celestial river always flows near it. There is a great and divine hermitage there, full of many kinds of ornaments. Narada, who possesses divine insight, went there for austerities. Seeing that hermitage, the tiger among sages performed austerities for a very long time. He was silent and sat firmly in *asana*. Pure in his intelligence, he practiced *pranayama*. The sage was in *samadhi* and the *vijnana*, 'I am the *brahman*', was generated. O *brahmanas*! The *brahman* was directly manifested before him. In this way, Narada, supreme among sages, engaged in austerities. As he performed the austerities, the mind of Shunasira[520] was tormented and agitated. He thought in his mind, 'The sage desires my kingdom.' Hari made efforts to bring about impediments. Shakra, the leader of devas, thought of Smara in his mind. Kama swiftly arrived there, along with his queen, who possessed an inclination similar to his, and the son.[521] Seeing that Kama had come, the lord, the king of the gods, addressed him. He was crooked in intelligence when it came to his selfish interests, and he spoke to him quickly. Indra said, 'O noble friend! O immensely valiant one! O one who always does what is good for me! Listen affectionately to my words and act so as to help me. Through your prowess, I have destroyed the pride of many ascetics. O friend! The stability of my kingdom has always been based on your favours. The sage Narada is tormenting himself through austerities in a cave in the Himalaya mountains. His mind has turned towards becoming the lord of the universe and he is firm in his control. I am scared that he may ask Vidhatri for my kingdom. Therefore, go there right now and create impediments in the path of his austerities.' Thus addressed by the great Indra, Kama went there, with his beloved Madhu.[522] Having gone there, in his pride, he thought of possible means. He quickly used all of his own skills. Vasanta also used all his own powers of intoxication. O excellent sages! But this did not cause the least bit of mental agitation to the sage. Through Mahesha's favours, his pride was destroyed. O Shounaka and others! Listen lovingly to the reason. Because

[520] One of Indra's names. Hari is also one of Indra's names.

[521] Smara, Madana or Kama is the god of love. His wife is Rati. It is not obvious what 'son' means. Kama and Rati's son is Harsha (joy) and that is the obvious meaning. But it could also mean Brahma's son, Vasanta (spring), who is Kama's friend.

[522] Madhu means spring, as well as the month of Chaitra. Here, it possibly means spring.

of Ishvara's favours, Smara had no powers. It was at this spot that Shambhu, Smara's enemy, had performed great austerities. It was at this spot that he had destroyed Kama, who used to disturb the austerities of sages. So that Kama might come back to life, Rati had entreated the gods. Requested by them, Shankara, who bestows prosperity on the worlds, had replied. 'O gods! After some time, Smara will come back to life again. But Smara's artifices will never work in this place. O immortals! The bit of ground that can be seen by people from this spot will be immune to the power of Kama's arrows. There is no doubt about this.' Since Shambhu had said this, Kama had made futile efforts against Narada. He quickly returned to Indra in heaven. Smara told him everything, about how he had no power against the sage. Madhu's beloved was then commanded to return to his own abode."'

"'The lord of the gods was astounded at this and praised Narada. He did not know about the true account and was confounded by Shiva's *maya*. All beings find it impossible to understand Shambhu's *maya*. Other than devotees who have surrendered their *atman*s to him, everyone in the universe is confounded. Through Isha's favours, Narada remained in that spot for a long time. When he thought that he had completed the austerities, the sage stopped. Thinking that he had defeated Kama himself, the lord among sages was proud. Confounded by Shiva's *maya*, he was deprived of true *jnana*. O supreme sages! Shambhu's great *maya* is blessed. It is blessed. Vishnu, Brahma and others cannot see its progress. Narada, supreme among sages, was also confounded by it. Insolent, he went quickly to Kailasa to report what he had done. Proud, the sage told Rudra about everything he had done. He took himself to be a great-souled one. Having conquered Smara, he thought that he was his own master. Hearing this, Shankara, who loves his devotees, spoke. He spoke to the ignorant one whose intelligence had been distorted because of his own *maya*. Rudra said, 'O son! O Narada! O wise one! You are blessed. But do not speak like this anywhere else, especially in front of Hari. Even if you are asked, you should not speak about what you have done, as you have done now. This is a secret. This must always be a secret and you must never speak about it. I am especially telling you this because I love you the most. You are Vishnu's devotee and anyone who is his devotee is my follower.' The Lord Rudra, the origin of creation, told him this in many ways. However, Narada was still confounded by Shiva's *maya* and did not pay heed to these beneficial words. The course of *karma* is powerful and even discriminating people cannot fathom it. Shankara's wishes can never be countered by people."'

"'The noble sage went to Brahma's world. Bowing down before Vidhatri, he told him how he had defeated Kama through the strength of his austerities. Hearing this, Vidhatri remembered Shambhu's lotus feet and got to know everything about the real reason. Therefore, he tried to restrain his son. Narada is supreme among those who possess *jnana*. But he was confounded by Shiva's *maya*. Therefore, he did not pay heed to the beneficial words Vidhatri had spoken. Insolence had sprouted firmly in his mind. Whatever Shiva wishes is what happens in the world. The entire universe is subject to his control and follows his words. With his intelligence destroyed, Narada swiftly went to Vishnu's world. With the sprout of insolence firm in his mind, he wished to tell him about what he himself had done. Vishnu saw that the sage Narada had arrived. He got up affectionately, advanced slowly towards him and embraced him. He made him sit down on his own seat. Hari remembered Shiva's lotus feet and desiring to destroy Narada's insolence, addressed him in these words. Vishnu said, 'O son! Where have you come from and why have you come here? O tiger among sages! You are blessed. Because of your arrival, I have become like a *tirtha*.' Hearing Vishnu's words, the proud sage, Narada, told him everything about what he had done. He was insolent and overwhelmed by pride. Hearing the sage's words, Vishnu remembered Shiva's lotus feet in his

heart and got to know everything about the reason for the pride.
Hari was Shiva's devotee, and his *atman* was immersed in Shiva.
Therefore, he devotedly joined his hands together in salutation,
and with his head lowered, praised Girisha Parameshvara. Vishnu
said, 'O lord of the gods! O Mahadeva! O Parameshvara! Please
show me your favours. O Shiva. You are blessed. Your *maya* is
blessed. It confounds everyone.' In this way, he praised Shiva,
the *paramatman*. He closed his eyes and meditated on his lotus
feet, before stopping. Knowing what Shankara was planning to
do, the preserver of the universe followed Shiva's instructions
and spoke pleasantly to the supreme sage. Vishnu said, 'O tiger
among sages! You are blessed. You are a store of austerities, and
your intelligence is extensive. O sage! Desire and delusion only
affect those in whom the three types of devotion do not exist.[523]
Because of that deviation, many kinds of miseries arise. But you
are faithfully devoted to *brahmacharya* and always possess *jnana*
and non-attachment. How can a deviation like desire arise in
you? You are intelligent and your mind does not suffer from any
deviation.' The excellent sage heard many such words of praise.
Smiling within his heart, he bent down and replied to Hari in
these words. Narada said, 'O lord! As long as you show me
your compassion, how can Smara have any powers over me?'
Saying this, the sage bent down before Hari and went wherever
he wanted to go.'"

Chapter 35-3.1(3) (Narada and the *Svayamvara*)

"The *rishi*s said, "O Suta! O immensely fortunate one!
O Suta! O Vyasa's disciple! We prostrate ourselves

[523] The three types of *bhakti* are *kirtana*, *shravana* and *manana*.

before you. O father! You have shown us your favours and narrated an extraordinary account. O father! What did Hari do after Narada had left? Where did Narada go? You should tell us that."'

Vyasa said, 'Hearing their words, the learned Suta, supreme among those who knew the accounts of the Puranas, remembered Shiva, who is behind every origin, and replied.'

'Suta said, "Vishnu is accomplished in the use of *maya*. When the sage Narada left, as he wished, he followed Shiva's wishes and swiftly extended his *maya*. He constructed a great city in the middle of the sage's path. It was one hundred *yojana*s in expanse and wonderful and extremely agreeable. It was more beautiful than heaven and was decorated with many kinds of objects. Excellent men and women, from all the four *varna*s, were amusing themselves. It was supreme. There, the prosperous King Shilanidhi was arranging for the *svayamvara*[524] of his daughter and there were great festivities. All kinds of princes assembled from the four directions. They were handsome, attired in many kinds of garments. They were eager that the maiden should choose them. Seeing this beautiful city, Narada was overcome with delusion. Full of curiosity and desire, he went to the king's gate. Seeing that the noble sage had arrived, King Shilanidhi made him sit on an excellent bejewelled throne. The king summoned his beautiful daughter, named Shrimati. He asked her to prostrate herself at Narada's feet. Seeing the maiden, the sage Narada was amazed and asked, 'O king! Who is this immensely fortunate maiden? She is like a daughter of the gods.' Hearing his words, the king joined his hands in salutation and replied, 'O sage! She is my daughter. Her name is Shrimati. The time has come to bestow the auspicious one and she is in search of a groom.

---

[524] In a *svayamvara*, a maiden herself chose her groom from assembled suitors.

She possesses all the auspicious signs, and the time has come
for her *svayamvara*. O sage! Please tell me affectionately about
her destiny, what has been ordained since birth. Please tell me
what kind of groom my daughter will get.' Thus addressed, the
tiger among sages was overwhelmed by desire and wanted her.
Narada addressed the king in these words. 'O lord of the earth!
This daughter of yours possesses all the auspicious signs. She is
immensely fortunate and blessed. Like Lakshmi, she is a store
of qualities. Her husband will certainly be a lord of everything,
a brave one who cannot be vanquished. He will be a lord,
like Girisha. He will be an excellent god who vanquishes even
Kama.' Telling the king this, the sage took his leave and went
away, wherever he willed. He was confounded by Shiva's *maya*
and overwhelmed with desire. In this mind, the sage started
to think, 'How can I possibly get her? In a *svayamvara* full of
kings, how can she possibly choose me? Every woman always
loves beauty. There is no doubt that if I show her such a form,
she will come under my control.' Thinking this, the excellent
sage made up his mind to assume Vishnu's form. Distracted by
desire, Narada quickly went to Vishnu's world. He prostrated
himself before Hrishikesha[525] and addressed him in these words.
'In private, I will tell you everything about what happened
to me.' Wishing to do what Shiva wanted, Shrisha Keshava
told the sage, 'Please tell me.' Narada replied, 'The excellent
King Shilanidhi is devoted to you. His daughter, Shrimati, is
large-eyed and beautiful in form. She is famous as someone
who confuses the worlds and is the most beautiful woman
in the three worlds. O Vishnu! I wish to marry her quickly.'
Following her wishes, the lord of the earth has organized a
svayamvara for her. From the four directions, thousands of
princes have arrived. If you grant me your form, I will certainly

[525] Vishnu. Shrisha (Shri's lord), Madhusudana and Keshava are
also Vishnu's names.

be able to obtain her. Unless I have your form, she will not place the garland of victory around my neck. O protector! Please grant me your form. I am your beloved servant. Please let it be such that the princess Shrimati chooses me.' Hearing the sage's words, Madhusudana laughed. Since he knew about Shankara's lordship, he was full of compassion and replied. Vishnu said, 'O sage! You can go wherever you want. I will do what is beneficial for you, just as a physician treats a person who is afflicted. After all, you are my beloved.' Saying this, Vishnu gave the sage the face of a monkey.[526] Having shown him his favours and given him this form, he vanished."'

'"Thus addressed, the sage was delighted that he had received Hari's form. He thought that he had been successful in his objective but did not comprehend the true intent. Narada, the excellent sage, swiftly went to the place where the svayamvara was being held, where all the princes had assembled. There was a divine assembly hall for the svayamvara, full of princes. O Indras among brahmanas! It resembled a second assembly hall of Shakra's. Narada went and sat down in the king's assembly. He sat there and thought, his mind full of delight, 'Since I am in Vishnu's form, there is no doubt that she will choose me.' The excellent sage did not know that his face was malformed. All the men assembled there only saw the sage in his former form. O brahmanas! The princes and others did not realize that there was a difference. To protect him, two of Rudra's ganas had arrived there. They assumed the forms of brahmanas and knew the secret about the difference. Taking the sage to be a fool, the two ganas approached him. As they conversed among themselves, they laughed at him. 'Behold Narada's form. It is as excellent as Vishnu's, but the face is that of a monkey. It is

[526] Hari is Vishnu's form and Narada asked for Hari's form. But the word hari also means monkey. Thus, ostensibly granting Narada his wish, Vishnu gave him the face of a monkey.

malformed and fearful. This one is confounded by desire and wants the king's daughter.' They addressed each other in these words and laughed at him. However, since he was overwhelmed by desire, though he heard their words, he did not comprehend the true meaning. Deluded by desire, the sage looked at Shrimati. At this time, the beautiful-limbed king's daughter left the inner quarters and arrived there, surrounded by women. Auspicious in qualities, she held a beautiful golden garland in her hand. As she stood there, in the midst of the *svayamvara* hall, she was as resplendent as Rama.[527] With the garland, the one who was excellent in her vows went around everywhere in the assembly hall. As she sought her desired groom, the princess was radiant. She saw the sage, with Vishnu's body and the face of a monkey and was angered. With a cheerful mind, she turned her gaze away and went elsewhere. She did not find anyone she desired in that *svayamvara* hall. She did not bestow the garland on anyone present there. Meanwhile, Vishnu arrived there, in the disguise of a king. She did not look at anyone else, but only looked at him. As she looked at him, her face, which was like a lotus, bloomed. The beautiful lady placed the garland around his neck. In the disguise of a king, the lord Vishnu accepted her and instantly vanished from the spot, returning to his own abode with her. All the princes lost any hopes of getting Shrimati. The sage still suffered from desire and was extremely distracted. His words faltered. Rudra's two *ganas*, accomplished in *jnana*, who were in the forms of *brahmanas*, spoke to him. The *ganas* said, 'O Narada! O sage! Your being confused by Madana is futile. You desire her but look at your own face. It is that of a despicable monkey.' Hearing their words, Narada was astounded. Confounded by Shiva's *maya*, he looked at his face in a mirror. Seeing that his face was like that of a monkey, he was filled with instant rage.

---

[527] Lakshmi.

Confounded, the sage cursed the two *gana*s, 'Since the two of you have laughed at me, you will be born as *brahmana*s. But though the seed will be that of a *brahmana*, your forms will be that of *rakshasa*s.' Hearing this, Hara's *gana*s, excellent in *jnana*, did not curse back in return. Since they knew the sage was deluded, they did not say anything. Those two *brahmana*s were indifferent. They returned to their own abodes, praising Shiva. They thought that everything is always determined by Shiva's wishes.'"

Chapter 36-3.1(4) (Narada Curses Vishnu)

'The *rishi*s said, "O Suta! O immensely fortunate one! O Suta! O immensely wise one! You have narrated an extraordinary account. Shambhu's *maya* is blessed. Everything mobile and immobile is under its control. The two *gana*s followed the wishes of Lord Shambu and departed. Distracted by desire, what did the angry sage Narada do?"'

'Suta replied, "Confounded, the sage cursed them, as he willed. Following Girisha's wishes, he looked at his face in a mirror and saw his own form. Because of Shiva's wishes, he did not understand.[528] But he remembered and decided Hari had done some deception. Full of rage that was impossible to tolerate, he went to Vishnu's world. Like a fire fed with kindling, he addressed him in angry words. Because of Shiva's wishes, his *jnana* was destroyed, and he used vile and taunting words. Narada said, 'O Hari! You are extremely wicked and deceitful. You bemuse the world. You cannot tolerate another person's enterprise and resort to filthy *maya*. Earlier, you

---

[528] He saw his natural form and did not know that he had a monkey's face.

assumed the form of Mohini and perpetrated a fraud.[529] You made the *asura*s drink *varuni* instead of *amrita*. O Hari! If Maheshvara Rudra had not taken pity on you and drunk the poison, all your *maya* would have been destroyed and would no longer be resplendent. O Vishnu! Any path that involves deception is especially liked by you. Your nature has never been virtuous, but the Lord has ensured that you are independent. Shiva, the *parmatman*, did not do what was right. Thinking of your power and strength and understanding what you do, he is repenting the independence he bestowed on you. Citing the *Veda*s he himself uttered, he has said that *brahmana*s are supreme. O Hari! Knowing this, today I will use my powers to instruct you, so that you never do something like this anywhere again. Till now, you have acted fearlessly because you have not come into contact with anyone who possesses superior spirit. O Vishnu! You will now receive the fruits of what you have yourself done.' The sage was still deluded by *maya*. Saying this, overcome with rage, he displayed a *brahmana*'s energy and cursed Hari. 'O Vishnu! For the sake of a woman, you agitated me and deceived me. You will now suffer distress in the very form in which you caused such deception. In that form, you will be born as a human on earth and suffer miseries. The face that you created will become your aide.[530] You will suffer miseries on account of being separated from a woman and will undergo great misery. Deluded by ignorance, you will generally follow the path a human takes.' Narada was himself deluded by ignorance and cursed Hari in this way. Praising

---

[529] At the time of the churning of the ocean, Vishnu assumed this form to deprive *asura*s of *amrita*. *Varuni* is liquor. Shiva drank the poison that emerged from the churning of the ocean and became blue in the throat.

[530] Since Vishnu had assumed the form of a king, he was born as King Rama, whose aide was Hanuman.

it since it had originated with Shambhu, Vishnu accepted the curse. Meanwhile, in his great pastime, Shambhu took away the delusion he had caused. With the *maya* of his delusion gone, Narada got back his *jnana*. When the *maya* vanished, he became as intelligent as he had been earlier. Narada was amazed in his mind. With his understanding restored, he was no longer agitated. Because of remorse, he repeatedly condemned himself. He also praised Shambhu's *maya*, which could also delude learned people. The sage got to know everything and realize that he had been confounded by *maya*. Narada, the greatest of Vishnu's devotees, fell down at Vishnu's feet. He presented himself before Hari and spoke these words. 'My evil intelligence has now gone. Confounded by evil intelligence, I have earlier addressed you in wicked words. O lord! I have also invoked a curse on you. Please make that futile. Otherwise, because of the great sin I have committed, I will certainly go to hell. O Hari! What can one do? I am your servant. Please command me, so that I can destroy all my sins and not go to hell.' Saying this, the supreme sage again fell down at Vishnu's feet. His intelligence was excellent now and he fell down, full of repentance."'

'"At this, Vishnu raised him up and addressed him in amiable words. Vishnu said, 'Do not suffer from remorse. There is no doubt that you are my greatest devotee. O son! Listen to what I say. This will certainly ensure a great benefit to you. Shiva's power will ensure that you do not go to hell. Confounded by your insolence, you showed disrespect to Shiva's words. He is the one who gave you such fruits. He is the one who bestows fruits of *karma*. Be certain in your mind that everything is the result of Shiva's wishes. Parameshvara Shankara is the lord who takes away insolence. He is the supreme *brahman*. He is the *paramatman*. He is the one who kindles understanding about *sacchidananda*. He is *nirguna*. He is without transformation. He is beyond *sattva*, *rajas* and *tamas*. He gathers up his own

maya and assumes three different forms. His *nirguna atman*
has the forms of Brahma, Vishnu and Mahesha. He is *nirguna*.
In his *nirguna* form, he is known as Shiva. He is Maheshvara,
the *paramatman*. He is the supreme *brahman*, without decay.
He is chanted about as the infinite Mahadeva. Vidhatri exists as
the creator to serve him, and I as the preserver of the universe.
He is always everything himself and assumes the form of Rudra
as the destroyer. In his form of Shiva, he is only a witness,
distinct from his *maya*. He is *nirguna* and does what he wills.
He indulges in his pastimes and shows favours to his devotees.
O Narada! O sage! Listen to an excellent means whereby you
will obtain happiness. He is the one who destroys every kind of
sin. He always bestows objects of pleasure and emancipation.
Casting aside all your doubts, praise Shankara's fame. Always,
single-mindedly, perform *japa* with the *stotram* that mentions
Shiva's one hundred names.[531] If you perform *japa* with that,
all your sins will be swiftly destroyed.' Having told Narada
this, full of compassion, Vishnu again spoke to him. 'O sage!
Do not grieve. You have done nothing. There is no doubt that
Shambhu did all this, as a result of his own wishes. He is the
one who took away your divine intelligence and made you
suffer on account of desire and insolence. Your mouth was an
instrument and Maheshvara used that to curse me. This is the
way he manifests his action in the world he himself has created.
He is the one who conquers death. He is like death unto Death.
He is intent on saving his devotees. There is no lord I love as
much as I love Shiva. He is the one who bestows happiness. He
is the Parameshvara who bestows every kind of power on me. O
sage! Worship him. Always offer homage to him. Hear and sing
about his fame. Always worship him. A person who approaches
Shankara in thought, words and deeds is known as learned. He
is spoken of as *jivanmukta*. Shiva's name blazes like a forest fire

[531] *Shatarudriya.*

and reduces mountains of great sins to ashes. This is the truth.
There is no doubt that this is the truth. Many kinds of miseries
have sin as the cause. Shiva's worship alone destroys them.
There is nothing else that destroys them completely. O sage! If
a person always seeks refuge with Shankara in thoughts, words
and deeds, he is pure in his *atman*. He is blessed and learned
and knows the *Veda*s. Many kinds of *dharma* are followed by
those who are eager for instant fruits. All of them have faith
in the worship of the destroyer of Tripura. O great sage! As
long as Shiva is worshipped, sins are destroyed. All the sins
on earth are destroyed. This is true. O sage! There are many
heaps of sins, the killing of a *brahmana* and others. As soon as
Shiva is remembered, they are destroyed. This is the truth. I am
telling you the truth. You have now obtained Shiva's name as a
boat to cross the ocean that is *samsara*. There is no doubt that
sins, the cause of *samsara*, will be destroyed. O great sage! For
beings, sins are the root cause of *samsara*. There is no doubt
that Shiva's name is an axe that severs it. If one is suffering from
the forest blaze of sins, one should drink the *amrita* of Shiva's
names. For those who are scorched by the forest blaze of sins,
there is no other means of finding peace. When the nectar of
Shiva's names showers down and floods, there is no doubt that
one does not grieve any longer amidst the forest conflagration
of *samsara*. Men who do not possess faith towards Shankara
suffer from attachment and hatred in their *atman*s. But even
people like that can suddenly obtain emancipation. However,
it is only if one has tormented oneself through austerities for an
infinite number of births that one develops devotion towards
Bhavani's[532] beloved. Devotion towards Shankara must be
generated. Any other ordinary course of action, which thinks
of worshipping others and ignores devotion towards Shiva, is
futile. If without thinking, a person ordinarily has devotion

[532] Bhavani means Parvati, Bhava's wife.

towards Shambhu, he can easily obtain emancipation. That
is my view. If a person has committed an infinite number of
sins, but possesses devotion towards Maheshvara, there is
no doubt that he is freed from all sins. This is just like trees
being reduced to ashes by a conflagration in the forest. In that
way, sins are burnt down by Shankara's names. If a person
constantly purifies his limbs with ashes and is eager to worship
Shiva, he crosses over the extremely difficult *samsara*, which is
so very difficult to cross. A man who is Virupaksha's[533] servant
is not touched by sins like stealing a *brahmana*'s possessions
or killing many *brahmana*s. Having looked at all the *Veda*s, it
has certainly been determined earlier that worshipping Shiva
is the best means of destroying *samsara*. Therefore, from now
on, following the norms and carefully, attentively, devotedly
and constantly, worship Samba Sadhashiva Maheshvara.
Lovingly, cover yourself from head to foot with *bhasma*. Using
the *mantra* with six *akshara*s, perform *japa* to Shiva, who
is famous in all the sacred texts. Full of devotion, following
the norms and using the *mantra*s, make efforts to devotedly
wear *rudraksha*, loved by Shiva, on all your limbs. Always
hear Shiva's account. Always speak about Shiva's account.
Carefully and repeatedly, worship Shiva's devotees. Without
any distraction, always seek refuge with Shiva. One always
obtains bliss through worshipping Shiva. Hold Shiva's lotus
feet within your pure heart. O supreme among sages! First visit
Shiva's *tirtha*s. Behold the infinite greatness of Shankara, the
paramatman. O sage! Later, go to Anandavana,[534] which is
loved most by Shambhu. See Vishveshvara there and devotedly
perform worship. In particular, when you prostrate yourself
and praise him, you will be freed from doubts. O sage! Indeed,
it is recommended that you should go there. Thereafter, to

---

[533] Virupaksha is one of Shiva's names.
[534] Kashi, literally, the forest of happiness.

accomplish your own desires and following my command, faithfully go to Brahma's world. O sage! In particular, prostrate yourself and praise Vidhatri, your own father. With a cheerful mind, ask him many things about Shiva's greatness. Brahma is foremost among Shiva's devotees, and he will happily make you hear about Shankara's greatness and tell you about the praise with one hundred names. O sage! From now on, become Shiva's devotee, one who seeks refuge with Shiva. You will obtain emancipation. Shiva will bestow a special benediction on you.' In this way, with a cheerful mind and affectionately, Vishnu instructed the sage. He remembered Shiva, bowed down and praised him, and vanished from the spot.'"

Chapter 37-3.1(5) (Narada's Visit to Kashi)

'Suta said, "O brahmanas! When Hari vanished, the excellent sage, Narada, wandered around the earth. Full of devotion, he saw Shiva lingams. Shambhu's two ganas got to know that Narada, divine in insight, was roaming around and that his inclinations were now pleasant. They approached him. Affectionately, the two ganas quickly touched his feet with their heads. They clasped his feet so that they might be freed from their curse and spoke to him. Shiva's two ganas said, 'O Brahma's son! O divine rishi! Listen cheerfully to our words. We are the ones who caused offence to you earlier and we are not really brahmanas. O brahmana! O sage! We are Hara's ganas, who caused you offence earlier. At the time of the svayamvara of the princess, your mind was confounded by maya, sent by Paresha.[535] You cursed us. Knowing that the time was not right, we thought that silence means life. We

---

[535] Parameshvara.

have reaped the fruits of our own deeds, and no one is to be blamed. O lord! Be pleased now and show us your favours.' The sage heard the words spoken by the devotee *ganas*, uttered affectionately. Suffering from remorse, he replied lovingly. Narada said, 'O Mahadeva's *ganas*! You are worthy of being respected by virtuous people. Now that I have been freed from delusion, listen to my words. They are true and will give you happiness. It is certain that because of Shiva's command, my intelligence deviated earlier. When I was deluded in every possible way, I used blades of *kusha* grass[536] to curse you. What I uttered was bound to happen. O *ganas*! However, listen to my words now. I will tell you how you will be saved from the curse. Please pardon my transgression. From the semen of a supreme sage and because of his command, you will be born as *rakshasas*. You will possess prosperity, strength and great power. You will be in control of your senses. You will be Shiva's devotees and you will rule over all the kings in the cosmic egg. When your death is caused by one of Shiva's manifestations, you will be reinstated in your own positions.' Hearing the words spoken by Narada, the great-souled sage, both Hara's *ganas* were delighted. They happily returned to their own abodes. Narada was also greatly delighted. As his mind was focused on Shiva's *dhyana*, he roamed around the earth and saw many Shiva *tirthas*."'

'"The sage reached Kashi, resplendent above all the others. It is loved by Shiva. It brings happiness to Shambhu. It is Shambhu's own form. Having seen Kashi, he accomplished his objective. He saw Kashinatha[537] and worshipped him. He was filled with great delight and supreme bliss. Successful in his objective, the supreme sage resided happily in Kashi.

---

[536] Often used before invoking a curse.
[537] The lord of Kashi, Shiva.

He prostrated himself before him[538] and devotedly recited his account, overwhelmed by love and affection. His mind constantly remembering Shiva, he then went to Brahma's world. His mind full of devotion towards Shiva, he wished to ask about Shiva's principles. Narada said, 'O Brahma! O one who know the nature of the *brahman*! O grandfather of the universe! O lord! Through your favours, I know everything about Vishnu's supreme greatness and *bhakti marga, jnana marga*, the extremely difficult *tapo marga, dana marga* and *tirtha marga*.[539] I have heard about these. But I do not know about Shiva's principles or about the due order and rules under which his worship has to be performed. O lord! Please also tell me about his different kinds of conduct. O father! How can Shiva be *nirguna* while Shankara is *saguna*? I do not know about Shiva's principles, and I am confounded by Shiva's *maya*. Before creation, how was Shambhu established in his own form? How does the lord sport in the midst of creation? At the end, how is the divinity Maheshvara established? How is Shankara Maheshvara, who bestows auspiciousness on the worlds, pleased with his devotees or with those who are devoted to others? What fruits does he bestow? O Vidhatri! Please tell me everything. I have heard that Bhagavan is instantly pleased. He is full of compassion and cannot bear to see great efforts made by his devotees. The three, Brahma, Vishnu and Mahesha, originated as the divinity Shiva's portions. Out of them, Mahesha possesses all the portions and is therefore like another Shiva himself. Please tell me about his manifestations and especially about his conduct. O lord! Please also tell me about Uma's manifestation and her marriage, in particular, their domestic life and pastimes. O unblemished one! Please tell

---

[538] Shiva.
[539] The respective paths of *bhakti, jnana, tapas* (austerities), donations and visiting *tirtha*s.

me everything else that is worth describing. O lord of subjects! In particular, please tell me about Shivaa's origin and marriage and Guha's birth. O lord! I have already heard about all this from many but am not satisfied. Therefore, I have sought refuge with you. Please show me your favours.' Hearing the words of Narada, who was born from his own body, Brahma, the grandfather of the worlds, replied in the following words."'

Chapter 38-3.1(6) (Mahapralaya and Vishnu's Origin)

‘ ‘‘Brahma said, 'O *brahmana*! O supreme among those who understand! You have asked a virtuous question. You have always been interested in the welfare of the worlds and this will bring benefit to the worlds. When all the worlds hear this, all their sins will be destroyed. Therefore, I will tell you about Shiva's *tattva*,[540] which is without decay. Neither I nor Vishnu truly know Shiva's *tattva*, or his supreme form. Nor does anyone else know. At the time of Mahapralaya,[541] everything mobile and immobile is destroyed. Everything is covered in darkness. The suns, the planets and the stars do not exist. There is no moon. There is no night or day. There is no fire, wind, earth or water. There is no Pradhana.[542] Everything is empty, devoid of energy. There is nothing that can be seen, nothing that can be described as sound or touch. There is nothing manifest in the form of smell or form. There is

[540] The word *tattva* means principles. But the sense of the true or essential nature, is not captured by the word 'principles'.
[541] The great dissolution that occurs at the end of Brahma's lifespan. The secondary dissolution occurs at the end of Brahma's day.
[542] Pradhana is the main cause behind material nature.

no taste and there are no directions. The only truth that exists
is darkness that cannot be penetrated with a needle. The only
thing that exists is what the sacred texts call 'the cause, or the
brahman'. In this situation, nothing can be described as existent
or non-existent. *Yogis* constantly perceive it in the space that is
within themselves. This is not something that can be perceived
through the mind or expressed in words. It has no name, no
form and no complexion. It is not thick or thin. It is not tall
or short. It is devoid of any notion of lightness or heaviness.
It has neither an increase nor a decrease. The sacred texts say
that it instantly envelopes everything. It is truth. It is *jnana*. It is
infinite. It is supreme bliss. It is splendid. It cannot be measured.
It is without foundation. It is without transformation and
without form. It is *nirguna*. *Yogis* are capable of approaching
it. It pervades everything and is alone the cause. It is beyond
doubt. It is without a beginning. It is devoid of *maya* and
hardships. It has no second. It is without a beginning or an
end. It has no development. It is pure consciousness. That
being the case, since it does not have an alternative, it cannot
be given a name or not be given a name. After some time, it
decided to have a second. Since it itself had no form, in its
pastimes, it decided to create an alternative that had form.
This was auspicious and possessed all the qualities of power.
It possessed every kind of *jnana*. It could go everywhere. It
possessed every kind of form. It could see everything. It was the
cause of everything. It should be worshipped by everyone. It is
the beginning of everything. It constantly purifies everything. It
thus thought of this manifested form of Ishvara, one that was
pure in form. The original entity is without a second, without
a beginning and without an end. It illuminates everything and
is in the form of consciousness. This is known as the supreme
and undecaying *brahman*, which can go everywhere. This is
without form. Having created the second, which has a manifest
form, it vanished. This manifested form is Sadashiva. Learned

ones, in ancient times and in current times, have spoken of it
as Ishvara. From his own portion, following his wishes and his
pastimes, Ishvara created Shakti. He created her from his own
body, but she did not harm his body in any way. This Shakti
is devoid of transformation and different names are used for
it—Pradhana, Prakriti, Maya, Gunavati, Paraa and the mother
of Buddhi *tattva*. That Shakti is spoken of as Ambika, Prakriti
and Ishvari. She is the mother of the three divinities and is the
prime cause. The auspicious one possesses eight arms and a
wonderful face. It is as if her face is always radiant with the
splendour of one thousand full moons. She is adorned with
many kinds of ornaments. She has many kinds of movements.
Devi holds many kinds of weapons, and her eyes are like full-
blown lotuses. Her energy cannot be imagined. She is the
womb of everything. This Maya is alone, but she has many
kinds of unions. The supreme Purusha is Ishvara, Shiva or
Shambhu, and he has no other lord above him. He holds the
Mandakini[543] on his head. He possesses three eyes and has the
moon on his forehead. He has five faces and a pleasant *atman*.
He possesses ten arms and wields a trident. He is as pure and
fair as camphor. His body is smeared with ashes. The *brahman*
assumed the form known as Kala and along with Shakti,
created the *kshetra* known as Shivaloka. This is the supreme
kshetra known as Kashika.[544] It is resplendent above everything
else and is spoken of as the place that bestows supreme *nirvana*.
In that beautiful *kshetra*, those two, in the form of supreme
bliss and in supreme bliss, sported. O sage! Even at the time of
pralaya,[545] that *kshetra* is never freed from Shiva and Shivaa.
Therefore, it is known as Avimukta.[546] Earlier, the wielder of

---

[543] Ganga.
[544] Kashi.
[545] Dissolution.
[546] Literally, never forsaken.

Pinaka[547] gave it the name of Anandavana, since the *kshetra* bestows bliss. It came to be known as Avimukta later. Shiva and Shivaa sported in Anandavana.'"'

"'"O divine *rishi*! They then wished that another being should be created. Shiva thought, "Let him bear this great burden. Let us reside in Kashi and only bestow *nirvana*. Through my favours, let him create, protect and dissolve. When he is created, we will be able to enjoy ourselves in Anandavana, with our minds not agitated by anything external adversely affecting our joy." Along with Shakti, Lord Parameshvara churned the ocean of his thoughts and gathered up the jewel of *sattva*, the coral of *rajas* and the crocodile of *tamas*. From a tenth portion on the left side of his ocean of nectar, he created a being who was the most handsome in the three worlds. Since there was an excess of *sattva guna*, this being was serene, as deep and fathomless as an ocean. O sage! He was endowed with forgiveness and there was no one who was his equal. His complexion was that of blue sapphire. He was glorious and his eyes were like lotuses. His form was golden, and he was clad in two excellent garments. He was endowed with great radiance and his arms were like two staffs. He could not be vanquished. That being prostrated himself before Shambhu Parameshvara and said, "O Lord! Give me a name and assign a task to me." Hearing these words, Lord Shankara Mahesha smiled and replied in a voice that rumbled like thunder. Shiva said, "Since you pervade everything, you will be known by the name of Vishnu.[548] But since you will bestow happiness on your devotees, you will have many other names too. Be steadfast and perform austerities, so that the supreme task can be accomplished." Saying this, he used his breath to breathe into him the *nigama*

---

[547] Pinaka is the same of Shiva's bow or trident.
[548] From the root *vish*, meaning someone who pervades everything.

texts.[549] Achyuta prostrated himself before Shiva and undertook extensive austerities. Along with Shakti and his companions, Parameshvara vanished. Achyuta tormented himself through austerities for twelve thousand divine years. However, he could not see his desired Lord, who is always auspicious to behold. Vishnu was filled with doubt. He lovingly thought of Shiva and remembered him in his heart. He wondered, "What will I do now?" Meanwhile, Shiva's auspicious voice was heard. "Since a doubt has presented itself, you should undertake austerities again." O *brahmana*! Hearing this, he tormented himself through extremely terrible austerities for a long period of time, following the path of *dhyana*. Following the path of *dhyana*, understanding arose in the being known as Vishnu. He was greatly delighted and amazed and thought, "What is truly great?" As a result of Shiva's *maya* and the exertion, many streams of water started to flow from Vishnu's limbs. O great sage! They covered everything in that great void. This water has the form of the *brahman* and if one touches it, sins are destroyed. The being Vishnu was exhausted and went to sleep on that water. Supremely happy, he spent a long period of time in that state of delusion. Thus, in conformity with the *shruti* texts, he got the name of Narayana.[550] Except for that Purusha, nothing else existed in nature then. Meanwhile, other *tattva*s emerged from the great-souled one. O wise one! O immensely intelligent one! Listen. I will tell you about them. Mahat came into being from Prakriti. The three *guna*s emerged from Mahat. As a result of differences between the three *guna*s, three kinds of *ahamkara* arose.[551] *Tanmatras*[552] were generated and so were the five gross elements. The organs of action resulted

---

[549] The *Veda*s.
[550] One whose abode (*ayana*) is water (*nara*).
[551] One associated with each of the three *guna*s.
[552] The five subtle elements.

and the organs of perception. O supreme among *rishi*s! I will
tell you the number of the *tattvas*. All those that originate from
Prakriti are insentient. Purusha is not like that. Together, there
are twenty-four *tattvas*.[553] Following Shiva's command, he[554]
accepted them and continued to sleep in what was a form of
the *brahman*.'"'

Chapter 39-3.1(7) (Dispute between Brahma and Vishnu)

'''Brahma said, 'As the divinity Narayana slept, an
excellent lotus sprouted from his navel. It was
gigantic. As a result of Shankara's wishes, it was suddenly
generated. The stalk was infinitely long, and the pericarp was
resplendent. It was infinite *yojana*s wide. It was infinite *yojana*s
tall. It was wonderful and radiant, resembling the dazzle of one
crore suns. It was supremely beautiful and wonderful, excellent
to behold. O child! Parameshvara Shankara carefully exerted
himself, as he had done earlier. Shambhu created me from the
right side of his body. O sage! Mahesha swiftly covered me
in his *maya*. He created us in his pastimes, and I originated
from the navel. O son! Since I was born in this way, I came to
be known as the one who was born from a golden womb.[555] I
possessed four faces and a red complexion. The Tripundraka
was on my forehead. Confounded by the *maya*, I did not know
anything other than the lotus. O son! My father had created

---

[553] Five organs of action, five sense of perception, five subtle
elements, *manas* (mind), *buddhi* (intellect),
ahamkara (ego) and Pradhana.

[554] Vishnu.

[555] Hiranyagarbha.

me from his own body, but my knowledge was weak. "Who am I? Where have I come from? What is the task that has been assigned to me? Whose son am I? Who has created me now?" These were the doubts that surfaced in my mind. "Why am I confused in this way? It should indeed be easy to obtain the knowledge. There is this lotus flower, and its place of origin must be down below. There is no doubt that my creator will be there." Thinking this, I began to climb down the lotus. O sage! I proceeded from one part of the stalk to another part of the stalk, and this continued for one hundred years. But I could not reach the excellent place from which the lotus had originated. I was again filled with doubt and was eager to climb up the stalk. O sage! Using parts of the stalk, I started to climb up the lotus. But just as I could not reach the root of the lotus, in my confusion, I couldn't find the top either. Using parts of the stalk, I wandered around again for one hundred years. After this, in a state of confusion, I stopped for a while. O sage! At this time, following Shiva's wish an extremely auspicious voice was heard from the sky and it destroyed my confusion. "Perform austerities." Hearing these words from the sky, I made efforts to torment myself through terrible austerities and did this for twelve years, so that I might be able to see my father.'''

''"Then, so as to show me his favours, Bhagavan Vishnu quickly arrived. He was four-armed, and his eyes were beautiful. He held a conch shell and the *chakra* as a weapon. He also held a mace and a lotus. All his limbs were as dark as the clouds, and he was attired in yellow garments. He wore a diadem and excellent ornaments. His pleasant face resembled a lotus. He resembled one crore Kandarpas[556] together. On seeing him, I was confused. Seeing his beautiful form, I was filled with great wonder. His complexion was both dark and

---

[556] Kandarpa is Kama's name.

golden. This four-armed form exists within all *atman*s. I saw him manifest himself in that form, with the existent and the non-existent[557] inside his *atman*. I saw the mighty-armed Narayana and was delighted. At the time, my mind was confused because of Lord Shambhu's *maya* and pastimes. Therefore, I did not recognize my own father and happily addressed him. Brahma said,[558] "Who are you?" Saying this, I used my hand to try and raise the eternal being. Since he did not wake up, I struck him even more sharply and firmly with my hand. At this, the one who was in control of himself arose shortly, though he was still lying down on his bed. Because of the sleep, when he looked at me, his eyes were like a wet lotus. As I stood there, Bhagavan Hari illuminated me with his radiance. Woken up by Brahma, he smiled once at me and spoke sweetly. Vishnu said, "Welcome. O child! Welcome. O grandfather! O immensely radiant one! Do not be scared. There is no doubt that I will give you everything you wish for." O bull among divine *rishi*s! He smiled first, before uttering these words. When I heard them, I was still bound in enmity because of *rajas*. I spoke to Janardana accordingly. Brahma said, "You are addressing me as 'child'. Though I am the one who destroys everything, you call me a 'child'. O unblemished one! You are smiling and speaking to me, as if you are the *guru* and I am the *shishya*. I am the creator of the worlds. I am the one who directly made Prakriti function. I am eternal and Aja.[559] I am Vishnu and Virinchi and I have originated from Vishnu. I am Vidhatri, the *atman* of the universe. I am the lotus-eyed Dhatri. You must quickly tell me why you have been overcome with confusion and have spoken to me in this way. The *Veda*s always speak of me as

---

[557] Alternatively, cause and effect. *Sat* and *asat* can be translated as either.

[558] Brahma is reporting what Brahma said then.

[559] Aja means without birth/origin.

Svayambhu Aja. I am the grandfather who is his own master.
I am the supreme Parameshthi." Hearing these words, Hari,
Rama's husband, became angry. Vishnu said, "I know that
you are the creator of the worlds. But to create and become
Dhatri, you have descended from my undecaying limbs. You
have forgotten the undecaying Jagannatha[560] Narayana. I am
Purusha, the *paramatman*. I am Puruhuta and Purushtuta.[561] I
am Vishnu, Achyuta and Ishana. The universe has originated
because of my powers. I am the mighty-armed Narayana. I am
the Ishvara who pervades everything. There is no doubt that
you have originated from the lotus in my navel. However, this
is not your fault. I have extended my *maya* over you. O one
with four faces! Listen to my true words. I am the lord of all
*deva*s. I am the creator, the preserver and the destroyer. There
is no lord who is my equal. O grandfather! I am supreme. I
am the supreme *brahman*. That is the truth. I am the supreme
light. I am the *paramatman* and I am the lord. Everything that
can be seen in the universe today, everything that is heard of,
mobile and immobile, know that all of that exists within me.
O four-faced one! It is I who created the twenty-four *tattva*s
that are manifest. Each small particle is bound to me. I have
created both anger and fear. In my power and pastime, I have
created your limbs and those of many others. I am the one
who created intellect and the three kinds of *ahamkara*. O one
born from a lotus! I created the *tanmatra*s and from those, the
mind, the body and the senses. In my pastimes, I created space
and the elements, and everything derived from the elements. O
lord of subjects! O Vidhatri! Understanding this, seek refuge
with me. There is no doubt that I will protect you from every
kind of misery." Hearing these words, Brahma was filled

[560] Lord of the universe.
[561] Puruhuta means someone who receives oblations first.
Purushtuta means someone who is praised first.

with rage. Confounded by *maya*, I reprimanded him and said, "Who are you? Why are you speaking a lot? These excessive words will lead to injury. You are not Ishvara nor are you the supreme *brahman*. Someone must certainly have created you." Deluded by *maya*, I started an extremely terrible battle with him. Because of the great Lord Shankara's *maya*, I fought with Hari. Thus, a clash that made the body hair stand up ensued between me and Hari. In the midst of that ocean of *pralaya*, the *rajas* caused us to be bound in enmity.'"

""'Meanwhile, a *lingam* appeared in front of us, so as to pacify the dispute and kindle understanding in us. It was covered with thousands of garlands of flames, and it resembled the fire of destruction. It was free of any increase or decrease and it had no beginning, middle or end. It was unmatched and beyond determination. It was the unmanifest origin of the universe. Bhagavan Hari was confounded by those thousands of flames. When I was also confounded, he told me, "Why do you want to contend with me now? A third one has now arrived, amidst the fight between the two of us. Where has this originated from? We should examine this object, which has fire as its origin. I will head downwards and ascertain the bottom of this pillar of fire. O lord of subjects! To examine it, you should use the force of the wind and make an effort to head upwards. You should proceed swiftly." Having said this, the one whose *atman* is in the universe, assumed his own form. He swiftly assumed the form of a boar. O sage! I assumed the form of a swan. Since then, I am called the great lord who is Hamsa-Hamsa.[562] A person who utters the words

---

[562] A *hamsa* (swan) is believed to have the power of discrimination, so that it can drink the milk from a mixture of milk and water. Brahma's mount is a swan. The word Hamsa is used for both the *paramatman* and the *jivatman* and for a supreme *sadhaka* who can discriminate between the two. The word Hamsa-Hamsa can be taken to be one who is supreme among such Hamsas.

246 SHIVA PURANA: VOLUME 1

"Hamsa-Hamsa" will also become a Hamsa. My complexion was a fiery white and I had wings on every side. In those earlier times, with the speed of thought and of the wind, I flew up and further up. Narayana, whose *atman* is in the universe, assumed an extremely white form. He was ten *yojana*s wide and one hundred *yojana*s long. He was as large as Mount Meru. His front tusks were white and sharp. His complexion was like the fire of destruction. His snout was long, and his roar was loud. His feet were short, and his multi-coloured body was firm and unmatched. Assuming the form of a boar, he swiftly headed downwards. In this way, for one thousand years, Vishnu kept going downwards. Since then, the worlds have known him as Shveta Varaha.[563] O *devarshi*! In terms of the measurement of time used by men, a *kalpa* passed. Using his powers, Vishnu headed downwards. Vishnu wandered around in different ways. However, the boar could not find the slightest indication of the root of the *lingam*. O destroyer of enemies! Till such time, I also explored upwards. Desiring to find the end, I quickly made every kind of effort. I was exhausted and was unable to find the end. Therefore, after some time, I headed downwards. In that way, the lotus-eyed Bhagavan Vishnu could not find the end. Gigantic in form, he swiftly arose, and it was if all *deva*s were in him. In front of us, behind us and in every direction, there was Parameshvara.[564] Along with me, he prostrated himself and remembered, "What is this? This has no form or name. It is devoid of *karma*. It has no sign, but it has the form of a *lingam*. It cannot be comprehended through the path of *dhyana*." Therefore, having reassured our minds, we did *namaskara*. Both Hari and I were certainly overcome by that extensive presence. "We do not know your form. O great lord! We do not know who you are. O Mahesha! We prostrate

[563] The white boar.
[564] In the form of the *lingam*.

ourselves before you. Please show us your form quickly." In this way, we spent one hundred autumns doing *namaskara*. O tiger among sages! Both of us were still full of pride.'"'

Chapter 40-3.1(8) (AUM)

' "Brahma said, 'O best among sages! In this way, with our pride gone, we wished to see the noble divinity. O sage! We constantly stood there. Bhava Shambhu, the protector of those who are afflicted, took pity on us. He is the one who takes pride away from those who are proud. He is the lord of everything and is without decay. At that time, a *nada* arose there, and its only attribute was the sound. The only characteristic of this "AUM" was its *pluta* attribute.[565] It was articulated exceedingly well by the best of the gods. "What is this great sound?" Thinking this, I stood there. Vishnu is revered by all. He is content in his heart and has no sense of enmity. He saw the eternal one emerge from the right side of the *lingam*. The letter "A" emerged first, followed by "U" and finally by "M". From the middle of "M" the *nada* extended till the end of "AUM". To the right of the first letter "A", he saw the solar disc. O *supreme rishi*! There was blazing fire above "U". There was the lunar disc in the middle of "M". Above this he saw the *brahman*, with a complexion like that of pure crystal. This was unsullied and was beyond the *turiya* state.[566]

---

[565] A short vowel sound is pronounced over a single *matra*, *matra* meaning a syllabic instant. A long vowel sound is pronounced over two *matras*. *Pluta* is protracted, pronounced over three *matras*.

[566] A living being has four states—waking, dreaming, sleeping and *turiya*. *Turiya* is the fourth state, when one perceives union between the human soul, *jivatman*, and the *brahman*.

It was without distinguishable form and beyond hardships. It was beyond the opposite pairs. It was alone and void, without any outside or inside. But it was inside the external and outside the internal. It was devoid of a beginning, a middle or an end. It was the source of bliss. It was truth, bliss and *amrita*. It was the supreme *brahman*, the refuge. "Where has this originated from?" He[567] wished to investigate the origin of this column of fire and descend this unmatched column of fire. Therefore, he immersed himself in this sound of the *Veda*s and meditated on the *atman* that pervades the universe. O *rishi*! At that time, a *rishi* arrived there and reminded him about the truth. Vishnu understood that this *rishi* was Parameshvara. He was Mahadeva, the supreme *brahman*, and had assumed this supreme form of Shabda Brahman.[568] Rudra is beyond thought and cannot be comprehended through words or the mind. They return, without reaching. He can only be expressed through that single *akshara*. That single *akshara* expresses him. He is *amrita* and the supreme cause. He is truth, bliss and *amrita*. He is the supreme *brahman*, greater than the greatest. In that single *akshara*, "A" is the seed for the illustrious one who was born from the egg.[569] In that single *akshara*, "U" stands for Hari, the supreme cause. In that single *akshara*, "M" stands for the illustrious Nilalohita.[570] The creator of creation is "A", the one who enchants is "U". "M" stands for the one who always grants favours. The lord known as "M" is the original seed, though the one known as "A" is spoken of as the seed. "U" is Hari, the womb and the lord of Pradhana and Purusha. But the original seed, the secondary seed, the womb and the sound are actually Maheshvara. According to his own wishes,

---

[567] Vishnu.
[568] Shabda Brahman means the sound AUM.
[569] That is, Brahma.
[570] Shiva's name, the blue-red one.

that original seed divides his *atman* and is established. The lord who is spoken of as the seed, represented by "A", arose from that original seed of the *lingam*. This was flung into the womb of "U" and spread in every direction. This became a golden egg, there being no other sign that could distinguish it. That divine egg floated on the water for many years. At the end of one thousand years, it divided into two and Aja[571] originated. The egg that floated in the water was struck by Ishvara himself. The extremely auspicious and golden upper part gave birth to the firmament, while the lower part became the earth, with its five characteristics.'"'[572]

'"'From that egg was born the four-faced one who is known as Kah.[573] He is the creator of all the worlds. The lord thus divided himself into three. Those who are supremely knowledgeable about the *Yajur Veda* refer to this as "AUM, AUM". Hearing the words of the *Yajur Veda*, the *Rig Veda* and the *Sama Veda* lovingly accepted this and spoke of the two of us as Hari and Brahma. In this way, according to our capacity, we got to know the lord of *deva*s. Using *mantra*s, we praised the divinity Maheshvara, the source of great prosperity. Meanwhile, along with me, the illustrious one who protects the universe saw another extraordinarily beautiful form. O sage! This had five faces and ten arms and was as fair as camphor. There were many kinds of brilliance in it, and it was adorned in many kinds of ornaments. It was extremely pervasive, extremely valorous and possessed all the signs of a great being. On seeing this supreme form, Hari and I were satisfied. At this, the illustrious Parameshvara Mahesha was pleased. Standing there, he smiled and told us about his divine form, which was

[571] Brahma.
[572] The five elements.
[573] Kah is Brahma's name, though the word is also applied to other divinities.

formed out of sound. "अ" stands for his head and "आ" is his forehead. "इ" is his right eye and "ई" is his left eye. "उ" is his right ear and "ऊ" is his left ear. "ऋ" is Parameshthi's right cheek and the long "ॠ" is his left cheek. "ऌ" and the long "ॡ" are his two nostrils. "ए" is his upper lip and "ऐ" is the lord's lower lip. "ओ" and "औ" are the two rows of his teeth. "अं" and "अ:" are the two palates of the lord of *deva*s who wields the trident. The five letters that begin with "क" are the five hands to the right. The five letters that begin with "च" are the five hands to the left. The five letters that begin with "ट" and the five letters that begin with "त" stand for his legs. "प" is said to be his stomach and "फ" is his right flank. "ब" is his left flank and "भ" is said to represent his shoulders. "म" is the heart of Shambhu Mahadeva, the *yogi*. "य", "र", "ल", "व", "श", "ष" and "स" are the lord's seven *dhatu*s.[574] "ह" is in the form of his navel and "क्ष" is said to be his nose. In this way, his form is full of sound. Though he doesn't possess *guna*s, these are the expressions of *guna*s in his *atman*. Seeing him, along with Uma, Hari and I were satisfied. In this way, we saw Mahesha Shiva, in his body of Shabda Brahman. Vishnu and I prostrated ourselves before him and looked upwards again. The Aumkara *mantra* has five parts[575] and is as pure as crystal. It is auspicious and has the thirty-eight *akshara*s inside it.[576] He arose in a form that was like a cloud, along with the powerful *gayatri mantra*, which when mastered, is a means to accomplish *dharma* and *artha*. It has twenty-four excellent *akshara*s and four supreme

---

[574] Plasma, blood, muscle, fat, bone, marrow and seminal fluid. These are known as the seven *dhatu*s.

[575] A, U, M, *bindu* and *nada*.

[576] One has to guess how this number of 38 is arrived at, since it is not immediately obvious. One possibility is 25 consonants, plus 4 sonorants, plus 4 conjunct consonants, plus 3 sibilants, ह and ळ. These *shloka*s are difficult to understand.

parts.[577] The *panchasita mantra*, with 30 auspicious *akshara*s and eight parts, is generally used for purposes of *abhichara*. The *mantra* from *Yajur Veda*, with 25 auspicious *akshara*s and eight parts, is used for happiness and peace. The excellent *mantra* with 61 *akshara*s and thirteen parts, with the word "*bala*" attached at the beginning, ensures origin, increase and destruction. Bhagavan Hari obtained supreme *panchakshara mantra*, *chintamani mantra*, *dakshinamurti mantra* and "*tattvamasi*" as Hara's great words[578] and performed *japa* with these. I and Bhagavan Vishnu were delighted in our minds at having seen him in his forms of parts; *akshara*s; *Rig*, *Yajur* and *Sama* hymns; Ishana; the highest form of Isha; the ancient one known as Purusha; the pleasant Aghora, who is in the heart; Sadashiva, who is always a secret; Mahadeva, with the beautiful feet; the one who is decorated with Indras among serpents; Shiva, with legs, eyes and hands on every side; Brahma's lord; and the cause of creation, preservation and destruction. We praised Samba Ishvara, who bestows boons, with supreme words.'"'

Chapter 41-3.1(9) (Shiva *Tattva*)

' "Brahma said, 'Maheshvara heard his own praise, uttered by Vishnu. Extremely pleased, the ocean of

---

[577] *Gayatri mantra* is usually written as *bhur bhuvah svah, tat savitur vareniyam, bhargodevasya dhimahi, dhiyo yo nah prachodayat*. But the *mantra* actually starts with *tat savitur vareniyam*. Thus, there are four lines, but the *mantra* proper has 8 × 3 = 24 *akshara*s.

[578] There are different *mantra*s that go by the name of *chintamani mantra*, including *gayatri mantra*. Dakshinamurti is Shiva's form as a teacher and there are different *mantra*s addressed to Dakshinamurti. '*Tattvamasi*' means 'You are that'.

compassion showed himself to us, along with his wife. He
had five faces and three eyes. He had matted hair and the
moon was on his forehead. He had large eyes and was fair in
complexion. His body was smeared with ashes. He was blue
in the throat and possessed ten arms. He was adorned with
ornaments everywhere. All his limbs were beautiful and there
was a Tripundraka formed with ashes on his forehead. We saw
the divinity Parameshvara in that form, along with his wife.
Along with me, the illustrious Vishnu used excellent words to
praise him again. At this, in the form of his breath, Hara gave
him the *nigama* texts. Mahesha, abode of compassion, was
pleased with Vishnu. He also bestowed on him *jnana* about
Hara, the *paramatman*. O sage! Out of his compassion, the
paramatman also gave me all this. Having obtained the *nigama*
texts, Vishnu was content. However, along with me, he joined
his hands in salutation and asked Maheshvara again. Vishnu
asked, "O divinity! How are you propitiated? O Lord! How
will I worship you? How should one perform *dhyana* on you?
How are you brought under control? O Mahadeva! We follow
your command. Please tell us what we should do. You are
cause and effect. O Shankara! For our pleasure, please instruct
us. O great ruler! O Lord! Please take pity on us and tell us all
this. Tell us everything else and make us understand. O Shiva!
We are your followers." Hearing these words, Bhagavan Hara
was pleased.'"

'"'The ocean of compassion was extremely pleased. He
cheerfully addressed us in these words. Shri Shiva said, "O
supreme among gods! I am indeed pleased with your devotion.
Behold me as Mahadeva and you will be freed from all your
fears. Always worship my *lingam* and perform *dhyana* on the
form that you see now. You must make efforts to undertake this
task. When I am worshipped in the form of the *lingam*, I am
pleased and bestow many kinds of fruits. I bestow on all people
the many kinds of things their minds desire. O best among

gods! Whenever there is hardship, you should worship my
lingam and the misery will immediately go away. O extremely
strong ones! I am the lord of everything. You have been from
my nature, from the left and the right of my body. This Brahma,
the grandfather of the worlds, was born from my right. I am the
paramatman and Vishnu originated from my left. I am pleased
with the two of you and I will give you the boon you wish for.
Through my command, may your devotion towards me be firm.
O wise ones! You should fashion my Parthiva image. When you
render many kinds of service to it, you will obtain happiness. O
Brahma! Carrying out my command, you are the one who will
create. O child! O Hari! O child! You will protect the mobile
and the immobile." The lord then told us about the auspicious
modes for worshipping him. Worshipped in that way, Shambhu
bestows many fruits. Hearing Shambhu's words, Hari and I
joined our hands in salutation. We prostrated ourselves and
replied to Mahesha. Vishnu said, "If you are pleased with
us, please bestow a boon on us. May we have constant and
undeviating devotion towards you. O father! Though you are
nirguna, in your pastimes, you assume an *avatara*[579] to help us.
You are supreme Parameshvara. O divinity! O lord of *deva*s!
The dispute between us has had an auspicious end since you
came here to settle the dispute." Hearing these words, Hara
spoke to Hari again, who stood there, with his head lowered
and his hands joined in salutation.'"

"'Shri Mahesha said, "Though I am *nirguna*, I become
saguna to undertake creation, preservation and destruction.
I am the supreme *brahman*, without any transformation. My
attribute is of being *sacchidananda*. O Hari! O Vishnu! I am
always *nishkala*. But for the sake of creation, preservation
and dissolution, I assume *guna*s and divide myself into three,

---

[579] *Avatara* is incarnation, with a root in descending or coming
down.

known as Brahma, Vishnu and Hara. O Vishnu! Along with
Brahma, you prayed that I might assume an *avatara*. Since I
am affectionate towards my devotees, I will make that wish
come true. O Brahma! My supreme form, one that resembles
the present one, will manifest itself from your body and will
be famous in the worlds under the name of Rudra. Born as my
portion, his capacity will be the same as mine and will not be
inferior. He is I. I am he. There is no difference in rules followed
for worship either. When fire comes into contact with water,
its qualities are not affected by that association. Like that, I am
not bound by any association with *guna*s. It is I in the form of
Shiva. I, Shiva, am also in the form of Rudra. O great sage![580]
One should not seek to make a difference between him and
me. They are essentially the same form. For the purposes of
the world, they have simply been divided into two. Therefore,
it should be known that there is never a difference between
Shiva and Rudra. When gold is made into an ornament, there
is no change in its substance. O god! There is a difference in
the name, not in the substance. Clay is the same, though it
may be used to fashion different vessels. The presence of the
cause in the effect is another example of this. This should be
known by all noble, learned and knowledgeable ones who
possess unsullied *jnana*. Understanding this, the two of you
should not see any difference. It is my substance and form of
Shiva that exists everywhere. I, you,[581] Aja and the one who
will be Rudra are really the same form. There is no difference.
Differences lead to bondage. But the eternal form of Shiva
belongs to me alone. This is always spoken of as the real cause.
It is truth, *jnana* and infinite. Knowing this in the mind, one
should always perform *dhyana* on this truth. O Brahma! Listen

---

[580] While Brahma can be addressed as a great sage, this is probably
an inconsistency and is meant for Narada.
[581] Vishnu.

to another secret that I will tell you about. The two of you have originated from Prakriti, but Rudra has not been born from Prakriti. I will be born in this form through Brahma's furrowed eyebrows. This Hara will be spoken of as naturally possessing *tamas guna*. It will also be known as *vaikarika ahamkara*. But the substance is *tamas* only in name, not actually. O Brahma! Because of this reason, you must do the following. O Brahma! You will be the creator and Hari will protect your creation. The one who will be born from my portion will be an agent for dissolution. This Devi Prakriti, who is Parameshvari, is known as Uma. Her Shakti, in the form of the goddess of speech, will find refuge with Brahma. Yet another Shakti will result from Prakriti, and she will find refuge with Vishnu. Her form will be that of Lakshmi. There will certainly be another portion known as Kali, who will seek refuge with me. For the purpose of undertaking her work, she will be born in the form of fire.[582] These are spoken of as the supreme and auspicious Devis or Shaktis. In due order, their tasks will certainly be creation, preservation and dissolution. O supreme among gods! They are portions of Prakriti, my beloved. Along with Lakshmi, you[583] should carry out your task. O Brahma! Following my command, along with the goddess of speech, born as Prakriti's portion, you should cheerfully undertake the task of creation. I will take the help of Kali, who is a portion of my beloved, who is greater than the greatest. In the form of Rudra, I will undertake the excellent task of dissolution. You will certainly be happy after having created the world, with its four *varna*s and *ashrama*s, all engaged in carrying out their many tasks. With *jnana* and *vijnana*, you will ensure benefit to the worlds. O Vishnu! Following my command, from now on, you will bestow emancipation on the world. The fruits obtained from

---

[582] Alternatively, light.
[583] Vishnu.

seeing you will be the same as the fruits obtained from seeing me.
This is the boon I am bestowing on you. This is the truth. There
is no doubt that this is the truth. Vishnu will be in my heart,
and I will be in Vishnu's heart. Those who draw a distinction
between the two do not know my mind. Hari was born from
my left limb, and Vidhatri was born from my right limb. Rudra,
the cause of the great dissolution and whose *atman* is in the
universe, will be born from my heart. I have divided myself
into three, known as Brahma, Vishnu and Bhava. For creation,
preservation and dissolution, these represent the three *gunas*—
rajas, *sattva* and *tamas*. But Shiva is directly distinct from the
*guna*s and is beyond Purusha and Prakriti. I am the supreme
brahman, eternal, infinite, complete and Niranjana. Hari, the
protector of the three worlds, has *sattva* outside and *tamas*
inside. Hara, who causes the dissolution of the three worlds,
has *tamas* outside and *sattva* inside. Vidhatri, the creator of the
three worlds, has *rajas* inside and outside. These are said to be
the *guna*s in the three divinities. Shiva is said to be devoid of
*guna*s. O Vishnu! Happily, protect the grandfather who will
undertake the task of creation *kalpa*. Following my command,
you will be worshipped in the three worlds. You and Vidhatri
will serve Rudra. The one will cause the dissolution of the
three worlds is Shiva's complete *avatara*. In the *kalpa* known
as Padma, the grandfather will be born as your son. You will
see me then and so will the one born from the lotus." Mahesha
Hara, full of unmatched compassion, said this. Extremely
pleased, Lord Sarveshvara again spoke to Vishnu.'"

Chapter 42-3.1(10) (Parama Shiva *Tattva*)

' '' 'Parameshvara said, "O Hari! O Vishnu! O one
who is excellent in vows! Listen to another of my

commands. You will always be revered and worshipped in all
the worlds. Whenever some unhappiness is generated in the
world created by Brahma, you will exert yourself to destroy
all these miseries. I will help you in all activities that are
difficult to undertake. I will slay your enemies when they are
unassailable and extremely fierce. O Hari! Assume many kinds
of *avatara*s and extend your excellent deeds in the world, intent
on becoming the supreme saviour. This Rudra will always
have a form that possesses *guna*s. There is no doubt that in
the worlds, he will carry out tasks that are impossible for you.
Rudra will meditate on you, and you will meditate on Hara.
There is no difference between you and Rudra. You are one.
You become Maha Vishnu because of this boon and because
of your pastimes. This is true. There is no doubt that this is
true. If a man who is devoted to Rudra criticizes you, all his
good merits will swiftly be reduced to ashes. O Purushottama!
Because of hatred towards you, he will descend into hell. O
Vishnu! This will happen because of my command. This is
true. There is no doubt that this is true. In this world, bestow
emancipation on men, especially objects of pleasure. Devotees
will meditate on you and worship you. Chastise and show your
favours."''"

"'Brahma continued, 'Having said this, he held me,
Vidhatri, and Hari by the hand.'"'

"''He told us, "In times of distress, always help. You will
control everyone. You will bestow objects of pleasure and
emancipation. Always be the best in accomplishing all the
objects of desire. Because of my command, be the breath of life
for everyone. O Hari! When there is a hardship, Rudra, who
originated from me, will be worshipped. Anyone who seeks
refuge with you certainly seeks refuge with me too. Anyone
who sees a difference between the two will certainly descend
into hell. In particular, hear about the lifespans of the three
divinities, Brahma, Vishnu and Hara. There should not be any

doubt about this. Four thousand *mahayugas*[584] will be spoken of as one of Brahma's days. After this, his nights are also of the same duration. Thirty days constitute a month and twelve months constitute a year. Brahma's lifespan is described as one hundred years. One of Brahma's years is said to be one of Vishnu's days. Vishnu will also live for one hundred years. One year for Vishnu will certainly be one day for Rudra. After Hara has lived for one hundred years, he is established in the form of Nara. He remains in this position as long as Sadashiva inhales with his mouth. When Sadashiva exhales, he[585] merges into Shakti. O best among gods! For embodied beings, Brahma, Vishnu, Hara, *gandharvas*, *uragas* and *rakshasas*, day and night is said to consist of twenty-one thousand and six hundred inhalations and exhalations. Six inhalations and exhalations amount to one *pala*. Sixty *palas* are one *ghati* and there are sixty *ghatis* in one day and night.[586] There is no measure of Sadashiva's inhalations and exhalations. Therefore, he is said to be undecaying. It is my command that you should protect this system and maintain all that has been created, with the many qualities, for that duration of time." Hearing Shambhu's words, along with me, Bhagavan Hari prostrated himself before the lord of the universe. He controlled himself and spoke slowly. Vishnu said, "O Shankara! O ocean of compassion! O lord of the universe! I have heard. Following your command, I will do all this. I will always meditate on you. It cannot but be otherwise. Earlier, I obtained all my strength because of you. O lord! Meditation on your supreme form will never be

---

[584] A *mahayuga* is a cycle of *satya/krita yuga*, *treta yuga*, *dvapara yuga* and *kali yuga*, with the intervening periods between these *yugas* also added. It amounts to 12,000 divine years.

[585] Nara.

[586] There are thus 2.5 *ghatis* in one hour and 2.5 *palas* in one minute.

far from my mind, not even for a tiny bit of time. O lord! If any of my devotees criticizes you, there is no doubt that he will reside in hell for an eternity. Your devotee will be greatly loved by me. If a person knows this, it will not be difficult for him to obtain emancipation. My greatness has certainly been enhanced by you. If I lack in qualities, please pardon that." Shambhu heard his excellent words. He told Vishnu, "I will happily pardon any deficiency in qualities." Saying this, the ocean of compassion showed Hari and me his compassion and touched us on all our limbs with his hands. Hara, who takes away all miseries, instructed us about different kinds of *dharma*. He bestowed many boons on us and told us about what was beneficial. After this, Shambhu, who loves his devotees and is full of compassion towards them, vanished from the spot as we looked on. Since then, Shambhu, who bestows objects of pleasure and emancipation, has been established in the *lingam* and the methods for worshipping a Prakrita *lingam* are said to have been established in the world. Maheshvara is himself the *lingam* and Mahadevi is the pedestal for the *lingam*. It is said that the entire universe dissolves into the *lingam*. In the presence of a *lingam*, if a person constantly reads this account of the *lingam* for six months, he assumes Shiva's form. There is no need to think about this. O great sage! If a person carries out any activity near a *lingam*, I am incapable of speaking about the fruits of his good deeds.'"'

Chapter 43-3.1(11) (Methods of Worshipping Shiva)

'The *rishi*s said, "O Suta! O immensely fortunate one! O Suta! O Vyasa's disciple! We prostrate ourselves before you. You have made us hear Shiva's wonderful account. It is supremely purifying. We have heard the auspicious and amazing account of the origin of the greatly divine *lingam*. Listening to its powers destroys all the miseries of this world. O ocean of compassion! Following the conversation between Brahma and Narada, please tell us about the methods of worshipping Shiva, whereby Shiva is pleased. *Brahmanas*, *kshatriyas*, *vaishyas* and *shudras* worship Shiva. How should they do this? Please tell us what you have heard from Vyasa's mouth."'

Vyasa said, 'Hearing the questions of the sages, he[587] happily told them everything. This is in conformity with the *Vedas* and bestows peace.'

'Suta replied, "O lords among sages! You have asked me a virtuous question about a secret. I will now tell you, according to my intelligence and according to what I have heard. What you have asked was formerly asked by Vyasa of Sanatkumara. Upamanyu heard it from him. Vyasa heard it from him.[588] For the welfare of the worlds, Vyasa made me study the methods of worshipping Shiva. Krishna heard it from the great-souled Upamanyu."'

'"Brahma said, 'O Narada! I will briefly tell you about worshipping the *lingam*. O sage! Even if I try for one hundred years, I am incapable of describing it in detail. This is Shankara's form—bliss, pure and eternal. If one worships it with supreme devotion, as fruits, one obtains everything one wishes for. There is no poverty, disease, misery or hardship as a result of the enemy. As long as one worships Shiva, the four kinds of sins do not exist.[589] When Shiva is worshipped,

---

[587] Suta.

[588] Upamanyu learnt from Sanatkumara and Vyasa learnt from Upamanyu. Vyasa's name is Krishna Dvaipayana.

[589] Since there are many sins, this refers to four major sins. Often, five major sins are listed. The number four probably refers to killing a *brahmana*, drinking, stealing from a *brahmana* and violating a *guru*'s bed. But some other listing may have been intended.

all miseries dissolve into the divinity. Every kind of happiness is obtained and subsequently, there is emancipation. For a human, happiness is mostly the result of offspring and similar things. When Mahadeva is worshipped, success is accomplished in all activities. Brahmanas, kshatriyas, vaishyas and shudras must follow the norms in the due order and worship Shankara. They will then be successful in everything that they desire. One must get up in the morning, at the time known as brahma muhurta.[590] Having remembered the guru, one must remember Shambhu. Having remembered the tirthas, one must perform dhyana on Hara. O sage! He must then remember me, the ones without decay[591] and the sages. Following the norms, he must then chant an auspicious stotram. Having got up, he must next pass his stool in the southern direction. It has been said that the prescribed norm for passing stool is in private. O sage! I will now tell you about this. Listen with an attentive mind. For purifying himself, a brahmana must clean himself with earth five times. A kshatriya must do it four times and a vaishya thrice. The norm for a shudra to purify himself is that he must use earth twice. Alternatively, he will carefully clean the anus once and the penis once. The left hand must be washed ten times and each of the feet seven times each. O son! Each of the hands must again be washed three times. Like shudras, women must use earth to clean themselves properly. After this, they will use earth to wash their hands and feet. Depending on the varna, a man will then use a twig to clean the teeth. For a brahmana, the length of the twig used to clean the teeth must

---

[590] A muhurta is a period of 48 minutes. Brahma muhurta is named after Brahma and is an auspicious time just before dawn, regarded as the last muhurta of the night. The precise hour depends on the time when the sun rises.
[591] The gods.

be twelve *angula*s. It must be eleven *angula*s for a king,[592] ten *angula*s for a *vaishya* and nine *angula*s for a *shudra*. These are said to be the measurements. What has been instructed by Manu[593] can be discarded only at the time of an emergency. O son! On *shashthi*,[594] *navami*s, days on which vows are being observed, Sundays and days of *shraddha*s, the cleaning of the teeth is forbidden. One must bathe following the norms. The due order must be followed in *tirtha*s. In specific places and at specific times, bathing must be done with *mantra*s.'"

""'Having first done *achamana*, one must wear a washed garment. He will be seated alone in a good spot and undertake the *sandhya* rites. Having undertaken the appropriate rites, he will then embark on the task of worship. One must steady the mind before entering the place where *puja* is to be performed. Having gathered together everything required for the *puja*, he will then seat himself on the seat. After having performed the due acts of *nyasa*, he will then follow the order for worshipping Hara. Ganadhisha, the guardians of the gates and the guardians of the directions must be worshipped first. After this, he must think of the pedestal. Alternatively, he can draw a lotus with eight petals. He will sit down, with the articles required for *puja* near him and make Lord Shiva sit down. He will then perform *achamana* thrice and wash his hands. He will perform *pranayama* thrice and meditate on Traymbaka in the middle. He has five faces and ten arms. His complexion is that of pure crystal. He is adorned in every kind of ornament and his upper garment is made out of tiger skin. If a man achieves *sarupya* with him, all his sins are burnt down. Having thus invoked Shiva, he will worship Parameshvara. He will purify his mind and in the due order, perform *nyasa* with the root *mantra*. Using

592 That is, a *kshatriya*.
593 In the Manu Samhita.
594 The sixth lunar day.

Pranava *mantra*, *nyasa* must be done in six limbs of the body.[595] After touching the heart, the *puja* will commence. Vessels must be thought of for offering *padya*, *arghya* and *achamaniya*. An intelligent person will follow the norms and place nine different pots. They must be placed on *darbha* grass and *darbha* grass will be used to sprinkle water over them. Cool water will be sprinkled over each of them. An intelligent person will chant Pranava *mantra*, look at the objects and sprinkle water over them. *Ushira*[596] or sandalwood paste can be used for *padya*. As is proper, powdered *jati*, *kankola*, *karpura*, the root of *vata* and *tamalaka*[597] will be sprinkled in the water for *achamaniya*. All the pots will be sprinkled with sandalwood powder. Alongside the lord of *deva*s, Nandisha[598] will be worshipped. Shiva will be worshipped with fragrances, incense and many kinds of lamps. Having purified the *lingam*, a man should cheerfully chant different *mantra*s, beginning with Pranava and ending with *namah*. Using Pranava, the seat must be conceived as being inside the lotus or the *svastika*. The undecaying eastern direction represents *anima*; the southern is *laghima*; the western is *mahima*; the northern is *prapti*; the south-eastern petal[599] is *prakamya*; the south-western is *ishitva*; the north-western petal is *vashitva*; the north-eastern is *sarvajnatva*;[600] and the pericarp is said to be Soma. Surya is below Soma and the fire is below that. In the due order, Dharma and the other

---

[595] If it is *kara nyasa*, the six will be the five fingers and the palm. If it is *anga nyasa*, the six will be the heart, the forehead, the crown of the head, the chest, eyes and around the head.

[596] *Ushira* is the root of the fragrant grass *Andropogon muricatus*.

[597] *Jati* is jasmine, *kankola* is the *ashoka* tree, *karpura* is camphor and *tamalaka* is the *tamala* tree. For the trees, powdered bark is used.

[598] Shiva's bull/attendant is Nandi/Nandisha/Nandishvara/Nandikeshvara.

[599] The directions refer to the eight petals of the lotus.

[600] Corresponding to *garima* of the *siddhi*s.

lords are thought of. In four undetermined directions, the three
gunas and Soma must be thought of. Parameshvara will be
invoked with the sadyojata mantra and made to sit down with
a mantra to Vamadeva. The sannidhya rite will be with Rudra-
Gayatri mantra and nirodha with Aghora mantra.[601] Ishana
will be worshipped with the mantra known as sarvavidya.[602]
Following the norms, padya, achamaniya and arghya must be
offered. Following the norms, Rudra must be bathed in water
mixed with fragrances and sandalwood powder. Following
the norms again, a vessel must be taken, mantras pronounced
over it, and he must be bathed with pancha gavya. After this,
to the pronouncement of Pranava mantra, he will be bathed
in cow's milk, curd, honey, sugar cane juice and ghee. If he
is worshipped in this way, he bestows everything desired.
Mahadeva's abhisheka will be done with auspicious objects,
while Pranava mantra is being chanted. The water in a vessel
will be sanctified with mantras and that water will be used
for the sprinkling. Purifying the water in the proper way, the
worshipper will strain it with a piece of white cloth. Until
the water has been sprinkled with sandalwood powder, one
should not use it for sprinkling. One must cheerfully worship
Shankara with beautiful rice. Many different kinds of flowers
must be used, and they should be rare—apamarga, karpura,
jati, champaka, patala, white karavira, mallika, kamala, utpala
and chandana.[603] Many kinds of vessels must be used to pour
streams of water over Parameshvara. The divinity Maheshvara

---

[601] Sannidhya means proximity and nirodha means confinement.
   [602] 27.35 of Vajasaneyi Samhita, stating that Ishana pervades the
universe.
   [603] Apamarga is Achyranthes aspera, champaka is a tree with
yellow and fragrant flowers, patala is Bignonia suaveolens, karavira is
a kind of tree, mallika is a kind of jasmine, kamala is a lotus, utpala is
blue lotus (or water lily) and chandana is sandalwood.

must be bathed in the proper way. If *mantras* are used to perform the *puja*, every kind of fruit is obtained.'"

"'O son! I will briefly tell you about the *mantras* that ensure success in every objective. Listen attentively. These *mantras* must be read or chanted from memory—the Rudra *mantra*; the Nila Rudra *mantra*;[604] auspicious *mantras* from the *Shukla Yajur Veda*; *mantras* used by *hotris*;[605] the *Atharvashirsha mantra*;[606] repetitions of *shanti mantras*;[607] *mantras* to Aruna[608] and those without reference to Aruna; desired *mantras* from *Sama Veda* used for vows to *devas*; the *rathantara mantra* from *Sama Veda*; *pushpa sukta*;[609] Mahamrityunjaya *mantra*; and the *panchakshara mantra*. The water must be poured one thousand times or one hundred and eight times. Mentioning the divinity's name, this must be done following the path indicated in the *Vedas*. Sandalwood paste and flowers must be placed atop Shiva. Chanting Pranava *mantra*, articles must be offered for freshening the mouth. After this, the *lingam* must be worshipped. The divinity is like crystal. He is *nishkala* and without decay. He is the cause behind all the worlds. All the worlds are pervaded by the supreme. He cannot be perceived by Brahma, Indra, Upendra[610] Vishnu and other *devas*. Those who know the *Vedas* know that he is spoken about in Vedanta

[604] From the Nila Rudra Upanishad.

[605] There were four classes of priests, though the classification varied over time. The *hotri* is the chief priest and is accomplished in the *Rig Veda*. The *adhvaryu* is the assistant priest and is accomplished in the *Yajur Veda*, though later, the *udgatri* came to be identified with the *Sama Veda*. In addition, there was the *brahmana* or *purohita*.

[606] The Ganapati *Atharvashirsha mantra* from Ganapati Upanishad.

[607] *Mantras* for peace.

[608] Surya.

[609] This probably means verses from *Shri Sukta*.

[610] Upendra is Vishnu's name.

as incomprehensible. He is without a beginning, a middle and an end. He is medication for every kind of disease. That which is known as Shiva *tattva* is present in Shiva's *lingam*. Following the norms, the *lingam* must be worshipped with Pranava *mantra*, incense, lamps, *naivedya*, beautiful betel leaves and the beautiful act of *niranjana*. That apart, with many kinds of *mantra*s, praise and *namaskara* must be done. *Arghya* must be offered, and flowers must be laid down at the feet. One must prostrate oneself before the lord of *deva*s and worship Shiva. One must then stand, with flowers held in *anjali*. Using *mantra*s, one must again pray to Ishana Shankara. "O Shankara! I have done this *japa* and *puja* knowingly or ignorantly. Through your favours, let it yield good fruits." Reading this, the flowers must be placed happily on Shiva. The norms will be followed for peace and benediction. One must next seek forgiveness from Shiva. Seeking forgiveness again, the act of *achamana* must be performed, along with *namaskara*. With *namaskara*, one must utter the *mantra* for the cleansing of sins. Thereafter, full of devotion, one must pray again. "May I have devotion towards Shiva. May I have devotion towards Shiva in every birth. May I have devotion towards Shiva. There is no other refuge. You alone are my refuge." When one prays to the lord of *deva*s in this way, every success is bestowed. The *puja* must be performed with supreme devotion and in a loud voice. Along with the family members, one must then do *namaskara*. If one happily undertakes this task, one obtains unmatched happiness. If a person is full of devotion towards Shiva and performs this *puja* every day, he obtains every kind of success at every step. He is born as an eloquent person and certainly obtains every desire in his mind. He does not suffer from disease, unhappiness or grief, artificial anxiety of any kind, crookedness, poison or any other hardship. If a person is supremely devoted towards Shiva, Shiva destroys his miseries. His good fortune increases, like the moon during *shukla paksha*. If he worships Shankara, there is no doubt that his good qualities increase. O supreme among sages! I have thus spoken to you about the method for worshipping Shambhu. O Narada! After this, what else do you wish to hear?'"'

Chapter 44-3.1(12) (The Essential and the Non-Essential)

' "Narada said, 'O Brahma! O Prajapati! O father! Since your mind is fixed on Shiva, you are blessed. Please explain all this to me in detail.'"'

'"Brahma replied, 'O son! On one occasion, I, born from a lotus, summoned the *rishi*s and the ones without decay[611] from all directions. I affectionately addressed them in excellent words. "If you have faith in eternal happiness, if you wish for success in meeting your desires, come with me to the shores of the ocean of milk." Hearing my words, they went along with me, to the place where Bhagavan Vishnu, who ensures welfare, was present. O sage! Having gone there, the gods joined their hands in salutation and prostrated themselves before Jagannatha Janardana, lord of *deva*s. Vishnu saw that Brahma and the other immortals had presented themselves. He remembered Shiva's lotus feet and addressed them in excellent words. Vishnu asked, "Why have Brahma, the gods and the *rishi*s come? What has happened? Out of love for you, please tell me what I should do?" Vishnu asked me and the gods this. We prostrated ourselves again and told him lovingly what needed to be done. In auspicious words, we told him about the task. The *deva*s said, "So that miseries are destroyed, who

---

[611] The gods.

should we serve every day?" Bhagavan is affectionate towards his devotees. Hearing these words, full of love and compassion, he spoke to the immortals and me. Shri Bhagavan said, "O Brahma! Listen. The gods have already heard all this earlier. Nevertheless, I will tell you and the *deva*s again. It has been seen and is being seen now. O Brahma and all *deva*s! Why is it being asked now? In every task and in every kind of way, one must always serve the divinity Shankara. He is the one who dispels all miseries. He has specially told Brahma and me this. Those who desire happiness must never give up worshipping him. A wonderful example of this has been seen and all of you have witnessed it. Having abandoned the worship of the divinity Maheshvara, lord of *deva*s, in the form of the *lingam*, Tara's sons were destroyed, along with their relatives.[612] I confounded them with my *maya*. My *maya* pushed them far away. Since they were without Shiva, all of them were destroyed. Therefore, manifested in the form of the *lingam*, Hara must always be worshipped. The supreme among *deva*s must be served with special devotion. Sharva's *lingam* must be worshipped by *deva*s, excellent *daitya*s, me and Brahma. How have you forgotten that? Whatever be the reason, his *lingam* must always be worshipped. O Brahma and gods! Sharva bestows every fruit that is desired. If a *muhurta* or a *kshana* is spent without worshipping Shiva, that is harmful, a great weakness, blindness and folly. If a person is full of great devotion towards Bhava, if his mind prostrates itself before Bhava and if he remembers Bhava, he does not have to undergo any sorrows. Those who wish for agreeable mansions, agreeable ornaments, women, satisfaction with riches, sons, grandsons and offspring, lack of disease in the body, status in the world, great fortune and

---

[612] Tara (Tarakasura) was killed by Skanda. Tara's sons were Tarakaksha, Vidyunmali and Kamalaksha. They possessed the three cities of Tripura and were destroyed by Shiva.

happiness in the world of the gods must be devoted towards
Parameshvara. The fruit of emancipation is also obtained.
This occurs because worship of Sadashiva accumulates good
merits. Full of devotion, those who constantly worship Shiva's
lingam obtain success in everything and are not served by sin."
Hearing this, *deva*s prostrated themselves before Hari. They
desired *lingam*s that full every kind of desire in men.'"'
""'O tiger among sages! Hearing this, Vishnu spoke to
Vishvakarma. "I am intent on saving beings. Follow my
instruction. O Vishvakarma! Construct Shambhu's auspicious
*lingam*s and give them to all the *deva*s." I told him, too. Asked
by me and Hari, Vishvakarma constructed *lingam*s, according
to entitlements, and gave them. O supreme among *rishi*s! I will
tell you about them. Listen. O sage! Shakra got one made out a
ruby; Vishrava's son[613] got one made out of gold; Dharma got
one made out of a yellow gem;[614] Varuna got a dark-blue Shiva;
Vishnu got one made out of yellow sapphire; Brahma got one
made out of gold; the Vishvadevas and Vasus got ones made
out of silver; the two Ashvins got Parthiva *lingam*s made out
of brass; the goddess Lakshmi got one made out of crystal; the
Adityas got ones made out of copper; King Soma got one made
out of pearl; Vibhavasu[615] got a *lingam* made out diamond;
Indras among *brahmana*s and their wives got *lingam*s made out
of earth; Maya got one made out of sandalwood; *naga*s lovingly
got those made out of coral; *devi*s got those made out of butter,
*yogi*s got those made out of ashes; *yaksha*s got those made out
of curd; and the shadow got a *lingam* made out of flour. It is
certain that Brahmani always worships a Shiva *lingam* made
out jewels. Bana and others worship a Parthiva *lingam* made
out of mercury. Vishvakarma gave such *lingam*s. All *deva*s and

---

[613] Kubera.
[614] Such as yellow sapphire.
[615] Agni.

*rishi*s worship these. Desiring their welfare, Vishnu had these *lingam*s given to *deva*s. He then told me, Brahma, the method to be used for worshipping the wielder of Pinaka. Hearing his words, my mind was assured and elated. I asked the excellent *deva*s to come to my own abode.'"

"'"O sage! Having gone there, I told all the *rishi*s and *deva*s about the proper method to be used for worshipping Shiva, so that everything desired is obtained. Brahma said,[616] "O *rishi*s and all the immortals! Full of great love, listen. I will affectionately tell you about the method for worshipping Shiva. This bestows objects of pleasure and emancipation. Among all beings, birth as a human is extremely difficult to obtain. O *deva*s and lords among sages! Within that, it is extremely rare to be born in a good lineage. It is even more difficult to be born as a *brahmana* who possesses good conduct and good merits. Having obtained this, it is said that one must undertake *karma* that gives satisfaction to Shiva. No one should violate the *karma* that is his by birth. As long as one possesses the riches, one must undertake the task of donations. *Tapo-yajna*[617] is superior to thousands of *karma-yajna*s. *Japa-yajna* is superior to thousands of *tapo-yajna*s. There is nothing superior to *dhyana-yajna*. *Dhyana* is the means for obtaining *jnana*. Through *dhyana*, a *yogi* can see whoever he wishes to remember. For a person who follows *dhyana-yajna*, Shiva is always near. A person who possesses *jnana* does not need to be purified through *prayashchitta*. O *brahmana*![618] Those who know about the *brahman* possess pure knowledge. Rites do not exist for them, and they do not need to think about happiness and unhappiness. O immortals! Those who possess knowledge are

[616] Brahma is reporting what he said earlier.
[617] Observing austerities.
[618] This is an inconsistency because it is a quote being reported to Narada.

always indifferent towards *dharma*, *adharma*, *japa*, oblations, *dhyana* and techniques of *dhyana*. The pure *lingam* represents undecaying Shiva and causes supreme bliss. He is *nishkala* and goes everywhere. It is known to *yogis* that he is established in their hearts. O *brahmanas*! *Lingams* are known to be of two types—external and internal. External ones are said to be gross and internal ones are subtle. Those who follow *karma-yajna* are intent on worshipping gross *lingams*. They cannot control their minds through subtle images and use gross ones. For a person to whom the *adhyatmika lingam* is not manifest, the gross *lingam* must be worshipped and not otherwise. For those who possess *jnana*, the undecaying and unblemished subtle *lingam* is manifest in the mind. Others who are not like that think the gross one is the best. In truth, for those who know, there is nothing to reflect on this. Shiva pervades the universe, as *nishkala* and *sakala*. This must be in each person's mind. Hence, if one possesses the *jnana* and is liberated, there is no harm in thinking of the alternative. For them, there are no rules about what should be done and what should not be done. A lotus in the water is not touched by the water. Like that, if a person with *jnana* is engaged in a householder's *karma*, he is not bound. However, until *jnana* has been generated in a man, it is that man's *karma* to worship the divinity, Shiva. This must be done to convince the world. The sun is one, but is seen in many kinds of ways, such as in different receptacles of water. O gods! O Brahma! Know that everything that is seen or heard in the world, existent or non-existent, has Shiva in the *atman*. What is reflected and thought about, in terms of differences, is because of water in the receptacles. This is what is said by all those who know the true meaning of the *Vedas*. Parameshvara himself moves around in all hearts. If a person possesses this knowledge, why does he need images? Those who lack such knowledge devise auspicious images. This is said to be the support a man needs to climb up to higher steps. Without such a support, it is difficult for him to climb up to higher steps. Using such an image as support, it is said that a man obtains the *nirguna*. It has been determined that one can obtain the *nirguna* through the *saguna*. In this way, images of all *deva*s bring about belief. This *deva* is great and must be worshipped. But without an image, of what use are fragrances, sandalwood and flowers? Hence, until *jnana* is generated, an image must be worshipped. If one lacks *jnana*, but still does not worship, downfall is certain. O *brahmana*s! Because of this reason, listen to the supreme truth. One must attentively undertake the *karma* earmarked for the category one has been born into. *Puja* and other things must be done for whatever one has devotion towards. Without *puja* and other things, sins will never be kept at a distance. As long as there is sin in the body, success is not obtained. When sin has left, one becomes successful in everything. If a piece of cloth is dirty, dyeing it does not make it better. It is only when it is washed and pure that a dye can be properly applied. In that way, proper worship of *deva*s makes the body clean. *Jnana* is generated and one is dyed with *jnana*. The true root of *vijnana* is unwavering devotion. The true root of *jnana* is also said to be devotion. The root of devotion is virtuous deeds and worship of the *deva* one wishes for. The root of this is said to be a good *guru* and the root of that is association with the virtuous. If one associates with virtuous people, one obtains a *guru*. From a *guru*, one obtains *mantra*s and methods of *puja*. Devotion results from *puja* and *jnana* is generated through devotion. *Vijnana* is generated through *jnana* and the supreme *brahman* manifests itself. When *vijnana* is generated, differences disappear. When differences disappear, one is freed from sorrows connected with the opposite pair of sentiments. When one is devoid of miseries connected with the opposite pair of sentiments, one assumes Shiva's form. Such a person does not know miseries associated with the opposite pair of sentiments. O gods and *rishi*s! There is nothing he should do or should not do. In this world, it is rare to find a person who does not follow *grahasthya ashrama*. If there is such a person, the sight of him destroys sins. Even the *tirtha*s praise a person who possesses such excellent *jnana*. All *deva*s and sages take him to be Shiva, with the supreme *brahman* in his *atman*. *Tirtha*s and earthen images of *deva*s take time to purify. A person who possesses *vijnana* purifies instantly. As long as one is in *garhasthya ashrama*, one should worship an image. One must cheerfully worship the best among the five *deva*s.[619] Alternatively, the worship of Shiva as the root and the single one is superior. O gods! When the root is sprinkled, all the branches are content. When the branches are completely content, the root is always content. O best among sages! In that way, when Shiva is satisfied, all the gods are satisfied. Those who possess subtle intelligence know this. When Shiva is worshipped, all the gods are worshipped. Therefore, one must worship the divinity Shankara, who brings benefit to the worlds. He is engaged in the welfare of all beings and bestows every fruit that is wished for.""'"

Chapter 45-3.1(13) (Description of Shiva's Worship)

' '' 'Brahma said, "After this, I will tell you about an excellent method of *puja*. O *rishi*s and all *deva*s! Listen. This ensures happiness and everything wished for. One must get up at *brahma muhurta* and remember Samba Shiva. Joining one's hands in salutation and with head lowered, one must pray. 'Arise. O lord of *deva*s! Wake up. O one who is

---

[619] Typically, these five are Shiva, Vishnu, Devi (Parvati), Surya and *Ishta devata* (the favoured *deva*).

stationed in the heart! Arise. O Uma's lord! Get up and bring
all that is auspicious to the entire universe. I know *dharma*, but
I do not have an inclination towards it. I know *adharma*, but
I do not refrain from it.[620] O Mahadeva! You are based in my
heart, and I do whatever you engage me in.' Having faithfully
uttered these words, one must remember the *guru*'s feet. To
release urine and excrement, one must then go out, in the
southern direction. Using earth and water, one must then clean
and purify the body. The hands and feet must be washed, and
the teeth cleaned. The teeth must be cleaned before the lord of
the day[621] rises. Using cupped hands, the mouth must be rinsed
sixteen times. O gods and *rishi*s! Devotedly and attentively,
the teeth must not be cleaned on the first *tithi* of the month,
shashthi, navami and Sunday. At a convenient time, one must
bathe in a river or at home. A man must never bathe against the
norms of the time and the place. On Sunday, *shraddha* days, at
the time of *sankranti*, during an eclipse, when great donations
are undertaken at a *tirtha*, on a day when one is fasting and
at a time of *ashoucha*,[622] one must not bathe in hot water. In
*tirtha*s and similar places, a man must devotedly bathe while
facing the sun. Oil must be applied on the limbs only after
considering the right order of days of the week. However, there
is no taint if one uses fragrant oil on the limbs every day. But
one should avoid a *shraddha* day, an eclipse, a day of fasting
or the first day of a *paksha*. Unless there is an eclipse, there is
no taint associated with using mustard oil. Depending on the
time and the place, one must follow the norms and have a bath,

---

[620] This is a famous statement. *Janami dharmam na cha me
pravrittih. Janami adharmam na cha me nivrittih.* Based on *Pandava
Gita*, this is usually attributed to Duryodhana.

[621] The sun.

[622] A time of impurity, such as when there is birth or death in the
family.

facing the north or facing the east. One should never bathe
wearing a garment that has been worn by another. Thinking
of *deva*s, one should bathe in a pure garment. In the night,
there is no harm in wearing another person's clothes. But they
must be cast off at the time of having a bath and washed. To
satisfy *deva*s, *rishi*s and ancestors, one should offer oblations
of water.[623] One must next wear a washed garment and do
achamana again."'"'

"'"'"O supreme among *brahmana*s! He must next go to a
pure place that has been smeared with cow dung. There, he
must devise an auspicious seat. It can be made out of a pure
piece of wood. Or it can be a place that is completely spread
with something. A colourful seat yields everything desired as
a fruit. Having chosen what is appropriate, it can be spread
with deerskin. Seating himself there, an intelligent person
will use ashes to draw Tripundraka. Tripundraka makes
japa, austerities and donations successful. If ashes are not
available, the mark can be made with water. Having drawn
Tripundraka in this way, a man must wear *rudraksha*. Having
undertaken his own rites, he must next worship Shiva. Using
*mantra*s, he must again perform *achamana* thrice. Or he can
do it once, saying that this is a drop of water from Ganga. For
worshipping Shiva, cooked food and water must be brought
there. According to one's capacity, all the other articles must be
placed nearby. Having patiently devised the place, there must
be a vessel for the *arghya* and another for fragrant water and
akshata. The vessel full of *upachara* must be placed on the right
shoulder, the *guru* remembered and his permission taken. In the
proper way, the *sankalpa* must be taken and the desires stated.
Thereafter, full of great devotion, one should worship Shiva
and his family. A *mudra* must be shown and using *sindura*[624]

---

[623] *Tarpana*.
[624] Vermilion.

and other articles, the destroyer of impediments worshipped, along with Siddhi and Buddhi.[625] Having worshipped him, one must again prostrate oneself before him. He bestows gains that are one hundred thousand times more. He must be addressed by his names in the dative case,[626] beginning with Pranava and ending with '*namah*'. Seeking his forgiveness, one must next worship the *deva* who is his brother.[627] He must be worshipped with great devotion, and one must prostrate oneself before him again. At the gate, Mahodara is always stationed as a doorkeeper.[628] Having worshipped him, Girija Sati must be worshipped next. Thereafter, Shiva must be worshipped with many kinds of sandalwood paste, *kumkuma*, incense, lamps and different kinds of *naivedya*. One must approach Shiva and perform *namaskara*. In the house, there may be a *lingam* made out of clay, gold, silver, some other metal, mercury or something else. One must again do *namaskara* to do this and worship this with great devotion. When this is worshipped, everyone else is worshipped."""

"""If the *lingam* is made out of clay, it must be established properly, following the norms. At home, one must always follow the rules in every kind of way. With *prana* invoked in the image, the act of purification against *bhutas* must be undertaken. In Shiva's temple, the guardians of the directions must be established and worshipped. At home, Shiva must always be worshipped with the root *mantra*. There are no rules about worshipping the gatekeepers. At home, the *lingam* is

---

[625] Ganesha is the destroyer of impediments. Siddhi and Buddhi are his personified wives.

[626] *Chaturthi* of grammar.

[627] That is, Kartikeya.

[628] Mahodara means the large-bellied one and is a name for Ganesha. Ganesha has already been worshipped and this may be a simple restatement. Alternatively, Mahodara is also one of Ganesha's *avatara*s.

worshipped since everything is established in it. At the time of worship, the divinity can be worshipped along with his various limbs and family members. But there are no rules about this. The worshipper must devise his own seat, near Shiva. He must face the northern direction and again do *achamana*. A man must wash his hands and do *pranayama* ten times, using the root *mantra*. Before starting the worship, he must certainly use his hands to display the five *mudras*. A man should undertake the worship only after showing the *mudras* in this way. The lamp must be shown, and one should do *namaskara* to one's *guru*. One should then be seated comfortably in *padmasana*, *bhadrasana*, *uttanasana* or *paryankasana*[629] and perform the rites. The cake used in the *puja* is a ball that makes one cross over. However, if the worship is being done in one's own house, this rule is not binding. Thereafter, the excellent *lingam* must be washed with the vessel used for *arghya*. With an attentive mind, one should gather together all the articles required for the *puja*. Then, a man must use *mantras* to perform *avahana* for the divinity. 'Parvati's supreme lord is seated on the summit of Kailasa. Shambhu's form is the one that has been stated before. He is *nirguna*, but the *gunas* are his form. He has five faces and ten arms. He has three eyes, and the bull is on his banner. He is as fair as camphor and his limbs are divine. He has matted hair and the moon is on his crest. His upper garment is made out of tiger skin. He is clad in the auspicious hide of an elephant. Vasuki and others are twirled around his body. He wields Pinaka and other weapons. The eight *siddhis* constantly dance around in front of him. His worshippers and devotees utter words "Victory. Victory." His energy is impossible to withstand. He is impossible to behold. *Devas* serve him. He is

---

[629] These are different postures (*asana*). Of these, *padmasana* and *bhadrasana* are seated postures. But *uttanasana* and *paryankasana* aren't.

the refuge for all beings. His pleasant face is like a lotus. The
Vedas and the sacred texts sing about him. Vishnu and Brahma
always praise him. Shiva is devoted to his devotees. He is bliss.
I am invoking him.' Having performed dhyana in this way,
one must think of a seat for Samba Shiva. In due order, the
dative case must be used for everything. Padya will be offered
to Shankara and arghya. After that, achamana will be done for
Shambhu, the paramatman. Thereafter, one must cheerfully
bathe Shankara with the five objects.[630] The appropriate
mantras from the Vedas will be used. Mantras will be addressed
to him by name, using the dative case. All the objects must
be offered with devotion. In this way, all the desired objects
will be offered to Sankara. Thereafter, Shiva must be bathed
with water.[631] Attentively, one must offer excellent fragrances,
sandalwood and unguents. Using fragrant water, one must
think of a continuous stream of water being poured. This must
be done with mantras from the Vedas or chanting the mantra
with six aksharas eleven times. Thereafter, it is time to wipe the
image with a piece of cloth. Then, achamaniya and a garment
must be offered. With many kinds of mantras, sesamum, barley,
wheat, mudga and gram must be offered to Shiva. Flowers
must be offered to the great-souled one who has five faces.
Meditating on each face, one should offer what is appropriate
and what one wishes—lotuses, shatapatras,[632] conch shells,
flowers, kusha flowers, dhatturas,[633] mandara flowers[634] that
have grown on trees and tulasi leaves. Bilva leaves are special.
The puja must be performed with great devotion. Shankara is

[630] Panchamrita.
[631] There are different kinds of bathing (snanam). Varuna snanam
is the one with water.
[632] Shatapatra is a lotus with one hundred petals.
[633] The white thornapple.
[634] Mandara is the coral tree.

affectionate towards his devotees. If nothing else is available, *bilva* leaves must be offered to Shiva. Every kind of worship is accomplished through the offering of *bilva* leaves. Full of great joy, powdered fragrances and excellent and fragrant oil of many kinds must be offered to Shiva. Then, one should happily offer incense, *guggula* and *aguru*.[635] A lamp lit with *ghee* must be offered to Shankara. Thereafter, reciting *mantra*s, one should devotedly offer *arghya* to him again. With devoted sentiments, one must then wipe the face with a piece of cloth. 'O Shankara! Give me beauty. Give me fame. Give me objects of pleasure. Give me objects of pleasure and emancipation as fruits. Please accept this *arghya*. I prostrate myself before you.' Next, many kinds of auspicious *naivedya* must be offered to Shiva. Without any delay, *achamana* must be lovingly done. Along with all the accompaniments, betel leaf must be offered to Shiva. Using a lamp with five wicks, *arati*[636] must be done. The lamp must be shown four times at the feet, twice at the navel, once at the face and seven times over the whole body. After this, uttering *mantra*s, *dhyana* must be done. A man will chant *mantra*s as many times as his knowledge allows. An intelligent person will perform *japa* with *mantra*s according to the path instructed by the *guru*. '*Mantra*s must be chanted according to the path instructed by the *guru*. In the matter of number of *mantra*s, a man will follow what he knows.'[637] Using many kinds of *stotram*s, he will praise Vrishadhvaja.[638] Then, he must slowly do *pradakshina* of Shiva. Following the norms, a man must do *sashtanga namaskara*. After this, with devotion, an *anjali* of flowers must be offered. 'This is for Shankara.

---

[635] *Aguru* is aloe.

[636] Waving of lamps before an image.

[637] The text repeats the same statement twice, the second time as a quote.

[638] Shiva's name, the one with the bull on his banner.

This is for Paresha. This is for satisfying Shiva. I have done this *puja*, knowingly and unknowingly. O Shankara! Show me your favours and grant me all the fruits. O Lord! As long as my breath of life exists, my mind is always immersed in you. O Gouri's lord! O Bhutanatha! Knowing this, be pleased with me. Those who stagger on the ground are supported by the ground alone. O lord! Those who cause you an offence find refuge in you.' Saying many such things, he will offer an *anjali* of flowers. He will prostrate himself several times and say, 'O lord of *deva*s! O Lord! Along with your family, return to your abode. O Lord! Please return again when it is time for *puja*. Full of love, depart now.' In this way, one should entreat Shankara, who is affectionate towards his devotees, many times. Having done the *visarjana* in the heart, the water must be sprinkled on the head. O sages! I have thus told you everything about worshipping Shiva. This bestows objects of pleasure and emancipation. O worthy ones! What else do you wish to hear?"'"

Chapter 46-3.1(14) (More Descriptions of Worship)

'The *rishi*s said, "O Vyasa's disciple! O immensely fortunate one! Please tell us the fruits conferred by Shambhu in worship with different kinds of flowers."'

'Suta replied, "O Shounaka and other *rishi*s! Listen lovingly. With great affection, I will now tell you everything about the determination regarding flowers and leaves. Vidhatri was formerly asked this by *maharshi* Narada. With great love, he told him about the determination regarding flowers and leaves."'

'"Brahma said, 'A person who desires prosperity should worship the divinity Shiva with lotuses, *bilva* leaves, *shatapatras* and *shankha* flowers.[639] O *brahmana*! If a person worships Shiva with one hundred thousand such flowers, his sins are destroyed and there is no doubt that he obtains prosperity. Twenty lotuses are said to amount to one *prastha*. One thousand *bilva* leaves are said to constitute half a *prastha*. One thousand *shatapatras* are said to constitute half a *prastha*. There are sixteen *palas* in a *prastha* and ten *tankas* are said to constitute one *pala*.[640] If these measures are weighed out on a pair of scales, every desire is accomplished. If a person has no desires, he becomes like Shiva. O lords among sages! A person who desires a kingdom must worship the divinity Shankara with ten crore Parthiva *lingams*. Flowers and unbroken paddy must be offered to Shiva's *lingam*. Sandalwood paste must be used, and water poured over the *lingam*. An appropriate *mantra* must be used and *bilva* leaves are excellent for the purpose. *Shatapatras*, lotuses and *shankha* flowers can also be used. It has formerly been said that these are special. Such worship is divine and always yields everything that is desired, in this world and in the next world. Incense, lamps, *naivedya* and *arghya* must be offered and *arati* done. After *pradakshina* and *namaskara*, one must seek forgiveness and do *visarjana*. Having done all these complements, people must be fed. If a person does this, Shankara bestows a kingdom on him. A man desiring importance must worship half the number.[641] A person desiring freedom from imprisonment must worship one hundred thousand. A person suffering from disease must worship half that number of Shiva *lingams*.[642] A person desiring a maiden must worship half that number of Shiva

---

[639] A *shankha* flower is *Clitoria ternatea*, the blue pea.
[640] *Pala* and *tanka* are measures of weight.
[641] That is, five crore *lingams*.
[642] That is, 50,000.

lingams.[643] A person desiring learning must worship half that number of Shiva *lingams.*[644] A person desiring eloquence in speech must worship Shiva with *ghee.* To uproot enemies, the same kind of worship is prescribed. To kill enemies, one hundred thousand *lingams* must be worshipped. To confound enemies, half that number is required. To conquer vassals, one crore *pujas* is praised. To subdue kings, ten thousand is prescribed. For fame and mounts, a number of one thousand is prescribed. A person desiring emancipation must devotedly worship Shambhu five crore times. A person desiring *jnana* must worship Shankara, who brings benefit to the worlds, one crore times. A person desiring to see Shiva must worship half that number. Alternatively, if a person wishes his desires to bear fruit, he can do *japa* with Mahamritunjaya *mantra.* After five hundred thousand such *japas,* Shiva shows himself. After one hundred thousand such *japas,* if he does a second one hundred thousand, he obtains the birth that he wishes for. If he does a third one hundred thousand, his desires are satisfied. If he does a fourth one hundred thousand, he sees Shiva. If he does a fifth one hundred thousand, there is no doubt that he obtains the fruits. When this *mantra* is used, the fruits obtained are one million times more.'''

''''A person desiring emancipation must worship with *darbha* grass. O supreme among *rishi*s! It should be known that the number to be worshipped is always one hundred thousand. A person desiring a long lifespan must worship with *durva* grass. A person desiring sons must worship with *dhattura* flowers. It is said that worship with *dhattura* that has red stems yields what is auspicious. A worshipper who uses *agastya* flowers[645]

---

[643] That is, 25,000.
[644] That is, 12,500.
[645] *Sesbania grandiflora*, often known as *agathi*. In Sanskrit, it is also known as *vangasena*.

obtains great fame. A person who worships with *tulasi* obtains objects of pleasure and emancipation as fruits. Influence is obtained through *arka* flowers and *kubjakalhara* flowers.[646] It is said that worshipping with *japa* flowers[647] brings death to enemies. *Karavira* drives away suffering from ailments. There is no doubt that ornaments are obtained through *bandhuka* flowers,[648] while mounts are obtained through *jati* flowers. Vishnu loves a person who worships with *atasi* flowers.[649] A man who worships with *shami* leaves obtains emancipation. If *mallika* flowers are used, Shiva gives him an auspicious woman. With *yuthika* flowers,[650] he will never lack crops or a house. With *karnikara* flowers,[651] he will obtain an abundance of garments. With *nirgundi* flowers,[652] the minds of people become pure. With one hundred thousand *bilva* leaves, all desires are satisfied. When garlands of beautiful flowers are used, prosperity and happiness are enhanced. There is no doubt that seasonal flowers bestow emancipation. *Rajika* flowers[653] bring about death to enemies. If one hundred thousand such flowers are offered to Shiva, great fruits are obtained. There is no flower that is not loved by Shiva. With the exception of *champaka* and *ketaka*,[654] everything can be offered. O excellent

[646] *Arka* is the sun plant. There is no flower immediately identifiable as *kubjakalhara*. *Kubja* is another name for *apamarga*, mentioned earlier. *Kalhara* is the white water lily. Perhaps *kubjakalhara* is meant to be taken as two separate words.

[647] China rose, hibiscus.

[648] A shrub (*Pentapetes phoenicia*) with red flowers, also known as *bandhujiva*.

[649] The flower of flax, *Linum usitatissimum*.

[650] Kind of jasmine.

[651] *Pterospermum acerifolium*, often known as *bayur*.

[652] *Vitex negundo* or Chinese chaste tree.

[653] *Brassica juncea*, the mustard plant.

[654] Alternatively, *ketaki*, screw pine.

one! After this, listen lovingly to the measurements of grain that must be used to worship Shankara, and the fruits obtained. When men use heaps of rice, prosperity results. O *brahmana*! With great devotion, unbroken grain must be offered to Shiva. There are one hundred thousand grains in six and a half *prastha*s, or two *pala*s. These must be used for worship. After first worshipping Rudra, a beautiful piece of cloth will be placed over Shiva's *lingam* and the excellent rice will be placed on this cloth. With fragrant flowers, a single *shriphala*[655] must be placed on top of this. When incense is added, the fruits of worship are obtained. After performing two Prajapatya ceremonies, a certain number of silver coins must be offered as *dakshina*. If this is not possible, *dakshina* must be given according to capacity. Twelve *brahmana*s must be fed thereafter. One hundred thousand such *puja*s must be performed, along with *mantra*s and all the accompaniments. It is said that the rule is to chant the *mantra* one hundred and eight times. The offering of one hundred thousand *pala*s of sesamum destroys great sins. There are one hundred thousand such seeds in eleven *pala*s. Desiring welfare, the worship must be conducted as described earlier. It is the task of men to feed *brahmana*s on the occasion. There is no doubt that miseries and great sins on account are instantly destroyed as a result. Worship of Shiva with one hundred thousand grains of barley is supreme. Eight and a half *prastha*s amount to one hundred thousand. The old measurement is two *pala*s. Worship with barley by sages enhances happiness in heaven. *Brahmana*s who desire fruits must undertake the Prajapatya rite. Shankara's *puja* with wheat is praised. If one does this with one hundred thousand grains, offspring increase. The earlier determination is that there are one hundred thousand grains in half a *drona*. If the divinity Shiva is worshipped with *mudga*, he bestows

[655] *Bilva* fruit.

happiness. Seven and a half *prastha*s amount to one hundred thousand grains, the ancient measure being of two *pala*s. Eleven *brahmana*s must also be fed. The *paramatman* is the one who supervises *dharma*. If the divinity is worshipped with *priyangu*,[656] *dharma*, *artha* and *kama* increase. A person who does such *puja* is always happy. The ancient measure is stated as one hundred thousand grains in one *prastha*. It is said that twelve *brahmana*s must be fed. It is said that worshipping Shambhu with *rajika* brings about the death of enemies. There are one hundred thousand *sarshapa* seeds[657] in twenty *pala*s. It is said that worshipping the divinity in this way brings about the death of enemies. It is wonderful to worship Shiva with the *adhaki* pulse.[658] Along with this, a cow and a bull must also be given. It is said that worshipping with pepper leads to the destruction of enemies. Shiva must be adorned with *adhaki* pulse and worshipped. This kind of worship brings many kinds of happiness and all the fruits. O supreme among sages! I have thus spoken about the measurement for grain. O lord among sages! Now lovingly hear about one hundred thousand flowers. There are one hundred thousand *shankha* flowers in one *prastha*. Vyasa, who knew about subtle measurements, instructed this. It is said that there are one hundred thousand *jati* or *yuthika* flowers in eleven *prastha*s. There are one hundred thousand *rajika* flowers in five and a half *prastha*s. There are one hundred thousand excellent *mallika* flowers in twenty *prastha*s. One hundred thousand sesamum flowers amount to less than one *prastha*. There are said to be one hundred thousand *karavira* flowers in two *prastha*s. The learned say that the measurement of *nirgundi* flowers is also

---

[656] Long pepper.
[657] Mustard seeds.
[658] *Arhar dal.*

that. The measurement of *karnikara* and *shirisha*[659] flowers is also that. There are one hundred thousand *bandhuka* flowers in ten *prasthas*. These are seen to be the different measures in which Shiva is worshipped by those who wish for every kind of desire to be met, prosperity and emancipation.'"'

"'I will next speak about the great fruits of *dhara puja*.[660] There is benefit to men even if they hear about this. Full of devotion, one should follow the norms and do Shiva's *puja*. After this, full of devotion, one must pour water over the *lingam*. A *dhara* of water brings auspiciousness and pacifies delirium and fever. This must be done with Shatarudriya *mantra*, *ekadasha* Rudra *mantra*,[661] performing *japa* on Rudra, Purusha *sukta*,[662] *shadanga* *mantra*,[663] Mahamrityunjaya *mantra* or *gayatri mantra*. This must begin with Pranava, use his name and end with "*namah*". As water is poured down, the *mantra* must be chanted. Such excellent *dhara puja* increases offspring and happiness. One must lovingly wear *bhasma* and add divine and auspicious objects to the water. If a person pours a *dhara* of *ghee* while one thousand *mantras* are chanted, there is no doubt that his lineage is extended. In this way, using the *mantras* mentioned by me, Shiva's worship must be undertaken. Lords among sages have said that *brahmanas* must be fed and the Prajapatya rite observed. In particular, one must always use a *dhara* of milk. Sugar will be added only when there is dumbness in intelligence. If a *dhara* is used as long as ten thousand *mantras* are chanted, the worshipper develops excellent intellect, similar to that of Brihaspati. If

---

[659] *Acacia sirissa.*

[660] When water or milk is poured over the *lingam*.

[661] A set of eleven *mantras*, one for each of the Rudras.

[662] *Purusha sukta*, also found in *Shukla Yajur Veda* and *Atharva Veda*, is hymn 10.90 of *Rig Veda*.

[663] To the six (*shada*) aspects (*anga*) of Shiva—consciousness, bliss, will, knowledge, action and eternal nature.

dhara puja is done, all miseries are destroyed—when magic is used against the person, when there is pain in the body without any reason, when any kind of sorrow increases on account of love and when there are incessant quarrels in one's own house. To chastise enemies, a *dhara* of oil must be poured over Shiva's *lingam*. If one does this extremely carefully, there is no doubt that one is successful. Fragrant oil increases objects of pleasure. Mustard oil certainly destroys enemies. By worshipping Shiva with money, one becomes king of the *yakshas*. A *dhara* of sugarcane juice poured over Shiva brings every kind of happiness. A *dhara* of Ganga water bestows the fruit of objects of pleasure and emancipation. For all of these, it is said that Mahamrityunjaya *mantra* must be chanted. The rule is to do this ten thousand times. Eleven *brahmanas* must be fed. O lord of sages! I have thus told you everything you asked me about. This brings success in the world and ensures benefit and the fulfilment of every kind of desire. I will now tell you about the rule for worshipping Shiva along with Skanda and Uma and about the fruits that are obtained if one does this devotedly. This is what I have heard. Such a person enjoys every kind of happiness and obtains auspicious sons and grandsons. He goes to Mahesha's world, which bestows every kind of happiness. He will be astride a *vimana* that is as resplendent as one crore suns, one that can go wherever it wills. He will be surrounded by Rudra's women, with songs and musical instruments. Until the deluge arrives, he will sport with Shiva's *bhutas*. After this, he will obtain undecaying *vijnana* and emancipation.'"'

Chapter 47-3.1(15) (Rudra's *Avatara*)

' "Narada said, 'O Vidhatri! O immensely fortunate one! O Vidhatri! O supreme among gods! You are blessed. You have now made me hear about Shiva's wonderful account, which is supremely purifying. I have heard about the auspicious, wonderful and immensely divine account about the origin of the *lingam*. Hearing about his powers destroys unhappiness. Please tell me what happened next, about his greatness of conduct. In particular, please tell me about the nature of creation.'"

'"Brahma replied, 'You have asked me a relevant question. I will briefly tell you about what happened next, as I heard it formerly. In the form of Shiva, the eternal divinity vanished. O Indra among *brahmana*s! Vishnu and I were filled with great happiness. I was in the form of a swan and Vishnu was in the form of a boar. With the desire that the worlds should be created, we withdrew from the spot.'"

'"Narada said, 'O Vidhatri! O Brahma! O immensely wise one! There is a great doubt in my heart. You are unmatched in your compassion. Please dispel it immediately. Why did the two of you assume the forms of a swan and a boar? Why did you ignore other forms? Please tell me the reason for this.'"

'Suta said, "Hearing the words of the great-souled Narada, Brahma remembered Shiva's lotus feet and replied affectionately."'

'"Brahma replied, 'A swan can constantly go upwards. That apart, like separating milk from water, it has the discrimination to distinguish truth from untruth. A swan possesses the discrimination to distinguish *jnana* from lack of *jnana*. That is the reason Brahma, the creator, assumed the form of a swan. O Narada! But despite assuming the form of a swan, I lost my sense of discrimination. Therefore, in that form of light, I could not discern Shiva's own form. How can *jnana* be generated in a person who wishes to embark on the task of creation? Therefore, despite assuming the form of a swan, I did not obtain a sense of discrimination. A boar can go constantly downwards. That is the reason Vishnu, who roams around in the forest, assumed the form of a boar. Alternatively, he thought of this form because he visualized the creation of a new *kalpa*. Vishnu became a boar because he wanted to turn the world into a forest. Since the day Hari assumed the form of a boar, the *kalpa* known as Varaha *kalpa* started. It is because of his[664] wishes that we assumed those two forms then. Since that day, the new *kalpa* known as Varaha *kalpa* commenced. O Narada! I have given you the answer to your question. Now listen. O sage! Remembering Shiva's lotus feet, I will describe the process of creation. Mahadeva vanished. Intent on carrying out his instructions, I, the grandfather of the worlds, engaged in *dhyana*. Prostrating myself before Shambhu, I acquired *jnana* from Hari. Filled with great bliss, I made up my mind to create. Vishnu also prostrated himself before Sadashiva. O son! Having instructed me, he vanished from the spot. Having obtained Shambhu's favours, Vishnu went outside the cosmic egg. He went to the city of Vaikuntha and started to reside there.'"

""'Desiring to create, I remembered Shiva and Vishnu. The water had already been created and I used that to offer oblations of water. Thereafter, twenty-four *tattva*s arose from the egg. O *brahmana*! The form of water could no longer be seen, and the form of Virat arose. I became full of doubts and tormented myself through extremely terrible austerities. For twelve years I engaged in *dhyana* on Vishnu. O son! At that time, Hari manifested himself. Full of great affection, he cheerfully touched my body and spoke to me. Vishnu said, "I am pleased with you. Please ask for a boon. There is nothing that cannot be given to you. O Brahma! Because of Shambhu's favours, I am capable of bestowing anything." Brahma said,[665] "O immensely fortunate one! This is appropriate. Shambhu has given me to you. O Vishnu! I prostrate myself before you. Therefore, it is appropriate that you should now give me what I ask for. This cosmic egg is in the form of Virat and possesses

---

[664] Shiva's.
[665] Brahma reporting what he told Vishnu.

twenty-four *tattvas*. But it has no consciousness and is seen to be insentient. O Hari! Through Shiva's favours, you have now manifested yourself before me. This egg has originated from Shankara. Please impart consciousness in it." The great Vishnu, who followed Shiva's instructions, was addressed in this way. Assuming his form of Ananta, he entered the egg. That Purusha possessed one thousand heads, one thousand eyes and one thousand feet. He touched the ground in every direction and pervaded the egg. When Vishnu entered the egg, I eulogized him properly. The egg, with the twenty-four *tattvas*, became sentient. Hari, the lord of the seven worlds, beginning with Patala,[666] was radiant. The Lord was himself Virat Purusha. For his own residence, the Lord with five faces created the beautiful city of Kailasa, where he is radiant with all his companions. O *devarshi*! When the cosmic egg is destroyed, Vaikuntha and Kailasa are never destroyed. O supreme among sages! I reside in Satyaloka. O son! Because of Mahadeva's command, I am engaged in the task of creation. As I desired to create, the evil creation manifested itself before me. O son! This was ignorance. It was *tamas*, cloaked as intellect. After this, with a pleasant mind, I created immobile objects. This was the primary creation. But because of Shambhu's command, I continued to meditate. I wanted to create those who were *sadhaka*s in their *atman*s. But the creation that resulted was full of misery and was downward in flow. I saw that this did not consist of *sadhaka*s.[667] Therefore,

---

[666] The seven nether regions.

[667] There are different layers of creation, described differently in different texts. As described here, the first one is *mukhya sarga* (primary creation), that of immobile objects; the second is *tiryaksrota* (flowing downwards), that of inferior animals; the third is *urddhvasrota* (flowing upwards), the creation of *deva*s; the fourth is *arvaksrota* (that which flowed subsequently) and is creation of humans; the fifth is *bhuta sarga*, the creation of elements. These five are known as *vaikrita* creations. The three *prakrita* creations are Mahat, subtle elements and *vikara*s (transformations).

instructed to create *sadhaka*s, I thought again. The *sattvika sarga*, or *urddhvasrota*, quickly resulted. This is known as the creation of *deva*s and is extremely pleasant. But I thought that this too was not of *sadhaka*s. Therefore, I again meditated on the lord within my *atman*. Through Shankara's command, the creation known as *rajas sarga* resulted. This is known as *arvaksrota*, the creation of humans, and has supreme *sadhaka*s. After this, because of Mahadeva's command, *bhuta sarga* resulted. I thus engaged in five kinds of creation. After this, Brahma is said to have brought about three *prakrita* creations. The first is creation of Mahat, while the second is the creation of subtle elements. The third is known as *vaikarika*. These are the three creations resulting from Prakriti. Taking *vaikrita* and *prakrita* together, there are eight kinds of creation. Koumara is spoken of as the ninth and it is both *vaikrita* and *prakrita*. I am incapable of explaining the differences between these. I must finally speak of the *dvija sarga*, which has served little purpose. In this Koumara *sarga*, this great creation of Sanaka and the others took place. Sanaka and the others were sons born through my mental powers and they are as revered as the *brahman*. There were five of these and they were full of supreme non-attachment.[668] Despite my instructions, those learned ones turned away from *samsara*. Their minds were fixed on *dhyana* about Shiva. Their minds did not turn towards creation. O supreme among sages! Indeed, they answered back. O Narada! On hearing this, I was overcome by delusion and filled with rage.'"

'"'O sage! When I was enraged and deluded, my mind was distracted. Because of the anger, drops of tears fell down from my eyes. At that time, when I thought of him in my mind, Vishnu quickly arrived there and enlightened me. Hari instructed me,

---

[668] Usually four names are given, Sanaka, Sananda, Sanatana and Sanatkumara. The fifth is Sujata.

"For Shiva's sake, perform austerities." O supreme among
sages! I engaged myself in great and fierce austerities. While I
was engaged in austerities for the sake of creation, from the spot
between my eyebrows and nose that is known as *avimukta*,[669]
Mahesha, who has three forms and is an ocean of compassion,
manifested himself. The lord of all portions assumed all his
portions and emerged as *ardhanarishvara*.[670] Shankara, the
one without birth, Uma's consort, himself emerged as a mass
of energy. He is omniscient, the creator of everything and
is known as Nilalohita. On seeing him, I prostrated myself.
Delighted and full of great devotion, I praised him. I said, "O
divinity! O lord of all *deva*s! Please create different kinds of
subjects." Hearing my words, Maheshvara, lord of *deva*s,
created many *gana*s of Rudras who were just like his own self.
I again told Isha Maheshvara Maharudra, "O divinity! Please
create subjects who suffer fear on account of birth and death."
Hearing my words, Mahadeva, the lord of compassion, laughed
at my words. O supreme among sages! He laughed and spoke
to me. Mahadeva said, "O Vidhatri! I will not create subjects
who suffer fear on account of birth and death. They are
submerged in an ocean of miseries because they are under the
subjugation of their own inauspicious *karma*. I save subjects
who are submerged in an ocean of grief. In my form as a *guru*,
I impart proper *jnana* to them. O Prajapati! Therefore, you
create all the subjects who will be overwhelmed by grief. Since
you are doing this after being commanded by me, you will not
be bound by *maya*." Telling me this, the prosperous Bhagavan
Nilalohita Hara swiftly vanished along with his *gana*s, as I
watched.'"

---

[669] The spot between the *bhru* (eyebrows) and *ghrana* (nose) is
known as *avimukta*.
[670] Half man and half woman.

Chapter 48-3.1(16) (Description of Creation)

' '' Brahma said, 'O Narada! I divided the five elements[671] and sound and the others and created the five gross elements of space, wind, fire, earth and water. I also created mountains, oceans, trees and other things, *kali* and the other *yuga*s and other measurements of time. O sage! Thereafter, I created other things, but was not satisfied. O sage! Therefore, I meditated on Samba Shiva and created *sadhaka*s. Marichi was created from my eyes, Bhrigu from my heart, Angiras from my head, Pulaha, the supreme sage, from *vyana*, Pulastya from *udana*, Vasishtha from *samana*, Kratu from *apana*, Atri from the ears and Daksha from *prana*.[672] I then created you from my lap and the sage Kardama from my shadow. I created Dharma, the means for accomplishing everything, from my resolution. O tiger among sages! Having created these *sadhaka*s, I decided I was successful. All these were created through Mahadeva's favours. O son! Following my command, Dharma, born out of my resolution, assumed the form of Manu and engaged the *sadhaka*s in their activities. After this, from different parts of my body, I created innumerable sons. O sages! I gave *sura*s, *asura*s and others their own forms.'''

''''Shankara was inside me. O sage! Urged by him, I split my body into two parts and assumed two forms. O sage! One half was a woman, and the other half was a man. Within her, he[673] created a couple, the best means of accomplishing every objective. The man was Svayambhuva Manu, the best instrument. The woman was known as Shatarupa, a *yogini*

[671] These were the subtle elements.
[672] *Prana* is the breath of life or the life force. *Prana* draws breath into the body, *apana* exhales it. *Vyana* distributes it through the body and *samana* assimilates it. *Udana* gives rise to sound.
[673] Shiva.

and an ascetic. O son! Following the rites of marriage, Manu
accepted the auspicious lady and they created subjects through
intercourse. Through her, he obtained two sons—Priyavrata
and Uttanapada. He also had three daughters, known as Akuti,
Devahuti and Prasuti. He bestowed Akuti on Ruchi and the
one in the middle⁶⁷⁴ on Kardama. He bestowed the youngest
daughter, Uttanapada's sister Prasuti, on Daksha. Prasuti
gave birth to those who spread over everything, mobile and
immobile. Akuti and Ruchi had twins, Yajna and Dakshina.
Through Dakshina, Yajna had twelve sons. O sage! Through
Devahuti, Kardama had many sons. Through Prasuti, Daksha
had twenty-four daughters. He bestowed thirteen of these,
Shraddha and others, on Dharma. O lord among sages!
Listen to the names of Dharma's wives—Shraddha, Lakshmi,
Dhriti, Tushti, Pushti, Medha, Kriya, Vasu, Buddhi, Lajja,
Shanti, Siddhi and Kirti.⁶⁷⁵ These are the thirteen. The eleven
younger and virtuous daughters, with excellent eyes, Khyati,
Sati, Sambhuti, Smriti, Priti, Kshama, Sannati, Anurupa, Urja,
Svaha and Svadha, were respectively married to Bhrigu, Bhava,
Marichi, the sage Angiras, Pulastya, Pulaha, Kratu, supreme
among *rishi*s, Atri, Vasishtha, Vahni⁶⁷⁶ and the ancestors.
Bhrigu and the other supreme *sadhaka*s accepted these
daughters, Khyati and the others. Thus, the three worlds, with
mobile and immobile objects, were filled everywhere. In this
way, following the commands of Ambika's lord and depending
on their *karma*, many beings were born. There were many bulls
among *brahmana*s too. In a different *kalpa*, Daksha is said to
have had sixty daughters. O Narada! Following the norms,
Daksha bestowed ten of these on Dharma, twenty-seven on the

⁶⁷⁴ Devahuti.
⁶⁷⁵ These are personified forms of attributes. For example,
Shraddha is faith.
⁶⁷⁶ Agni.

moon, thirteen on Kashyapa, four on the supremely beautiful
Tarkshya and two each on Bhrigu, Angiras and Krishashva.
They had many offspring, who spread over everything mobile
and immobile. O supreme among sages! Following the norms,
Daksha bestowed ten daughters on the great-souled Kashyapa.
Their offspring spread over the three worlds, mobile and
immobile. There was no space, mobile or immobile, that was
empty. Beginning with the nether regions of Patala and all
the way up to Satyaloka, the offspring born from Daksha's
daughters, *devas*, *rishis*, *daityas*, trees, birds, mountains and
herbs covered everything mobile and immobile. Everything
in the cosmic egg was covered. Nothing was empty. In this
way, following Shambhu's command, Brahma completed the
creation in the proper way.'"'

'"'Rudra always protected Sati at the tip of his trident.
Earlier, Shambhu, who pervades everything, created her for
the sake of his austerities. Thereafter, for the task of the
worlds, she was born through Daksha. To save his devotees,
he engages in many pastimes. Shiva is said to have divided
himself into three—Vaikuntha from the left flank, I from the
right flank and Rudra from the heart. Vishnu, Rudra and I
are said to represent the three *gunas*. Shiva is the supreme and
undecaying *brahman*. He is himself always without *gunas*.
Vishnu is said to represent *sattva*, I *rajas* and Rudra *tamas*.
But this is only the way the world perceives our activities.
The reality is different. Vishnu represents *sattva* on the
outside but has *tamas* inside. Rudra represents *tamas* outside
but has *sattva* inside. O sage! I represent *rajas* everywhere,
inside and outside. The divine goddess[677] is *rajas* in nature.
Sati's form is *sattva*, while Lakshmi is full of *tamas*. These
are known to be the three supreme forms of Shivaa. In this
way, Shivaa became Sati and married Shankara. At her

---

[677] That is, Sarasvati.

father's sacrifice, she gave up her own body. She did not accept it again but returned to her own abode. As a result of the prayers of *deva*s, Shivaa was born again as Parvati. Having performed extremely extensive austerities, she got Shiva back again. O lord among sages! She is known by many names—Kalika, Chandika, Bhadra, Chamunda, Vijaya, Jaya, Jayanti, Bhadrakali, Durga, Bhagavati, Kamakhya, Kamada, Amba, Mridani and Sarvamangala. All of these names bestow objects of pleasure and emancipation. They vary according to qualities, acts and forms. She is generally known as Parvati. Devi and Deva possess all the *guna*s and divide themselves into the three *guna*s. Together, they engage in many wonderful acts of creation. O supreme among sages! I have thus described to you the process of creation. Following Shiva's command, I created the entire cosmic egg. Shiva is the supreme *brahman*. We three divinities are said to be his forms. Vishnu, Rudra and I differ in forms because of qualities. The *paramatman* is both *saguna* and *nirguna*. He rules himself and amuses himself with Shivaa in the beautiful region of Shivaloka. Rudra is his complete *avatara* and is said to be Shiva himself. The one with five faces resides in his beautiful abode of Kailasa. When the cosmic egg is destroyed, he is not destroyed.'"'

Chapter 49-3.1(17) (Gunanidhi's Conduct)

'Suta said, "O lords among sages! Hearing Brahma's words, Narada bent down humbly and again questioned him."'

'"Narada asked, 'When did Shankara, who is affectionate towards his devotees, go to Kailasa? How did he develop a friendship with the great-souled Kubera? What does Hara, completely auspicious in form, do there? Please tell me all this. I am filled with great curiosity.'"'

"'Brahma replied, 'O Narada! Listen. I will tell you about the conduct of the one with the moon on his crest, how he went to Kailasa and how he developed a friendship with Dhanada.[678] In the city of Kampilya,[679] there was a person named Yajnadatta, born in a lineage that performed *soma* sacrifices. He was Dikshita[680] and was accomplished in the knowledge of performing sacrifices. He was wise and knew the *Veda*s and Vedanta. He was accomplished in Vedanta and other things. He was revered by the king and was generous in many ways. He was famous. He was engaged in tending to the sacrificial fire and studying the *Veda*s. He had a son named Gunanidhi, who was handsome and beautiful in his limbs. His form was like the lunar disc. He initiated this son. After *upanayana*, he received a lot of knowledge of the eight kinds.[681] However, his father did not know that he engaged in gambling. He took a lot of wealth from his mother and handed this over to other gamblers. He was friendly with them. He gave up the conduct of *brahmana*s. He turned away from bathing at the time of the *sandhya*s. He criticized *Veda*s and the sacred texts. He criticized *deva*s and *brahmana*s. He ignored the conduct indicated in the *smriti* texts and indulged in singing and the playing of musical instruments. He was bound in love towards actors, heretics and mimics. Though his mother sent him to his father, he didn't go. He[682] was Dikshita and so was she. While she was engaged in her household tasks, he would

[678] Lord of riches, Kubera.

[679] Described as the capital of Panchala, specifically, South Panchala. Identified with Kampil, in Farrukhabad district of Uttar Pradesh.

[680] Meaning initiated.

[681] The *Veda*s, metaphysics, governance, professional knowledge, Itihasa, rituals, logic and *dharma*. This is the usual list given of the eight.

[682] Yajnadatta.

occasionally ask her about Gunanidhi, his son. "O fortunate one! I don't see him at home. What is he doing?" On every such occasion, she would tell him, "He has just gone out. He has been engaged in bathing and worshipping *devas*. For the sake of studying, he has gone out with two or three friends." Though she had been initiated, since he possessed only one son, she deceived in this way. Her Dikshita husband did not know anything about this act of hers. Till the age of sixteen years, he had all the *samskaras*, ending with *keshanta*, done. In this way, Yajnadatta initiated his son. Following the rules of the *grihya sutras*,[683] he got his son married. O Narada! Every morning, the mother would wake up her son, Gunanidhi. Her heart full of affection, she would make him sit down and gently chastise him. "O son! Your father is great-souled, but he is prone to swift rage. If he gets to know of your conduct, he will chastise me and you. Every day, I hide your wicked deeds from your father. O son! Because of his good and virtuous conduct, he is revered by people. O son! Good conduct and association with virtuous people is wealth for *brahmanas*. How is it that your mind is not happily drawn towards such good behaviour? Your forefathers were learned, initiated into the performance of *soma* sacrifices. Therefore, they were revered in this world. Give up the association with wicked people and associate with those who are virtuous. Fix your mind on virtuous learning and follow the conduct worthy of *brahmanas*. In beauty, fame, noble lineage and good behaviour, be like your father. Therefore, why don't you give up this wicked conduct that you love? You are nineteen years old now and she[684] is sixteen years old. Accept her and protect her properly. Be devoted towards your father. Your father-in-law possesses qualities and good conduct. He must always be respected by you. O son!

[683] Texts that set out rules and rituals for householders.
[684] Gunanidhi's wife.

Therefore, why don't you give up this wicked conduct? O son! Your maternal uncles are also unmatched in learning, good conduct and lineage. You are not scared of them either. Both of your lineages[685] are pure. Look around our house at the other *brahmana* boys. Inside the house, look at your father's *shishya*s. They are humble. O son! If the king hears about your wicked conduct, he will cease to respect your father and may even take away his means of subsistence. So far, people thought that all your acts were those of a child. But hereafter, they will stop speaking of you as having been initiated. All of them will abuse your father and me. They will utter wicked words, saying that the son has taken after his mother's conduct. Your father is not a sinner. He follows the path of the *shruti* and *smriti* texts. Maheshvara is my witness that my mind has always been fixed on his feet. Since bathing after my season,[686] I did not see the face of any wicked person. But destiny is powerful. That is the reason I have given birth to you." Every instant, the mother tried to instruct the evil-minded one. However, he did not give up *adharma*. A person addicted to vices cannot be made to understand easily. Hunting, liquor, slander, falsehood, theft, gambling and prostitutes are vices that have shattered many men. Extremely evil-minded, he grabbed anything he could see inside the house, garments, pots and other things and took them away for purposes of gambling.'"'

'"'On one occasion, he stole a valuable ring, set with stones, belonging to his father. He handed it over to a gambler. By chance, the Dikshita saw it on the hand of a gambler. The Dikshita asked, "Where did you get this ring?" When asked once, the gambler didn't answer. When asked again, he replied, "O *brahmana*! Why are you accusing me of having indulged in theft? I got this ring from your son, who gave it to me.

---

[685] Paternal and maternal.
[686] Before conceiving Gunanidhi.

Earlier, I won from him his mother's garment. He has not only
given me this ring. There are many other objects he has given
other gamblers. He has given gems, pots, garments, cosmetic
articles and colourful vessels made out of bronze and copper.
Every day, gamblers strip him naked and bind him. There is
no gambler on earth who is as unskilled as he is. Your son is
foremost among gamblers. O *brahmana*! How is it that you did
not know about this till today? He is accomplished in unfair
means and deception." When he heard this, he hung his head
down under the burden of shame. He covered his head with
his garment and entered his own house. Dikshita Yajnadatta
was addicted to the rites mentioned in the *shruti* texts. He
spoke to his wife, who was extremely devoted to her husband.
Yajnadatta said, "O one who has been initiated! Where is that
cunning son, Gunanidhi? Let it be. What do I have to do with
him? Where is my auspicious ring? When you applied unguents
on my body, you took that ring off. Please bring that bejewelled
ring quickly and give it to me." Hearing these words, the lady
who had been initiated was scared. She was engaged in rites
connected with the midday bath and replied, "I am anxiously
engaged in collecting articles required for worshipping *deva*s.
O one who loves guests! The time for attending to guests is
passing. I am eager to finish cooking the food now. While
engaged in placing it in vessels, I have forgotten where I have
kept it." Dikshita replied, "You have always spoken the truth,
but you are a mother who has given birth to a false son.
Whenever I asked you where the son has gone, you told me
that he had just gone out. You had told me that he had gone
out with two or three friends for the sake of studying. O wife!
Where is the red piece of cloth I gave you? After getting it, you
always kept it in the house. Give up your fear and please tell
me the truth. Now, I do not see the bejewelled vase I gave you.
Where is the tripod covered with a threaded piece of cloth? I
gave that to you too. Where is the bronze pot from the south?

Where is the copper one from Gouda? Where is the ivory
hangar from which curios used to hang? Where is the statue
from the mountainous regions? It was wonderful and was as
radiant as the moon. It was ornamented with the image of a
lady holding a lamp. What is the need to speak a lot? You have
been born in a noble lineage. Being angry with you is futile. I
will eat only after I have married again. Since the wicked one
has defiled the lineage, I am without offspring now. Get up
and bring me some water. I will offer him oblations of water
mixed with sesamum.[687] It is better for men not to have sons
than to have wicked sons who are the worst of the lineage. For
the sake of the lineage, I will forsake him now. This is eternal
good policy." Following the daily rituals, Dikshita bathed.
On that very day, he accepted the hand of the daughter of a
learned *brahmana*.'"'

Chapter 50-3.1(18) (Gunanidhi's Virtuous End)

' ' Brahma said, 'Hearing what had happened, Dikshita's
son reprimanded himself for what he had done
earlier. Considering all this, he left for some other place. A
long period of time passed after the departure of Yajnadatta's
son. Having been abandoned, the wicked Gunanidhi lost all
sense of enterprise. He thought a great deal. "Where will I go?
What will I do? I am not learned. Nor do I possess a great
deal of riches. In a different country, only a wealthy person
can find happiness, though a wealthy person will be scared of
thieves. There are impediments in every direction. I was born in
a lineage of those who officiated at sacrifices. How will I face
this great hardship? Alas! Destiny is powerful and binds us to

---

[687] Behaving as if Gunanidhi was dead.

karma. Since there is no one I know, I cannot even beg. Nor do I possess any riches. Who will provide me refuge? Before the sun rose, my mother always used to feed me sweet food. Who will I ask now? My mother isn't here either." O Narada! In this way, he thought a lot. Extremely miserable, he sat down under a tree and the sun set.'"'

'"'There was a man who was Maheshvara's devotee. At this time, he emerged out of the city, carrying offerings with him. He had fasted on Shiva Ratri. To worship Ishana, he carried many kinds of divine objects and was surrounded by his own relatives. With his intelligence fixed on Shiva, the devotee entered Shiva's temple. With an excellent mind, he worshipped Shankara in the appropriate way. The *brahmana* who was Yajnadatta's son inhaled the fragrance of cooked food. He had been cast away by his father and he was without his mother. He was hungry and arrived there. "It is night. This cooked food has been brought for Shiva and I will take it when Shiva's devotee's go to sleep. It is chance that all these many and great offerings have been brought." Having assured himself in this way and having found support, he sat down at the door to Shambhu's temple. He witnessed the great *puja* devised by the devotees. Having completed the singing and the dancing, the devotees slept. So as to steal the *naivedya*, he entered Bhaga's chamber. In the dim light of the lamp, he looked at the cooked food. So as to get better illumination, he tore half of his garment and placed it on the lamp. Yajnadatta's son lovingly seized Shiva's *naivedya*. Suddenly happy, he grabbed the many kinds of cooked food. Having seized the cooked food, he quickly went outside. He struck a sleeping person with his foot, who woke up in rage. "Who is this? Who is running away quickly? Seize him. Grab him." Filled with great fear, that person screamed in this way. While he was running away in fear, the guards of the city arrived. In a short while, they bound him and killed him.

O sage! Yajnadatta's son could not eat the *naivedya*, which
should not be eaten.'"'

""'However, he either possessed the strength of accumulated
good deeds, or Shiva showed him favours. Yama's terrible
servants arrived, with nooses and clubs in their hands. They
wished to bind him and take him to Samyamani.[688] However,
Shiva's attendants also arrived, wearing garlands that had
nets with bells. With tridents in their hands, they arrived, to
take him away astride a divine *vimana*. Shiva's *gana*s said,
"O Yama's servants! Release the *brahmana*. He is extremely
devoted to *dharma*. This *brahmana* does not deserve to be
punished. All his accumulated sins have been burnt down."
Hearing the words spoken by Mahadeva's *gana*s, King Yama's
servants were extremely surprised. Full of fear, Yama's servants
looked towards Shambhu's *gana*s. Yama's servants prostrated
themselves and said, "O *gana*s! This *brahmana* is extremely
wicked in conduct. He transgressed his family's conduct. He
turned away from his father's words. He deviated from truth
and purity. He did not bathe at the time of the *sandhya*s. He
stayed away from good *karma* and went so far as to transgress
by taking away offerings made to Shiva. You can directly see it
yourself. He does not deserve to be touched by the likes of you.
He ate offerings made to Shiva. He violated offerings made
to Shiva. Even if a person touches someone who gives Shiva's
offerings away to others, that is a sin. Even if the breath of life
is stuck in the throat, it is better to look at or drink poison than
to touch supreme offerings made to Shiva or his possessions.
You are the ones who determine *dharma* and there is no one
like you. O *gana*s! Nevertheless, listen to us. He does not
possess the least bit of *dharma*." Hearing the words spoken by
Yama's servants, Shiva's servants remembered Shiva's lotus feet
and replied to those attendants. Shiva's servants said, "Shiva's

[688] Yama's city.

dharma is subtle. Those like you only notice gross objectives.
What are objectives? Objectives are those perceived by those
with subtle vision. O servants! Listen carefully to the *karma*
that Yajnadatta's son has done. The shadow of a lamp fell on
top of the *lingam*, and he countered this. In the night, he cut
off a piece of his own garment and made a wick for the lamp.
O servants! There is yet another act of supreme *dharma* that
was done. In that connection, though inadvertently, he heard
Shiva's names being chanted. He saw devotees perform many
different kinds of *puja*. At that time, he was fasting, and his
mind was also focused. Let him go to Shiva's world with us.
As Shiva's follower, he will enjoy great objects of pleasure for
some time. After that, with his sins cleansed, he will become the
king of Kalinga. This *brahmana* has certainly become supreme
among those Shiva loves. There is no need to say anything
more. Return wherever you came from. O Yama's messengers!
With extremely pleasant minds, return to their own abode."
O lord among sages! Hearing these words, Yama's messengers
retreated and all of them left for Yama's world. O sage! The
servants told Death everything that Shambhu's messengers had
said about *dharma*. Dharmaraja said, "O servants! All of you
listen attentively to my words. Placing my instructions at the
forefront, follow them lovingly. O servants! In the world, you
must always avoid those who wear Tripundraka and white
ashes. They must never be brought here. O servants! You must
avoid all those who smear their limbs with white ashes. They
must never be brought here. You must avoid those who are
dressed like Shiva, whatever be the reason. They must never
be brought here. In the world, those who wear *rudraksha*s and
those who wear matted hair must all be avoided. They must
never be brought. You must avoid those who assume Shiva's
garb in the course of their livelihoods. All these must never be
brought here. Even if people don Shiva's garb in insolence or in
deceit, they must all be avoided and must never be brought."

In this way, Yama commanded his own servants. All of them were surprised and smiled silently. They agreed.'"'

'"'The *brahmana* was freed from Yama's attendants. Pure in mind, along with the *gana*s, he quickly went to Shiva's world. There, he enjoyed all the objects of pleasure and served Shiva and Shivaa. After this, he was born as the son of Arindama, the king of Kalinga. He was known as Dama and he was devoted to serving Shiva. Even as a child, along with other children, he was devoted to Shiva. In due course, when he became a youth and his father died, he obtained the kingdom. Delighted, he spread Shiva's *dharma* everywhere. King Dama was indomitable and knew of only one kind of *dharma*. The former *brahmana* donated lamps for each of Shiva's temples. He summoned all the village headmen who resided in his kingdom and told them to arrange for lamps in all of Shiva's temples. Otherwise, he would truly punish them. "The *shruti* texts have said that Shiva is satisfied through the donation of lamps. Therefore, without any reflection, you must arrange for lamps to be lit in every Shiva temple that exists in your villages. There is no doubt that if you violate my order, I will cut off your head." As a result of this fear, lamps were lit in every Shiva temple. Following this *dharma* alone for as long as he lived, King Dama accumulated a great deal of *dharma*. In due course, he came under the subjugation of the *dharma* of time. The desire to light many lamps remained ignited in his mind. He became the lord of Alaka[689] and only sought the wicks of lamps. Thus, in the course of time, even the least bit done for Shiva bears fruits. Knowing this, those who seek great happiness should serve Shiva's tasks. Dikshita's son always ignored every kind of *dharma*. Through the intervention of destiny, he stole objects from Shiva's temple. Because of his own selfish motives, he used a lamp to illuminate the top of Hara's *lingam*. Consequently,

---

[689] Kubera's capital.

he obtained the kingdom of Kalinga and was always devoted to *dharma*. All this happened because he fasted and lit a lamp in Shiva's temple. O lord among sages! Consider. He became a guardian of the worlds. Despite following human *dharma*, that is the pleasure that he now enjoys. I have thus described the conduct of Gunanidhi, Yajnadatta's son. Listening to this gives Shiva satisfaction and bestows everything that is desired. O son! All *deva*s are in Shiva, and I will tell you exactly how he became Shiva's friend. Listen attentively.'"'

Chapter 51-3.1(19) (Shiva's Friendship with Kubera)

❝ ❝ Brahma said, 'Earlier, in Padma *kalpa*, I, Brahma, had a son through my mental powers. He was Pulastya and Pulastya's son was Vishrava. Vishrava had a son named Vaishravana, who enjoyed the city of Alaka, built by Vishvakarma. Formerly, he had engaged in fierce austerities and had worshipped the three-eyed divinity. That *kalpa* ended and the *kalpa* known as Megavahana started. Shrida,[690] Yajnadatta's son, performed austerities that were impossible to tolerate. He knew the power of devotion consequent to offering only lamps to Shambhu. With this illumination in his mind, in those earlier times, he reached the city of Kashika. Using that jewel of illumination in his mind, he chanted *mantra*s to the eleven Rudras. He was full of unmatched devotion. With deep love, he was unwavering in his *dhyana*. Surrounded by the fire of his austerities, he obtained union with Shiva, the great vessel. Desire, anger and other great impediments were

---

[690] That is, Gunanidhi.

like insects that were burnt down and shunned. He controlled his breath of life, which became pure. His vision became pure. He established Shiva's *lingam* and full of virtuous sentiments, worshipped it with flowers. Until he was reduced to skin and bones, he continued to torment himself through austerities. He tormented his body for a hundred thousand years. Pleased in his mind, along with Vishalakshi,[691] the divinity Vishveshvara himself looked at the lord of Alaka, who resembled an immobile pillar, with his mind fixed on the *lingam*. He said, "O lord of Alaka! I will grant you a boon. Ask for it." At this, the store of austerities opened his eyes and looked. It was if one thousand suns had risen together. Indeed, the radiance was greater than that of one thousand suns. He saw Uma's beloved Shrikantha[692] standing in front of him, with the moon on his crest. That energy overwhelmed the energy of his eyes and he closed them. He addressed the divinity who is lord of *deva*s, the one who is beyond anything the mind can approach. "O Lord! Please grant me the capacity to see your feet. O protector! That I have been able to see you is itself a sufficient boon. O Isha! O Shashishekhara![693] What will I do with any other boon? I prostrate myself before you." Hearing these words, Uma's lord, lord of *deva*s, granted him capacity to see and touched him with the palm of his hand. Yajnadatta's son opened his eyes and having opened the capacity, first looked at Uma. "Who is this lady near Shambhu? She is beautiful in all her limbs. Has she tormented herself through austerities that are greater than mine? How wonderful is her beauty! How wonderful is her love and good fortune! How wonderful is her great prosperity!" O son! In this way, he said this several times. He looked at her with an improper glance and repeatedly uttered these words.

---

[691] The large-eyed one, Parvati.
[692] Beautiful in throat, Shiva's name.
[693] Shiva's name, one with the moon on his crest.

Because of looking at the lady in this way, his left eye burst. At this, Devi spoke to the divinity. "Who is this wicked ascetic? He is looking at me with an improper glance and is asking me to surpass the strength of his austerities. He is again looking at me, with an improper glance in his right eye. He is jealous of my beauty, love, good fortune and prosperity." Hearing Devi's words, her lord laughed. "O Uma! This is your son. There is nothing improper in his glance. He is glancing at the power of your austerities and is describing it." Addressing Devi in this way, Isha spoke to him again. "O child! I am satisfied with your austerities. I will bestow a boon on you. You will be the lord of *nidhi*s and the lord of *guhyaka*s.[694] O one who is excellent in vows! You will be Rajaraja and the king of *yaksha*s and *kinnara*s. You will always be Dhanada and will be the lord of *punyajana*s. You will always have a friendship with me, and I will reside near you. O friend! I will increase your delight and live near Alaka. Come. Prostrate yourself at your mother's feet." The great devotee, Yajnadatta's son, was greatly delighted in his mind. Thus, the divinity Shiva bestowed a boon on him. He then told Shivaa, "O Deveshi![695] Please show him your favours. This ascetic has been born from your limbs." Hearing Shambhu's words, with a pleased mind, Parvati, the mother of the universe, spoke to Yajnadatta's son. Devi said, "O child! May you always possess unblemished devotion towards Bhava. Since your left eye burst out, you will be Ekapinga.[696] The boons the divinity bestowed on you will come to pass. O son! Since you were jealous of my beauty, you will be named

---

[694] *Guhyaka*s are semi-divine species, companions of Kubera. So are *kinnara*s (*kimpurusha*s). *Nidhi*s are treasures and Kubera is their lord. Kubera is also known as Dhanada, the lord of riches. Rajaraja is Kubera's name. *Punyajana* means virtuous people. *Saptajana* is a synonym. These were seven sages who were originally *rakshasa*s.

[695] Parvati's name.

[696] Yellow in one eye.

Kubera."[697] Along with Devi, the divinity Maheshvara thus bestowed boons on Dhanada. Vishveshvara then went to his own abode. In this way, in ancient times, Dhanada acquired the friendship of Shri Shambhu, who resided near Alaka, in Shankara's abode in Kailasa.'"'

Chapter 52-3.1(20) (Shiva's Departure for Kailasa)

" "Brahma said, 'O My Narada! O sage! O excellent one! Through the strength of Kubera's austerities, hear about how Shiva went to Kailasa, best among mountains. Having granted him the boon of lordship over *nidhi*s, he left for his own excellent abode. Vishvesha,[698] having granted the boon to Kubera, thought in his mind. "My own form has been born from Aja[699] and is capable of undertaking the complete task of dissolution. I will adopt that form and go to Kailasa, abode of *guhyakas*. Rudra has originated from my heart and is a complete portion of the *nishkala brahman*. He is unblemished and no different from me and should be served by Hari, Brahma and the others. Therefore, in that form, I will become Kubera's well-wisher and reside with him, indulging in my pastimes and undertaking great austerities." Thinking this, following Shiva's wishes, Rudra was eager to go. He sounded his drum and that let out an excellent *nada*. Using that sound to help him, he summoned everyone in the three worlds, that wonderful sound imparting speed to their arrival. Hearing this, Vishnu, Brahma and other gods, sages, *agama* and *nigama*

---

[697] One with a malformed body.
[698] The same as Vishveshvara.
[699] Brahma.

texts in embodied from and *siddha*s went there. All the gods and *asura*s went there, along with all the festivals. All the *pramatha*s[700] went, wherever they might have been. There were immensely fortunate leaders of the *gana*s, revered by all the worlds. I will tell you about their number. Listen attentively. Ganeshvara Shankakarna went there, with one crore *gana*s; Kekaraksha went with ten crores and Vikrita with eight; Vishakha went with sixty-four crores and Pariyatraka with nine; Sarvantaka went with six and the handsome Dundubhi with eight; Jalanka, bull among *gana*s, went with twelve crores; Samada and the handsome Vikritanana went with seven each; Kapali went with five and the auspicious Sandaraka with six; Kanduka and Kundaka went with one crore each; Vishtambha and Chandratapana went with eight each; Mahakesha, leader of *gana*s, was surrounded with one thousand crores; Kundi, Vaha and the auspicious Parvataka had twelve each; Kala, Kalaka and Mahakala had one hundred each; Agnika went with one hundred crores and Abhimukha with a crore; Adityamurdha and Dhanavaha went with one crore each; Sannaha and Kumuda with one hundred crores each; Amogha, Kokila and Sunmantraka with one crore each; Kakapada with six crores and the lord Santanaka with six crores; Mahabala, Madhupinga and Pingala with nine crores each; Nila, Devesha and Purnabhadra with ninety crores each; and the immensely strong Chaturvakra with seven crores. Surrounded by crores, thousands of crores, hundreds and twenties, Sarvesha[701] went there, preparing to go to Kailasa. Kashthaguda, Sukesha and Vrishabha went with sixty-four crores each, while Chaitra, Nakulisha and Svayamprabhu went with seven crores each. Lokantaka, Diptatma, the lord Daityantaka, the divine Bhringi, Riti, the handsome Devadevapriya, Ashani, Bhanuka

---

700 *Pramatha*s are Shiva's attendants.
701 Meaning presumably Shiva, the lord of everything.

and Sanatana went with sixty-four crores each. Ganadhisha Nandishvara and Mahabala went with one hundred crores each. There were other immensely strong and innumerable leaders of *gana*s. Each of them possessed one thousand hands and wore matted hair and diadems. All of them were adorned with the crescent moon. They were blue in the throat and three-eyed. They were ornamented with necklaces, earrings, bracelets and crowns. They resembled Brahma, Indra and Vishnu and possessed *anima* and other qualities. They were as radiant as crores of suns. All these lords of *gana*s went there. There were other great-souled leaders of *gana*s, sparkling in their radiance. Greatly delighted, they went there, desiring to see Shiva.'"

"'Having gone there, they saw Shiva. They prostrated themselves and uttered supreme praises. With Vishnu at the forefront, all of them joined their hands in salutation and bowed their heads down. Along with Vishnu and the others, Mahesha Parameshvara lovingly went to Kailasa, to the great-souled Kubera. When Shambhu arrived, Kubera affectionately worshipped him. Along with his family members, he devotedly offered him many offerings. To please Shiva, he also worshipped Vishnu and the other *deva*s, the *gana*s and Shiva's followers. Delighted in his mind, Shambhu embraced Kubera and inhaled the fragrance of his head. With all the others, he resided near Alaka. The lord instructed Vishvakarma to construct mountains as residences, as each deserved, for the many devotees, his own as well as those of others. O sage! Obeying Shambhu's command, Vishvakarma quickly went there and constructed many such. Shambhu was delighted. Because of Hari's prayer and to show favours to Kubera, he went to Mount Kailasa. At an excellent *muhurta*, Parameshvara entered his own abode. He gives pleasure to everyone and is a protector who is devoted towards his devotees. Vishnu and all the other gods were delighted. The sages and the *siddha*s were delighted at Shiva's consecration. In due order, with many kinds of offerings in their hands, they worshipped him. Performing *niranjana* in front of him, they engaged in great festivities. O sage! On that auspicious occasion, flowers were showered down. Extremely happy, *apsara*s sang. Others danced. Sounds of "Victory" were pronounced from the sky and everything was cleansed. Everyone was extremely enthusiastic, and happiness was enhanced. Seated on the throne, Shambhu was even more resplendent. Vishnu and the others looked at him and served him, as was proper. All the gods and others praised him separately. Their words were full of deep meaning, and they praised Shankara, who brings benefit to the worlds. Hearing the praises, Shiva was delighted in his mind and gave them whatever they wished for. Lord Sarveshvara happily gave them the boons they desired in their hearts. O sage! After this, on Shiva's command, all of them returned to their own respective abodes. Along with Vishnu, I was delighted at having obtained what I wished for. Shambhu asked me and Vishnu to sit down. Immensely happy, Parameshvara showed us his favours and addressed us in many kinds of ways. Shiva said, "O Hari! O Vidhatri! O sons! I love you the most. O best among gods! You will always be entrusted with the creation and preservation of the three worlds. Following my command, return to your own abodes. You will always be without fear. I will always look after you and bestow happiness on you." We heard Shambhu's words and commands and prostrated ourselves before him. Happy in our minds, Hari and I returned to our own abodes. At that time, Shankara cheerfully made the lord of *nidhi*s sit down. He clasped him by the hand and addressed him in auspicious words. Shiva said, "O friend! You have conquered me with your love, and I have become your friend. O umblemished one! Go to your residence. Be without fear. I will always be your aide." Hearing Shambhu's words, Kubera was delighted in his mind. Obeying that command, full of joy, he went to his own abode. Along with his *gana*s, Shambhu remained in

Kailasa, supreme among mountains. He is engaged in *yoga* and performs *dhyana*, as he wills. Sometimes, he meditates on his own *atman*. Sometimes, he engages in *yoga*. Sometimes, as his mind desires, he cheerfully recounts Itihasa to his *ganas*. Sometimes, in excellent spots in Kailasa, Maheshvara amuses himself with the *ganas*. He knows about pastimes and happily engages in many such. Shankara Parameshvara thus assumed the form of Rudra. Though supreme among *yogis*, he engaged in pastimes on that mountain. Parameshvara spent some time without a wife. After that, he obtained Daksha's daughter as a wife. Maheshvara amused himself with Sati, Daksha's daughter. O *devarshi*! Following the norms observed in the world, he was happy. O lord among sages! I have thus described Rudra's *avatara* to you, about his arrival in Kailasa and his friendship with the lord of *nidhis*. I have also described his inner pastimes and they extend *jnana*. As fruits, they always yield everything that is desired, in this world and in the next one. If a person controls himself and reads or hears this account, he obtains objects of pleasure in this world and emancipation in the next one.'"'

This ends Srishti Khanda.

Sati Khanda (The Section on Sati)

Chapter 53-3.2(1) (Sati's Conduct in Brief)

' "Narada said, 'O Vidhatri! Through Shankara's favours, you know everything. You have narrated extraordinary and auspicious accounts about Shiva and Shivaa. I have heard Shiva's supreme account, uttered from your lotus-like mouth. O lord! But I am not satisfied and wish to hear more. Earlier, you described Rudra as being Shankara's complete portion. O Vidhatri! You said the controlled Mahesha made an abode in Kailasa. The *yogi* is the destination of the virtuous and deserves to be served by Vishnu and all the gods. The great lord is indifferent and always sports, devoid of the opposite pairs of sentiments. He married the supreme lady and became a householder again. Because of Hari's prayers, he happily married Mangala,[702] who was herself an ascetic. At first, she was Daksha's daughter. Later, she became the daughter of the mountain. With a single body, how is it held that she was the daughter of two? How did Sati become Parvati and unite with Shiva again? O Brahma! You should tell me about all this and about other things.'"

'Suta said, "Hearing his words, Brahma immersed his *atman* in the divinity Shankara. With a delighted mind, he spoke these words."'

---

[702] The auspicious one, Parvati's name.

315

'"Brahma said, 'O son! O best among sages! I will tell you the auspicious account. There is no doubt that when you hear this, your birth will be successful. Earlier, I saw my own daughter, Sandhya, in the company of her sons. O son! I suffered from the arrows of desire and there was a deviation in me.[703] The supreme lord, the great *yogi* Rudra, was remembered by Dharma. O son! He reprimanded me and my sons and returned to his own abode. I am the one who utters the *Vedas*. Yet, I was foolish in intelligence. I fell prey to delusion and *maya* and acted against Paramesha Shambhu. Deluded by Shiva's *maya*, along with my sons, I foolishly sought many different ways to make him deviate. O lord among sages! But because of Shambhu's great powers, all these were countered, and these attempts proved to be futile. When I did not succeed, along with my sons, I remembered Rama's lord. Rama's lord told me about Shiva's *tattva*s and kindled my understanding. I cast aside my jealousy. However, I was still deluded and did not give up deceit. I served Shakti and managed to generate her pleasure. Daksha was my own son. So as to confound Hara, I created her as the daughter of Daksha and Asikni Virini.[704] Uma became Daksha's daughter and performed austerities that were impossible to tolerate. Wishing to ensure benefit to her own devotees, full of devotion, she became Rudra's wife. With Uma, Rudra, the supreme lord, was attracted towards becoming a householder and engaged in his pastimes. With an intelligence that did not deviate, he confounded me even at the time of his own marriage. He is independent. He assumed a body and came to marry her. He then returned to his own

[703] Brahma lusted after his own daughter Sandhya, the personified form of *sandhya*.

[704] There is no consistency about the name of Daksha's wife. Her name is usually given as Prasuti. But it is also given as Asikni, who was also known as Virini (Virani).

mountain and pleasured himself, confounding many. O sage! As he sported with her, a long period of time passed. Shambhu, the destination of the virtuous, is indifferent. However, he seemed to spend time in seeking happiness.'"'

"'"Because of Rudra's own wishes, a sense of rivalry was generated in Daksha. He was deluded by the *maya* and became extremely foolish and extremely proud. As a result of its powers, Daksha turned extremely insolent, confounded in intelligence. As a result of this delusion, he criticized the greatly serene and indifferent one a lot. Because of his pride, Daksha performed a sacrifice without Hara. He invited all the *deva*s, Vishnu, me and all the other lords. Since he was full of rage, he did not offer any oblations to Rudra there. Since he was deluded by destiny, he did not invite his own daughter, known by the name of Sati. She wasn't invited by her father, whose mind was confounded by *maya*. The immensely virtuous Shivaa possessed excellent *jnana* and engaged in her own pastimes. The proud Daksha hadn't invited her. Nevertheless, taking Shiva's permission, Sati went there, to her father's house. She was dishonoured and also noticed that Rudra wasn't offered a share. Reprimanding everyone, she gave up her body there. Hearing this the divinity, lord of *deva*s, was filled with intolerable rage. Uprooting a strand of his matted hair, he gave birth to Virabhadra. He was created, along with *gana*s, and asked, "What will I do?" He was instructed to first insult everyone and then destroy the sacrifice. Commanded in this way, with many forces, Ganadhisha went there. Full of great strength and valour, he descended violently. Following the command, the *gana*s created great havoc there. They chastised everyone. No one was spared. The supreme *gana* made efforts and defeated Vishnu and the immortals. He cut off Daksha's head and offered it as an oblation into the fire. He caused great havoc and quickly destroyed the sacrifice. He then returned to his own mountain and prostrated himself before Lord Shambhu. While the world of *deva*s looked on,

Virabhadra and others, Rudra's companions, destroyed the sacrifice. O sage! It should be known that this is the policy sanctioned in the *shruti* and *smriti* texts. When Rudra is enraged, how can there be sparkling happiness in the world?'"'

"'"After this, hearing his praise, Rudra was pleased. Compassionate towards the distressed, he satisfied everyone. The great-souled one became as compassionate as he had been earlier. Mahesha Shankara sported in many kinds of pastimes. Daksha was brought back to life, and everyone was honoured. Because of Shankara's compassion, the sacrifice was undertaken again. O sage! In particular, all the *deva*s and the entire universe worshipped Rudra there, at the sacrifice, and were extremely pleased. A blaze arose from Sati's body and brought happiness to the world. It fell down on the mountain. It brought happiness and was worshipped. This became known as Jvalamukhi[705] and yields everything that is desired. Seeing the supreme Devi there destroys all sins. Even now, to obtain all wishes as fruits, people worship her there. They follow the norms and undertake great festivities there. Later, Devi Sati became the daughter of the Himalayas. She became famous under the name of Parvati. She again practiced difficult austerities and was united with her husband, Paramesha. O lord among sages! I have thus told you everything you asked me about. If one listens to this, there is no doubt that one is cleansed of all sins.'"'

Chapter 54-3.2(2) (Kama's Origin)

'Suta said, "O residents of Naimisha! Hearing these words, the best among sages again asked about accounts that destroy all sins."'

[705] There is such a temple in Kangra district in Himachal Pradesh.

'"Narada said, 'O Vidhatri! O immensely fortunate one! O Vidhatri! O great lord! I have heard Shambhu's auspicious account flowing out from your mouth, which is like a lotus. But I am not content. Therefore, tell me everything about Shiva's auspicious account. O creator of the universe! I wish to hear Sati's divine account recited. How was the auspicious Sati born from Daksha's wife? How did Hara's mind turn towards accepting a wife in marriage? In ancient times, because of her rage with Daksha, how did Sati give up her body? Having died, how was she born again as the daughter of the Himalayas? How did Parvati undertake fierce austerities and how did her marriage take place? How did she come to acquire half the body of the one who destroyed Smara?[706] O immensely intelligent one! Please tell me all this in detail. In dispelling doubts, there is no one like you, nor will there ever be.'"

'"Brahma replied, 'O sage! Listen to everything about Sati and Shiva's auspicious account. This is extremely divine and purifying. Among all secrets, it is the supreme secret. O sage! In earlier times, Shambhu himself narrated this to Vishnu, his noble devotee. When he was asked with great devotion, he did this for the sake of benefit to others. After this, I asked the intelligent Vishnu, Shiva's supreme devotee. O supreme among sages! Out of his love for me, he told me in detail. I will describe that ancient account about Shiva and Shivaa. As fruits, it bestows everything that is wished for. Originally, the divinity Shiva was *nirguna* and without any other alternative. Separated from Shakti, he had no form. He was only consciousness, beyond the existent and the non-existent. Along with Shakti, the lord assumed a second form, one that possessed *guna*s. O *brahmana*! United with Uma, he acquired this divine form. But greater than the greatest, he was still indifferent. Vishnu was born from his left side and I, Brahma,

[706] Shiva.

was born from his right side. O supreme among sages! Rudra originated from his heart. Sadashiva divided himself into three forms—Brahma was the creator, Vishnu was the preserver and Rudra was the destroyer. I, Brahma, the grandfather of the worlds, worshipped him and embarked upon the task of creating all the subjects, gods, *asura*s and all the others. I created the Prajapatis, Daksha as the foremost, and supreme gods. I thought of myself as the best of all and was extremely pleased. O sage! I, Brahma, created Marichi, Atri, Pulaha, Pulastya, Angiras, Kratu, Vasishtha, Narada, Daksha, Bhrigu and other great lords as my mental sons. At that time, from my mind was born a beautiful lady, beautiful in all her limbs. She was named Sandhya, Divakshanta, Sayam and Sandhyajapantika. She was extremely beautiful. Her excellent eyebrows charmed even the minds of the sages. In the world of *deva*s, among mortals and in the nether regions, there was no one who was her equal. She was complete in all the qualities and there was no woman like her in the three periods of time.[707] Seeing her, I raised her up, my mind full of many kinds of thoughts. My sons, Daksha, Marichi and other creators of subjects, also thought like me.'"

""'O supreme among sages! From Brahma's mental thoughts, a handsome man originated. He was extremely wonderful. His complexion was golden. His chest was broad, and his nose was excellent. His thighs, hips and calves were round. He had waves of blue hair. His enchanting eyebrows touched each other. His face was like the full moon. His broad chest was like a door, radiant with body hair. His large form was like that of a cloud or an elephant. He was attired in blue garments. His hands, eyes, face, feet and fingers had a tinge of red. He was slender at the waist and his teeth were beautiful. His fragrance was like that of an intoxicated elephant. His eyes were like the petals of a blossoming lotus, with eyelashes

[707] The past, the present and the future.

as fragrant as the filament. His throat was like a conch shell and his banner bore the mark of a fish. He was tall and his mount was a *makara*.[708] His weapons were five flowers, and his powerful bow was decorated with flowers.[709] He was handsome. He cast sidelong glances and his eyes darted around. O son! A fragrant wind started to blow, and he was served by *shringara rasa*.[710] On seeing him, all my sons, Daksha and the others, were extremely curious. Their minds were filled with great wonder. The minds of my sons quickly became deviant. O son! With their minds overwhelmed by desire, they lost their patience. The man saw me, Vidhatri, the creator and lord of the universe. He lowered his shoulders down in humility and prostrated himself. The man asked, "O Brahma! What will I do? Please engage me in a task. O Vidhatri! Please give me a task that is auspicious and appropriate, so that I am respected as a man. Give me pride, an appropriate place and a wife. O lord of the three worlds! O creator and lord of the universe! Please tell me." I heard the great-souled man's words. For a while, the creator was surprised and could not say anything. But he controlled his mind properly and cast aside his wonder. Brahma instructed the man, Kama, about his task. Brahma said, "In this form, with arrows made out of five flowers, you will delude men and women and carry on the eternal task of

---

[708] *Makara* is a mythical aquatic creature, loosely translated as crocodile/shark. Kama is known as Minaketu (with the fish on his banner) and Makaradhvaja (with *makara* on his standard).

[709] Kama's arrows are made out of five flowers—*aravinda* (lotus), *ashoka*, *chuta* (mango), *navamallika* (jasmine) and *nilotapala* (blue lotus). His bow is made out of sugarcane.

[710] *Rasa* means taste. But in this context, it means the emotional flavor, or state of mind. Eight (or nine) *rasa*s are described—*shringara* (romance), *hasya* (laughter), *roudra* (fury), *karuna* (compassion), *bibhatsa* (disgusting), *bhayanaka* (terrible), *vira* (heroic), *adbhuta* (extraordinary) and *shanta* (peace).

creation. There are many beings in the three worlds, *deva*s
and others, mobile and immobile objects. None of them will
be able to withstand your powers. I, Vasudeva and Sthanu[711]
Purushottama will come under your subjugation. What need
be said about others who have life? Invisible in form, you will
always enter the hearts of beings. You will yourself create a
sensation of pleasure and carry on the eternal task of creation.
Your flowery arrows will always find an easy target in minds.
You will always be able to madden all beings. Thus, I have
engaged you in the task of carrying creation forward. These
sons of mine will tell you about the nature of your names."
Saying this, the best among gods looked towards the faces of
his own sons and in a short while, seated himself on his seat
on the lotus.""'

Chapter 55-3.2(3) (Kama's Curse)

" "Brahma said, 'All the sages, my sons, Marichi as the
foremost, glanced towards my face and understood
my intention. They understood other things too and gave him
names. Daksha and the other creators gave him a place and a
wife. Marichi and the other foremost *brahmana*s determined
his names. Together, my sons spoke to the man. The *rishi*s said,
"As soon as you were born, you churned our minds and also
that of Vidhatri. Therefore, you will be famous in the world as
Manmatha.[712] O one who originated from the mind! You will
be able to assume any form you wish. There will be no one in
the world who is your equal. Therefore, you will be famous

[711] Shiva.
[712] One who agitates the mind.

as Kama.[713] Since you will intoxicate, you will be known as Madana.[714] Since you were insolent when you were born, you will be Darpaka. In the world, you will also be famous as Kandarpa.[715] Among all *devas*, there will be no one who is your equal in energy. Hence, every place is your habitation. You will pervade everything. O best among men! Daksha, the first among Prajapatis, will fulfil your wish and give you a beautiful lady as a wife. When Brahma meditated, a beautiful lady was born. Therefore, she will be famous as Sandhya.[716] The lovely one will possess the complexion of a *mallika*." He was born from the mind accepted the flowers as his weapons. He made up his mind that he would remain hidden. His arrows are said to be *harshana, rochana, mohana, shoshana* and *marana*.[717] Even sages are deluded by these.'"

""""Brahma has instructed me about my eternal task.[718] Vidhatri told me this, in the presence of the sages. Therefore, that is what I will do. All the sages, and Prajapati himself, is present here. Right now, they will be witnesses to my decision. Brahma spoke words about Sandhya, and she is also present here. I will test her to carry out my task and use her to delude." Thinking this, the one who originated the mind made up his mind. He fixed flowers made out of arrows on a bow that was also made out of flowers. He carefully adopted a posture for shooting and drew on his bowstring. Kama, supreme among archers, drew it with great force. As he was ready with the bow, an extremely fragrant wind started to blow. O best among sages! As it blew,

---

[713] From wish or desire.

[714] One who intoxicates.

[715] *Darpa* means insolence. Brahma is known as Kah. Since he showed his insolence (*darpa*) to Kah, Kama is Kandarpa.

[716] From the root word for *dhyana*.

[717] Respectively, delighting, appealing, deluding, drying up and killing.

[718] These are Kama's thoughts.

it caused delight to everyone. Using sharp arrows made out of flowers, he confused and confounded Vidhatri and all the sons who were born through mental powers. O sage! I and all the sages were deluded. Together, we experienced a great deviation in our minds. As a result of this distortion, all of us repeatedly looked at Sandhya. Desire increased. A true woman is one who ignites such intoxication. Thus, all of us were repeatedly deluded by Madana, until we lost control over our senses. With my senses heightened, I, Vidhatri, glanced towards her. At that time, he struck me with his five arrows. Because she was struck by Kandarpa's arrows, she too repeatedly looked at me. As a result of such sentiments, she cast enchanting glances towards me. Sandhya was naturally beautiful, but these mental sentiments made her even more radiant. Her body seemed to be made out of waves of the divine river. Full of such sentiments, Sandhya enticed Prajapati. O sage! Though I was full of *dharma*, I desired her. O best among *brahmanas*! All the other sages, Marichi, Atri and others, Daksha and others, also suffered from this transformation in the senses. Madana saw that I, Daksha, Marichi and others were in this state and so was Sandhya. He paid even greater attention to his task. "This is the task that Brahma instructed me to undertake. I can accomplish it easily." This is what he thought. Seeing that his brothers and father had been reduced to this wicked state, Dharma remembered Shambhu, the lord who protects *dharma*."'

""Shankara is the one who protects *dharma*. Dharma, who was born from Aja,[719] remembered him in his mind and praised him with many kinds of words. Dharma said, "O lord of *devas*! O Mahadeva! O protector of *dharma*! I prostrate myself before you. O Shambhu! You are the one who engineers creation, preservation and destruction. Brahma

[719] Brahma.

is the creator, Vishnu is the preserver and in the form of Hara, you bring about dissolution. They possess the three *guna*s of *sattva*, *rajas* and *tamas*. O Lord! You are devoid of *guna*s. O Shiva! You are *nirguna*. You are yourself the fourth, superior to Prakriti. You are *nirguna* and without transformation. You are accomplished in many pastimes. Save me. O Mahadeva! Save me. This is a sin that is impossible to traverse. The intelligence of my father and my brothers has turned evil." The supreme lord, Mahesha, was thus praised by Dharma. The one who has an origin in his own *atman*, arrived there quickly, so as to protect Dharma. From the sky, Shambhu saw Vidhatri in that state. In his mind, he laughed at me, Daksha and the others. In mock laughter, he praised all of us and laughed out aloud. O best among sages! Vrishadhvaja shamed us and spoke. Shiva said, "Alas! O Brahma! How has this feeling of desire been generated through seeing your daughter? This is not worthy of those who follow the *Veda*s. A daughter, a sister and a brother's wife are like a mother. Therefore, a learned person should never look at them with evil eyes. This is the determined path of the *Veda*s, which are located in your mouth. O Vidhatri! At the slightest twinge of desire, how have you forgotten that? O Brahma! O one with four faces! Generate fortitude in your mind. O Vidhatri! For some inferior desire, how have you forgotten that? Daksha, Marichi and the others practice *yoga* in solitude and always see Aditya's light. How have their minds become attracted to a woman? Kama is limited in intelligence and doesn't know about the right time. Kama is evil-souled. How has he become so powerful now, using his arrows to cause transgressions? If a person's constant fortitude is disturbed by a beautiful woman and if his mind is agitated and submerged, shame on his learning." Hearing his words, I, who am Shiva's form in this world, was filled with twice the amount of shame. In that instant, I perspired all over my limbs. O sage! I controlled my senses and gave up that transgression. Though I still desired Sandhya, who was the form of desire, I was scared.'"'

'"O supreme among *brahmana*s! From beads of my sweat that fell down on the ground, the category of ancestors known as Agnishvattas were generated.[720] These ancestors had complexions that were like masses of collyrium. Their eyes were like blooming lotuses. They were sacred and complete ascetics. They were supreme and turned away from *samsara*. There are said to be sixty-four thousand of these. O sage! In that way, there are said to be eighty-six thousand Barhishads. From the beads of sweat that fell down on the ground from Daksha's body, a beautiful woman originated. She possessed all the qualities. She was slender in the limbs and symmetrical at the waist. It is said that her body hair was fine. Her body was delicate, and her teeth were excellent. She was as radiant as molten gold. She was beautiful in all her limbs and her face was like a lotus or the full moon. She was famous under the name of Rati, and she was capable of confounding even sages. With the exception of Kratu, Vasishtha, Pulastya and Angiras, all the other six, Marichi and the others,[721] could restrain the functioning of their senses. For these four, their semen fell down on the ground. O supreme among sages! Other categories of ancestors were born from these. They were named Somapas, Ajyapas, Kalinas and Havishmats. All of them are collectively known as Kavyavahas. Somapas were Kratu's sons, Kalinas

---

[720] There are different categories of ancestors, Agnishvatta, Barhishad, Soumya, Ajyapa, Havishmats and Kalinas. For example, Ajyapas accept oblations of *ghee*, Soumyas (Somapas) accept *soma*. While on earth, Agnishvattas did not perform fire sacrifices. Barhishads seated themselves on *barhi* grass. Havishmats accept oblations. *Kavya* stands for oblations to ancestors in general. Kavyavahas are those who convey such oblations.

[721] A list of ten has earlier been given of sages born through Brahma's mental powers.

those of Vasishtha, the sons of Pulastya were spoken of as Ajyapas and Havishmats were the sons of Angiras. O Indra among *brahmanas*! As soon as these categories of ancestors, Agnishvattas and others, were born in this world, they were revered as Kavyavahas. To accomplish this purpose, Sandhya gave birth to the ancestors. Since Shambhu glanced at her, she was freed of taints and devoted herself to tasks of *dharma*. Meanwhile, having shown his favour to all the *brahmanas* and having protected *dharma* in the proper way, Shambhu swiftly vanished. I, the grandfather of the worlds, was ashamed at Shankara's words. With furrowed eyebrows, I looked at Kandarpa in rage. Glancing towards my face, Manmatha discerned my intentions. O sage! He quickly withdrew his arrows. He was also scared of Pashupati. O sage! However, born from the lotus, I was still full of rage. My glance was like a fire that blazes extremely strongly. O supreme among *brahmanas*! "Kandarpa is deluded in his insolence. The fire that originates from Bhava's eyes will burn him down. Mahadeva will perform this extremely difficult deed." In the presence of the large numbers of ancestors and sages who had controlled their *atmans*, this is what Vidhatri said about Kama's destruction. Rati's husband was scared at this and immediately cast aside his arrows. Hearing about this extremely terrible curse, he showed himself. O sage! He spoke to me, Brahma, and my sons, Daksha and the others. He had lost his insolence and Sandhya and the large number of ancestors heard him. Kama said, "O Brahma! Why have you invoked this extremely terrible curse on me? O lord of the world! You follow the path of law and I have not committed any offence against you. O Brahma! I have only undertaken the task you asked me to do. That being the case, this curse is not appropriate. I have done nothing contrary. You told me that you, Vishnu, Shambhu and everyone else would be susceptible to my arrows. I only tested this. O Brahma! I am innocent and I have not committed a crime. O divinity! O lord of the universe! Given the agreement, this curse is terrible." Madana had already controlled himself, but I wanted to subdue him a bit more. Therefore, hearing his words, I, Brahma, the lord of the universe, replied. Brahma said, "There is a reason why I cursed you. Sandhya is my daughter and you ignited desire by targeting her and me. O one who originated from the mind! I have now been pacified and I am telling you that you should give up your fear. Listen to me and be happy. Do not be suspicious. O Madana! The fire that emanates from Bhava's eyes will reduce you to ashes. But he will be swiftly pacified, and you will easily get your body back again, when Hara takes a wife. That is when you will regain your body." I, grandfather of the worlds, thus raised Madana up. As the Indras among sages watched, he vanished. Hearing my words, Madana, and the sons born through my mental powers, were happy. They returned to their own homes.'"

Chapter 56-3.2(4) (Kama's Marriage)

' "Narada said, 'O Vidhatri! O lord who created the worlds! O Vishnu's *shishya*! O immensely wise one! You have narrated something extraordinary, about the *amrita* of Shiva's pastimes. O father! Now please tell me about what occurred thereafter. If I am hearing something about Shambhu's account, I am full of devotion.'"

' "Brahma replied, 'Shambhu returned to his own abode and I, Vidhatri, vanished. Daksha remembered my words and spoke to Kandarpa. Daksha said, "O Kandarpa! She has been born from my body and possesses beauty and all the qualities. Since she possesses qualities that are similar to yours, accept her as a wife. This greatly energetic one will be your companion. Following *dharma*, she will obey you, as you wish." She was born from the beads of sweat on his body. Saying this, he placed her, giving her the name of Rati, in front of Kandarpa. O Narada! After marrying her, Smara was delighted. Daksha's daughter was beautiful, capable of confounding even sages. Madana looked at his own auspicious wife, known as Rati. He was pierced by his own traits and was charmed and delighted with Rati. She was fair and her radiance resembled lightning. She was cheerful and her eyes were like those of a doe. Her sidelong glances were intoxicating. His wife, Rati, was like that. Looking at her eyebrows, Madana was filled with doubt. "Vidhatri has placed these on her so that my bow can be surpassed." O supreme among *brahmanas*! On seeing the swift speed of her sidelong glances, he no longer had any faith in the speed of his own weapons. Her breath was naturally fragrant. On inhaling this, Madana gave up all faith in the Malaya breeze.[722] Madana looked at her face, which resembled the full moon. He noticed the desirable qualities and could see no difference between her face and the moon. Her two breasts were golden, resembling the buds of a lotus. She possessed shining nipples, which seemed to be surrounded by bees. Her breasts were firm and raised. From between the two breasts, an auspicious and slender necklace, marked with signs of the moon, hung down, extending up to her navel. As Kama looked at her limbs, he forgot his own bow made out of flowers, surrounded by swarms of bees. Her navel was deep and was surrounded on four sides by soft skin. He looked at her lotus face, with lips that resembled red fruit. Her waist was slender. Her body was golden and possessed the radiance of an altar. Kama looked at the woman. Her two thighs were soft and delicate, extending like the trunks of plantain trees. Kama looked at her beauty and her strength, resembling his own. The soles and sides of her two feet and her toes were

---

[722] The fragrant breeze from Mount Malaya carries the scent of sandalwood and flowers and kindles love.

tinged with red. Full of love, the one who was born from the
mind looked at her. She was a person who would help him in his
work. There were red nails, resembling *kimshuka* flowers,[723] on
her two hands. Her fingers were round and beautiful, slender at
the tips. Her lovely arms were like a couple of lotus stalks. They
were gentle and soft and possessed the sheen of red coral. Her
charming mass of hair was like blue clouds, resembling the tail
of a *chamari* deer.[724] Such was the radiance of Smara's beloved.
When Ganga flowed from the snow-clad mountains, Mahadeva
accepted her. Like that, with eyes dilated in wonder, he accepted
the woman named Rati. Her beautiful hands held a *chakra* and
a lotus. They resembled the stalks of lotuses. The curves of her
eyebrows seemed to be surrounded by billowing waves. Her
eyes were like blue lotuses, tossed around on the tides of her
glances. Her body hair was like moss along the banks, while her
mind was like the trees along the banks. The lower part of her
navel was like a pond. The beautiful lady was enchanting in all
her limbs. She was the abode of every kind of charm. She was
as beautiful as Rama. She was adorned with twelve ornaments
and possessed the sixteen arts of *shringara*.[725] She bemused all

[723] *Kimshuka* is a tree with orange-red flowers, flame of the forest,
Butea frondosa.

[724] *Chamara* (*chamari* is the feminine) is a kind of deer.

[725] The twelve ornaments probably refer to armlets, bracelets,
necklace, earrings, diadem, finger rings, anklets, ornaments on the
hair, on the waist, on the forehead, on the nose and on the wrist.
Sixteen arts of *shringara* refer to the sixteen steps of beautification—
washing and dressing the hair, an ornament for the braiding of the
hair, the vermilion mark, a *tilaka* mark on the forehead, collyrium
on the eyes, a nose ring, earrings, a necklace, armlets, bangles, the
colouring of the hands, wearing rings on the fingers, wearing a ring on
the thumb, wearing an ornament around the waist, wearing anklets
and wearing toe rings. Though there is agreement on sixteen steps,
drawing on an analogy with the sixteen phases of the moon, the listing
of the sixteen steps isn't consistent.

the worlds and illuminated the ten directions. Madana saw that Rati was like this and was eager to accept her. He was full of love, just as Hrishikesha felt excellent love for Lakshmi. Kama was besotted and forgot about the terrible curse Vidhatri had imposed on him. Therefore, in the midst of his joy, he did not tell Daksha about this. O son! There were great festivities and they enhanced happiness. My son, Daksha, was more delighted than anyone else. Kama obtained great happiness and all his miseries were gone. Rati, Daksha's daughter, obtained Kama and rejoiced. Along with her, Smara was also radiant, like a cloud in the evening, when it is united with delightful lightning. Just as a *yogi* with insight clasps knowledge to his chest, full of delusion, Rati's consort embraced Rati. Having obtained her excellent husband, Rati was also radiant, like Kamala[726] on having obtained Hari. She resembled the full moon.'"'

Chapter 57-3.2(5) (Sandhya's Story)

'Suta said, "The excellent sage heard Brahma's words and rejoiced. Delighted in his mind, he remembered Shankara."'

'"Narada said, 'O Brahma! O Vidhatri! O immensely fortunate one! O Vishnu's *shishya*! O immensely wise one! You have recounted the wonderful pastimes of the one who wears the moon on his head. Having obtained a wife, Madana happily went to his own abode. Daksha went to his own house and so did you, the creator. Your sons, born through mental powers, also returned to their own residences. Where did Sandhya, Brahma's daughter and the mother of the ancestors,

---

[726] Kamala is Lakshmi, so named because she is seated on a lotus.

go? What did she do, and which man did she marry? Please tell me in detail everything about Sandhya's conduct.'"'

'Suta said, "Hearing the words of Brahma's intelligent son, Brahma, who knows the truth, devotedly remembered Shankara."'

'"Brahma answered, 'O sage! Hear everything about Sandhya's auspicious conduct. O sage! Hearing this, all virtuous ladies always obtain everything they wish for. In ancient times, Sandhya was my daughter, born through mental powers. Performing austerities and giving up her body, she was born as Arundhati. The intelligent one was born as the daughter of Medhatithi, best among sages. Following the words of Brahma, Vishnu and Mahesha, she observed vows and obtained the great-souled Vasishtha, praised for his vows, as a husband. She is foremost among those who are devoted to their husbands and obtains a great deal of worship even now.'"'

'"Narada asked, 'How did Sandhya torment herself through austerities? Where and for what purpose? How did she give up her body and become Medhatithi's daughter? What was ordained by the divinities, Brahma, Vishnu and Shiva? How did she obtain the great-souled Vasishtha, praised for his vows, as a husband? O grandfather! Please make me hear all this in detail. I am eager to know about Arundhati's character. Please tell me the truth about this.'"'

'"Brahma said, 'On seeing my own daughter, Sandhya, my mind was quickly enticed by desire. Scared of Shiva, I abandoned her. Agitated by Kama's arrows, Sandhya's mind had also wavered. This also happens to great-souled *rishi*s who have controlled their minds. She heard Bharga's words and the way he laughed at me. She realized that she had wavered and that she had caused offence to the *rishi*s. She had seen how Kama used similar sentiments to repeatedly confound the sages. On seeing this, Sandhya was extremely miserable at the prospect of her getting married. O sage! At the time, I, Brahma, cursed Madana. Shiva left for his own residence, and I also vanished. O supreme among sages! Sandhya was filled with great intolerance. My daughter reflected on this and performed *dhyana*. The spirited one quickly started to meditate on what had taken place earlier. Remembering all this, at the time, Sandhya thought about what should be done. Sandhya said, "As soon as I was born, my father saw my youth and goaded by Madana, was attracted towards me and loved and desired me. Behold the state of the sages born through mental powers. They had cleansed their *atman*s. But on seeing me, they violated the norms, and their minds were filled with desire. The evil-souled Madana managed to agitate my mind as well. Consequently, on seeing all the sages, my mind was greatly agitated. The wicked Madana repeated the fruits of what he himself had done. That is the reason, in front of Shambhu, the grandfather cursed him. I am wicked. I have also committed a crime and must reap the fruits. I wish to quickly find a means to purify myself of those fruits. On seeing me, my father and my brothers were filled with desire. On seeing this, I also desired them. Therefore, since I caused it, I am the greater sinner. On seeing them, I also violated the rules and was filled with desire. I behaved towards my own relatives as I would naturally do towards a husband. Having committed the sin, I must myself perform the *prayashchitta*. I will follow the path of the *Veda*s and offer myself as an oblation into the fire. I alone will establish an ordinance on earth, so that no person with a body is filled with desire immediately on birth. For this purpose, I will torment myself through extremely terrible austerities. I will establish the ordinance. After that, I will give up my body. This is the body, for which, my own father desired me. This was also true of my brothers. There is no need for this body. As a result of this body, my father naturally felt inclinations of desire. Therefore, this cannot be a means for accomplishing good deeds." Thinking this in her mind, Sandhya left for the best of

mountains. She went to the place known as Chandrabhaga,[727]
because River Chandrabhaga is there.'"

"'I got to know that Sandhya had gone there, towards that
supreme mountain. I, Brahma, spoke to my son, Vasishtha, who
had controlled himself through austerities. He was in control of
his *atman*. He knew everything. He was a *yogi* who possessed
jnana. He was accomplished in the Vedas and the Vedangas.[728]
At the time, he was seated near me. Brahma said, "O Vasishtha!
O son! Go to my spirited daughter, Sandhya. She has made up
her mind to perform austerities. Go and initiate her in the proper
way. O supreme among sages! You should pardon the wicked
desire she earlier felt on seeing you. She was filled with desire
towards all of you and towards me as well. That was an act
she had done earlier. It is as if she had done it in earlier life and
after death, has forgotten it. Since she wished to give up her life,
she no longer has such feelings towards any of you. She follows
ordinances and is performing austerities so as to establish an
ordinance. To perform austerities, the virtuous lady has gone
to the mountain known as Chandrabhaga. O father! She does
not know anything about performing austerities. Therefore,
instruct her, so that she can accomplish what she wants. O sage!
Give up this form and assume a different form. Instruct her
about performing austerities. She has seen this form of yours
earlier and might be ashamed. Therefore, you should assume a
different form." O Narada! Out of pity, I instructed Vasishtha
in this way. The sage agreed with what I had said and went to
Sandhya's presence. He saw that divine lake, which was as full
of qualities as Lake Manasa was. Vasishtha saw Sandhya on

---

[727] Chenab. The mountain in question is the Himalayas.

[728] *Vedanga* means a branch of the Vedas, and these were six
kinds of learning that were essential to understand the Vedas—
shiksha (phonetics), *kalpa* (rituals), *vyakarana* (grammar), *nirukta*
(etymology), *chhanda* (metre) and *jyotisha* (astronomy).

the banks of that lake. She was radiant on the banks of that lake, bright with lotuses. It resembled the evening sky when the rise of *nakshatras* has taken place. Seeing her there, the sage was filled with eagerness and good sentiments. He saw the lake, known as Brihallohita.[729] River Chandrabhaga originates from that range and flows towards the southern ocean. The sage went there and saw the summit of that large mountain. The river breaks through the western ridge of the mountain known as Chandrabhaga, just as the Ganga flows from the Himalayas towards the ocean. Vasishtha saw Sandhya on Mount Chandrabhaga, on the shores of Lake Brihallohita."'"

"'"He spoke to her affectionately. Vasishtha said, "O fortunate one! Why have you come to this secluded mountain? Whose daughter are you? What do you wish to do? If it is not a secret, I wish to hear this. Your face has the complexion of the full moon but has no expression." Hearing the words of the great-souled Vasishtha, she looked at the great-souled one, who blazed like a fire. He had matted hair and it was as if the radiance of *brahmacharya* was personified in him. Sandhya lovingly prostrated herself and spoke to the store of austerities. Sandhya said, "The purpose for which I came to this mountain has already been achieved. Please listen to me. O lord! Since I have seen you, from that very sight, success will be ensured. O *brahmana*! I came to this desolate mountain to perform austerities. I was born as Brahma's daughter and am known by the name of Sandhya. If you are interested and if you can tolerate me, please instruct me. This is what

---

[729] Brihallohita means the large Lohita. Though regarded as a tributary now, the Lohita (Louhitya or Lohit) river is identified with the Brahmaputra. The Vayu Purana says that the river Louhitya originates from Lake Lohita, which is at the foot of the mountain known as Lohita or Hemashringa. This is to the south-east of Kailasa. Chandrabhaga actually consists of two rivers, Chandra and Bhaga, both of which have sources near the Bara-lacha la pass.

I wish. There is nothing that is a secret. Without knowing
about the techniques for austerities, I have come to this forest
meant for austerities. Worrying about this, I was drying up
and my mind was trembling." Hearing her words, Vasishtha,
who knew about the *brahman* and had himself accomplished
everything, did not ask anything else. She had controlled her
atman and was ready to embark on austerities. In his mind,
he remembered Shankara, who is affectionate towards his
devotees. Vasishtha said, "He is the supreme and great energy.
He is supreme and great austerities. He is supreme and the
most worthy of worship. In your mind, meditate on Shambhu.
He is the single and original cause for those who seek *dharma*,
artha, *kama* and *moksha*. He alone is the cause of the universe.
Worship Purushottama. O one with an auspicious face! Use
this *mantra* to worship Shambhu, lord of *deva*s. There is no
doubt that through this, you will obtain everything. '*Aum
namah Shankaraya Aum*.'[730] Through this, and using silence,
austerities will commence. Listen attentively to me. Bathing
must be done in silence. Hara's *puja* must be done in silence.
In the first and the second of the six *kala*s in a day, food must
only be in the form of water.[731] One must fast in the third of the
six *kala*s. This must continue until the austerities are over and
the rites must be undertaken at the end of each of the six *kala*s.
This is known as austerities in silence and yields the fruits of
brahmacharya. O lady! This yields everything that is desired.
This is true. There is no doubt that this is the truth. You
should desire to accept this instruction and wish to think about
Shankara. If he is pleased with you, he will soon give you what
you wish for." Vasishtha sat down and told Sandhya about the

[730] 'AUM. I prostrate myself before Shankara. AUM.'
[731] *Kala* means part/portion. Here, the day is divided into six
*kala*s, each lasting for four hours.

rites for austerities. Having explained what was proper, the sage vanished from the spot.'"'

Chapter 58-3.2(6) (Sandhya's Austerities)

' '' Brahma said, 'O noble son! O immensely wise one! Hear about Sandhya's great austerities. If one hears about this, there is no doubt that accumulated sins are destroyed in an instant. Having instructed her about the rites for austerities, Vasishtha returned to his own house. Having learnt about the rites required for austerities, Sandhya was delighted. Her garb was like that of a person who rejoices mentally. On the shores of Lake Brihallohita, she commenced her austerities. As an instrument for the austerities, she used the *mantra* uttered by Vasishtha. Full of devotion, she used that *mantra* to worship Shankara. Single-minded in attention, she performed those great austerities. She thought of Shambhu alone and a cycle of four *yuga*s passed. Shambhu was pleased and content at her austerities. He showed his form to her, inside her and outside in the sky. He manifested himself in the form that she had been thinking about. She saw the lord in front of her, in the form that she had thought about him. Shankara's pleasant face was serene, and she was delighted. "What am I capable of saying? How will I praise Hara?" Full of these great thoughts, she closed her eyes. Though her eyes were closed, Hara entered her heart. He bestowed divine *jnana*, divine words and divine sight on her. She obtained divine *jnana*, divine sight and divine words. She directly saw Durga's[732] lord. She praised the lord of the universe.'"'

---

[732] Durga is Parvati.

""'Sandhya said, "You are without form. You can be perceived through *jnana*. You are supreme. You are not gross, subtle, or high. Internally, *yogis* think of you. You are the creator of the universe. In that form, I prostrate myself before you. You are everything. You are serene. You are sparkling. You are indifferent. You can be reached through *jnana*. You are self-illuminated. You are without transformation. You are spoken of as the road to heaven. You are the path that is beyond darkness. You are pleased. I prostrate myself before that supreme form of yours. You are alone. You are pure. You are radiant. You are without origin. You are consciousness. You are bliss. You are naturally without transformation. You are eternal joy. You are truth. You are prosperity. You are pleased. I prostrate myself before that glorious form of yours. Your form can be thought of as knowledge. You are different from all that is sentient. Your form is the *atman*, and you can easily be meditated on in that way. You are the substance. You are the distant shore. You are the most purifying among those who purify. I prostrate myself before that form of yours. Your form is pure. Your form is agreeable to the mind, adorned with jewels. You are clear and as fair as camphor. In your hands, you hold what is desired, freedom from fear, a trident and a skull. You are full of *yoga*. I prostrate myself before that form of yours. The sky, the earth, the directions, the water, the fire and time are your forms. I prostrate myself before that form of yours. Pradhana and Purusha emerged from your form. But you are not manifest in your form. I prostrate myself before you. O Shankara! I prostrate myself before you. You create as Brahma. You preserve as Vishnu. You destroy as Rudra. I prostrate myself before you. I bow down before you. O cause behind all causes! You are the one who bestows divine *amrita*, *jnana* and prosperity. You are the one who bestows prosperity inside everything. Illumination is your form. You are greater than the greatest. There is no other station in the universe that is superior to yours. The earth, the directions, the sun, the moon, the one born from the mind, space and everything inside and outside originated from your navel. I prostrate myself before that Shambhu. I bow down before you. You are supreme. You are the *paramatman*. Hara is known through all the different kinds of knowledge. You are the truth. You are the *brahman*. You are the supreme *brahman*. You are the object of all reflection. You have no beginning, no middle and no end. The universe originated from you. O divinity! How can I praise the Hara who cannot be approached through words or the mind? Brahma, *deva*s and sages who are stores of austerities are unable to describe his forms. How can he be described by me? I am a woman. O lord! You are *nirguna*. How can your *guna*s be known to me? Indra, the gods and *asura*s do not know your form. I prostrate myself before Mahesha. I prostrate myself before the one who is full of *tamas*. O Shambhu! Please show me your favours. O lord of *deva*s! I repeatedly prostrate myself before you." Hearing her words of praise, Parameshvara was greatly pleased.'"'

'"'Shankara, who is affectionate towards his devotees, was satisfied. Her body had been clad in bark and deerskin, but was now covered in long strands of matted hair that hung down from her head. The auspicious one was radiant. Her face resembled a lotus covered in front. On seeing this, Hara was filled with compassion and spoke to her. Maheshvara said, "O fortunate one! I am pleased with your austerities and supreme praise. O one auspicious in wisdom! Ask for a boon now. Let the boon be anything that is in your mind, anything that accomplishes the purpose. O fortunate one! I will grant it to you. I am pleased with your vows." Hearing Mahesha's words, her mind was pleased. Rejoicing, Sandhya repeatedly prostrated herself before him. Sandhya said, "O Maheshvara! If a boon is to be given to me out of affection, if I am worthy of being given a boon, if I have been purified of that sin and if the divinity is pleased with my present austerities, let the first boon granted to me be as follows. O lord of *deva*s! This firmament is full of desire. But as soon as a being is born, let the being not succumb to it. Let me also choose the boon that no other woman should become, or will ever become, as famous in the three worlds as I am. Let nothing created by me succumb to desire or fall down in any way. O protector! Let my husband be someone who will be my well-wisher. Let any man who looks at me with desire lose his manliness. Let him become a eunuch." Hearing her words, Shankara, affectionate towards his devotees, spoke to her. She had been cleansed of her sins and he was greatly pleased with her. Maheshvara said, "O goddess! O Sandhya! Listen. Your sins have been reduced to ashes. I have cast aside my anger towards you. Because of your austerities, you have become pure. O fortunate one! I will grant you every boon you have asked for. O Sandhya! I am extremely pleased with your austerities, and I will grant you every boon. For any embodied being, the first quarter will be infancy and the second quarter will be childhood. The third quarter will be youth and the fourth quarter will be old age. With these divisions in the lifespan, desire will only surface in the third quarter. In some cases, it will happen at the end of the second quarter. Because of your austerities, I will establish this ordinance in the world. As soon as an embodied being is born, the being will not suffer from desire. You will become a *sati*[733] in this world. No one in the three worlds will be like you or will ever be like you. Without accepting your hand in marriage, if any person looks at you with eyes of desire, he will immediately become weak and impotent. Your husband will be immensely fortunate, possessing beauty and austerities. Along with you, he will live for seven *kalpa*s. These are the boons you have asked from me, and I have granted them to

---

[733] A chaste and virtuous woman, devoted to her husband.

you. I will also tell you about something that transpired in your former life. It has been pledged that you will give up your body in the fire. I will tell you how to ensure this. You must certainly act in this way. The sage Medhatithi is performing a sacrifice that will last for twelve years. He has lit all the blazing fires. Therefore, you must act without delay. In a hermitage of ascetics, on the banks of River Chandrabhaga and in the valley of this mountain, Medhatithi is performing this great sacrifice. Go there easily, without being noticed by the sages. Through my favours, you will become his daughter, born from the fire. If you have ever thought of a desirable groom and husband in your mind, think of him as you give up your own body in the fire. O Sandhya! While you performed those fierce austerities on the mountain, a cycle of four *yuga*s has passed. After *krita yuga* and in the first part of *treta yuga*, Daksha had daughters. They possessed eloquence and good conduct and were married appropriately. He bestowed twenty-seven daughters[734] on the moon. But ignoring the others, Chandra loved Rohini the most. Because of this, Daksha cursed Chandra in rage. At the time, all the *deva*s assembled near you. O Sandhya! However, since your mind was fixed on me, you could not see Brahma and the *deva*s. You regained your sight later. Meanwhile, to free Chandra of his curse, Vidhatri created Chandranadi.[735] At that time, Medhatithi arrived there. There is no one who is his equal in austerities. There has not been nor will there ever be. He is the one who has started the sacrifice, with *jyotishtoma* and other great rites. A great fire has been lit. Give up your own body there. You are extremely pure now and all your desires have been accomplished. O ascetic lady! I have done all this to accomplish a certain purpose. O immensely fortunate one! Go to that great sage's sacrifice and act accordingly."

[734] The twenty-seven *nakshatra*s. Rohini *nakshatra* is Aldebaran.
[735] The moon's river, that is, Chandrabhaga.

Having indicated what was beneficial for her, the lord of *deva*s
vanished from the spot.'"'

Chapter 59-3.2(7) (Arundhati Marries Vasishtha)

" " **B**rahma said, 'O sage! Having granted the boon,
Shambhu vanished. Sandhya went to the place where
the sage Medhatithi was. Because of Shambhu's favours, she
was not noticed by anyone. She remembered the *brahmachari*
who had instructed her about austerities earlier. O great
sage! Following the words of Parameshthi and to instruct
her in austerities, Vasishtha had earlier assumed the form
of that *brahmachari*. In her mind, Sandhya remembered the
brahmana brahmachari who had instructed her in austerities
and accepted him as a husband. A fire had been kindled for
that great sacrifice. Because of Shambhu's favours, she was not
noticed by the sages. Vidhatri's daughter happily entered the
fire and her body immediately merged into the cakes offered
into the fire. She was burnt along with the cakes, her fragrance
unnoticed. Because of Shambhu's instructions, the fire burnt
her body and conveyed it, in pure form, into the solar disc.
To cause pleasure to *deva*s and ancestors, Surya divided her
body into two parts and placed them on his chariot. O lord
among sages! The upper part of her body became the morning
sandhya, placed between night and day. The remaining part of
her body became the evening *sandhya*, placed between day and
night. This always pleases *deva*s and ancestors. Before the sun
rises, but when the sun is about to rise, that period is known
as morning *sandhya* and brings pleasure to *deva*s. When the
sun has set and assumes the tinge of a red lotus, this period is
known as evening *sandhya* and brings pleasure to ancestors.
The protector, Shambhu, is full of compassion. Therefore, he

has given embodied beings her *prana*, her mind and her divine body. When the sacrifice of the sages was over, the sage[736] found this daughter in the middle of the fire. Her radiance was like that of molten gold. Full of joy, the sage accepted this daughter, born from the sacrifice. The sage bathed her and placed her on his lap. The great sage gave her the name of Arundhati. Surrounded by his disciples, he was filled with great joy. She never obstructed *dharma*, for any reason whatsoever. That is the reason she obtained this name, which made her famous in the three worlds.[737] The sage completed the sacrifice successfully and obtained this treasure of a daughter. O divine *rishi*! Along with his disciples and offspring, he reared this beloved daughter in his hermitage. The lady grew up in the supreme hermitage of the sage. It was located on the banks of Chandrabhaga and was known as Tapasaranya.[738] When she attained five years of age, as a result of her qualities, the virtuous one purified Chandrabhaga and Tapasaranya. Brahma, Vishnu and Maheshvara arranged for her marriage with Vasishtha, Brahma's son. The marriage was concluded with great enthusiasm and enhanced delight. O sage! All the gods and sages were filled with great delight. From the water that flowed out of the hands of Brahma, Vishnu and Maheshvara, seven rivers originated, Shipra[739] and others. They are supremely purifying. Arundhati was supremely virtuous, supreme among all virtuous wives. O sage! Having obtained Medhatithi's daughter, Vasishtha became even more radiant. Through her, he obtained auspicious and excellent sons, Shakti and others. O supreme among sages! She obtained Vasishtha

---

[736] Medhatithi.

[737] *Rundhan* is to block. Someone who does not do this is Arundhati.

[738] Literally, forest of ascetics.

[739] Also known as Kshipra.

as her beloved and was radiant. O supreme among sages! I
have thus told you about Sandhya's conduct. This is sacred,
purifying and divine. It yields everything desired as fruits.
If a man or woman listens to this, auspicious in vows, that
person obtains everything wished for. There is no need to think
about this.'"

Chapter 60-3.2(8) (Description of Vasanta)

'Suta said, "Hearing the words of Prajapati Brahma, Narada
was delighted in his mind and spoke."'

'"Narada said, 'O Brahma! O Vidhatri! O immensely
fortunate one! O Vishnu's *shishya*! O immensely wise one! O
Shiva's devotee! You are blessed. You are the one who shows
the path to the supreme truth. You have made me hear this
excellent and divine account and it increases devotion towards
Shiva. You have told me about Arundhati's conduct and
who she was earlier. O one who knows about *dharma*! Now
please tell me about Shiva's sacred and supreme conduct. It
is excellent, destroys sins and bestows all that is auspicious.
Having obtained a wife, Kama was delighted and left. Sandhya
left for austerities and the others also departed. What happened
thereafter?'"

'Suta said, "Hearing the words of the *rishi*, who had
cleansed his *atman*, Brahma was delighted even more and
spoke these words."'

'"Brahma replied, 'O Narada! O Indra among *brahmana*s!
Hear devotedly about his auspicious conduct and about Shiva's
pastimes. Since you serve Shiva, you are blessed. O son! Since I
had also been deluded earlier, I vanished from the spot. Suffering
from the poison of Shambhu's words, I constantly thought
about this. I thought for a long time. My mind was still deluded

by Shiva's *maya*. Because of my jealousy towards Shiva, listen to what I did. I will tell you. I went to the place where Daksha and the others were. On seeing Madana, along with Rati, I felt slightly happy. O Narada! Full of joy, I addressed Daksha and the other sons. Deluded by Shiva's *maya*, I addressed them in these words. Brahma said, "O Daksha! O Marichi and the other sons! Listen to my words. After listening, think of a means to dispel my misery. Just because he saw the desire for a woman, Shambhu reprimanded me and you. He is a great *yogi* and he reprimanded us in many ways. I am tormented by that misery and cannot find the slightest bit of peace. Therefore, we must endeavour to act so that he accepts a wife. When he accepts a wife, I will be happy and will no longer be miserable. But on thinking about it, I arrive at the conclusion that this wish is extremely impossible to accomplish. As soon as he saw that I desired a woman, Shambhu censured me, in front of the sages. How will he accept a wife? Which woman in the three worlds will be fixed in his mind, so that he abandons the path of *yoga*? Who will delude him? Even Manmatha is not capable of deluding him. He is a complete *yogi* and does not tolerate even the name of a woman. Until Hara is pierced by those arrows, this creation will be middling. No one can counter his words. On earth, there are great *asura*s who are bound in *maya*. Some are bound in that created by Hari and some are bound in that created by Shambhu. Shambhu has turned away from *samsara*. That is the reason he has no attachment towards a woman. That being the case, there is no doubt that we can do nothing about the matter." Telling my sons this, I looked at Daksha and the others. Full of joy, I then spoke to Madana, along with Rati. Brahma said, "O Kama! You are foremost among my sons and have brought pleasure in every possible way. O one who is devoted to his father! Along with your wife, now listen affectionately to my words. O one who originated from the mind! With this companion, you are radiant. With

you as a husband, she is also extremely radiant. This is like
Hrishikesha with his wife, Hari with Rama. This is like the
night united with the moon and the moon united with the
night. In that way, placing matrimony at the forefront, the two
of you are radiant. O child! For the welfare of the universe, if
you succeed in deluding the wielder of Pinaka, you will become
the standard of the world and the standard of the universe.
You must act swiftly, so that Shambhu's mind turns towards
accepting a wife. Go wherever he goes, to desolate and pleasant
spots, mountains and rivers. Take her with you and make
efforts to delude Hara, who has turned away from women.
With your exception, there is no one who can delude him. O
one who originated from the mind! When love is generated in
Hara, it is only then that your curse will be pacified. Therefore,
do what is beneficial for you. Bhava Maheshvara, the noble
yogi, will save you only when he desires a beautiful woman and
feels attachment for her. Hence, you must make unmatched
efforts to delude Hara. When you delude Maheshvara, you will
become a standard for the universe." I am his father and the
lord of the universe.'"

""'Manmatha heard my words and spoke to me, the
lord of the universe. Manmatha said, "O lord! I will act in
accordance with your words and delude Shambhu. But where
is the beautiful woman who will be my weapon? O lord! Create
her. When Shambhu is deluded by me, he has to be deluded
by her. O Vidhatri! It is now your task to devise a supreme
means of ensuring this." When Kandarpa said this, I, Vidhatri,
and Prajapati[740] thought about the matter. "Who will delude
him?" As I thought about this, I exhaled my breath. Vasanta[741]
was born from this, adorned with his clusters of flowers. He
resembled a red lotus, and his eyes were like a blossoming lotus.

[740] Meaning Daksha.
[741] Spring.

His face was like the full moon when it rises in the evening. He possessed an excellent nose. His feet were arched, like bows. His hair was dark and curly. He was adorned in a pair of earrings, and he resembled the sun at dawn. His stride was like that of an elephant. His arms were thick, and his shoulders were raised. His throat was like a conch shell. His chest was extremely broad, and his face was round. He was handsome in all his limbs. His complexion was dark everywhere and he possessed all the auspicious signs. He was wonderful to behold and could enchant everyone. He enhanced desire. Vasanta, a store of flowers, was born in this way. A fragrant breeze started to blow, and all the trees were in bloom. Hundreds of cuckoos called sweetly, in the *panchama* note.[742] Lotuses bloomed in lakes and clear ponds. On seeing that this excellent being had originated in this way, Hiranyagarbha[743] addressed Madana in these sweet words. Brahma said, "O Manmatha! He will always be your aide. He will do everything possible to please you. Just as the wind is a friend to the fire and helps in every possible way, he will always be your friend and will follow you. Since he is the cause for residing, he will be known as Vasanta.[744] His task will be to follow you and delight people. *Shringara* will reside in him. The breeze from Malaya will reside in him. He will be your well-wisher in every kind of sentiment and will be under your control. Just as they are your friends, the sixty-four arts, feigned indifference and others, will be

---

[742] The seven notes are *shadaja, rishabha, gandhara, madhyama, panchama, dhaivata* and *nishada,* that is, *sa-re-ga-ma-pa-dha-ni.* Cuckoos are believed to call in the *panchama* note. Other than being the fifth, the *panchama* note is believed to originate from the wind in five parts of the body—navel, thighs, heart, throat and head.

[743] One born from the golden egg, Brahma.

[744] From the root for residing. Presumably, this means the residing of love and desire.

Rati's friends.[745] O Kama! With all these aides, Vasanta being the foremost, along with Rati, make great efforts to delude Mahadeva. O son! After having reflected properly, I will use my mind to attentively fashion the woman who delude charm Hara." Kama was thus addressed by me, the eldest among the gods. He rejoiced, and along with his wife, prostrated himself at my feet. He also prostrated himself before Daksha and all my sons, born through mental powers. Manmatha then went to the place where Shambhu, the *atman*, was.'"'

Chapter 61-3.2(9) (Kama's Powers and His Aides)

‘ ‘‘Brahma said, 'Along with his followers, Manmatha went to Shiva's abode. O lord among sages! Hear about his conduct and the wonderful account. The immensely brave Manmatha, the creator of delusion, went there. With his natural powers, he deluded beings. To delude Hara, Vasanta also exhibited his powers. O sage! All the trees flowered at the same time. Along with the one who originated from the mind, Rati made many efforts. All the beings came under subjugation, but not Shiva, the lord of *gana*s. O sage! The efforts made by Vasanta and Madana were futile. Bereft of his pride, he returned to my abode. He prostrated himself before me, Vidhatri. O sage! Despondent, bereft of pride and in piteous tones, he spoke to me. Kama said, "O Brahma! Shambhu is

[745] Sixty-four arts are mentioned as skills of *kama kala*, such as in Vatsyayana's *Kamasutra* (listed in the third chapter of the first book). These include skills like singing, playing of musical instruments, dancing, writing, drawing, tailoring, cooking, knowledge of languages, solving puzzles and so on.

devoted to *yoga* and cannot be deluded. I do not possess the strength, nor does anyone else, to delude Shambhu. O Brahma! Along with my friends, I made many kinds of efforts. Rati also tried everything. But against Shiva, all those were unsuccessful. O Brahma! O father! O sage![746] Hear about the many kinds of attempts we made to delude Hara. Shambhu was in *samadhi* and had controlled his senses. I tried to agitate Rudra with a fragrant breeze that was cool and forceful. It always causes delusion. I used that against the three-eyed Mahadeva, who was in *samadhi*. I fixed my own five arrows to the bow. Along with my companions, I circled around him. As soon as I entered, all beings came under my control. But along with his *gana*s, the lord Shankara was unperturbed. O Vidhatri! When the lord of *pramatha*s went to the Himalayas, I, Rati and Vasanta also went there. When Rudra went to Meru, Nagakeshara[747] or Kailasa, I also went there. On the occasions when Hara got out of his *samadhi*, I arranged for a pair of *chakravaka* birds[748] to be placed in front of him. O Brahma! I arranged for those birds to repeatedly make gestures with their brows and indulge in many kinds of excellent activities couples engage in. Along with my companions, I placed many kinds of animals and birds in front of Nilakantha Mahadeva, seeking to entice and delude him. Couples of peacocks engaged in such amorous activities, seeking to entice him. They exhibited many kinds of gaits, in front of him and along his sides. My arrows could not find any weakness in him. O lord of the worlds! I am telling you the truth. I do not have the capacity to delude. Vasanta also made efforts to bring about delusion. O immensely

---

[746] Since Kama is speaking to Brahma and not to Narada, this is an inconsistency.

[747] Identified with Mount Naga in the Fergana range in Central Asia.

[748] *Chakravaka* is the Brahminy duck.

fortunate one! Hear about that. This is true. I am telling you the truth. At the place where Hara was, he made many kinds of flowers bloom—*champaka, keshara, bala, karana, patala, nagakeshara, punnaga, kimshuka, ketaki,* fragrant *mallika* and clumps of *kurubaka.*[749] The lakes were filled with blossoming lotuses and Malaya breeze blew. He made efforts to make the hermitage in the mountains very fragrant. Flowering creepers were made to twine around the trees, as if they were resting on the laps of trees, deep in love. On seeing the trees laden with flowers and on inhaling the fragrant breeze, even sages come under the subjugation of desire, not to speak of others. But it is true that no reason for Shambhu's delusion was noticed. Shankara did not exhibit any feeling towards me, not even one of rage. On seeing all this and learning about his sentiments, I will refrain from making any attempt to delude Shambhu. That is what I am telling you. When he gives up his *samadhi,* we cannot remain in the vision of his sight, not even for an instant. We are incapable of remaining there. Who will delude Rudra? His eyes blaze like the fire. With his mass of matted hair, he is fierce. O Brahma! He is like a horned animal. On seeing this, who is capable of standing before him?" I, the four-faced one, heard the words uttered by the one who originated from the mind. Though I wished to, I could not say anything. I remained immersed in thoughts. The one who originated from the mind was incapable of deluding Hara. O sage! Hearing his words, I was filled with great misery.'"

'"From my sighs, many strong beings emerged. As soon as they originated, they lolled their tongues. Those lolling tongues were fearful. All of them played on innumerable musical instruments. There were drums and many other things.

---

[749] *Keshara* (also known as *nagakeshara*) is a flowering tree, *bala* is a kind of jasmine, *karana* probably means *karnora* (oleander), *patala* is rose, *punnaga* is white lotus and *kurubaka* is amaranth.

There was a terrible and loud roar. Emerging from my deep
sighs, those gigantic beings stood in front of me, Brahma. They
said, "Kill. Slice." Hearing their words of "Kill" and "Slice",
addressed to me, Vidhatri, Kama started to speak to me. O
sage! Seeing those many beings, Madana spoke to me. Smara
restrained those beings who stood in front of Brahma. Kama
said, "O Brahma! O lord of subjects! O one who engineered
every kind of creation! Who are these brave ones who have
originated? They are extremely cruel and terrible. O Vidhatri!
What task will they embark on? Where will they be established?
What are their names? Where will they be employed? Please
tell me that. Employ them in your own tasks. Give them a place
to reside in. Give them names. O lord of *devas*! After that,
show me your compassion and assign an appropriate task to
me." O sage! Hearing his words, I, the creator of the worlds,
spoke to Madana and instructed him about his task. Brahma
said, "As soon as they originated, they uttered the word 'Kill'.
Since they repeatedly said this, their names will be Maras.[750]
These beings will always create impediments for creatures. O
Kama! However, since they are addicted to desire, they will
not prevent you from your tasks. O one who originated from
the mind! Their primary task will be to follow you. There is
no doubt that they will always be your aides. Wherever you
go, engaged in your task, they will always go there and act as
your aides. They will cause confusion in the senses and make
people come under the subjugation of your weapons. They will
always impede learned ones who follow the path of *jnana*."
O supreme among sages! Hearing my words, along with Rati
and his great follower,[751] his face turned somewhat cheerful.
Hearing these words, all those beings surrounded me and
Madana on every side. Having surrounded us, each of them

[750] From the root word for killing.
[751] Vasanta.

assumed whatever form he wished. Brahma spoke to Smara affectionately and instructed him. "To delude Hara, go again, along with these aides. Along with these Maras, make efforts to distract his mind, so that Shambhu is deluded and seeks to accept a wife." Hearing these words, Kama spoke to me again. O *devarshi*! Realizing how important this was, he prostrated himself and addressed me in words full of humility. Kama said, "I have already made proper efforts to delude him. O father! However, he was not deluded, and it will not happen now. However, since I think your views are important, I will go there again with my wife and with these Maras. I will follow your command. But I am certain that there will be no delusion. O Vidhatri! I am scared that he will reduce my body to ashes." O lord among sages! Saying this, along with Spring, Rati and the large number of Maras, Kama went to Shiva's abode. As was the case earlier, the one who originated from the mind exhibited his powers. He and Vasanta used their intelligence to devise many kinds of means. The large number of Maras also made diverse efforts. But there was no delusion of any kind in Shambhu, the *paramatman*. At this, Smara again returned to my residence. The large number of Maras had lost their pride. They were depressed and stood there. O son! Having lost his enthusiasm, Kama prostrated himself and stood in front of me, along with the Maras and Spring, all of whom had lost their pride. He said, "O Vidhatri! We made even greater efforts than we did last time. However, he was immersed deep in *dhyana* and there was no delusion. Since he is full of compassion, my body was not reduced to ashes. My earlier good merits may also have been a reason. The lord was indifferent. O one who originated from a lotus! If you wish that Hara should take a wife, you should think of some other means. Having lost my pride, this is what I think." Saying this, along with his companions, Kama returned to his own residence. Smara prostrated himself before me and remembered Shambhu, the one who is affectionate towards the distressed and the one who dispels pride.'"'

Chapter 62-3.2(10) (Conversation between Brahma and Vishnu)

❝❝ Narada said, 'O Brahma! O Vidhatri! O immensely fortunate one! Since your mind is attached to Shiva, you are blessed. You have spoken about the excellent conduct of Shankara, the *paramatman*. Along with those beings and along with Rati, Kama returned to his own residence. What happened then and what means did you resort to? Please tell me that now.'"'

'"Brahma replied, 'O Narada! With a great deal of love, listen to the conduct of the one who wears the moon on his crest. As soon as a man hears about this, he becomes indifferent. With his companions, Kama returned to his own residence. Hear from me about what happened next and about his conduct.[752] O Narada! Having lost my pride, there was great surprise in my heart. My wishes not having been met, my mind was filled with unhappiness. My mind grieved in many kinds of ways. How will he accept a woman? Shankara is indifferent and has conquered his *atman*. He is devoted to *yoga*. O sage! In this way, having lost my pride, I reflected in many kinds of ways. Full of devotion, I remembered Hari. I was born from his body, and he has Shiva in his *atman*. I praised him with auspicious hymns and my words were full of distress. Hearing this, the lord swiftly manifested himself in front of me. He was four-armed, and his eyes were like lotuses. He held a conch shell, a

---

[752] Shiva's conduct.

lotus and a mace. He was clad in dazzling yellow garments and his complexion was dark. Hari always loves his devotees. On seeing him in that form, I repeatedly sought refuge with him. I praised him again, in words full of love. My voice choked with tears. Hari heard the praise and was extremely pleased. He takes away the miseries of his devotees and Brahma had sought refuge with him. He spoke to me. Hari said, "O Vidhatri! O Brahma! O immensely fortunate one! You are the creator of the worlds, and you are blessed. Why have you remembered me now? Why have you praised me? What is the great misery you face? In front of me, tell me now. I will pacify everything. There is no need to reflect on this." Brahma replied, "O lord of *deva*s! O Rama's lord! O one who bestows honours! Listen to my words. Hearing this, show me your compassion. Act so as to take away my grief. I sent Kama to delude Rudra. O Vishnu! He went, surrounded by his companions and relatives, along with the Maras. He made many kinds of efforts, but they were unsuccessful. He is a *yogi* who is impartial in outlook, and he was not deluded." Hearing these words, Hari was surprised and spoke to me. He knows everything and possesses every kind of *jnana*. He is knowledgeable about Shiva's *tattva*s. Vishnu said, "O grandfather! How is it that you developed this kind of inclination? O Brahma! Use your intelligence to reflect on everything and tell me the truth." Brahma replied, "O father! Listen to what happened. Your *maya* deludes everyone and the entire universe succumbs to it. This leads to happiness and misery and everything else. Because of this, I got ready to commit a sin. O lord of *deva*s! Listen to what happened. Following your command, I will tell you. At the beginning of creation, ten sons were born to me, Daksha and others. An extremely beautiful woman was born from my speech. Dharma was born from my chest, Kama was born from my mind and the others were born from parts of my body. O Hari! When I saw the daughter who had been born, I was filled with delusion.

Confounded by your *maya*, I looked at her with a wicked glance. At that instant, Hara arrived there and reprimanded me and my sons. Taking himself to be the supreme lord, he rebuked all of us. He possesses *jnana*. He is a *yogi*. He is the lord of serpents, and he has conquered his senses. O Hari! Even though he manifested himself as my son, he rebuked me to my face. This is my great misery and I have now stated it in your presence. If he accepts a wife, I will be happy and the sorrows in my mind will be destroyed. O Keshava! That is the reason I have sought refuge with you." Hearing the words of Brahma, that is me, Madhusudana laughed.'"

'"'He delighted me by speaking to me, the creator. Vishnu said, "O Vidhatri! Listen to all my words, so that all your confusion is dispelled. This is supreme in meaning and is in conformity with the *Veda*s and the *agama* texts. O Vidhatri! How has this great folly generated in your mind? You are the one who uttered all the *Veda*s. You are the creator of all the worlds. Yet, you have turned evil-minded. Cast off this lassitude. Let your intelligence not be such that your mind is wicked. What do all the *Veda*s say? Who do they praise? With a virtuous mind, remember that. O evil-minded one! You think of Parameshvara Rudra as your own son. O Vidhatri! Though you are the one who uttered the *Veda*s, you have forgotten all *vijnana*. Taking Shankara to be an ordinary god, you hate him. Your good intelligence has left. Instead, evil intelligence has arrived. I will tell you about the truth and the determination. Listen with a virtuous intelligence. He is the one whom the *nigama* texts have described as the true cause of creation. Shiva is the creator of everything, the preserver and the destroyer. He is greater than the greatest. He is the supreme *brahman*. He is the supreme lord. He is *nirguna* and eternal. He cannot be ascertained. He is without transformation. He is the *paramatman*. He is without a second. He does not decay. He is infinite. He is the destroyer. He is the lord who pervades

everything. He is Parameshvara. For purposes of creation,
preservation and destruction, he divides himself into the three
gunas. He is spoken of as Brahma, Vishnu and Mahesha. But
he is beyond sattva, rajas and tamas. He is distinct from maya.
He is accomplished in maya, but he is indifferent towards
maya. He possesses gunas but is independent of them. He finds
bliss within himself. He does not have an alternative. He finds
delight within his own atman. He is without the opposite pair
of sentiments. His excellent image is under the control of his
devotees. He is a yogi who is always engaged in yoga. He is
the one who shows the path of yoga. He takes away pride. He
is the lord of the worlds. He is always affectionate towards
the distressed. Such is the lord, and you think of him as your
own son. Give up such wicked jnana and seek refuge with him.
With all your heart worship Shambhu. That is the way he is
satisfied. O Brahma! If there is a thought in your mind that
Shankara should take a wife, perform excellent austerities.
Remember Shiva. Perform dhyana on Shivaa, with the
objective of accomplishing your desire. If Deveshi is pleased,
every task will be accomplished. If Shivaa assumes gunas and
takes an avatara, if she becomes someone's daughter in this
world, then she will certainly become his wife. O Brahma!
Command Daksha to make efforts to perform austerities with
devotion, so that she is born as his daughter, for the sake of
becoming Shiva's wife. O son! It is well known that both Shiva
and Shivaa are under the control of their devotees. Though
they are forms of the supreme brahman, following their
own wills, they assume gunas and are born." At that time,
addressing me in this way, my lord remembered Shiva, his
own lord. Having obtained his compassion, he obtained jnana
and spoke to me. Vishnu continued, "O Vidhatri! Remember
the words that Shankara had spoken earlier on his own when
we had been born and had entreated him. You have forgotten
all of that. Shambhu's maya is truly blessed. You have been

confounded in every way by that. Other than Shiva, no one can fathom it. Shiva is *nirguna*. But out of his own will, he assumed *guna*s and was born. Through his own powers and in his own excellent pastimes, he created me and you. At that time, Lord Shambhu instructed you to embark on the task of creation. O Brahma! The undecaying and original cause gave me the task of preservation. Having obtained our stations, we bowed our heads and joined our hands in salutation. We said, 'O Sarvesha! You should also assume *guna*s and take an *avatara*.' Thus addressed, the lord smiled and was filled with compassion. The one who is accomplished in many kinds of pastimes was extremely pleased and looked up at the firmament. He said, 'O Vishnu! O Vidhatri! My supreme form will manifest itself from my body and will be famous in the world under the name of Rudra. He is my complete form and must always be worshipped by both of you. He will ensure everything wished for. He will be the lord of dissolution and the controller of *guna*s. Without any differentiation, he will practice excellent *yoga*. All three divinities are my forms. But in particular, Hara is complete. O sons! Uma will also have three kinds of forms. Under the name of Lakshmi, she will be Hari's wife. As Sarasvati, she will be Brahma's wife. In her complete form, she will be named Sati and will become Rudra's wife.' Having shown his compassion and having said this, Maheshvara vanished. We were filled with joy and returned to our respective abodes to engage in our respective tasks. O Brahma! In the course of time, we acquired our wives, but not Shankara. He has himself taken an *avatara* as Rudra and resides in Kailasa. O lord of subjects! Shivaa will also take an *avatara* under the name of Sati. One should devise a means and make efforts so that this task is carried out." Having shown me great compassion and having said this, Vishnu vanished. I rejoiced greatly and my jealousy went away.'"'

Chapter 63-3.2(11) (Durga's Praise and Brahma's Boon)

‘ ‘‘Narada said, ‘O Brahma! O father! O immensely wise one! O supreme among eloquent ones! Please tell me what happened after Vishnu departed. O Vidhatri! What did you wish to do?’’’’

‘‘‘Brahma replied, ‘O noble son of a *brahmana*! Listen attentively. When Bhagavan Vishnu departed, I will certainly tell you what I did. She is pure. She is the form of the supreme *brahman*. True knowledge and false knowledge are in her *atman*. I praised Devi Jagaddhatri[753] Durga, who is always loved by Shambhu. She pervades everything. She is eternal and without a support. She is without agitation. She is the mother of the three divinities. She is grosser than the grossest but is without a form. "O Deveshi! You are consciousness. You are supreme bliss. Your form is that of the *paramatman*. Be pleased with me and accomplish my task. I prostrate myself before you." O sage! In this way, I praised Yoganidra.[754] O *devarshi*! Chandika manifested herself in front of me. She had a beautiful form, with the gentle hue of collyrium. She was four-armed and divine. She was astride a lion and one of her hands was in *varada mudra*. Her hair was adorned with pearls and jewels. Her face was like the autumn moon. The sparking moon was on her forehead. She was three-eyed and beautiful in all her limbs. The nails on her lotus feet were radiant. O sage! I saw Uma, Shiva's Shakti, in front of me. Full of devotion, I lowered my lofty shoulders. I prostrated myself and praised her. Brahma said, "I bow down. I prostrate myself before the one who has the form of *pravritti* and *nivritti* in the universe.

---

[753] The mother of the universe.
[754] The goddess who is the sleep (*nidra*) of *yoga*.

You are the form of creation and preservation. You are the excellent power behind mobile and immobile objects. You are the one who confounds everyone. You are Shri, always a garland around Keshava's image. As someone who holds up the universe, everything is inside you. Earlier, you were Maheshi, the cause behind creation. You are the destroyer of the three worlds. You are beyond the *gunas*. You are the agreeable one who is inside *yogis*. You are the substance in *paramanus*.[755] I prostrate myself before you. You are perceived in the hearts of *yogis*. You manifest yourself in the path of *dhyana* followed by *yogis*. You are illumination, purity and non-attachment. The many kinds of knowledge find a refuge in you. You are hidden and not manifest. Your form is infinite. You are radiant. As time, you pervade the universe. You are responsible for the seed of transformation. You are eternal. But you are also the *gunas* in all kinds of beings. O Shivaa! You are the refuge of the three *gunas*, but you are also beyond them. They are spoken of as *sattva*, *rajas* and *tamas*. But you are without transformation and these three originate in you. In the form of the *gunas*, you are the single cause behind the universe. The *brahman* is inside you. You create, preserve and destroy. You are the seed of the entire universe. You are known as one whose form is *jnana*. You are always engaged in the welfare of the universe. O Shiva's wife! I prostrate myself before you." Hearing my words, Kali, the creator of the worlds, was pleased. The creator and mother of the universe addressed me in words that were like those spoken by ordinary people. Devi asked, "O Brahma! Why have you praised me? Please tell me. If anyone has abused you, please quickly tell me. I have manifested myself in front of you. I will certainly accomplish your objective. Therefore, let me know what you wish, and I will certainly do what you want."''"

---

[755] Atoms.

'"Brahma said, 'Brahma replied, "O Devi! O Maheshani! Listen and take pity on me. You know everything about my wish. Nevertheless, since you have commanded me, I will tell you. O Deveshi! Earlier, your husband, Shiva, manifested himself through my forehead. Known as Rudra, he is a *yogi* and resides in Kailasa. The lord of beings is performing austerities. He is alone and without a second. He is without a wife and is indifferent. He has no second. O Sati! Since he does not look at anyone else, please bemuse him. With the exception of you, no one else will be able to entice his mind. Therefore, assume a form that will bemuse Hara. O Shivaa! Become Daksha's daughter and Rudra's wife. You assume the form of Lakshmi and cause delight to Keshava. For the welfare of the universe, act like that. Merely because I looked at a woman with eyes of desire, Vrishadhvaja rebuked me. O Devi! How will he voluntarily take a woman? If Hara does not accept a wife, how will this auspicious creation continue? He is the cause behind the beginning, the middle and the end. But he is indifferent. That is the reason I am overcome by thoughts. To ensure benefit, there is no other refuge but you. For the benefit of the universe, please go through this hardship. Vishnu is incapable of confounding him, or Lakshmi, or the one who originated from the mind or I. O mother of the universe! There is no one other than you who can do this. O one who is divine in form! O Maheshvari! Therefore, become Daksha's daughter. Because of my devotion, become the wife of the *yogi* and entice Ishvara. O Deveshi! On the shores of the ocean of milk, Daksha is performing austerities. He is firm in his vows and has fixed his mind on you." Shivaa heard my words and started to think. Surprised in her mind, the mother of the universe spoke to me. Devi said, "O one who uttered the *Veda*s! O one who created the universe! This is an extremely great wonder. O one who possesses great *jnana*! O Vidhatri! What is a person like you saying? O Vidhatri! Great delusion has been generated in your mind and that is the cause of misery. Hara is indifferent and you desire to confound him. O Vidhatri! You are seeking a boon from me so as to delude Hara. What gain will occur as a result of this? He is without delusion and without an alternative. Shambhu is spoken of as the supreme *brahman*. He is *nirguna* and without transformation. I am always his servant. I always follow his commands. In his complete form, Shiva has the name of Rudra. Though he is independent, to save the devotees, Parameshvara has manifested himself in this form. Lord Shiva is Hari and Vidhatri. He is not inferior to anyone else. He is lovingly engaged in *yoga*. He is the lord of *maya* but does not succumb to *maya*. He is greater than the greatest. O Brahma! You think of him as a son, as an ordinary god. That is the reason, deluded by ignorance, you wish to confound him. This is the truth. Yet, if I do not grant a boon, there will be deviation from the policy of the *Veda*s.[756] What will I do, so that Lord Maheshvara is not angry with me?" Reflecting this, Shivaa remembered Mahesha in her mind. Having obtained Shiva's permission, Durga spoke to me. Durga said, "O Brahma! Everything that you have said is the truth. Other than me, there is no one in this world who can entice Shankara. If Hara does not take a wife, then eternal creation cannot continue. What you have stated is certainly true. I will therefore make efforts so that Hara takes a wife. O Vidhatri! I will entice him myself. I will assume the form of Sati and remain under his control. I will become his beloved, just as the immensely fortunate Lakshmi is Vishnu's. O Vidhatri! Through his favours, I will make efforts so that he remains under my control. In the form of Sati, I will be born through Daksha's wife. O grandfather! Through my pastimes, I will then serve Shankara. Just as other creatures on earth are subservient to their wives, through my devotion, Hara will also become subservient to a woman."

---

[756] When a boon is sought, it must be given.

Shivaa, the mother of the universe, addressed me in this way. O son! While I looked on, she vanished from the spot. When she had vanished, I, the grandfather of the worlds, went to my own sons and described to them everything that had occurred.'"'

Chapter 64-3.2(12) (Daksha's Boon)

' ' "Narada said, 'O Brahma! O wise one! O unblemished one! O supreme among Shambhu's devotees! You have properly described to me Shiva and Shivaa's conduct. This has done me good, and my birth has been purified. Please tell me now about the austerities Daksha, firm in his vows, practiced. What boon did he obtain from Devi and how did she become Daksha's daughter?'"'

'"Brahma replied, 'O Narada! Listen. You are blessed. All the sages regard you with devotion. I will tell you about how Daksha, excellent in his vows, tormented himself through austerities and obtained a boon. Because of my instruction, the extremely intelligent and great lord, Daksha, controlled himself and started to worship Devi, the mother of the universe, so that his wish could be satisfied. He went to the northern shore of the ocean of milk and fixed her in his heart. Wishing to directly see Ambika, he started to torment himself through austerities. Daksha performed austerities for three thousand divine years. Firm in his vows, he controlled his *atman*. He subsisted on air. He fasted. He subsisted on water. He only ate leaves. He spent his time in this way, thinking of the one who pervades the universe. He spent time in such austerities, devoting to performing *dhyana* on Durga. Excellent in his vows, he followed many different *niyama*s and worshipped Devi. O supreme among sages! Daksha observed *yama* and other rites. He worshipped the mother of the universe and

is the boon that has been granted to you, for every secondary cycle of creation. I will become your daughter and will become Hara's beloved." Maheshani spoke in this way to Daksha, the foremost among the Prajapatis. While Daksha looked on directly, she instantly vanished. When Durga had vanished, Daksha was delighted that she would become his daughter. He returned to his own abode.'"'

Chapter 65-3.2(13) (Daksha Curses Narada)

" " Narada said, 'O Brahma! O Vidhatri! O immensely wise one! O eloquent one! O supreme among eloquent ones! Daksha returned home happily. What happened next?'"'

"'Brahma replied, 'Cheerful in his mind, Daksha Prajapati returned to his own hermitage. Following my command, he undertook many kinds of mental creation. On seeing that his creation of subjects was not being extended, Daksha Prajapati reported this to his father, me, Brahma. Daksa said, "O Brahma! O father! O lord of subjects! O lord! These subjects are not increasing. Everything I have created remains stable. O lord of subjects! What will I do? How can they flourish on their own? Please tell me about the means and there is no doubt that I will create subjects." Brahma replied, "O Daksha Prajapati! O son! Listen to my supreme words and act accordingly. O best among gods! Shiva will ensure what is beneficial. O Prajapati! Panchajana's daughter is beautiful. O lord of subjects! Her name is Asikni.[758] Accept her as your wife. Through the *dharma* of intercourse with a beautiful woman, create subjects

---

[758] Asikni is sometimes known as Virani (Virini), Virana's daughter.

SHIVA PURANA: VOLUME 1

again. Through this method, many beautiful women will be born." Following my command and the *dharma* of physical intercourse, he married Virana's daughter and had subjects through her. Through his own wife, Virini, Daksha Prajapati had sons who were known as Haryashvas. O sage! All these sons were identical in *dharma* and conduct. They were always devoted to their father and followed the path indicated in the *Veda*s. O son! Following the words spoken by their father, so as to create subjects, Daksha's sons went to the western direction to perform austerities. They went to the supremely purifying *tirtha* of Lake Narayana, at the place where the divine River Sindhu has a confluence with the ocean. As soon as they touched the water, their intelligence was kindled. The *dharma* of Paramahamsas[759] completely cleansed their impurities. So as to increase subjects, those excellent ones practiced austerities there. Daksha's sons were firm in their resolve to obey their father and controlled themselves. O Narada! You got to know that they were performing austerities for creation. You went there and repeatedly addressed them lovingly, creating an impediment. "O Haryashvas! O Daksha's sons! Without having seen the world, how have you embarked on this task of creation?" You affectionately told them this. The Haryashvas heard your words attentively. Intent on creation, all of them thought about this a lot. "How can a person understand his father's command if he does not comprehend what the excellent sacred texts say about *nivritti*? Having understood, how can one trust the *guna*s and engage in creation?" Having determined this, all those sons, with excellent intelligence, prostrated themselves before you and embarked on the task of circumambulation. They followed the path of *nivritti*. O sage! O Narada! With your mind fixed on Shambhu, you wandered around the worlds. You were indifferent and your mind was fixed on following Mahesha.

[759] Supreme Hamsas or *sadhaka*s.

A long period of time elapsed and my son, Prajapati, got to know his sons had been destroyed because of what Narada had done. Confounded by Shiva's *maya*, Daksha repeatedly grieved a lot. "Many sons are a reason for sorrow." I went and cheerfully comforted Daksha, my son. I told him about serenity and that destiny was powerful. Comforted by me, through Panchajana's daughter, Daksha had one thousand sons known as Sabalashvas. Obeying their father and firm in their vows, so as to become successful in the creation of subjects, they followed the direction traversed by their brothers. When they touched the water, their sins were destroyed, and they became sparkling. They tormented themselves through great austerities there. They were excellent in their vows and meditated on the *brahman*. O Narada! Knowing that they were about to embark on the creation of subjects, you went there. Remembering the path followed by Ishvara,[760] you repeated your earlier words to them. O sage! Infallible in your insight, you showed them the path followed by their brothers. Those sons followed the path traversed by their brothers and you went upwards. My son, Daksha Prajapati, saw many kinds of evil portents. He was amazed and miserable in his mind. He heard a repetition of what you had done earlier and was extremely sad. He grieved because his sons had been destroyed. As a result of his great misery on account of his sons, he lost his senses. At that time, as an act of destiny and to show compassion towards him, you went there. But angry at you, Daksha addressed you in wicked words. Daksha was overwhelmed by sorrow and his lips quivered in rage. As soon as you approached, he addressed you in shameful and reprehensible words. Daksha said, "O foremost among wicked ones! O one who bears the marks of a virtuous person! What have you done? You have showed my sons the path of a mendicant, one that is not

---

[760] Of indifference.

virtuous. They have not been freed from their three debts.[761] You have created impediments for them, both in this world and in the next one. This is not beneficial. You are cruel and deceitful. Without repaying the three debts, if a man leaves the house, abandoning his father and his mother, and embarks on *sannyasa* in the pursuit of *moksha*, he heads downwards. You are cruel, without any sense of shame. You take away fame from the minds of children. Foolish in intelligence, why do you roam around amidst Hari's attendants? O worst of the worst! You have repeatedly caused me injury. Therefore, as you roam around the worlds, you will never be able to remain stationary in any one place." Though you are revered by the virtuous, in his sorrow, Daksha cursed you in this way. Confounded by Shiva's *maya*, he did not understand Ishvara's desire. O sage! Indifferent in your intelligence, you accepted the curse. All *sadhaka*s who follow the *brahman* accept it in this way and take it on themselves.'"'

Chapter 66-3.2(14) (Sati's Birth and Childhood)

' "Brahma said, 'O divine sage! Meanwhile, knowing about your conduct, I, the grandfather of the worlds, was greatly delighted and swiftly arrived there. As had been the case earlier, I comforted Daksha. Using my discrimination, I attracted his love and made him extremely affectionate towards you. O noble sage! Full of great love, I comforted you, my son who is loved by *deva*s. Having assured both of you, I returned

---

[761] To *deva*s, *rishi*s and ancestors. The first two are respectively paid through worship and studying, the third requires the generation of offspring.

to my own residence. Comforted by me, through his own
wife, Daksha Prajapati had sixty revered daughters, who were
extremely fortunate. Attentive, he married them to Dharma and
others. O lord among sages! I will tell you about them. Listen
with great love. O sage! In the proper way, Daksha bestowed
ten daughters on Dharma. He bestowed thirteen on the sage
Kashyapa and twenty-seven on the moon. He bestowed two
daughters each on Bhrigu, Angiras and Krishashva. The others
were bestowed on Tarkshya. The offspring of these daughters
filled the three worlds. I am scared of describing this in detail.'"

'"'Some say that Shivaa was the eldest, others that she was
in the middle. Still others say that she was the youngest of them
all. All three views are correct in different *kalpa*s. When the
daughters were born, along with his wife, Daksha Prajapati
cheerfully meditated on the mother of the universe. He praised
her in words full of love, his voice faltering. He prostrated
himself repeatedly and humbly joined his hands in salutation.
Devi was delighted at this and reflected in her mind. "So as
to keep my promise, I will take an *avatara* through Virini."
O supreme among sages! Having decided this in her mind,
the mother of the universe told Daksha this and he became
radiant. At an auspicious *muhurta*, Daksha happily deposited
his seed in his wife. Full of compassion, Shivaa started to
reside in the mind of Daksha's wife. All the signs of pregnancy
started to show. O son! Virini became even more radiant and
was happy in her mind. Through the powers of Shivaa residing
within her, she exhibited all the extremely auspicious signs. In
accordance with his lineage, prosperity and the *shruti* texts,
with a lofty mind, Daksha happily performed all the excellent
rites, *pumsavana* and the others. Along with those rites, there
were great festivities. As they desired, Prajapati donated riches
to *brahmana*s. Meanwhile, Hari and the other gods got to
know that the goddess Virini had conceived and were filled
with joy. All of them arrived there and praised the mother of

the universe. They repeatedly prostrated themselves before the one who ensures the welfare of the worlds. Delighted in their minds, they praised Daksha Prajapati and Virini in many kinds of ways and returned to their own abodes. O Narada! Through those nine months, the customary rites were observed. O sage! When the tenth month was completed, Shivaa manifested herself before her mother. The *muhurta* was full of bliss and the moon, the planets and the stars were favourable. As soon as she was born, Prajapati was filled with great joy. On seeing her great energy, he thought that this was indeed Devi. Flowers were showered down from above and the clouds showered down water. O lord among sages! As soon as she was born, the directions instantly turned serene. The gods assembled in the firmament and played on auspicious musical instruments. The fires blazed in serenity. Everything was extremely auspicious.'"

'"'On seeing that the mother of the universe had been born through Virini, Daksha joined his hands in salutation and prostrating himself, devotedly praised her in many ways. Daksha said, "O Maheshani! I prostrate myself before you. O Jagadamba![762] O eternal one! O Mahadevi! O true one! O one whose form is the truth! Please show me your compassion. O Shivaa! O serene one! O Mahamaya! O Yoganidra! O one who pervades the universe! O one who brings about everything that is auspicious! Those who know the *Veda*s speak about you and I prostrate myself before you. Formerly, you are the one who engaged Vidhatri in the creation of the universe, and he always does that. I prostrate myself before the supreme Maheshvari, the mother of the universe. You are the one who engaged Vishnu in the preservation of the universe, and he always does that. I prostrate myself before the supreme Maheshvari, the mother of the universe. You are the one who engaged Rudra in the destruction of the

---

[762] Mother of the universe.

universe, and he always does that. I prostrate myself before the supreme Maheshvari, the mother of the universe. *Sattva, rajas* and *tamas* are your forms and you are the one who always does everything. You are Devi, the mother of the three divinities. O Shivaa! I prostrate myself before you. O Devi! You are supreme. In their *atman*s, there are those who think of you as both *vidya* and *avidya*.[763] Objects of pleasure and emancipation are always in the palms of their hands. O Devi! O Shivaa! Those who directly see you, the purifying one, are certain to obtain emancipation. You are the one who manifests *vidya* and *avidya*. O mother of the universe! Those who praise you as Bhavani, Ambika, Jaganmayi and Durga obtain everything." Shivaa, the mother of the universe, was praised by the intelligent Daksha in this way. She spoke to Daksha, so that her mother[764] could not hear. She confounded everyone else, so that no one other than Daksha could hear. Parameshvari Shivaa told him the truth. Devi said, "O Prajapati! To obtain me as a daughter, you had worshipped me earlier. Your wishes have now been met. Continue with your austerities." Having spoken to Daksha in this way, Devi used her own *maya* and assumed the form of an infant, crying near her mother. Hearing her weeping, the women spoke in agitated tones and full of love and respect, the servant maids arrived there. Seeing the form of Asikni's daughter, all the women rejoiced. All the inhabitants of the city uttered words of "Victory". Along with singing and the playing of musical instruments, there were great festivities. Having seen the auspicious face of their daughter, Daksha and Asikni were filled with joy. Following the norms of his lineage and the *shruti* texts, Daksha performed all the rites. He made donations to *brahmana*s and gave riches to others. As was

---

[763] Respectively, knowledge and lack of knowledge (ignorance).
[764] Virini.

appropriate, there was singing and dancing everywhere. Many auspicious musical instruments were played. Hari and all the other *devas*, along with their companions, and large numbers of sages arrived to join the appropriate festivities. They saw Daksha's daughter, Parameshvari, the mother of the universe. All of them bent low humbly and praised her through auspicious hymns. Delighted, all of them uttered words of "Victory". Rejoicing, they specially praised Daksha and Virini. Following their instruction, Daksha named her Uma. Since she possessed *sattva* and all the other *gunas*, she was praised, and he was filled with delight. Later, the worlds got to know her under other names. Those names bring everything that is auspicious. In particular, they destroy miseries. With his hands joined in salutation, Daksha bowed down before Hari, me and all the immortals and sages. Full of devotion, he praised and worshipped us. At this, Vishnu and all the others praised him. Remembering Shiva and Shivaa, they happily returned to their own residences. The mother purified the daughter in the proper way. Following the norms used for feeding infants, she offered her breasts and other things. The great-souled Daksha and Virini reared her. She grew, like the digits of the moon during *shukla paksha*. O supreme among *brahmanas*! Even when she was a child, all the pure and virtuous qualities entered her, like all the agreeable digits enter the moon. Amidst her friends, she followed her own sentiments and conduct. She would repeatedly etch images of Bharga. As a child, Shivaa sang excellent songs, but always remembering Sthanu, Hara, Rudra, the chastiser of Smara. Every day, the couple found that her unmatched compassion increased. Even in her childhood, she was constantly and repeatedly filled with devotion. As a child, she possessed all the qualities and illuminated her own household. She constantly and repeatedly brought satisfaction to her parents.'"

Chapter 67-3.2(15) (Nanda Vows and Shiva's Praise)

' "Brahma said, 'O Indra among sages! On one occasion, I saw Sati standing next to her father. All the essence of the three worlds was with her. After bowing down to her father, Sati saw us and honoured both you and me. Following the customs of the world, she cheerfully and devotedly prostrated herself. After the prostration was over, Sati saw you, Narada, and I, seated on the seat given by Daksha. I humbly spoke to her. "O Sati! The omniscient lord of the universe desires you and you desire him. Obtain the divinity as your husband. He has not accepted anyone else, he does not accept anyone else and he will not accept anyone else as a wife. O auspicious one! Such a person, without equal, will be your husband." O Narada! Having said this, we again remained in Daksha's residence for a long time. Then, granted permission by him, we returned to our respective abodes. On hearing this, Daksha was no longer anxious and was filled with delight. He thought he had obtained a daughter who was Parameshvari herself. When she was a girl, she engaged in charming pastimes, affectionate towards her devotees. Having voluntarily assumed the form of a human, she passed this stage of being a girl. When childhood was over, Sati was in the early phase of youth. Her body was radiant, and she was enchanting in all her limbs. Daksha, lord of the worlds, saw that she had attained the early stage of youth. He wondered, "How will I bestow this daughter on Bharga?" She also desired that she be bestowed on Bharga. Knowing what her father wanted, she approached her mother. Humble in her intelligence, Sati Parameshvari sought her mother Virini's permission to perform auspicious austerities for Shankara.'"'

""'Sati was firm in her vow that she would obtain Mahesha as a husband. Having obtained her mother's permission, she worshipped him in her own house. In the month of Ashvina, on Nanda *tithi*,[765] she bowed down before Hara and devotedly worshipped him with cooked rice mixed with molasses and salt. She spent the month in that way. On *chaturdashi* in the month of Kartika, she remembered Parameshvara and worshipped him with *apupas* and *payasam*. On *ashtami* in *krishna paksha* in the month of Margashirsha, Sati worshipped Hara with cooked barley mixed with sesamum and spent the days in this way. On *saptami* in *shukla paksha* in the month of Pousha, Sati stayed awake at night and worshipped Shiva in the morning with cooked rice and *krisara*.[766] On *pournamasi*[767] in the month of Magha, she stayed awake in the night. On the banks of a river, wearing wet clothes, she worshipped Shankara. On *amavasya*[768] in the month of Phalguna, she stayed awake in the night and undertook a special worship, offering *bilva* leaves in every *yama*. On *chaturdashi* in *shukla paksha* in the month of Chaitra, day and night, she remembered Shiva and worshipped him with *palasha* and *damana* flowers.[769] She spent the month in this way. On *tritiya* in *shukla paksha* in the month of Vaishakha, Sati worshipped Rudra with cooked rice mixed with sesamum and spent the month in this way. On the night of *pournamasi* in the month of Jyeshtha, she

---

[765] *Tithi*s (lunar days) are divided into five groups—Nanda (1st, 6th and 11th), Bhadra (2nd, 7th and 12th), Jaya (3rd, 8th and 13th), Rikta (4th, 9th and 14th) and Purna (5th, 10th and 15th). Nanda is for happiness, Bhadra for good fortune, Jaya for victory, Rikta for emptiness (for negative acts, like cleansing) and Purna is for completion.

[766] *Krisara* is a dish made out of sesamum and grain.

[767] The day of the full moon.

[768] The day of the new moon.

[769] *Damana* is *Artemisia*.

worshipped Shankara with garments and *brihati* flowers[770] and fasted through the month. On *chaturdashi* in *shukla paksha* in the month of Ashadha, she wore dark clothes and worshipped Rudra with *brihati* flowers. On *ashtami* and *chaturdashi* in *shukla paksha* in the month of Shravana, she worshipped Shiva with sacred threads and auspicious garments. On *trayodashi* in *krishna paksha* in the month of Bhadra, she used many kinds of flowers and fruits to worship and subsisted only on water on *chaturdashi*. She restrained her diet and used many kinds of seasonal flowers and fruits to spend the months worshipping Shiva and performing *japa* on him. On every day and every month, Sati was devoted to worshipping Shiva. Devi, who had voluntarily assumed a human form, was firm in her vows. In this way, completely controlled, she completed the entire Nanda vow. Full of love, Sati's mind was fixed on Shiva and not on anyone else.'"'

'"'O sage! Meanwhile, all the *deva*s and sages, with me and Vishnu at the forefront, arrived to witness Sati's austerities. Having arrived, *deva*s saw Sati, an embodied form of success. She was completely immersed in performing *dhyana* on Shiva, having attained a state of *siddhi*. Delighted, all the gods joined their hands in salutation and bowed down to Sati. The sages bent their shoulders down. Vishnu and the others were delighted in their minds. Vishnu and all the gods and *rishi*s were extremely happy. They praised Sati's austerities and were amazed at it. The sages and gods again prostrated themselves before Sati. They immediately went to the supreme mountain of Kailasa, loved by Shiva. With Lakshmi, Bhagavan Vasudeva happily approached Hara. I also approached, with Savitri.[771] Having gone and seen the lord, with great respect, we prostrated ourselves. Humbly clasping our hands together,

---

[770] *Solanum indicum.*
[771] Meaning the goddess of speech.

we praised him with many kinds of hymns. The *deva*s said, "We prostrate ourselves before Bhagavan, who is everything mobile and immobile. He is Purusha, Mahesha, Paresha, the great *atman*. You are the original seed of everything. You are supreme consciousness. You are the *brahman*. You are without transformation. You are the Purusha who is beyond Prakriti. You are the one who created this universe. You are the one who illuminates it. You are the one from whom everything originated. You are the one in whom everything is established. You are the one who controls everything. You are superior to all this. You are supreme and indifferent. You are the great lord. You see all this within your own *atman*. We bow down before that Svayambhu. Your vision is not impeded. You are the supreme witness. You are in all *atman*s. You have many different kinds of forms. You are supreme *brahman*. It is your *atman* that heats. We seek refuge with you. *Deva*s, *rishi*s and *siddha*s do not know about his state. How are other beings worthy of knowing him or understanding him? Greatly virtuous people attached to emancipation wish to see his state. Those unblemished ones observe the vow of *salokya*, so that they can obtain that excellent destination. There is nothing that leads to misery there, birth and other transformations. However, in your *maya*, you accept all these and show compassion towards them. We prostrate ourselves before Paresha, who is extraordinary in his deeds. We prostrate ourselves before the *brahman*, the *paramatman* who cannot be approached through words. You are without form. You possess a pervasive form. You are supreme and infinite in your potency. You are the lord of the three worlds. You are a witness to everything. You go everywhere. We prostrate ourselves before the one whose *atman* provides the illumination. You are *nirvana*, bliss and prosperity. *Jnana* is in your *atman*. We prostrate ourselves before the pervasive Ishvara. When one ceases to perform *karma*, you are easily obtained. We prostrate ourselves before the lord of *kaivalya*. We prostrate ourselves before the eternal Purusha Paresha. *Kshetrajna* is a form of your *atman*.[772] You are the cause behind every kind of perception. You are the great one who controls everything. We prostrate ourselves before the foundation of Prakriti. We bow down before the eternal Purusha Paresha. We prostrate ourselves before the three-eyed and five-faced one who is always illuminated. You are the witness to all the senses and the *gunas*. We prostrate ourselves before the one who is without a cause. We bow down to the one who is the cause of the three worlds. We prostrate ourselves before the one who bestows emancipation. O one who swiftly bestows emancipation! O one who saves those who seek refuge! O one who is an ocean of learning of all the *agama* texts! O Parameshthi! O destination of devotees and *gunas*! We prostrate ourselves before you. You are the heat that is latent in the *arani* of the *gunas*. O Maheshvara! We prostrate ourselves before you. O one whose form is impossible for the foolish to reach! O one who is always there in the hearts of the learned! O one who frees animals from the noose! O one who bestows emancipation on devotees! O self-illuminated one! O eternal one! You are infinite in your learning. O one without decay! O one who is the complete witness! You are without transformation. You are the foundation for supreme prosperity. There are those who pursue the four *purusharthas*. There are those who desire a virtuous end. Please show them your compassion. O Bhava! We prostrate ourselves before you. Show us your favours. Your devotees desire you alone and nothing else. They only sing about your supremely auspicious conduct. You are without decay. You are the supreme *brahman*. You are the lord whose form is not manifest. You are complete

---

[772] *Kshetra* is the physical body, *kshetrajna* is one who knows about the *kshetra*, that is, the *atman*.

and can be reached through the *yoga* of *adhyatma*.[773] We praise
you. You are beyond the senses. You are without support. You
are the cause and support everything. You are infinite. You
are the original. You are subtle. We prostrate ourselves before
the lord of everything. Hari and all the other *deva*s, the worlds
and mobile and immobile objects possess slight differences in
names and forms but have all been created as your portions.
This is said to be like flames from the fire or rays from the sun
emerging, residing and disappearing. All these flows are minor.
You are not a *deva*. You are not an *asura*. You are not a mortal.
You are not inferior species. You are not a bird. O lord! You
are not a man or a woman. You are not a eunuch. You are
nothing existent or non-existent. You are what remains after
all this has been negated. You create the universe. You preserve
the universe. You dissolve the universe. The universe is your
atman. We prostrate ourselves before that Ishvara. *Yogi*s who
have restrained *karma* through *yoga* see you, because their
consciousness has been purified through *yoga*. O lord of *yoga*!
We bow down before you. We prostrate ourselves before the
one whose force is impossible to withstand. You are the three
Shaktis. The three are in you.[774] We prostrate ourselves before
the pleasant one who preserves. We prostrate ourselves before
the one who is infinite in potency. O Ishana! The wicked senses
find it impossible to reach you. You are beyond all paths. You
are engaged in saving your devotees. We prostrate ourselves
before the one whose rays are hidden. According to capacity,
we meditate on your *atman*. Enough. Those with foolish
intelligence cannot know you. Your greatness cannot be
surpassed. We prostrate ourselves before you, the great lord."

---

[773] Transcendental knowledge about the *paramatman* and the
jivatman.
[774] The three are Brahma, Vishnu and Rudra and the three Shaktis
are Sarasvati, Lakshmi and Uma.

In this way, Vishnu and all the other gods praised Mahadeva. With their shoulders lowered in virtuous devotion before the lord, they then remained silent.'"'

Chapter 68-3.2(16) (Brahma and Vishnu Pray to Shiva)

‘ ‘‘Brahma said, 'Shankara heard the praise uttered by Hari and the others. The origin of creation was pleased and smiled. Hara saw that Brahma and Vishnu had arrived, along with their wives. He addressed them in the appropriate way and asked them about the reason why they had come. Rudra said, "O Hari! O Vidhatri! O *devas*! O sages! O sons! Without any fear, tell me the true reason for your arrival here. Why have you come here? What task must be accomplished now? I wish to hear everything. My mind has been pleased at your praise." O sage! Thus asked and goaded by Vishnu, I, the grandfather of all the worlds, addressed Mahadeva. "O lord of *devas*! O Mahadeva! O ocean of compassion! O lord! Please listen to the reason why we have come here, along with the gods and the *rishi*s. O Vrishadhvaja! There is a special reason for our arrival and praise. We seek the appropriate help from you. Otherwise, all will not be well with the universe. O Maheshvara! Some *asura*s must be killed by me, some must be killed by Hari and there are others who have to be killed by you. O great lord! Some will be killed by the son who results from your seed. There will be *asura*s who can only be killed through *maya*. O Shambhu! Hence, the gods can obtain ultimate happiness only through your favours. Until all the terrible *asura*s are destroyed, the welfare of the universe will always be subject to fear. You are always engaged

in *yoga*, devoid of attachment and hate. Thus, since they are
the subjects of your compassion, some can never be killed by
you. O Vrishadhvaja! O Isha! Until they are restrained, how
can the equilibrium of creation, preservation and destruction
be constantly maintained? It will always be unstable. The tasks
of creation, preservation and destruction are carried out by us.
That there is no difference in our forms can only be perceived
by those who are free from *maya*. We are one in form. The
differences only because there are differences in the tasks. Had
a difference in tasks not existed, there would have been no
need for differences in forms. The *paramatman*, Maheshvara,
is one, but divides himself into three. The reason behind this is
maya. The lord is independent in his pastimes. Hari was born
from his left side, I from the right. You were born from Shiva's
heart and are Shiva's complete form. We thus originated in
three forms and our powers and forms are different. O eternal
one! You know in your heart that we are the sons of Shiva
and Shivaa. To perform our tasks, Vishnu and I were born
along with our wives. O lord! Following your command, we
are engaged in performing our tasks for the worlds. For the
welfare of the universe and to ensure the happiness of the gods,
you should accept a beautiful and auspicious lady as your wife.
O Mahesha! Please listen to something else. I have remembered
what transpired earlier. In ancient times, in your form as Shiva,
you yourself told us this. 'O Brahma! This is my supreme form,
and it will manifest itself from your body. It will be known in
the worlds under the name of Rudra. Brahma will carry out the
task of creation. Hari will carry out the task of preservation. In
the form of Rudra, I will assume *guna*s and will carry out the
task of dissolution. I will carry out the excellent task carried
out in the worlds of taking a woman as a wife.' I have thus
remembered what you yourself said. Now please fulfil your
pledge. O lord! It was your instruction that I should be the
creator. Hari will be the one who preserves. To carry out

dissolution, Shiva himself has manifested through your form. Without you, we are incapable of carrying out our respective tasks. We carry out our tasks for the worlds. But you are alone. Please accept a woman. The one who resides on the lotus is Vishnu's companion and Savitri is mine. O Shambhu! In that way, accept a beloved now." Hearing the words spoken by me, Brahma, in front of Hari, Hara, the lord of the worlds, had a smile on his face.'"

"'Ishvara said, "O Brahma! O Hari! I always love you the most. Indeed, on seeing you, I have been filled with joy. The two of you are distinguished among the gods and are indeed the lords of the three worlds. Since you are engaged in Bhava's tasks, what you have said is important. O best among the gods! However, it is not appropriate for me to marry. It is known that I am a *yogi* who is indifferent, always engaged in *yoga*. I follow the virtuous path of *nivritti*. I find delight in my own *atman* and am without blemish. I possess the body of an *avadhuta*.[775] I possess *jnana*. I am myself the witness and am devoid of desire. I am without transformation, never enjoying objects of pleasure. I am always regarded as impure and inauspicious. That being the case in the world, what need do I have of a woman? Please tell me. I am only immersed in *yoga*. I always experience bliss. A man devoid of *jnana* desires many things. In the world, it is known that marriage is the reason for a great bondage. Therefore, I have no inclination towards it. This is true. I am telling you the truth. I have no interest in *pravritti*. But I have thought about this, without any selfish motive. Therefore, for the welfare of the universe, I will do what you have said. I think your words are weighty. In addition, I must fulfil my pledge. Since I am always controlled

---

[775] An *avadhuta* is an ascetic who has renounced all worldly attachments. However, it also has the nuance of someone who has been cast off from society and has been excluded by it.

by my devotees, I will marry. O Hari! O Brahma! However, in conformity with my pledge, hear about the kind of woman I will accept. This is in accordance with my words. She must be capable of accepting parts of my energy. For the sake of a wife, please indicate a *yogini* whose form is desirable. She must be a *yogini* and must be united with me in *yoga*. She must be a desirable woman who engages in acts of desire with me. Shiva is without decay. Learned ones who know the *Vedas* describe him as one whose form is energy. They think about that eternal one. When I immerse myself in thinking about the *brahman*, the beautiful lady must not be a cause for any impediments and must not destroy the meditation. You, Vishnu and I are portions of Shiva, whose form is the *brahman*. We are extremely fortunate, and it is appropriate that we should meditate on him. O one who resides on a lotus! It is because I have thought about this that I have stayed away from marriage. Therefore, tell me about a wife who will always follow what I practice. O Brahma! There is yet another part of my pledge that you must hear about. If she does not trust me, or trust what I say, I will abandon her." Hearing the words spoken by Hara, Vishnu and I smiled and were delighted in our minds. I humbly replied, "O lord! O Mahesha! Following the path indicated by you, I will happily tell you about such a woman. O lord! She is Uma. To accomplish the task, she has been born in a different form. O lord! In ancient times, she divided herself into two, as Sarasvati and Lakshmi. The beautiful Padma[776] is to Vishnu what Sarasvati is to me. To ensure the welfare of the worlds, she has now assumed a third form. O lord! She has been born as Daksha's daughter and her name is Sati. She will be an appropriate wife for you, and she will ensure your welfare. O lord of *devas*! For your sake, firm in her vows, she is tormenting herself through austerities. She desires to obtain

[776] One seated on a lotus, Lakshmi.

you as a husband. Sati is great in her energy. O Maheshvara! Show your compassion towards her. Go and grant her the boon. Full of affection, grant her the boon and marry her. She is appropriate. O Shankara! Hari, I and all *deva*s also desire this. Satisfy our wishes and let us lovingly witness the festivities. This will be extremely auspicious for the three worlds and will bring about happiness. There is no doubt that it will dispel every kind of anxiety that anyone suffers from." After my words were over, Achyuta Madhusudana spoke to Ishana, who is affectionate towards his devotees and assumes different forms in his own pastimes. Vishnu said, "O lord of *deva*s! O Mahadeva! O Shankara! O reservoir of compassion! There is no doubt that what Brahma has said represents everything that I have to say. O Mahesha! Show your compassion towards me and act accordingly. Cast a favourable glance towards the three worlds and be its protector. Marry her." O sage! After saying this, the intelligent Bhagavan Vishnu was silent. The lord, who is affectionate towards his devotees, smiled as a result of this praise. He agreed. Having obtained his permission, the sages and gods and both of us were greatly delighted. Taking leave of Isha, we departed, along with our wives.'"'

Chapter 69-3.2(17) (Sati Gets the Boon)

' "Brahma said, 'I have thus told you how all *deva*s exhibited their supreme devotion towards Shambhu. O sage! Now hear lovingly to how Shivaa obtained a boon. On *ashtami* in *shukla paksha* in the month of Ashvina, Sati fasted again. She devotedly worshipped the lord of everything. The Nanda vow was completed in this way and the day of *navami* arrived. As she was immersed in *dhyana*, Hara manifested himself before her. He was handsome in all his limbs and fair

in complexion. He had five faces and three eyes. The moon
was on his crest, and he had a pleasant appearance. He was
blue in the throat and had four arms. He held a trident and the
brahman was in him. His hands were in the *varada* and *abhaya*
*mudra*s. He was smeared in ashes and radiant. The celestial
river dazzled on his head. He was handsome in all his limbs.
He was the embodiment of great grace. His face resembled one
crore moons. His beauty was like that of one crore Smaras
taken together. His form was such that it was agreeable in
every possible way to women. Sati saw her beloved lord, Hara,
in front of her. She worshipped his feet and lowered her face
in bashfulness. Mahadeva spoke to Sati, who had observed the
virtuous vow. He desired her as a wife and wished to bestow on
her the fruits of her austerities. Mahadeva said, "O Daksha's
daughter! O one who is excellent in vows! I am pleased with
your vows. Please ask for a boon. I will grant you whatever
is your wish." Mahadeva, the lord of the universe, knew her
sentiments. Nevertheless, because he wished to hear her words,
he asked her to ask for a boon. However, she was embarrassed
and was incapable of stating what was in her heart. She tried
to express her wish but was again enveloped in shame. Though
she heard Shiva's beloved words, she was overwhelmed by
love. Understanding this, Shankara, affectionate towards his
devotees, was pleased. He again quickly said, "Ask for a boon.
Please ask for a boon." Since Shambhu knew about Sati's
devotion and virtuous inner sentiments, he was attracted to
her. After making efforts to suppress her shame, Sati spoke
to Hara. "O one who bestows boons! Please grant me the
boon I desire, without any impediments."[777] Vrishadhvaja is
affectionate towards his devotees. Therefore, without waiting
for her to finish her words, he told her, "Be my wife." Hearing

---

[777] The word *vara* means boon, as well as groom. Hence,
implicitly, Sati asked for the groom of her choice.

these words, which were the substance of her desired fruits and thoughts, she was silent. But she was delighted at having obtained her desired boon. The one with the beautiful smiles stood in front of Hara, who was filled with love. She expressed her sentiments through gestures, and these served to increase desire. *Shringara rasa* gathered together all these sentiments and swiftly entered their hearts. O *devarshi*! As soon as it entered, they followed the pastimes of ordinary people and glowed, like the conjunction between Chitra *nakshatra* and the moon.[778] Having obtained Hara, Sati was radiant, with a gentle glow, like that of a mass of collyrium. She sparkled like crystal and resembled a line of clouds near the moon. Dakshayani[779] repeatedly spoke to Hara, who is affectionate towards his devotees. She was pleased. She joined her hands in salutation and lowered her head. Sati said, "O lord of *devas*! O Mahadeva! O lord! O lord of the universe! Informing my father, please follow the rites and accept me in marriage." Mahesha is affectionate towards his devotees. Hearing Sati's words, he looked at her with eyes full of love and agreed. Knowing this, Dakshayani devotedly bowed down before Shambhu. Having obtained his permission, with an enchanting gait and full of joy, she returned to her mother.'"'

'"'Hara returned to his hermitage on the plains of the Himalayas. Since he was separated from Dakshayani, with difficulty, he devoted himself to *dhyana*. Having composed his mind, Shambhu Vrishadhvaja thought of following the customary practices of the world. O *devarshi*! He mentally thought of me. Mahesha, the wielder of the trident, thought of me. As soon as he thought of me, goaded by the urge to

---

[778] On the night of the full moon in the month of Chaitra, the moon transits through Chitra *nakshatra* (Spica). The word 'Chitra' means the bright one.

[779] Daksha's daughter.

ensure Hara's success, I quickly presented myself in front
of him. Hara, the *yogi*, was on the plains of the Himalayas.
O son! Along with Sarasvati, I presented myself there. O
devarshi! The lord saw me, along with Sarasvati. Since he
was bound in love to Sati, Shambhu was eager and spoke.
Shambhu said, "O Brahma! In the matter of marriage, I have
shown a selfish motive. Because of that selfishness, a sense of
ownership manifests itself before me now. Sati Dakshayani has
devotedly worshipped me. Because of the powers of the Nanda
vow, I have bestowed a boon on her. O Brahma! She asked me
for the boon that I should be her husband. Satisfied in every
possible way, I told her that she would be my wife. At this, Sati
Dakshayani told me, 'O lord of the universe! Accept me after
informing my father.' O Brahma! Satisfied with her devotion,
I pledged that I would do this. O Vidhatri! She returned to
her mother, and I have come here. Therefore, follow my
instructions and go to Daksha's residence. Tell Daksha that
he should bestow his daughter on me. Do everything so that I
am no longer separated from Sati. O one who is accomplished
in every kind of knowledge! Assure Daksha." Having said this
in the presence of me, the Prajapati, Mahadeva quickly looked
at Sarasvati. He was suffering from the pangs of separation.
Thus commanded by him, I had become successful in my
objective and was happy. I replied to the lord of the universe,
who is affectionate towards his devotees. Brahma said, "O
Bhagavan Shambhu! O Vrishadhvaja! After due reflection, it
has been determined that what you have said is the primary
interest of *deva*s, and mine too. Daksha will himself bestow his
daughter on you. In his presence, I will tell him what you have
said." Having told this to Mahadeva, the lord and master of
everything, on a swift chariot, I went to Daksha's residence.'"

'"Narada asked, 'O Vidhatri! O wise one! O immensely
fortunate one! O eloquent one! O supreme among eloquent
ones! After Sati returned home, what did Daksha do?'"'

'"Brahma replied, 'Having tormented herself through austerities, Sati obtained her desired boon. Returning home, she prostrated herself before her father and her mother. Her friends told her father and mother everything, about how Maheshvara had been satisfied at Sati's devotion and how he had bestowed a boon on her. Through the mouths of the friends, her mother and father heard everything. They were filled with supreme joy and organized great festivities. Generous of mind, they gave desired objects to *brahmanas*. Great-minded Virini donated to others, the blind and the distressed. Virini embraced her daughter, who had enhanced their delight. She happily inhaled the fragrance of her head and repeatedly praised her. After some time had passed, Daksha, supreme among those who knew about *dharma*, wondered about how his daughter might be bestowed on Shambhu. "Pleased, Mahadeva had come here. But he has returned. For the sake of my daughter, how might he be brought back again? Can I easily send someone to Shambhu? That is not right. If he refuses, I will suffer the pangs of failure. Alternatively, shall I worship Vrishadhvaja? He has himself been satisfied with my daughter's devotion. She made efforts to worship him and obtain what she desired. Shambhu has given her the boon that he will be her husband." As Daksha was thinking this, I suddenly presented myself in front of him, along with Sarasvati. Seeing me, his father, Daksha prostrated himself and stood there. As is natural, he offered me an appropriate seat. Though Daksha was overcome with thoughts, he was happy and quickly asked me, the lord of all the worlds, the reason why I had arrived there. Daksha asked, "O creator! Why have you come here? O *guru* of the universe! Is it that you are showing me your great favours? O creator of the worlds! It is out of affection towards your son? Please tell me. Is there some other reason behind your coming to my residence? I am delighted to see you." O supreme among sages! My son,

Daksha, asked me this. I smiled and addressed Prajapati in
words that delighted him. Brahma said, "O Daksha! Listen
to the reason why I have come to you. I desire your benefit
and it is something I want too. Your daughter has worshipped
Mahadeva, the lord of the universe. The time has arrived to
implement her desired boon. It is certain that Shambhu has
sent me here, for the sake of your daughter. I will present
before you the course of action that is best for you. Listen.
Having bestowed the boon, Rudra has left. However, since
he left, because of separation from your daughter, Shankara
has not been able to find any peace. Though he made repeated
efforts with every kind of flowery arrow, Madana did not
find a weakness in Girisha. However, having now been
pierced by Kama's arrows, he has abandoned thinking about
the *atman*. Like an ordinary person, he is agitated, thinking
about Sati. Separated from her, he forgets himself and utters
words in front of his *gana*s. 'Where is Sati?' They tell him that
she is not there. O son! Earlier, this is what I, you, Madana
and Marichi and other great sages desired. That objective
has now been accomplished. Your daughter has worshipped
Shambhu. He resides in the Himalaya mountains, thinking
about her, searching for her and desiring her. Full of *sattva*,
she worshipped him through many kinds of vows. Just as
Sati worshipped Shambhu, he worships her now. Daksha's
daughter has been intended for Shambhu. Therefore, without
any delay, one must accomplish the objective and bestow
her on him. Using Narada, I will have him brought to your
residence. She was intended for him. Bestow her on him."
Hearing my words, my son rejoiced. Filled with joy, Daksha
uttered words of assent. O sage! I happily went to the place
where Girisha was, eager to follow the practices of the world.
Narada also went there. Daksha, his wife and daughter
obtained their wishes. It was as if they had been filled with
nectar.'"

Chapter 70-3.2(18) (Bestowing of the Daughter)

" "Narada asked, 'What occurred after you went to Rudra? O father! What did you tell him? What did he himself do?' "

" 'Brahma replied, 'With a happy mind, I went to Parameshvara, who was then residing in the Himalaya mountains. I wanted to bring Mahadeva. Vrishadhvaja saw that I, the creator of the worlds, was approaching. His mind was filled with repeated doubts about whether he would get Sati. In his pastimes, Hara had happily assumed the ordinary conduct of people. As a result of Sati's devotion, he quickly spoke to me, like an ordinary person. Ishvara said, "O best of the gods! What has your son done about bestowing Sati on me? Tell me. Otherwise, Manmatha will shatter my inside. O best of the gods! This pang of separation from Sati rushes and strikes me alone. It does not touch her; she still sustains her life. O Brahma! Tell me what I must do. O Vidhatri! Sati is always present. There is no difference between her and me. Tell me what must be done to get her." I heard Rudra's words, which were deeply in conformity with customary conduct. O Narada! O sage! I spoke to Shiva and comforted him. Brahma answered, "O Vrishadhvaja! Hear what my son has said about Sati. Understand that whatever you wanted to achieve has been accomplished. 'My daughter will be bestowed on him. It is for him that she has been born. That is my desire and your words have reinforced it. In addition, my daughter has herself worshipped Shambhu for this purpose alone. He is asking for me for the one whom I must bestow on Hara. Let him come to me at an auspicious *lagna*[780] and excellent *muhurta*. O Vidhatri!

---

[780] *Lagna* is the specific *rashi* (zodiacal sign) which is on the horizon at that time.

When Shambhu comes and asks me for alms, I will give my daughter to him.' O Vrishadhvaja! Daksha spoke to me in this way. At an auspicious *muhurta*, go to his house and bring her here." O sage! Rudra, affectionate towards his devotees, was following the conduct of ordinary people. He heard my words, smiled and answered. Rudra said, "Along with you and Narada, I will go to his house. O creator of the universe! Therefore, you and I should remember Narada. Also remember your own sons born through mental powers, Marichi and the others. O Vidhatri! Along with them and the *gana*s, I will go to Daksha's abode." Devoted to the conduct of ordinary people, this is the way Isha instructed me. I remembered you, Narada and Marichi and the other sons. As soon as I remembered, you and all the sons born through mental powers swiftly arrived and were happy to see me. As soon as Rudra remembered, Vishnu, king among Shiva's devotees, swiftly arrived. He was astride Garuda and was accompanied by Kamala and his own soldiers. It was *shukla paksha* in the month of Chaitra. The divinity of the *nakshatra* was Bhaga.[781] As soon as the sun arose on *trayodashi*, Maheshvara left. All the large number of gods were with him, Brahma and Vishnu leading the way. Shankara left along with the sages and was resplendent along the path. As he left, *deva*s and others arranged for festivities along the way. The minds of Hara's *gana*s were filled with joy and they also did this. Obeying Shiva's wishes, all his appropriate ornaments went with him—the hides of an elephant and a tiger, the snakes, his matted hair and the crescent moon. With Vishnu leading the way and on his powerful bull, Hara, the *yogi*, reached Daksha's residence in a short while. Daksha's body hair stood

---

[781] The *nakshatra* was Uttara Phalguni (Denebola). *Nakshatra*s have divinities associated with them and that for Uttara Phalguni is Bhaga. The names of these divinities used to be the former names of the *nakshatra*s.

up in delight. Along with all his own relatives, he humbly arrived and welcomed him. Daksha himself honoured the large number of gods. In due order, the best among sages were seated along the side. Daksha invited Shiva inside the house, along with all his companions, the gods, the *gana*s and the sages. Pleased in his mind, Daksha himself offered Sarveshvara Hara an excellent seat, following the norms and honouring him. Full of devotion and observing the appropriate norms, he worshipped Vishnu, me, the *brahmana*s, the gods and all the *gana*s. Daksha worshipped them in the appropriate way, using objects of worship and in front of the assembled mental sons, made the announcement. After this, my son, Daksha, happily looked at me, his father. He prostrated himself and said, "O lord! It is your task to conduct the marriage ceremony." Delighted in my mind, I agreed. Thereafter, we arose and conducted all the rites, when the *muhurta* was auspicious and the *lagna* was such that the planets were powerful. Full of joy, Daksha bestowed his daughter Sati on Shambhu. Following the norms of marriage, Vrishadhvaja happily accepted the hand of Dakshayani, whose limbs were beautiful. I, Hari, you, the gods, the sages and the *gana*s prostrated ourselves and praised and satisfied the lord of the gods. There were great festivities, accompanied by singing and dancing. All the sages, *gana*s and gods were filled with great joy. Daksha, my son, was successful in the bestowing of his daughter. Shiva and Shivaa were happy and everything was an abode of all that is auspicious.'"'

Chapter 71-3.2(19) (Shiva's Pastimes)

' "Brahma said, 'Having bestowed his daughter on Hara, following the norms, Daksha gave her various

items as dowry.[782] Extremely happy, he donated many kinds
of riches to brahmanas. Along with Kamala, the one who has
Garuda on his banner[783] got up and approached Shambhu. He
joined his hands in salutation and spoke. Vishnu said, "O lord
of devas! O Mahadeva! O ocean of compassion! O lord! O
father! You are the father of the universe and Sati is the mother
of everything. In your pastimes, you always assume avataras
to ensure the welfare of the virtuous and to chastise those who
are crooked. The eternal shruti texts say this. O Hara! She is
dark blue, like gentle collyrium. With Dakshayani's radiance,
you have become even more resplendent. You are the opposite
of Padma and me.[784] Along with Sati, protect devas, humans
and the virtuous. O Shambhu! For those who are in samsara,
let everything be auspicious. O lord of all beings! If anyone
looks at her, or hears about her, with eyes of desire, my request
is that you should kill that person." Hearing Vishnu's words,
Parameshvara laughed. The one who knows everything told
Madhusudana that it would be that way. O lord among sages!
Hari returned to his own abode, but I remained there. Keeping
the matter secret, I organized for the festivities. I approached
Sati and had all the practices of the grihya sutras performed.
The decreed fire rites were observed in great detail. Following
the instructions of me, the preceptor and the brahmanas, Shiva
and Shivaa happily did pradakshina of the fire. O supreme
among brahmanas! There were great festivities there. There was
singing and dancing and the playing of musical instruments,
bringing joy to everyone. Thereafter, an extraordinary event
occurred. O son! It was very strange. I will tell you. Listen.

---

[782] The word youtaka [here dowry] means a woman's private and
individual property.
[783] Vishnu.
[784] Padma (Lakshmi) is fair and Vishnu is dark, while Shiva is fair
and Sati is dark.

Shambhu's *maya* is impossible to understand. It confounds the universe, *devas*, *asuras*, humans and mobile and immobile objects. Earlier, I wished to delude Shambhu through deceitful means. O son! In his pastimes, Shankara deluded me now. If a person tries to harm another, it is he who is harmed instead. There is no doubt about this. Therefore, it is held that a man should not harm another. O sage! As Sati was performing *pradakshina* of the fire, her two feet could be seen below her garment, and I saw them. Desire overwhelmed my mind and I looked at Sati's limbs. O best among *brahmana*s! I was confounded by Shiva's *maya*. The more eagerly I looked at Sati's beautiful limbs, the more I was afflicted by desire. O sage! I looked at Daksha's daughter, who was devoted to her husband. With my heart overwhelmed by desire, I wished to see her face. However, because she was ashamed of Shambhu, she did not show her face. As a result of her bashfulness, I could not see her face. I thought of a means whereby I might be able to see her. Greatly afflicted by desire, I thought of using strong smoke. I flung heaps of wet kindling into the fire. Since there was little *ghee* and a lot of wet kindling, swirls of smoke arose and covered every direction. There was darkness around the sacrificial altar. The lord, Parameshvara Mahesha indulges in many kinds of pastimes. Suffering from the smoke, he covered his eyes with his hands. O sage! At this, I raised the garment and looked at Sati's face. I was suffering the pangs of desire inside and looked at her. O son! I repeatedly looked at Sati's face. I was no longer in control of myself, and my senses were in a whirl. As I looked at her, my semen quickly oozed out. Four drops, resembling snowflakes, fell down on the ground. O sage! I was silent but was immediately scared and astounded. So that no one might see, I covered the semen. However, with his divine sight, Bhagavan Shambhu got to know. Since the semen had oozed out, he was filled with rage and spoke to me. Rudra said, "Why have you committed this reprehensible and

contemptible sin? At the time of my marriage, you have looked
at my beloved's face with eyes of desire. You thought that
Shankara would never get to know about this act. O Vidhatri!
There is nothing in the three worlds that is unknown to me.
How can this remain a secret? O foolish one! Just as there is oil
in sesamum seeds, I am amidst everything in the three worlds,
mobile and immobile." He loved Vishnu and saying this, he
remembered Vishnu's words. So as to kill Brahma, Shankara
raised his trident.'"'

'"'O supreme among *brahmana*s! When Shambhu raised
his trident to kill me, Marichi and the others uttered sounds
of lamentation. Shankara blazed and filled with fear, the large
number of *deva*s and all the sages praised him. The *deva*s said,
"O divinity! O Mahadeva! O divine one! You are affectionate
towards those who seek refuge. O lord of those who protect!
O Maheshvara! Save Brahma and show him your compassion.
O Mahesha! It is held that you are the father of the universe
and Sati is the mother. O lord of gods! Hari, Brahma and
all the others are your servants. The pastimes you engage
in are extraordinary. O lord! Your *maya* is wonderful. O
Ishvara! Other than a person who is your devotee, everyone
is confounded by it." Maheshvara, lord of *deva*s, was filled
with rage. The anxious and distressed *deva*s and sages praised
him in many kinds of ways. Scared, Daksha quickly arrived
in front of the lord of beings and raising his hands, pleased,
"Don't. Please don't." Maheshvara glanced at Daksha, who
was in front of him. He remembered Hari's words and replied
in disagreeable words. Maheshvara said, "O Prajapati! I
have pledged to do what my devotee, Vishnu, has requested
me. Vishnu told me, 'O lord! Anyone who looks at Sati with
eyes of desire must be killed by you.' Those words can't be
falsified, and I must kill Vidhatri. Why did Brahma look at
Sati with eyes of desire? He has also committed a crime by
releasing his semen. Hence, I must kill him." Full of wrath,

Mahesha, lord of *deva*s, said this. Everyone, *deva*s, sages and humans, trembled. There were great sounds of lamentation and despondency everywhere. I had wanted to delude him but had myself been confounded. Vishnu is extremely loved by Mahesha and is discriminating about what must be done. The intelligent one prostrated himself before Rudra and praised him. Shankara is affectionate towards his devotees, and he praised him through many kinds of hymns. He quickly arrived in front and restrained him through these words. Vishnu said, "O lord of beings! Please do not kill Vidhatri. He is the lord and creator of the universe. You are affectionate towards those who seek refuge, and he has sought refuge with you. I am a devotee who is greatly loved by you and am described as the king of all your devotees. Please listen to what is in my mind and show me your compassion. O protector! Please listen to another reason that is full of grave import. O Mahesha! Please show me your compassion and reflect on this. O Shambhu! The one with the four faces has been manifested so that he may create subjects. If the creator of subjects is killed, there will be no one like him. O protector! We three divinities are forms of Shiva. Following your command, we repeatedly undertake tasks of creation, preservation and destruction. O Shambhu! If he is killed, who will carry out your task? O lord of dissolution! Therefore, you should not kill the creator. O lord! For your sake, it is he who devised an excellent means so that Shivaa might become Sati, Daksha's daughter." Mahesha heard Vishnu's pleading. Firm in his vows, he replied so that everyone might hear. Mahesha answered, "O divinity! O divine one! O Rama's lord! O Vishnu! I love you as much as my own life. O son! Please do not restrain me from killing this wretch. I will carry out the pledge you yourself requested me about earlier. The one with the four faces has committed a great sin and is wicked. I will kill him. I will myself create all subjects, mobile and immobile. Alternatively, using my own energy, I

will create another creator. I must kill Vidhatri and fulfil my
pledge. I will create another creator! O lord! Please do not
restrain me." Hearing Girisha's words, Achyuta smiled within
himself and again spoke to him, restraining him. Achyuta said,
"You are Purusha, and it is appropriate that you should fulfil
your pledge. O Isha! O lord! But please reflect on this. One
cannot kill one's own self. O Shambhu! We three divinities are
part of your own *atman* and are not different. We are the same
form and are not distinct. Please reflect on the truth of this."
Shambhu heard the words of Vishnu, his great favourite. He
spoke again, describing his distinctive inclination. Shambhu
said, "O Vishnu! O lord of all my devotees! How can Vidhatri
be part of my *atman*? He can be seen as different, directly
standing in front." In front of everyone, Mahesha spoke in
this way, with a view to instructing. The one with Garuda on
his banner spoke, satisfying Mahadeva. Vishnu replied, "O
Sadashiva! Brahma is not different from you, and you are not
different from him. O Parameshvara! I am not different from
you, and you are not different from me. O Parameshvara!
O Sadashiva! You are omniscient and know everything.
Nevertheless, you wish to hear everything through my mouth.
O Isha! Following your command, I will speak. Let all the gods
and sages hear about Shiva's *tattva* and fix it in their minds. O
lord! We three divinities are parts of the resplendence. We are
insignificant parts of the significant whole. Who are you? Who
am I? Who is Brahma? You are the *paramatman*. For purposes
of creation, preservation and destruction, we are three distinct
parts. Thinking of yourself within your *atman*, in your own
pastimes, you assumed these forms. The *brahman* is one. The
three of us are *saguna* parts. This is like a single body possessing
a head, a neck and other parts. O Hara! The three of us are
Isha's limbs. You are the sparkling radiance and possess your
own abode. You are ancient and hidden. You are not manifest.
You are infinite in form. You are eternal. You are devoid of

lofty and other adjectives. Everything is Shiva." O lord among
sages! Hearing these words, Mahadeva was extremely pleased
and did not kill me.'"

Chapter 72-3.2(20) (Description of Sati's Marriage)

' " Narada said, 'O Brahma! O Vidhatri! O immensely
fortunate one! O supreme among Shiva's devotees!
O lord! You have made me hear about Shambhu's wonderful
conduct and it ensures everything that is auspicious. O father!
Please describe what happened thereafter. The conduct of Sati
and the one who wears the moon on his crest is divine and
destroys all the heaps of sins.'"

"'Brahma replied, 'Shankara is compassionate towards his
devotees and refrained from killing me. Devoid of fear, everyone
was pleased and happy. All the sages lowered their shoulders,
joined their hands in salutation and prostrated themselves.
They devotedly praised Shankara and cheerfully uttered words
of "Victory". O sage! At this time, I was also delighted and
lost my sense of fear. I devotedly praised Shankara, using many
auspicious hymns. The lord Shambhu, who indulges in diverse
types of pastimes, was pleased in his mind. O sage! While
everyone heard, he addressed me in the following words. Rudra
said, "O Brahma! O son! I am pleased with you. Get rid of
your fear. Follow my command without any fear. Touch your
head with your hand." The lord Shambhu indulges in diverse
types of pastimes. Hearing his words, I touched myself, Kah,
and in that posture, prostrated myself before Vrishadhvaja. As
soon as I touched myself, Kah, with my hand, in that position,
I assumed the form of his mount, the bull. Full of shame in all
my limbs, I stood there, my face facing downwards. Indra and

all the other immortals stood around and saw me in that form.
Full of shame, I prostrated myself before Maheshvara. I praised
him and said, "Please pardon me. Please forgive me. O lord!
Please tell me about a *prayashchitta* so that I can purge myself
of this sin. Chastise me in the proper way, so that this sin leaves
me." I prostrated myself before Shambhu and addressed him
in this way. Sarvesha is affectionate towards his devotees. He
was extremely pleased and spoke to me. Shambhu replied,
"With me astride you, you will worship me in this form. With
a cheerful mind, you will perform austerities and be devoted
to worshipping me. You will become famous everywhere on
earth under the name of Rudrashira.[785] Full of energy, you will
perform every kind of rite for *brahmanas*. Discharge of semen is
something that humans do. Since you have done that, you will
become human and roam around on earth. If anyone sees you
roaming around earth in this form and asks, 'What is this on
Brahma's head?' you will reply, 'It is the destroyer.' If a person
commits the sin of outraging another person's wife, as soon as
he eagerly hears everything you have done, he will be instantly
freed. As you continue to tell people what you have done, you
will gradually be purified of your sin. O Brahma! This is the
prayashchitta I have decided for you. In the world, people will
laugh at your extremely reprehensible deed. When you were
overcome by desire, I saw your semen fall down in the middle
of the altar. It will not remain there. Four drops of semen fell
down on the ground. Those will become clouds of dissolution
in the firmament." Meanwhile, in front of *deva*s and *rishi*s,
clouds instantly emerged from the semen. O son! Samvartaka,
Avarta, Pushkara and Drona—these are the four great clouds
that bring about dissolution. As soon as Shiva wishes, they
thunder and release torrents of water. O best among sages!
Those clouds spread throughout the firmament and roar

---

[785] Rudra's head.

loudly. They thunder loudly and envelope the firmament. After this, Shankara and Devi Dakshayani were pacified and quickly turned extremely serene.""'

""'O sage! Following Shiva's command, I lost my fear and completed the remaining marriage rites. Flowers showered down on the heads of Shiva and Shivaa. O best among sages! Everyone, *deva*s and *gana*s, rejoiced. There was singing and musical instruments were played. Full of devotion, noble *brahmana*s chanted from the *Veda*s. Rambha and other celestial women lovingly danced. O Narada! There were great festivities and loud exclamations by wives of *deva*s. Parameshvara, the lord of sacrificial rites, was pleased. As I joined my hands in salutation, following the practices of ordinary people, he spoke to me. Ishvara said, "O Brahma! You have conducted all the marriage rites exceedingly well and I am pleased with you. What *dakshina* will I give to you, the *acharya*? O eldest among the gods! Ask for it, even if it is extremely difficult to obtain. O immensely fortunate one! Tell me quickly. There is nothing that I will not give you." O sage! Hearing Shankara's words, I joined my hands in salutation. Humbly, I repeatedly prostrated myself before Isha and spoke. Brahma said, "O lord of *deva*s! O Mahesha! If you are pleased with me and if I am worthy of being given a boon, then you should cheerfully do what I am asking you to do. O Maheshvara! To purify men from their sins, please always remain established in this altar, in your present form. O Shashishekhara! O Shankara! So as to destroy my own sins, I will set up my hermitage near it and perform austerities. O Hara! If any man on earth comes here and devotedly visits on Sunday, in the month of Chaitra, in *shukla paksha*, when the *nakshatra* is Uttara Phalguni,[786] let all his sins be destroyed. Let his store of good merits increase and become extensive and let all his ailments be destroyed. If any

---

[786] The text uses the word 'Bhaga'.

woman is unfortunate, barren, one-eyed or ugly, as soon as she
sees this, let her certainly become free of those taints." Hearing
my words, the lord Shiva, who ensures every kind of happiness,
was pleased in his mind and uttered words of assent. Shiva
said, "For the welfare of the worlds, along with my wife, Sati,
I will remain established in this altar. O Vidhatri! I will act
in accordance with your request." Saying this, along with his
wife, Bhagavan Vrishadhvaja created an image from his own
portion and established himself in altar.'"'

'"'Parameshvara Shankara, affectionate towards those
who are his own, then wanted to leave, along with his wife,
Sati, and sought Daksha's permission. Meanwhile, the
intelligent Daksha bent down in humility and joined his hands
in salutation. Happy, he praised Vrishadhvaja. Vishnu and
all the other gods, the sages and the *gana*s bowed down and
praised him in many kinds of ways, cheerfully uttering sounds
of "Victory". Taking leave of Daksha, Shambhu made Sati sit
on the bull. Happily, the lord himself sat on the bull and left
for the slopes of the Himalayas. Her teeth were excellent, and
her smile was beautiful. As she sat on the bull with Shankara,
she was radiant, resembling the dark mark at the end of the
moon. Vishnu and all the other gods, Marichi and the other
*rishi*s, Daksha and all the other people were confounded
and remained immobile. Some of them played on musical
instruments, others sang. They chanted about the pure fame of
Shiva and Shivaa and followed Shiva happily. Midway along
the path, full of pleasure, Daksha took Shambhu's leave. Full
of love, along with his *gana*s, Shambhu reached his abode.
Though Vishnu and the other gods had been released by
Shambhu, full of joy and devotion, they followed Shiva. Will
all his *gana*s and with his wife, Sati, Shambhu reached his own
abode and saw the beautiful Himalaya mountains. Having
reached, he lovingly honoured all *devas*, sages and others a lot
and cheerfully released them. Taking Shambhu's leave, Vishnu

and all the other gods and sages bent down and praised him, returning to their own respective abodes. Shiva was delighted with his wife, Daksha's daughter. Following the customs of the world, he sported on the slopes of the Himalayas. O sage! Along with Sati and his *ganas*, Shiva reached his own residence and saw Kailasa, supreme among mountains. I have thus told you everything that happened earlier, about the marriage of the one who uses the bull as a mount, towards the end of Svayambhuva *manvantara*. After worshipping Vrishadhvaja, if a person eagerly hears this account at the time of a marriage or before starting a sacrifice, all his impediments for marriage and every kind of rite are destroyed. As a result of listening to this auspicious account, all rites are always free from obstructions. The bride is happy and possesses the qualities of good fortune and good conduct. If she lovingly listens to this auspicious account, she is chaste and has sons.'"'

Chapter 73-3.2(21) (Sati and Shiva's Sport)

" "Narada said, 'O father! O unblemished one! O one who knows everything! You have spoken well. We have heard about the great, wonderful and auspicious conduct of Shiva and Shivaa. We have heard the complete account of the marriage, and this destroys every kind of delusion. This bestows a person with supreme *jnana* and makes him the excellent reservoir of all that is auspicious. However, I still wish to know about Shiva and Shivaa's auspicious conduct. O immensely wise one! Because of your unmatched compassion towards me, please describe it.'"

'"Brahma replied, 'O sage! It is appropriate that you have wished to hear about the one who is compassionate. O amiable one! You have goaded me into describing Shiva's pastimes.

He married Devi Sati, Daksha's daughter and the mother of the three worlds. He went to his own residence. Hear about what he cheerfully did thereafter. Along with his own *ganas*, Hara reached his own delightful abode. O *devarshi*! There, he lovingly descended from the bull. As is right, Sati's friend entered his own residence. O *devarshi*! Extremely happy, Shiva practiced the norms of the world. Having obtained Dakshayani and having reached his own residence, Virupaksha released Nandi[787] and the other *ganas* from the cave in the mountain. The lord, an ocean of compassion, was following the practices of ordinary people. He addressed Nandi and the others in pleasant words. Mahesha said, "O *ganas*! Immediately leave my presence, but lovingly remember me in your minds. You will not come to me until I remember you." Vamadeva addressed his own *ganas*, Nandi and the others, in this way. Those immensely forceful and immensely valiant ones departed in various directions."'"

""'Ishvara was left with the radiant one. In private and extremely happy, he sported with Dakshayani. Sometimes, he gathered beautiful wildflowers and making a garland with these, placed it around Sati's neck, in place of a necklace. Sometimes, when Sati was looking at herself in a mirror, Hara followed her and saw his own face reflected in it. Sometimes, he played with her earrings, taking them off, cleaning them himself and putting them back on again. Sometimes, Vrishadhvaja applied red colour, as bright as the fire, on her feet, making her naturally red feet completely red. There are words that cannot be spoken in front of many. Hara whispered them into her ears and looked at her face. He never went far from her. If he left, he immediately returned. While she was thinking of something, he approached from the rear and covered her eyes. Vrishadhvaja

---

[787] In these sentences, the text repeatedly says *nadi* (river). We have corrected it to Nandi.

used his *maya* and disappeared. When she became scared and agitated, he would suddenly embrace her. Her two nipples were like the buds of golden lotuses. He used musk to make marks resembling bees around these. Hara suddenly took her necklace off her two breasts and repeatedly touched and kneaded them with his hands. He repeatedly took off her bracelets, bangles and rings and embracing her, put them back in their respective places. While she looked on, he suddenly touched the areolas on the tips of her peaked breasts and remarked, "This is known as Kalika. This is your friend, who bears the same complexion as you."[788] Sometimes, Pramathadhipa[789] became senseless with desire. Full of joy, he addressed his beloved in endearing words of love. Shankara gathered lotuses and other beautiful flowers and lovingly adorned her limbs with ornaments made out of flowers. Maheshvara, affectionate towards his devotees, sported with Sati in all the beautiful groves in the mountains. He didn't go anywhere without her. Without her, he didn't do anything. Without her, Shankara did not obtain the least bit of peace. He spent a long period of time in the groves on Mount Kailasa. He then went to the slopes of the Himalaya mountains and of his own will, remembered Smara. As soon as Kama reached Shankara's presence, Vasanta entered there and following the lord's commands, spread his powers everywhere. There were flowers on all the trees. All the creepers bloomed. There were blossoming lotuses in the water and bees buzzed around the lotuses. As soon as he entered, the beautiful Malaya breeze started to blow, bearing with it the fragrant and intoxicating scent of fragrant flowers. There were radiant *palasha* flowers, resembling the crescent moon in the evening. The trees rejoiced and bore flowers, Kama's weapons. Dazzling lotuses bloomed

---

[788] Since this *shloka* is terse, we have expanded it a bit, to make the meaning clear.

[789] Lord of *pramatha*s, Shiva.

in the lakes. With an excellent face, the divinity of the wind generated delusion. There were *nagakeshara* flowers, golden in hue, on the trees. Pleasant in appearance, they bloomed near Shankara, resembling Madana's banner. In those ancient times, the breeze was fragrant with the scent of clove creepers and deluded those whose minds were full of desire. Divine tones wafted through the mango trees, their leaves resembling flames of fire. It was as if, urged by Madana, they had become couches for Madana's arrows.[790] There were radiant and spotless flowers blossoming in the water, as if lying down on beds of *kusha* grass. They were like the minds of sages, in which, the supreme illumination had become manifest. As soon as the ice came into contact with the sun's rays outside, like hearts, it melted and became water. The moon was clear, not obstructed by mist and resembled a beautiful and radiant woman, in the company of her beloved. At that time, on that excellent spot on earth, Mahadeva easily sported with Sati for a very long time, in the groves and along the rivers. O sage! Dakshayani was just as radiant as him and without her, Hara couldn't find any peace, not even for an instant. In matters of intercourse, Devi Sati brought pleasure to his mind. She entered Hara's limbs and seemed to drink up his juices. Her entire body was ornamented with garlands of flowers that he had fashioned himself and this gave her newer pleasures. Hara glanced at her with smiling eyes and conversed with her. Her husband instructed Girija[791] in matters connected with the *atman*. Hara remained there and drank up the nectar from her moon-like face. In many general and specific ways, he never wavered from that slender-limbed one. Like a giant tusker that has been bound and is incapable of movement, he was bound to the fragrance of her lotus face, her beauty, her pleasantries and her qualities. In this way,

---

[790] The mango trees were ready to bloom.
[791] Parvati, the daughter of the mountain.

along with Daksha's daughter, Mahesha sported every day, in
the groves and plains of the Himalaya mountains. O divine
rishi! While he sported there, measured in years of the gods,
twenty-five years passed.'"'

Chapter 74-3.2(22) (More on Sati and Shiva's Sport)

' "Brahma said, 'Vrishadhvaja was on the slopes of
Mount Kailasa. On one occasion, when the clouds
arrived, Daksha's daughter spoke to him. Sati said, "O divinity!
O divine one! O Mahadeva! O Shambhu! O one who I love
like my own life! O protector! O one who bestows honours!
Please listen to my words and act accordingly. The clouds have
arrived, and it is a time that is extremely difficult to tolerate.
There are masses of clouds with many kinds of hues. Their
singing can be heard in the sky and in the directions. Speedy
gusts of wind are blowing, washing the *kadamba* flowers[792]
and gathering up the drops of water, thus enticing the heart.
The clouds are thundering loudly and releasing torrents of
water. They are tinged with flags made of lightning. They are
fierce and are agitating our minds. The sun cannot be seen and
the lord of the night[793] is shrouded in clouds. The day seems
to be night and causes distress to those who suffer pangs of
separation. Goaded by the wind, the clouds do not remain in
one place and are scattered. O Shankara! It seems as if they
will fall down on the heads of people. Struck by the wind,
large trees seem to be dancing in the sky. O Hara! On seeing
this, cowards are scared, and desire is kindled. The clouds in

---

[792] A flower that blossoms at the time of the rains.
[793] The moon.

the sky are like masses of blue collyrium and flocks of cranes swiftly follow them, resembling foam on the Yamuna. At the end of the day, a dark circle can be seen, resembling the blazing Vadavamukha fire in the ocean.[794] O Virupaksha! Crops have started to sprout in the courtyards of temples. I need not speak about crops sprouting elsewhere. There are dark, silver and red masses of clouds on the Himalayas and Mandara and they resemble birds on the ocean of milk. There is an unmatched radiance on the *kimshuka* flowers, but they have lost their fragrance. It is as if, in times of prosperity and adversity, Lakshmi has forsaken virtuous people and is serving those who are crooked. On every forest in Mandara, the repeated calls of peacocks and their extended tails indicated their constant delight. *Chataka* birds[795] stand like travellers on the paths, calling in sweet tones, eager to drink up the drops of rain and quench the heat. Behold the wickedness of the clouds. They seem to be touching my body with their hands but are also covering the peacocks and *chataka*s that follow them. On seeing that even the sun has been conquered, peacocks and *saranga* birds[796] have happily gone to Lake Manasa, far away from this lord of mountains. At a time like this, even crows and *chakoras*[797] build nests. If you don't have hope, how can you possibly find peace? O wielder of Pinaka! Let us not suffer from this great fear on account of the clouds now. Listen to my words and quickly construct a residence for us. Let it be on Kailasa, the Himalaya mountains or the great Kashi on earth. O Vrishadhvaja! You should construct an appropriate home." In this way, Dakshayani spoke to Shambhu more than once.

---

[794] Vadavamukha fire is the subterranean fire, in the shape of a mare's (*vadava*) head (*mukha*).

[795] The *chataka* bird is believed to survive on raindrops.

[796] Cranes or flamingoes.

[797] Partridges.

He laughed and the beams of the moon on his head seemed to smile. The great-souled and omniscient Parameshvara spoke to Devi Sati with a smile quivering on his lips, comforting her. Ishvara said, "O beautiful one! O beloved! To bring you pleasure, it is my task to construct a home for you, one that the clouds will never be able to reach. O beautiful one! Even at the time of the monsoon, the clouds only swirl around the buttocks of the mountain and never approach the summit. O Devi! Like that, they generally clean Kailasa's feet. They never reach or proceed above that. Nor do the clouds ever reach above the summit of Mount Sumeru. Pushkara, Avarta and others only reach up to Jambu's[798] foundation. Choose the summit of any of these Indras among mountains. Quickly tell me which of these appeals to you as a home. On any of these mountains in the Himalayas, you will be able to eagerly roam around, as you wish and appropriately enjoy yourself. Swarms of bees with golden wings will fan you with that breeze and their excellent buzzing sound will be like sweet songs. As you roam around, as you wish on the grounds of that jewel-studded mountain, *siddha* women will eagerly offer you a beautiful seat and bring you fruits and other things that you want. Daughters of the king of serpents, mountain maidens, *naga* maidens and *kinnara* women will always help you in every possible way, accompany you and give you joy. The women will look at your unmatched beauty and excellent face and will no longer be able to tolerate their own beauty. Though they are beautiful in form, they will no longer have any respect for their bodies, their beauty and their qualities. With unblinking eyes, they will always look at you. Menaka, the wife of the king of the mountains,[799] is famous in the three worlds because of her beauty and qualities. She too will constantly entreat you and bring pleasure to your

[798] Meaning, Jambu*dvipa*.
[799] The Himalayas.

mind. There are many women in the residence of the king of
the mountains, extensive in their beauty. Pleased with your
qualities, they will seek you out with joy and honour you,
imparting instruction to you, though there is no need for that.
O beloved! Is that where you want to go? The power of spring
is constantly felt there. There are wonderful groves, filled with
the delightful calls of cuckoos. In the Himalayas, Indra among
mountains, there are many varied waterbodies, filled with cool
water. Hundreds of excellent lotuses blossom there. There are
green meadows and trees that yield every object of desire, so
that they are known as *kalpavrikshas*.[800] You will always see
flowers, horses and elephants and cows in the pastures. The
place is surrounded by sages and even the predatory beasts are
calm. O Mahamaya! There are many kinds of animals, and it is
like a temple of *deva*s. It is radiant with crystal, gold and silver.
It is ornamented with Manasa and other lakes. There are golden
buds and blooming lotuses, with stems made out of jewels. The
water is inhabited by innumerable porpoises,[801] turtles and
*makara*s. There are gallinules and blue lotuses. O Deveshi! All
these release fragrance and pollen. The waterbodies are full of
clear, sparkling and fragrant water. The shores are beautiful,
adorned with green moss. Abandoning their own nature, the
branches of the trees seem to be dancing. They are adorned with
cranes and *chakravaka* birds, intoxicated by the god of love.
There are sweet and maddening sounds of the buzzing of bees.
They ignite desire in the guardians of the directions, Vasava,[802]
Kubera, Yama, Varuna, Agni, Nirriti, Vayu and Ishana.[803] The
abode of the gods and the lovely cities of these guardians are on
the lofty summit of Meru. They are served by Rambha, Shachi,

[800] The same as *kalpadruma*s, trees that yield every object of desire.
[801] *Shishumara.*
[802] Indra.
[803] The guardians of the eight directions.

Menaka and others.[804] Among all these mountains, do you desire this mountain? It is extremely beautiful and represents the essence of all the great mountains. There, the goddess Shachi, along with her friends and large numbers of *apsaras*, will always assist you, in every appropriate way. Alternatively, Kailasa, Indra among mountains, is my constant abode. Do you desire a residence there, ornamented by the city of the lord of riches? That place is as resplendent as the full moon and is washed by the waters of Ganga. In the valleys and summits there, maidens constantly utter sounds of the *brahman*. There are diverse types of animals there and hundreds of waterbodies filled with lotuses. O beautiful one! The summit of Sumeru possesses every kind of virtuous quality. Which region does your mind desire? Tell me quickly and I will build a residence for you there." Hearing Shankara's words, Dakshayani slowly spoke to Mahadeva, expressing her own preferences.'"'

'"'Sati said, "Along with you, I wish to reside on the Himalayas. Without any delay, please arrange for a residence on that great mountain." Hara was greatly in love with her. Hearing her words, along with Dakshayani, he went to the summit of the Himalayas. He went to the beautiful summit, beyond the reach of birds. Large numbers of *siddha* women resided there and there were lakes and forests. There were wonderful and beautiful lotuses, and the summit was variegated with jewels. Shambhu, Sati's friend, reached that place, which resembled the rising sun. It was covered with clouds that resembled crystal. It was radiant with grass and trees. There were colourful flowers and lakes. There were blossoms on the tips of the branches, surrounded by buzzing bees. Clumps of lotuses and blue lotuses bloomed. The place resounded with the calls of *chakravakas*, *kadambas*,[805] swans,

---

[804] *Apsaras*. This Shachi seems to be an *apsara*, different from Indra's wife.

[805] A kind of goose.

shankus,[806] intoxicated cranes, curlews and peacocks. Male cuckoos sang in melodious voices. *Turangavadanas*,[807] *siddhas*, *apsaras*, *guhyakas*, *vidyadhara* women, goddesses and *kinnara* women sported there. There were married women and maidens from the mountains, who played on lutes, *trikamas*,[808] drums and kettledrums. Beautiful *apsaras* danced with enthusiasm. There were beautiful goddesses, beautiful ponds and beautiful fragrances. The groves were always adorned with blossoming flowers. On that beautiful abode on the king of the mountains, along with Sati, Vrishadhvaja sported for a very long time. That place was like heaven. With Sati, Shankara happily sported for ten thousand divine years. Sometimes, Hara went to a different spot. Sometimes, on the summit of Meru, he surrounded himself with gods and goddesses. Sometimes, he went to the many continents, gardens and forests on the surface of the earth. However, having gone there, he returned and happily sported with Sati. Whether it was night or day, he did not sacrifice. Nor did he perform austerities or think of the *brahman*. It was Sati alone who caused pleasure to Shambhu's mind. Sati constantly looked towards Mahadeva's face. Mahadeva also constantly looked towards the face of Daksha's daughter. In this way, in association with each other, the tree of love was nourished. Kali and Shiva nurtured it with their sentiments.'"

Chapter 75-3.2(23) (Power of *Bhakti*)

' " Brahma said, 'Sati sported in this way with Shankara. She was content and non-attachment resulted. One

---

[806] A kind of goose.

[807] With the face of a horse, another name for *kinnaras*.

[808] Probably a musical instrument in the shape of a triangle.

day, Devi Sati approached Shiva in private. She devotedly prostrated herself before him, joining her hands upwards in salutation. Sati, Daksha's daughter, bowed down before the lord, who was extremely pleased. She devotedly joined her hands in salutation and humbly addressed him in these words. "O divinity! O divine one! O Mahadeva! O lord! O ocean of compassion! O one who saves the distressed! O great *yogi*! Please show me your compassion. You are the lord who is the supreme Purusha. You are beyond *sattva*, *rajas* and *tamas*. You are *nirguna* and *saguna*. You are the indifferent witness. You are the great lord. Since I was born as woman who became your beloved and sported with you, I am blessed. O Hara! When I was born, because of your affection towards your devotees, you became my husband. O protector! I spent many years in supreme sport with you. O Mahesha! I am satisfied and my mind has turned away from that. O Devesha! O Hara! I wish to know the supreme *tattva* that ensures happiness, whereby living beings easily cross over the miseries of *samsara*. How do living beings who are addicted to material objects obtain the supreme destination? O protector! How can they transcend *samsara*? Please show me your compassion and tell me about that principle." O sage! Full of devotion, Sati asked Shankara this. Maheshani is the original Shakti. She did this only for the sake of saving the living.'"'[809]

'"'Shiva's intellect is devoted to *yoga*, and he is indifferent. As a result of his own wishes, he assumed a form and became her husband. Hearing her words, he was extremely happy and spoke to Sati. Shiva replied, "O Devi! O Dakshayani! O Maheshvari! I will tell you about the supreme *tattva*, following which, a person is emancipated. Listen. O Parameshvari! Know that the supreme *tattva* is *vijnana*. The intellect is purified than and nothing else is remembered then, other than, 'I am the

---

[809] She knew and had no reason to ask.

brahman.' O beloved! This knowledge is extremely difficult
to obtain. 'I am directly the constant *brahman* and there is
nothing that is superior to this.' This sentiment is rare in the
three worlds. It can only be gained through *bhakti* towards me,
which bestows objects of pleasure and emancipation. *Bhakti*
can easily be obtained through my favours and is said to be
of nine types. There is no difference between *bhakti* and *jnana*
and a person who follows *bhakti* always obtains happiness.
O Sati! In a person who opposes *bhakti*, there is no *vijnana*.
O Devi! As a result of the power of *bhakti*, there is no doubt
that I go to the homes of those who are inferior and lowly,
even to those who are devoid of a proper *jati*. O Devi! It is said
that *bhakti* is of two types, *saguna* and *nirguna*, following the
norms and natural. It is also said to be superior and inferior.
Based on whether it is continuous or intermittent, there are also
two differences. Of the two, it is said that continuous *bhakti*
is of six types. The learned also know of differences based on
whether it is prescribed, or not prescribed. Thus, there are many
kinds of *bhakti*, described elsewhere. O beloved! As described
by sages, know that there are nine aspects to *bhakti*. I will
narrate these nine aspects to you. O Daksha's daughter! Listen
lovingly. O Devi! Constant hearing, chanting, remembering,
tending, serving, worshipping, prostrating, friendly conduct
and surrender[810]—the learned know these as the nine aspects.
O Shivaa! Their sub-divisions are said to be of many types. O
Devi! Listen to the separate characteristics of these nine aspects.
When a devotee offers up his mind to me, that bestows *bhakti*
and emancipation. Always seated in a steady posture on a seat,
when a person always honours my account, drinking it in, and
that causes delight to his body and other parts, that is said to be
hearing. When a person visualizes my origin and deeds inside

---

[810] Respectively, *shravanam, kirtanam, smaranam, sevanam,
dasyam, archanam, vandanam, sakhyam* and *atmarpanam.*

his heart and lovingly recites, that is said to be chanting. O Devi! When a person constantly sees me pervading everything everywhere, offering freedom from fear to the worlds, that is said to be remembering. At the time of sunrise, if a person performs the appropriate service to me, in thought, words and deeds, that is said to be tending. If a person uses all the senses to serve me all the time, enjoying the beloved *amrita* in the heart, that is said to be serving. Depending on his fortune, if a person always behaves like a servant towards me, the *paramatman*, offering me *padya* and the other sixteen *upacharas*, that is worshipping. Uttering the *mantras* in words, gradually moving on to *dhyana* in the mind and doing *sashtanga pranama* on the ground, that is known as prostrating. 'Anything good or bad that Ishvara does to me is always for my welfare.' This belief is the sign of friendly conduct. Lovingly dedicating the body and everything else and retaining nothing for one's own self, that is known as surrender. These nine aspects bestow *bhakti* towards me, objects of pleasure and emancipation. These generate *jnana* and are extremely loved by me. There are said to be many sub-divisions of *bhakti* towards me. Nurturing a *bilva* tree can be regarded as one of those. O beloved! These aspects and sub-divisions of *bhakti* towards me are best of all. They lead to *jnana* and non-attachment. A person is radiant because it leads to emancipation. The fruits of all tasks are always obtained. I love such a devotee as much as I love you. A person who constantly holds me in his heart is extremely loved by me. There is no path in the three worlds that brings as much of happiness as *bhakti* does. O Deveshi! Out of the four *yugas*, this is especially true in *kali yuga*. In *kali yuga*, *jnana* and non-attachment have assumed the form of old men, bereft of joy. O Devi! They have become old because no one who accepts them is born. In *kali yuga*, and indeed in all the *yugas*, *bhakti* directly yields fruits. There is no doubt that I always succumb to its powers and come under its subjugation. If a man on earth

possesses *bhakti* towards me, I always help him. There is no
doubt that I punish any enemy who causes him impediments.
O Devi! I protect my own. For the sake of my devotee, I was
overcome with rage and burnt down Kala with the fire that
emerged from my eyes.[811] O Devi! Indeed, in ancient times, for
the sake of my devotees, I defeated Ravi. I became extremely
angry and seizing my trident, conquered him.[812] O Devi! For
the sake of a devotee,[813] I became angry and abandoned Ravana
and his followers, showing no partiality towards him. O Devi!
For the sake of a devotee, when Vyasa was grasped by wicked
intelligence, I became angry and asked Nandi to chastise him
with a rod, expelling him from Kashi.[814] O Deveshi! What is
the need to speak a lot? I am always under the control of my
devotees. There is no doubt that I am always under the control
of a man who acts in such a way." Sati, Daksha's daughter,
heard this about the greatness of *bhakti*. She was delighted in
her mind and happily prostrated herself before Shiva.'"'

'"'Full of virtuous devotion, she again asked about the sub-
divisions of *bhakti*. This is described in the sacred texts and
brings pleasure to the worlds. It leads to the salvation of living
beings. In particular, she asked about the greatness of *yantra*,
mantra and the sacred texts and many other aspects of *dharma*
that lead to the salvation of living beings. Hearing Sati's
question, Shankara's mind was pleased. Extremely happy,
he described everything about the salvation of living beings.
Maheshvara, the supreme divinity, spoke about the greatness
of *yantra*s, as described in the sacred texts and their five

---

[811] To protect Markandeya, Shiva burnt down Yama (Kala).
[812] To protect Mali and Sumali, Shiva vanquished Ravi (Surya).
[813] Rama. Ravana was also Shiva's devotee.
[814] This devotee is Vishnu. Vyasa committed the crime of thinking
that Vishnu is superior to Shiva. He was punished by Nandi.

parts.[815] He described the Itihasa accounts and the greatness of devotees. O lord among sages! He spoke about the *dharma* of *varna*s and *ashrama*s and the *dharma* of men. He told her about the greatness of the *dharma* of sons and wives and the eternal *dharma* of *varna*s and *ashrama*s. He told her about the sacred texts of medicine and the sacred texts of astronomy, both of which bring happiness to living beings. He also explained to her the many supreme sacred texts of astrology.[816] Exhibiting compassion, Mahesha described the truth about all these. Sati and Shiva know everything. This was done for the welfare of the three worlds. For the welfare of the worlds, they assumed bodies with virtuous qualities and sported in many kinds of ways in Kailasa, in the Himalayas and other places. They are actually forms of the supreme *brahman*.'"'

Chapter 76-3.2(24) (Rama's Test)

'"'Narada said, 'O Brahma! O Vidhatri! O lord of subjects! O immensely wise one! O one who shows compassion! I have heard about Shankara's fame and the auspicious account of Sati and Shankara. Now, full of great affection, tell me more about their excellent fame. As a couple located there, what else did Shiva and Shivaa do?'"'

'"Brahma replied, 'O sage! Full of love, hear from me about the conduct of Sati and Shiva. Adopting the practices of ordinary people, they constantly engaged themselves in pastimes. O sage! Thereafter, Mahadevi Sati was separated from her husband, Shankara. Those who possess excellent

---

[815] The *bija mantra*s, associated with the five elements.

[816] *Samudrika shastra*, reading of marks on the body, or sometimes, palmistry.

intelligence say this. Sati and Isha are always united, like a word and its meaning. O sage! That being the case, how could separation have taken place? All of this occurred because they were indulging in their pastimes. Isha and Sati followed the ways of the world. Daksha's daughter said that at the time of her father's sacrifice, her husband abandoned her. Since Shambhu did not show her the affection, she gave up her body. The one named Sati manifested herself again in the Himalayas. Having become Parvati, she obtained Shiva again and married him.'"'

'Suta said, "Hearing Brahma's words, Narada asked Vidhatri about Shiva and Shivaa's great fame."'

'"Narada said, 'O Vishnu's devotee! O immensely fortunate one! O Vidhatri! Please tell me in detail about Shiva and Shivaa's conduct when they followed the ways of the world. For what reason did Shankara abandon his beloved wife, whom he loved more than his own life? O father! Tell me about this. I think this is extraordinary. On the occasion of his sacrifice, why did your son dishonour Shiva? Having gone to her father's sacrifice, how did she cast aside her body? What happened thereafter? What did Maheshvara do? Please tell me all this. Full of devotion, I wish to hear.'"'

'"Brahma answered, 'O son! O Narada! Full of great love, listen, along with the sages. You are a noble son. O immensely wise one! Hear about the conduct of the one who wears the moon on his crest. Having bowed down before Mahesha, served by Hari and the other gods, I will tell you about the extremely wonderful conduct of the supreme *brahman*. Everything is Shiva's pastime. The lord displays many kinds of pastimes. He is independent and indifferent. Sati is also like that. O sage! Otherwise, who is capable of performing such deeds? He is the supreme *brahman*. He is Parameshvara, the *paramatman*. Shri's lord, I and all the gods always worship him. So do the great-souled *siddha* sages, Sanaka and the others. O son! Happily, Shesha always sings about the fame of the lord Shiva Shankara but is unable to complete it. If one is confused about all the *tattva*s, this is because of his pastimes. No blame is attached to this. Pervading everything, he is the one who urges this.'"'

""'On one occasion, along with Sati, Rudra Bhava was roaming around the three worlds. Accomplished in pastimes, astride the bull, he wished to visit. Having wandered around the earth, right up to the girdle of the ocean, he reached Dandakaranya. Devoted to the pledge of truth,[817] the lord showed Sati the beauty of the earth there. Hara saw Rama there. Along with Lakshmana, he was searching for his beloved Sita, who had been deceitfully abducted by Ravana. His mind suffering from the pangs of separation, he was exclaiming, "Alas, Sita!" Repeatedly weeping, he was casting his eyes around, in this direction and that. His heart wishing to get her back, he was asking about where she might have gone. Because of the evil effects of Kuja[818] and other planets, his intelligence had been destroyed. Lacking any shame, he was overwhelmed by grief. The brave one was born in *surya vamsha*. He was the son of King Dasharatha. He was Bharata's elder brother. He was bereft of joy and had lost his radiance. Hara has no desires. He happily bestows boons on those he loves. Extensive in his intelligence, he saw Rama wandering around in the forest, along with Lakshmana. Remaining invisible, he exclaimed, "Victory to you." He did not show himself and remained hidden. In this way, Shankara, affectionate towards his devotees, addressed Rama in the forest. Witnessing this, Sati was confounded by Shiva's pastimes. Extremely surprised and deluded by Shiva's *maya*, she spoke to Shiva. Sati said, "O divinity! O divine one! O supreme *brahman*! O Sarvesha! O Parameshvara! All the gods,

---

[817] Perhaps a pledge to show her the earth.
[818] The text uses the word Mars.

Hari, Brahma and the others, always serve you. Everyone must
prostrate before you. You must be served by everyone. You must
always be meditated upon. When one makes efforts, you can
be known through Vedanta. You are without transformation.
You are the supreme lord. O protector! Who are these two
men, suffering from the pangs of separation? Suffering and
distressed, they are roaming around in the forest, though they
are brave and wield bows. Why were you delighted when you
saw the older one, as dark blue as a lotus? You were delighted
and extremely pleased, behaving like a devotee. O husband! O
Shankara! I have a doubt about this, and you should dispel it.
O lord! A master does not prostrate himself before a servant."
Devi Sati Shivaa is the primordial Shakti. She is Parameshvari.
Nevertheless, overwhelmed by Shiva's *maya*, she asked the lord
Shiva. Hearing Sati's words, Parameshvara Shankara laughed.
Accomplished in pastimes, he spoke to Sati. Parameshvara
answered, "O Devi! O Sati! Listen lovingly to the truth. There
is no deceit in the matter. Because of the power of the boon,[819]
I affectionately prostrated myself before him. These are the
brothers Rama and Lakshmana, revered as valiant ones. O
Devi! They are wise and have been born in *surya vamsha*, as
Dasharatha's sons. The fair-complexioned younger brother is
Lakshmana, who has been born as a portion of Shesha. The
elder one is Rama, born as Vishnu's complete portion. He
is incapable of suffering. To protect the virtuous and ensure
our welfare, he has taken an *avatara* on earth." Saying this,
Shambhu, the lord who bestows prosperity, stopped. Despite
hearing Shambhu's words, her mind did not trust them. Shiva's
maya is powerful and confounds the three worlds. Knowing
that her mind did not believe this, the eternal Shambhu
addressed her in the following words. The lord is accomplished
in pastimes. Shiva said, "O Devi! If your mind does not believe,

[819] Bestowed by Shiva on Rama.

listen to my words. Using your own intelligence, test Rama. O Sati! O beloved! Act so that your confusion is destroyed. He is standing there, under the *vata* tree. Go and become his examiner." Following Shiva's command, Sati went there.'"'

"'Ishvari wondered, "How will I test Rama, who is roaming around in the forest? I will assume Sita's form and go to Rama's presence. If Rama is Hari, he will know everything, not otherwise." Thinking this, she assumed Sita's form and approached Rama. Overcome by delusion, Sati approached, so as to test him. On seeing Sati in Sita's form, the descendant of the Raghu lineage discerned the truth and smiled. He bowed down and did *japa* with Shiva's name. Rama said, "O Sati! My love for you is great. Please tell me. Why has Shambhu not come with you? Without your husband, why have you come here alone, to this forest? O Sati! Why have you given up your own form and assumed this form? O Devi! Please show me your compassion and tell me the reason." Hearing Rama's words, Sati was amazed. She remembered what Shiva had said and realized it was true. She was extremely ashamed. Understanding that Rama was Vishnu, she assumed her own form. Remembering Shiva's feet in her mind, with a pleased mind, Sati replied. "The lord Shiva is roaming the earth, along with me and the *gana*s. The self-ruling Parameshvara came here, to this forest. He saw you here, accompanied by Lakshmana, searching for Sita. You were separated from Sita and your mind was suffering. While you, who are Vishnu's form, stood near the root of the *vata* tree, he came and prostrated himself before you. Full of great joy, he praised your greatness. On seeing this unblemished form, he was filled with supreme delight, a joy greater than the one he obtains when he sees you, Hari, in your four-armed form. When I heard Shambhu's words, my mind did not accept them. O Raghava! Therefore, following what he told me, I wanted to test you. O Rama! I have now got to know your nature as Vishnu. I have seen your great lordship.

O immensely intelligent one! I no longer harbour any doubts.
Nevertheless, listen to me. Why did he prostrate himself before
you? Please tell me the truth about that. Dispel my doubt about
this, so that I can quickly become happy." Hearing her words,
Rama's eyes dilated in joy. He remembered Lord Shambhu and
was flooded with even greater delight. O sage! Without Sati's
permission, he did not approach Shambhu. However, Raghava
spoke to Sati again, describing his greatness.'"

Chapter 77-3.2(25) (Sati's Separation)

‘‘‘Rama said, "O Devi! In ancient times, on one
occasion, Shambhu, who bestows great prosperity,
summoned Vishvakarma to his own region, greater than the
greatest. He made him construct a beautiful shed for his cows,
an appropriate and extensive residence and an excellent throne
there. To removed impediments, Shankara made Vishvakarma
construct a great and divine umbrella, excellent and extremely
wonderful. He quickly invited Shakra and the large number
of *deva*s, *siddha*s, *gandharva*s, *naga*s, all the texts containing
instructions, all the *agama* texts, Vidhatri and his sons, the
sages, all the goddesses and the *apsara*s, who brought many
kinds of objects. To undertake the auspicious rites, sixteen
maidens were brought from each of the categories of *deva*s,
*rishi*s, *siddha*s and serpents. O sage![820] Many kinds of musical
instruments, primarily *veena*s and *mridanga*s[821] were played.
With the playing of musical instruments and excellent singing,
festivities were organized. All the appropriate objects required
for the consecration of a king were brought, including all

---

[820] Since Rama is speaking, this is clearly an inconsistency.
[821] Kind of drum.

the herbs. Five pots were filled with water taken directly from *tirtha*s. His *gana*s brought every other kind of divine article. Shankara arranged for the loud utterance of sounds of the *brahman*. With a delighted mind, he invited Hari from Vaikuntha. O Devi! Maheshvara was delighted at his complete devotion. At an auspicious *muhurta*, Mahadeva made Hari sit down on that excellent throng. Lovingly, he adorned him with every kind of ornament. A beautiful crown was fixed, and all the auspicious arrangements were made. Mahesha himself consecrated him, in that pavilion that was like the universe. He bestowed all his prosperity on him, including that which should not be given away. The self-ruling Shambhu is affectionate towards his devotees. He praised him. He is pervasive and independent. However, he is affectionate towards his devotees and can be conquered by boons he has bestowed. He addressed Brahma, the creator of the worlds, in these words. Mahesha said, 'O lord of the worlds! All of you listen. From now on, following my instructions, I will prostrate myself before Hari Vishnu and so should all of you. O son![822] All *deva*s should prostrate themselves before Hari. Following my command, Hari will be extolled in the *Veda*s, just as I am.' Saying this, Rudra prostrated himself before the one who has Garuda on his standard. He is affectionate towards his devotees and bestows boons. He was pleased at Vishnu's devotion. Since then, Hari has been worshipped by Brahma and all *deva*s, *asura*s, sages and *siddha*s. Extremely pleased and affectionate towards his devotees, Mahesha bestowed great boons on Hari and the residents of heaven. Mahesha said, 'Following my command, you will be the creator, preserver and destroyer of the worlds. You will bestow *dharma*, *artha* and *kama*. You will chastise those who follow wicked policy. You will be the

---

[822] Since Rudra was born from Brahma, this can be translated as father too. The word used is *tata*.

lord of the universe. You will be worshipped by the universe.
You will be immensely strong and valiant. In battle, you will be
invincible against everyone, even me. I will voluntarily bestow
three Shaktis on you. Accept them. You will be independent in
the three worlds and will have the power of diverse kinds of
pastimes. O Hari! Indeed, I will make efforts to chastise those
who hate you. O Vishnu! I will bestow excellent *nirvana* on your
devotees. Accept my *maya*, which even the gods find impossible
to comprehend. It confounds the universe and renders it bereft
of consciousness. O Hari! You are my left hand and Vidhatri
is my right. You and Vidhatri will become the creator and the
preserver. There is no doubt that Rudra is my heart and that I
am he. You must certainly worship him and so must Brahma
and the others. While stationed here, you will preserve the
entire universe. In particular, you will assume many *avatara*s
and always devise diverse means of preservation. In my world,
you will have a place that is full of great prosperity. It will be
extremely radiant and will be known as Goloka. O Hari! You
will have *avatara*s on earth who will be those who protect.
They will certainly be my devotees. On seeing them, I will
be delighted and will treat them with affection.' Thus, Hara
himself bestowed unlimited prosperity on Hari. Thereafter, as
he willed, Umapati[823] sported on Kailasa, with his own *gana*s.
Since then, Lakshmi's lord has assumed the garb of a cowherd.
The lord of *gopa*s, *gopi*s[824] and cattle was extremely happy
and wandered around. Since then, Vishnu has been pleased
in his mind and has protected the entire universe. Following
Shiva's command, so as to become the agent of preservation,
he assumed many kinds of *avatara*s. Now, following Shiva's
command, he has assumed four different *avatara*s. They are—I,
Rama, Bharata, Lakshmana and Shatrughna. O Devi! Obeying

[823] Uma's consort, Shiva.
[824] A *gopa* is a cowherd, *gopi* is the feminine.

my father's command, with Sita and Lakshmana, I have now come to the forest and am distressed because of what destiny has done. Using some means, the roamer in the night[825] has abducted my wife, Sita. I am separated from my relatives in this forest and am searching for my beloved. Since I have had the good fortune of seeing you, all will be well. O mother Sati! There is no doubt that you will show me your compassion. O Devi! There is no doubt that I will obtain the supreme boon of getting Sita back. Through your favours, I will kill the wicked *rakshasa* who has caused me grief. It is my good fortune that both of you have decided to show me your compassion now. Any man on whom you bestow the boon of your compassion is blessed." Having said many such things, he prostrated himself before Sati Shivaa. Taking her permission, the descendant of the Raghu lineage roamed around in the forest.'"'

'"'Sati heard the words of Rama, who had controlled his *atman*. Having witnessed the devotion in his heart towards Shiva, she praised him. Remembering her own acts in her mind, she suffered from great grief. Distressed and pale, she returned to Shiva's presence. As she travelled along the path, Devi repeatedly thought. "I had evil thoughts about Rama and did not pay heed to Shiva's words. Having returned to Shankara's presence, what answer will I give him?" Suffering from repentance, she thought a lot in this way. Having reached Shambhu's presence, in her heart, she prostrated herself before Shiva. Her face was distressed. She was anxious with sorrow. Her radiance had faded. On seeing that she was miserable, Hara asked if all was well. He affectionately asked her, "Have you completed the test?" Hearing Shiva's words, she lowered her face and said nothing in reply. Distressed and miserable, she stood there, near him. Mahesha is a great *yogi*, accomplished in many kinds of pastimes. He meditated

---

[825] *Rakshasa*, that is, Ravana.

and understood what was going on in the mind of Daksha's
daughter. He remembered the pledge that he had himself made
to Hari when he was angry with him.[826] Rudra always keeps
the pledge he makes to someone who asks. He is one who
speaks about *dharma*, acts in accordance with *dharma* and
always protects *dharma*. The lord was distressed and thinking
about it in his mind, spoke. Shiva said, "If my love towards
Daksha's daughter remains as great as it was earlier, I will
destroy the purity of my pledge, even if I act in accordance
with the practices of the world." Thinking about this in many
kinds of ways, in his heart, he abandoned Sati. The one who
protects the *dharma* of the *Veda*s did not destroy his pledge.
Thus, in his mind, Parameshvara distanced himself from Sati.
The lord returned to his own mountain bound by the pledge
of separation he had made. As they travelled along the path, a
voice from the sky spoke to Maheshvara. Everyone heard this,
especially Daksha's daughter. The voice from the sky said, "O
Paramesha! You are blessed. You have adhered to the truth of
your pledge. There is no one like you in the three worlds. You
are the great lord. You are a great *yogi*." Hearing this voice
from the sky, Devi, who had lost her radiance, asked Shiva. "O
Parameshvara! O protector! Please tell me. What is the pledge
you have made?" The lord Girisha, who always does what
brings welfare, was asked this by Sati. He did not speak about
his own pledge, which he had made in front of Hari earlier. At
this, Sati meditated on Shiva, her husband, whom she loved
more than her own life. O sage! She understood everything
about the reason why her beloved had abandoned her. She
grieved a lot but immediately understood that Shambhu had
made up his mind to forsake her. She sighed repeatedly. Shiva
comforted himself and kept what was in his mind about her
a secret. Though, outwardly, the lord spoke a lot, he kept his

[826] That he would not marry a woman who disbelieved his words.

own pledge from Sati. When he reached Kailasa with Sati, they conversed about many things. The *yogi* fixed himself on his own supreme form and entered *samadhi*. Sati remained in that residence, extremely distressed in her mind. O sage! No one understood the conduct of Shiva and Shivaa. O great sage! A long period of time passed, and they remained in that state. Having used their powers to assume bodies, they followed the ordinary practices of the world. Thereafter, suffering from great affliction, Girisha abandoned his *dhyana*. Realizing this, Sati, the mother of the universe, went to the spot. With her heart shattered, Devi bowed down before Shiva. Shambhu, pervasive in his intelligence, gave her a seat in front of him. They happily conversed about many kinds of agreeable things. Indulging in such pastimes, he managed to immediately dispel her sorrow. He got her former happiness back, but he did not abandon his own pledge. O son! For Shiva, who is Parameshvara, this is not extraordinary. Nor need it be commented upon. O sage! The sages speak about this account of Shiva and Shivaa. Some who are not learned, ask, "How could they be separated?" Who knows the supreme meaning of Shiva and Shivaa's conduct? They sport as they will and always act according to that. Sati and Shiva are always connected to each other, like a word and its meaning. Their union and separation are possible and can happen only if they so will it.'"'

Chapter 78-3.2(26) (Conflict between Shiva and Daksha)

' "Brahma said, 'In ancient times, all the great-souled sages happened to undertake a great sacrifice in Prayaga. All the *siddha*s, Sanaka and other celestial *rishi*s, *deva*s, Prajapatis and learned ones who knew about the

brahman assembled there. Along with my companions, I went
there too. The *nigama* and *agama* texts, in extremely radiant
and embodied forms, accompanied me. With this wonderful
assembly, there were great festivities. They debated *jnana*, as
described in many sacred texts. O sage! At that time, the lord
Rudra, the lord who brings benefit to the three worlds, arrived
there, to ensure welfare. Bhavani and the *gana*s were with him.
On seeing Shiva, all the gods, *siddha*s and sages devotedly
bowed down before the lord and praised him, as did I. Full
of joy, as instructed by Shiva, they seated themselves in their
respective places. They were satisfied at having seen the lord
and described this as their own good fortune. At that time, the
lord Daksha, the lord of Prajapatis, arrived there voluntarily.
He was extremely happy and extremely radiant. Daksha
prostrated himself before me and when I instructed him, seated
himself. He regarded himself as the revered lord of the universe.
He was proud and only knew about the truth externally. All
the gods and *rishi*s praised Daksha and prostrated themselves
before him. They honoured the one who was superior in
energy. They humbly joined their hands in salutation. The
supreme lord, Maheshvara, rules himself and indulges in many
kinds of pastimes. He did not budge from his seat and did
not bow down before Daksha. On seeing that Hara did not
bow down, my son was mentally displeased. Daksha Prajapati
suddenly became angry with Rudra. Full of great pride, he cast
a cruel glance towards Rudra, the great lord. While everyone
heard, bereft of *jnana*, he spoke loudly. "All these gods and
*asura*s bowed down before me. So did the noble *brahmana*s
and *rishi*s. Who is this wicked person who takes himself to be
great-minded? He is surrounded by *preta*s and *pishacha*s. He
is shameless and resides in cremation grounds. Why has he not
prostrated himself before me now? He is devoid of rites. He is
served by *bhuta*s and *pishacha*s. He is intoxicated, devoid of
norms. He always condemns good policy. He is a heretic and

an evil person. He is wicked in conduct, like an insolent person who criticizes when he sees a *brahmana*. Though he is old, he is always engaged in intercourse with his wife. Therefore, I will prepare myself to curse him now." Having said this, the extremely crooked person was filled with rage. He addressed Rudra in these words. Daksha said, "O noble *brahmanas*! O gods! Listen. This person deserves to be killed by me. I will expel this Rudra from sacrifices. He is beyond *varnas* and has a disgusting form. Along with *devas*, he does not deserve a share. He resides in cremation grounds. He is devoid of nobility of birth." Hearing Daksha's words, Bhrigu and many others, who held the same view about Rudra being a wicked person, reprimanded him.'"

'"'Nandi heard these words and his eyes rolled around in rage. With the intention of cursing Daksha, the *gana* immediately spoke to him. Nandishvara said, "O deceitful one! O extremely foolish one! O Daksha! Your intelligence is evil. If my lord, Mahesha, is kept away from a sacrifice, how will it be completed? As soon as he is remembered, all sacrifices are rendered successful. The *tirthas* are rendered pure. How can you curse that Hara? O Daksha! O evil-minded one! In your fickleness as a *brahmana*, you are seeking to curse him in vain. O wicked one! You have laughed at the great lord, Rudra, in vain. He is the one who creates this universe, preserves it and at the end, destroys it. O worst among *brahmanas*! How have you cursed Rudra Mahesha?" Prajapati was censured in this way by Nandi. Full of rage, Daksha cursed Nandi. Daksha said, "All Rudra's *ganas* will be expelled from rites of the *Vedas*. You will be abandoned by *maharshis* and those who follow the path of the *Vedas*. You will be addicted to heretical views. You will be devoid of virtuous conduct. You will be addicted to drinking liquor. You will have matted hair and will wear ashes and bones." Daksha cursed Shiva's servants in this way. Hearing this, Nandi, loved by Shiva, was filled with great

rage. He instantly replied to Daksha, who was insolent and
exceedingly crooked. The energetic Nandi, Shilada's son,[827]
was loved by Shiva. Nandishvara said, "O Daksha! O deceitful
one! O one with evil intelligence! You cursed Shiva's servants
in vain. Because of your fickleness as a *brahmana*, you do not
know about Shiva's *tattva*. Bhrigu and the others are wicked
in intelligence. They are foolish and have laughed at the great
lord, Mahesha. Taking themselves to be *brahmana*s, they are
insolent. *Brahmana*s like them, who turn away from Rudra,
are deceitful. With the power of Rudra's energy, I am cursing
them. You will speak about the *Veda*s, but you will only know
about the meaning of the *Veda*s externally. These *brahmana*s
will always say that nothing else exists.[828] They will be addicted
to desire and pursue heaven. They will be full of rage, avarice
and insolence. Without any shame, these *brahmana*s will
always be beggars. While placing the path of the *Veda*s at the
forefront, these *brahmana*s will act as officiating priests for
*shudra*s. They will be poor and will always receive gifts. All of
them will receive from the wicked and go to hell. O Daksha!
Some of them will always become *brahma-rakshasa*s.[829] Anyone
who hates and abandons Shiva, taking Parameshvara to be an
ordinary god, will be evil in intelligence and will never know the
truth. They will always pursue mysterious *dharma* in homes,
wishing for happiness and carnal pleasures. They will debate
the eternal *Veda*s and lay down norms for rituals. Daksha's
pleasant face will vanish. He will become an animal and forget
the path of the *atman*. He will always deviate from *karma*.
He will soon come to have a goat's head." After Ishvara was
cursed by Daksha and the *brahmana*s were angrily cursed by
Nandi, great sounds of lamentation arose. Hearing this, I, the

---

[827] The sage Shilada prayed to Shiva and obtained Nandi as a son.
[828] These *shloka*s are reminiscent of Bhagavat Gita 2.42-43.
[829] A *brahmana* who is born as a *rakshasa*.

creator of the *Veda*s and one who knew about Shiva's *tattva*, repeatedly reprimanded Bhrigu and the other *brahmana*s in grave words.'"'

"'"Hearing Nandi's words, Ishvara laughed. Sadashiva addressed him in sweet words, kindling his understanding. Sadashiva said, "O Nandi! O immensely wise one! Listen. You should not act in rage. In your confusion, you thought that I had been cursed and cursed the lineage of *brahmana*s in vain. I am directly present in the *akshara*s in the *mantra*s of the *Veda*s. The *sukta*s are full of me. The *atman* is present in all *sukta*s and in all those with bodies. Therefore, a person who knows about the *atman* must never curse in rage. With a wicked intelligence, no one must ever curse the *Veda*s. I have not been cursed now. You should understand the truth. O extremely intelligent one! Be calm. Enlighten Sanaka and the others. I am the sacrifice. I am the rites of the sacrifice. I am all the limbs of the sacrifice. I am the *atman* of the sacrifice. I am the one who is devoted to sacrifices. I am also the one who is outside the sacrifice. Who is this? Who are you? Who are they? In truth, I am everything. You have forgotten this understanding and have cursed the *brahmana*s in vain. Use *jnana* about the truth to extract the essence from this *prapancha*. O immensely intelligent one! Understand this and get rid of your rage." In this way, Shambhu kindled understanding in Nandikeshvara. He obtained a great sense of discrimination and became serene. He lost his rage. Shiva thus swiftly enlightened his own *gana*, whom he loved more than his own life. Along with his *gana*, he cheerfully returned to his own abode. Daksha was still full of rage. Surrounded by the *brahmana*s, he returned to his own residence, but his heart was full of hatred for Shiva. Daksha remembered how, full of great anger, he had cursed Rudra. Foolish in intelligence and giving up his devotion, he greatly criticized those who worshipped Shiva. I have thus spoken about Daksha's wicked intelligence vis-à-vis Shambhu, the *paramatman.* O son! Hear about what he did with this wicked intelligence subsequently. I will tell you.'"

Chapter 79-3.2(27) (Commencement of the Sacrifice)

‘ "**B**rahma said, 'O sage! On one occasion, he started a great sacrifice. All the gods and *rishi*s arrived there and consecrated themselves. For purposes of the sacrifice and confounded by Shiva's *maya*, all the unblemished *maharshi*s arrived there—Agastya, Kashyapa, Vamadeva, Bhrigu, Dadhichi, the illustrious Vyasa, Bharadvaja, Goutama, Paila, Parashara, Garga, Bhargava, Kakupa, Sita, Sumantu, Trika, Kanka, Vaishampayana and many other sages. They went there happily, along with their wives and sons, to my son Daksha's sacrifice. All the large number of gods, the extremely prosperous guardians of the worlds and all other unblemished ones went to help in whichever way they could. I, the creator of the world, was honoured and invited from Satyaloka, along with my sons and companions and the embodied forms of the *Veda*s. With a great deal of affection, Vishnu was invited from Vaikuntha and was taken to the sacrifice, along with his attendants and companions. There were other deluded ones who went to the sacrifice. The evil-souled Daksha welcomed all of them. Tvashtri[830] created divine, extremely expensive, large and extremely radiant mansions and these were given to them. As each deserved, all the lords were honoured and kept there. Along with Vishnu and me, they were radiant. The great sacrifice was conducted in the *tirtha* of Kanakhala.[831]

[830] The architect of the gods.
[831] Kanakhala in Haridwar district.

Bhrigu and the others were made *ritvijas*.[832] Along with the large number of Maruts, Vishnu himself presided. I, Brahma, was there, to indicate how the rites of the three[833] should be followed. The guardians of the worlds became the gatekeepers and guards. Along with their attendants, they held weapons, and this excited curiosity. The personified form of a sacrifice itself arrived there, in the form of the sacrifice. All the great and best sages were those who held up the *Veda*s. The sacrificial fire divided itself into thousands of parts, so that it could swiftly receive the oblations offered at the great festival of the sacrifice. Eighty-six thousand *ritvijas* offered oblations. Sixty-four thousand divine *rishi*s functioned as *udgatri*s. Narada and others were *adhvaryu*s and *hotri*s. The *saptarshi*s recited separate chants. Daksha himself invited *gandharva*s, vidyadharas, large numbers of *siddha*s, large numbers of *aditya*s and their companions and innumerable excellent *naga*s and their followers to his sacrifice. There were large numbers of *brahmana rishi*s, royal *rishi*s, divine *rishi*s and kings, with their friends, advisers and soldiers. There were the best of Vasus and all the *ganadevata*s.[834] All of them went to the sacred sacrifice. Daksha arranged for all the auspicious requirements and consecrated himself for the sacrifice. Having had the auspicious benedictions pronounced, along with his wife, he was extremely radiant. The evil-souled Daksha did not invite Shambhu to the sacrifice. Deciding that he was a Kapali,[835]

---

[832] *Ritvijas* are officiating priests. Though the classification varied over time, there were four types of *ritivijas*. The *adhvaryu* chanted hymns from the *Yajur Veda*, the *hotri* chanted hymns from the *Rig Veda*, the *udgatri* chanted hymns from the *Sama Veda* and the *brahmana* chanted hymns from the *Atharva Veda*.

[833] The three *Veda*s.

[834] Deities (*devata*) who appear in groups (*gana*).

[835] One who holds or wears a skull, an expression used for an inferior person. Kapali is also Shiva's name.

he did not invite him to the sacrifice. This was despite the fact that his beloved daughter, Sati, was Kapali's wife. Since Daksha could not see her qualities, she too, was not invited to the sacrifice. In this way, the great festival of Daksha's sacrifice commenced.'"'

'"'There, all the revered ones were engaged in tasks connected with the sacrifice. Meanwhile, Dadhichi, Shiva's devotee, did not see the lord Shankara there and was mentally agitated. He spoke the following words. Dadhichi said, "O foremost among *devas* and *rishis*! Listen cheerfully to my words. Why has Shambhu not come to this great festival of the sacrifice? All the lords of the gods, the best of sages and the guardians of the worlds have arrived. Despite this, without the great-souled wielder of the trident, the sacrifice is not resplendent. Greatly learned ones praise him as the one who ensures everything auspicious. He is the ancient being, Vrishadhvaja Paresha, blue at the throat. He cannot be seen here. Daksha knows that he changes everything inauspicious into the auspicious. In the three worlds, the supreme and ancient one makes everything auspicious. Therefore, it is our task to invite Paramesha here. Let Brahma, the lord Vishnu, Indra, the guardians of the worlds, the *siddhas* or the *brahmanas* quickly bring Vishnu's lord here now. For the sacrifice to be complete in every way, Shankara must be brought. Everything goes where the divinity Maheshvara is. Therefore, Shambhu, along with Dakshayani, must be quickly brought. It is Shambhu, the *paramatman*, who makes everything pure. O lords of gods! The *paramatman* must be brought here, along with Amba. As soon as one remembers his name, everything becomes well. Therefore, every attempt must be made to bring Vrishadhvaja. If Shankara is brought, this sacrifice will be purified. Otherwise, it will remain incomplete. I am telling you the truth." Hearing his words, Daksha was filled with rage. The foolish one, evil in intelligence, spoke quickly and seemed to laugh at these words. "Vishnu is the foundation of all *deva*s and eternal *dharma* vests in him. I have invited him in the proper way. What else is needed for the sacrificial rites? All the *Veda*s, sacrifices and various kinds of rites are established in him. That Vishnu has come here. Brahma, the grandfather of the worlds, has come here, accompanied by the *Veda*s, the *Upanishad*s and the various *agama* texts. The king of the gods has himself come, along with large numbers of gods. All of you *rishi*s, devoid of sins, have come here. They are like serene receptacles of everything required for a sacrifice and they have come. All of them are firm in their vows and know the *Veda*s and the truth about the meanings of the *Veda*s. Since they are here, what is the need for Rudra? O *brahmana*![836] Urged by Brahma, I bestowed my daughter on him. O *brahmana*! Hara lacks a lineage. He does not have a father or a mother. He is the lord of *bhuta*s, *preta*s and *pishacha*s and is insufferable.[837] The foolish one has created himself. He is immobile, silent and envious. He is unworthy of this rite. That is the reason I have not brought him now. Therefore, you should never utter such words again. The task of all of you is to make my great sacrifice successful." Hearing his words, while *deva*s and sages heard, Dadhichi replied in words that were full of substance. Dadhichi answered, "Without Shiva, this great event is no

---

[836] Addressed to Dadhichi.

[837] A *preta* is a ghost, the spirit of a dead person or simply something evil. A *bhuta* has the same meaning. Strictly speaking, there are differences between *preta*, *bhuta* and *pishacha* (one who lives on flesh). A *preta* is the spirit (not necessarily evil) of a dead person before the funeral rites have been performed. A *bhuta* (not necessarily evil again) is the spirit of a dead person who has had a violent death and for whom, proper funeral rites have not been performed and may not even be performed. A *pishacha* (necessarily evil) is often created deliberately through evil powers. But the three terms are often used synonymously.

longer a sacrifice. In particular, your destruction will occur here." Saying this, Dadhichi emerged from Daksha's sacrificial arena and swiftly left for his own hermitage. The foremost devotees of Shankara and those who followed the views of Shiva's devotees also left for their own hermitages, after having pronounced instant curses. When these sages and others had left the sacrifice, the evil-minded Daksha laughed and spoke to the sages who hated Shiva. Daksha said, "The *brahmana* who loves Shiva, by the name of Dadhichi, has departed. Others who are like him have also left my sacrifice. Consequently, since this has become even more auspicious, I approve of this in every possible way. O lord of *deva*s, gods and sages! I am speaking the truth. They have lost their senses and are wicked. They speak what is false and are deceitful. They are beyond the pale of the *Veda*s and are evil in conduct. They should be cast away from sacrificial rites. With Vishnu at the forefront, all of you speak about the *Veda*s. O *brahmana*s and gods! You will soon render my sacrifice successful." Hearing his words and deluded by Shiva's *maya*, all the gods and *rishi*s performed that sacrifice to the gods. O lord of sages! I have thus described how the sacrifice was cursed. I will now tell you about the events that led to the destruction of the sacrifice. Listen lovingly.'"

Chapter 80-3.2(28) (Sati's Journey)

' "Brahma said, 'When the gods and rishis were leaving for the festival of Daksha's sacrifice, at that time, Devi was on Mount Gandhamadana. Under a canopy that had bathrooms,[838] surrounded by her friends, Dakshayani Sati

---

[838] *Dharagriha*, that is, a bathroom with some kind of shower or waterjet.

was engaged in many kinds of sports. While happily engaged
in her sports, Devi Sati saw Rohini headed towards Daksha's
sacrifice. Seeing her in that state, with her hair parted,[839] Sati
quickly spoke to Vijaya, the foremost among her friends, one
whom she loved more than her own life and one who ensured
her welfare. Sati said, "O best friend! O one whom I love
more than my own life! O Vijaya! Where is Rohini going
with Chandra? Ask quickly." Addressed by Sati in this way,
Vijaya swiftly went to their presence. In the appropriate way,
she asked the moon, "Where are you going?" Having heard
Vijaya's words first, he affectionately told her everything,
about the festival of Daksha's sacrifice and other things.
Hearing this, Vijaya was alarmed and quickly returned
to Devi. She told Sati everything that the moon had said.
Hearing this, Devi Kalika Sati was amazed. Not knowing
and not remembering any reason for this,[840] she thought in
various ways. "Daksha is my father. Virini is my mother. I am
their daughter Sati, and I am not wicked. Why have they not
invited me? Have they forgotten me, their beloved daughter? I
will lovingly ask Shankara about the reason for this." Having
thought about this and having made up her mind, she went
there. Devi Dakshayani left Vijaya, her best friend, there. She
quickly went to Shiva's presence. She saw him in the midst
of the assembly, along with many ganas—Nandi and other
immensely valiant ones, the foremost leaders and leaders of
groups. Daksha's daughter saw her lord and husband Ishana
there. To ask him about the reason, she swiftly reached
Shankara's presence. Full of love, Shiva took up his beloved
on his own lap. He showed her a great deal of respect and
addressed her in delightful words. Shambhu is Sarvesha and

---

[839] Meaning Rohini was dressed up.

[840] Obviously, Shiva had not told Sati about the conflict with
Daksha.

engages in many kinds of pastimes that yield pleasure. Amidst
the *gana*s, he quickly addressed Sati lovingly. Shambhu asked,
"Why have you come here, in the midst of this assembly?
You seem to be surprised. O slender-waisted one! With a
great deal of affection, tell me the reason." O lord among
sages! When Mahesha spoke to her in this way, Sati Shivaa
quickly prostrated herself before her lord and joined her
hands in salutation. Sati said, "I have heard that my father
is organizing a great sacrifice. All the gods and *rishi*s have
assembled at that great festival. Why does going to my father's
great sacrifice not appeal to you? O divinity! O lord of *deva*s!
O lord! Please tell me everything. The *dharma* of well-wishers
is that they must associate with well-wishers. O Mahadeva!
A well-wisher does what enhances delight. O lord! Therefore,
you must now make every effort to go with me to my father's
sacrificial arena. O husband! That is my request." Hearing
Sati's words, the divinity Maheshvara was pierced yet again
by the arrows of Daksha's words. Nevertheless, he replied
in courteous words. Maheshvara answered, "O Devi! Your
father, Daksha, hates me in particular. I have been respected
by all the foremost gods and *rishi*s. But there are other foolish
ones who are devoid of *jnana*. They have gone to your father's
sacrifice. O Devi! Without being invited, if a person goes to
someone else's house, he is dishonoured and that is worse
than death. In such a situation, even if a person like Indra
goes to someone else's house, he demeans himself. What need
be said of others? Such a journey will be inimical. Therefore,
especially you and I should not go to Daksha's sacrifice. O
beloved! I have told you the truth. People are not hurt by
arrows shot by enemies as much as they are hurt when their
hearts are pierced by wicked words uttered by one's own.
They strike at the inner organs. That is my view. O beloved!
Those who are deceitful do not perceive that they strike at
their own positions when they abuse those who possess the

six qualities,[841] learning and others. That is the view of the virtuous." The great-souled Mahesha addressed Sati in this way. She was filled with rage and spoke to Shiva, supreme among eloquent ones. Sati replied, "O Shambhu! O lord of everything! You are the one who makes a sacrifice successful. My father has committed an evil act by not inviting you there now. O Bhava! However, I wish to know everything about the sentiments of that evil-souled one and also those of the evil-souled gods and rishis who have assembled there. O lord! Therefore, I will go to my own father's sacrifice. O lord! O Maheshvara! Please grant me permission to go there." Bhagavan Rudra was thus addressed by Devi. Shiva himself knows everything and is a witness to everything. He is the one who ensures welfare. Having seen, he addressed Sati. Shiva said, "O Devi! If that is what appeals to you, you must certainly go. O one who is excellent in vows! With my permission, you must quickly go to your father's sacrifice. Ascend this Nandi, the bull who will be lovingly decorated. He will be ornamented in greatly resplendent fashion and possesses many qualities." Thus addressed by Rudra, Sati ascended that ornamented bull. Ornamented properly, Sati left for her father's residence. The *paramatman* gave her many great and radiant gifts, excellent umbrellas and *chamaras*, superb garments and ornaments. Obeying Shiva's command, sixty thousand of Rudra's *ganas* cheerfully went with her, full of curiosity about that great festival. As they left, in every direction, great festivities were organized by Sati and Shiva's beloved *ganas*, Vamadeva and others. Eagerly, the *ganas* chanted about Shiva and Shivaa's fame. Delighted, those immensely valiant ones, loved by Shiva, leapt around like children. As the mother of the universe departed, everything

[841] Usually learning, purity, truthfulness, compassion, liberality and non-violence. But the listing isn't uniform.

was extremely beautiful. Joyous sounds of happiness filled
the three worlds.'"'

Chapter 81-3.2(29) (Sati's Words)

" "Brahma said, 'Dakshayani went to the place where
the extremely radiant sacrifice was being performed
by enthusiastic gods, *asura*s and Indras among sages. She saw
her father's extremely radiant and beautiful house, full of
extraordinary objects and large numbers of gods and *rishi*s.
While she was still at the gate, Devi got down from her seat
astride Nandi and quickly went inside, to the place where the
sacrifice was being held. On seeing that Sati had come, her
illustrious mother, Asikni, and her sisters received her in the
appropriate way, with affection. However, on seeing her,
Daksha did not show the least bit of affection. Confounded by
Shiva's *maya*, and out of fear, nor did any of the others. O sage!
Extremely surprised at everyone's behaviour, Devi Sati bowed
down before her father and mother. In that sacrifice, she saw
the shares of *deva*s, Hari and others. But since no share had
been arranged for Shambhu, Sati was filled with intolerable
rage. Full of severe and complete anger, Sati glanced at Daksha
and everyone who had caused such dishonour with a cruel
glance, as if she was going to burn them down. Sati asked,
"How is it that the extremely auspicious Shambhu has not
been invited? He is the one who purifies the entire universe and
all its mobile and immobile objects. He is the sacrifice. He is
the best among those who know about sacrifices. He is part of
a sacrifice. He is the *dakshina* of a sacrifice. He is the performer
of a sacrifice. How can there be a sacrifice without Shambhu?
As soon as he is remembered, everything is sanctified. Anything
done without him is not sanctified. All the articles used, the

havya and the *kavya*,[842] are full of him. How can a sacrifice be done without Shambhu? Did you wish to disrespect Shiva, taking him to be an ordinary god? O worst among fathers! You have now become full of confused intelligence. Vishnu, Brahma and other *deva*s serve Maheshvara and obtained their own positions as a result of that. You do not know Hara. When Shambhu, their own lord, is not present, how have Vishnu, Brahma and other gods and the sages come to your sacrifice?" Having said this, Parameshani, with Bhava in her *atman*, spoke separately to Vishnu and all the others, reprimanding them. Sati said, "O Vishnu! Do you not know the truth about Mahadeva? The *shruti* texts speak about his *saguna* and *nirguna* forms. There are many occasions when Maheshvara has extended his helping hand to you. O Hari! In the past, for your sake, he instructed many, Shalva being the foremost.[843] O one with evil intelligence! Despite that, your mind has not been filled with *jnana*. Without Shiva, your own lord, being present, you desire a share in Daksha's sacrifice. You[844] had five faces earlier and were insolent. Sadashiva reduced you to four faces. Have you forgotten that so quickly? O Indra! Don't you know about Mahadeva's valour? Hara had ruthlessly reduced your thunderbolt to ashes.[845] O gods! Don't you know about Mahadeva's valour? O Atri, Vasishtha and other sages! What have you done? On an earlier occasion, the lord was roaming around in Daruvana,[846] begging for alms. At that time, you sages cursed Rudra, in his form as a mendicant.

---

[842] Respectively, oblations offered to gods and ancestors.

[843] This is a reference to King Shalva, Shiva's devotee, who hated Krishna and fought against him.

[844] This is spoken to Brahma.

[845] When Indra had attacked Shiva with his *vajra*.

[846] Daruvana or Darukavana is named after a demon named Daruka and his wife Darukaa, really the latter. The *lingam* is identified as the Nageshvara *jyotirlingam* in Dvaraka.

Have you forgotten what Rudra did when you cursed him? His *lingam* burnt down the entire universe, with its mobile and immobile objects. All of you, Vishnu, Brahma and the gods and the sages, have been filled with foolishness. You have come to a sacrifice that does not have Shambhu. Even if one uses everything accumulated in the *Vedas*, the *Vedangas*, the words of the sacred texts and Vedanta, one will not be able to obtain complete understanding of Shambu." With her heart shattered, Sati, the mother of the universe, spoke many such angry words. Hearing these words, the minds of Vishnu and all *devas* and sages were agitated and filled with fear. They remained silent.'"'

'"'However, Daksha heard his daughter's words. He glanced towards Sati with a cruel glance and addressed her in angry words. Daksha said, "Why are you speaking so much? There is nothing for you to do here now. You can go or stay. O fortunate one! Why have you come here? The learned know that your husband, Shiva, is inauspicious. He doesn't have a lineage. He is outside the pale of the *Vedas*. He is the king of *bhutas*, *pretas* and *pishachas*. O daughter! Therefore, knowing this, I have not invited Rudra, who wears evil attire, to this sacrifice and this assembly of *devas*, *rishis* and learned ones. Urged by Vidhatri, I bestowed you on this evil and wicked person. Rudra is evil-souled and haughty. He does not know the true meaning of anything. O one with the sweet smiles! Therefore, cast aside your rage and be calm. Since you have come to this sacrifice, accept what is given to you." Daksha addressed his daughter, Sati, worshipped by the three worlds, in this way. Seeing that her father was full of such contempt, she became extremely angry. She wondered, "How can I return to Shankara? I desire to see Shankara. But if he asks me, what will I say in reply?" Full of anger, Sati, who gives birth to the three worlds, sighed. She replied to her father, the evil-minded Daksha. Sati said, "Those who criticize Mahadeva and listen to such criticism will go to hell and remain there, until the moon and the sun exist. Therefore, I will cast aside my body and enter the fire. O father! Having heard this disrespect shown to my lord, what is the point of my remaining alive? In particular, if a person possesses the capacity to slice off the tongue of a person who utters the intolerable criticism of Shambhu, there is no doubt that he is purified. If he doesn't possess the capacity, a supreme and learned person should cover his ears and leave the spot. He will be purified. That is the best way to avoid going to hell." She spoke about this policy of *dharma* and repented. With a mind full of grief, she remembered Shankara's words. Enraging Daksha even more, Sati addressed all *deva*s and sages, Vishnu and the others, in these determined words. Sati said, "O father! Having criticized Shambhu, you will repent later. You will undergo great hardships in this world and face pain thereafter. The *paramatman* is loved. There is no one in the world he does not love. Other than you, who can hate and be adversarial towards Sharva? However, it is not surprising that those who are jealous should indulge in such great criticism. The great dust from his feet destroys *tamas* and makes everything auspicious. In any connection, even if men utter the two *askhara*s in Shiva's name once,[847] all their sins are swiftly destroyed. His deeds are sacred and unblemished, but you hate Shiva. Shambu is Sarveshvara. His command cannot be crossed. Alas! You are crooked. Like bees, the mind searches out his lotus feet. They are full of the essence of the *brahman* and bestow everything. If one lovingly tends to them, one obtains everything. All the noble people in the world instantly serve Shiva, lovingly. O foolish one! But you hate him. You will suffer infinite bonds. He is spoken of as auspicious.[848] Other

[847] Shi + va.
[848] The word Shiva means auspicious.

than you, have other learned people, Brahma and Sanaka and other sages, regarded Shiva as inauspicious? He wears matted hair. He resides in cremation grounds and holds a skull. Ashes are his ornament. Knowing this, those who are pervasive in intelligence love him. They affectionately touch his feet and place that dust on their heads. The sages know that these are the ornaments of Parameshvara Shiva. The *Veda*s speak of two kinds of rites—*pravritti* and *nivritti*. Learned ones reflect on these two kinds of conduct. They are contrary to each other, and both cannot be followed simultaneously. But Shambhu is the supreme *brahman* and these rites do not touch him in any way. Let us never follow the footsteps of my father and do what he does. The trails of smoke that emerge from your sacrificial pavilion are not the path of supreme liberation. The *lingam* that is not manifest is always served by *avadhuta*s. O father! O one with wicked intelligence! You should not show any pride. What is the need to speak a lot? You are wicked, with every kind of evil intelligence. I have no further need of a body that originated from you. Shame on such a greatly futile life, which has originated from a person who is crooked. A learned person must specially avoid any association with such a person. Bhagavan Vrishadhvaja has said that you have given me your *gotra*. Therefore, my name has abruptly come to be Dakshayani and my mind is greatly distressed on this account. Therefore, I will cast aside this body, born from you. It stinks and is always contemptible. Hence, I will certainly give it up now and obtain what ensures happiness. O gods! O sages! All of you listen to my words. Evil in your minds, you have perpetrated an act that is evil in every possible way. All of you are foolish. You are addicted to criticizing Shiva and picking quarrels with him. Hara will certainly punish and restrain all of you." In that sacrifice, Sati spoke these words to Daksha and the others. She mentally remembered Shambhu, whom she loved more than her own life.'"

Chapter 82-3.2(30) (Sati Gives up Her Life)

‘ ‘‘Narada said, 'Sati, loved by Shankara, was silent. O Vidhatri! What happened after that? Out of affection, please tell me.'’’

‘‘Brahma replied, 'Lovingly remembering her own husband, Devi Sati was silent. Tranquil in her mind, she quickly sat down on the ground, in the southern direction. She sipped water and purified herself, covering herself in her garment. She closed her eyes and remembering her husband, entered the path of *yoga*. Wan of face, she maintained equilibrium between the two breaths of life—*prana* and *apana*. From the *chakra* in the navel, she raised *udana* up. Using her intelligence, Sati raised it up to her heart, then to her throat and finally to the middle of her eyebrows. The unblemished one was loved by Shankara more than his own life. In this way, angry at Daksha, Sati suddenly gave up her own life. Resorting to the path of *yoga*, she held the pure breath of life and burnt her body. She thought of her own husband's feet and nothing else. With her intelligence fixed on the path of *yoga*, that is all Sati saw. Purified of sins, the body was reduced to fire. O best among sages! Following her own wish, she instantly reduced it to ashes. Loud exclamations were uttered by those who witnessed this on earth and from the sky. There were extraordinary and wonderful sounds of lamentation, causing fear to the gods and others. "Alas! Devi Sati, supremely loved by Shambhu like a divinity, has given up her life. Which extremely wicked person has enraged her? Alas! Behold the extremely wicked thing that Daksha has done. He is Prajapati's son and is the lord of all mobile and immobile objects. Alas! The spirited Devi Sati was distressed in her mind. The virtuous should always look at Vrishadhvaja's beloved with eyes full of respect. Shame on Prajapati, who hates the *brahman* and has intolerance in his heart. He will obtain endless ill fame on earth. His daughter was born from his own body, and he proceeded to hate Shambhu. When he dies, because of his crime, he will enjoy great miseries in hell." Witnessing this extraordinary act of Sati giving up her own body, people spoke in this way. Her attendants were instantly filled with wrath. They stood up and raised their weapons. All the *gana*s, who were stationed at the door, were filled with anger. The lord Shambhu's attendants were extremely strong and were enraged. They lamented and uttered words of "Shame." The valiant leaders of Shankara's *gana*s uttered such loud words of lamentation. Those loud sounds of lamentation enveloped the directions. All *deva*s and sages present there were filled with fear. Consulting each other, all the angry *gana*s raised their weapons up. They created destruction and the sounds of their weapons spread in the directions. Some of them were filled with grief and used their weapons to slice their own limbs. O *devarshi*! With those extremely sharp weapons, which could take away lives, others sliced their own heads and faces. In this way, when Dakshayani died, twenty thousand *gana*s died along with her. It was extraordinary. When these *gana*s were destroyed, the remainder of the great-souled Shankara's *gana*s stood up and raised their weapons. Angry, they rushed forward to kill Daksha. O sage! Seeing that they were swiftly advancing and were going to destroy the sacrifice, the illustrious Bhrigu uttered *mantra*s from *Yajur Veda* and offered oblations into the *dakshinagni* fire. When Bhrigu offered these oblations, thousands of[849] giant *asura*s known as the Ribhus arose. They were exceedingly valiant. O lord among sages! They used liquids on fire[850] as weapons and there was an extremely terrible clash between them and the *pramatha*s. Even hearing about it makes

---

[849] Ribhus, also known as Vibhus, are divinities whose notion has evolved over time.

[850] Alternatively, flaming torches.

the body hair stand up. The Ribhus were extremely brave. They were full of the energy of the *brahman* and slaughtered the *pramatha*s, who could no longer endeavour, in every direction. Slaughtered in this way, Shiva's *gana*s swiftly fled. This extraordinary event occurred as a result of the wishes of Shiva and Mahashakti. Witnessing this, the *rishi*s, *deva*s, Shakra and the others, the large number of Maruts, the Vishvadevas, the Ashvins and the guardians of the world were silent. From every direction, some beseeched the lord Vishnu. They were anxious and repeatedly consulted the one who removed impediments. Some, with good intelligence, thought for a long time about the consequences of what had been done and were greatly anxious. The gods, Vishnu and others had repeatedly heard the sounds of destruction. In this way, there were impediments to the sacrifice of the evil-souled one. O sage! Daksha was Brahma's relative and hated Shankara.'"'

Chapter 83-3.2(31) (A Voice from the Firmament)

Brahma said, 'O lord among sages! Meanwhile, a voice was heard from the firmament. While Daksha and the others heard, it spoke the truth. The voice from the firmament said, "O Daksha! O evildoer! O one who is addicted to insolent conduct! O immensely foolish one! What have you done? This deed will bring disaster. You did not act according to the words of Dadhichi, king among Shiva's devotees. That was the yardstick for ensuring every kind of happiness and auspiciousness. O foolish one! But you did not do that. After invoking an intolerable curse on you, the *brahmana* departed from the sacrifice. Even then, you did not comprehend anything. You are foolish in your mind. Why did you not treat your own daughter with great affection? The auspicious Sati came to your house of her own accord. O one who is weak in knowledge! Why did you not worship Sati and Bhava? You were deluded and haughty since you are Brahma's son. Sati must always be worshipped. She is the one who destroys all sins. She is the mother of the worlds. She ensures welfare and is half of Shankara's body. Sati must always be worshipped. She bestows every kind of good fortune. Maheshvari bestows everything auspicious on her own devotees. If Sati is constantly worshipped, she destroys the fear of *samsara*. Devi bestows what the mind desires and takes away every kind of calamity. If Sati is constantly worshipped, she bestows fame and prosperity. She is supreme Parameshani and confers objects of pleasure and emancipation. Sati is the mother of the universe. She protects the universe. She is the primordial Shakti. At the end of the *kalpa*, she destroys the universe. Sati is the mother of the universe. She is Vishnu's enchanting mother. She is described as the mother of Brahma, Indra, the moon, the fire, the sun and *deva*s. Sati is the one who bestows the fruits of austerities, *dharma* and donations. Mahadevi is Shambhu's Shakti. She is the slayer of the wicked. She is greater than the greatest. Such is Devi Sati, and you did not offer a share to the one whose beloved wife she is. In your folly, you have acted in a wicked way. Shambhu is Paramesha. He is the lord of everything. He is greater than the greatest. He deserves to be worshipped by Brahma, Vishnu and the others. He bestows every kind of welfare. Desiring to see him, *siddha*s torment themselves through austerities. Desiring to see him, *yogi*s engage in *yoga*. The sight of Shankara is said to yield great fruits—infinite wealth and grain and success in sacrifices. The lord Shiva is the creator of the universe. He is the lord of every kind of knowledge. He is the supreme and primordial lord of knowledge. Among everything auspicious, he is the most auspicious. O crooked one! You have shown disrespect to his Shakti. Therefore, your sacrifice will be destroyed. If someone who should be worshipped is not worshipped, the consequence is inauspicious. Shiva should have been worshipped, but you did not worship him. Every day, with delight, Shesha bears the dust from his feet on his one thousand hoods. Sati is that Shiva's Shakti. With constant love, Vishnu worshipped his lotus feet and performed *dhyana* on them. That is how he obtained the status of being Vishnu. Sati is the beloved of that Shambhu. With constant love, Brahma worshipped his lotus feet and performed *dhyana* on them. That is how he obtained the status of being Brahma. Sati is the beloved of that Shambhu. With constant love, Indra and the other guardians of the worlds worshipped his lotus feet and performed *dhyana* on them. That is how they obtained their respective positions. Shiva is the father of the universe. Sati Shakti is the mother of the universe. O foolish one! Not having honoured her, how will you obtain what is good for you? Since you did not devotedly worship Bhavani and Shankara, misfortune will cross your path. Calamities will cross your path. Without worshipping Shiva Shambhu, how could you aspire for welfare? What is this indomitable pride that you possess? Your pride will now be destroyed. Since Sarvesha has turned away from you, what will *deva*s do for you? I do not see how they can help you in any possible way. If *deva*s try to help you now, they will be destroyed, like moths by a fire. Your face will burn, and your sacrifice will be destroyed. Anyone who helps you will also be swiftly burned. If any of the immortals seeks to help this evil-souled one, he will now confront the inauspicious. That is a pledge. Therefore, let all the immortals leave this sacrificial pavilion. Otherwise, in every possible way, they will now be destroyed. Let all the others, the sages and *naga*s, also leave this sacrifice. Otherwise, in every possible way, they will now be destroyed. O Hari! Leave this sacrificial pavilion quickly. Otherwise, in every possible way, you will now be destroyed. O Vidhatri! Leave this sacrificial pavilion quickly. Otherwise, in every possible way, you will now be destroyed." The voice from the firmament, which ensures every kind of welfare, spoke in this way to everyone who was present in the sacrificial arena. O son! Hearing this voice from the firmament, Hari and all the other gods and the sages and others were filled with wonder.'"'

Chapter 84-3.2(32) (Virabhadra's Origin)

'‘"Narada asked, 'After hearing this voice from the firmament, what did the ignorant Daksha do? What did the others do? What occurred? Shiva's *gana*s were defeated by the strength of Bhrigu's *mantra*s. What did they do? Where did they go? O immensely intelligent one! Please tell me.'"'

'"Brahma replied, 'Hearing the voice from the firmament, the gods and all the others were astounded. They did not say anything. Confused, they remained there. The brave remnants of Shiva's *gana*s were made to flee by the strength of Bhrigu's *mantra*s. They went and sought refuge with Shiva. After lovingly prostrating themselves before the infinitely energetic Rudra, they told him everything that had occurred. The *gana*s said, "O lord of *deva*s! O Mahadeva! We have sought refuge with you. Please save us. O protector! Please listen affectionately to everything connected with Sati. O Mahesha! The extremely evil-souled Daksha was insolent. Without any discomfort, he dishonoured Sati and did not show her any affection. The wicked and insolent Daksha gave *deva*s a share but did not give you a share. Instead, he uttered harsh words. O lord! Seeing that you were not given a share in the sacrifice, Sati became angry. Censuring her father in many ways, she gave up her body. In shame, ten thousand of the *gana*s died there. They sliced off their limbs with weapons. We, the others, were enraged. Armoured and fearful in appearance, we powerfully rushed forward to destroy the sacrifice. However, using his own powers, Bhrigu abused us and countered us. O lord who holds up the universe! We have come here to seek refuge with you. Please grant us freedom from fear. We are scared that we will be killed. O great lord! In particular, we have witnessed the dishonour exhibited by Daksha and the others at the sacrifice. They are wicked and extremely insolent. They are foolish in intelligence. Do what you want with them." O Narada! In this way, they told him everything connected with Sati.'"'

'"'Hearing the words of his own *ganas*, the lord remembered Narada, so that he might quickly hear everything that had occurred. O *devarshi*! O one with divine sight! You swiftly went there. Having devotedly prostrated yourself, you stood there, your hands joined in salutation. The lord praised you and asked you about Sati's account, about what had transpired after she went to Daksha's sacrifice. O son! Asked by Shambhu, with Shiva in your *atman*, you told him everything that had happened at Daksha's sacrifice. O sage! Ishvara heard the truth, spoken through your mouth. Rudra, extremely terrible in his valour, was instantly angered. Rudra, the destroyer of the worlds, plucked out a strand from his matted hair and seething in rage, flung it on top of the mountain. O sage! The strand from the lord's matted hair divided into two parts. There was a mighty roar, like the terrible sound heard at the time of the great dissolution. O *devarshi*! From the first part of that strand of matted hair, the immensely strong Virabhadra arose. He was extremely terrible and was foremost among the *ganas*. He covered the entire earth and extended ten *angulas* above it. He stood there, lofty, resembling the fire of dissolution. He possessed two thousand arms. As the great Rudra sighed in rage, one thousand *jvaras* and thirteen *sannipatas* were generated.[851] Mahakali originated from the other part of the strand of matted hair. O son! She was extremely fearful and was surrounded by crores of *bhutas*. All these embodied forms were cruel and harsh, causing terror to the worlds. They blazed in their own energy and burnt everything down.'"'

'"'The valiant Virabhadra prostrated himself before Parameshvara. Skilled in the use of words, he joined his hands in salutation and spoke the following words. Virabhadra said, "O great Rudra! O extremely terrible one! O one with the sun and the moon as your eyes! What is my task? O lord! Quickly command me about what I must do. O Ishana! Are the oceans to be dried up in an instant? O Ishana! Are the mountains to be crushed in an instant? O Hara! Is the universe to be reduced to ashes in an instant? Are the gods and lords among sages to be reduced to ashes in an instant? O Shankara! Are all the worlds to be destroyed? O Ishana! Is my task one of causing violence to all beings? O Maheshvara! Through your favours, there is nothing that I am incapable of doing. There has been no one who is my equal in valour, nor will there ever be. O lord! Instruct me about my task and send me. Through your favours, I will swiftly accomplish that task. O Shankara! Through your command, even the inferior can cross over the ocean that is the world. Am I therefore not capable of crossing an ocean that is full of great adversity? O Shankara! Sent by you, even a blade of grass is capable of easily accomplishing a great task. There is no doubt about this. O Shambhu! Through your pastimes, any task meets with success. Therefore, through your favours, send me. O Shambhu! A strength like mine has been obtained through your favours. O Shankara! Without your favours, who can be strong? Without your command, not even a blade

---

[851] *Jvara* is fever and *sannipata* is aggravation caused by disequilibrium in three *doshas* or humours in the body, *vata*, *pitta* and *kapha*.

of grass can be moved. One is incapable. There is no doubt that
this is the truth. O Shankara! All *deva*s and others are subject
to Shambhu's control. I am controlled in that way. All those
with bodies are controlled. O Mahadeva! I prostrate myself
before you. I prostrate myself again. O Hara! Now, swiftly
dispatch me to successfully accomplish whatever you desire. O
Shambhu! My right limbs are throbbing repeatedly.[852] O lord!
Dispatch me. I will be victorious today. For some reason, there is
a special kind of enthusiasm and delight. O Shambhu! My mind
is fixed to your lotus feet. There has been something auspicious
at every step that I have taken. If a person has firm devotion
towards Shambhu, the refuge of everything auspicious, that
ensures auspiciousness for him, and he is always victorious."
The lord of auspiciousness heard these words and was content.
Pronouncing benedictions, he said, "O Virabhadra! May you
be victorious." Maheshvara said, "O son! O Virabhadra! With
an excellent mind, listen to my words. Make efforts to do this
and that will bring satisfaction to me. Daksha, the crooked
son of Vidhatri, is engaged in the task of organizing a sacrifice.
In particular, he opposes me. He is immensely proud and has
become ignorant now. Along with everything that accompanies
the sacrifice, reduce that sacrifice to ashes. O supreme among
*gana*s! After that, return quickly to my abode. If there are any
gods, *gandharva*s, *rakshasa*s or others there, swiftly reduce
them to ashes too. If Vishnu, Brahma, Shachi's consort or
Yama are there, make efforts to bring all of them down. If
gods, *gandharva*s, *yaksha*s or others are there, quickly and
violently, reduce them to ashes too. If anyone is there, crossing
the pledge Dadhichi made about me, make determined efforts
to blaze against them. The *pramatha*s will go with you. In their
confusion, if Vishnu and the others are present, they will be
attracted with *mantra*s and quickly burnt down. Those who

[852] An auspicious sign.

are insolent and remain there, crossing the pledge made to me, they act against me. They will be blazed in garlands of fire. Blaze and reduce to ashes those who are present at the place of Daksha's sacrifice, along with their wives and material objects. After that, swiftly return. When you go there, it is possible that the Vishvadevas will lovingly praise you. Even then, like a fire, swiftly blaze against them. If *deva*s have acted in a contrary way, surround them with garlands of flames. Perform *dhyana* on me, your protector, and swiftly blaze against them, using a fiery form. O brave one! Blaze against Daksha and everyone else, their wives and relatives. After this, toying with Daksha, drink water."[853] With eyes coppery-red in rage, the protector of the ordinances of the *Veda*s, Kala's[854] enemy and everyone's lord, spoke these words to the immensely valiant one, before stopping.""'

Chapter 85-3.2(33) (Virabhadra's March)

' "Brahma said, 'Virabhadra lovingly heard Shri Mahesha's words. He was extremely satisfied and prostrated himself before Maheshvara. He bowed his head down and accepted the command of the lord of *deva*s, the wielder of the trident. After this, Virabhadra quickly left for the sacrifice. To increase the dazzle, Shiva dispatched crores of *gana*s. Along with them, the immensely valiant one resembled the fire of dissolution. Those powerful *gana*s proceeded ahead of Virabhadra. Brave *gana*s also followed him at the rear, exciting curiosity. Along with Virabhadra, there were hundreds of thousands of *gana*s. These were companions in

---

[853] Don't drink any water before accomplishing the task.
[854] Yama's.

the form of time and destiny and in appearance, all of them resembled Rudra. The great-souled Virabhadra wore attire and ornaments that were like those of Hara, and he was with these *ganas*. He possessed one thousand firm arms, resembling the king of serpents. Powerful and terrifying, he was astride a chariot. There were so many chariots that two thousand *nalvas*[855] of ground were covered. Ten thousand lions made efforts to pull the vehicles. Like that, there were many powerful lions, tigers, *makaras*, fish and thousands of elephants to act as those who protected the flanks. To destroy Daksha's sacrifice, Virabhadra advanced quickly. Released by *kalpavrikshas*, there was a shower of flowers. The *ganas* praised the brave one, who was engaged in carrying out the task instructed by Shipi.[856] As the festivity of the march commenced, there was curiosity everywhere. Along with the large number of *bhutas*, Mahakali advanced to destroy Daksha. The nine Durgas were with her—Kali, Katyayani, Ishani, Chamunda, Mundamardini, Bhadrakali, Bhadra, Tvarita and Vaishnavi. To destroy Daksha's sacrifice, *dakinis*, *shakinis*, *bhutas*, *pramathas*, *guhyakas*, *kushmandas*, *parpatas*, *chatakas*, *brahma-rakshasas*, *bhairavas* and *kshetrapalas* emerged swiftly.[857] These brave ones were intent on obeying Shiva's command. There were sixty-four categories of *yoginis*.[858] To destroy Daksha's sacrifice, they rushed forth, enraged. O Narada! Hear about the numbers of the *ganas*. There were large numbers. The foremost among

[855] A *nalva* is a measure of distance, equal to 400 *hastas* or cubits.

[856] Shipi is Shiva's name and also that of Vishnu.

[857] In this context, these are different types of demons and demonesses.

[858] The number of *yoginis* varies, but is usually given as sixty-four, or groups of sixty-four. The names also vary. Often, *yoginis* are linked with *matrikas*, though the names/numbers of *matrikas* also vary. Each *matrika* is associated with seven other *yoginis*. With eight *matrikas*, there are 8 × 8 *yoginis*. But this taxonomy is not consistent.

them were extremely strong and full of fortitude. Ganeshvara
Shankukarna advanced with ten crores. Kekaraksha had ten
crores and Vikrita had eight. Vishakha had sixty-four crores
and Pariyatrika had nine. The brave Sarvankaka had six crores
and so did Vikritanana. Jvalakesha, bull among ganas, had
twelve crores. Samadjjiman had seven crores and Dudrabha
had eight. Kapalisha had five crore ganas and Sandaraka had
six. Kotikunda had crores and crores. The brave Vishtambha,
supreme among ganas, had eight crores. O son! Sannada and
Pippala each had one thousand crores. Aveshana had eight
crores and Chandrapatana also had eight crores. Mahavesha,
leader of ganas, had one thousand crores. O sage! Kundi had
twelve crores and so did Parvata, the excellent gana. They
advanced to destroy Daksha's sacrifice. Kala, Kalaka and
Mahakala advanced towards Daksha's sacrifice, each with
one hundred crores. Agnikrit had one hundred crores and
Agnimukha had one crore. Adityamurdha and Ghanavaha
each had one crore. Sannaha had a hundred crore ganas and
Kumuda had a crore. Amogha and Kokila, lord of ganas,
each had crores and crores. O son! Kashthagudha, Sukeshi,
Vrishabha and Sumantraka, lord of ganas, each advanced
with sixty crores. Kakapadodara, supreme among ganas, and
Santanaka, bull among ganas, each had sixty crores. Mahabala
and Pungava had nine crores each. O son! Madhupinga, leader
of ganas, departed with ninety crores. Nila and Purnabhadra
also had that number each. Chaturvakra, leader of ganas,
departed with one hundred crores. Kashthaguda, Sukesha
and Vrishabha had sixty-four crores each.[859] Virupaksha,
leader of ganas, had sixty-four crores. Talaketu, Shadashya
and Panchasya, leader of ganas, had the same number each.
O sage! Samvartaka, the lord Kulisha, Lokantaka, Diptatma,
Daityantaka, Bhringiriti, Devadevapriya, Ashani and Bhalaka

---

[859] This sentence is unnecessary repetition.

each had sixty-four thousand *gana*s. Following Shiva's command, the valiant Virabhadra, lord of all those who are brave, advanced, surrounded by crores and thousands of crores, hundreds and twenty times that number. As the valiant one rapidly marched, thousands of crores of *bhuta*s and three crores of canine *gana*s born from the body hair proceeded with him. There was the loud sound of drums and many kinds of sounds from conch shells. There were many kinds of horns. All these emerged from Hara's mouth and matted hair. In that great festival, many kinds of musical instruments were played. The sound spread everywhere and tied everything in a pleasant bond. O great sage! In this way, Virabhadra marched with his army and many pleasant portents were repeatedly seen.'"'

Chapter 86-3.2(34) (Bad Omens)

' " Brahma said, 'Along with the *gana*s, Virabhadra advanced in this fashion. Daksha and the gods witnessed bad omens. As Virabhadra and the *gana*s marched, there were diverse evil portents of the three types.[860] These signified the destruction of the sacrifice of *deva*s and *rishi*s. Daksha's left eye, arm and thigh throbbed. O son! There were many such inauspicious indications, suggesting hardships of many kinds. There was an earthquake at the place where Daksha's sacrifice was taking place. At midday, Daksha saw extraordinary *nakshatra*s. The directions turned extremely dirty, and the sun seemed speckled. The environment was besieged with one thousand terrifying signs. *Nakshatra*s, blazing like lightning and the fire, fell down. Some *nakshatra*s moved

---

[860] Relating to *adhidaivika* (destiny), *adhibhoutika* (nature) and *adhyatmika* (one's own nature).

diagonally. Others descended, facing downwards. Thousands
of vultures arrived and touched Daksha's head. Shadows from
the wings of vultures darkened the sacrificial pavilion. Jackals
howled towards the top of the sacrificial ground. Netraka[861]
showered down meteors and white scorpions were born from
these. Harsh winds started to blow and there were showers of
dust. Insects[862] arose and were whirled around, trembling in
the wind. The new pavilion constructed for Daksha's sacrifice
by *devas* and Daksha was flung upwards by the gust of wind.
Daksha and all the others repeatedly vomited blood, lumps of
flesh and stakes. It was extraordinary. The lamps flickered, as
if they had been struck by the wind. Everyone was miserable,
as if struck by showers of weapons. The eyes of Daksha and
the others resembled lotuses growing in the forest. But at that
moment, they seemed to have been struck by showers during
the monsoon or struck by showers of hail. Suddenly, they
resembled lotuses at night or lotuses at the time of early dawn.
Devas seemed to shower down blood and the directions were
covered in darkness. In particular, the directions blazed and
terrified everyone. In this way, the gods and others witnessed
diverse evil portents. O sage! Vishnu and the others were filled
with great fear. Some shrieked "Alas! We have been killed."
They fell down on the ground, senseless. They were like trees
along the banks, struck by the force of a river. They fell down
immobile on the ground, like cruel snakes that had been killed.
Like balls, they fell down on the ground and rose up again.
Tormented and scorched, they wept like female ospreys. Their
words and the sounds of their weeping mingled with each other.
All of them, including Vishnu, were anxious and their power
was impeded. Anxious, they clung to each other's throats and
seemed to move like tortoises. Meanwhile, a disembodied voice

[861] An evil star or planet.
[862] Specifically, locusts.

spoke and was heard by all *deva*s present there, particularly
by Daksha. The voice from the sky said, "O Daksha and the
other extremely foolish ones! You are wicked in intelligence.
Originating from Hara, great miseries that cannot be countered
will descend on you. The foolish ones, *deva*s and others, present
here, will utter words of lamentation. There is no doubt that
they will confront great miseries." Hearing the voice from the
sky and witnessing the evil portents, Daksha was filled with
fear. This was also true of other *deva*s. Daksha trembled
and his mind turned numb. He went and sought refuge with
Vishnu, his own lord, the destroyer of enemies. Overwhelmed
by fear and insensible, he prostrated himself and praised him.
He spoke to Vishnu, the lord of *deva*s, who is affectionate
towards those who are his own.'"'

Chapter 87-3.2(35) (Vishnu's Words)

' " ' "Daksha said, "O lord of *deva*s! O Hari! O Vishnu!
O friend of the distressed! O ocean of compassion!
You should protect me and my sacrifice. You are the one who
protects a sacrifice. You are the sacrifice. You are the one who
performs the sacrifice. You are the *atman* of the sacrifice. O
lord! Please show me your compassion and ensure that this
sacrifice is not shattered."'"'

'"Brahma continued, 'In this way, Daksha lovingly told
him many things. His mind overwhelmed with fear, he fell
down at his feet. Daksha's mind was suffering, and Vishnu
raised him up. He heard the words of the evil-minded one
and remembered Shiva. He remembered his own lord, Shiva
Mahesha Parameshvara. He knew about Shiva's *tattva*. Hence,
he kindled understanding in Daksha. Hari said, "O Daksha!
Listen. I will tell you the truth. Listen to my words. They are

like a great *mantra* and are beneficial to you in every possible way. They will bring you happiness. O Daksha! You did not know the truth and you have shown disrespect to the lord of everything, Shankara, the *paramatman*. If Ishvara is dishonoured, every task becomes futile in every possible way. In fact, there is a calamity at every step. When those who should not be worshipped are worshipped, and those who should be worshipped are not worshipped, poverty, death and fear—these three occur. Therefore, every possible effort must be made to honour Vrishadhvaja. Since Mahesha has been dishonoured, a great fear has presented itself. Though we possess powers, we have no powers now. Because of your bad policy, this has happened. I am telling you the truth." Hearing Vishnu's words, Daksha was filled with worries. His face turned pale. He sat down on the ground and was silent.'"

'"'Meanwhile, sent by Rudra, Virabhadra, the leader of *gana*s, arrived at Daksha's sacrifice, along with the soldiers. Some followed him at the rear, others arrived through the sky. There were others who enveloped all the directions and sub-directions. These brave *gana*s followed Sharva's command. They were fearless and like Rudra in valour. There were innumerable, such supremely valiant ones, and they roared like lions. Their loud roars echoed in the three worlds. Dust covered the firmament, and the directions were enveloped in darkness. Terrified, the earth, along with its seven *dvipa*s, mountains and forests, quaked. All the oceans were agitated. Those great soldiers were like that, signifying the destruction of the worlds. Seeing this, the immortals and others were astounded. Witnessing the arrival of the soldiers, Daksha's agitated face turned red. Like a rod, accompanied by his wife, he fell down at Vishnu's feet. Daksha said, "With you as my strength, I embarked on this great sacrifice. O Vishnu! O great lord! You are the yardstick in accomplishing any virtuous task. O Vishnu! You are the witness to rites and the one who protects sacrifices. You are the womb of the *dharma* of the *Veda*s. O great lord! You are the *brahman*. O lord! Therefore, you must devise a means to save my sacrifice. Who other than you is capable? You are the lord of everything." Daksha had turned himself away from Shiva's *tattva*s and was miserable at the time. Hearing his words, Vishnu addressed him in the following words, kindling understanding in him.'"'

"'"Vishnu said, "O Daksha! I will devise a means to protect your sacrifice. My pledge of protecting truth and *dharma* is famous. What you have said is the truth. However, you have committed a transgression. O Daksha! Listen. I will tell you now. Cast your cruel intelligence aside. There was a wonderful incident in Naimisha *kshetra* and it occurred in an instant.[863] O Daksha! Don't you remember it now? Has your evil intelligence made you forget it? Among those present here, who is capable of protecting you against Rudra's rage? O Daksha! If anyone protects an evil-minded person like you, he will meet with no approval. O evil-minded one! You do not see what should be done and what should not be done. Just because one is capable, a rite doesn't always find success. Understand that your own *karma* does not take place because of your own capacity. Other than Sha[864] Ishvara himself, no one else can bestow *karma*. If a person is devoted to Ishvara and is serene and full of faith in his mind, Shiva bestows on him the fruits of *karma*. If men resort to *jnana* alone and are not devoted to Ishvara, they go to hell for one hundred crores of *kalpa*s. After this, in birth after birth, they are bound in the nooses of *karma*. As a result of *karma* alone, they are cooked in hell. Virabhadra, the one who crushes enemies, is the leader of Rudra's *gana*s. He has originated from the fire of Rudra's rage and has arrived at this sacrifice, along with the *gana*s. There is no doubt that

---

[863] *Nimesha* is the twinkling of an eye.
[864] Sha is one of Shiva's names.

he has come here for our destruction. Indeed, there is nothing
that he is incapable of doing. There is no doubt that all of
us will be set ablaze. There is no doubt that the great lord's
heart will be pacified only after that. In my confusion, I have
also deviated from the pledge given to Shri Mahadeva. Since
I have remained with you, together with you, I will also face
miseries. O Daksha! I no longer possess the capacity to counter
this. I have transgressed the pledge and have opposed Shiva.
Those who oppose Mahesha cannot find happiness in the three
periods of time.[865] Hence, together with you, there is no doubt
that I will also face miseries now. My Sudarshana *chakra* is
incapable of striking him. It is a *chakra* that originated with
Shiva and is used by Shiva for purposes of dissolution. Even
if Virabhadra had not been here, Ishvara's *chakra* would have
slain us now. Having done that, it would have swiftly returned
to Hara's presence. Even after I transgressed the pledge made
to Shiva, the *chakra* remained with me and was not suddenly
withdrawn. That only indicates his supreme compassion. After
this, it is certain that the *chakra* will no longer remain with me.
Now, with its garland of flames, it will swiftly depart. We must
quickly worship Virabhadra, with great affection. However,
he is suffused with great anger and may not save us. Alas! An
untimely act of dissolution has suddenly come upon us. Alas! A
destruction has presented itself before us now. Alas! In the three
worlds, there is no one who can be a refuge now. In the worlds,
who will provide refuge to a person who hates Shankara? Even
when the body is destroyed, Yama's pain will remain. That
leads to many kinds of miseries and is impossible for us to bear.
On seeing a person who hates Shiva, Yama himself gnashes his
teeth. He makes such a person fall into a pot filled with heated
oil. It cannot but be otherwise. After saying all this, I should
have adhered to the supreme pledge and left. Nevertheless, as

---

[865] The past, the present and the future.

a consequence of my association with wicked people, I did not leave swiftly. Even if we seek to run away from this place, Sharva's devotee will use his weapons to drag us back. There is no place that Shri Virabhadra's weapons cannot go to, heaven, earth or the nether regions. Such are the powers of all the *gana*s of Shri Rudra, the wielder of the trident. This is certain. Earlier, in Kashi, Shri Kalabhairava had playfully used the tips of his nails to sever Brahma's fifth head. This is certain."'"

'"Brahma continued, 'Having said this, the lotus-faced Vishnu remained there, full of distress. Meanwhile, Virabhadra reached the sacrificial pavilion. While Govinda was speaking, that ocean of soldiers arrived, along with Virabhadra. The gods and others watched.'"'

Chapter 88-3.2(36) (Conversation between Vishnu and Virabhadra)

'"Brahma said, 'While Vishnu was saying this, Indra laughed at him. Accompanied by the other gods, the one with the *vajra* in his hand wished to fight. Thus, Indra mounted his elephant and Anala[866] mounted a goat. Yama was astride a buffalo and Nirriti was on a *preta*. The one with the noose[867] was astride a *makara* and the one who goes everywhere[868] was astride a deer. Kubera attentively armoured himself and mounted Pushpaka.[869] Large numbers of other powerful gods, *yaksha*s, *charana*s and *guhyaka*s mounted their own respective mounts. Witnessing their preparations,

---

[866] Agni.
[867] Varuna.
[868] Vayu.
[869] Kubera's *vimana*.

along with his wife, the red-faced Daksha approached them
and spoke to them. Daksha said, "On the basis of your
strength, I started this great sacrifice. O immensely radiant
ones! You are the yardsticks in accomplishing all virtuous
tasks." Hearing Daksha's words, all *deva*s, along with Vasava,
swiftly emerged, ready to do battle. All the large number of
powerful *deva*s fought. Shakra and the other guardians of the
worlds were confounded by Shiva's *maya*. There was a great
battle between *deva*s and *gana*s. Using sharp javelins and iron
arrows, they fought against each other. In that great festival of
a battle, conch shells and drums were sounded. There was the
loud sound of battle drums, kettledrums and smaller drums.
That loud sound stoked the pride of the gods. Accompanied by
the guardians of the worlds, they started to slaughter Shiva's
servants. O tiger among sages! With the power of Bhrigu's
*mantra*s, Indra and the other guardians of the worlds forced
Shambhu's *gana*s to retreat. To rout them, perform a sacrifice
for *deva*s and satisfy those who had been consecrated for the
sacrifice, Bhrigu performed a sacrifice. Seeing that his own
side had been defeated, Virabhadra was filled with rage. He
asked *bhuta*s, *preta*s and *pishacha*s to remain at the rear.
Astride a bull, the immensely strong one himself led from
the front. Seizing a giant trident, he brought down the gods.
With great force, all the *gana*s used tridents to slay *deva*s,
*yaksha*s, large numbers of *sadhya*s, *guhyaka*s and *charana*s.
Some were sliced into two. Others were uprooted with swords
and clubs. The *gana*s used other weapons to shatter the gods.
Defeated in this way, all of them resorted to running away.
Abandoning each other, *deva*s fled to heaven. Only Shakra and
the other guardians of the worlds remained, eager to fight in
that terrible battle. They were immensely strong and resorted
to their fortitude. In the field of battle, Shakra and the other
*deva*s gathered together and bending down in humility, spoke
to Brihaspati. The guardians of the worlds said, "O *guru*!

O Brihaspati! O father! O immensely wise one! O ocean of compassion! Please tell us quickly. How can we possibly be victorious?" Hearing their words, Brihaspati made efforts to remember Shambhu. He then spoke to the great Indra, whose knowledge was weak. Brihaspati replied, "Everything that Vishnu spoke about earlier has come true now. O Indra! I will expand on that. Listen attentively. There is a lord of sacrifices who bestows the fruits of every act. The lord does not do anything himself. He gets it done through the apparent agent. All the *mantra*s, herbs, *abhichara*s, ordinary tasks, *karma*, Vedas, *mimamsas*[870] and many other sacred texts based on the *Veda*s are incapable of knowing Isha. All the ancient ones have said this. Mahesha himself cannot be known through any of these texts associated with the *Veda*s. He can only be known if one seeks refuge in *bhakti*. That is the great learning. Through supreme serenity and a vision that is indifferent in every possible way and through his favours, Sadashiva can indeed be known. Having examined it, I will now tell you what should be done and what should not be done. O lords of gods! This will ensure your success. Listen to what is good for you. O Indra! As a result of your childishness, always accompanied by the other guardians of the worlds, you came to Daksha's sacrifice. What will you do with this prowess? These extremely angry *gana*s have Rudra as their aide. They have come to create impediments to the sacrifice and there is no doubt that they will accomplish this. There is no means to counter it in any way. There will be impediments and the sacrifice. This is the truth. I am telling you the truth." Thus, the residents of heaven heard Brihaspati's words. Along with Vasava, all the guardians of the worlds were filled with thoughts. Surrounded by the extremely valiant *gana*s, Virabhadra remembered Shankara in

[870] Meaning examination and inquiry. A school of philosophy (*darshana*).

his mind and spoke to Indra and the other guardians of the
worlds. Virabhadra said, "O foolish ones! Expecting to receive
a gift, all of you arrived here. I will now give you a return
gift.[871] Come near me. I will give you that *avadana*. O Shakra!
O Shuchi![872] O Bhanu![873] O Shashin![874] O lord of riches! O one
with the noose in the hand![875] O Vayu! O Nirriti! O Yama! O
Shesha! O large number of gods! You are indeed discriminating.
O supreme among wicked ones! I will grant you *avadana* and
satisfy you now." Addressing them in this way, full of rage,
Virabhadra, foremost among the *gana*s, immediately struck
them with sharp arrows. All the gods, Vasava and the other
lords among gods, were struck by these arrows. They fled in
the ten directions.'"'

'"'When the gods and the guardians of the worlds had
departed, with the *gana*s, Virabhadra approached the sacrificial
arena. All the *rishi*s were scared and wished to quickly inform
Rama's consort about this. Extremely anxious, they spoke
urgently. The *rishi*s said, "O lord of *deva*s! O Rama's consort!
O Sarveshvara! O great lord! Please save Daksha's sacrifice.
There is no doubt that you are the sacrifice. You are the one who
performs the sacrifice. The sacrifice is your form. You are the
limb of the sacrifice. You are the protector of the sacrifice. Please
save this sacrifice. Protect it. Other than you, there is no one
who can protect it." Hari heard the words uttered by the *rishi*s,
who said them in fear. Vishnu wished to fight with Virabhadra.
The four-armed one armoured himself. In his hand, he wielded
the *chakra* as a weapon. Along with the immortals, the

---

[871] *Dana* is a gift. The gods came to the sacrifice, expecting *dana*.
Virabhadra promised them *avadana*, the word means a heroic act. But
it also means to cut into pieces.
[872] The pure one, Agni.
[873] Surya.
[874] Chandra.
[875] Varuna.

immensely strong one emerged from the sacrificial arena. With the trident in his hand, Virabhadra was surrounded by many *gana*s. He saw the great lord Vishnu, armoured and desiring to fight. Seeing him, Virabhadra furrowed his eyebrows and forehead. He faced him, the way the Destroyer faces a sinner, or the lord of deer[876] faces an elephant. Virabhadra, the crusher of enemies, looked at Hari. Angry and surrounded by brave *gana*s, he swiftly spoke to him. Virabhadra said, "O Hari! You have violated the pledge you made to Mahadeva. How is it that your mind is full of insolence now? What has happened to you? Do you possess the strength to violate Shri Rudra's pledge? Who are you? Who in the three worlds will save you? Why did you come here? We do not know the reason for that. How did you become a saviour of Daksha's sacrifice? Please explain that. Have you not seen what Dakshayani did? Have you not heard what Dadhichi said? You also came to Daksha's sacrifice to receive gifts. O mighty-armed one! Therefore, I will give you *avadana* too. O Hari! I will use the trident to shatter your chest. Why did you come into my presence? Who will save you now? I will bring you down on the surface of the earth and burn you with fire. After burning you, I will swiftly crush you now. O Hari! O evildoer! O worst among those who have turned away from Mahesha! Do you not know about Shri Maharudra's purifying greatness? O mighty-armed one! Despite that, you are stationed in front of me, desiring to fight. If you still wish to stand here, I will convey you to the state you were formerly reduced to." Hearing the intelligent Virabhadra's words, Vishnu, lord of gods, was pleased and smiled as he spoke. Vishnu said, "O Virabhadra! Standing in front of you, I will tell you. Listen. Do not speak of me as someone who has turned away from Rudra. I serve Shankara. Earlier, for the sake of the sacrifice, Daksha had repeatedly beseeched me. He

---

[876] A lion.

did not know the truth and was firm in his devotion towards *karma*. I am subservient to my devotees, just as Maheshvara is. O father! Daksha is my devotee. That is the reason I have come to this sacrifice. O brave one! O one who has originated from Rudra's rage! Listen to my pledge. Your energy is like that of Rudra. O lord! You are the reservoir of great power. I will counter you. You can also counter me. Whatever is going to happen, will happen. I will exhibit my valour." When Govinda said this, the mighty-armed one laughed. He said, "I am extremely pleased that you are loved by our great lord." Hence, Virabhadra, foremost among the *gana*s, was extremely pleased and laughed. In words of assurance, he humbly spoke the truth to the divinity Vishnu. Virabhadra said, "O great lord! I said that to test your sentiments. I will now tell you the truth. Please listen attentively. You are just like Shiva. Shiva is just like you. O Hari! Following Shiva's command, this is what the *Veda*s say. All of us follow Shiva's command. We serve Shankara. O Rama's lord! Nevertheless, urged, we speak to each other without affection." Hearing Virabhadra's words, Achyuta laughed and addressed Virabhadra in the following words. Vishnu said, "O immensely brave one! Without any hesitation, fight against me. With your weapons striking me all over my body, I will return to my own hermitage." He ceased speaking and armoured himself for the clash. Accompanied by his own *gana*s, the immensely strong Virabhadra also armoured himself.'"'

Chapter 89-3.2(37) (Destruction of the Sacrifice)

" "Brahma said, 'In the battle with Vishnu, the immensely strong Virabhadra remembered Shankara, the remover of all hardships, in his mind. The one who could crush all enemies mounted his divine chariot. He took up his supreme weapons and roared like a lion. The powerful Vishnu blew loudly on his own large conch shell, Panchajanya, delighting those on his own side. Hearing the blare of the conch shell, *deva*s who had abandoned the field of battle and had fled earlier, returned again. Roaring like lions, the powerful guardians of the world, together with Vasava, fought against Virabhadra and his *gana*s. The duels between the *gana*s and the guardians of the worlds were fearful. It was tumultuous and they roared like lions. Shakra fought with Nandi and Anala with Ashman.[877] The powerful Kubera fought against Kushmandapati. Indra struck Nandi with the *vajra*, which had one hundred spikes. Nandi used his trident to strike Shakra back between the breasts. Those two powerful ones cheerfully fought against each other. Wishing to defeat each other, Nandi and Shakra struck each other in different ways. Full of anger, Shuchi struck Ashman with a javelin. He also powerfully struck Pavaka back with a sharp trident. Mahaloka, foremost among *gana*s, fought against Yama. In that tumultuous clash, the brave one remembered Mahadeva and was happy. Chanda, supreme among strong ones, approached Nirriti. He fought with his supreme weapons and discomfited Nirriti. The immensely strong and brave Munda was Varuna's equal. He fought with an excellent spear and amazed the three worlds. Vayu struck Bhringi with his greatly energetic weapon. The powerful Bhringi struck Vayu back with a trident. The brave and powerful Kushmandapati meditated on Maheshvara in his heart and clashed against Kubera. The great leader of *bhairavi*s[878] was surrounded by a circle of *yogini*s. She shattered all the *deva*s and drank up their blood. It was extraordinary. In

---

[877] The text states Vaishnava. This is a typo. A few sentences later, it becomes clear that this is meant to be Ashman.

[878] That is, Mahakali.

a similar way, Kshetrapala also devoured the bulls among gods.
Kali also shattered and drank up the blood of many. At this,
the immensely energetic Vishnu, the slayer of enemies, started
to fight. He flung his *chakra* with great force, and it seemed to
burn the ten directions. Kshetrapala saw that the *chakra* was
advancing with great force. The brave and powerful one rushed
to the spot and violently devoured it. Vishnu, the destroyer
of enemy cities, saw that the *chakra* had been devoured. He
seized the enemy by the throat and forced him to vomit it out.
Having got his own *chakra* back, the immensely honourable
one, who alone preserves the world, was filled with great rage.
Angry, the immensely powerful one picked up many kinds of
weapons and fought against those brave ones. In that great
battle, Vishnu cheerfully fought against them. He exhibited
his terrible valour and hurled many tumultuous weapons.
Bhairava and the others fought a lot. The supremely energetic
ones were angry and unleashed many weapons. Seeing that they
were fighting against the infinitely energetic Hari, the powerful
one[879] withdrew from his own duel and fought against him.
Vishnu raised his greatly energetic *chakra* and consequently,
he fell down senseless. After this, Bhagavan Madhava fought
against Virabhadra. The clash between the two was extremely
terrible and made the body hair stand up. O sage! As a result
of the powers of *yoga* of Vishnu, lord of *deva*s who lies down
on the water, many brave warriors originated from his body.
Their number was innumerable. They were extremely terrible
and held conch shells, *chakra*s and maces in their hands. They
also roared and fought against Virabhadra. These hordes were
as powerful as Vishnu and held many types of weapons. All
of them were brave and as radiant as Narayana. However,
he remembered Lord Shiva and using his trident, struck
them and reduced them to ashes. As if playing in the field of

[879] This seems to mean Bhairava.

battle, the immensely strong Virabhadra then struck Vishnu on the chest with a trident. O sage! Violently struck in this way, Purushottama Hari lost his senses and fell down on the ground. A wonderful energy then arose from the sacrifice, and it resembled the fire of dissolution. It was fierce and consumed the three worlds, causing terror even among the brave. The prosperous lord arose again, his eyes red with rage. The bull among beings stood there, ready to strike with his *chakra*. That *chakra* was extremely terrible, as radiant as the sun at the time of destruction. However, Lord Shiva bestowed freedom from fear on Virabhadra and he was not distressed in his mind. O sage! As a result of the powers of Shambhu, the lord of *maya*, the immensely radiant *chakra* was numbed and did not move at all from Hari's hand. Virabhadra, leader of *gana*s, spoke to Vishnu. "Remain stupefied in this fashion, like the summit of a mountain." O Narada! In this way, Vishnu was stupefied by Virabhadra. In his mind, the wielder of the Sharnga bow recited *mantra*s used to free oneself from stupefaction. In this way, Rama's lord was freed from the stupefaction. O sage! He angrily seized his own Sharnga bow and arrows. O sage! However, in that very instant, Virabhadra used three arrows to strike the Sharnga bow in Hari's hand and severed it into three parts. A voice told Vishnu that the radiance of the great *gana*s was impossible to withstand. Knowing this in his mind, he vanished from the spot. He got to know everything that was going to happen, as a result of what Sati had done. It was impossible for anyone else to tolerate. Therefore, he remembered the self-ruling Shiva, the lord of everything, and returned to his own world. Suffering and grieving on account of my son, I too went to Satyaloka. Extremely miserable, I wondered about what I should do.'"

""'Vishnu, I, *deva*s and sages departed. All those who were left at the sacrifice were vanquished by the *gana*s. The sacrifice itself witnessed the calamity and the destruction of

the great sacrifice. Therefore, extremely terrified, it assumed
the form of a deer and fled. As it fled in the form of a deer
through the sky, Virabhadra seized it and sliced off its head.
After this, the brave one, the great *gana*, seized Prajapati
Dharma, Kashyapa, Arishtanemi, the lord of sages, along with
his many sons, the sage Angiras, Krishashva and Datta, bull
among sages. He flung them down and kicked them on their
heads with his feet. Using the tips of his hands, the powerful
Virabhadra sliced off the tips of the noses of Sarasvati and
the mother of *devas*.[880] The other *devas* and others were
flung down on the surface of the ground and crushed. His
eyes were full of rage. Virabhadra crushed the foremost *devas*
and sages. Even after this, he was not pacified. He was like
the king of serpents, wrath easily roused. Virabhadra seized
the enemy, just as a maned lion seizes a forest elephant. He
then looked around in various directions, examining, "Who
else is here?" Meanwhile, the powerful Manibhadra uprooted
Bhrigu. He kicked him on the chest with his feet and tore off
his beard. With great force, Chanda uprooted Pushan's teeth.
When Hara had been cursed earlier, he had exhibited them in
joy. In rage, Nandi plucked out Bhaga's eyes and flung them
down on the ground. When Daksha had uttered the words
of the curse earlier, he had used these to wink at him. The
leaders of the *ganas* caused discomfiture to Svadha, Svaha,
Dakshina, Mantras, Tantras and others present there.[881]
In wrath, the *ganas* showered down excrement and spread
this over the sacrificial fires. Those brave *ganas* rendered
the sacrifice impure. Scared of these powerful ones, Daksha
had hidden himself inside the sacrificial alter. Virabhadra
commanded that he should be dragged out from there. He
seized him by the head and using a sword, tried to sever his

---

[880] That is, Aditi.
[881] In their personified forms.

head. However, because of his powers of *yoga*, it could not be sliced off. He got to know that the head could not be severed with any *astra* or *shastra*. Therefore, he kicked him in the chest with his feet and used his hands to tear off the head. Daksha was wicked and hated Hara. Virabhadra, foremost among *gana*s, flung his head into the fire pit. As he wandered around, with the trident in his hand, Virabhadra was radiant. The angry Ranaksha and Samvarta resembled mountains and blazed. However, Virabhadra easily killed them. In rage, he flung them into the fire, like moths hurled into a blazing fire. Virabhadra saw that the foremost on Daksha's side had been burnt. He roared in laughter and the sound filled the three worlds. He was surrounded by a prosperity that befits all heroes. A divine shower of flowers rained down from Nandana[882] on Virabhadra and his *gana*s. Fragrant and cool breezes blew gently, bearing pleasant scents and causing happiness. At the same time, excellent celestial drums were sounded. Having accomplished his supreme task, the brave one returned to Kailasa as quickly as the sun, the firm destroyer of all darkness. Seeing that Virabhadra had succeeded in his task, Shambhu was pleased in his mind. Parameshvara made him the leader of the valiant *gana*s.'"'

Chapter 90-3.2(38) (Conversation between Kshuva and Dadhichi)

'Suta said, "Hearing the words of the infinitely intelligent Vidhatri, Narada, supreme among *brahmana*s, was amazed and happily asked again."'

---

[882] The celestial garden.

'"Narada asked, 'Daksha's sacrifice was taking place in Shiva's absence. What was the reason for Hari and the gods to go there, where there was bound to be dishonour? Please tell me. Did Hari not know about Shambhu's powers of dissolution? Like an ignorant person, why did he fight with the *gana*s? I still have a doubt about this. O ocean of compassion! Please dispel it. O lord! Please tell me about Shambhu's conduct. It fills the mind with enthusiasm.'"'

'"Brahma replied, 'O noble *brahmana*! Listen cheerfully to the conduct of the one who wears the moon on his crest. What you have asked about dispels every kind of doubt. In ancient times, Hari was cursed by the sage and that made him lose his *jnana*. Therefore, to help Kshuva, he went to Daksha's sacrifice, along with the immortals.'"'

'"Narada asked, 'Why did Dadhichi, the excellent sage, curse Vishnu? How did Hari harm him by helping?'"'[883]

'"Brahma answered, 'It is said that the extremely energetic King Kshuva was born. He was the friend of Dadhichi, the immensely radiant Indra among sages. In connection with austerities, there was a prolonged debate between Kshuva and Dadhichi. This occurred in earlier times and caused a great deal of harm. It is famous in the three worlds. Dadhichi was Shiva's devotee and knew the *Veda*s. He said, "Among the three *varna*s, there is no doubt that *brahmana*s are the best." King Kshuva heard the words of Dadhichi, the great sage. He was confounded by the insolence of prosperity. Kshuva replied, "In his body, a king holds the eight guardians of the world. Therefore, a king is best. He is the lord of *varna*s and *ashrama*s. The *shruti* texts state that all *deva*s exist in the king, who is supreme. O sage! Thus, I am that divinity. Therefore, a king is superior to a *brahmana*. O Chyavana's son! Reflect

---

[883] Helping Kshuva.

on this.[884] Therefore, I must not be disrespected and must be worshipped in every possible way by you." The excellent sage heard Kshuva's views. These were contrary to the *shruti* and *smriti* texts. Bhargava was filled with great rage. O sage! The immensely energetic one felt that his pride had been hurt and was angry. Dadhichi struck Kshuva on the head with his left fist. Kshuva struck Dadhichi with the *vajra* and severed him. After this, evil in intelligence, the lord of the world roared angrily. Struck by the *vajra*, Bhargava fell down on the ground, dead.'"'

'"'When Kshuva did this, the extender of the Bhargava lineage remembered Shukra.[885] The *yogi* arrived at the spot where Dadhichi's body was lying down. Shukra joined the two parts that had been severed by Kshuva. Bhargava[886] joined the two parts, so that the body became as it had been earlier. The foremost among Shiva's devotees, the one who initiated the knowledge about conquering death, then spoke to Dadhichi. Shukra said, "O son! O Dadhichi! Worship the lord, Sarveshvara Shiva. Hear the excellent Mahamrityunjaya *mantra*, stated in the *shruti* texts. I will state it to you.[887] 'We worship Tryambaka, the father and lord of the three worlds. He is the father of the three *mandala*s,[888] Maheshvara of the three *guna*s. He is in the three *tattva*s, the three fires and divides himself into three in everything. He is in the three

---

[884] Oddly, Dadhichi is described as Chyavana's son, here and later. Dadhichi's father was Atharvan, identified with the Bhrigu lineage.

[885] Shukracharya, the preceptor of the demons, who knew the art of bringing the dead back to life.

[886] Shukracharya's father was Bhrigu.

[887] As stated here, the *mantra* is different from, and an expansion of, the standard Mahamrityunjaya *mantra*.

[888] Since the word *mandala* can have different meanings, we have not translated it.

parts of the day, the three arms and divides himself into three
in everything. Mahadeva is in the three divinities. He is the
fragrance that enhances nourishment. He is everywhere in all
beings. He is the one who has created the three *gunas*. He is
in the senses and in everything else, *devas* and *ganas*. Like
the fragrance in flowers, he is the fragrance in gods. He is
the lord of the immortals. He is the nourishment in Prakriti.
Therefore, Purusha and Prakriti are two. He is in Mahat and
every kind of transformation. He is in Vishnu, the grandfather
and the sages. He is in the senses of *devas*. Therefore, he is
the one who enhances nourishment.' O supreme among
brahmanas! O one excellent in vows! O great sage! He is the
immortal divinity, Rudra. Therefore, worship him through
deeds, austerities, studying, *yoga*, *dhyana*, *japa*, truth and
every other means. He is the most subtle. He is himself the
noose of death. Like a cucumber, the lord is the cause of
bondage and emancipation.[889] It is my view the Mritasanjivani
mantra is the best.[890] Follow the *niyamas*, remember Shiva and
happily perform *japa* with this. Day and night, drink water
after using this *mantra* to perform *japa* and offer oblations. If
dhyana is performed in Shiva's presence, there is no fear from
death. After having done *nyasa* and everything else, follow the
norms and worship Shiva. If the norms are eagerly followed,
Shankara is pleased. He is affectionate towards his devotees.
I will tell you about *dhyana*. *Japa* must be performed after
dhyana. Until the *mantra* ensures success through Shambhu's
powers, an intelligent person will use it. 'Along with Girija, I
worship the three-eyed one, the conqueror of death. Holding
two pots of water in her two hands, she sprinkles water on his

[889] The cucumber remains tied to the bond of the plant or is freed.
[890] The same as the Mahamrityunjaya *mantra*. *Mritasanjivani*
means something that brings the dead back to life.

head.[891] She holds two other pots of water in her two other hands. He holds a string of *rudraksha* beads, a deer and a lotus in his hands. The moon on his head exudes nectar all over his body.'" Shukra himself instructed Dadhichi, supreme among sages. O son! He remembered Lord Shankara and returned to his own abode.'"'

"'"Hearing his words, the great sage, Dadhichi, remembered Shiva. Full of great joy, he went to the forest to perform austerities. Having gone there, he followed the norms and used Mahamrityunjaya *mantra*. He cheerfully used that to perform *japa*. He remembered Shiva and tormented himself through austerities. He used the *mantra* to perform *japa* for a very long time and used austerities to worship Shankara. Using Mahamrityunjaya *mantra*, he satisfied Shiva. Shambhu is affectionate towards his devotees. His mind was pleased as a result of the *japa*. O great sage! Pleased, he manifested himself in front of him. Seeing his own lord, Shambhu, the lord among sages was delighted. Full of devotion, he prostrated himself in the proper way. He joined his hands in salutation and praised him. O son! Shiva was pleased at this and was pleased with the sage who was Chyavana's son. Extremely pleased, he said, "Ask for a boon." Hearing Shambhu's words, Dadhichi, supreme among devotees, humbly joined his hands in salutation and spoke to Shankara, who is affectionate towards his devotees. Dadhichi answered, "O lord of *deva*s! O Mahadeva! Please grant me three boons—the *vajra* should be in my bones, I should be incapable of being killed and I should never be distressed in any way." Hearing these words, Parameshvara was happy and granted him the three boons, agreeing to what Dadhichi had said. Having obtained the three boons from Shiva, the great sage was delighted. The one

---

[891] These sentences are convoluted, and some liberties have been taken.

who followed the path of the *Vedas* quickly went to Kshuva's abode. He had obtained the excellent boons that he could not be killed, the *vajra* would be in his bones and he would never be distressed. He kicked the Indra among kings on the head with his feet. King Kshuva became angry. In particular, he was insolent because Vishnu had shown him his favours. He struck Dadhichi on the chest with the *vajra*. The *vajra* could not destroy the great-souled Dadhichi. This was because of Paramesha's powers and Vidhatri's son[892] was amazed.'"'

'"'He quickly went to the forest and worshipped Hari Mukunda, Indra's younger brother.[893] Because of Mahamrityunjaya *mantra* and because Dadhichi served the one who was a refuge of the distressed, he had been vanquished by him. Bhagavan Madhusudana was satisfied at his worship. Astride Garuda, he showed himself before him in his divine form. Using his divine sight, he saw the divinity, Janardana. He prostrated himself before the one who was astride Garuda and praised him with eloquent words. He praised the divinity who was the unconquerable lord, the one who was worshipped by the lord of the gods and others. Full of devotion, he looked at Janardana, prostrated his head and spoke to him. The king said, "O Bhagavan! There is a *brahmana* known as Dadhichi. He is humble and knows *dharma*. Earlier, he used to be my friend. But because of the powers of Sarvesha Shankara, he cannot be killed in any possible way. He has worshipped Mahadeva, the unblemished one who conquers death. In an assembly, he dishonoured me and kicked me on the head with his left foot. The great ascetic, Dadhichi, struck me with force. In his pride, he told me that he is not frightened of anyone. O Hari! Having obtained the excellent boon of conquering death,

---

[892] Meaning Kshuva.

[893] As sons of Aditi, Vishnu (Upendra) was Indra's younger brother.

his insolence is unmatched." Knowing that the great-souled Dadhichi could not be killed, Hari remembered Mahesha and his unmatched powers. Remembering this, Hari quickly spoke to Kshuva, Vidhatri's son. "O Indra among kings! *Brahmana*s have nothing to be scared about. O lord of the earth! In particular, Rudra's devotees have nothing to fear. If I cause unhappiness to the *brahmana*, he will curse me and the gods. O Indra among kings! As a result of his curse, I and the lords of the gods will be destroyed at Daksha's sacrifice. But I will rise up again. O Indra among kings! Therefore, nothing will be achieved by undertaking any sacrifice. O Indra among kings! I will make efforts so that you can defeat Dadhichi." Hearing what Hari had said, King Kshuva uttered words of assent. Delighted, he remained there, anxious to achieve his mind's desire.'"'

Chapter 91-3.2(39) (Clash between Vishnu and Dadhichi)

' "Brahma said, 'Bhagavan is affectionate towards his devotees. To do something for Kshuva, he assumed the form of a *brahmana* and went to Dadhichi's hermitage. The *guru* of the universe honoured the *brahmana rishi*, Dadhichi, and spoke to him. To accomplish Kshuva's task, he resorted to deception and spoke to the Indra among Shiva's devotees. Vishnu said, "O Dadhichi! O *brahmana rishi*! O one engaged in worshipping Bhava, the one without decay! I am asking you for a boon. You should grant it to me." Dadhichi, supreme among Shiva's devotees, was thus entreated by the lord of *deva*s, who wished to accomplish Kshuva's objective. He quickly addressed Hari in these words. Dadhichi said, "O *brahmana*! I know what you wish for. You have come here to accomplish Kshuva's task. You are Bhagavan Hari and have used your *maya* to come here in the form of a *brahmana*. O lord of *deva*s! O Janardana! Through the favours of Rudra, I always possess knowledge about the three periods of time, the past, the present and the future. O one who is excellent in vows! I know you as Hari Vishnu. Give up this state of being a *brahmana*. You have been worshipped by King Kshuva, who is deceitful in his intelligence. I know you as Bhagavan Hari, who is affectionate towards his devotees. Abandon this deceit. Remember Shankara and assume your own form. Since I am engaged in worshipping Bhava, why should anyone be scared of me? Basing yourself on the truth, you should make efforts to speak to me. With my intellect addicted to remembering Shiva, I do not utter a lie. There is no one in the universe I am scared of, *deva*s, *daitya*s or anyone else." Vishnu replied, "O Dadhichi! O one who is excellent in vows! All your fears have been destroyed. This is because you are devoted to worshipping Bhava and know everything. I bow down before you. At least once, you should say that you are frightened. Because of my request, tolerate Kshuva, Indra among kings." Hearing Vishnu's words, the great sage laughed. Dadhichi, supreme among Shiva's devotees, was fearless and replied. Dadhichi said, "I do not have the slightest fear of anyone. This is directly because of the powers of Shambhu, the wielder of Pinaka and the lord of *deva*s." Hearing the sage's words, Hari became angry. He raised his *chakra* and stood there, wishing to burn down the excellent sage. However, the extremely terrible *chakra* had no effect on the unperturbed *brahmana*. This happened because of Isha's powers, in the king's presence. Seeing that the *chakra* had been repulsed, Dadhichi smiled and spoke to Vishnu, who was himself the cause behind existence and non-existence. Dadhichi said, "O Bhagavan Vishnu! In ancient times, you made efforts and obtained the extremely terrible *chakra*, known as Sudarshana. But this is Bhava Shambhu's

chakra, and it will not kill me. O Bhagavan Hari! Be angry
with me and use every kind of weapon against me. Please make
efforts to use *brahmastra*, arrows and every other weapon."
Hari heard his words and saw that he was only human,
without any vigour. One by one, he angrily unleashed every
possible weapon. The *devas* lovingly sought to help Vishnu.
With their intelligence distorted, they fought against that single
brahmana. From every direction, they quickly hurled their own
respective *astras* and *shastras*. Shakra and others, on Hari's
side, hurled these on Dadhichi, with great force. Remembering
Shiva, Dadhichi grasped some *kusha* grass in his fist and hurled
this at all the *devas*. With the *vajra* in his bones, he could
control everyone. O sage! As a result of Shankara's powers,
that *kusha* in the sage's fist became a trident that blazed like
the fire of destruction. It made up its mind to burn down *devas*,
with their weapons and their crests. Shiva's weapon blazed in
every direction, surpassing the fire at the end of a *yuga* in its
radiance. There were various weapons that had been hurled by
devas, Narayana, the moon and others. All these prostrated
themselves before the crest of that weapon. With their valour
destroyed, all *devas* and residents of heaven fled.'"
    ""'Scared, Hari, supreme among those who used *maya*,
alone remained there. From his own body, Bhagavan Vishnu
Purushottama created hundreds of thousands of divine beings,
who were just like him in appearance. Those brave ones,
Vishnu's companions, also fought against the solitary *devarshi*,
Dadhichi, who possessed Shiva in his *atman*. In the battle, he
fought against those several companions of Vishnu. Dadhichi,
Shiva's excellent devotee, violently burnt all of them down.
Hari was astounded at what the sage Dadhichi had done.
The universe is his form, and he is accomplished in the use
of great *maya*. Hence, in Hari's body, Dadhichi, the excellent
brahmana, directly saw thousands of *devas* and other beings.
There were crores of beings and crores of entities. There

were crores of eggs in the one whose body was the universe. Chyavana's son saw all these things there. He spoke to the lord Vishnu Jagannatha, the one without origin who is praised by the universe. Dadhichi said, "O mighty-armed one! Give up this *maya*. On reflection, this is only an illusion. O Madhava! I also know of thousands of things that are impossible to understand. Behold attentively and see the entire universe inside me. I will bestow divine insight on you, and you will see yourself, Brahma and Rudra." Saying this, the sage showed him everything inside in his own body. The entire body of Chyavana's son was full of Shambhu's energy and the universe was inside him. Dadhichi, supreme among Shiva's devotees, remembered Shankara in his mind. The intelligent one was without fear. He laughed and spoke to Vishnu, lord of *deva*s. Dadhichi said, "O Hari! What power do your *maya* or *mantra*s have? Therefore, you should wish to fight properly and make efforts without using these." Vishnu heard the words of the fearless sage, who was infused with Shambhu's energy. He became angry with the sage. *Deva*s returned again to help the divinity Narayana, who desired to fight against the powerful sage, Dadhichi. At this time, Kshuva came to their presence. He restrained the one born from the lotus, Hari and the gods and made them cease. He heard my words and those of Hari. "The *brahmana* has not been vanquished. Go near the sage and prostrate yourself before him." Even more distressed, Kshuva went to the lord of sages. He honoured Dadhichi and helpless, beseeched him. Kshuva said, "O tiger among sages! Be pleased. You are the crest of Shiva's devotees. May Paramesha show his favours. He cannot be seen if one is in the company of wicked people." Hearing the words of the king and those of the large number of gods, Dadhichi, ocean of austerities, showed them his favours. However, the sage then saw Rama's lord and others and his rage agitated him. Remembering Shiva in his heart, he cursed Vishnu and the others. Dadhichi said, "*Deva*s, along with Indra of the gods, lords among sages, the divinity Vishnu and his companions, will be burnt down by the fire of Rudra's rage." Having cursed the gods in this way, the sage looked towards Kshuva and spoke to him. "O Indra among kings! A supreme *brahmana* deserves to be worshipped by *devas* and kings. O Indra among kings! *Brahmanas* possess the strength of Vishnu's powers." Clearly stating this, the *brahmana* entered his own hermitage. Kshuva honoured Dadhichi and returned to his own home. Vishnu went to his own world and the gods to wherever they had come from. Since then, that place has become a *tirtha* and is known as Sthaneshvara.[894] A person who goes to Sthaneshvara attains *sayujya* with Shiva. O son! I have briefly told you about the dispute between King Kshuva and Dadhichi and about how Brahma and Vishnu were cursed that they would be without Shiva. If a person constantly recites this account about the dispute between Kshuva and Dadhichi, he conquers untimely death. When he dies, he goes to Brahma's world. If a person always recites this before entering a field of battle, he does not suffer fear of death and is victorious.'"

Chapter 92-3.2(40) (Sight of Shiva)

" "Narada said, 'O Vidhatri! O immensely wise one! O Vidhatri! O one who shows the path about Shiva's *tattva*! You have made me hear the wonderful account about Shiva's pastimes. It is extremely wonderful. The brave Virabhadra destroyed Daksha's sacrifice and went to Mount Kailasa. What happened after that?'"

'"Brahma replied, 'The large number of *devas* and the sages were all vanquished. With their limbs mangled by

---

[894] In Kurukshetra (Thanesar).

Rudra's soldiers, they went to my world. They bowed down before me, Svayambhu, and repeatedly praised me. They specifically told me everything about their hardships. Hearing their words, I suffered grief on account of my son. With my mind afflicted, I anxiously thought. "What should be done? So as to ensure happiness of *deva*s, which task must be swiftly undertaken? How can Daksha be brought back to life? How can the sacrifice of the gods be completed?" O sage! I reflected on this in many kinds of ways and could not find any peace. Full of devotion, I remembered Vishnu and obtained the appropriate *jnana*. Therefore, with *deva*s and sages, I went to Vishnu's world. We bowed down. Having bowed down, we praised him in many kinds of ways and reported the hardship. "O lord of *deva*s! O Rama's consort! O Vishnu! O one who ensures happiness for *deva*s! We, *deva*s and sages, have sought a certain refuge in you. He was performing a sacrifice. Please make all the gods and sages happy. Please act so that the sacrifice is completed." Hearing the words of me, Brahma, Rama's lord, distressed in his mind, remembered Shiva. With Shiva in his *atman*, he replied. Vishnu replied, "An offence committed against an energetic person is not conducive to welfare. Such an offence leads to many kinds of miseries. All the gods have committed a crime against Parameshvara Shiva. O Vidhatri! They have appropriated a share that belongs to another, that of Shambhu. With pure minds, all of you must seek his favours. You should clasp Shiva's feet and obtain his supreme favours. When that divinity is angry, he destroys the entire universe. With his command, the guardians of the world and the sacrifice will be revived. Therefore, without any harsh words, one should quickly seek to please the divinity. He will pardon the offence the extremely evil-souled Daksha has committed, directed against his heart. O Vidhatri! This is the great means, and the only one, to ensure peace. I think that Shambhu must be satisfied. I am telling you the truth. I, you, the other gods, the sages and those with bodies do not know his *tattva* and his measure. Nor do we know the extent of his strength and valour. He rules himself and is supreme. He is the *paramatman*. O Vidhatri! What other means can there be to bring success to foolish ones who have opposed the supreme one? O Brahma! Along with all of you, I will also go to Shiva's abode. I have also committed an offence against Shiva, and I will certainly seek forgiveness from Girisha." This is what Vishnu instructed me, Brahma, and the immortals. Along with *deva*s, he made up his mind to go to the mountain.'"

'"'With the immortals, sages and the lords of subjects, Hari Vishnu went to that auspicious and supreme mountain, Shiva's abode. This was a spot that was greatly loved by the lord. It was constantly full of *kinnara*s, those who were not humans, *apsara*s, *yogi*s and *siddha*s. It was extremely lofty. There were many kinds of jewels on the summits, and it was beautiful in every direction. There were many colourful minerals and diverse trees and creepers. It was populated by large numbers of many kinds of animals and there were diverse birds. There were many waterfalls full of water, frequented by celestial and *siddha* women. With those they loved, they sported in the many lakes. There were many caves and summits. It dazzled with many wild species of trees that were silvery in hue. It was populated with large creatures, tigers and others, but they were devoid of any signs of cruelty, infused with Sarvesha's sentiments. It was divine and gave rise to great wonder. Ganga originated from Sati's region and made the place even more sacred. The sparkling river emerged from Vishnu's feet and purified everything. Such was the mountain known as Kailasa, loved by Shiva. On seeing it, *deva*s, Vishnu and the others and the lords among sages were filled with wonder. Near that place, they saw the beautiful city known as Alaka. This was the sparkling and extremely divine city of Kubera, Rudra's friend. Near that, they saw the grove Sougandhika, full of every kind of celestial

tree. It was extraordinary. There were two divine and purifying
rivers that flowed outside it—Nanda and Alakananda. Even if
one saw these, sins were destroyed. Every day, celestial women
came from their own regions to bathe there and drink the
waters. Full of desire, they sported there with the men. The
gods passed beyond the city of the lord of *yakshas* and the
grove Sougandhika. They reached Shankara's *vata* tree. The
tree extended constant shade all around it but had no roots.[895]
It was one hundred *yojanas* tall and there were no nests on it. It
was devoid of heat. They saw that extremely sacred, extremely
purifying and beautiful tree. After this, there was the divine
place where Shambhu practiced *yoga*. It was excellent and
served by *yogis*. The *vata* tree was immersed in great *yoga* and
could only be seen by those desiring to seek refuge in *moksha*.
Vishnu and the other gods saw Shiva seated there. He was
always happily served by Vidhatri's sons, great *siddhas* and
Shiva's devotees, who were themselves the images of serenity
and tranquillity. His friend, Kubera, the lord of *guhyakas* and
rakshasas, was also there. He was also specifically served by
his own *ganas* and their kin. Parameshvara's radiant form was
one desired by ascetics. Shiva's affection extended towards
these well-wishers. With *bhasma* and other things, he was
extremely resplendent. O sage! You were urging him by asking
him excellent questions about *jnana* and he was replying. He
was seated on a seat made of *kusha* grass and all the virtuous
people heard. His left leg was placed over his right thigh and
knee. A string of *rudraksha* beads was in his hand and his other
hand was in *tarka-mudra*.[896] Such was Shiva and Vishnu and

---

[895] It was without hanging roots.

[896] Literally, this means the posture adopted for debating and
arguing. The tip of the thumb touches the index finger. The other
fingers are close together and are held out straight. *Tarka-mudra*
specifically refers to the position of the hands, rather than the overall
posture. It is also known as *jnana-mudra*.

the other gods saw him. All of them quickly joined their palms
in salutation and prostrated themselves. On realizing that I and
Vishnu had arrived, Rudra, the refuge of the virtuous, arose.
The lord lowered his head in greeting. Vishnu and all the other
divine beings paid obeisance at Shiva's feet. They bent down,
just as Vishnu does to Kashyapa, the virtuous refuge of the
worlds. The gods and Vishnu showed every affection and
spoke to him, worshipped by gods, *siddha*s, the lords of *gana*s
and *maharshi*s.'"'

Chapter 93-3.2(41) (*Devas* Praise Shiva)

' '' '' 'Vishnu and the others said, "O lord of *deva*s! O
Mahadeva! O lord who has decreed the customs of
the world! As a result of your compassion, we know that you
are the *brahman*, Ishvara Shambhu. O father! Why are you
confounding us through your supreme *maya*? O Parameshvara!
You are impossible to fathom and always delude men. Purusha
and Prakriti are the seed and the womb of the universe.
However, you are beyond them. You are the supreme *brahman*,
impossible to reach through words and thoughts. You are the
one who weaves his strands and creates and protects the
universe, like a spider with its web. O Shiva! You sport with
Shakti, who is your own form. O Ishana! Full of compassion,
you are the one who created the sacrifice. You used Daksha as
a strand. You are always the lord of the three.[897] You populated
the worlds and established the ordinances, followed by
*brahmana*s accomplished in the path of the *Veda*s, pure, firm
in their vows and full of faith. O lord! Auspicious sacrifices
bring happiness to the doer and to others. Inauspicious acts can

[897] The three *Veda*s.

lead to benefits, mixed results or adverse effects. You are the
one who always bestows the fruits of every *karma*. All the
shruti texts have said that you are the source and lord of fame.
Those who only undertake extensive *karma* with wicked wishes
are inferior in intelligence. Full of jealousy, those foolish ones
oppress others with harsh words. O lord! Though such *devas*
should be killed, you should not slay them. You are Bhagavan
Paramesha. O supreme lord! You should show them
compassion. We prostrate ourselves before Rudra, the serene
one. You are the *brahman* and the *paramatman*. You are
Mahesha with the matted hair. We prostrate ourselves before
that great radiance. You are the creator of the universe. You
are the creator of the creator. You are the great-grandfather.
The three *guna*s are in your *atman*, but you are *nirguna*. You
are beyond Purusha and Prakriti. We prostrate ourselves before
Nilakantha, the creator and the *paramatman*. You are the
universe. You are the seed of the universe. You are the cause of
bliss in the universe. You are Aumkara, Vashatkara[898] and the
initiator of every enterprise. You are Hantakara and
Svadhakara. You are the one who always partakes *havya* and
kavya. O one who is devoted to *dharma*! How could you have
broken up the sacrifice? O Mahadeva! O lord! You do what is
beneficial for *brahmanas*! How could you have destroyed the
sacrifice? You are the protector of *brahmanas*, cattle and
dharma. O lord! At the end, you are always the refuge of all
beings. O Bhagavan Rudra! You possess the splendour of an
infinite number of suns. We prostrate ourselves before you. We
prostrate ourselves before Bhava, the divinity who is in juices

---

[898] *Vashat* is the exclamation made at the time of offering an
oblation. Vashatkara means the act of uttering *vashat*, or the one who
says it. Similarly, *Svadha* is said at the time of offering oblations to the
ancestors and *hanta* is a benediction, also uttered when presenting an
offering to a guest.

and water. We always prostrate ourselves before Sharva, the fragrant one who exists in the form of the earth. We prostrate ourselves before the extremely energetic Rudra, who exists in the form of fire. O Isha! In the form of wind and touch, we prostrate ourselves before you. We bow down. You are Pashupati. You are the performer of the sacrifice. You are the creator. O Bhima! In the form of space and the principle of sound, we prostrate ourselves before you. We prostrate ourselves before Mahadeva, who is Soma and *pravritti*. We prostrate ourselves before Ugra, who is the form of the sun, the *yogi* who undertakes *karma*. We prostrate ourselves before the destroyer of Kala. We prostrate ourselves before the wrathful Rudra. We prostrate ourselves before the terrible Shiva, the auspicious Shankara. As Ugra, you control all beings. For us, you are the auspicious. You cause yourself to pervade the universe. You are the *brahman*. You are the destroyer of afflictions. You are Ambika's lord. We prostrate ourselves before Uma's lord. You are Sharva, existing in every form. You are Purusha, the *paramatman*. You are beyond manifestations of cause and effect. You are the great cause. We prostrate ourselves before the one who is born in many extensive forms in the world. We prostrate ourselves before Nila, Nilarudra, Kadrudra and Prachetas. You are the divinity who is Midushtama.[899] We prostrate ourselves before the one who is pervaded by rays. We prostrate ourselves before the one who is the greatest. You always slay the enemies of *deva*s. You are the extremely energetic Tara, Sutara and Taruna. We prostrate ourselves before the divinity with the tawny hair. We prostrate ourselves before Mahesha. You are Shambhu of the *deva*s. You are absolution. You are the *paramatman*. We prostrate ourselves before the supreme one. We prostrate ourselves before the one who is dark in the throat. You are golden. You

[899] Shiva's name.

are Paresha. We prostrate ourselves before the one who has a golden body. You are Bhima, terrible in form. You are engaged in terrible deeds. You smear your body with *bhasma*. The *rudraksha* is your ornament. We prostrate ourselves before the short one, the tall one. We prostrate ourselves before the one who is a dwarf. We prostrate ourselves before the divinity who can kill from a distance. We prostrate ourselves before the one who can kill from the front. You possess a bow and a trident. We prostrate ourselves before the one who wields a mace and a plough. To destroy *daitya*s and *danava*s, you wield many kinds of weapons. We prostrate ourselves before Sadya, Sadyarupa and Sadyojata. We prostrate ourselves before Vama, Vamarupa and Vamanetra. We prostrate ourselves before Aghora, Paresha and Vikata. You are Tatpurusha, the protector and the ancient Purusha. You are the one who bestows the *purushartha*s. You are the one who follows vows. You are Parameshthi. We prostrate ourselves before Ishana. We prostrate ourselves before Ishvara. We bow down. You are the *brahman*. Your form is the *brahman*. We prostrate ourselves before the one who is himself the *paramatman*. For all those who are wicked, you are fierce and control them. For us, you are auspicious. You are the one who swallowed the *kalakuta* poison and protected *deva*s and others. You are Vira, Virabhadra, one who wields the trident and protects the brave. You are the great Mahadeva. We prostrate ourselves before Pashupati. Valour is your *atman*. You are excellent learning. You are Srikantha, wielder of Pinaka. We prostrate ourselves before the infinite one. We prostrate ourselves before the subtle one. You are the death of anger. You are the supreme Paramesha. You are greater than the greatest. We prostrate ourselves before the pervasive one who is greater than the greatest. We prostrate ourselves before the one whose form is the universe. We prostrate ourselves before Vishnukalatra, Vishnukshetra, Bhanu, Bhairava, Sharanya, Tryambaka and

Viharin. You are Mrityunjaya. You are grief. You are the three
gunas. The *gunas* are in your *atman*. The sun and the moon are
your eyes. You are the bridge behind every cause. You are the
one who pervades the entire universe with your energy. You
are the supreme *brahman*. You are without transformation.
You are consciousness, bliss and illumination. O Maheshvara!
All the gods, with Brahma, Vishnu, Indra, the moon and others
as the foremost and all the sages originate in you. Since you
divide the radiance in your body into eight different parts, you
are known as Ashtamurti.[900] You are the original Isha, full of
compassion. The wind blows because it is scared of you. The
fire burns because it is scared of you. The sun heats because it
is scared of you. Because it is scared of you, death rushes
around everywhere. You are an ocean of compassion.
O Mahesha! Please be pleased with us. O Parameshvara! Please
save us. You have always saved us from calamities. We
are insensible. O protector! O ocean of compassion!
We have always been protected by you. O Shambhu! In that
way, please save us now from many kinds of fears. O protector!
Please show us your favours quickly and save the sacrifice and
Daksha Prajapati. O Durga's lord! It is incomplete. Please
restore Bhaga's eyes. Let the performer of the sacrifice come
back to life. Let Pushan's teeth grow back. Let Bhrigu's beard
be as it used to be earlier. O Shankara! *Devas* and others have
had their bodies mangled, through weapons and stones.
Through your favours, let all of them be healthy. O protector!
You will get a complete share. Vasishtha, the performer of the
sacrifice, will earmark a share of the sacrifice as belonging to
Rudra. There will never be a violation of this." Stating this,
along with Prajesha,[901] Ramesha joined his hands in salutation

---

[900] Bhava, Sharva, Rudra, Pashupati, Ugra, Mahadeva, Bhima
and Ishana.

[901] Lord of subjects, Brahma.

and prostrated himself on the ground like a rod, seeking forgiveness.'"''

Chapter 94-3.2(42) (End to Daksha's Misery)

' '' Brahma said, 'Brahma's lord,[902] Prajesha and all the sages entreated Shambhu in this way. Parameshvara was pleased. The ocean of compassion smiled and comforted Vishnu and the other *deva*s. Showing a great favour, Paramesha replied. Shri Mahadeva said, "O excellent gods! Listen attentively to my words. O ones! You have indeed spoken the truth. I have always tolerated your wrath. I do not describe, or think about, sins committed by children. I wield the rod of chastisement over those who are overwhelmed by my *maya*. I did not cause the breaking up of Daksha's sacrifice. If a person hates others, this invariably happens to the person. One must never act so that there is suffering to others. If a person hates others, that effect is felt on the person himself. At the sacrifice, Daksha's head was severed. Let him have the head of a goat. With restored eyes, Mitra[903] will be able to behold his share of the sacrifice. O sons! Pushan used his teeth to devour food offered at sacrifices. However, he will now perform sacrifices with broken teeth. I have spoken the truth. Bhrigu opposed me. Let him have a goat's beard. I will restore their natural bodies on *deva*s who opposed me. Let the arms of the Ashvins and the hands of Pushan act as mounts for the other *adhvaryu*s. Since I am pleased with you, I have spoken thus." Full of compassion, Paramesha said this and ceased. He is the overlord and divinity of all mobile and immobile objects. He is the one who ensures

902 Vishnu.
903 That is, Bhaga.

the following of the *Veda*s. All the gods heard what Shankara had said. Along with Vishnu, all of them were content and uttered words of praise.'"'

""'Shambhu summoned me, Vishnu, gods and *rishi*s. Full of joy, we proceeded again to the sacrifice of the gods. At Shambhu's request, Vishnu and the other gods went to Kanakhala, to Prajapati's sacrificial arena. There, Rudra saw what Virabhadra had done. The sacrifice, and specifically *deva*s and *rishi*s, had been destroyed. In the field of battle, Svaha, Svadha, Pushti,[904] Tushti, Dhriti, Sarasvati, all the other *rishi*s, ancestors, fires and many others, *yaksha*s, *gandharva*s and *rakshasa*s—had been mutilated, wounded and killed. He saw that the sacrifice was also like that and summoned Virabhadra, the extremely brave leader of *gana*s. The lord smiled and spoke to him. "O Virabhadra! O mighty-armed one! What have you done here? O son! You have swiftly imposed a great punishment on *deva*s, *rishi*s and others. O son! Quickly bring Daksha here. He is the one who undertook an inauspicious sacrifice and brought about such consequences." When Shankara said this, Virabhadra swiftly brought the headless torso and flung it down in front of Shambhu. Shankara, who brings welfare to the worlds, saw that the torso was without a head. O supreme among sages! He laughed and spoke to Virabhadra, who was standing in front of him. "Where is the head?" Thus addressed, the lord Virabhadra replied, "O Shankara! I have offered the head as an oblation into the fire." Hearing Virabhadra's words, the lord Shankara affectionately told *deva*s to do what he had already told them earlier. Everything was done exactly as Bhagavan Bhava had said. I and Vishnu quickly told Bhrigu and the others. A sacrificial animal was tethered to the sacrificial post. Following Shambhu's excellent instruction, that goat's head was joined to Prajapati's torso. After the

[904] The text reads Pushan but should probably read Pushti.

head had been fixed, Shambhu cast a favourable glance and
Prajapati instantly got back his life, as if he had been asleep.
When he got up, he saw Shambhu, the ocean of compassion,
in front of him.'"'

'"'Daksha's intelligence was pleasant now. He stood there
affectionately now, with his mind extremely happy. Earlier,
his mind had been tainted by great enmity towards Hara.
But as he looked at Shiva now, it was as clear as the autumn
moon. He wished to praise Bhava. But as a result of his love,
he was incapable. He was incapacitated because of his anxiety.
Besides, he remembered his daughter. Full of shame, but with
a delighted mind, Daksha eventually prostrated himself and
praised Shiva Shankara, who brings welfare to the worlds.
Daksha said, "I prostrate myself before the divinity who
bestows boons and deserves to be worshipped. The eternal
Maheshvara is a reservoir of *jnana*. I prostrate myself before
Ishvara Hara, the lord of *deva*s. He always bestows excellent
happiness and is the only relative the universe possesses. I
prostrate myself before the lord of the universe. The universe
is his form. He is ancient. The *brahman* is a form of his
own *atman*. I prostrate myself before Sharva Bhava, the one
who conceives the world. He is greater than the greatest. I
bow down before Shankara. O lord of *deva*s! O Mahadeva!
Please show me your compassion. I prostrate myself before
you. O Shambhu! O ocean of compassion! Please pardon my
offence now. O Shankara! Under the pretext of chastising me,
you have shown me a favour. I was crooked and foolish in
intelligence. I did not understand your *tattva*. I have now got
to know your *tattva*. It is my view that you are above everyone
else. Vishnu, Brahma and the others serve you. O Maheshvara!
You are known through the *Veda*s. For the virtuous, you are a
kalpavriksha. Against the wicked, you always wield the rod of
chastisement. You are the self-ruling *paramatman*. You bestow
the desired boons on devotees. From your mouth, you created

*brahmana*s first, so that they might uphold learning, austerities and vows and comprehend the truth about the *atman*. You are like a cowherd who protects animals. You take up the rod against the wicked. You are the one who protects the ordinances. O Parameshvara! In the form of abusive words, I have pierced you with arrows. Consequently, immortals who are favourably disposed towards me were distressed. You are Bhagavan Shambhu, the friend of the afflicted. You are greater than the greatest. O one who is affectionate towards devotees! You are satisfied through the extensive deeds you yourself undertake." Full of humility, Prajapati praised Mahesha Shankara, the great lord who brings welfare to the worlds, in this way. Pleased in his mind, Vishnu also praised Vrishadhvaja. His voice choked with tears. He joined his hands in salutation and prostrated himself properly. Vishnu said, "O Mahadeva! O Mahesha! O one who is the cause of favours to the worlds! You are the supreme *brahman*. You are the *paramatman*. You are the friend of the afflicted. You are an ocean of compassion. You pervade everything. You follow your own inclinations. O lord! Your fame is known through the *Vedas*. You have shown us every kind of benevolent favour. Daksha is my devotee. Earlier, he was crooked and criticized you. O Mahesha! Since you are indifferent, you should pardon that now. O Shankara! In my folly, I also committed an offence against you. I took his side and fought against Virabhadra and the *gana*s. You are the lord. You are the supreme *brahman*. O Sadashiva! I am your servant. Like a father does, I should always be nurtured by you." Brahma said, "O lord of *deva*s! O Mahadeva! O lord who is an ocean of compassion! You are the self-ruling *paramatman*. You are the undecaying Paramesha, without a second. O divinity! O Ishvara! You have shown a favour to my son. You did not consider the disrespect shown towards you. Please save Daksha's sacrifice. O lord of *deva*s! Please be pleased. Please counter every curse. You are the one who kindles understanding in me and urges me. You are also the one who counters." O great sage! Mahesha was praised in this supreme way. I joined my hands in salutation and lowered my head in humility. Shakra and the other *deva*s and the guardians of the worlds, excellent in intelligence, praised the divinity Shankara, whose pleasant face was like a lotus. Similarly, pleased in their minds, all the *deva*s, *siddha*s, *rishi*s and lords of subjects cheerfully praised Shankara. So did the minor gods, the assistant priests and *brahmana*s. Full of great devotion, they prostrated themselves and praised him separately."'

Chapter 95-3.2(43) (Arranging Daksha's Sacrifice)

'"Brahma said, 'Ramesha, I, gods and *rishi*s praised him in this way and so did the others. Mahadeva was pleased. Shambhu cast a glance of compassion towards the *rishi*s and gods. He comforted Brahma and Vishnu and spoke to Daksha. Mahadeva said, "O Daksha! O Prajapati! I am pleased with you. Listen to my words. Though I am self-ruling and the lord of everything, I am always under the control of my devotees. There are four kinds of people, virtuous in deeds, who always worship me. O Daksha Prajapati! A succeeding category is superior to a preceding one. They are—the afflicted, the inquisitive, those who desire *artha* and as the fourth, those who possess *jnana*. The first three are ordinary, while the fourth is special. Therefore, it is said that I love a person with *jnana* the most. There is no one who is loved more by me. This is the truth. I am telling you the truth. A person who possesses *jnana*, knows about the *atman* and is accomplished in Vedanta and the *shruti* texts, can reach me. Those who are limited in intelligence endeavour to reach me without *jnana*.

Foolish men are addicted to *karma* and seek to obtain me through *Veda*s, sacrifices, donations and austerities. They never succeed. You wished to cross over *samsara* through *karma* alone. That is the reason I was angered and caused the destruction of your sacrifice. O Daksha! From now on, think of me as Parameshvara. Possess supreme *jnana* in your intellect and then control yourself and undertake *karma*. O Prajapati! In addition, with virtuous intelligence, listen to my words. For the sake of *dharma*, I will tell you about this secret. I will tell you about *saguna*. Brahma, Vishnu and I are the supreme cause behind the universe. But in my *atman*, I am Ishvara. I am the witness. I am the one who sees, devoid of attributes. O sage![905] I enter my own *maya*, which consists of the *guna*s. I create, preserve and destroy the universe and assume descriptions appropriate to the tasks. However, I am supreme and without a second. My *atman* is only that of the *brahman*. The ignorant see differences in the entities, Brahma, Ishvara and so on. A man does not regard his head, hands and other limbs as separate from his own self. Those who are immersed in me do not see differences in beings. O Daksha! If a person sees that the three divinities exist in the *atman*s of all beings and that they are one, he obtains peace. If a person, worst among men, possesses intelligence that differentiates between the three divinities, he resides in hell for as long as the moon and stars exist. A discriminating person who is immersed in me worships all *deva*s. He obtains the *jnana* that leads to eternal emancipation. Without devotion towards Vidhatri, there cannot be devotion towards Vishnu. Without devotion towards Vishnu, no devotion towards me is generated." The lord Shankara, the lord of everything, spoke in this way. Everyone present there heard the words uttered by the one who shows compassion. "If

---

[905] While Daksha can be addressed as a sage, it is likely that this is meant for Narada and has crept in.

Hari's devotee criticizes me, or if Shiva's devotee criticizes him, both of them will be cursed and will never obtain the truth." Mahesha's words brought happiness. O sage! Hearing his words, everyone present there, gods and sages, were delighted. Daksha was extremely happy and became devoted to Shiva. Along with his family, the gods and others, he formed the view that Shiva was the lord of everything. They praised Shambhu, the *paramatman*. Shambhu, satisfied in his mind, bestowed boons on them.'"'

'"'Serene in his intelligence, Daksha, Shiva's devotee, quickly performed *japa* to Shiva. O sage! Through Shiva's favours, the sacrifice was completed. He gave shares to all the gods and a complete share to Shiva. Having obtained Shambhu's favours, he donated to *brahmana*s. Following the norms, the great task of *deva*s was completed. Along with the *ritvija*s, Daksha Prajapati completed everything in the proper way. O lord among sages. In this way, Daksha's sacrifice was completed through the favours of Shankara, who is a form of the supreme *brahman*. All the *deva*s and *rishi*s praised Shankara's fame. Content and full of great joy, they returned to their own respective abodes. Vishnu and I were filled with great delight and returned happily to our own respective abodes. We sang about Shambhu's extensive glory, which always brings everything that is auspicious. Daksha affectionately honoured Mahadeva, the goal of the virtuous. Extremely happy, with his own *gana*s, he returned to Mount Kailasa. Having returned to his own mountain, Shambhu remembered his beloved Sati. He told the most important of his *gana*s about her account. Having spoken about her account, the one who possessed *jnana* spent a long period of time. However, the lord then resorted to the path followed by ordinary people and desired to see her. O sage! The lord never follows wrong policy. He is the supreme *brahman* and the goal of the virtuous. How could he be deluded? How could he grieve? How could be suffer from such great aberration? I, or Vishnu, can never know the truth about this, nor can others, like sages, *devas*, humans and *yogi*s. This is Shankara's infinite greatness, impossible for even the learned to comprehend. Through his favours, without any effort, a devotee, full of true devotion, can get to know. There is not the least bit of aberration in Shiva, the *paramatman*. By following this kind of a path, he merely instructs the worlds. O sage! By reading this, or hearing it, all the intelligent people in the world obtain a virtuous destination and divine and excellent happiness in the world hereafter. Thus, Dakshayani Sati gave up her own body. She was born again, as the daughter of the Himalayas and his wife, Mena. This is famous. She again performed austerities and obtained Shiva as her husband. Shivaa became Gouri. Beautiful in her limbs, she engaged in wonderful pastimes with him. I have thus described the extremely wonderful account of Sati's conduct. This is divine and bestows objects of pleasure and emancipation. It confers everything that is desired. This unblemished account is sacred and supremely purifying. It bestows the fruits of heaven, fame, a long life and sons and grandsons. O son! Full of devotion, men who listen to it, or full of faith, make it heard, accomplish every kind of *karma*. In the world hereafter, they obtain the supreme destination. If a person reads or teaches this auspicious account, he enjoys every object of pleasure. At the end of these pleasures, he obtains emancipation.'"'

This ends Sati Khanda.

Parvati Khanda

Chapter 96-3.3(1) (Himachala's Marriage)

"Narada asked, 'O Brahma! After Devi Dakshayani Sati gave up her body in her father's sacrifice, how did the mother of the universe become the daughter of the mountain? How did she undertake fierce austerities and obtain Shiva as a husband? I am asking you this specifically. Please explain it completely to me.'"

"'Brahma replied, 'O tiger among sages! Listen to Shivaa's excellent account. It is divine and supremely purifying. It is auspicious and destroys every sin. Devi Dakshayani Parameshvari, in her pastimes, was happily sporting in the Himalayas with Hara. At that time, Mena, loved by Himachala,[906] knew that she would become her daughter. Therefore, like a radiant mother, she wished to nurture her with every kind of nourishment. Parameshvari Dakshayani went to her father's sacrifice and angry, gave up her own body. O sage! At that time, Mena, loved by Himachala, desired to worship Devi, who resides in Shiva's world. Sati's heart desire

---

[906] The Himalayas in personified form. The word Himalayas is used both in animate and inanimate forms. Mena/Menaka was Himachala's wife.

was, "I will become her daughter." Having given up her body, her mind was determined to become the daughter of the Himalayas. When the time arrived, Devi Sati, praised by all *devas*, who had given up her body, happily became Menaka's daughter. Named Parvati, instructed by Narada, Devi went through austerities that were impossible to tolerate and again obtained Shiva as a husband.'"

'"Narada said, 'O Brahma! O Vidhatri! O immensely wise one! O supreme among eloquent ones! Please tell me about Menaka's origin, marriage and conduct. Devi Sati was born as Menaka's daughter. Therefore, she is blessed. That lady, devoted to her husband, is blessed and should be revered by everyone.'"

'"Brahma replied, 'O sage Narada! Hear about the origin, marriage and conduct of Parvati's mother. It is sacred and enhances devotion. In the northern region, there are the great Himalayas, lord of mountains. O best among sages! That mountain is greatly energetic and enjoys prosperity. It is famous in two forms, divided as mobile and immobile. I will briefly describe his own subtle form. He is embedded and stationed, extending from the eastern to the western ocean. He is beautiful and is the reservoir of many jewels. He is like a measuring rod on earth. He is full of many kinds of trees and there are diverse colourful summits. He is frequented by lions, tigers and other animals. Many happy ones always reside there. He is fierce, the reservoir of snow. He is colourful, with many kinds of wonders. He is resorted to by *devas*, *rishi*s, *siddha*s and sages and he is loved by Shiva. There are places for austerities. Pure in his *atman*, he is great-souled and purifying. He bestows success in austerities. He is the store of many auspicious minerals. Such is his beautiful and divine form, handsome in all his limbs. He is the untransformed portion of Vishnu. He is the emperor over all kings among mountains and is loved by the virtuous. To establish his lineage, extend *dharma* and with a desire to enhance the welfare of *devas* and ancestors, the mountain wanted to marry. At that time, *deva*s thought about all their selfish interests. O lord among sages! They approached the divine ancestors and spoke to them lovingly. The *deva*s said, "O ancestors! Pleased in your minds, all of you listen to our words. If you wish to accomplish the task of *deva*s, you must quickly do this. Your eldest daughter is named Mena and she is auspicious in form.[907] With a great deal of happiness, get her married to the great mountain, the Himalayas. In this way, there will be great gains to everyone. At every step, your miseries and those of the immortals will be destroyed." Hearing these words, the ancestors remembered how their daughters had been cursed and replied in words of assent. Following the excellent rites, their bestowed their daughter, Mena, on the Himalayas. There were great festivities on the occasion of this auspicious marriage. Hari and other *deva*s, the sages and everyone else arrived there, remembering Vamadeva and fixing their minds on Bhava. They organized festivities and gave away many kinds of donations. They praised the divine ancestors and also praised Himachala. All the *deva*s and lords among sages were filled with great delight. Thereafter, remembering Shiva and Shivaa, they returned to their own respective abodes. Having obtained wonderful gifts and having obtained his beloved in a marriage, the lord of mountains happily returned to his own residence. O lord among sages! I have lovingly described to you the excellent marriage that took place between Mena and the Himalayas. This brings happiness. What else do you want to hear?"'"

[907] Mena was born as a daughter to the ancestors. There were three daughters—Mena, Dhanya and Kalavati. Since they didn't recognize and show respect to Sanaka, Sananda, Sanatana and Sanatkumara, they were cursed that they would be born on earth. In addition, Mena would become wife of the Himalayas and be Parvati's mother. These incidents will be described in the next chapter.

Chapter 97-3.3(2) (An Earlier Account)

‘ ‘‘ **N**arada said, 'O Vidhatri! O wise one! Now, full of affection, please tell me about Mena's origin. Please dispel my doubt and also tell me about the curse.'''

'"Brahma replied, 'O Narada! O noble son! O greatly intelligent one! Along with the sages, lovingly use your sense of discrimination to hear about Mena's origin. I will tell you. O sage! Earlier, I have told you about my son, known by the name of Daksha. For purposes of carrying forward creation, sixty daughters were born to him. He had them married to Kashyapa and other grooms. O Narada! You know all that. Now listen to what I will tell you now. Among them, the daughter known as Svadha was bestowed on the ancestors. She had three extremely fortunate daughters and they were the embodiments of *dharma*. O lord among sages! Hear their sacred names. These are extremely auspicious and always remove every kind of impediment. The eldest daughter was named Mena. Dhanya was the one in the middle and Kalavati was the youngest. All these were born through the mental powers of the ancestors, they were not born from the womb. However, following the customary practice, they were regarded as Svadha's daughters. When people utter their excellent names, they obtain everything that they wish for. These mothers of the world are always supremely worshipped by the world. They are supreme *yoginis*, reservoirs of *jnana*. They could go anywhere in the three worlds.'''

'"'O lord among sages! On one occasion, the three sisters went to Shvetadvipa, desiring to see Vishnu's world.[908] They prostrated themselves before Vishnu and full of devotion, praised him. Obeying his command, they remained there,

[908] One of the seven *dvipas* into which the world is divided.

where a great assembly was taking place. O sage! At that time, Brahma's *siddha* sons, Sanaka and the others, went there. They bent down before Hari and praised him. Obeying his command, they remained there. Seeing Sanaka and the other sages, everyone present quickly got up. They bent down and honoured the ones who are worshipped by *deva*s and others in the worlds. O sage! However, deluded, the three sisters did not stand up. Because of destiny and *paramatman* Shankara's *maya*, they were rendered immobile. Shiva's great *maya* confounds all the worlds. Everyone in the universe is subservient to it and this is known as Shiva's wish. It has many names and is spoken of as *prarabdha*.[909] But it is nothing other than Shiva's wish. There is no need to think about this. Having come under its subjugation, they did not show any respect and only remained there, surprised. Sanaka and the other lords among sages saw the state they were in. Though they possessed *jnana*, they succumbed to great and intolerable rage. Sanatkumara, lord among *yogi*s, was confounded by Shiva's wish and spoke angrily. He invoked a curse as punishment. Sanatkumara said, "Because of your pride, you did not get up and bow down to us. Since you were deluded by human sentiments, you will go far away from heaven. Your *jnana* was deluded. Hence, you will become human women. Reflecting the power of your own deeds, you will reap this kind of fruit." Hearing this, the three virtuous ones were extremely surprised. They lowered their heads and fell down at his feet. The daughters of the ancestors said, "O noble sage! You are an ocean of compassion. You should be pleased with us now. We were foolish and did not prostrate ourselves before you. There was no thought behind this. O *brahmana*! O great sage! We have reaped the consequence. It is not our fault. Please show us your favours, so that we can return to heaven again." O son! Hearing their

[909] *Prarabdha karma, karma* that has ripened.

words, the sage spoke. Pleased in his mind, Shiva's *maya* also urged him to lift the curse. Sanatkumara replied, "O three daughters of the ancestors! Listen to my words with happy minds. My words will destroy your misery and bring you happiness in every possible way. The eldest one will become the beloved wife of the Himalayas, the mountain that is Vishnu's portion. Parvati will be her daughter. The second, Dhanya, will be a *yogini* and will be Janaka's beloved. Mahalakshmi will be her daughter, under the name of Sita. The youngest, Kalavati, will be the beloved of Vrishabhana, the *vaishya*. At the end of *dvapara yuga*, Radha will be her daughter. As a result of a boon bestowed by Parvati, along with her husband, *yogini* Menaka will go to Kailasa, the great destination, in her body. Siradhvaja, born in Janaka's lineage, will be blessed with Sita.[910] He will be *jivanmukta* and a great *yogi*. He will go to Vaikuntha. Kalavati will enjoy herself with Vrishabhana. She will be a *jivanmukta* and there is no doubt that, along with her daughter, she will go to Goloka. Without a calamity, how does one achieve greatness anywhere? For those with good *karma*, the misery goes away and that power leads to happiness that is extremely difficult to obtain. All of you, daughters of the ancestors, will enjoy yourselves in heaven. As a result of seeing Vishnu, your *karma* has been exhausted." Having said this and having lost his rage, the lord among sages spoke again. In his mind, he remembered Shiva, who bestows *jnana* and confers objects of pleasure and emancipation. "Affectionately, listen to something else. My words always ensure happiness. You will be blessed and loved by Shiva. You will be instantly revered and worshipped. Mena's daughter will be Parvati, the Devi who is the mother of the universe. Having undertaken austerities that are extremely difficult to tolerate, she will become Shambhu's

[910] Siradhvaja was Sita's father. All the kings in the lineage were known as Janaka.

beloved. Dhanya's daughter, known as Sita, will become Rama's wife. Adopting the practices of the world, she will enjoy herself with Rama. Kalavati's daughter, Radha, is one who directly resides in Goloka. She will become Krishna's wife and will be bound to him in love that will remain a secret." After saying this, the illustrious sage, Sanatkumara, was praised and along with his brothers, vanished from the spot. O son! The three sisters, daughters born to the ancestors through their mental powers, were freed from their sins. Having obtained happiness, they swiftly returned to their own abode.'"

Chapter 98-3.3(3) (Prayer to Devi)

' "Narada said, 'O Vidhatri! O wise one! O immensely intelligent one! O supreme among eloquent ones! O great and virtuous *guru*! What happened after this? You have described an extraordinary account, about what happened to the auspicious Mena earlier. I have heard the complete account about the excellent marriage. After having married Mena, what did the mountain do next? Please tell me that. How was Parvati, mother of the universe, born? How did she undertake intolerable austerities and obtain Hara as her husband? Please tell me all this and Shankara's fame in detail.'"

'"Brahma replied, 'O sage! Listen lovingly to Shankara's excellent and auspicious fame. If one hears this, a person who kills a *brahmana* is purified and obtains everything that he desires. O Narada! After marrying Mena, when the mountain returned home, there were great festivities in the three worlds. Himachala was also greatly pleased and arranged for supreme festivities. With a virtuous intelligence, he performed supreme worship of *brahmana*s and many kinds of relatives. All the *brahmana*s were satisfied and pronounced excellent

benedictions. They returned to their own respective residences
and so did the many kinds of relatives and others. With Mena
bringing happiness to the home, Himachala was extremely
happy and amused himself in Nandana and other groves
and other excellent spots. O sage! Meanwhile, *devas*, Vishnu
and all the others, and the great-souled sages approached the
mountain. Seeing that *deva*s had come, the mountain happily
prostrated himself. Full of devotion, he followed the norms and
praised them greatly. He lowered his head and joined his hands
in salutation. He devotedly praised them. The great mountain's
body hair stood up and he shed tears of joy. Extremely happy
and pleased in his heart, Himalaya mountain prostrated
himself. O sage! Having prostrated himself, he spoke to Vishnu
and the other gods. Himachala said, "Today, my birth has been
rendered successful. My great austerities have been rendered
successful. Today, my *jnana* has been rendered successful.
All my rites have been rendered successful today. I have been
blessed today. My entire dominion is blessed. My family is
blessed. There is no doubt that my wife and everyone else is
blessed. All of you have collectively come here, together. Take
me to be your own servant and affectionately tell me about
your command." Hearing the great mountain's words, the
gods, Hari and the others, were happy. They thought that their
own task would be accomplished and spoke. The *deva*s said,
"O Himachala! O immensely wise one! Listen to our beneficial
words. All of us will happily tell you about the reason why
we have come. O mountain! The mother of the universe was
Daksha's daughter earlier. Having become Rudra's wife,
she sported on earth for a very long time. When her father
dishonoured her, Sati remembered her own pledge. The mother
gave up her body and returned to her own abode. O Himalaya
mountain! This is known in the world, and you know it too. As
a result of this, there will be a great gain to the large number of
*deva*s. In every way, all the gods will be under your control."

Hearing the words of Hari and the other gods, the lord of mountains was pleased in his mind and agreed, speaking to them affectionately. With a great deal of love, they instructed him about the proper method.'"'

'"'They themselves went and sought refuge with Uma, Shankara's wife. They remained in an excellent spot, and controlling their minds, remembered the mother of the universe. The gods prostrated themselves and devotedly praised her in many kinds of ways. The *deva*s said, "O Devi Uma! O mother of the universe! O one who resides in Shiva's world! O Sadashiva's beloved! O Durga! O Maheshvari! We prostrate ourselves before you. You are Shri. You are Shakti. You are the one who purifies. You are serene. You are supreme nourishment. You are pure. You are Mahat. Your form is not manifest. Full of devotion, we prostrate ourselves before you. O Shivaa! O one who ensures auspiciousness! O pure one! O gross one! O subtle one! O refuge! You are delighted with inner learning and good learning. We prostrate ourselves before you. You are faith. You are fortitude. You are prosperity. You are inside everything. Your radiance enters the sun. You yourself illuminate the universe. Everything that exists in the universe, every living entity in the universe that moves, from Brahma to a blade of grass, is pervaded by you. We prostrate ourselves before you. You are *gayatri*, the mother of the *Veda*s. You are *savitri*. You are Sarasvati. You are the conduct of the entire universe. You assume the form of the three kinds of *dharma*.[911] In all beings, you are sleep, hunger, satisfaction, thirst, beauty, complexion and contentment. You always bring every kind of joy. For those who perform goods deeds, you are Lakshmi. For those who are wicked, you are always Jyeshtha.[912] For the

[911] The three *Veda*s.
[912] Meaning, the elder one. Alakshmi, the goddess of adversity, is regarded as Lakshmi's elder sister.

entire universe, you are peace. You are the mother who nurtures
lives. Your form is inside all beings. You are the essence of the
five elements. You are the one who upholds justice. Your forms
exist in good policy and transactions. You are the songs of the
Sama Veda. You are the chords of the *Yajur Veda*. You are
the oblations of the *Rig Veda*. You are the measurements of
the *Atharva Veda*. You are the ultimate objective. You are the
power of *tamas* that exists in all the gods. You are the power of
rajas that exists in the qualities of Vidhatri. The universe is your
form. We have heard of you as the one who creates. We praise
you. Cruel *samsara* is like an ocean, and you are the one who
counters its miseries. You are the sacred thread that enables us
to cross over. You are accomplished in pastimes, and you are
the one who protects *ashtanga yoga*. You always love to reside
in the Vindhya mountains.[913] We prostrate ourselves before
you. She always holds up the nose, eyes, face, arms, chest and
mind of living beings and extends happiness. The extremely
fortunate one makes the universe go to sleep, for the sake of
its preservation and protection. May she be pleased with us."
Maheshani Uma Sati, the mother of the universe, was praised
by all of them in this way. With happy minds, they waited,
desiring to see her.'"

Chapter 99-3.3(4) (Comforting the Gods)

" " Brahma said, 'Devi Durga, the destroyer of afflictions,
was praised by *deva*s in this way. The mother of the
universe appeared in front of the *deva*s. Extremely resplendent,
she was astride a divine chariot, studded with jewels. It was
extremely wonderful and was adorned with nets of bells. A

[913] As Vindhyavasini, she resides in the Vindhyas.

supreme and soft spread was laid on it. The dazzle of her beautiful limbs surpassed that of one crore suns. She was like a supreme image, in the midst of her own mass of energy. Mahamaya, who always sports with Sadashiva, is without a parallel. She possesses the three *guna*s. She is *nirguna*. She is eternal. She resides in Shiva's world. She is the mother of the three divinities. She is Chandi Shivaa, the destroyer of every kind of affliction. She is the mother of everyone. She is the great slumber. She is the one who saves all people. As a result of the powers of that great mass of energy, the gods could not see Shivaa.[914] Desiring to see her, the gods praised her again. They instantly obtained her compassion. Vishnu and the large number of *deva*s, wishing to see her, saw the mother of the universe. All the residents of heaven were filled with great joy. They repeatedly prostrated themselves. In particular, they extolled her. *Deva*s said, "O Shivaa! O Sharvani! O Kalyani! O Jagadamba! O Maheshvari! O destroyer of all afflictions! All the gods bow down before you. O Deveshi! All the *Veda*s and sacred texts do not know you. O Shivaa! Your greatness is beyond thoughts and words. In their fear, the *shruti* texts are always agitated and define you as what you are not.[915] What need be said about others? As a result of their devotion, devotees obtain your compassion and know you in many kinds of ways. Devotees who seek refuge with you never suffer from any kind of fear. O Ambika! We are always your servants. Listen affectionately to what we will tell you. O Devi! O Mahadevi! We, the inferior ones, will describe it to you. O one loved by Hara! You were formerly born as Daksha's daughter. You destroyed the great vanity of Brahma and the others. As a result of your pledge, when your father dishonoured you, you

---

[914] The text states that they could see Shivaa. In view of what follows, there is a negative missing.

[915] She is not this, she is not that and so on.

gave up your body. You caused grief to Hara and returned to your own abode. O Maheshvari! But the task of *deva*s has not yet been carried out completely. We, *deva*s and sages, are anxious and have sought refuge with you. O Maheshani! Make us well and satisfy our wishes completely. O Shivaa! Let Sanatkumara's words come true. O Devi! Descend on earth and become Rudra's wife again. Perform the appropriate pastimes and let us be well and happy. Let Rudra, who is in Mount Kailasa, also be happy. Let everyone be happy. Let all miseries be destroyed." Full of love, Vishnu and all the other immortals said this and were silent. They stood there, humble in appearance and full of faith.'"

'"'Hearing the praise of the immortals, Shivaa was extremely pleased. She remembered her own lord, Shiva, and understood the entire reason for their arrival. Devi Uma spoke. Affectionate towards her devotees, she smiled at them, led by Rama's lord. Uma said, "O Hari! O Vidhatri! O *deva*s! O sages! Your distress has gone. All of you listen to my words. There is no doubt that I have been pleased. My conduct is such that it brings happiness everywhere in the three worlds. I am the one who induced delusion in Daksha and did everything else. There is no doubt that I will take a complete *avatara* on earth. There are many reasons for this. Full of great affection, I will tell you about them. O *deva*s! In earlier times, full of great devotion, Himachala and Mena served me, in my body as Sati, like a father and a mother. Even now, they constantly serve me with great devotion. This is especially true of Mena. There is no doubt that I will become their daughter. Like you, Rudra wishes that I should assume an *avatara* in Himachala's house. Therefore, I will descend in that way and there will be an end to miseries. All of you return to your own respective abodes. You will shortly obtain happiness. I will assume an *avatara* and becoming her daughter, bestow happiness on Mena. I will become Hara's wife. However, that is my great secret. Shiva's pastimes are wonderful. They delude even those who possess *jnana*. O gods! On witnessing my father's disrespect and the fact that my husband had not gone to the sacrifice, I gave up my body as Daksha's daughter. Since then, my husband, Rudra, has assumed the traits of the fire of destruction. Thinking of me alone, he quickly became Digambara.[916] He saw Sati's rage when she went to her father's sacrifice. The one who knows about *dharma* decided that I had given up my body out of love for him. Therefore, he turned into /became a *yogi* and discarded his home. He followed a conduct that is contrary to customary practice. Maheshvara could not tolerate the separation from Sati. Immensely miserable on my account, he assumed inappropriate attire. He discarded all the excellent pleasures that result from desire. O Vishnu! O Vidhatri! O sages! O gods! There is more. Listen. The pastimes of the great lord, Mahesha, protect the world. Full of love and suffering from the separation, he started to wear a garland made out of my bones. However, though he possesses understanding, he could not find peace anywhere. The lord Rudra roamed around here and there, as if he was not Isha. He always roamed around here and there, incapable of distinguishing between proper and improper. The lord Hara desired to indulge in such pastimes, illustrating what lovers go through. As if he was overwhelmed by the pangs of separation, he uttered the words of a lover. In reality, Parameshvara is without transformation, without distress and can never be conquered. My lord, Shiva, is complete. He is the lord of *maya* and is the lord of everything. Otherwise, what is the need for him to be deluded by desire? Why did he swiftly succumb to transgressions? The lord is not touched by *maya*. The lord Rudra desires to accept my hand

---

[916] Literally, with the directions as garment, naked. But implying someone who is indifferent to the home and material objects. Digambara is one of Shiva's names.

again. O gods! Therefore, I will assume an *avatara* on earth, in the house of Mena and Himachala. To provide satisfaction to Rudra, I will descend and follow customary worldly practice, with Himachala and his wife, Mena. I will become a devotee and practice extremely intolerable austerities, becoming Rudra's beloved. I will accomplish the task of *deva*s. This is true. There is no doubt that this is the truth. All of you return to your own residences and constantly worship Bhava. Through his compassion, there is no doubt that all your miseries will be destroyed. He will become compassionate, and his compassion always bestows what is auspicious. Since I am his wife, I am revered and worshipped in the three worlds." Jagadamba spoke to *deva*s in this way. O son! As they looked on, Shivaa vanished and swiftly returned to her own world. Vishnu and all the gods and sages rejoiced. They bowed down in her direction and returned to their own respective residences. O lord of sages! I have thus described Durga's excellent conduct. It always bestows happiness on men and gives them objects of pleasure and emancipation. If a person controls himself and constantly hears it, makes it heard, reads it or makes it read, he obtains everything that he wishes for.'"'

Chapter 100-3.3(5) (Mena's Boon)

' ' 'Narada said, 'Devi Durga vanished and returned to her own abode and the large number of immortals also left. What happened after that? How did Mena and the lord of mountains torment themselves through great austerities? O father! How did Mena obtain a daughter? Please tell me that.'"'

'"Brahma replied, 'O noble *brahmana*! O best among sons! Listen to the great account. I will prostrate myself before Shankara, which always enhances devotion, and then tell you. O son! When the large number of gods instructed them and departed, the lord of mountains and Menaka tormented themselves through supreme austerities. Day and night, the couple thought of Shivaa and Shambhu. Full of devotion in their minds, they constantly worshipped in the proper way. The mountain's beloved was filled with great joy and worshipped Devi and Shiva. She donated to *brahmana*s and constantly satisfied them. Desiring to have a child, for twenty-seven years, commencing in the month of Chaitra, she worshipped Shivaa for a month. She fasted on *ashtami* and donated sweetmeats, offerings, cakes, *payasam* and fragrant flowers on *navami*. In Oushadhiprastha,[917] on the banks of the Ganga, she fashioned Uma's earthen image and using many kinds of objects, worshipped this. On some days, she fasted. On some days, she observed vows. On some days, she subsisted on air. On some days, she only subsisted on water. For twenty-seven years, Menaka's mind was fixed on Shivaa and full of great joy and exuding radiance, she spent this time. At the end of twenty-seven years, Uma, Shankara's beloved, the mother of the universe, the one who pervades the universe, was extremely pleased. Devi was satisfied at the great devotion. Therefore, to show her favours, Parameshvari manifested herself in front of Mena. Her body possessed divine limbs and she was in the midst of a circle of energy. She smiled, showed herself to Mena and spoke.'"'

'"'Devi said, "O extremely virtuous one! Ask for the boon that is in your mind. O beloved of the mountain! I am extremely pleased with your austerities. O Mena! You have resorted to austerities and vows. I will give you what you ask for, everything that you wish for." Menaka saw Devi Kalika in front of her. On seeing her, she prostrated herself and

---

[917] A mountain near Kailasa, where many kinds of herbs and medicinal plants were found. The capital of Himachala's kingdom.

addressed her in the following words. Mena said, "O Devi! I have now directly seen your form. I desire to extol you. O Kalika! Therefore, be pleased. Kalika confounds everyone." When Mena addressed her in this way, pleased in her mind, she embraced Menaka with her arms. Menaka obtained great *jnana*. With eloquent words and full of devotion, she praised the auspicious Kalika, who had appeared in front of her. Mena said, "O Mahamaya! O Jagaddhatri! O Chandika! O one who holds up the worlds! O Mahadevi! O one who bestows everything that is desired! I prostrate myself before you. You are the one who bestows eternal bliss. You are *maya*. You are Yoganidra. You are the one who gives birth to the universe. O one who is always a *siddha*! O one who wears a garland of auspicious lotuses! I prostrate myself before you. O maternal grandmother![918] O constant bliss! O one who destroys grief for devotees! O one who is an ideal for women! O one who assumes the form of intelligence in living beings! You are the cause behind the severance of bonds for mendicants. How can someone like me sing about your powers? You are the violence mentioned in the *Atharva Veda*. May you always grant me everything that I desire. Though large numbers of beings are united with sentiments of temporary and permanent and the *tanmatras*, you are beyond them. You are their power and are always eternal in form. You are a woman who is capable of being united with *yoga* at the right time. You are the mother of the earth. The universe is you. You are the eternal Prakriti, and you are beyond that. You bring everything under control. Your form is the *brahman*. You are always full of *sattva*. O mother! Be pleased with me now. You are the fierce power in the fire. You are the power of scorching in the sun's rays. You are the many kinds of delight in the moon's beams.

---

[918] By extension. Mena's mother was Svadha and Svadha has different origins, depending on the text.

I extol you. I prostrate myself before Chandi. You are loved by virtuous women. To those who hold up their seed, you are eternal. For the entire universe, you are desire. That is the way Hara thinks of you. O Devi! You are the endeavour behind creation, preservation and destruction and accordingly, you assume different forms. You are the reason behind Brahma, Achyuta and Sthanu assuming bodies. Please be pleased with me now. I prostrate myself before you again." In this way, she praised Durga Kalika again.'"'

""'Thus addressed, Devi asked Menaka to seek the desired boon. Uma said, "O Himachala's beloved! I love you more than my own life. There is no doubt that I will give you what you ask for. There is nothing that cannot be given to you." Menaka, loved by the mountain, heard the words Maheshani spoke and they were like nectar. Content, she replied. Mena said, "O Shivaa! Victory, victory to you. O wise one! O Maheshvari! O mother of the world! If you think that I deserve to be given a boon, I will ask you for a boon. Then, I will ask for a boon again. O mother of the universe! Let my first boon be that I should have one hundred sons. Let them be valiant and possess long lifespans. Let them possess prosperity and success. After that, let me have a single daughter, possessing beauty and qualities. Let her bring joy to both the lineages.[919] Let her be worshipped in the three worlds. O Shivaa! To accomplish the task of *devas*, become my daughter. O mother of the world! Become Rudra's wife and indulge in your pastimes." Hearing what Menaka said, pleased in her mind, Devi replied. Smiling first, she fulfilled her wishes with her words. Devi answered, "You will have one hundred sons who will be full of valour. The first one to be born will be foremost in valour. Satisfied with your devotion, I will be born as your daughter. Since all the gods have served me, I will perform the task of *devas*." Jagaddhatri Kalika Parameshvari

---

[919] The father's and the mother's.

spoke in this way. As Menaka looked on, Shivaa vanished from the spot. O son! Having obtained the desired boon from Maheshani, Menaka was filled with infinite delight and all the sufferings because of the austerities were destroyed. Pleased in her mind, the virtuous one prostrated herself in Sati's direction. Uttering the word "victory", she entered her own residence and informed her husband about the excellent boon. Through good omens and his intelligence, he already knew this but her excellent words reinforced that. Hearing Mena's words, the lord of the mountains was delighted. He lovingly praised his beloved and her devotion towards Shivaa. O sage! In the course of time, they engaged in intercourse. Mena conceived and the foetus increased every day. She gave birth to the excellent son, Mainaka, who deserved to be enjoyed by *naga* women. Subsequently, he was bound in a wonderful pact of friendship with the ocean. O *devarshi*! When the slayer of Vritra became angry and severed the wings of the mountains, his excellent wings remained and his limbs could not be harmed.[920] He was supreme among the one hundred sons, immensely strong and valiant. He was foremost among mountains and was instated as the Indra of mountains. There were great and wonderful festivities in Himachala's city. The couple was filled with supreme joy and their sorrows were over. They donated to *brahmana*s and gave wealth to others. For both of them, the love for Shiva and Shivaa became greater.'"

Chapter 101-3.3(6) (Parvati's Birth)

‘ "Brahma said, 'For the sake of the birth and to accomplish the task of *deva*s, full of love and

---

[920] Earlier, mountains had wings. These wings were sliced off by Indra, but Mainaka's remained.

affection, the couple remembered the mother of the world. Earlier, because of her father, Chandika had used *yoga* to give up her body. She now desired to be born through the mountain's beloved. She cheerfully bestows everything desired and wanted to make her own words come true. Therefore, with all her portions, Maheshvari entered the mountain's mind. Extremely delighted, he became radiant, with a resplendence that had not existed earlier. With a mass of energy, the great-minded one was as unassailable as the fire. At an extremely auspicious time, the mountain immersed himself in *samadhi* and deposited Shivaa's entire portion in his beloved. Through Devi's favours, the mountain's wife meditated and fixed her mind on the mountain, who was now a reservoir of compassion and happiness, and conceived. The refuge of the entire universe now resided inside the mountain's beloved. Therefore, Mena became even more radiant, as if she was in the midst of a circle of energy. Mena showed the signs of being pregnant and this increased her husband's joy. The auspicious one was happy that she had conceived one who would bring the desired happiness to *deva*s. Since her body was weak, she could not don all her ornaments. Her face was like a *lodhra* flower,[921] resembling the time of the night when there are few *nakshatra*s and the moon is waning. O sage! When he inhaled the fragrance of her mouth, bearing the scent of the earth, in private, the lord of mountains wasn't satisfied, and his love increased. The mountain asked her friends, "Does Mena desire any object? Because she is embarrassed, she does not ask me for anything." In her difficult state of pregnancy, whenever she desired anything, he would see that it was quickly brought. There was nothing in the three worlds he would not do. As she passed beyond the first stage of pregnancy, her body turned heavier. Mena was as radiant as a young creeper, sprouting

---

[921] The lotus bark tree, implying that her face was pale.

new leaves and flowers. The mountain considered his pregnant queen was like the earth, with an abode of treasures inside its womb, or the *shami* tree, with fire hidden inside it. His mind delighted with his wife, the wise one performed all the appropriate rites, as befitted his own riches, his uplifted state and the *shruti* texts.'"'

"'At the right time, he felt that Mena was about to deliver. She resembled the sky covered with clouds and along with physicians, he had her placed in the delivery chamber. Looking at his beloved, auspicious in all her limbs, the lord of mountains rejoiced. Since the mother of the universe was in her womb, she was extremely energetic at the time. O sage! At that time, Vishnu and the other *deva*s and sages arrived and praised Shivaa, who was still inside the womb. *Deva*s said, "O Durga! Victory to you. O wise one! O Jagadamba! O Maheshvari! Victory to you. You are truthful in your vows. You are supremely devoted to the truth. You are *trisatya*.⁹²² Your form is the truth. You are established in truth. You are extremely pleased with the truth. You are the womb of truth. You are the truth. You are truth amongst everything that is true. Your sight is truth. We are afflicted and have sought refuge with you. O Shiva's beloved! O Maheshani! O destroyer of the misery of *deva*s! O mother of the three worlds! O Sharvani! O pervasive one! O one affectionate towards devotees! O lord of the three worlds! Manifest yourself. Accomplish the task of *deva*s. O Maheshvari! It is because of your favours that all of us have a protector. All those who are happy obtain that excellent happiness from you. O Amba! Without you, nothing in the three worlds is beautiful." In this way, they lauded Maheshani, who was still inside the womb, in many kinds of ways. With pleased minds, *deva*s then returned to their own respective abodes.'"'

⁹²² Truth in its three aspects of thoughts, words and deeds.

""'Nine months were complete, and the tenth month arrived. It was evident that the progress of Kalika Jagadamba in the womb was over. An excellent time arrived, and the planets and the stars were serene. The sky was clear, and all the directions were radiant. There were auspicious signs on earth, with its forests, villages and oceans. Lotuses bloomed in lakes, rivers and ponds. O lord among sages! The various kinds of breezes that blew were pleasant to the touch. All the virtuous people were delighted and there was misery amongst the wicked. Gods assembled in the firmament and sounded their drums. Flowers were showered down and excellent *gandharvas* sang. *Vidyadhara* women and *apsaras* danced in the sky. In the sky, *devas* and others organized grand festivities. At this time, in her entire potency, Devi Shivaa Sati appeared before Mena in her own form. The season was Vasanta, the month was Madhu,[923] it was *navami* and the *nakshatra* was Mrigashira. Like Ganga from the lunar disc, she was born at midnight. Like Lakshmi emerging from the ocean, at the right time, Shivaa emerged from Menaka's womb in her own form. As soon as she was born, Bhava was pleased. A slow and heavy breeze started to blow, bearing auspicious fragrances. There was a shower of flowers, followed by a shower of rain. The fires that blazed were serene and the clouds rumbled. As soon as she was born, everything in Himachala's city turned pleasant and all miseries were destroyed. At that time, Vishnu and all the other gods arrived. They were happy and delighted and wished to see Jagadamba. They praised Shivaa Amba Kalika, desired by Shiva. She is Mahamaya, divine in form. She resides in Shiva's world. The *devas* said, "O Jagadamba! O Mahadevi! O one who bestows every kind of success! You are the one who always accomplishes tasks of *devas*. We prostrate ourselves before you. O one who is affectionate towards devotees! In every possible

[923] Chaitra.

way, you bring welfare to *deva*s. You have satisfied Mena's
wish. Now please satisfy that of Hara." Extolling Shivaa in
this way, Vishnu and the other *deva*s prostrated themselves.
Delighted, they praised the destination of the virtuous and
returned to their own respective abodes. O Narada! When
Devi was born, Menaka looked at her and rejoiced. She was
dark, with a complexion like the petals of a blue lotus. On
looking at her divine form, the mountain's beloved obtained
jnana. Knowing that this was Parameshani, she delightedly
praised her. Mena said, "O Jagadamba! O Maheshani! You
have shown great compassion. O Ambika! Radiant, you have
manifested yourself in front of me. O Shivaa! Among all
Shaktis, you are the original one. You are the mother of the
three worlds. O Devi! You are Shiva's beloved. You are always
supremely praised by all *deva*s. O Maheshani! Show me your
favours and remain in my *dhyana* in the form in which you
have appeared before me. But otherwise, assume my daughter's
form." Hearing the words of Mena, the mountain's wife, Devi
Shivaa happily replied to the mountain's beloved. Devi said, "O
Mena! Earlier, you were engaged in serving me well. Extremely
pleased with your devotion, I appeared before you, to grant
you a boon. 'Ask for a boon.' Hearing my words, you asked for
an excellent boon and said, 'O Mahadevi! Become my daughter
and ensure the welfare of the gods.' Affectionately granting
you the boon, I returned to my own abode. O beloved of the
mountain! With the time having arrived, I have become your
daughter. So that I remain in your memory, I have assumed
the divine form now. Otherwise, had I assumed a mortal form,
you would not have realized it was me. The two of you can
think of me as a daughter or in my divine form. I will reside
with you. Show me affection. Subsequently, you will obtain a
destination with me. Engaging in wonderful pastimes on earth,
I will accomplish the task of *deva*s. I will become Shambhu's
wife and save virtuous people." Shivaa Ambika said this and

was silent. While her mother looked on lovingly, using her own
maya, she instantly assumed a daughter's form.'"'

Chapter 102-3.3(7) (Parvati's Childhood Pastimes)

‘ ‘‘**B**rahma said, 'In front of Mena, the immensely
radiant one assumed a daughter's form. Resorting to
practices of the world, she started to cry. O sage! As she lay
down on the couch in the delivery chamber, her great radiance
spread in every direction and made the lamps burning in the
night seem dim. Hearing the beautiful sound of her cries, all
the women of the household were eager and happy. Full of
joy, they quickly arrived there. A messenger from the inner
quarter swiftly informed the mountain about Parvati's birth,
an auspicious incident that brought happiness and would
accomplish the task of *deva*s. On hearing the auspicious news
of his daughter's birth from the messenger, there was nothing
that the mountain could not instantly give the messenger, even
his white umbrella.[924] Along with the priest and a *brahmana*,
the mountain happily went there. He saw his extremely
radiant and beautiful daughter. Her excellent and pleasant
radiance was dark, like the petals of a blue lotus. Seeing
a daughter like that, the lord of mountains rejoiced. All the
citizens present, men and women, rejoiced. There were great
festivities, and many musical instruments were sounded. There
were auspicious songs and courtesans danced. He donated
to *brahmana*s and performed the decreed *jatakarma* rites.
Himachala arrived at the gate and organized great festivities.

[924] One of the signs of royalty.

Pleased in his mind, he donated riches to those who sought them. At a *muhurta* believed to be good, along with the sages, Himachala named his daughter Kali and also gave her other names that bring joy. With a great deal of love and affection, he donated to *brahmana*s. Along with singing, he arranged for many types of festivities. Organizing the festivities, along with his wife, the mountain repeatedly looked at Kali. Though he possessed many sons, she made him rejoice. In the home of the king of mountains, Devi Shivaa grew up, like the Ganga during the monsoon or the moon during autumn. Devi Kalika was beautiful in all her limbs and was charming to behold. Every day, she grew more and more beautiful, like *kala*s being added to the moon's disc. As was appropriate for the lineage, she was known by the name of Parvati.[925] She loved all the relatives and was a friend to everyone. She possessed the qualities of good conduct. O sage! Her mother tried to restrain Kalika from performing austerities, exclaiming, "Uma!"[926] Hence, subsequently, the one with the beautiful face came to be known on earth as Uma. Although he possessed sons, the mountain's eyes were not satisfied from looking at the child known as Parvati. She possessed all the signs of good fortune. O lord among sages! During spring, there are an infinite number of flowers. However, swarms of bees are especially attracted towards mango blossoms. Mount Himalaya was adorned and purified by her, just as learned men are by polished speech. A lamp in the house obtains greater radiance because of the leaping flames and those who follow the virtuous path by the Ganga. That is what happened to the mountain because of Girija. In her childhood, amidst her friends, the daughter repeatedly played on the sandy bed of the Ganga with artificial balls. O sage! The time then arrived for Devi Shivaa to receive

---

[925] Parvata's (mountain's) daughter.
[926] Uma = U + *ma*, meaning, 'Oh! Don't!'

her instructions. With joy and attention, she learnt the various forms of learning from a virtuous *guru*. In the autumn, swans return to the divine river.[927] In the night, radiance returns to the herbs. In that way, she got back the learning from her former life. I have thus described some of Shivaa's sports. O sage! I will now describe her other pastimes. Listen lovingly.'"'

Chapter 103-3.3(8) (Conversation between Narada and Himalaya)

' " Brahma said, 'Narada possesses *jnana* about Shiva. He is supreme among those who know about Shiva's pastimes. Sent by Shiva, he happily arrived in Himachala's house. O sage! On seeing you, the lord of mountains bent down and worshipped you. He summoned his daughter and asked her to fall down at your feet. O lord among sages! Mount Himachala prostrated himself again and spoke to you. Thinking that he should follow the norms, he joined his hands in salutation and repeatedly lowered his head. Himalaya said, "O sage! O Narada! O lord with *jnana*! O Brahma's supreme son! You are omniscient. You are compassionate and engaged in the welfare of others. Please tell me about the qualities and taints of the daughter who has been born to me. Whose beloved will my fortunate daughter become?" Addressed in this way by Himalaya, lord of mountains, the noble sage examined Kalika's palm and particularly, her limbs. O son! You are wonderfully accomplished in the use of words. You possess *jnana* and know about the end of everything. Pleased in his mind, Narada spoke to the mountain. Narada said, "This daughter, yours and

[927] Ganga.

Mena's, will grow like the digits of the moon, starting with the first *kala*. O king of mountains! She possesses all the auspicious signs. She will bestow infinite happiness on her husband. She will extend the fame of her parents. She will be greatly virtuous. She will always bring great happiness to everyone. O mountain! Your daughter's palm bears all the extremely auspicious signs. There is only one inauspicious line. Hear the truth about its consequences. This is about her husband. He will be a naked *yogi*. He will be without *guna*s and without desire. He will be without a father and a mother. He will not be respected and will be attired in inauspicious clothes. Her husband will be like that." Hearing his words, the couple took them to be true. Therefore, Mena and Himachala were unhappy. O sage! However, hearing the same words, Shivaa Jagadamba formed the view that it was Shiva who possessed these attributes. There was joy in her heart. Shivaa thought that Narada's words could not be false. Therefore, she turned her love and mind towards Shiva's two feet.'"

""'O Narada! With sorrow in his mind, the mountain spoke to you. "O sage! This is a reason for great sorrow. What can be done?" O sage! You are accomplished in the use of words. Hearing his words, you addressed him in auspicious words that filled him with joy and great wonder. Narada said, "O mountain! Listen lovingly to my words. My words are true and are never false. The lines in the palm are drawn by Brahma. They can certainly not be false. Hence, there is no doubt that she will have a husband like that. However, listen lovingly to the means whereby you will obtain happiness. The lord Shambhu, who assumes a form full of pastimes, is a groom like that. In him, the wicked qualities become good qualities. Taints in such a lord do not lead to grief. They only cause misery in a person who is not such a lord. The sun, the fire and Ganga can be cited as instances of this. Therefore, use your discrimination and bestow your daughter, Shivaa, on

Shiva. Shiva is the Sarveshvara who should be served. He is the undecaying lord who has no transformation. There is no doubt that Shiva's favours can be quickly obtained. Specifically, this can be accomplished through austerities. Let Shivaa observe austerities. In every possible way, Shiva, everyone's Ishvara, is an appropriate person. He cannot be destroyed, not even with the *vajra*. He is the one who keeps Brahma under this control." O *brahmana*! O sage! O son! You again spoke these auspicious words to the king of mountains, delighting him. "She is meant to be Shambhu's beloved, and Hara will always be favourably disposed towards her. He is extremely virtuous and excellent in her vows. She will extend the happiness of her parents. She will become an ascetic and make Shambhu's mind devoted to her. He will marry no woman other than her. A love like theirs has not existed in the past. It does not exist now. Nor will it exist in the future. O best among sages! Together, they will accomplish the task of the gods and bring those who are dead back to life. O mountain! This maiden will be half of Ardhanarishvara Hara. Their union will give rise to delight. Satisfying Mahesha, everyone's lord, through the power of her austerities, your daughter will take half of Hara's body. Satisfying Hara through her austerities, she will have a golden hue and will become Svarnagouri.[928] Your daughter will become fairer than lightning. This daughter will be famous under the name of Gouri. She will deserve to be worshipped by all *deva*s, Hari, Brahma and the others. O supreme among mountains! You should not bestow her on anyone else. This is a secret of the gods and must never be divulged." O *devarshi*! O Narada! O sage! O one who is accomplished in the use of words! Hearing your words, Himalaya addressed you in the following words. "O sage! O Narada! O wise one! O one who brings happiness! There is something I have to say. Please listen to it lovingly

---

[928] Golden Gouri.

and act accordingly. It has been heard that Mahadeva is in control of his *atman* and that he has abandoned attachment. He is constantly engaged in austerities and even *deva*s cannot approach him. He is following the path of *dhyana* and his mind is immersed in the supreme *brahman*. O *devarshi*! How can he made to deviate from *that*? I have a great doubt about this. The supreme *brahman* is without decay, like the burning wick of a lamp. His own form is known as Sadashiva, without transformation, without origin and beyond the *brahman*. He is *nirguna* and *saguna*. He is without any distinctive attribute and without desire. He always looks towards the inside and not towards anything outside. O sage! This is what we have always lovingly heard from the mouths of *kinnara*s, when they have come here. Why should they lie? Their words must be true. We have also heard that, formerly, the one known as Hara had entered into a pledge. Hear my words about this. 'O Dakshayani! O beloved Sati! I will not accept anyone other than you as a wife. The words I have spoken are true.' In earlier times, this is the pledge he made to Sati. How can he himself render that false and accept someone else?" In your presence, the mountain said this and was silent. O *devarshi*! O son! Hearing this, you told him the truth. Narada answered, "O king of mountains! O immensely intelligent one! You should not worry on this score. In earlier times, your daughter, Kali, used to be Daksha's daughter. Her name was Sati and she always brought everything that was auspicious. Sati, Daksha's daughter, became Rudra's beloved. At her father's sacrifice, she was dishonoured and witnessed Shankara being dishonoured. Full of rage, Sati gave up her own body. Ambika Shivaa has been born in your home again. There is no doubt that Parvati will be Hara's wife." You explained all this in detail to the mountain, Parvati's earlier form and conduct. All this about Kali's earlier account increases delight. Hearing this from the mouth of the sage, the mountain, his wife and his sons no longer had any doubts. When Kali heard this account from Narada's mouth, she lowered her head in shame, but there was an extended smile on her face. Hearing about her conduct, the mountain touched her with his hand. Inhaling the fragrance of her head for a long time, he made her sit down on his own seat. O sage! On seeing her seated there, you spoke again, delighting the king of mountains, Menaka and their sons. "O king of mountains! Why have you made her sit on your throne? Her seat will always be Shambhu's thigh. Having obtained Hara's thigh as a seat, your daughter will go to a place that no eye and mind can reach." O Narada! Speaking these words to the lord of mountains, you immediately happily went to heaven. The mind of the king of mountains was filled with delightful joy. He returned to his home, full of every kind of wealth and prosperity.'"'

Chapter 104-3.3(9) (The Dream)

' "Narada said, 'O Vidhatri! O father! You are supreme among Shiva's devotees. O wise one! Out of compassion towards me, you have described a wonderful account and have increased my joy even more. O Vidhatri! I, the possessor of divine sight, went to my own abode. O father! What happened after that? Out of compassion towards me, please tell me that now.'"'

'"Brahma replied, 'O sage! After you went to heaven, a period of time elapsed. On one occasion, Mena approached the mountain and prostrated herself. The mountain's beloved stood there and humbly spoke to her husband. The virtuous lady loved her daughter more than her own life and she spoke to the lord of mountains. Mena said, "Because of my feminine nature, I have not been able to understand the sage's words

completely. One should marry a daughter to a handsome
groom. If a marriage is conducted according to this, it always
brings unprecedented happiness. Let the mountain's daughter
have a groom who possesses good qualities and is from a good
lineage. O beloved! I love my daughter more than my own life.
This is how she will be happy. I prostrate myself before you. Let
her obtain a good groom and be extremely happy." He heard
the words of his wife, who had fallen down at his feet. Her face
was bathed in tears. The mountain, supreme among wise ones,
raised her up and spoke to her. Himalaya said, "O Menaka! O
queen! Listen. I will tell you the truth. Give up your confusion.
Do not make the sage's words false. If you love your daughter,
instruct your daughter affectionately. With her mind fixed in
devotion, let her perform austerities for Shankara. O Menaka!
Thus pleased, Shiva will accept Kali's hand. Everything will
be auspicious then. What Narada said about the inauspicious
will be destroyed. In Sadashiva, everything inauspicious turns
auspicious. Therefore, so that your daughter can obtain
Shiva, quickly instruct her about austerities." Hearing the
mountain's words, Mena became exceedingly happy. She went
to her daughter, intending to instruct and turn her inclination
towards austerities. Menaka saw that her daughter's limbs
were delicate. She was distressed and her eyes quickly filled
with tears. The mountain's beloved was unable to instruct
her daughter. Parvati instantly understood what her mother
intended. Devi Kalika, Parameshvari who knows everything,
repeatedly comforted her mother and immediately spoke to her.
Parvati said, "O mother! O immensely wise one! Listen. Show
me your compassion. In the night, at *brahma muhurta* when
the sun rises, I had a dream. I will tell you about it. O mother!
Full of love and compassion, a *brahmana* ascetic instructed
me to perform austerities for Shiva." Hearing these words,
Menaka quickly summoned her husband there. She told him
everything about the dream their daughter had seen. Hearing

about the dream seen by their daughter from Menaka, the lord
of mountains was extremely happy. He addressed his beloved
in gentle words. The lord of mountains said, "O beloved!
Towards the end of the second half of the night, I too had a
dream. With a great deal of joy, listen to it. I will lovingly tell
you. There was a supreme ascetic, possessing excellent limbs,
just as Narada had said. He cheerfully arrived on the outskirts
of the city, so as to perform austerities. Taking my daughter
with me, full of great joy, I went there. I got to know that
this was the lord Shambhu, the groom Narada spoke about. I
instructed our daughter to serve that ascetic. I asked him to give
her what she asked for, but he did not agree. There was a great
discussion between them on *samkhya* and Vedanta. Thereafter,
obeying his command, my daughter remained there. Hiding the
desire in her heart, she devotedly served him. This is the dream
I saw. O one with the beautiful face! I have told you about it. O
beloved! For some time, I think we must test the consequences
of this. I have certainly understood that this is the appropriate
course of action for us." O lord among sages! The king of
mountains spoke to Menaka in this way. Pure in their minds,
they decided to wait and test the consequences.'"'
    ""'A few days passed. Paramesha is the goal of the
virtuous. Separation from Sati had led to severe unhappiness
in him, and he wandered around, here and there. With a few
*gana*s, the lord arrived there, so as to perform austerities. His
mind was overwhelmed by love for Sati and stricken because
of the separation from her. While he himself engaged in
austerities there, along with two of her friends, Parvati always
served him cheerfully. The lord Shambhu does not suffer from
transgressions. The gods sent Smara to delude him and though
pierced by his arrows, he was not affected.[929] Instead, with the
fire that emerged from his eyes, he burnt Smara down there.

---

[929] These sentences don't really belong here.

Remembering the words I had spoken, he was enraged and vanished. After some time, he destroyed Girija's pride. As a result of her great austerities, Maheshvara was pleased. To show his favours to Vishnu, Rudra resorted to customary practices of the world. He married Kali and many kinds of auspicious things resulted. O son! I have thus briefly told you about the lord Shankara's supremely divine conduct. What do you wish to hear again?"'"

Chapter 105-3.3(10) (Bhouma's Origin)

"'Narada said, 'O Vishnu's disciple! O immensely fortunate one! O Vidhatri! O supreme among Shiva's devotees! O lord! Full of affection, you should speak to me about Shiva's pastimes in detail. Separated from Sati, what did Shambhu do? To perform austerities, when did he go to the excellent slopes of the Himalayas? Please fulfil my wishes by telling me how the auspicious conversation between Shiva and Shivaa occurred? Having performed austerities, how did Parvati obtain Shiva Shambhu? O Brahma! You should tell me about all these and about Shiva's other conduct. This is auspicious and yields great joy.'"

'Suta said, "The supreme lord of the worlds heard Narada's question. Extremely happy, Vidhatri remembered Shiva's lotus feet and spoke."'

'"Brahma replied, 'O devarshi! O Shiva's noble devotee! Hear lovingly about his glory. It is purifying and brings everything that is auspicious. It enhances supreme devotion. Suffering from separation from his beloved, Shambhu returned to his own mountain. In his heart, he remembered his beloved Devi Sati, whom he loved more than his own life. Grieving, he summoned his ganas and happily described her qualities, which increased love, to them. He thus exhibited the customary practices of the world. The directions were his garments. He abandoned the virtuous path followed by householders. Accomplished in every kind of pastime, he roamed around the worlds again. Miserable at being separated from Sati, he could not see her anywhere. Shankara, who bestows welfare on his devotees, returned to the mountain. He made efforts to fix his mind in *samadhi*. *Samadhi* destroys miseries. When he did this, he saw his own undecaying form. He remained stationary in this way for a long time, destroying the three *gunas*. He is the supreme *brahman*, without transformations. The lord is himself the lord of *maya*. After many years passed, he gave up this state of *samadhi*. I will now quickly tell you what happened thereafter. As a result of the exertion, drops of sweat emerged from the lord's forehead. They fell down on the ground and a wonderful child emerged from this. He was four-armed, with a red complexion. O sage! He was charming in appearance. He was handsome and his radiance was not of this world. He was energetic and impossible for others to withstand. In front of Paramesha, the child started to cry. Bhava behaved towards him as an ordinary being would towards his own child. The earth thought about this for a very long time and assumed a beautiful body. Full of fear, she appeared there, before Shankara. Like a mother, she quickly took the child up on her lap. She happily fed him the milk that was flowing from her breasts all over her body. As if she was playing with her own son, she smiled and lovingly kissed his face. In Sati's absence, to do what would be good for Paramesha, she behaved like the child's mother. On witnessing her conduct, Shambhu was amused. Hara knows what is inside everyone. Knowing that this was the earth, he smiled and spoke to her. "O earth! You are blessed. Lovingly nourish this child of mine. This extraordinary child has emerged from drops of perspiration that fell down on you. He will be supreme and extremely energetic. O earth! This child was born from my exertion. Nevertheless, since you have shown him love, he will become famous on earth under your own name. He will always be free from the three types of distress. This child of yours will possess qualities but will bestow what is inauspicious.[930] He will bestow happiness on me. But for householders, he will bestow what he wills." Having said this, he stopped, his mind somewhat free of the pangs of separation. Rudra is indifferent and loves the virtuous, but he was following customary practices of the world. The earth accepted Shiva's command. The earth quickly returned to her own residence. At having obtained a son, she was filled with great joy. The child, known as Bhouma, swiftly became a youth. In Kashi, he served Lord Shankara for a very long time. As a result of Vishveshvara's favours, the earth's son obtained the status of becoming a planet. He swiftly attained the divine world, a supreme region beyond Shukra's world. Shambhu's conduct, after his separation from Sati, has thus been described. O sage! Now listen lovingly to how Shambhu engaged in austerities.'"'

Chapter 106-3.3(11) (Shiva and the Mountain Meet)

' "Brahma said, 'Shakti, worshipped by the worlds, grew up as the mountain's daughter. Born in Himalaya's house, the virtuous one attained eight years of age. Distressed on account of separation from Sati, Girisha knew about her birth. O Narada! Knowing about this, he was delighted internally. At the time, Shambhu was engaged in following the practices of the world. Therefore, he made up his mind and

[930] As the earth's child, Mangala (Mars) is known as Bhouma and is regarded as an inauspicious planet.

wished to perform austerities. There is an excellent place in the Himalayas, known as Gangavatara. In ancient times, Ganga descended there, flowing from Brahmapura.[931] O sage! She destroys all sins and is supremely purifying. Along with a few serene *ganas*, Nandi and others, he went there to bathe. Hara controlled himself and remaining there, started his austerities. He single-mindedly fixed his thoughts on his own *atman*. His consciousness is the source of *jnana*. He is eternal, in the form of illumination and without any affliction. He pervades the universe. He is consciousness and bliss. He is without a second and requires no support. When Hara immersed himself in *dhyana*, some of the *pramatha*s also engaged in *dhyana*. So did some of the *ganas*, Nandi, Bhringi and others. Some other *ganas* served Shambhu, the *paramatman*. Others became doorkeepers, remaining silent and not conversing.'""

""'Meanwhile, hearing that Shankara had come to Oushadhiprastha, Mount Himalaya affectionately arrived there. Along with his companions, the lord of mountains prostrated himself before Lord Rudra. He honoured him and worshipped him. Full of joy, he joined his hands in salutation and praised him. Himalaya said, "O lord of *devas*! O Mahadeva! O Kapardin![932] O Shankara! O lord! As the lord of the worlds, you are the one who protects the three worlds. O divinity! O lord of *devas*! I prostrate myself before you. You are the one who assumes the form of a *yogi*. You are *nirguna*. I bow down before you. In your pastimes, you become *saguna*. O one who resides in Kailasa! O Shambhu! O one who roams around the worlds! I prostrate myself before Paramesha, the

---

[931] Gangavatara should be Gomukh, at the foot of the Gangotri glacier. In that case, Brahmapura will be higher up. However, if Brahmapura is identified with Vairatapattana in Dhikuli in Uttarakhand, Gangavatara might be Gangadvara or Haridvara.

[932] One with matted hair, Shiva.

one who engages in pastimes and wields the trident. You are a complete abode of qualities. You are without transformations. I prostrate myself before you. You are without wishes. You are the one who abandons. You are the patient one. You are the *paramatman*. You are the one who bestows internal enjoyment. You are affectionate towards people. I prostrate myself before you. O lord of the three *guna*s! O lord of *maya*! O *brahman*! O *paramatman*! You deserve to be served by Brahma, Vishnu and others. Vishnu and Brahma are your own forms. You are the one who created Brahma and Vishnu. O one who is affectionate towards devotees! I prostrate myself before you. You are engaged in austerities. You are the place for austerities. You bestow the fruits of good austerities. You love austerities. O serene one! I bow down before the one whose form is the *brahman*. You are the one who determined the norms for worldly transaction and behaviour. You possess *guna*s! I prostrate myself before Paresha, the *paramatman*. O Mahesha! Your pastimes cannot be understood. They bring happiness to those who are virtuous. Your own form is one that is controlled by devotees. You are subservient to your devotees. You undertake *karma*. O lord! It is my good fortune that you have come here. You have become my protector. You are described as one who is affectionate towards those who are distressed. Today, my birth has been rendered successful. Today, my life has been rendered successful. Since you have arrived here, today, everything has been rendered successful. O Maheshvara! Know that I am your foremost servant. Command me. With single-minded intelligence, I will serve you and obtain great joy." Maheshvara heard the words of the lord of mountains. He opened his eyes a little and saw the mountain and his companions.'"

'"'Vrishadhvaja saw the lord of mountains and his companions. Immersed in *dhyana* and *yoga*, the lord of the universe seemed to smile as he spoke. Maheshvara said, "I

came to this secluded spot so that I could torment myself
through austerities atop you. Act so that no one can approach
near me. You are great-souled and a store of austerities. The
sages always seek refuge with you. So do *devas*, *rakshasas* and
other great-souled ones. *Brahmanas* and others always reside
here, constantly purified by the Ganga. You do a good deed
to all the others and are the master and lord of mountains. I
will perform austerities in this spot, in Gangavatara. I have
controlled my *atman* and have happily sought refuge with the
king of mountains. O mountain! In my austerities, let there
be no cause for impediment. O best among mountains! That
is what you must do now, ensure it in every possible way. O
supreme among mountains! This is the greatest service you
can do for me. Make efforts to ensure it and when it is over,
cheerfully return to your own residence." Having said this,
the protector of the world was silent. The king of mountains
prostrated himself before Shambhu and spoke these words.
Himalaya said, "O lord of the universe! O Parameshvara! I
have worshipped you. I have myself come to you now. You are
located in my kingdom and there is nothing I cannot give you.
You cannot be obtained, even when *devas* make efforts and
engage in great austerities. That Mahesha has arrived here on
his own. There is no one who is superior to me. There is no one
whose good merits are superior to mine. You have come and are
going to engage in austerities on my slopes. O Parameshvara!
I consider myself to be superior to Indra of the gods. You are
the one who bestows fortune and you have shown me a favour
and have come here, along with your *ganas*. O lord of *devas*!
You are self-ruling. Perform your supreme austerities without
any impediments. I am your servant and will serve you. O
lord! I will always be there for you." Saying this, the lord of
mountains quickly returned to his own residence. He lovingly
reported this incident to his beloved. O Narada! He summoned
all his relatives and companions. The lord of mountains told

them about the truth. Himalaya said, "From today, none of you should go to Gangavatara. Let this be an instruction for anyone who is in my capital. I am telling you the truth. If any person goes there, he will be extremely crooked, and I will impose specific punishment on him. I have spoken the truth." O sage! He swiftly told all his companions about this rule. After this, the mountain made excellent efforts. Listen. I will tell you.'"

Chapter 107-3.3(12) (Shiva and the Mountain Converse)

" "Brahma said, 'The lord of mountains collected an excellent pile of flowers and fruits. Taking his daughter with him, he approached Gangavatara. Having gone there, he prostrated himself before Jagannatha, who was immersed in supreme *dhyana*. In his mind, he performed the wonderful act of bestowing his daughter, Kali, on him. With all the flowers and fruits, he made his daughter stand ahead of him. Placing his daughter in front, the king of mountains spoke to Shambhu. Himalaya said, "O Bhagavan! O Chandrashekhara! My daughter is eager to serve you. Since she desires to worship you, I have brought her here. Along with her two friends, let her always serve Shankara. O protector! Please show me your favours and grant her the permission to do that." At this, Shankara looked at her. She was in the first bloom of youth. Her face was like a fully blown blue lotus or like the full moon. She was attired in an auspicious garment and every kind of charm was spread throughout her body. Her throat was like a conch shell and her eyes were large. Her beautiful ears were radiant. Her graceful arms were like the stalks of lotuses. Her breasts were thick and firm, and her nipples were like the buds of blue lotuses. With a slender waist, she dazzled, and her stomach was beautiful, with three lines. Her two beautiful feet were like lotuses that grew on the land.[933] She was like a crest among beautiful women. The sight of her was capable of agitating the minds of sages who were immersed and bound in *dhyana*. O son! Her beautiful form was such that it could make those engaged in *tantra* and *mantra* deviate. She enhanced desire. On seeing her, the great *yogi* quickly closed his eyes and meditated on his own excellent form. He is the supreme and undecaying truth, beyond the three *guna*s. The lord of everything saw her in that form. Desiring to engage in austerities, the lord closed his eyes. Kapardin was adorned with the crescent moon as an ornament. He is the one who is known through Vedanta and was in his supreme posture. Himachala was filled with doubt. Distressed in his mind, he lowered his head down. The lord of mountains, supreme among those who are eloquent in the use of words, spoke these words to the single friend the universe has. Himachala said, "O lord of *deva*s! O Mahadeva! O abode of compassion! O Shankara! O lord! I have sought refuge with you. Please open your eyes and look at me. O Shiva! O Sharva! O Mahesha! O lord who ensures happiness to the universe! O Mahadeva! You are the one who destroys every hardship, and I am bowing down before you. O lord of *deva*s! All the *Veda*s and sacred texts do not know you. Your greatness is always beyond thoughts and words. Therefore, all the *shruti* texts say little about you. In their fear, they say what you are not, not what you are. What need be said of others? Many devotees know you. That is because they have devotion and have obtained your compassion. For devotees who seek refuge with you, there never is any reason for confusion. Please listen lovingly to me now. I am your servant. O divinity! O father! In my ignorance and since I am inferior, I dare to state it. O Mahadeva!

---

[933] *Sthalapadma, Hibiscus mutabilis.*

O Shankara! As a result of your favours, I have been fortunate.
O protector! I prostrate myself before you. Taking me to be
your servant, please show me your compassion. O lord! Every
day, I will come here to see you, along with this daughter.
O lord! Please grant us the permission." Hearing these words,
Maheshvara opened his eyes.'"'

'"'Having given up his *dhyana*, the lord of *deva*s thought a
little and spoke these words. Maheshvara said, "O mountain!
Do come every day to see me. But leave the maiden in your
house. She cannot see me." Shivaa's father heard Mahesha's
words. The mountain lowered his shoulders and spoke to
Girisha in this way. Himachala said, "Please tell me why I
should not come here with her. Why is she unworthy of serving
you? I do not know the reason." Shambhu Vrishadhvaja
laughed and spoke to the mountain. In particular, he showed
him the worldly conduct followed by bad *yogi*s. Shambhu
said, "This maiden possesses beautiful hips. She is slender and
auspicious, and her face resembles the moon. She should not be
brought to my presence. I am repeatedly forbidding you. Those
who are accomplished in the *Veda*s have said that a woman is
the form of *maya*. In particular, this is true of a young woman.
She creates impediments for ascetics. I am an ascetic and *yogi*,
always unaffected by *maya*. O mountain! What need do I have
for association with a woman? Supreme ascetics resort to you.
Therefore, you should not say such things again. You are wise
and possess *jnana* about the *dharma* of the *Veda*s. O mountain!
You are supreme among learned ones. Association with them
leads to attachment and destroys non-attachment. That leads
to deviation from austerities. O mountain! Therefore, ascetics
should not associate with women. This is the root of great
attachment towards material objects and destroys *jnana* and
non-attachment." Maheshvara, the great *yogi*, said this many
times. After this, Lord Girisha, supreme among great *yogi*s,
stopped. O divine *rishi*! Hearing these beneficial words of

Shambhu, indifferent and cruel, Kali's father was somewhat agitated. But he remained silent. Bhavani also heard the words spoken by the ascetic and saw that the lord of mountains was agitated. She reflected on these and prostrated herself before Shiva. She then started to speak the following words.'"'

Chapter 108-3.3(13) (Conversation between Parvati and Parameshvara)

‘ ‘‘ ‘Bhavani said, "You are a *yogi* and an ascetic. What did you tell the king of mountains? O lord! O one who is accomplished in *jnana*! O lord! Hear the reply from me. O Shambhu! You possess the strength of austerities and are undertaking great austerities. Since you are great-souled, your intelligence turns towards tormenting yourself through austerities. Know that Prakriti is the strength behind all *karma*. Everything is created, preserved and destroyed through her. Who are you? Who is subtle Prakriti? O Bhagavan! Reflect on this. Without Prakriti, who is Maheshvara, with the *lingam* as his form? You are always revered by beings. They revere you and perform *dhyana* on you. But it is said that Prakriti is in all their hearts. Reflect on this." Hearing Parvati's words, Mahesha, engaged in the great task, was pleased in his mind. He smiled and spoke these words. Maheshvara said, "I will destroy Prakriti with my supreme austerities. In truth, devoid of Prakriti, I will remain as Shambhu. The task of the virtuous is not to ever accept Prakriti. They should establish themselves as indifferent, devoid of customary worldly conduct." O son! Engaged in customary worldly conduct, Shambhu said this. Kali smiled within her heart and replied in these sweet words. Kali answered, "O *yogi*! O Shankara! O lord! Based on what you have said, how can you say that there is no Prakriti and that you are beyond her? Please reflect on the truth of this statement, as is appropriate. Everything is incessantly bound by Prakriti. There is nothing that can be said or done without her. In your mind, you should know that every act of speaking or doing is based on Prakriti. Everything heard, everything eaten, everything seen and everything done—all that is done by Prakriti. It is futile to say that is a false statement. If you are superior to Prakriti, why are you tormenting yourself through austerities? O lord! You are Shambhu and you are now on Mount Himalaya. O Hara! You do not know your own self. You have been swallowed by Prakriti. O Isha! If you do not know yourself, why are you tormenting yourself through austerities? O *yogi*! What need do I have to engage in this argument with you? The learned say that inference, without direct perception, is no proof.[934] For embodied beings, as long as perception is based on the senses, all that is based on Prakriti. That is the comment of those who possess *jnana* in their intellect. O lord of *yoga*! What is the need to speak a lot? Listen to my supreme words. You are Purusha and I am Prakriti. This is the truth. There is no doubt that this is the truth. It is through my favours that you have assumed this form, consisting of *guna*s. Without me, you are without attributes and are incapable of doing anything. You are under the control of someone else. You are under the subjugation of many kinds of *karma*. How are you indifferent? How are you not touched by me? O Shankara! If you have spoken true words, that you are beyond Prakriti, you should have no reason to fear my presence." Shiva heard her words, which were in conformity with the sacred texts of *samkhya*. He replied to Shivaa in words that were in conformity with Vedanta. Shri Shiva replied, "O Girija! O one who upholds the *sankhya* view! O one excellent in speech! If this is what you say, unrestricted, serve me every

---

[934] The basic principle of *samkhya*.

day. But if I am the indifferent *brahman*, the one who is known through Vedanta, the Parameshvara who is the lord of *maya*, and all this is my *maya*, what will you do then?" Telling Girija this, the lord spoke to the mountain again.'"'

'"'He is the one who delights his devotees. He is the one who shows favours to his devotees. Shiva said, "O mountain! Here, on your extremely beautiful slopes, I will engage in supreme austerities. I roam around on earth to display my supreme nature, full of bliss. O lord of mountains! You should grant me permission to undertake these austerities. Without your permission, no one is able to undertake the least bit of austerities." Hearing the words of the lord of *deva*s, the wielder of the trident, Himalaya prostrated himself and addressed Shambhu in the following words. Himalaya said, "Everything in the universe, *deva*s, *asura*s and humans, belongs to you. O Mahadeva! Who am I? I am inferior. Nevertheless, I wish to tell you something."[935] Himalaya said this to Shankara, who brings welfare to the worlds. He smiled at the king of mountains and affectionately asked him to leave. Having obtained Shankara's permission, Himalaya returned to his own house, along with Girija, though he wanted to see him every day. Even without her father, along with her two friends, Kali went to Shankara's presence every day. Full of great devotion, she served him. O son! On the instructions of Mahesha, who issues pure commands, none of the *gana*s, Nandishvara and the others, prevented her. The conversation between Shiva and Shivaa about *samkhya* and Vedanta is auspicious and always brings happiness. If one thinks about it properly, there is no difference between them.'"'

'"'Shankara showed respect to the words of the king of the mountains. The lord of the earth allowed his daughter to

[935] As will be evident, a request that his daughter should serve Shiva.

remain near him. The lord of the earth spoke these words to
Kali and her two friends. "Serve me every day. You can come,
go and remain, without any fear." Telling Devi this, Hara
accepted her service. He is the great *yogi* who is indifferent.
The lord engages in many kinds of pastimes. Such is the great
patience and fortitude excellent ascetics possess. Even if they
face impediments, they do not succumb to those impediments.
O lord among sages! With his attendants, the king of
mountains returned to his own city. He was filled with delight
in his mind. Hara engaged in *dhyana* and *yoga*. He lovingly
immersed his mind in the *paramatman* and thought about it,
without any impediments. Along with her two friends, Kali
served Chandrashekhara Mahadeva every day. She came, went
and remained. She washed Shambhu's feet and drank the water
after washing his feet. She wiped his body with a garment
purified in the fire. She worshipped him in the proper way,
using sixteen kinds of *upachara*. Every day, before returning
to her father's house, she prostrated herself repeatedly. In this
way, Shivaa served Shankara, who was immersed in *dhyana*.
O supreme among sages! A long period of time elapsed.
Sometimes, along with her two friends in Shankara's hermitage,
Kali sang beautiful songs, with excellent *tala*.[936] This enhanced
desire. Sometimes, she herself collected *kusha* grass, flowers
and kindling. Along with her two friends, she always cleaned
the place. Sometimes, she remained in the home of the one
who wears the moon. Full of surprise and desire, she looked at
Chandrashekhara. The lord of *bhuta*s engaged in austerities in
that secluded spot. He looked at her and thought of her. Though
Kali was in embodied form and was present near him, Girisha
did not accept her as his wife. She was the store of a great deal
of charm, enough to confound sages. But Mahadeva repeatedly
saw that she was in control of her senses. Full of compassion,

---

[936] *Tala* is the measurement of time in music.

he saw that she was constantly engaged in serving him. He thought, "Let Kali observe vows and perform austerities. I will accept her when she has lost all seeds of pride." Thinking this, the lord of *bhuta*s quickly immersed himself in *dhyana*. Ishvara is a great *yogi*. The lord engages in great pastimes. Shiva, the *paramatman*, was immersed in *dhyana*. O sage! There was no other thought in his mind. Every day, Kali devotedly served Shambhu and always thought about the great-souled one's form. Every day, Hara, immersed in *dhyana*, saw Kali standing there. He forgot his earlier thoughts about her. Though he saw her, he did not really see her. Meanwhile, following Brahma's instructions, Shakra and other *deva*s and sages affectionately sent Smara there. They were suffering from the depredations of the extremely valiant *asura*, Taraka. They desired to unite Kali and Rudra. Having gone there, Smara tried every one of his means. Hara's mind was not agitated. Instead, he reduced him to ashes. O sage! Following his commands, Parvati lost her pride. The virtuous one practiced great austerities and obtained Shiva as her husband. After this, Parvati and Parameshvara were satisfied and extremely happy. Engaged in the welfare of others, they accomplished the task of the gods.'"

Chapter 109-3.3(14) (Taraka and Vajranga's Origin)

" "Narada said, 'O Vishnu's disciple! O Shiva's great devotee! O Vidhatri! You have spoken well. This is the supreme account about Shiva and Shivaa. O Brahma! Who was the *asura* who oppressed *deva*s? Whose son was he? Please tell me how he was connected with Shiva. How did Shankara, in control of himself, reduce Smara to ashes? Full of affection, please tell me all this. The lord's conduct is extraordinary. For the sake of being happy, how did Shivaa engage in fierce austerities? How did the primordial Shakti, who is beyond the universe, obtain Shambhu as her husband? O immensely intelligent one! Please tell me all this, specifically and in detail. My *atman* is in Shiva. I am full of devotion and am your own son.'"'

'"Brahma replied, 'O noble son! O immensely wise one! O divine *rishi*! O one praised for his vows! Remembering Shankara, I will tell you everything that occurred. Listen. O Narada! First hear about Taraka's origin. *Deva*s made great efforts to kill him and sought refuge with Shiva. My son was the noble Marichi, and his son was Kashyapa. Kashyapa married thirteen of Daksha's daughters. Diti was the eldest of these two wives and she had two sons. The elder one was Hiranyakashipu and the younger one was Hiranyaksha. In the form of Nrisimha and the boar, Vishnu killed these two *daitya*s.[937] They had caused great misery to *deva*s, who were now happy and free of fear. Diti was miserable and went and sought refuge with Kashyapa. Excellent in her vows, she served him devotedly and conceived again. Knowing this, the great Indra, great in his enterprise, looked for an opportunity and found it. He entered her womb and repeatedly severed the foetus with his *vajra*. Because of the power of her vows, the foetus did not die. She was sleeping at the time. As a result of destiny, seven times seven sons were born.[938] These sons became *deva*s and all

---

[937] *Daitya* means Diti's son. In the Nrisimha/Narasimha *avatara*, Vishnu killed Hiranyakashipu. In the *varaha avatara*, Vishnu killed Hiranyaksha. Hiranyakashipu and Hiranyaksha were twins. Sometimes, Hiranyaksha is described as the younger one. Sometimes, it is the other way around.

[938] The number of Maruts varies but is usually given as 49. Indra sliced the foetus into seven parts and then sliced each of these seven into seven parts. Indra needed a weakness (in Diti's observance of vows) to be able to penetrate her womb. On one occasion, she went to sleep without washing her feet and that was Indra's opportunity.

of them were known as Maruts. The king of *deva*s honoured
them and took them to heaven with him. Diti was tormented
because of what she had herself done and served her husband
again. As a result of her supreme service, the sage was greatly
pleased. Kashyapa said, "Be pure and perform austerities for
ten thousand of Brahma's years. After that, you will have an
unmatched son." O sage! Full of devotion, Diti completed
these austerities. Through her husband, she conceived and
obtained the kind of son she desired. Diti's son was like the
immortals and was named Vajranga. Befitting his name, he
was born brave, powerful and strong.[939] Obeying his mother's
instructions, the son immediately used force to seize the king
of the gods. He also punished the gods in diverse ways. On
seeing the miseries inflicted on Shakra and the others, Diti was
happy. The immortals, Shakra and the others, suffered miseries
because of what they themselves had done.'"

"'I am always engaged in the welfare of *deva*s. Along with
Kashyapa, I quickly went to him and spoke to him in gentle
words, persuading him to release the *deva*s. Having released
*deva*s, Vajranga spoke to me affectionately. He was Shiva's
devotee and was pure in his *atman*. He was indifferent and
pleasant in his intelligence. Vajranga said, "In order to accomplish
his selfish objective, the wicked Indra killed my mother's son.
He has now reaped the fruits of that act. Let him rule over his
own kingdom. O Brahma! I did all this because of my mother's
command. I have no desire to enjoy any of the objects of pleasure
in the world. O Vidhatri! O supreme among those who know
the *Veda*s. Please tell me about their essence, so that I am always
happy, indifferent and pleasant in my intelligence." O sage! On
hearing his words, I replied, "These are spoken out of sentiments
of *sattva*. I will happily create a beautiful woman who represents
their essence." Her named was Varangi and I bestowed her on

[939] Vajranga means one whose limbs are like the *vajra*.

Diti's son. After this, extremely happy, I returned to my own
residence, as did Kashyapa, his father. The *daitya*, Vajranga,
was full of sentiments of *sattva*. He gave up *asura* sentiments.
He had no feelings of hatred and was happy. But there were
no *sattva* sentiments in Varangi's heart. The virtuous lady was
full of desire and devotedly served her husband in many kinds
of ways. As a result of her service, her great lord was quickly
satisfied. Her husband, Vajranga, addressed her in these words.
Vajranga said, "O beloved! Tell me what you desire. What
is in your heart?" Hearing this, she bowed down before her
husband and told him about her wish. Varangi said, "O virtuous
husband! If you are pleased with me, please give me a son. Let
him be extremely strong and a conqueror of the three worlds.
Let him cause misery to Hari." Hearing the words spoken by
his beloved, he was amazed and agitated. His heart was full of
sentiments of *sattva*, and he had no sense of hatred. He spoke,
full of *jnana*. "O beloved! You wish to have enmity with the
gods. This does not appeal to me. What will I do? Where will I
go? How will I ensure that my pledge is not destroyed? If I satisfy
my beloved's wish, the three worlds will constantly suffer and so
will the *deva*s and the sages. But if I do not fulfil my beloved's
wish, I will go to hell. In both cases, *dharma* will be violated.
That is what we have heard." O sage! In this way, Vajranga was
whirled around in a conflict of *dharma*. He used his intelligence
to reflect on the strengths and weaknesses of both options. O
sage! Following Shiva's wishes, the learned one told his wife
that he agreed with what she had said. That is what the king
of *daitya*s told his beloved. To accomplish this, he engaged in
extremely difficult and fierce austerities, directed towards me.
Extremely cheerful, he conquered his senses and did this for
many years. O dear one! As a result of his great austerities, I
showed myself to him, to bestow a boon on him. Pleased in my
mind, I said, "Ask for a boon." Vajranga was happy to see me,
the lord, stationed in the sky. He prostrated himself and praised

me in many kinds of ways, asking for the boon his beloved desired. Vajranga said, "O lord! Please grant me a son who will bring great benefit to his mother. Let him be extremely strong and extremely powerful. Let him be extremely capable and a store of austerities." O sage! Hearing his words, I said that it would be that way. Remembering Shiva, I returned to my own abode, though I was somewhat distracted.'"'

Chapter 110-3.3(15) (Tarakasura's Austerities and Kingdom)

' "Brahma said, 'After this, full of love for him, Varangi conceived. Inside her, the extremely energetic foetus developed for many years. When the due time was over, Varangi delivered a son. He was gigantic in size and extremely valiant. His radiance blazed in the ten directions. At that time, there were great and evil portents, the cause of hardships. When Varangi's son was born, the gods were miserable. O son! There were bad omens on earth, in the firmament and in heaven, causing fear in all the worlds. They signified the three kinds of hardship. I will tell you about them. Meteors showered down and there were bolts of lightning. They were fearful and made large sounds. What arose caused agitation in the hearts and was the cause of misery. The earth, along with its mountains, quaked. All the directions blazed. The waters in all the rivers were agitated, especially those in the oceans. Blinding gusts of wind shrieked and blew, harsh to the touch. They uprooted large trees and dust was like standards on the winds. O Indra among *brahmanas*! Rahu repeatedly obscured the sun and covered it with clubs.[940] All this indicated great fear and

---

[940] Clubs on the solar disc are a mark of impending disaster.

unhappiness. At that time, storms issued forth from the cavities in mountains. They thundered like chariots and caused terror. Jackals and owls howled in extremely hideous tones, vomiting fire through their mouths. The terrible and inauspicious sound of jackals howling could be heard inside villages. Raising up their heads, dogs seemed to sing, as they barked and wept, uttering many kinds of sounds. O son! Groups of asses ran around here and there, braying harshly. Maddened, they dug up the ground with their hooves. Terrified in their minds, birds flew up from their nests. They shrieked, anxious in their minds, and could not find perches anywhere. The animals seemed to be stricken and did not remain in one place. Full of fear, they wandered around, releasing urine and excrement in settlements and forests. The terrified cows had tears in their eyes and could not be milked. The fearful clouds showered down pus. Images of *deva*s were uprooted and seemed to weep. Trees fell down, even though there was no wind. The planets fought in the sky. O supreme sage! In this way, there were many evil portents. The people did not know what was happening and thought that the world was being submerged.'"'

'"'Prajapati Kashyapa gave the *asura* a name. He thought about it and named the immensely energetic one Taraka. The immensely valiant one suddenly manifested his own virility. He grew and his body was as strong as iron. His size was like a lord of mountains. *Daitya* Taraka was extremely strong and valiant. To perform austerities, the great-minded one sought his mother's permission. He possessed the strength of *maya* and could delude with his *maya*. Having obtained the permission, he made up his mind that he would undertake austerities so as to conquer all the *deva*s. Obeying the instruction of his senior, he went to the forest of Madhu.[941] Having been instructed in the proper way, he followed the norms and tormented himself

---

[941] Madhuvana, the region around Mathura.

through extremely terrible austerities. He raised both arms up, stood on one leg and gazed at the sun with his eyes. Firm in his mind and firm in his vow, he performed austerities for one hundred years. He touched the ground only with his big toe and stood like that for one hundred years. Taraka, the lord and king of *asuras*, was firm in his resolve and tormented himself through austerities. For one hundred years, he only subsisted on water. For one hundred years, he only subsisted on air. For one hundred years, he immersed himself in water. For one hundred years, he performed austerities on land. For one hundred years, he was inside a fire. For one hundred years, he was upside down. For one hundred years, he used the palm of his hands to support himself on the ground.[942] O sage! For one hundred years, he used his feet to suspend himself from the branch of a tree. For one hundred years, he was suspended with his face facing downwards, drinking only pure smoke. In this way, the king of *daitya*s tormented himself through hardships, as part of excellent austerities. Pursuing his wish, he undertook austerities in the proper way. It is impossible to tolerate hearing about them. O sage! As he tormented himself in this way, a great mass of energy issued from his head and swirled everywhere, causing great calamities. It went to the world of *deva*s and almost burnt it down. O sage! All *deva*s and *rishi*s suffered from great miseries. Indra, lord of *deva*s, was filled with great fear. "Someone is performing austerities and desires to usurp my position. The lord will rob the universe of its support." He was full of uncertainty and having decided, could not find any peace.'"

""'All the gods and *rishi*s consulted among themselves. Scared and distressed, they came to my world and presented themselves before me. Their minds were suffering. All of

---

[942] That is, he was upside down. In the earlier case, he probably hung upside down.

them prostrated themselves before me and praised me. They joined their hands in salutation and reported everything to me. I used my intelligence to determine the reason behind all this. To bestow a boon, I went to the place where the *asura* was tormenting himself. O sage! I told him, "Ask for a boon. You have tormented yourself through fierce austerities. There is nothing that cannot be given to you." Hearing my words, Taraka, the great *asura*, prostrated himself and extolled me. He then asked me for an extremely terrible boon. Taraka said, "O one who bestows boons! If you are satisfied with me, what can I not accomplish? O grandfather! Therefore, hear about the boon I seek from you. O lord of *deva*s! If you are pleased with me and if a boon is to be given to me, show me your compassion and please grant me two boons. O great lord! In all the three worlds that have been created by you, there should not be a single man who is my equal in strength. If a son born through Shiva's seed becomes a commander and hurls weapons against me, let my death occur only then." O lord among sages! This is what the *daitya* told me then. Granting him such boons, I swiftly returned to my own world. The *daitya* obtained the excellent boons he desired. Extremely pleased, he went to the city known as Shonita.[943] Following the command of Shukra, the *guru* of the *asura*s, the great *asura*, accompanied by other *asura*s, was instated in the kingdom of the three worlds. Thus, the great *daitya* became the leader of the three worlds. He had his own orders implemented and oppressed mobile and immobile objects. In the right way, Taraka ruled over the kingdom of the three worlds. He protected the subjects, but oppressed gods and others. Taraka *daitya* seized jewels from Indra and other guardians of the worlds and out of fear, they

---

[943] Shonitapura was later the capital of Banasura. Tezpur, in Assam, is in the district of Sonitpur.

gave those to him. Scared, Indra gave him Airavata.[944] Kubera
gave him his nine *nidhi*s.[945] Varuna gave him his white horses.
The *rishi*s gave *kamadhenu*. Scared of him, Surya gave him the
divine Ucchaihshrava.[946] Wherever an auspicious object was
seen, he pursued it and quickly seized it. The three worlds were
devoid of substance. O sage! Scared, the ocean gave him all the
jewels. Without being tilled, the earth provided all the crops
that subjects desired. The sun heated mildly, so that he did not
suffer. The moon's light was always seen, and the breeze was
always agreeable. The evil-souled *asura* seized all the objects
that belonged to *deva*s, ancestors or others. He subjugated
the three worlds and became Indra himself. He became the
wonderful lord, without a second, and ruled over the kingdom.
He removed all *deva*s and installed *daitya*s in their places. He
engaged *deva*s in his own personal tasks. O sage! Restrained
in this way, all the *deva*s, with Shakra at the forefront, sought
refuge with me. They were without a protector and were very
agitated.'"'

Chapter 111-3.3(16) (Assuring the *Deva*s)

❝ ❝ **B**rahma said, 'Thus, all the gods prostrated themselves
before the lord of subjects. Oppressed by Taraka,
full of great devotion, they praised me. I heard the praise and
understood the heart of the matter. I was extremely pleased
and replied to the residents of heaven. "O gods! Welcome. I

---

[944] Indra's elephant.

[945] The names of Kubera's nine *nidhi*s (treasures) are Mahapadma,
Padma, Shankha, Makara, Kacchapa, Mukunda, Kunda, Nila and
Kharva.

[946] The horse.

hope you are exercising your rights without any impediments. Why have all of you come here? Please tell me." Hearing my words, all the residents of heaven bent down. Suffering from Taraka and distressed, they bent down and spoke to me. *Devas* said, "O lord of the worlds! Because of your boon, Taraka *daitya* has become insolent. Using force, the deceiver has seized our positions and has taken them over himself. Don't you know about the misery that has presented itself? So that the misery can be swiftly destroyed, we have sought refuge with you. Wherever we might be, he causes impediments for us, day and night. Wherever we run away, we see Taraka there. O lord of everything! All our miseries stem from Taraka. O father! We are suffering greatly. Agni, Yama, Varuna, Nirriti, Vayu and all the other guardians of the worlds have come under his subjugation. All of them follow the *dharma* of humans. All of them offer him tribute. They are never independent and serve the great *daitya*. Constantly under his subjugation, *deva*s are suffering in this way. All of us are engaged in doing what he wishes. We obtain our subsistence from him. The immensely strong *daitya*, Taraka, has seized all our women and the large number of *apsara*s. No sacrifices are going on. The ascetics are not performing austerities. Donations and other *dharma* do not exist anywhere in the worlds. His commander is an extremely wicked *danava*, Krouncha. He has gone to the nether region of Patala and is constantly causing impediments to the subjects there. O creator of the universe! Taraka is evil and has no compassion in him. The deceitful one has forcibly seized the three worlds. We will go wherever you instruct us to go. O protector of the world! Our enemies, the *asura*s, have barred us from our own places. We have no refuge other than you. You are the ruler, creator and saviour. All of us have been scorched by the fire known as Taraka and are very agitated. All our cruel attempts have been robbed of energy, like a *sannipata* fever against which medicinal herbs possess no energy. Our hopes of victory were based on Hari's Sudarshana *chakra*. However, hurled against his throat, it was ineffective, like an offering of flowers around a divinity's throat." O sage! I heard the words spoken by the gods.'"'

"'I replied to all the gods in words that were appropriate for the occasion. Brahma said, "The *daitya* known as Taraka has become successful because of my words. O residents of heaven! It is not appropriate for him to be killed by me. His death from a source that has led to his prosperity is not appropriate. A person who has reared a poisonous tree cannot himself become the reason for its severance. Shankara is the appropriate person to do every task for you. But he can be the cause. He is himself not capable of countering him. I have myself determined the means for destroying the wicked one known as Taraka. I will tell you about the means whereby this can be brought about. Taraka cannot be killed by me, or by Hari or Hara. Thanks to my boon, no other god can do this. I am telling you the truth. O gods! If a son is born through Shiva's energy, he alone can kill the *daitya* known as Taraka, no one else. O best among gods! I have told you about the means. Act according to what I have said. There is no doubt that success will be obtained through Mahadeva's favours. Earlier, Sati Dakshayani gave up her body. She has now been born through Menaka's womb. This is known to you. Girisha will certainly accept her hand. O residents of heaven! Therefore, act in accordance with this means. Thus, make excellent efforts so that his seed is discharged into Parvati, Menaka's daughter. Shambhu is someone who holds up his seed. There is no one else who is capable of doing this. Everyone else is weak and lacks the strength. The daughter of the king of the mountains is now in the prime of youth. While Hara is performing austerities on Mount Himalaya, she constantly serves him. Because of the words of her father, Himalaya, Kali Shivaa is there. Along with her two friends, she is serving Parameshvara, who is immersed in *dhyana*. She is the most beautiful woman in the three worlds. Standing in front of him, she worships him. Mahesha is immersed in *dhyana* and there is no distraction in his mind. Kali must become Chandrashekhara's wife. O gods! Without any delay, make excellent efforts so that this comes about. I will myself go to the spot where Taraka *daitya* is. I will restrain him from his wicked deceit. O immortals! Now return to your own abodes." Having said this to the gods, I quickly approached the *asura* known as Taraka. Extremely cheerfully, I addressed him in the following words. Brahma said, "You are ruling over our kingdom of heaven, which is full of the essence of energy. This exceeds what you desired when you tormented yourself through excellent austerities. I bestowed an excellent boon on you but did not bestow the kingdom of heaven on you. Therefore, you should abandon heaven and rule over a kingdom on earth. There too, you can undertake all deeds that are worthy of *deva*s. O best among *asura*s! Without thinking about it, this is what you should do." I said this and kindled understanding in the *asura*. After this, I remembered the auspicious Shiva, the lord of everything, and vanished from the spot. Taraka abandoned heaven and went to earth. He established himself in the city known as Shonita and ruled over the entire kingdom. Having heard my words, all the *deva*s prostrated themselves before me. Cheerful, they went to Shakra's region. Having gone there, they met Shakra. They controlled themselves and consulted among themselves. Cheerful, all the Maruts addressed Maghavan[947] in these words. *Deva*s said, "There must be liking and desire in Shambhu for Shivaa. O Maghavan! This is what must be done. This is what Brahma has said." Everything that transpired was reported to the lord of the gods. Having reported everything, all the *deva*s happily returned to their own respective abodes.'"

[947] Indra.

Chapter 112-3.3(17) (Conversation between Indra and Kama)

"" **B**rahma said, 'When all *deva*s had departed, Shakra remembered Smara. Oppressed by the *daitya* Taraka, he was distressed in his mind. Immediately, Kama, loved by Rati, arrived there, along with Vasanta. The lord who could conquer the three worlds was accompanied by Rati. Smara prostrated himself and stood in front of him. O son! The great-minded one joined his hands in salutation and spoke to Shakra. Kama asked, "What task has arisen? Why have you remembered me? O lord of *deva*s! Please tell me the truth about that. I have come here to perform your task." Hearing Kandarpa's words, the lord of gods cheerfully praised him and said that this was most proper. Shakra said, "Since you are ready to commence on my work, you are virtuous. O Makaradhvaja![948] Since you are ready to do this, you are blessed. With you ready and in front of me, listen to the words I speak. This is a task meant for you and not for anyone else. It is true that I have many great friends. O Smara! However, you are a virtuous friend and there is no one who is your equal. O son! This excellent *vajra* has been constructed for my victory. But when the *vajra* fails, there is no one other than you. Who is more loved than the person who does something beneficial? Therefore, you are the best of friends, and you must carry out my task. Because of destiny, an impossible misery has arisen. Other than you, there is no one else who can dispel it. A person who donates is tested at the time of a famine, a brave person in the field of battle. A friend is tested at the time of a calamity and a woman when the family is incapacitated. O son! A friendship that is not false is tested in adversity, when a difficulty presents itself and

[948] With a *makara* on the standard, Kama.

when the friend is not present.[949] O son! This is the test of good affection. There is no other way, and I am telling you the truth. I face a hardship that cannot be countered by anyone else. O noble friend! Hence, your test has presented itself now. This is not a task that will bring happiness to me alone. There is no doubt that this is a task for all the gods too." Makaradhvaja heard the words spoken by Maghavan. He first smiled and then spoke words that were deep with affection. Kama said, "Why are you speaking like this? I will not reply to you. When a person is naturally helped, people do not see it or speak about it. At the time of a hardship, if a person speaks a lot, what is he going to accomplish? O great king! O lord! Nevertheless, listen to my words. I am always your friend. I will bring down the enemy who is performing extremely terrible austerities so as to take away your position. In an instant, using the glances of beautiful women, I will make *deva*s, *rishi*s and *danava*s deviate. Men do not even enter into my reckoning. Fling the *vajra* and many other weapons far away. O friend! When I am present, what task will they accomplish? There is no doubt that I can make Hari and Brahma deviate. There is no need to mention others. I can bring down even Hara. I possess five gentle arrows that are made out of flowers and the three segments of my bow are made out of flowers. The bowstring is made out of bees. My beloved is my strength and Vasanta is known as my adviser. I possess five kinds of strength and the store of nectar is my friend.[950] Shringara is the commander of my forces and gestures and emotions are my soldiers. O Shakra! All of them are gentle and I am also like that. An intelligent person uses those who can accomplish the task. Engage me in all the tasks

---

[949] That is, what the friend says behind one's back.
[950] The store of nectar is the moon, and the five kinds of strength are the five arrows.

that are appropriate for me." Hearing these words, Shakra was extremely happy.'"'

"'"He spoke words of affection to Kama and his beloved, both of whom bring pleasure. Shakra said, "O one who originated from the mind! I will tell you about the task that is in my mind. In truth, you are the person who is capable of accomplishing it, not anyone else. O Kama! O supreme among friends! Listen. I will tell you. O one who originated from the mind! I will tell you about the reason why I wished to see you today. There is a great *daitya* known as Taraka. He has obtained a wonderful boon from Brahma. Having become invincible, he is causing misery to everyone. He has oppressed the worlds and has destroyed *dharma* in many kinds of ways. All the gods and all the *rishi*s are miserable. To the best of their capacity, all the *deva*s have already fought against him. But all their weapons have been rendered futile. The noose of the lord of the waters was shattered. Hari's Sudarshana *chakra* was rebuffed. Vishnu hurled it at his throat, but it was thwarted. The lord of subjects has indicated that this evil-souled one will only die at the hands of the son born from the seed of Shambhu Ishvara, the great *yogi*. This is the virtuous task that you must make great efforts to undertake. O friend! Then we, *deva*s, will be supremely happy. Thus, I have told you what will bring happiness to all the worlds. Remember the *dharma* of friends in your mind and undertake this task now. Shambhu is engaged in great austerities on the king of mountains. There is no desire in the lord. Parameshvara rules himself. Along with her two friends, Parvati is there. We have heard that because of her father's command, she remains there and serves him. Shiva is controlled in his *atman*. There is no doubt that your task is to constantly smite him, so that his mind turns towards her. If you do this, you will become famous, and all miseries will be destroyed. You will be permanently established in this world, not otherwise." Hearing this, Kama's face resembled a full-blown lotus. He lovingly told the lord of *deva*s that there was no doubt that he would do this. He replied in words that indicated his assent. Confounded by Shiva's *maya*, Kama instantly accepted the task. Along with his wife and Vasanta, he cheerfully went to the place where the lord of *yoga* was tormenting himself through supreme austerities.'"'

Chapter 113-3.3(18) (Kama's Disturbances)

' " Brahma said, 'Confounded by Shiva's *maya*, the proud Smara went there. He remained there, spreading the enticing *dharma* of spring everywhere. O lord among sages! Vasanta's *dharma* spread everywhere around Oushadhiprastha, the place where Mahesha was performing austerities. O great sage! The trees in the groves blossomed. O lord among sages! This happened because of his special powers. There were fragrant flowers on mango and *ashoka* trees, igniting lamps of desire. Bees swarmed around white lotus flowers and especially overwhelmed people with desire. The sweet calls of cuckoos, extremely charming and pleasant to the mind, also ignited lamps of desire. O sage! Many kinds of sounds were made by the bees, and these too were charming and ignited desire. The moon spread its beautiful beams in every direction. These seemed to be messengers between pairs of lovers. Even amongst the proud, these were signs that the time for love had arrived. A virtuous and pleasant breeze blew, not liked at all by those who were separated from their lovers. In this way, Vasanta extended himself, overwhelming everyone with desire. The residents of the forest and the sages found this to be extremely intolerable. O sage! The insentient succumbed to these pangs of love. How can one describe sentient ones who possessed life? Such were the extremely intolerable powers of spring. They ignited desire

among all beings. O son! Hara saw that spring had arrived at
the wrong time. The lord, who had assumed a body in his own
pastimes, thought that this was a great wonder. However, the
one who engages in pastimes was not moved and continued
with his extremely difficult austerities. The lord is in control of
himself. Hara is the one who dispels miseries. When Vasanta
extended everywhere, along with Rati, Kama stood on the left,
affixing an arrow made out of mango blossoms. He extended
his powers and confounded everyone. On seeing Kama with
Rati, who will not get deluded? With soldiers in the form of
shringara, they indulged in acts of love. Using gestures and
emotions, they approached Hara. Madana is usually inside the
mind and does not manifest himself outside. But he showed
himself. He could not see any weakness in Shambhu, through
which, he could enter. Smara could not find a weakness in the
supreme *yogi*, Mahadeva. He was confused and filled with
great fear. Shankara was immersed in *dhyana*. The eye on his
forehead blazed, resembling fiery flames. Who was capable of
approaching him?"'

'"'At that time, along with her two friends, Shivaa arrived
there. To worship Shiva, she brought many flowers. There are
many kinds of great beauty in the world that are described.
It is certain that what existed in Parvati surpassed them all.
There were superb seasonal flowers that she held. How can
their beauty be described, even in one hundred years? As
soon as the mountain's daughter approached Shiva, for an
instant, Shankara broke out of his *dhyana*. Having found his
opportunity, Madana was initially delighted. Rejoicing, he
held his arrow and stood by Chandrshekhara's side. O sage!
As if to help Kama, along with sentiments of *shringara* and
the fragrant one,[951] Parvati approached Hara. To enhance the
interest of the wielder of the trident in her, Smara drew his bow

[951] Spring.

and quickly affixed the arrow made of flowers. He steadied himself and released it. As she always did, she approached Shiva. She prostrated herself, worshipped him and stood there. Parvati saw that the lord Girisha was staring at her. As a result of the bashfulness of her feminine nature, she covered her limbs. The lord remembered the boon that Vidhatri had bestowed on her earlier. O sage! Therefore, Shiva started to happily describe her limbs. Shiva said, "Is that your face, or is it the moon? Are those your eyes, or are they lotuses? Are those your eyebrows, or is that the great-souled Kandarpa's bow? Is that your lower lip, or is that a *bimba* fruit? Is that your nose, or is it a parrot's beak? Is that your voice, or is that a cuckoo's call? Is that your waist, or is it a sacrificial altar? Can her gait be described? Can her beauty be described? Can the flowers be described? Can her garments be described? Every kind of beauty and charm that has been created and fashioned, exists together in this woman's limbs. There is no doubt about that. Parvati, extraordinary in beauty, is blessed. In the three worlds, there is no woman who is equal to her in beauty. She is a store of excellent charm. She is radiant in her wonderful limbs. She will confound the sages. She will extend great happiness." In this way, he repeatedly described her limbs, thinking about the excellent boon that Vidhatri had bestowed. After this, he stopped. Shankara slipped his hand inside her garment and moved it. As a result of her feminine nature, she was ashamed and moved away. She covered her limbs and repeatedly looked at him. O sage! Shivaa smiled and glanced deeply at him, causing great intoxication. Witnessing her movements, Shambhu was bemused. Maheshvara, the lord of great pastimes, spoke these words. "As soon as one sees her, there is great joy. If one embraces her, what will the pleasure be?" He thought about this only for an instant, honouring Girija. Supremely indifferent, the great *yogi* collected himself and spoke. "How extraordinary is this conduct? How has this delusion come over me? Ishvara, the lord of beings, has succumbed to this distraction because of desire. I am Ishvara, yet I wished to touch someone else's limbs. How helpless will an inferior being be? What are the things such a person will not do?" Having thus turned indifferent, he prevented her from sitting down on the couch. How can there be a downfall for Paresha, who is in all *atmans*?"''

Chapter 114-3.3(19) (Kama's Destruction)

'' ''Narada asked, 'O Brahma! O Vidhatri! O immensely fortunate one! What happened after that? Show me your favours and tell me about the account that destroys all sins.'''

'''Brahma replied, 'O son! Hear about what occurred thereafter. Out of affection towards you, I will tell you about Shiva's account. It brings joy. On witnessing the distraction that had come about in his fortitude, the great *yogi*, Maheshvara, thought about this in his mind and was filled with great wonder. Shiva said, "While I was engaged in excellent austerities, how did this impediment originate? Who has performed this wicked deed and agitated my mind? I have expressed affection towards someone else's wife. This has contravened *dharma*. It has transgressed the ordinances of the *shruti* texts." The great *yogi*, Paramesha, the destination of the virtuous, thought in this way. Full of suspicion, he looked in different directions. He saw Kama standing on the left, the bow, with an arrow affixed, drawn. Foolish in intelligence and proud, he wished to release his arrow. Girisha, the *paramatman*, saw Kama standing in this way. O Narada! He was filled with rage and wished to destroy him, that very instant. O sage! Standing in the sky and holding his bow and arrow, Kama released his weapon, infallible and unerring,

at Shankara. However, against the *paramatman*, the infallible
weapon failed. It was pacified by the enraged Parameshvara.
When his weapon was rendered unsuccessful by Shiva,
Manmatha was filled with fear. He saw the lord who conquers
death standing in front of him and trembled. Agitated by fear, he
remembered all the gods, Shakra and the others. O tiger among
sages! Smara had failed in his objective. O lord among sages!
Kama remembered Shakra and other *deva*s and all of them
arrived. They bowed down and praised Shambhu. All the *deva*s
praised the angry Hara. A great blazing fire issued from his third
eye, from the middle of his forehead. The flames of fire blazed
upwards, as dazzling as the fire at the time of dissolution. It
swiftly shot up into the sky and then fell down on the ground. It
whirled around and fell down on the ground. Before the Maruts
could say, "Please pardon, please forgive", it reduced the wicked
Madana to ashes. When the valiant Smara was killed, *deva*s were
filled with grief. Agitated, they wept and shrieked loudly, "What
has happened?" The daughter of the king of the mountains was
distressed and her limbs turned pale. Taking her friends with
her, she returned to her own residence.'"

'"As a result of sorrow on account of her husband's death,
Rati immediately lost her senses and fell down, as if she was
dead. When she regained her senses, Rati was greatly agitated.
She lamented in many loud words. Rati said, "What will I do?
Who will I go to? What have *deva*s done? The gods summoned
my husband here and destroyed him. Alas! O protector! Alas!
O Smara! You brought me happiness. You were a husband I
loved more than my own life. Alas! What has happened here?
Alas! O one most loved!" In this way, she lamented and spoke
many kinds of words. She flung her hands and feet around
and tore out her hair. O Narada! On hearing her lamentation,
all the residents of the forest were filled with great sorrow,
even those immobile. Meanwhile, Shakra and all the other
*deva*s remembered Maheshvara and spoke words of assurance

to Rati. The *deva*s said, "Take some ashes and keep them safely. Make efforts to give up your fear. The lord will revive your husband and you will get your beloved back again. He is the one who bestows happiness. He never causes misery to anyone. Everyone, even a *deva*, enjoys the fruits of own deeds. Do not grieve in vain." In this way, all the *deva*s comforted Rati and approached Shiva. They devotedly sought to placate Shiva and addressed him in these words. The *deva*s said, "O Bhagavan! O Shambhu! O lord! Please listen to our words. O one affectionate towards those who seek refuge! O Mahesha! Please show compassion. O Shankara! Full of affection, please reflect on what Kama did. O Maheshvara! Kama did not do this because his own selfish motive. O lord! The wicked Taraka was oppressing *deva*s and everything else. O protector! O Shankara! Know that the task was done for that reason and not for any other purpose. O divinity! The virtuous Rati is alone and is lamenting in her misery. O Girisha! Please comfort her in every possible way. You have destroyed Smara. O Shankara! In your rage, if you had really wished to destroy, you would have destroyed all the *deva*s along with him. On witnessing Rati's misery, *deva*s have almost been destroyed. Therefore, you must act to dispel Rati's grief." Hearing their words, Bhagavan Shiva was pleased. He addressed all the *deva*s in these words. Shiva said, "O *deva*s and all the *rishi*s! Listen lovingly to my words. There can be no counter to what has occurred as a result of my rage. Until Krishna takes an *avatara* on earth and becomes Rukmini's husband, Kama, Rati's lord and husband, will be Ananga.[952] When Krishna and Rukmini are in Dvaraka and have sons, Kama will be born to them, and his name will be Pradyumna. There is no doubt that this will happen. As soon as the son is born, Shambara will seize him. Abducting him, Shambara, supreme among *danava*s, will

---

[952] Without a body (*anga*).

fling him into the ocean. Taking him to be dead, the foolish
one will return to his city in vain. O Rati! Until then, you will
remain happily in his city.[953] You will get back your husband
Pradyumna there. Uniting with you, Kama will kill Shambara
in a battle. O *deva*s! Under the name of Pradyumna, he will
be happy with his wife. Taking various objects, along with
her, he will return to his own city.[954] O *deva*s! These are my
true words." Hearing the words Shambhu had spoken, *deva*s
were comforted somewhat. They prostrated themselves, bent
down, joined their hands in salutation and spoke. The *deva*s
said, "O lord of *deva*s! O Mahadeva! O lord who is an ocean
of compassion! O Hara! Please revive Kama quickly and save
Rati's life." Hearing the words of the immortals, Parameshvara
was pleased. The ocean of compassion and the lord of everything
spoke again. Shiva said, "O *deva*s! I am extremely pleased and
will revive him within me. Kama will become one of my *gana*s
and will always sport. O gods! This account should not be told
in front of anyone. Return to your own places. I will destroy
every kind of misery." Saying this, while *deva*s lauded him,
Rudra vanished. All the *deva*s were pleased and lost their fear.
They were comforted by Rudra's words. O sage! Following
what he had said, they returned to their own respective abodes.
As instructed, Kama's wife went to that city. O lord of sages!
As instructed by Rudra, she waited for the time.'"

Chapter 115-3.3(20) (The Vadava Fire)

' "Narada said, 'O Vidhatri! There was a blazing fire
that issued from Hara's eye. Where did it go? Please

[953] Reborn as Mayavati in Shambara's household.
[954] Pradyumna will return to Dvaraka with Shambara's possessions.

tell me that and also tell me about the conduct of the one who wears the moon on his head.'""

'"Brahma answered, 'A fire emerged from Shambhu's third eye and swiftly reduced Kama to ashes. It blazed everywhere and destroyed everything. There were great lamentations in the three worlds, among mobile and immobile entities. O son! All *devas* and *rishis* quickly sought refuge with me. Agitated and anxious, they told me everything. They prostrated themselves, lowered their heads, joined their hands in salutation and praised me. Hearing this, I remembered Shiva and remembered the reason for everything. To save the three worlds, I humbly went there. Wishing to burn, that blazing fire was like a garland of ignited flames. However, because of Shambhu's favours, I possessed the energy to pacify it. Full of rage, the fire desired to burn down the three worlds. O *rishi*! O amiable one! O sage! That blaze was in the form of a mare's head. As a result of Shiva's wish, I, the lord of the universe, gathered up the fire that was in the form of a mare's head. For the welfare of the worlds, I went to the ocean. O sage! On seeing me arrive, the ocean joined its hands in salutation. The store of jewels assumed a human form and approached me. The ocean prostrated himself and praised me in the proper way. Extremely happy, he spoke to me, the grandfather of all the worlds. The ocean asked, "O Brahma! O lord of everything! Why have you come here? I will happily carry out your command. Know me to be your servant." Hearing the ocean's words, I was filled with joy. Remembering Shankara, for the welfare of the worlds, I replied to him. Brahma said, "O son! O extremely intelligent one! O one who brings joy to all the worlds! Listen. I have been sent here by Shiva's will, lodged in my heart. O ocean! I will happily tell you. This is the rage of the great lord, Mahesha, and has assumed the form of a mare. Having swiftly burnt down Kama, it wished to burn down everything. The gods suffered and because of Shankara's will, quickly entreated me. O son! I quickly went there and pacified

the pure fire. It assumed the form of a mare and taking it, I
have come here. O store of water! O store of compassion! I am
instructing you. This rage of Mahesha's has assumed the form
of a mare. It is blazing at the mouth. Hold it until the deluge
arrives. O lord of rivers! When I come here and reside with you,
release it then. It is Shankara's extraordinary rage. Its food will
always be your water. Make efforts to hold it, so that it does not
sink within you." Hearing what I had said, the ocean certainly
acted in accordance with that. No one else was capable of
accepting Rudra's *vadava* fire. Assuming the body of a mare,
the pure fire entered the ocean. It blazed like a garland of flames
and aided by the wind, consumed the torrent of water. O sage!
Satisfied in my mind, I returned to my own abode. The ocean,
divine in form, prostrated himself before me and vanished. The
entire universe was well, free of the fear that had arisen. O sage!
*Deva*s and sages were happy.'"'

Chapter 116-3.3(21) (Narada's Instruction to Parvati)

" "Narada said, 'O Vidhatri! O father! O immensely
wise one! O Vishnu's disciple! O creator of the
three worlds! You have narrated a wonderful account about
the great-souled Shankara. The fire that issued from Shambhu's
third eye reduced Smara to ashes and entered the ocean. What
happened after that? What did Devi Parvati, the daughter of
the mountain, do? Where did she go with her friends? O ocean
of compassion! Please tell me that.'"

"'Brahma replied, 'O son! O immensely wise one! Hear
about the conduct of the one who wears the moon on his crest.
My lord brings great welfare. Hear lovingly. The fire that issued
from Shambhu's eye purified Madana. At that time, a loud and

wonderful sound arose and filled the firmament. Hearing that loud sound and seeing that Kama was burnt down, she was scared. Agitated, with her two friends, she returned to her own house. Himalaya and his family were amazed at hearing this sound. Remembering that his daughter had gone there, he was unhappy. The lord of the mountains saw that his daughter was extremely agitated and was miserable. Separated from Shambhu, she was weeping. The lord of the mountains approached her. Using his hands, he wiped the tears from her eyes. He told the auspicious one, "Do not be scared. Do not weep." Himalaya, the lord of mountains, quickly took up his daughter and placed her on his lap. She was extremely agitated. He comforted her and took her to his own residence. When Smara was burnt down, Hara disappeared and on account of being separated from him, Shivaa was very distressed. She could not find any peace. Shivaa went to her father's house and met her mother. The daughter of the mountain thought that she had been born again. She criticized her own beauty and exclaimed, "Alas! I have been undone." Though her friends tried to make her understand, the daughter of the Indra among mountains would not understand. Whether she was sleeping, drinking, bathing, walking or amidst her friends, Shiva could not find any joy. "Shame on my beauty, birth and deeds." Saying this, she constantly remembered what Hara used to do. In this way, suffering from separation from Shambhu, Parvati's mind was distressed. Unable to find any joy, she kept saying, "O Shiva! O Shiva!" With her mind on the wielder of Pinaka, she resided in her father's house. O son! Shivaa repeatedly grieved and lost her senses. The king of the mountains, Menaka and the sons, Mainaka as the foremost, tried to comfort her. But she was dispirited and did not forget Hara.'"

"'"O divine sage! O intelligent one! Engaged by the slayer of Bala[955] and roaming around as you wished, you arrived

---

[955] That is, Indra.

on the slopes of the Himalayas. The great-souled mountain worshipped you. Seated on an excellent seat, you asked about his welfare. The lord of mountains told you everything about his daughter's conduct, about how she had served Hara and how Hara had burnt down Kama. O sage! Hearing this, you told the lord of mountains, "Worship Shiva." Advising him in this way, you stood up and remembered Shiva in your mind. O sage! You are loved by Shiva. You possess *jnana* and are engaged in the welfare of the worlds. Taking your leave from him, you quickly went and met Kali in private. Having met Kali, interested in her welfare, you affectionately kindled understanding in her. O supreme among all those who possess *jnana*! You addressed her in the following words. Narada said, "O Kali! Listen to my words. I am compassionate and am telling you the truth. They are beneficial in every possible way and are bereft of deviations. They will lead to great happiness. You served Mahadeva without engaging in austerities. He is the one who shows compassion. Since you were proud, he destroyed it. The lord Maheshvara is a great *yogi* and is indifferent towards you. He is affectionate towards his devotees. But having burnt Smara, he left you. Therefore, you should engage in excellent austerities and worship Ishvara for a long time. Once you have cleansed yourself through austerities, Rudra will accept you a second time. Never abandon Shankara Shambhu. O Devi! You will not accept any husband other than Shiva." O sage! Hearing these words, Kali, the mountain's daughter, sighed in relief. She joined her hands in salutation and spoke to you cheerfully. Shivaa said, "O lord! You are omniscient and are engaged in the welfare of the worlds. O sage! Give me a *mantra* that can be used for worshipping Rudra. In the absence of a virtuous *guru*, no rite is ever successful. I have heard this earlier. This is the eternal truth stated in the *shruti* texts." Hearing Parvati's words, the excellent sage followed the norms and instructed her about Shambhu's *panchakshara mantra*.[956] O sage! You used your words to awaken faith in her. O sage! You told her about the powers of this king of *mantra*s, the greatest of them all. Narada said, "O Devi! Hear about the supreme and extraordinary powers of this *mantra*. As soon as he hears it, Shankara is greatly pleased. This *mantra* is the emperor of all *mantra*s and yields what is wished for. It is greatly loved by Shankara and bestows objects of pleasure and emancipation. O extremely fortunate one! If one uses this properly to perform *japa* and worship, there is no doubt that quickly and without any delay, Shiva manifests himself before that person. Think of his form and follow the *niyama*s. O Shivaa! Use the *akshara*s of the *mantra* to perform *japa* and Shiva will be swiftly satisfied. O virtuous one! Practice austerities in this way. Maheshvara can be obtained through austerities. Every fruit can be obtained through austerities, not in any other way." Narada, loved by Shiva, said this to Kali at that time. Engaged in the welfare of *deva*s, as you wished, you then went to heaven. O Narada! Hearing your words and having obtained the excellent *panchakshara mantra*, Parvati rejoiced.'"'

Chapter 117-3.3(22) (Parvati's Austerities)

' ''Brahma said, 'O divine sage! After you departed, happy in her mind, Parvati thought that Hara could be obtained through austerities. Therefore, she made up her mind to perform austerities. She summoned her two friends, Jaya and Vijaya. She used her two friends to seek permission from her father and her mother. They first went to the father, Himalaya, lord of mountains. They prostrated themselves and humbly

---

[956] *Na + mah + Shi + va + ya = Namah Shivaya.*

asked him. The two friends said, "O Himalaya! Hear now what your daughter has said. She wants to act so that her body, her beauty and her lineage are rendered successful. This can be accomplished through austerities. No other means can be seen. O best among mountains! Therefore, grant her the permission now. Affectionately allow Girija to leave for the forest, so as to perform austerities." O supreme among sages! The two friends asked in this way. The king of mountains reflected deeply on what Parvati had said and answered. Himalaya replied, "This appeals to me. If it appeals to Mena too, there can be nothing better than this. There is no doubt that this will bring success to our lineage. If it appeals to the mother too, what can be more auspicious than this?" They heard the words the father uttered. Taking his permission, the two friends next went to the mother. Having gone to the mother, they prostrated themselves, clasped their hands together in salutation and affectionately reported Parvati's words. The two friends said, "O queen! O mother! We prostrate ourselves. Listen to your daughter's words. If you are pleased with what you hear, please act accordingly. Your daughter wishes to perform supreme austerities for Shiva. She has obtained permission from her father for these austerities. She is now asking you. O one devoted to your husband! She desires to render her own beauty successful. If your permission is obtained, she will torment herself through austerities." O lord among sages! Saying this, the two friends were silent. Distressed in her mind, Mena did not agree to these words. Hence, Parvati herself spoke to her mother. She clasped her hands together and with humility in her mind, remembered Shiva's lotus feet. Parvati said, "O mother! In the morning, I will leave, so as to perform austerities and obtain Maheshvara. Please grant me permission to leave for the forest where austerities will be performed, for the sake of austerities." Hearing her daughter's words, Mena was miserable. The virtuous lady was dejected and called her daughter close to

her. Mena said, "O daughter! O Shivaa! O Parvati! If you are
unhappy and wish to torment yourself through austerities,
then perform those austerities at home. Do not go out. Where
will you go to undertake austerities? All *devas* exist in my
home. There are all the *tirthas* and many kinds of *kshetras*.
O daughter! Do not commit this rash act. You should never
go outside. What did you accomplish earlier? What will you
accomplish now? O child! Your body is delicate. Austerities
are great and difficult. Hence, you should not go outside to
perform austerities. We have never heard of women going to
hermitages to accomplish their wishes. O daughter! Therefore,
you should not wish to leave and perform austerities." The
mother restrained the daughter in many such ways. However,
without worshipping Maheshvara, she did not experience
any joy. Since Mena restrained her from going to the forest
and performing austerities, as a result of that reason, Shivaa
obtained the name Uma then. Mena, loved by the mountain,
got to know that Shivaa was miserable. O sage! Therefore, she
instructed Parvati that she could go and perform austerities. O
supreme among sages! The one who was excellent in her vows
obtained her mother's permission. Remembering Shankara,
Parvati felt great happiness. Delighted, Shivaa prostrated
herself before her mother and her father. She remembered
Shiva and along with her two friends, prepared to torment
herself through austerities. She made up her mind to cast aside
the many and diverse garments. She quickly wore bark and tied
a beautiful girdle made out of *munja* grass. She gave up her
necklace and wore excellent deerskin. To undertake austerities,
she went to Gangavatarana.'"[957]

    ""'On the slope of the Himalayas, Gangavatarana was the
place where Shambhu had performed *dhyana* and had burnt

---

[957] The same as Gangavatara.

down the one who originated from the mind.⁹⁵⁸ That slope in
the Himalaya mountain was seen to be devoid of Hara. O son!
Kali Parvati, the mother of the universe, remained there. That
is the place where Shambhu had tormented himself through
extremely difficult austerities earlier. She remained there for
a while, suffering from the pangs of separation. Shivaa, the
daughter of the mountain, wept, "Alas! Hara." She lamented
in great misery, her thoughts full of that grief. After a long
time, Parvati resorted to her fortitude and got rid of the
confusion. Himalaya's daughter consecrated herself for the
niyamas. She performed austerities in the great and excellent
tirtha known as Shringi. Because of her austerities, it came to
be known as Gouri-Shikhara.⁹⁵⁹ O sage! Shivaa planted many
beautiful trees there, so that she could test the fruits of her
austerities.⁹⁶⁰ The beautiful one purified the ground and created
an altar. She started austerities that were difficult for even
sages to undertake. She controlled her senses with her mind
and undertook supreme austerities in that spot. In the summer,
day and night, she had a fire blazing around her. In the midst
of this, she constantly performed *japa* with the *mantra*. During
the rainy season, she remained properly seated on the bare
ground. She remained on the slope of the mountain, constantly
drenched by the downpour of rain. Full of devotion, during the
winter, she remained inside the water. She did it when there was
ice. She did this during the night. She fasted. In this way, she
observed austerities, performing *japa* with the *panchakshara*
mantra. Shivaa meditated on Shiva, who bestows everything
that is desired. Every day, whenever there was an opportunity,

⁹⁵⁸ Kama.
⁹⁵⁹ Both *shringi* and *shikhara* mean peak. Gouri-Shikhara is
identified as Mount Gaurishankar, in that part of the Himalayas that
is in Nepal.
⁹⁶⁰ To test whether they would bear fruit.

along with her friends, she tended to the trees she had planted, imagining that they were guests. There were cold winds, rain, intolerable heat and many other things. With an excellent mind, she tolerated all these. There were many hardships, but she ignored them. O sage! Her mind was only fixed on Shiva. In the first year, she only ate fruit. In the second year, she only ate leaves. In this way, progressively, Devi spent an unlimited number of years in austerities. Shivaa, Himalaya's daughter, stopped eating even leaves. Without eating anything, Devi engaged in austerities. Himalaya's daughter discarded even leaves from her food. Therefore, *devas* gave Devi the name of Aparna.[961] Parvati stood on one leg and remembered Shiva. She engaged in those great austerities, performing *japa* with the *panchakshara mantra*. She was clad in tattered bark. She had masses of matted hair. With her mind fixed on Shiva, she surpassed even sages in her austerities. Performing austerities and thinking of Maheshvara, Kali spent three thousand years in that hermitage. In that spot, Hara had tormented himself through austerities for sixty thousand years and Shivaa thought about this. "Does Mahadeva not know about the *niyama*s I am following now? Have I not been following his path for a long time? In customary practices, in the *Veda*s and in the chants of the sages, Girisha Shankara is always spoken of as someone who knows everything. He is in all *atman*s and can see everything. He is the divinity who bestows every kind of prosperity and is aware of every kind of sentiment. He always bestows everything that a devotee desires. He destroys every kind of hardship. I have cast aside every kind of desire and devoted myself to Vrishadhvaja. Let Shankara therefore be pleased with me. Full of devotion and following the norms, I have always performed *japa* with the *panchakshara mantra*

---

[961] Aparna = *a* (without) + *parna* (leaf).

Narada spoke to me about.[962] Let Shankara therefore be
pleased with me. I have been without any transgressions and
have devoted myself to Shiva Sarveshvara, as I have been
instructed. Let Shankara therefore be pleased with me." As she
tormented herself with those austerities for a very long time, she
constantly thought in this way. Her face was cast downwards,
and she was without any transgressions. She wore bark and
her hair was matted. She tormented herself through austerities
that were difficult for even sages to undertake. Remembering
what she had done, men were filled with great wonder. They
reverentially assembled there and thought that they were
blessed to have witnessed it. All of them used this as a role
model for instruction. "It is said that benefit is obtained by
following the path of *dharma* shown by the seniors and those
who are great. There are no fixed yardsticks for austerities. The
learned always revere every act of *dharma*. Having seen, and
heard about, these austerities, which other person will engage
in austerities? In this world, there haven't been austerities that
have surpassed these, nor will there ever be." Conversing in this
way, all of them greatly praised Shivaa's austerities, even those
who possessed hardened bodies. Happy, all of them returned to
their own respective abodes. O *maharshi*! Now hear about the
great power of her austerities. Parvati Jagadamba performed
great, wonderful and supreme austerities. There were creatures
who were naturally opposed to each other. When they arrived
at her hermitage, because of her powers, they always lost their
natural animosity. Lions and cows were always full of love

---

[962] We have deviated from the text. The text should be translated
as 'the *mantra* from the Narada *tantra*', with Narada *tantra* interpreted
as one of the versions of the Narada/Naradiya Purana (Samhita). It
seems to us that this unnecessary complication is the result of some
distortion in the text at some point. A simpler statement will suffice,
as in our translation.

for each other. Because of her greatness, they did not make
each other suffer. O best among sages! This was also true of
cats and rats. Though they are naturally enemies, they never
showed any transgressions there. The trees were full of fruit
and there were many kinds of grass. O supreme among sages!
Many kinds of flowers always blossomed in that forest, which
came to resembled Kailasa. They assumed these forms because
of the success in her austerities.'"'

Chapter 118-3.3(23) (Attempts to Dissuade Parvati)

'"Brahma said, 'O lord among sages! In this way,
to obtain Shiva, Parvati engaged in austerities. A
long period of time passed, but Hara did not show himself.
Parvati had made up her mind to persevere. Along with his
wife, sons and ministers, Himalaya came there and spoke to
Parameshvari. Himalaya said, "O immensely fortunate one!
O Parvati! Enough of austerities. Do not make yourself suffer
any more. O child! Rudra is not to be seen. There is no doubt
that he is indifferent. You are slender, delicate in your limbs.
There is no doubt that these austerities will confound you. This
is the truth. I am speaking the truth. O one with a beautiful
complexion! Therefore, get up from here and go to your own
house. What do you have to do with Rudra? In earlier times,
he burnt down Smara. Since he is indifferent, Hara will not
come here and accept you. O Deveshi! Since he will not come,
why are you hankering after him? It is impossible to grasp the
moon in the sky. O unblemished one! Like that, Shambhu is
impossible to reach. You should know that." Along with the
mountain, Mena, the virtuous lady, also said the same thing. So
did other mountains like Meru, Mandara, Mainaka, Krouncha

and others. So as to dissuade Girija, who was beyond suffering, many kinds of arguments were advanced. The slender one, engaged in austerities, was addressed in this way. Pleasant in her smiles, she smiled and spoke to Himalaya. Parvati said, "O father! O mother! O relatives! Have you forgotten what I told you earlier? Listen to me. I still have the same pledge. Mahadeva is indifferent. In his rage, he burnt down Smara. However, Shankara is affectionate towards his devotees, and I will satisfy him with my austerities. All of you return cheerfully to your own respective abodes. He will be propitiated. There is no need to reflect on this. He burnt Madana. He burnt the forest in this mountain. However, using only my austerities, I will bring him here. Sadashiva can always be properly served through the great strength of austerities. O immensely fortunate ones! Know that this is the truth. I am telling you the truth." Girija Shivaa, the young daughter of the king of the mountains, excellent in speech, quickly spoke to her father Himachala, Menaka, Mainaka and her relatives, Mandara and others and was silent. The golden lord of mountains and the other mountains were addressed by Shivaa in this way. They possessed a sense of discrimination and listened to what she had said. They were extremely surprised and repeatedly praising her, returned to wherever they had come from.'"'

'"'When they had departed, intent on her supreme objective and surrounded by her friends, she tormented herself through even greater austerities. O best among sages! When she tormented herself through these great austerities, all mobile and immobile objects in the three worlds, *deva*s, *asura*s and humans, *yaksha*s, *kinnara*s, *charana*s, *siddha*s, *sadhya*s, sages, *vidyadhara*s, giant *uraga*s, *guhyaka*s and the Prajapatis were scorched. They suffered greater and greater miseries but did not know the reason for this. All of them, Shakra and the others, were agitated. They consulted their *guru*s and assembled on Sumeru. Their limbs scorched by the austerities, they sought refuge with me, Vidhatri. They lost their radiance and were agitated. All of them swiftly prostrated themselves and praised me with identical voices. The *deva*s said, "You have created everything in the universe, mobile and immobile. O lord! We are being scorched and we do not know the reason. O Brahma! O lord! You should tell us the reason. All *deva*s are being scorched. Other than you, we have no other protector." Hearing their words, I remembered Shiva in my heart. Having reflected on this in my mind, I understood that all this was the consequence of Girija's austerities. Everything in the universe was being scorched because of this. Affectionately taking them with me, I quickly went to the ocean of milk to inform Hari about this. Having gone there, I saw Hari, radiant on his comfortable set. Along with the gods, I prostrated myself. Joining my hands in salutation, I praised him and spoke. "O great Vishnu! Protect us. Save us. Those being scorched have sought refuge with you. As a result of Parvati's fierce austerities, all of us are being greatly scorched." Rama's lord, who was lying down on his couch of Shesha, heard the words I spoke on behalf of the residents of heaven and replied. Vishnu said, "I know that all of this has been caused by Parvati's austerities. Along with you, I will now go to Parameshvara. We will beseech the divinity to accept Girija. O immortals! For the welfare of the worlds, he should accept her hand in marriage. The lord of *deva*s, the wielder of Pinaka, should bestow this boon on Shivaa. We must now strive to act so that he does this. Therefore, we must go to the place where the great lord, Rudra, is present. He bestows everything that is supremely auspicious and confronting these fierce austerities, we must go to him." Hearing Vishnu's words, all the gods were extremely scared of the one who brings about dissolution. In his rage, he had burnt down the rash Kama. The *deva*s said, "He is supremely terrifying. When enraged, he blazes like the fire of destruction. All of us cannot approach the immensely

radiant Virupaksha. Invincible in his valour, earlier, he burnt
Madana down. Full of rage, there is no doubt that he will burn
us down in that way." Rama's lord heard the words spoken
by Shakra and the others. O sage! Hari comforted all the gods
and spoke to them. Hari answered, "O gods! Listen cheerfully
and attentively to my words. He will not burn you down. He is
the lord who destroys fears *deva*s suffer from. All of you have
a sense of discrimination. It is my view that along with me, you
should seek refuge with the extremely radiant Shambhu. He is
the one who ensures everything auspicious. Shiva is the ancient
Purusha. He is the lord whose form should be worshipped. He
is supreme and ancient. He is the *paramatman* and his form is
worshipped through austerities. He is greater than the greatest.
We must seek refuge with him." The *deva*s were addressed in
this way by the greatly powerful Vishnu. Along with Vishnu,
they left, desiring to see the wielder of Pinaka. But first, they
went to the hermitage of the daughter of the mountain, wishing
to see her austerities. Vishnu and all the others were immensely
curious, and it was along the way. They witnessed Parvati's
excellent austerities. Everything was pervaded by her energy.
They prostrated themselves before the mother of the universe.
Engaged in austerities, her form was full of energy. Having
witnessed her austerities, the personified form of success,
the gods praised her. They then went to the place where
Vrishadhvaja was. O sage! Having gone there, *deva*s sent you.
They watched Hara, who had reduced Kama to ashes, from
a distance. Narada, who had no fear, approached Shiva's
place. In particular, he is Shiva's devotee and was pleased to
see the lord. O sage! He returned and carefully ushered the
*deva*s, Vishnu and others, into Shankara's presence. Vishnu
and all the others went and saw the lord, Shiva. The one who
is affectionate towards his devotees was comfortably seated,
with a pleasant appearance. Surrounded by *gana*s, Shambhu
was seated in a posture of *yoga*. Though his form is that of

Parameshvara, he was seated in a form of austerities. Vishnu and the other gods, the *siddha*s and the lords among sages prostrated themselves. Using hymns from the *Veda*s and the Upanishads, they praised him.'"'

Chapter 119-3.3(24) (Shiva Agrees to the Marriage)

' '' 'The *deva*s said, "We prostrate ourselves before the divinity Rudra, the destroyer of Madana. We praise the one who is extensive in radiance. We prostrate ourselves before the one who has three eyes. We bow down. We prostrate ourselves before the one clad in hides, the terrible one, the one with the terrible eyes. We bow down before you. We prostrate ourselves before the powerful Mahadeva, the lord of the three worlds. You are the protector of all the worlds. You are the father and the mother. You are Ishvara. You are Shambhu, Isha and Shankara. In particular, you are compassionate. You are the creator of all the worlds. O lord! You should save us. O Maheshvara! Other than you, who is capable of destroying miseries?"''''

'"Brahma said, 'Hearing the words of the gods, Nandikeshvara was filled with great compassion and lovingly informed Shambhu. Nandikeshvara said, "O noble divinity! Vishnu and large numbers of gods, sages and many *siddha*s have come here to see you. They have an objective in mind. They are being chastised by noble *asura*s. Having suffered great defeat, they have come to you as the great refuge. O Sarvesha! You should save the gods and the sages. You are specially spoken of as the friend of the distressed. You are affectionate towards your devotees." Full of great compassion, Nandi informed Shambhu in this way. Gradually, he withdrew from his great *dhyana* and slowly opened his eyes. Isha Shambhu, the *paramatman* who knows everything, withdrew from his *samadhi* and spoke to all the gods. Shambhu asked, "O lords among gods! O Hari, Brahma and all the others! Why have all of you come to my presence? Quickly tell me the reason." Hearing Shambhu's words, all the *deva*s were filled with great joy. They glanced towards the excellent face of Vishnu, so that he might explain the reason. Vishnu is a great devotee. Desiring the welfare of *deva*s, he explained the great task that needed to be performed for *deva*s. I have already spoken about it. "O Shambhu! What Taraka has done to *deva*s is extremely unusual. Their miseries have become greater and greater. All the *deva*s have come here to tell you about this. O Shambhu! The son born from you, and no one else, will kill the *daitya* Taraka. O Mahadeva! Please reflect on what I have said and show your compassion. I prostrate myself before you. O lord! Please save *deva*s from the misery wrought by Taraka. O divinity! O Shambhu! Hence you should accept Girija with your right hand. Please accept the hand of the great-minded one, when it is offered by the Indra among mountains." Hearing Vishnu's words, Shiva was pleased. Immersed in *yoga*, he showed himself, the destination of the virtuous, to all of them. Shiva said, "If I accept Devi Girija, beautiful in all her limbs, all the Indras among gods, sages and *rishi*s will be full of desire and will not possess the capacity to follow the other path. As soon as I accept Durga's hand, Smara will revive. To accomplish everyone's task, I burnt down Madana, following Brahma's words. O Vishnu! Hence, there is nothing to think about. When deciding what to do and what not to do, one should remember this in one's mind. All of you and Indra of the *deva*s should not be rash. O Vishnu! Having burnt down Kama, I performed an extremely great act for the gods. Along with me, all of you should be determined to be free of desire. Like me, all the gods can make efforts to undertake supreme austerities and perform extremely difficult deeds. O gods! Since there is no Madana, you can immerse yourselves in *samadhi*. You are indifferent and are filled with great bliss. O Vidhatri! O Hari! O great Indra! O *deva*s! All of you have forgotten what Smara did earlier. You should not forget. O gods! Madana is a great archer and is deceitful. In earlier times, he destroyed the *dhyana* you have been engaged in. Kama leads to hell and anger results from it. Delusion results from anger and anger destroys austerities.[963] Since you have given up desire and anger, you have become best among gods. All of you should think about my words and not act in a contrary way." Having made them hear this, Bhagavan Mahadeva Vrishadhvaja asked the gods, Vidhatri, Vishnu and the sages to speak. Shambhu was silent and immersed himself in *dhyana* again. He was as immobile as he had been earlier, surrounded by the *gana*s. Immersed in his own *atman*, Shambhu thought about his *atman* and nothing else. He is without blemish, without false appearances, without transformations and without ailments. He is greater than the greatest. He is eternal. He is without a sense of ownership and without impediments. He is beyond expressions of speech. He is *nirguna* and can be reached through *jnana*. He is beyond the supreme. Resorting to *dhyana*, he thought about his own supreme form. He was submerged in supreme bliss, with many types of prosperity. All the residents of heaven saw that Sarvesha was immersed in *dhyana*. Hari, Shakra and the others bowed down before Nandi and asked. The *deva*s said, "What will we do now? He is indifferent and has immersed himself in *dhyana*. You are Shambhu Shankara's friend. You know everything. You are a pure attendant. O lord of *gana*s! What means can be used to please Girisha? We have sought refuge with you. You should tell us about the means." *Deva*s, sages, Hari and others asked him this.'"

---

[963] This *shloka* is similar to Bhagavat Gita 2.62-63.

""'Nandi, Shambhu's beloved *gana*, replied to the gods. Nandishvara said, "O Hari! O Vidhatri! O Shakra and the other immortals! O sages! Listen to my words. This will satisfy Shiva. If you are rash enough to insist that Shiva should accept a wife, you should be extremely miserable and should lovingly praise him. O gods! Mahadeva cannot be conquered through ordinary devotion. But if the devotion is proper, Parameshvara will do even what he should not do. O gods led by Vidhatri and Vishnu! All of you should do this. Otherwise, without any delay, return along the path you used to come here." O sage! Hearing his words, Vishnu and the gods thought that they should agree to his. Full of great joy, they praised Shankara. "O lord of *deva*s! O Mahadeva! O ocean of compassion! O lord! Save us from this great calamity. We have sought refuge with you." Thus, the gods praised Shankara in many kinds of ways. With their minds overwhelmed by love, all of them wept in loud tones. Hari and I addressed him in many piteous tones. Full of supreme devotion, we remembered Shambhu in our minds. The gods, Hari and I praised Shambhu a lot. As a result of affection towards his devotees, Maheshvara stopped his *dhyana*. Pleased in his mind, Hara spoke to Hari and the others, delighting them. Shankara, affectionate towards his devotees, glanced at them with eyes full of compassion. Shankara asked, "O Hari! O Vidhatri! O Shakra and other *deva*s! Why have all of you come to me together? Now that you are in front of me, tell me the truth." Hari replied, "O Mahesha! You are omniscient. O lord of everything! You are inside everything. Don't you know what is in our minds? Nevertheless, following your command, I will tell you. O Mrida![964] As a result of Tarakasura, we have suffered diverse miseries. It is for everyone's sake that the gods have sought to please you. Shivaa has been born, as the daughter of Mount Himalaya. His death will come about

[964] Shiva's name.

through the son born to you and her, not through anyone else. This is the boon Brahma bestowed on that *daitya*. Since he cannot be killed by anyone else, he has caused impediments to the entire universe. Following Narada's instructions, Shivaa has been engaged in performing difficult austerities and her energy has pervaded everything in the three worlds, mobile and mobile. O Parameshvara! Please go there and bestow a boon on her. O lord! Destroy the sorrows of *deva*s and bring us happiness. O Shankara! There is great enthusiasm in my heart and in those of *deva*s to witness your marriage. Please act accordingly. O one who is greater than the greatest! You had granted Rati a boon. The time has come for you to quickly make your pledge come true." Having told him this, Vishnu, *deva*s and *maharshi*s prostrated themselves before him. All of them stood in front of him and used many kinds of hymns to praise him. Shankara, who is subservient to his devotees, heard the words of the *deva*s. The one who protects the ordinances of the *Veda*s smiled and quickly replied. Shankara said, "O Hari! O Vidhatri! O *deva*s! Listen affectionately to everything I say. What I will say is appropriate and it flows from a sense of discrimination. The ordinances say that it is not good for men to marry. The firm bonds of marriage are described as a great fetter. There are many wicked associations in the world. But association with a woman is worse than all of them. One can save oneself from every kind of bondage, but one cannot free oneself from association with a woman. Even if one is firmly bound with bonds made out of iron and wood, one can free oneself from those fetters. However, if one is firmly bound to a woman, one can never free oneself. The attachment to material objects increases those great bonds. When a person is attached to material objects, it is impossible for him to free himself, even in his dreams. Therefore, a wise person who desires happiness must cast aside every kind of material object. Material objects are said to be like poison. Material objects destroy a person.

O Indra! Even if one converses with a person who is attached
to material objects, one instantly falls down. Preceptors have
said that material objects are like *sita*, *tali* and *varuni* liquor.[965]
I know all this and specifically, I possess *jnana*. However, I
will act so that your wishes come true. I am subservient to
my devotees. Because of this subservience, I will perform every
kind of task. I am famous in the three worlds as one who does
what should not be done. I made the pledge made to the king of
Kamarupa come true and saved King Sudakshina when he was
imprisoned by Bhima.[966] I am Tryambaka[967] in my *atman* and
bring happiness, but I caused hardship to Goutama. I cause
misery to those who are wicked, especially those who curse
others. I am full of sentiments of affection towards my devotees
and for the sake of the gods, I drank poison. O gods! I have
always made efforts to remove every affliction *deva*s face. I have
made efforts and have gone through many kinds of sufferings
for devotees. To remove the miseries of sage Vishvanara, I
became Grihapati.[968] O Hari! O Vidhatri! What is the need
to speak a lot? I am telling you the truth. All of you know the
truth about my pledge. Whenever devotees face a calamity, at

[965] Types of liquor. *Sita* liquor is made out of some form of sugar
or molasses, while *tali* liquor is made from palm.

[966] Bhima was a demon who imprisoned the king of Kamarupa,
Sudakshina. Sudakshina was Shiva's devotee. When Sudakshina
prayed to Shiva, Shiva killed Bhima and saved Sudakshina. Kamarupa
is identified with Assam, though the Bhimashankara temple is near
Pune. Tryambakeshvara *lingam* is also in Maharashtra, near Nasika.
The sage Goutama cursed Indra, was punished by Shiva and was
saved when he prayed to Shiva and Godavari was brought down to
earth. This story is narrated in detail in Brahma Purana.

[967] Brahma, Vishnu and Rudra exist within Mahadeva.

[968] The sage Vishvanara's wife, Shuchismati, prayed that she
might have a son resembling Shiva. Vishvanara worshipped Shiva in
Kashi and Grihapati (literally, lord of a household) was born as his
son. Grihapati eventually became the *garhapatya* fire.

that very instant, I swiftly take away every kind of calamity. I know everything about the misery that has arisen on account of the *asura* Taraka, and I will take it away. This is the truth. I am telling you the truth. I do not have any kind of inclination towards pleasures. Nevertheless, for the sake of having a son, I will marry Girija. O gods! Without any fear, all of you return to your own residences. I will accomplish the task. There is no need to think about this." Having said this, Hara was silent and immersed himself in *dhyana*. O sage! Vishnu and all the *deva*s returned to their respective abodes.'"'

Chapter 120-3.3(25) (Test by the *Saptarshis*)

' ' "Narada asked, 'Happy, *deva*s, Vidhatri, Vishnu and the sages departed. What happened after this? O father! What did Shambhu do? After what interval of time did he go to bestow the boon? How did it happen? To please me, tell me.'"'

'"Brahma replied, 'Brahma and other *deva*s returned to their own residences. To test her austerities, Bhava immersed himself in *samadhi*. He immersed himself in his own *atman* and thought of his own *atman*. He is greater than the greatest. He is self-ruling. He is devoid of *maya*. He is without impediments. Bhagavan Ishvara Vrishadhvaja is truly like that. His movements cannot be discerned. Hara Parameshvara is the source of prosperity.'"'

'"'O son! Girija was tormenting herself through supreme austerities. Rudra was filled with great wonder at her austerities. He was dislodged from his *samadhi*. It cannot but be otherwise for someone who is subservient to devotees. Hara, the cause of prosperity, remembered the seven sages, Vasishtha and the others. As soon as they were remembered, the seven sages

swiftly arrived there. Their faces looked pleased and all of
them praised their good fortune in many kinds of ways. Full of
delight, they prostrated themselves before Mahesha and praised
him. They clasped their hands and lowered their shoulders,
their words faltering. The *saptarshi*s said, "O lord of *deva*s!
O Mahadeva! O ocean of compassion! O lord! Since we have
been remembered by you now, we are extremely blessed. Why
have you remembered us? Please command us. O lord! We are
like your servants. We bow down before you. Show us your
compassion." The ocean of compassion heard what they said.
He smiled and spoke, his eyes dilating like blossoming lotuses
in delight. Maheshvara replied, "O seven sages! O sons! Listen
to my words. All of you possess *jnana* and are discriminating.
You do what is beneficial for me. Deveshi Parvati Girija is
performing austerities now. Firm in her resolve, she is on the
mountain known as Gouri-Shikhara. O *brahmana*s! She desires
me as her husband and is served by her friends. She has given
up all desires and is determined to pursue this objective and
nothing else. O excellent sages! Follow my command and go
there. With love towards me in your minds, act so that you test
the firmness of her resolve. In every kind of way, use deceitful
words and be harsh. O ones excellent in vows! Following my
command, there is no doubt that you should do this." Thus
instructed, the sages quickly went there.'"

'"'The mother of the universe, the mountain's daughter,
was there, blazing in her radiance. They saw Shivaa, the direct
personified form of success in austerities. Her form was one
of pure energy and as a result of that great energy, she was
resplendent. Mentally, the seven *rishi*s, excellent in their vows,
prostrated themselves before her. They bent down and spoke
to her, specially worshipping her. The *rishi*s said, "O Devi! O
daughter of the mountain! Listen. Why are you tormenting
yourself through austerities? Is there any god you desire?
What fruits do you wish for now?" Devi Shivaa, the daughter

of the Indra among mountains, was addressed in this way by
the *brahmanas*. Though it was a great secret, since they were
in front of her, she replied, telling them the truth. Parvati
answered, "O lords among sages! With affection in your
hearts, listen to my words. I have used my own intelligence to
think and decide and I will tell you about that. When you hear
my words, you will laugh, considering this to be impossible. O
brahmanas! I hesitate to describe it to you. But what else can I
do? This mind is helpless and is firmly focused on achieving a
great task. Indeed, this is like wishing for a great foundation,
with lofty walls, in the water. Having obtained the instructions
of the divine *rishi*, I am engaged in these firm austerities. My
wish is that Rudra should become my husband. My mind is
like a fledgling bird without wings that wishes to rashly fly
into the sky. Let Lord Shankara, the ocean of compassion,
fulfil that desire." Hearing her words, the sages laughed.
Though they loved and honoured Girija, they spoke deceitful
and false words. The *rishi*s said, "In vain do you pride yourself
on your learning. O daughter of a mountain! You do not
know about the conduct of the *devarshi*. He is thought to
be learned but is cruel in his mind. Narada is crooked in his
speech, seeking to agitate the minds of others. If one listens to
his words, there is harm in every possible way. With excellent
intelligence, listen to a wonderful historical account. Out of
love for you and to make you understand, we will gradually
tell you. Listen. Daksha is Brahma's son. Following his father's
command, through his wife, he had ten thousand sons. He
loved them and asked to undertake austerities. The sons left
in the western direction and went to Lake Narayana, having
pledged to perform austerities. Narada went there. There, the
sage Narada made them listen to wicked advice. Following
his instructions, none of them returned to the father's home.
Hearing this, Daksha became angry, but his father calmed
his mind. He had another one thousand unmatched sons.

Following their father's command, these sons also went there, so as to perform austerities. Narada went their again and imparted his own advice. When he instructed them in this way, they too followed the path their brothers had taken. They did not return to their father's house and followed the conduct of mendicants. O daughter of a mountain! Such good conduct of Narada's is famous. Hear about something else he does. It causes non-attachment among men. Earlier, there was a *vidyadhara*, known as Chitraketu. He gave him advice and made his home empty.[969] He gave his advice to Prahlada and made him suffer greatly at the hands of Hiranyakashipu. He causes confusion in the intelligence of others. Using his own knowledge, whenever the sage says something, one hears it, and it is pleasant to the ears. However, the person quickly leaves his own house and generally follows the conduct of a mendicant. Though Narada's body always blazes, his *atman* is full of filth. Since we have resided with him, we know this especially well. Since one does not know that it always eats fish, a stork is described as virtuous. A person always knows the conduct of someone he resides with. You are revered as a person who is wise. But you have also accepted his advice. You have become a fool and are undertaking these austerities in vain. O child! You are undertaking such extensive austerities for a person who is always indifferent. He is without transformations. There is no doubt that he is Madana's enemy. He has a form that is inauspicious. He is shameless. He does not possess a home or a lineage. He wears evil clothing and associates with *preta*s and *bhuta*s. He is naked and wields a trident. He is crooked and will use his own *maya* to destroy your *vijnana*. You have been confounded by apparently virtuous words and are engaged in these austerities. If you get

[969] Instructed by Narada, King Chitraketu gave up the life of a householder. The story is told in Bhagavata Purana.

such a groom, what happiness will you obtain? O Deveshi! O
daughter of a mountain! You should think about this yourself.
He first married the virtuous lady Sati, Daksha's daughter,
who possesses excellent intelligence. However, the foolish one
could only maintain her for a few days. Finding a taint in her,
the lord himself gave her up. Without any taints and sorrows
on account of this, he continued to meditate on his own form.
He is alone, without anyone else. He is pursuing *nirvana* and
does not associate with anyone else. O Devi! How can any
woman put up with him? Follow our instructions. Give up this
wicked intelligence and return home. O immensely fortunate
one! As soon as you leave us, you will find welfare. Vishnu is
the appropriate groom for you. The lord possesses all the good
qualities. He resides in Vaikuntha and is Lakshmi's lord. He is
accomplished in many kinds of pastimes. We will arrange for
you to marry him, and you will obtain every kind of happiness.
O Parvati! Give up this rashness and be happy." Parvati, the
mother of the universe, heard these words.'"

'"She laughed and spoke again to the sages who were
accomplished in *jnana*. Parvati said, "O lords among sages!
According to your *jnana*, you have spoken the truth. O
*brahmana*s! But I will not free myself from my rashness. Since
I have been born from a mountain, my body is naturally hard.
Use your excellent intelligence to think about this. You should
not restrain me. I will never give up the words of the divine
rishi. They are like medication. Those who are accomplished
in their knowledge of the *Veda*s say that the words of *guru*s
are like medication. There are those who are firm in their
minds that the words of *guru*s are the truth. In this world
and in the next one, they obtain supreme happiness, never
unhappiness. There are those whose minds are such that they
do not accept the words of *guru*s as the truth. In this world
and in the next one, they experience unhappiness, never
happiness. O *brahmana*s! In every kind of way, the words

of *guru*s must not be ignored. Whether I reside in a home or not, my rashness will always give me happiness. O supreme among sages! There is a hidden meaning in what you have said. Let me use my discrimination to briefly describe it to you. You have described Vishnu as an abode of *guna*s and as one who sports. That is true. Sadashiva is spoken of as one without *guna*s. There is said to be a reason for this. Shiva is the *brahman*. He is without transformations. He assumes different forms for his devotees. He does not wish to display the customary signs of lordship. Therefore, he assumes a form that is the greatly loved objective of Paramahamsas. Shambhu finds supreme bliss in his form as an *avadhuta*. Beautiful ornaments are found in those who are contaminated by *maya*, not in those who have found the *brahman*. The lord is *nirguna* and without origin. He is devoid of *maya*, and his great movements cannot be discerned. O *brahmana*s! Shambhu's favours are not bestowed on the basis of *dharma* and *jati*. Through my *guru*'s favours, I know about Shiva's true nature. O *brahmana*s! If Shiva does not marry me, I will always remain as one who is not wed. This is the truth. I am speaking the truth. Even if the sun rises in the western direction, even if Meru moves, even if the fire becomes cold and even if a lotus blooms on the rocky summit of a mountain, I will not deviate from my rashness. I am speaking the truth." Saying this, the mountain's daughter quickly prostrated herself before the sages. She stopped and indifferent in her mind, remembered Shiva. Understanding that Girija was firm in her determination, the *rishi*s uttered words of "Victory" and pronounced excellent benedictions over her. Pleased in their minds, the sages prostrated themselves before Devi. O sage! Having tested her, they quickly returned to Shiva's abode. Having gone there, they bent down before Shiva and reported what had occurred. Having obtained his permission, they lovingly returned to their own world.'"

Chapter 121-3.3(26) (Shivaa's Conversation with Jatila)

' '' Brahma said, 'The sages returned to their own world. Shankara, the lord who bestows prosperity, wished to test Devi's austerities himself. Using the pretext of testing her, satisfied in her mind, Shambhu wished to see her. He therefore assumed the form of a Jatila[970] and went to Parvati's forest. His form was that of an extremely aged *brahmana*. He was pleased in his mind and blazed in his energy. He held an umbrella and a staff. He saw Devi standing there, surrounded by her friends. Pure, Shivaa stood on the platform, resembling the moon's *kala*s. Shambhu, in the form of a *brahmachari*, looked at Devi. Affectionate towards his devotees and pleased, he approached her. Shivaa Devi saw the *brahmana* approach, extraordinary in his energy. Using every kind of object used for worship, she worshipped him. Full of great joy, she worshipped and honoured him, following the norms. Cheerful, Parvati respectfully asked about the *brahmana*'s welfare. Parvati asked, "You are in the form of a *brahmachari*. Who are you and why have you come here? Please tell me. O supreme among those who know the *Veda*s! You have illuminated the forest with your radiance." The *brahmana* replied, "I am an intelligent *brahmana* whose body is aged. I wander around as I will and have come here. I am an ascetic who brings happiness and does good turns to others. There is no doubt about this. Who are you? Whose daughter are you? Why are you performing austerities, impossible for even sages to accomplish, in this desolate forest? You are not a child nor are you aged. You are a beautiful and radiant woman in her youth. Without a husband, why are you performing these fierce austerities in the forest?

---

[970] An ascetic with matted hair.

O fortunate ascetic lady! O Devi! Are you the companion of an ascetic who does not tend to you in the forest and has gone elsewhere? Tell me. Which lineage have you been born in? Who is your father? What is your conduct? Your form suggests great fortune. Why are you interested in austerities in vain? Are you the one from whom the *Vedas* originated? Is your beautiful form that of Lakshmi or Sarasvati? Which of the two are you? I am not interested in debating the matter." Parvati said, "O *brahmana*! I am not one from whom the *Vedas* originated. I am not Lakshmi or Sarasvati. I am Himachala's daughter, and my name is Parvati now. Earlier, in a different birth, I was born as Daksha's daughter and was named Sati. Since my father abused my husband, I used *yoga* to give up my body. In this birth, I obtained Shiva. However, because of destiny, he did not accept me. He abandoned me and having reduced Manmatha to ashes, departed. When Shankara left, I could not conquer my torment. O *brahmana*! I left my father's house and arrived at the banks of this celestial river to perform extremely firm austerities. I have practiced hard austerities for a very long time but have not obtained the one whom I love more than my own life. I was about to enter the fire. But on seeing you, I stopped for a short while. Please leave. Since Shiva has not accepted me, I will enter the fire. Wherever I may be born, I will only accept Shiva as a groom." Having said this, Parvati entered the fire that was in front of her. Standing in front of her, the *brahmana* repeatedly tried to restrain her.'"'

'"'As soon as she entered the fire, because of Parvati's powers, the fire instantly became like sandalwood paste. She stood inside it for a while and then leapt up into the air. Shiva, in the form of the *brahmana*, suddenly laughed and spoke to the one with the beautiful form. The *brahmana* said, "O fortunate one! Your austerities are wonderful. I have not understood anything. Your body has not been burnt by the fire. Nor have you obtained what your mind desired. O Devi!

It is evident that your wish has not been fulfilled. Tell me what is in your mind. The noble *brahmana* who stands before you can bestow every kind of happiness. O Devi! In the proper way, tell me everything. Since a friendship has developed with you, you should not keep anything a secret. O Devi! What is the boon that you desire? I am asking you. Please tell me about your wish. O Devi! Since austerities exist inside you, all the fruits can be seen. Whether your austerities are for someone else or for some other objective, you have cast away the accumulated jewels in your hand and have stored bits of glass. You possess this kind of beauty. Why have you rendered it futile? Having cast aside many kinds of garments, you have worn hides instead. Tell me the reason for all this. What is the truth behind your austerities? Hearing this, a noble *brahmana* like me will be filled with joy." When she was asked by him in this way, Ambika urged her friend. Excellent in her vows, she used her mouth to recount everything. Parvati sent her friend Vijaya, whom she loved more than her own life. She knew about the excellent vows and spoke to Jatila. The friend said, "O virtuous one! Listen. I will tell you about Parvati's supreme conduct. If you wish to hear about it, I will tell you everything about the reason for her austerities. I am the friend of the daughter of the king of mountains, Mount Himachala. She is the daughter of Menaka and is known by the name Parvati. She has been named Kali. She has not married anyone and does not desire anyone other than Shiva. The virtuous lady has observed austerities for three thousand years. O virtuous one! O supreme among *brahmana*s! I will tell you about the reason why my friend started such austerities. Listen. Ignoring *deva*s, Indra as the foremost, Hari and Brahma, Parvati desires to obtain the wielder of Pinaka as her husband. In earlier times, my friend planted many trees. O *brahmana*! All of them have grown and have yielded flowers and fruit. To render her beauty a success, to become an ornament to her father's lineage, to show a favour to Kama and for the sake of Mahesha, as instructed by Narada, my friend has tormented herself through these terrible austerities. O ascetic! Why has her desire not met with success? O best among *brahmana*s! I have thus told you about the wish that is in my friend's mind. To please you, I have described it to you. What else do you desire to hear?" O sage! Hearing Vijaya's true words, Jatila Rudra laughed and spoke the following words. Jatila said, "The friend has said this. But I imagine this must be in jest. O Devi! If this is true, you should use your own mouth to tell me about it." The *brahmana* Jatila said this. Using her own mouth, Devi Parvati replied to the *brahmana*.'"'

Chapter 122-3.3(27) (The *Brahmachari*'s Deceptive Words)

'''"Parvati said, "O Indra among *brahmana*s! O Jatila! Hear everything about my conduct. What my friend has stated is the truth. It is not otherwise. In thoughts, words and deeds, I have directly regarded Shankara as my husband. This is the truth and there has been no falsity in my conduct. I know that this objective is extremely difficult to obtain. How can I possibly get it? Nevertheless, my mind is eager, and I am tormenting myself through these austerities." Having spoken these words to him, Girija remained there. Having heard Parvati's words, the *brahmana* replied. The *brahmana* said, "Until now, I have had a great desire to know the object that Devi desires. Why is she undertaking these great austerities? O Devi! Having heard everything through your lotus face, I have got to know everything. I am leaving this place and will go elsewhere. You can do what you want. You should not say anything to me. Our friendship will be futile. One should however happily say that, what happens, depends on the deed." Having spoken these words, he got ready to go. However, Devi Parvati prostrated herself and addressed the *brahmana* in the following words. Parvati said, "O Indra among *brahmana*s! Why are you leaving? Remain here and give me beneficial advice." Thus addressed, the one who was holding the staff remained and spoke to her.'"'

"'The *brahmana* said, "O Devi! Full of devotion, you have asked me to stay, and you wish to hear. So that you become wise, I will tell you the truth about everything. Because of my *dharma* as a *guru*, I know everything about Mahadeva. I will tell you the truth, as it is. Listen attentively. Mahadeva is Vrishadhvaja. He smears himself with ashes and has matted hair. His garments are the hide of a tiger. He covers himself with the hide of an elephant. He holds a skull, and many snakes are coiled all around his limbs. Poison has left a mark on him. He eats what should not be eaten. He has malformed eyes, and he is awful to behold. His birth is not known. He is always devoid of the enjoyments of a home. He is naked and has ten arms. He is always surrounded by *bhuta*s and *preta*s. What is the reason you desire he should be your husband? O Devi! Where has your *jnana* gone? Reflect on this and tell me. Earlier, I have heard about his terrible vow. If you are inclined to hear, listen to it attentively now. The virtuous Sati was Daksha's daughter. In earlier times, she accepted the one who rides a bull as her husband. Their destined union is known. Since she was Kapali's wife, Daksha abandoned Sati. Shambhu was deprived of obtaining a share at sacrifices. As a result of the dishonour, Sati was overwhelmed by great rage. She gave up her beloved life and she abandoned Shankara too. You are a jewel among women. Your father is the king of all the mountains. You should have a worthy husband. Why are you tolerating these fierce austerities because of him? Handing over a golden coin, you wish to accept a piece of glass. Giving up pure sandalwood

paste, you desire to smear yourself with mud. Giving up the
energy of the sun, you are wishing for a firefly. Giving up
silk cloth from China,[971] you desire a garment made out of
hide. Giving up residing in a home, you hanker for residence
in the forest. O Deveshi! Giving up excellent and valuable
treasures, you desire a lump of iron. Giving up Indra and the
other guardians of the worlds, you are devoted to Shiva. What
you are doing now is seen to be against the recommendations
of the world. You are one with eyes like the petals of a lotus
and he is three-eyed. Your face is like the moon and Shiva is
said to have five faces. The braid of hair on your head is as
radiant as a divine serpent. Shiva is known to be famous for
his matted hair. You have sandalwood paste on your limbs and
Shiva has ashes. You have a beautiful girdle and Shiva has the
hide of an elephant. You have divine ornaments and Shankara
has serpents. You move around with *devas*, he loves to move
around with *bhutas*, amidst sacrifices made to them. You are
associated with the sound of *mridanga*, he with a *damaru*.[972]
You are associated with the melodious sound of a *bheri*, he
with the inauspicious sound of a horn. You are associated the
sound of a *dhakka*, he with inauspicious yells from the throat.
There can be no comparison between your excellent beauty and
Shiva. If he possessed any objects, why should he be naked?
His mount is a bull, and he possesses nothing else. In terms of
what brings happiness to women through qualities in a groom,
Virupaksha is said to possess not even one of those qualities.
That is the reason Hara burnt down your beloved Kama. It
is also evident that he showed you disrespect, by leaving you
and going elsewhere. His *jati* is not known. One does not see
any learning or *jnana* in him. His aides are *pishacha*s. Poison

---

[971] *Chinamshuka.*
[972] *Damaru* is a small drum, shaped like an hourglass. *Bheri* is a
kettledrum. *Dhakka* is a large drum that can be played on both sides.

is seen in his throat. He is always alone. In particular, he is without attachment. Therefore, you should not fix your mind on Hara. Where is your necklace and where is his garland of skulls? There are divine unguents on your body, his body is smeared with ashes. O Devi! Between your form and that of Hara, everything is contrary. Your wish does not appeal to me but do what you want. It is evident that you yourself wish for everything evil. Withdraw your mind from him. Otherwise, do whatever you want." Parvati heard these words spoken by the *brahmana*. Mentally angry because Shiva had been greatly criticized, she spoke to the *brahmana*.'"'

Chapter 123-3.3(28) (Parvati Sees Shiva's Form)

' '' 'Parvati said, "Until now, I thought that someone else had come. Now I have got to know everything and also that you cannot be killed. O divinity! What you have said is known. It is not true. There are no contrary words in anything that you have said. There are occasions when Maheshvara is seen in that kind of garb. He is the supreme *brahman*. In his own pastimes, he assumes those kinds of forms. In the form of a *brahmachari*, you have tried to deceive me. You came here and addressed me with deceptive words and bad arguments. In particular, I know about Shiva's own nature. After proper reflection, I will speak about Shiva's *tattva*. He is actually the *nirguna brahman*. But there are reasons why he assumes a *saguna* form. How can he have a *jati*? He is *nirguna*, though the *guna*s are in his *atman*. Sadashiva is the foundation for every kind of learning. Since he is the complete *paramatman*, what does he have to do with learning? In ancient times, at the beginning of the *kalpa*, Shambhu used the form of his breath to bestow the *Vedas* on Vishnu. Where is there a lord who is as great as him? He is the primordial being, before anyone else. How can one measure his age? Prakriti was born from him. He is the cause behind Shakti. If a person lovingly and constantly worships Shakti and Shankara, the undecaying Shambu always bestows the three kinds of Shakti[973] on that person. A living being who worships him becomes fearless and conquers death. Therefore, he is famous in the three worlds under the name of Mrityunjaya. Vishnu obtained his status as Vishnu because of his favour. Brahma obtained his status as Brahma and *devas* obtained their status as *devas*. Whenever the king of *devas* goes to see Shiva, he has to honour *bhutas* and others, those who guard Shiva's gates. Otherwise, his crown is always struck with staffs and shattered. Since he is himself the great lord, he does not need many people on his side. His form is benevolent. If one serves him, everything can be obtained. Does the divinity Sadashiva desire me? In this world, if a person is poor for seven lives and serves Shankara, Lakshmi herself serves him. The eight *siddhis* always dance before him and satisfy him, lowering their faces. How can welfare be difficult for him to obtain? Though Shankara does not serve anything auspicious, as soon as one remembers him, everything auspicious results. Through the power of worshipping him, every type of desire is obtained. How can there be an aberration in a person who is always without transformations? If Shiva's auspicious name is constantly in a person's mouth, as soon as other people see him, they are always purified. You have said that ashes from a funeral pyre are impure. In that case, why do *devas* smear it on their limbs and wear it on their bodies? The divinity assumes *gunas* and becomes the creator, preserver and destroyer of the world. But Shiva's true nature is *nirguna*. How can it be known? Shiva

---

[973] Power of lordship, good counsel and enterprise. However, this can be interpreted in other ways too.

is the *paramatman*. His form is that of the *brahman*, without
*guna*s. With their faces turned outwards, how can people know
him? Those who are wicked in conduct, sinners and those who
have moved away from *deva*s cannot know Shiva's *nirguna*
form. In this world, if a person does not know about Shiva's
tattva and criticizes him, all the store of good merits he has
accumulated since birth is reduced to ashes. You have criticized
the infinitely energetic Hara. Since I have worshipped you, I
have also become a sinner. Having seen someone who hates
Shiva, one should bathe, wearing one's clothes. Having seen
someone who hates Shiva, one must perform *prayashchitta*. O
wicked one! You have said that you know Shankara. However,
no one knows the eternal Shiva with certainty. Whatever be
Rudra's form, he is extremely handsome. I desire the eternal
one, who is without transformation. He is loved by the
virtuous. Vishnu, Brahma or anyone else is not the great-souled
one's equal. What need be said of other immortals? All *deva*s
are subservient to time.[974] Having used my own intelligence to
reflect on this, I have got to know the true *tattva*. I have come
to this forest and am following these extensive austerities for
Shiva's sake. He is Paramesha Sarvesha, affectionate towards
his devotees. He is the one who shows favours to the distressed
and I desire to obtain him."''"

'"Brahma continued, 'O sage! Having said this, Girija,
the daughter of the king of the mountains, stopped. With
mind that was indifferent, she meditated on Shiva. Hearing
Devi's words, the *brahmachari brahmana* started to say
something again. However, Girija quickly spoke to her
friend, Vijaya. Her mind and inclinations were fixed on
Shiva. She had turned away from any criticism of Shiva.
Girija said, "O friend! Make efforts to restrain this worst
among *brahmana*s. He has made up his mind to speak again

---

[974] In the course of time, they face destruction.

and will criticize Shiva. A person who criticizes Shiva is a sinner. But a person who hears such criticism also becomes a sinner. Those who criticize Shiva should always be killed by Shiva's devotees. If that person happens to be a *brahmana*, one should shun him and quickly leave the spot. This wicked person will criticize Shiva again. Since he is a *brahmana*, he cannot be killed. But he must be shunned and must not be seen in any way. Without any delay, let us leave this place and go away, so that no conversation with this wicked person occurs again." O sage! As soon as Uma said this and stepped forward, Shiva manifested himself and embraced his beloved. He created his own fortunate form, the one Shivaa had used to perform *dhyana* on Shiva. Shiva showed himself and spoke to Shivaa, whose face was cast downwards. Shiva said, "Leaving me, where are you going? I will not let go of you again. I am pleased with you. Please ask for a boon. There is nothing that cannot be given to you. You have bought me with your austerities. From today, I am your servant. You have bought me with your beauty and from that instant, I wanted to be united with you. Give up this shame. You are my eternal wife. O Girija! O Maheshvari! Use your virtuous intelligence to reflect on this. I have tested you in many kinds of ways, but you are firm in your mind. Please pardon those offences. I have been following the pastimes of the world. In the three worlds, I do not see a beloved like you. O Shivaa! I am subservient to you in every possible way. Let your wish meet with success. O beloved! Come to me. You are my wife, and I am your groom. With you, I will quickly go to my residence on that excellent mountain." When the lord of *deva*s said this, Parvati was delighted. She cast aside the hardship on account of austerities, just as one throws away something old. O supreme among sages! All her exhaustion was destroyed. Whenever the fruits are obtained, a being's former exhaustions are destroyed.'"

Chapter 124-3.3(29) (Conversation between Shiva and Shivaa)

‘ ‘‘Narada asked, 'O Brahma! O Vidhatri! O extremely fortunate one! What happened after that? I wish to hear everything. Please tell me about Shivaa's glory.'"'

"'Brahma replied, 'O *devarshi*! Listen. I will happily tell you everything. This account destroys great sins. It increases devotion to Shiva. O *brahmana*! Hearing the words of Hara, the *paramatman*, and beholding his form, which caused bliss, Parvati rejoiced. The extremely virtuous one spoke to the lord, who was standing near her. Devi Shivaa was extremely happy, and her eyes dilated in joy. Parvati said, "O Devesha! You are my lord. Have you forgotten how, in earlier times, you destroyed Daksha's sacrifice, when he performed it deceitfully? To accomplish a task for *deva*s, I have been born from Mena. O divinity! O Devesha! Taraka has caused them miseries. O Devesha! O Ishana! O lord! If you are pleased with me and if you are going to show me your compassion, please become my husband. Act in accordance with my words. Taking your permission, I will return to my father's house. Let your pure and supreme fame be known there. O protector! O lord! You should go to Himachala. You are accomplished in pastimes. Become a mendicant and ask me from him. You should do this to establish your fame in the worlds. When my father agrees to everything, you should assume the role of a householder. Urged lovingly by the *rishi*s and surrounded by his own relatives, there is no doubt that my father will act in accordance with your words. In earlier times, when I was Daksha's daughter, my father[975] had bestowed me on you. But you had not married me in accordance with the rites. My father, Daksha, did not

---

[975] The father at that time, Daksha.

worship the planets. Therefore, in connection with the planets, there was a great lapse. O lord! Hence, you should follow the decreed rites for marriage. O Mahadeva! This is to accomplish the task of *deva*s. One must certainly follow the rites for the marriage. Let Himalaya also know that his daughter has completed the austerities successfully." Hearing her words, Sadashiva was extremely pleased.'"'

'"'He seemed to smile, as he lovingly addressed Girija in the following words. Shiva said, "O Devi! O Maheshani! Listen to my supreme words. Let all the auspicious and appropriate rites be carried out, without deviations. O one with the beautiful face! Brahma and all other beings are temporary. O beautiful one! Know that everything that can be seen is subject to destruction. The absolute is one and is *nirguna* but assumes *guna*s. It is self-luminous and like moonlight, others obtain their radiance from it. O Devi! I am self-ruling, but you have made me subservient to you. You are Prakriti Mahamaya. You are the one who does everything. This entire universe has been created out of *maya*. Through his own intellect, the supreme *atman* holds everything up. He is the *paramatman* and is in all *atman*s. Because his *atman* becomes attached, surrounded by the *gana*s, he undertakes this excellent creation. What are planets? What are the several seasons? What are the other planets you have spoken about? O Devi! O Shivaa! O one who is beautiful in complexion! The two of us have created these differences in *guna*s and tasks. We have created the universe for the welfare of devotees, driven by sentiments of affection towards devotees. You are the subtle Prakriti. You have *sattva*, *rajas* and *tamas* within you. You are accomplished and pervasive. You are always *saguna* and *nirguna*. O slender-waisted one! I am in the *atman*s of all beings. I am without attachment and without desire. Depending on what a devotee wishes, I assume an image. O daughter of a mountain! I will not go to your father, Himalaya. I will never become a mendicant and ask for you. O daughter of the Indra among mountains! Even if a man is great-souled, even if he possesses great and superior qualities, as soon as he says, 'Please give', he becomes inferior. O fortunate one! Knowing this, please tell me what is good for us. O fortunate one! I will follow your command. Do what you wish." The virtuous Mahadevi, with eyes like lotuses, was addressed in this way. Full of devotion, she repeatedly prostrated herself before Shankara and spoke. Parvati said, "You are the *atman*, and I am Prakriti. There is no need to reflect on this. We are self-ruling, but we are subservient to our devotees. We are both *nirguna* and *saguna*. O Shambhu! O lord! You should make efforts to act in accordance with my words. O Shankara! If you ask for me from Mount Himalaya, you will bestow good fortune on him. O Mahesha! Please show me your compassion. I am always your devotee. O lord! From one birth to another birth, I am always your wife. You are the *brahman*, the *paramatman*. You are *nirguna* and beyond Prakriti. You are without attachment and without desires. You are the self-ruling Parameshvara. Nevertheless, attentive towards saving devotees, you become *saguna*. You are accomplished in many kinds of pastimes and your *atman* is always engaged in sport. O Mahadeva! O Maheshvara! I know you in every possible way. O omniscient one! What is the point of speaking a lot? Please show me your compassion. Perform your great and wonderful pastimes and extend your fame in this world. O lord! People will sing about it and cross this ocean that is the world." Saying this, Girija repeatedly prostrated herself and stopped. She lowered her shoulders before Mahesha and joined her hands in salutation. Addressed by her in this way, the great-souled Maheshvara thought that he would mimic the practices of the world and agreed. He laughed and happily agreed to do that. Extremely delighted, Shambhu vanished. He went to Kailasa, his mind suffering from the pangs of separation from Kali. Having gone

there, Mahesha told Nandi and the others everything that had
transpired. He was filled with great joy. Hearing this, Bhairava
and all the other *gana*s were filled with great happiness and
organized great festivities. O *brahmana*! O Narada! Everything
there was extremely auspicious. All sorrows were destroyed.
Everything was full of joy.'"'

Chapter 125-3.3(30) (Parvati's Return)

" "Narada said, 'O Vidhatri! O father! O immensely
fortunate one! You are blessed. You possess insight
about the ultimate objective. As a result of your favours, you
have made me listen to this wonderful account. When Hara
left for his own mountain, what did the extremely auspicious
Parvati do? Where did she go? O extremely intelligent one!
Please tell me that.'"'

'"Brahma replied, 'O son! Full of great joy, listen to
what happened after Hara returned to his own residence.
Remembering Shiva, I will tell you. Parvati had rendered
her beauty successful. Conversing about Mahadeva with
her friends, she returned to her father's residence. Hearing
that Parvati was returning, Mena and Himachala were
overwhelmed with delight. They ascended a divine vehicle and
left. The priest, citizens, many friends, relatives and several
others went with them. All the brothers, Mainaka as the
foremost, also went, uttering exclamations of "Victory". They
were filled with great exultation. Auspicious and radiant pots
were placed along the royal road, filled with sandalwood paste,
aguru, *kasturi*[976] and branches laden with fruit. Along with the
priest, there were *brahmana*s and sages who chanted about the

---

[976] Musk.

brahman. There were female dancers and well-decorated kings among elephants. In every direction, there were the trunks of plantain trees. Along with their husbands and sons, there were women, holding lamps in their hands. Collectively, groups of *brahmanas* pronounced auspicious benedictions. Many kinds of musical instruments were sounded and there was the sound of conch shells. At this time, Durga approached near her own city.'"'

'"'Devi entered the city and saw her parents again. They were extremely happy and rushed forward to meet her, their minds overwhelmed with joy. Kali and her friends were also over-joyed and prostrated themselves before them. They pronounced complete benedictions over her and clasped her to their breasts. They exclaimed, "O child!" Full of love, they cried. Women who served her and other women rejoiced. The wives of her brothers were extremely happy and embraced her. "A great task has been completely accomplished by you and it will save the lineage. All of us have been sanctified through your virtuous conduct." In this way, all of them praised her. They rejoiced and prostrated themselves before her. Rejoicing, they honoured and worshipped Shivaa with sandalwood paste and fragrant flowers. At this time, the delighted *deva*s gathered in the sky, astride their *vimana*s. They showered down auspicious flowers and praised her with hymns. All of them placed her on a beautiful and excellent chariot. The *brahmana*s and all the others were happy and made her enter the city. Showing a great deal of respect, her friends and other women made Shivaa enter the house, the *brahmana*s leading the way. The women performed her ablutions, while *brahmana*s pronounced benedictions. O lord among sages! Himalaya and her mother, Menaka, were delighted. Himalaya thought that his *ashrama* as a householder had been rendered successful. A daughter is superior to a wicked son. He also applauded Narada with words of praise. The Indra among mountains gave riches to

*brahmana*s and *bandi*s.[977] He made *brahmana*s read auspicious
texts and there were great festivities. O sage! The parents were
delighted to see their daughter. Full of joy, the brothers and
the sister gathered together in that arena. O son! Himalaya
was happy and extremely pleased in his mind. He lovingly
honoured everyone and left for the Ganga, to have a bath.'"'

'"'Shambhu is affectionate towards his devotees and
engages in excellent pastimes. At this time, he assumed the
form of an excellent dancer and approached Menaka. He
held a horn in his left hand and a *damaru* in the right. He
had a *kantha*[978] on his back and was attired in red garments.
He was accomplished in singing and dancing. In that form of
an excellent dancer, he delighted Menaka's companions. He
danced well and sang many kinds of extremely melodious
songs. With a melodious tune, he blew on the horn and
played on the *damaru*. He performed many kinds of great
and wonderful acts. On seeing him, all the citizens, men and
women, aged and young, assembled there. O sage! Hearing
his beautiful singing and witnessing his charming dancing, all
of them suddenly lost their senses, including Mena. Though
Durga also became unconscious, she saw Shankara within her
heart. His radiant form was exceedingly handsome, with the
trident and all the other signs. He was adorned with ashes and
wore a beautiful garland of bones. The three eyes blazed on
his forehead. His sacred sacrificial thread was made out of
a serpent. Maheshvara was fair in complexion, and he kept
saying, "Ask for a boon." He is the friend of the distressed and
is an ocean of compassion, enchanting in every possible way.

---

[977] The *suta*s were charioteers, as well as raconteurs of tales.
*Magadha*s were minstrels and bards. So were *bandi*s. But *magadha*s
seem to have also composed, while *bandi*s sung the compositions of
others.
    [978] A patched garment worn by mendicants and *yogi*s, sometimes
used to store things.

Witnessing Hara Isha within her heart, she prostrated herself. She made up her mind to ask for the boon and said, "Please become my husband." With pleasure, Shiva, within her heart, gave her the boon and disappeared. The mendicant started to dance again.'"'

""'Mena's mind was filled with affection. She lovingly placed some excellent jewels in a golden vessel, so as to give these to him. The mendicant did not accept these but asked for Shivaa instead. Engaged in his pastimes, he started to sing and dance again. Hearing his words, Mena was greatly surprised and became angry. She rebuked the mendicant and was about to throw him out. Meanwhile, the noble mountain returned from the Ganga. He saw the mendicant in his courtyard, in the form of a man. Hearing everything from Mena's mouth, he was also greatly angered. He issued instructions that the dancer should be thrown out. O excellent sage! However, his great energy blazed like a great fire, and it was impossible to touch him. No one was capable of throwing him out. O son! The mendicant was accomplished in many pastimes. He displayed his own infinite powers to the mountain. The mountain saw that he quickly transformed himself into Vishnu's form. He wore a diadem and earrings. He was four-armed and clad in yellow garments. The wielder of the mace is offered flowers and other things at the time of worship. He saw all these on the mendicant's body and head. After this, the lord of mountains saw the four-faced creator of the universe, red in complexion and reading suktas from the shruti texts. He next saw him in the form of Surya, the eye of the universe. Seeing all this instantly, the king of mountains marvelled. O son! He next saw the great, beautiful and wonderful form of Rudra, great in his energy and smiling, accompanied by Parvati. Thereafter, the form became one that was only energy, without form, without blemish, without attributes and without desire. It was extremely wonderful and without form. In this way, he

saw many kinds of forms there. He was greatly surprised and
immediately filled with supreme bliss. Since he would not accept
anything else, the mendicant, the source of all prosperity, asked
for Durga as alms. Confounded by Shiva's *maya*, the Indra
among mountains did not agree to this. Not accepting anything
else, the mendicant vanished. After this, Mena and the lord of
mountains realized that the Lord Shiva had deceived them and
had returned to his own residence. Thinking about Shiva, the
two of them were filled with great devotion towards him. He is
the divine one who bestows great emancipation. He is the one
who bestows every kind of bliss.'"'

Chapter 126-3.3(31) (Shiva's *Maya* and the *Brahmana*)

' "Brahma said, 'O Narada! Shakra and all the other *deva*s
got to know about their supreme and unwavering
devotion towards Shiva. They thought. The *deva*s said, "The
mountain is single-minded in his devotion. If he bestows his
daughter on him, he will immediately obtain *nirvana* and
vanish from Bharata. He is a store of jewels, and he will leave
the earth and disappear. It is certain that any statement about
this land being a store of jewels will be falsified. He will give up
his immobile form and assume a divine form. If he bestows his
daughter on the one who holds a trident, he will go to Shiva's
world. There is no doubt that he will attain *sarupya* with
Mahadeva. There, he will enjoy excellent objects of pleasure
and attain emancipation." Having consulted among themselves
in this way, all the gods were greatly confused and decided
to send their *guru*.[979] O Narada! Thus, full of humility and

[979] Brihaspati is the *guru* of the gods.

affection and desiring to accomplish their objective, Shakra and all the other *deva*s went to their *guru*'s residence. Having gone there, all the *deva*s, along with Vasava, bowed down before the *guru*. They affectionately told the *guru* everything that had happened. The *deva*s said, "O *guru*! To accomplish our task, please go to Himalaya's house. Having gone there, please criticize the wielder of the trident. Durga will not accept any groom other than the one who holds Pinaka. If he bestows his daughter unwillingly, he will still reap the complete fruits but only after a while. For the moment, let the mountain remain on earth. O *guru*! He is the store of many jewels. Let him remain on earth." Hearing what *deva*s said, the *guru* remembered Shiva's name. He covered his hands with his ears and did not agree. After this, Brihaspati, pervasive in his intelligence, remembered Mahadeva. Shaming them repeatedly, he replied to the noble *deva*s. Brihaspati said, "All of you *deva*s are selfish and destroy the objectives of others. If I criticize Shankara, I will certainly go to hell. O gods! One of you should go to the mountain. Make the Indra among mountains understand what you wish for. Let him bestow his daughter reluctantly and happily remain in Bharata. If he bestows his daughter devotedly, he will certainly obtain emancipation. Subsequently, let all the *saptarshi*s go and make the mountain understand. Durga will not accept any groom other than the wielder of Pinaka. Alternatively, let all the gods, along with Vasava, go to Brahma's world. Tell him everything. He will accomplish your task." Having heard this and discussed the matter, all the gods came to my assembly. They bent down and humbly and affectionately, reported everything. O sage! I am the one who utters the *Veda*s. I heard the words of *deva*s about criticizing Shiva. I lamented and addressed the gods. Brahma said, "O children! Criticism of Shiva is extremely difficult to tolerate. I am incapable of doing that. It destroys prosperity and beauty. Its form is that of a seed that brings about calamity. O gods! Go to Kailasa and satisfy

Shankara. Let him quickly go to Himalaya's house. Let him go to the lord of mountains and criticize himself. The criticism of others leads to destruction. But it is held that criticizing one's own self contributes to fame." Hearing my words, devas were happy and prostrated themselves before me. They quickly went to Kailasa, the mountain that is known as the lord of mountains. Having gone there, they saw Shiva. They lowered their heads and prostrated themselves. Joining their hands in salutation, all the gods praised Hara. The devas said, "O lord of devas! O Mahadeva! O abode of compassion! O Shankara! We have sought refuge with you. Show us your compassion. We prostrate ourselves before you. You are affectionate towards your devotees. You are the lord who is always engaged in carrying out the tasks of devotees. You are the one who saves the distressed. You are an ocean of compassion. You are the one who saves devotees from calamities." Mahesha was thus praised by all the devas, along with Vasava. They lovingly told him everything that had happened. Hearing the words of devas, Maheshvara consented. He smiled and comforted the devas and made them return. All the devas were delighted and returned to their own residences. They were of the view that they had accomplished their objective and praised Sadashiva.'"'

'"'Bhagavan Mahesha is affectionate towards his devotees. He is indifferent and is the lord of maya. He left for the residence of the lord of mountains. At that time, he was happily seated in an assembly of mountains. He was surrounded by his relatives and Parvati was also there. At that time, Sadashiva arrived. He held a staff and an umbrella. He was attired in divine garments and there was the radiant mark of a tilaka on his forehead. He held a string of threaded crystals in his hand. He wore a shalagrama around his neck. The brahmana was attired in the garb of a virtuous person. He was devotedly performing japa with Hari's name. On seeing him, Himalaya and all his companions stood up. Exhibiting devotion towards the guest,

like rods, they prostrated themselves on the ground in front of
him. Full of devotion, Parvati prostrated herself before the lord
whom she loved like her own life, disguised in the form of a
brahmana. Recognizing him in her mind, Devi was filled with
great joy and praised him. O son! Happily, Shiva, in the form
of the *brahmana*, pronounced his benedictions over everyone.
These were especially bestowed on Shivaa, so that she might
obtain the desire of her heart. The *brahmana* happily accepted
madhuparka[980] and everything else, offered with great love by
the mountain who has ice all over his body. Mount Himalaya,
supreme among mountains, asked about his welfare. O sage!
Observing the proper norms, he worshipped the Indra among
*brahmana*s with a great deal of affection. The lord among
mountains then asked, "Who are you?" The Indra among
*brahmana*s quickly responded to the Indra among mountains
in affectionate words. The Indra among *brahmana*s said, "O
best among mountains! I am a *brahmana* who is devoted to
Vishnu and am supreme among intelligent ones. I roam around
on earth and my profession is that of a matchmaker. I can
go wherever I wish. Through the powers of my *guru*, I know
everything. I am pure in my *atman* and am engaged in ensuring
the welfare of others. I am an ocean of compassion and remove
transgressions. I have got to know that you wish to bestow
your daughter on Hara. She is divine and supreme in form,
resembling a lotus. She possesses all the auspicious signs. He is
without support and associates with no one. He is malformed
and possesses no qualities. He resides in cremation grounds and
his form is like that of a predator who catches snakes. He is a
yogi, and the directions are his garments. His limbs are terrible,
and he wears snakes as ornaments. His name and lineage are
not known. His conduct is vile, and he has nothing to amuse.

[980] *Madhuparka* is a mixture of honey and water, customarily
offered to a guest.

His body is smeared with ashes. He is prone to rage and has no
sense of discrimination. His age is not known. He always wears
extremely terrible matted hair. He is a refuge for all those who
wander around. He is a mendicant who wears a garland of
snakes. He is devoted to a wicked path. He is deceitful and has
abandoned the path of the Vedas. O mountain! This intention
of yours will certainly not bring about anything auspicious.
O supreme among those who possess jnana! O one born into
Narayana's lineage![981] Understand this. For the rite of bestowing
Parvati, he is not a worthy recipient. As soon as they hear about
this, the mouths of great people will break into smiles. O lord
of mountains! Behold. He does not have a single relative. You
are a store of great jewels, and he possesses no riches. O lord
of mountains! You should quickly make efforts to consult your
relatives, Menaka, your sons and learned people—everyone
other than Parvati. O supreme among mountains! Medication
never appeals to a person suffering from disease. Instead, such
a person likes bad food, which always causes even greater
affliction." Having said this, the brahmana ate quickly. Serene
Shiva engages in many kinds of pastimes. He cheerfully left for
his own abode.'"

Chapter 127-3.3(32) (Arrival of Saptarshis)

' ' "Brahma said, 'Hearing the brahmana's words, Mena's
heart was shattered. Tears of sorrow flowed from her
eyes, and she spoke to Himalaya. Mena said, "O Indra among
mountains! Listen to my words. They will lead to happiness.
Ask the supreme among all Shiva's devotees about what the

---

[981] Since Himalaya was the son of Brahma, who originated from
Vishnu.

brahmana has said. The *brahmana* who is devoted to Vishnu has criticized Shambhu. O lord among mountains! Hearing his words, my mind is very distressed. O lord among mountains! Therefore, I will not bestow my daughter on Shiva. He is wicked in form and conduct and our daughter possesses all the auspicious signs. If you do not pay heed to my words, I will certainly die. I will immediately leave the house or devour poison. Using a rope, I will tie Ambika to my neck and leave for the desolate forest. I will submerge myself in the great ocean. But I will not bestow my daughter on him." Having quickly said this, grieving, Mena entered the chamber of sorrow.[982] She threw aside her necklace. She lay down on the ground and wept.'"

'"'O son! Meanwhile, Shambhu's mind was agitated by the pangs of separation, and he instantly remembered the seven *rishi*s. As soon as all these *rishi*s were remembered by Shambhu himself, they immediately arrived there, resembling *kalpavriksha*s. Arundhati, in the form of success personified, also arrived there. On seeing them, dazzling like the sun, Hara stopped in his *japa*. O sage! The best among *rishi*s stood in front of Shiva. They lowered their heads and praised him. The ascetics thought that they had become successful in their objective. Extremely surprised, they stood there, prostrating themselves again. They joined their hands in salutation and spoke to Shiva, revered by the worlds. The *rishi*s said, "O best of all! O great king! O emperor of the residents of heaven! How can we even describe our complete and supreme good fortune? Formerly, we have tormented ourselves through three kinds of austerities.[983] We have studied the excellent *Veda*s. Formerly, we have offered oblations into the fire and visited

---

[982] *Kopalaya*, a special chamber that women (particularly queens) entered when they were angry.

[983] *Tapas* (austerities) are of three types—*tamasika* (torturing the physical body), *rajasika* (undertaken with a motive) and *sattvika* (done naturally).

many *tirtha*s. Because of what we have done in thoughts, words and deeds, we have accumulated some good merits. But since you have remembered us, everything has been obtained now. You have shown us a favour by remembering us. If a man constantly worships you, he is always successful in his objective. How can one describe the good merits of those whom you remember? O Sadashiva! Since you have remembered us, we have become the best of all. When people wish, you don't usually show yourself. O lord! It is extremely difficult to see you. It is like fruit stooping down for a dwarf, like sight to a person born blind, like a dumb person becoming eloquent, like a poor person seeing a store of treasure, like a lame person crossing a supreme mountain and like a barren woman giving birth. Since we have seen you today, from now on, the world will worship and respect us as lords among sages. You have yourself granted us refuge at your feet. What is the need to speak a lot about this? O lord of *deva*s! O Ishvara of all *deva*s! Through seeing you, we have become revered in every possible way. If you show us your compassion and instruct us about a supreme task, we will become complete. We are your servants. Please give us an auspicious task that is appropriate." Shambhu Maheshvara, who was following the customary conduct of the world, heard their words and replied in pleasant words. Shiva said, "*Rishi*s must always be worshipped, especially those like you. O *brahmana*s! There is a reason why I have remembered you. You know that I am always engaged in doing good turns. In particular, if anything needs to be done for the welfare of the worlds, it must be accomplished. *Deva*s are suffering miseries on account of the extremely evil-souled Taraka. Since Brahma has granted him a boon, what can I possibly do against that unassailable one? O supreme *rishi*s! My eight forms are spoken about.[984] They manifest themselves for the welfare of others,

[984] Bhava, Sharva, Rudra, Pashupati, Ugra, Mahadeva, Bhima and Ishana.

not for a selfish objective. I desire to marry Shivaa. She has tormented herself through extremely difficult austerities that are difficult for even supreme *rishi*s to undertake. Following Parvati's words, I assumed the form of a mendicant and went to the mountain's residence. Accomplished in pastimes, I purified Kali. On getting to know that I am the supreme *brahman*, full of great devotion, the couple wished to follow the rites of the *Veda*s and bestow their daughter on me. Urged by *deva*s, to diminish their devotion, I assumed the form of Vishnu's devotee and criticized myself. O sages! Hearing this, they were distressed and are no longer interested in bestowing their daughter on me. Therefore, you must certainly go to Himachala's house. Having gone there, kindle understanding in the supreme mountain and his wife. Speak to them words that are in conformity with the *Veda*s. Do everything so that the excellent task is accomplished. O excellent ones! I desire to marry their daughter. I have agreed to marry her and have already granted her that boon. What is the need to speak a lot about this? There must be understanding in Himalaya. For the welfare of *deva*s, Mena must also be made to understood. Whatever method you devise will be more than enough. This is your task, and you will obtain a share in the good merits of the task." All the sages were free of any blemish. Having heard these words, since the lord had shown them his favours, they were filled with joy. "We are blessed. We have been successful in every possible way. He is revered by all and specially worshipped by Brahma and Vishnu. Since he accomplishes every objective, he is worshipped. He is the one who is sending us and that sending is for a task that will bring happiness to the world. He is held to be the lord of the worlds, the father and the mother. Any association with him always increases, like the waxing moon." Having said this, the divine *rishi*s bowed down before Shiva. Making their path through the sky, they went to Himalaya's city.'"'

""'On seeing that divine city, the *rishi*s were extremely surprised. They described themselves as having been sanctified and conversed with each other. The *rishi*s said, "Having seen Himalaya's city, we are blessed and have been sanctified. Shiva has engaged us for a task that concerns *deva*s. This excellent city is seen to be superior to Alaka, heaven, Bhogavati and Amaravati.[985] There are extremely beautiful houses, made out of many kinds of excellent crystal. There are wonderful arenas, made out many different kinds of jewels. In every house, there are wonderful *suryakanta* and *chandrakanta* gems.[986] Celestial trees have grown. Gates and Lakshmi can be seen in every house. There are many kinds of wonderful *vimana*s, yoked to parrots and swans. There are wonderful canopies, and the gates are covered with cloth. There are many kinds of waterbodies and ponds. There are wonderful groves, frequented by happy people. All the men are like *deva*s and all the women are like *apsara*s. In *karma bhumi*,[987] the followers of Puranas undertake many kinds of sacrifices, desiring to obtain heaven. Since they have abandoned Himalaya's city, all these efforts are in vain. O *brahmana*s! Men wish for heaven only as long as they have not seen this. What is the need for heaven?' The *rishi*s described the city in this way. All of them went to Himalaya's house, which possessed every kind of prosperity. From a distance, Himalaya saw those seven extremely energetic sages, resembling the sun, arriving through the sky. He was filled with great wonder. Himalaya said, "These seven, resembling the sun, are approaching me. I must now make efforts to worship the

---

[985] Alaka is Kubera's capital, Bhogavati is the capital of the *naga*s and Amaravati is Indra's capital.

[986] *Suryakanta* is the sunstone, believed to burst into flames under the influence of the sun's rays. *Chandrakanta* is the moonstone, believed to melt under the influence of the moon's beams.

[987] Bharatavarsha is known as *karma bhumi*.

sages. When such great-souled ones arrive in any householder's house, they bestow happiness. We are blessed." Meanwhile, they descended from the sky and stood on the ground. Seeing them in front of him, so as to show them honour, Himalaya advanced. He joined his hands in salutation, lowered his shoulders and prostrated himself before the *saptarshi*s. Showing a great deal of respect, he worshipped them. To ensure the welfare of Himalaya, lord of the mountains, the *saptarshi*s clasped him by the hand and with pleasant faces, pronounced auspicious words of benediction over him. Full of devotion, he placed them in front and said, "Since you are in front of me, my status as a householder has been blessed." Saying this, he offered them seats. When they were seated, he himself stood there, waiting for their command. Himalaya spoke to the sages, who were full of resplendence. Himalaya said, "I am blessed. My tasks have been accomplished. My birth has been rendered successful. People regard me as someone to be seen. I am held to be equal to many *tirtha*s. But you, who are forms of Vishnu, have come to my house. You are complete in all your objectives. Why have you come to an inferior person's house? Nevertheless, I am like a servant. Is there any task that needs to be done? Please show me your compassion and tell me about it. May my birth yield excellent fruits."'''

Chapter 128-3.3(33) (Assuring the Mountain)

''' 'The *rishi*s said, "Shiva is said to be the father of the universe. Shivaa is held to be the mother of the universe. Therefore, your daughter should be bestowed on the great-souled Shankara. O mountain full of ice! If you do this, your birth will be successful. Amongst all the *guru*s in the world, there is no doubt that you will become the greatest *guru*."

O lord among sages! On hearing the words of the *saptarshis*, the king of mountains joined his hands in salutation. Prostrating himself, he addressed them in these words. Himalaya said, "O immensely fortunate *saptarshis*! Following the wishes of Girisha, I have already pledged to do what you have spoken about. However, recently, a *brahmana* who follows the *dharma* of worshipping Vishnu arrived here. He cheerfully uttered words that were directed against Shiva. Since then, Shivaa's mother has lost her senses. She no longer wishes to get her daughter married to Rudra, a *yogi*. Extremely tormented, she has gone to the chamber meant for rage. Her clothes are dirty. She is extremely obstinate. O *brahmanas*! Though I have tried to make her understand, she does not understand. To tell you the truth, I have also lost my senses. I do not wish to bestow my daughter on Mahesha, who has the form of a mendicant." Confounded by Shiva's *maya*, the king of mountains said this. O sage! After this, he remained in the midst of the sages, silent. All the seven *saptarshis* applauded Shiva's *maya*. So that Menaka might understand, they sent Arundhati to her. Instructed by her husband, Arundhati, the one who confers *jnana*, quickly went to the spot where Mena and Parvati were. Having gone there, she saw Mena lying down, senseless with grief. The virtuous one carefully addressed her in sweet and beneficial words. Arundhati said, "O Menaka! O virtuous lady! Please get up. I am Arundhati and I have come to your house. The seven sages, who are full of compassion, have also come." Hearing Arundhati's voice, Menaka quickly got up. She lowered her head and addressed the one who was like Padma in her energy. Mena said, "How wonderful! What sanctification for us! Our births have been rendered successful. The daughter-in-law of the creator of the universe and Vasishtha's wife has come here. O goddess! What is the reason for your arrival here? Please tell me specifically. I am like your servant maid. Please show me and my daughter your compassion." When

Menaka said this, the virtuous lady used many kinds of words to make her understand. She then happily returned to the place where the *rishi*s were. All of them were accomplished in the use of words. Remembering Shiva's two feet, they affectionately made the lord of mountains understand. The *rishi*s said, "O Indra among mountains! Listen to our words. They will ensure welfare. Bestow Parvati on Shiva and became the Destroyer's father-in-law. He is Sarvesha and does not seek. In connection with the task of destroying Taraka, Brahma strove to get him to ask. Shankara is supreme among *yogi*s and was not eager to take a wife. Since Vidhatri beseeched him, the divinity agreed to accept your daughter. Your daughter tormented herself through austerities and he made a pledge to her. Thus, there are two reasons behind the Indra among *yogi*s agreeing to marry." Hearing the words of the *rishi*s, Himalaya laughed. But he was also slightly frightened. Therefore, when he spoke, it was full of great humility. Himalaya replied, "I do not see any royal possessions with Shiva. He has no prosperity he can depend on. He does not possess relatives and kin. He is a *yogi* who is not attached, and I do not wish to bestow my daughter on him. You are the sons of the one who created the *Veda*s. Please tell me your decision. If a father does not bestow his daughter on a groom who is worthy, as a result of desire, confusion, fear or greed, he is destroyed and goes to hell. That is the reason I do not wish to bestow my daughter on the wielder of the trident. O *rishi*s! However, whatever be your decision, let that be carried out." O lord among sages! Hearing Himalaya's words, Vasishtha, accomplished in the use of words, spoke to him.'"

'"Vasishtha said, "O lord of mountains! Listen to my words. They will bring benefit in every possible way. They are not against *dharma*. In truth, they will ensure happiness in this world and in the next one. O mountain! Whether it is in customary practice or whether it is in the *Veda*s, words are of three types. Using his pure insight of *jnana*, a person who knows the sacred texts knows all this. Using his sharp intelligence, an enemy utters words that are beautiful to hear now, though they lead to falsehood and harm later. Such words are never beneficial. A person who is devoted to *dharma* and is compassionate will utter words that cause displeasure now but lead to happy consequences later. He uses these to kindle understanding in a friend. But the best kind of words, those that are desirable, are those which are like nectar as soon as they are heard and lead to happiness for all time to come. They are beneficial and have truth as their essence. O mountain! Those who know *nitishastra*[988] thus say that there are three kinds of speech. Among these three types, tell me which kind of speech you wish to hear. Shankara, lord of the gods, is devoid of the prosperity Brahma created. His mind is immersed in the ocean of true *jnana*. When he is the lord of *jnana* and bliss, why should he hanker after objects created by Brahma? A householder bestows his daughter on a person who possesses riches and a kingdom. If a father bestows a daughter on a miserable person, he is like a person who kills his daughter. Since Kubera is his servant, who takes Shankara to be a miserable person? Through the pastime of bending his eyebrows, he can create. He is the creator, preserver and destroyer. He is the *nirguna paramatman*. He is the supreme lord, beyond Prakriti. He has three forms. For purposes of creation, he is Vidhatri. Known as Brahma, Vishnu and Hara, he creates, preserves and destroys. Brahma resides in Brahma's world. Vishnu resides on the shores of the ocean of milk. Hara has a home in Kailasa. All these are Shiva's manifestations. Prakriti, originating from Shiva, also has three forms. In her pastimes, she creates these forms, though she has many other manifestations too. As the goddess of speech, she has originated from the divinity's mouth. Originating from his chest, she is in

[988] Texts on good policy.

the form of Lakshmi, with every kind of prosperity. Shivaa's energy is manifest in the power of all *devas*. She destroyed all the *danavas* and bestowed prosperity on *devas*. In another *kalpa*, she was born from the womb of Daksha's wife. Named Sati, she obtained Hara. Daksha bestowed her on him. Hearing criticism of her husband, she used *yoga* to give up her body. Through Mena's womb, that Shivaa has now been born to you. O mountain! From one birth to another birth, Shivaa is Shiva's wife. From one *kalpa* to another *kalpa*, she assumes the form of intelligence and is the supreme mother of those who possess *jnana*. She is always born in the form of Siddhaa and confers *siddhi*. *Siddhi* is her form. Hara himself devotedly wears the ashes and bones from Sati's funeral pyre. Therefore, voluntarily bestow this auspicious one on Hara. Otherwise, she will go the place where her beloved is and bestow herself. Witnessing the innumerable hardships your daughter went through, the lord of *devas* assumed the form of a *brahmana* and went to the place where she was performing austerities. He made a pledge to her. Having bestowed a boon on her, he returned to his own residence. O mountain! That was the reason why Shambhu sought Shivaa from you. Both of you possessed devotion towards Shiva in your hearts and accepted the proposal. O lord of mountains! How has this opposite view come upon you? When he was beseeched by *devas*, the lord quickly sent us, the *rishis* and Arundhati, to your presence. We were to instruct you, so that you might bestow Parvati on Rudra. O mountain! If you do this, you will obtain great happiness. O Indra among mountains! Even if you do not voluntarily bestow Shivaa on Shiva, the power of destiny will ensure that their marriage takes place. O son! At the end of the austerities, Shankara bestowed that boon on Shivaa. Nothing contrary to Ishvara's pledge can be thought of. O mountain! In this entire world, if a person devoted to Shiva makes a promise, it can never be violated. What need be said about Isha himself?

In his pastimes, the great Indra single-handedly sliced off the wings of mountains. In her pastimes, Parvati shattered Meru's summit. O lord of mountains! One should not destroy all one's riches for a single person. Indeed, the eternal *shruti* texts state that for the sake of the family, a single individual should be cast aside. When fear presented itself on account of a *brahmana*, King Anaranya protected his prosperity by bestowing his own daughter on the *brahmana*. Scared that the *brahmana* might invoke a curse, his *gurus*, the best among his kin and people who knew about good policy and the sacred texts immediately made him understand. O king of mountains! You should also bestow your daughter on Shiva and save the large number of your relatives and your family. You should also do this for the gods." Hearing Vasishtha's words, he smiled outwardly, but his heart was dejected. He asked about that king's account. Himalaya asked, "O *brahmana*! In what lineage was King Arananya born? How did he bestow his daughter and save his entire prosperity?" Hearing the mountain's words, Vasishtha, pleased in his intelligence, told the mountain about the king's account. This brings happiness.'"'

Chapter 129-3.3(34) (Anaranya's Conduct)

' '' 'Vasishtha said, "King Anaranya, lord of men, originated from the lineage of the fourteenth Manu, known as Indra Savarni. Anaranya, best among kings, was a lord of the earth who ruled over the seven *dvipa*s. He was powerful and was the son of Mangalaranya. He was particularly devoted to Shambhu. With Bhrigu as the priest, he performed one hundred sacrifices. Though the gods offered him the status of Indra, he did not accept it. O Himalaya! One hundred sons were born to him. He also had a beautiful daughter named Padma, resembling the one who makes her home on the lotus.[989] He loved his one hundred sons, but he loved his daughter even more. O supreme among mountains! The king's feelings towards her were like that. The king had five beloved queens, whom he loved more than his own life. All these wives possessed every kind of fortune. In her father's house, the daughter attained the prime of youth. He sent letters, so that he might obtain an excellent groom for her."""'

'"""'"On one occasion, the *rishi* Pippalada was eager to return to his own hermitage. In that desolate spot for performing austerities, he saw a *gandharva*. He was with his wife and his mind was immersed in the ocean of *shringara rasa*. Skilled in *kama shastra*[990] and full of love, he was amusing himself. Seeing this, the tiger among sages was filled with desire. His mind was no longer interested in austerities. Instead, his thoughts turned towards obtaining a wife. This is what happened to the sage Pippalada. Some time passed, but his mind was churned by desire. On one occasion, the lord among sages went to the river Pushpabhadra[991] to have a bath. He saw a maiden Padma, as beautiful as Padma.[992] The sage asked the people who were around, 'Who is this maiden?' Scared of being cursed, the people bowed down and replied. The people said, 'She is Anaranya's daughter, and her name is Padma. She is like another Rama. This beautiful lady is a store of qualities and the best among kings have sought her.' The sage heard the words of the people, who spoke the truth. His mind was agitated, and he desired her. Having bathed, the sage

---

[989] Lakshmi.

[990] *Kama shastra* texts are about love and sensual pleasures.

[991] A river that is also known as Pushpavaha.

[992] The maiden's name was Padma. The second Padma means Lakshmi.

followed the norms and worshipped his *ishta deva*,[993] Shiva. O
mountain! Desiring her, he went to Anaranya's assembly, so as
to seek alms. On seeing the sage, the king was filled with great
fear and prostrated himself. He offered him *madhuparka* and
other things and devotedly worshipped him. In his desire, the
sage accepted everything and asked for the maiden. The lord of
the earth was silent and was unable to say anything. The sage
said, 'O lord among kings! Give me this maiden. Otherwise, in
an instant, I will reduce everything to ashes.' All the attendants
were overwhelmed by the sage's energy. The king and his
attendants looked at the *brahmana*, who was suffering from
old age, and wept. Hearing his words and unable to decide
what should be done, all the queens wept. The chief queen, the
maiden's mother, was overwhelmed by grief and lost her senses.
The minds of all the sons were also filled with sorrow. O lord
of mountains! Everyone associated with the king was thus filled
with grief. At that time, a wise *brahmana*, best among *guru*s,
arrived before the king, along with the intelligent *purohita*. The
king prostrated himself in front of them and wept. He told
them everything and quickly asked them about what should
be done. The king's *guru* and the learned *brahmana*, who was
the priest, were both knowledgeable about the sacred texts on
good policy. They made the king, the grief-stricken queens and
the maiden, who was the king's daughter, understand. The
instructed him about excellent policy that would ensure benefit
to everyone. The *guru* and the priest said, 'O immensely wise
king! Listen to our beneficial words. Do not grieve. Along with
the family members, turn your minds towards the sacred texts.
O king! Today, or at the end of a year, the maiden must be
bestowed on a worthy groom, a *brahmana* or someone else
who is distinguished. In the three worlds, we do not perceive a
recipient as worthy as a *brahmana*. Bestow your daughter on

[993] Desired god, tutelary deity.

the sage and save all your prosperity. O king! If all prosperity is going to be destroyed on account of a single person, a person should give up that person and save everything else, unless that person happens to be someone who has sought refuge.' Hearing the words of the wise ones, the king lamented repeatedly. However, he bestowed his ornamented daughter on that Indra among sages. O mountain! Following the norms of marriage, the sage accepted the maiden Padma, who was like Padma herself. Happy, he returned to his own abode. Having bestowed his daughter on an old man, the king gave up everything. His mind was full of distress. However, he collected himself and went to the forest to perform austerities. O mountain! When her beloved husband left for the forest, the beautiful chief queen grieved over her husband and her daughter and gave up her life. Without the king, the revered sons and the servants lost their senses. Thinking that the king was dead, all the other people grieved. Having gone to the forest, Anaranya performed austerities for Shankara. Having devotedly worshipped him, he went to Shiva's world and was freed from all ailments. The king's eldest son was named Kirtimat and he was devoted to *dharma*. He ruled over the kingdom and protected the subjects, as if they were his sons. O mountain! I have thus told you about Anaranya's auspicious account. He bestowed his daughter, saved his lineage and obtained all the riches. O king of mountains! You should also bestow your daughter on Shiva, save your entire lineage and make all the gods subject to your control."'"

Chapter 130-3.3(35) (Padma and Pippalada)

' "Narada said, 'O father! After hearing about Anaranya's conduct and about how he bestowed his daughter, what did the excellent mountain do? Please tell me that.'"

'"Brahma replied, 'The lord of mountains heard about Anaranya's conduct and about how he bestowed his daughter. He joined his hands in salutation and again asked Vasishtha. The lord of mountains said, "O Vasishtha! O tiger among sages! O Brahma's son! O ocean of compassion! You have described Anaranya's extremely wonderful conduct to me. Anaranya's daughter obtained the sage Pippalada as her husband. Her conduct brings delight. What did she do after that?"'"

'""Vasishtha replied, 'Pippalada was supreme among sages, but he was exceedingly old in age. He returned to his own hermitage, accompanied by the lady who was Anaranya's daughter. Extremely happy, the ascetic resided there. He was not excessively dissolute. O supreme among mountains! In that forest, he always followed his own *dharma*. Anaranya's daughter also faithfully served the sage in thoughts, words and deeds, just like Lakshmi serving Narayana.'"'"

'""On one occasion, the one with the excellent smiles was going to the celestial river to have a bath. Along the path, she saw Dharma, who had used his *maya* to assume a man's form. He was astride a chariot studded with jewels and he was adorned with many kinds of ornaments. He was handsome and in the prime of youth. His radiance was like that of Kamadeva. On seeing the beautiful Padma, the lord Vrisha[994] spoke to her. He wished to determine the inner thoughts of the sage's wife. Dharma said, "O beautiful one! You are as beautiful as Lakshmi. You deserve a king. You are extremely young and beautiful. Youth is fixed in you. The sage Pippalada is old, suffering from old age. O one with the beautiful limbs! I am telling you the truth. In your presence, he lacks any radiance. The *brahmana* is engaged in austerities. He is without pity and

[994] Dharma.

wishes to die. Abandon him and look at me. I am an Indra
among kings and am skilled in intercourse. I am afflicted by
Smara. O beautiful one! A lady obtains this auspicious beauty
as a consequence of what she has done in her past life. All
that becomes successful only when one embraces a man of
taste. I am loved by one thousand beautiful women. I am
accomplished in *kama shastra*. O beloved! Abandon your
husband and make me your servant. Find pleasure with me
in secluded groves, beautiful mountains and the banks of
rivers. Render your birth successful." Having said this, he got
down from his own chariot. He was eager to clasp her by the
hand. The lady, devoted to her husband, spoke to him. Padma
answered, "Go far away. O wicked king! Go far away. If you
look at me with eyes of desire, you will be instantly destroyed.
Pippalada is best among sages. His body has been purified
through austerities. How can I abandon him and serve a person
who is lascivious and addicted to desire, conquered by women?
If one touches a person conquered by women, all good merits
are destroyed. A person conquered by women is extremely
wicked. His sight is sinful. Even if a man constantly performs
virtuous rites, if he is conquered by women, he remains impure.
All the ancestors, *deva*s and humans censure him. If a person's
mind is firmly fixed on women, what use are *jnana*, great
austerities, oblations, worship, learning and donations to him?
Your sentiments towards me should have been those towards a
mother, but you have addressed me in words befitting a wife.
Therefore, because of my curse, you will be destroyed within a
short while." Hearing the virtuous lady's curse, Dharma gave
up his form as a king. The lord of *deva*s assumed his own form
and trembled as he spoke. Dharma said, "O mother! Know
that I am Dharma, the *guru* of all *guru*s who possess *jnana*.
O virtuous one! My mind is such that I always look upon
another person's wife as a mother. Desiring to know your inner
thoughts, I came to your presence. Though I knew what was

in your mind, destiny goaded me. O virtuous one! By seeking to chastise me, you have not done anything contrary. Ishvara has determined that those who deviate from the right path must be punished. He is the supreme one, who alone is capable of bestowing joy and misery on everyone. He is responsible for prosperity and adversity. I prostrate myself before that Shiva. He is the one who determines friendship, enmity, love and quarrels. He is the creator, and he is the destroyer of this creation. I prostrate myself before that Shiva. In ancient times, he is the one who made milk white, made water cool and gave fire the power to burn. I prostrate myself before that Shiva. He is the one who originally created Prakriti, Mahat and the others, Brahma, Vishnu and Mahesha. I prostrate myself before that Shiva." Having said this, Dharma, the *guru* of the universe, stood in front of her. He was satisfied at her devotion towards her husband but did not say anything.'""'"

'""""'O mountain! Padma, the virtuous lady who was the king's daughter and was loved by Pippalada, was surprised to know that this was Dharma. Padma replied, "O Dharma! You are the witness to all the deeds that are performed. O lord! To know what was in my mind, why did you resort to deception? O *brahmana*! Because of everything I have done, no crime attaches to me. O Vrisha! Because of my feminine nature and because I did not know, I have cursed you in vain. I am thinking about what can be done now. When my mind settles down, perhaps it will occur to me. The sky, the directions and the winds can be destroyed, but a virtuous lady's curse is never destroyed. O king of *deva*s! In *satya yuga*, all the time, night and day, you were radiant with all your four legs, like the moon on a full moon night.[995] O best among gods! In *tretya yuga*, one of the feet will be destroyed. O lord! You will lose

[995] As *yuga*s progress, Dharma progressively loses one of its feet (one quarter). Here, this is attributed to Padma's curse.

a second foot in *dvapara yuga* and a third in *kali yuga*. At the end of *kali yuga*, all your legs will be destroyed. When *satya yuga* arrives, you will be complete again. In *satya yuga*, you will be pervasive, but in the others, only partially. This will be the respective arrangements in the *yugas*. Let these words of mine be true and bring pleasure to you. O lord! I will leave to serve my husband. You should go to your own residence." Hearing her words, Vrisha was satisfied. Vidhatri's son spoke to the virtuous lady who had spoken to him. Dharma said, "As a result of your devotion towards your husband, you are blessed. O chaste lady! May you be well. To save your husband, accept this boon. Let your husband become young. Let him be devoted to *dharma* and accomplished in intercourse. Let him possess all the qualities and be handsome. Let him be eloquent in speech and let his youth always remain stable. Let him live forever, with a lifespan greater than that of Markandeya. Let him possess riches more than those of Kubera. Let his prosperity be greater than that of Shakra. Let him be Shiva's devotee, equal to Hari himself. Let him be a greater *siddha* than Kapila. Let him be Brihaspati's equal in intelligence and Vidhatri's equal in serenity. As long as you are alive, you will share in your husband's good fortune. O lady! You will be fortunate in this way and your youth will be steady. You will have ten sons who will possess the qualities. They will live forever and will surpass your husband. There is no doubt about this. O virtuous lady! Your home will possess every kind of prosperity. It will always be radiant and will surpass Kubera's residence." O supreme among mountains! Dharma said this and stood there. She performed *pradakshina*, prostrated herself and returned to her own residence. Pronouncing benedictions over her, Dharma left for his own home. In every assembly he went to, he praised Padma. In private, she always sported with her husband, who had become young. Later, she had sons who exceeded her husband in qualities. The couple obtained every kind of happiness. In this world and in the next world, they found peace and every kind of happiness was enhanced. O Indra among mountains! This ancient history about the couple has been recounted to you and you have heard it lovingly and affectionately. Using your intelligence, bestow your daughter, Parvati, on Ishvara. O Indra among mountains! Along with your wife, Mena, shed the wicked sentiment. In a week's time, there will be an extremely auspicious and rare moment. The lord of the *lagna* will be in his *lagna*. Chandra and his son[996] will be in a happy conjunction with Rohini *nakshatra*. The moon and the stars will be in pure states. Monday in the month of Margashirsha will be free of all taints. All the good planets will be auspicious, and the bad planets will not cast an inauspicious glance. If bestowed on a good husband at this time, her husband will live for long and she will have good fortune. O mountain! Your daughter, Girija, is Jagadamba Ishvari, who is the original Prakriti. Bestow her on the father of the universe and be successful in your objective."'''''

"'Brahma concluded, 'O tiger among sages! Vasishtha, supreme among those who possess *jnana*, said this and stopped. He remembered Shiva, the lord who engages in many kinds of pastimes.'''

Chapter 131-3.3(36) (Words of the *Saptarshi*s)

' "Brahma said, 'Hearing Vasishtha's words, Himalaya, his wife and his companions were amazed. The lord of mountains spoke to the mountains. Himalaya said, "O Meru, king of mountains! O Sahya! O Gandhamadana! O Mandara! O Mainaka! O Vindhya! O all the Indras among

[996] Budha (Mercury).

mountains! Listen to my words. This is what Vasishtha has
said. We must reflect on what should be done. Determine
everything in your minds and tell me." Hearing his words, the
mountains happily made their determination. With Sumeru as
the foremost, they spoke to Himalaya. The mountains said,
"What is the point of consultation now? One should act.
The immensely fortunate one has been born to accomplish
a task for *deva*s. Shivaa, who has taken an *avatara*, must be
bestowed on Shiva. She has worshipped Rudra and Rudra has
also said this." Hearing the words of Meru and the others,
Himachala was very happy. Within her heart, Girija smiled.
Using many reasons, Arundhati made Mena understand. She
used many words and cited many historical accounts. Finally,
Menaka, the mountain's wife, understood and was pleased in
her mind. She fed the sages, Arundhati and the mountains and
then ate. Having obtained *jnana*, the supreme mountain served
the sages. He was pleased and happy, his confusion having
been destroyed. He joined his hands in salutation and spoke.
Himachala said, "O immensely fortunate *saptarshi*s! Listen
to my words. Hearing everything about Shiva and Shivaa's
account, my confusion has gone. Everything that I possess, my
body, my wife Mena, my sons and my daughter, my prosperity
and my success, belong to Shiva and not to anyone else." Saying
this, he looked lovingly at his daughter. He adorned her limbs
with ornaments and then placed these in the laps of the *rishi*s.
Delighted, the king of mountains spoke to the *rishi*s again. "I
have made up my mind that this is the share I am going to
give to him." The *rishi*s replied, "O mountain! Shankara is a
mendicant, and you are the one who is going to give. The alms
are Devi Parvati. What can be more wonderful than that? The
ends of your peaks are going to follow this kind of course. O
lord of all the mountains! You are supreme in every possible
way. You are blessed." Having said this, the sages, free of all
blemishes, pronounced benedictions over the maiden and said,

"May you bring pleasure to Shiva." They touched her with their hands and said, "May you be fortunate. Just as the moon waxes during *shukla paksha*, may your qualities increase." Saying this, all the sages happily gave the mountain flowers and fruit, settling the matter.'"'

'"'The pleasant-faced Arundhati delighted Mena. The extremely virtuous lady spoke to her about Shiva's qualities and tempted her. Following the customary practice of the world, excellent auspicious rites were performed, smearing the mountain's beard with turmeric paste and *kumkuma*. Having fixed an excellent *lagna*, on the fourth day, the contented sages congratulated each other and went to Shiva's presence. Having gone there, they bent down and praised Shiva with various hymns. Vasishtha and all the other sages spoke to Parameshvara. The *rishi*s said, "O lord of *deva*s! O Mahadeva! O Paramesha! O great lord! Cheerfully listen to our words, about what your servants have done. O Mahesha! Using many kinds of hymns and ancient accounts, we have made the king of mountains and Mena understand. There is no doubt about this. The Indra among mountains has given his word about bestowing Parvati and it will not be violated. Along with *deva*s and *gana*s, leave for the marriage. O Mahadeva! O lord! Leave swiftly for Himachala's house. For the sake of a son, follow the norms and marry Parvati." Mahesha was intent on following the customary practices of the world. Hearing their words, his mind was pleased. He smiled and spoke. Mahesha said, "O immensely fortunate ones! I have never heard about a marriage ceremony or seen one. You should specifically speak to me about the norms for this." They heard Mahesha's auspicious words, which were in conformity with customary practice. They smiled and replied to Sadashiva, lord of *deva*s. The *rishi*s said, "Specially invite Vishnu and his attendants. Cheerfully invite Brahma and his sons, *deva* Shatakratu, all the large number of *rishi*s, *yaksha*s, *gandharva*s, *kinnara*s,

*siddha*s, *vidyadhara*s and large numbers of *apsaras*. O lord!
Invite all the others affectionately. There is no doubt that they
will accomplish everything." Having said this, the seven *rishi*s
cheerfully took his leave. They left for their own respective
abodes, praising Shankara's conduct.'"'

Chapter 132-3.3(37) (Invitations and Arrival for the Wedding)

' ' "Narada said, 'O father! O wise one! Please show me
your compassion. When the *saptarshi*s departed,
please tell me what Mount Himalaya did.'"'

'"Brahma answered, 'O lord among sages! The seven sages
and Arundhati departed. I will tell you what Himachala did. He
took his leave of his brothers, Meru and the other mountains.
Along with his beloved sons, Himalaya, lord among mountains,
rejoiced. Extremely happy and full of joy, he requested his
own priest, Garga, to draw up the *lagna patrika*.[997] He had
this *patrika* and many kinds of objects, happily offered by his
relatives and himself, sent to Shiva. Those people went to Shiva
in Kailasa. They gave Shiva the *patrika* and applied the mark
of a *tilaka* on his forehead. The lord specially honoured them,
as is appropriate. All of them were delighted in their minds
and returned to the mountain's presence. The people who had
gone were particularly honoured by Mahesha. Seeing this, the
mountain was extremely happy, and his mind was delighted.
Rejoicing, he invited his own relatives. They brought joy and
arrived from all the different regions. Lovingly, he had objects
of gold fashioned. He collected many kinds of objects, required

---

[997] This sets out the *lagna* for the marriage. Stated simply, it is a
wedding invitation, with those auspicious details indicated.

for the marriage. Heaps of rice, parched and flattened rice, molasses, sugar and salt were collected. Tanks were constructed for milk, *ghee* and curd. There was barley and other kinds of grain, sweetmeats and sweetmeats in the shape of balls.[998] He had tanks constructed for *shashkulis*,[999] *svastikas*,[1000] sugar, sugar cane juice that tasted like *amrita*, *ghee* that would be offered into the fire and *asava*.[1001] Arrangements were made for cooking large amounts of extremely tasty rice. There were side dishes that would appeal to *gana*s and *deva*s. There were many kinds of priceless garments, purified in the fire. There were different types of gems and jewels and gold and silver. In the proper way, all these objects were gathered together. On an auspicious day, the mountain started the auspicious rites. The mountain's women performed the cleansing rites for Parvati. The *brahmana* women in the city observed the customary worldly practices. Adorning themselves in ornaments, they performed the auspicious rites. Having undertaken the auspicious rites first, there were many kinds of festivities. Cheerful in his mind, Himalaya also performed the auspicious rites. He was happy in every possible way and was eager for his relatives to arrive.'"'

'"'Meanwhile, the invited relatives arrived, along with their wives, sons and companions. O *devarshi*! Hear attentively about the mountains who came. This increases love towards Shiva, and I will describe it briefly. Mount Mandara is an abode of *deva*s. He has a large and divine form. Because of the many jewels, he was radiant, and he arrived with his companions. He had carefully gathered together many jewels and great gems. He was handsome, attired in excellent garments and ornamented.

[998] Respectively, *pishtaka* and *ladduka*.
[999] A kind of rice gruel.
[1000] A kind of cake.
[1001] A type of liquor.

He was resplendent in every possible way and came with his wife and sons. Astachala[1002] is divine in his *atman*. Generous in intelligence, he arrived with many kinds of objects as gifts. Udayachala,[1003] extremely handsome, happily arrived, bringing with him gems and jewels. Malaya, king among mountains, arrived with his family. He was very happy, and his excellent companions came with him. The mountain named Durdura, divine in form, cheerfully arrived with his wife and many companions. O son! Nishada was extremely radiant and went to Himachala's house. His mind was delighted, and he arrived with his companions. The immensely fortunate Mount Gandhamadana affectionately went to Himachala's house, with his wives and sons. Karavira, full of great prosperity, and Mahendra, best among mountains, went to Himalaya. Pariyatra is a store of gems and jewels. Happy in his mind and extremely radiant, he arrived with his companions, sons and wives. Krouncha, king among mountains, was accompanied by a large retinue of attendants. He went to Himalaya with his family and companions. The best among mountains brought many gifts. Mount Purushottama came with his companions. He went to Mount Himachala with great gifts. Full of joy, Nila playfully went to Himalaya's house. He was with his sons and women and brought various objects. Trikuta,[1004] Chitrakuta,[1005] Venkata,[1006] Shrigiri,[1007] Gokamukhi and Narada[1008] arrived in Himalaya's house. The auspicious Vindhya, best among

---

[1002] Mountain behind which the sun sets.

[1003] The sun rises from behind Mount Udayachala.

[1004] In Lanka.

[1005] This range extends beyond Uttar Pradesh and Madhya Pradesh.

[1006] Venkatadri/Venkatachalam, near Tirumala in Chittoor district.

[1007] Srisailam in Kurnool district.

[1008] Name of a mountain.

mountains happily arrived with his wife and sons, full of great
prosperity. Kalanjara, the great mountain, was filled with
great joy. With many companions, he happily went to Mount
Himalayas. Kailasa, the great mountain, was filled with great
joy. He arrived, showing a favour to everyone, since the
lord resided atop him. O *brahmana*! There were many other
mountains from other *dvipa*s.[1009] All the mountains went to
Himachala's house. O sage! The mountains arrived since
they had been invited earlier. All of them happily arrived, for
Shiva and Shivaa's marriage. All the rivers arrived, adorned in
many kinds of ornaments. All of them, Shona, Bhadra and the
others, were extremely radiant and very happy. They arrived
for Shiva and Shivaa's marriage. They were divine in form and
happily arrived for Shiva and Shivaa's marriage—Godavari,
Yamuna, Brahmastri[1010] and Venika. To attend the marriage
of Shiva and Shivaa, they came to Mount Himalaya. Ganga
was extremely happy and was bedecked in many ornaments.
Divine in form, she went to Shiva and Shivaa's marriage.
Narmada is supreme among rivers and is Rudra's daughter.
Delighted and full of great joy, she quickly went to Shiva and
Shivaa's marriage. From every direction, everyone arrived in
Himachala's house. The divine city became full and dazzled
in every possible way. There were great festivities. Banners
fluttered on the many gates. There were many types of radiant
canopies to guard against the sun. Full of joy and affection,
Himalaya honoured and welcomed them in various ways, as
was due to each. He arranged separate residences for them.
They were completely satisfied with the many kinds of objects
that were offered.'"

[1009] There are seven *dvipa*s. What has been described so far is
from Jambudvipa.
[1010] Meaning Sarasvati.

Chapter 133-3.3(38) (Construction of the Pavilion)

' '' **B**rahma said, 'O supreme among sages! After this, Himalaya, lord of mountains, happily went about decorating his city in wonderful ways for the great festivities. The roads were cleaned and sprinkled with water. They were decorated and looked extremely radiant. Plantain trees were planted, and auspicious objects placed at every door. An arena was constructed, with plantain trees as pillars. Cords were used to bind cloth around them, and they were decorated with leaves from trees. The gates were extremely radiant, with garlands of *malati* flowers.[1011] Radiant, sacred and auspicious objects were placed in the four directions. Full of great joy on account of his daughter, the Indra among mountains carried out all these things. In determining appropriate auspicious rites, the immensely powerful Garga was given prime importance. He[1012] affectionately invited Vishvakarma and had him construct an extremely large pavilion, with a beautiful altar and other things. O divine *rishi*! It extended for ten thousand *yojana*s. It was full of wonderful objects and possessed many auspicious signs. All the agreeable mobile and immobile objects could be seen inside this. It was extraordinary in every possible way and there were many wonderful articles. Sometimes, the mobile objects depicted surpassed the immobile ones. Sometimes, the immobile objects depicted surpassed the mobile ones. Sometimes, spots with water surpassed those with land. In other places, it was the other way round. Even learned people could not distinguish what was land and what was water. In places, there were artificial lions. In others, there were artificial arrays of cranes.

[1011] A kind of jasmine with white flowers.
[1012] Himalaya.

In places, there were extremely beautiful artificial peacocks. In some places, artificial women danced, along with artificial men. Looking at these artificial creations, people were confused. In this way, there were beautiful artificial doorkeepers. With bows raised in their hands, they were immobile, but resembled the mobile and real ones. An extremely wonderful artificial image of Mahalakshmi was created and placed at the gate. She possessed all the auspicious signs and it seemed as if she had herself emerged from the ocean of milk. There were artificial elephants and horses, fashioned to resemble real ones. There were artificial horse-riders and elephant-riders too. There were charioteers on chariots, full of great wonders. There were other vehicles and foot soldiers. But all these were artificial. O sage! In this way, Vishvakarma created these to confuse people. The minds of *deva*s and sages were delighted at this. O sage! Nandi was designed, to stand there as a great doorkeeper. But it was an image. He was as pure as crystal and was just like the real Nandi. There was the immensely divine Pushpaka, adorned with jewels. It was radiant and extremely beautiful, decorated with pure new sprouts, and the immortals were seated on it. On the left, there were two sparkling elephants, saffron in hue. They were extremely radiant and possessed four tusks each. They were sixty years of age and caused dread. In that way, there were two extremely radiant horses, as bright as the sun. They were divine, adorned with whisks. They were decorated with divine ornaments. There were the armoured guardians of the worlds, adorned with the best of jewels. Vishvakarma created each *deva*, exactly as he truly was. He did this with all the *rishi*s too, Bhrigu and others, stores of austerities. He fashioned other gods and other *siddha*s. Vishnu and all his companions were there, including the one known as Garuda. All these were artificially created and were extremely wonderful and handsome. O Narada! I was also artificially created, surrounded by my sons, the *Veda*s and the *siddha*s.

I was reciting hymns. With his attendants, Shakra was astride the elephant, Airavata. But he was artificially created and resembled the full moon. O *devarshi*! What is the need to speak a lot? Urged by Himalaya, Vishvakarma created all the various gods. In this way, he created a pavilion that was divine in form. It was large and full of many wonders, confusing the *devas*. Instructed by the lord of mountains, the immensely intelligent Vishvakarma carefully crafted residences for the gods and others to dwell in. There were large and divine couches, extremely radiant and extremely wonderful. They caused pleasure and Vishvakarma created these. In an instant, he fashioned the wonderful seven worlds. These were radiant and divine and were for Svayambhu's[1013] residence. In this way, the extremely sparkling and divine Vaikuntha was constructed for Vishnu. He constructed it in an instant and it was full of great wonders. In that way, he constructed a divine, wonderful and excellent residence of the lord of the immortals. Vishvakarma created it such that is possessed every kind of prosperity. He constructed beautiful residences for the guardians of the worlds. They were divine, wonderful and large and brought them pleasure. In that way, one by one, he constructed colourful residences for all the immortals. Vishvakarma was extremely intelligent and had obtained a great boon from Shambhu. To satisfy Shiva, he constructed all these in an instant. In that way, he constructed an extremely radiant, supreme and wonderful residence for Shambhu, worshipped by the best of *devas*. It sparkled greatly and possessed all of Girisha's signs. Vishvakarma thus created Shivaloka. It was greatly resplendent and full of great wonders. It was extraordinary and he did this to satisfy Shiva. In this way, following customary practices, everything was done. This having been done, Himachala happily waited for Shambhu's arrival. O *devarshi*! I have thus told you the complete account

[1013] Brahma's.

of what Himalaya did. This brings joy. What else do you wish to hear?'"

Chapter 134-3.3(39) (*Devas* Arrive)

❝❝Narada said, 'O Vidhatri! O father! O immensely wise one! O Vishnu's disciple! I bow down to you. O ocean of compassion! In truth, you have made us hear about a wonderful account. I now wish to hear about the conduct of the one who wears the moon on his crest and about his extremely auspicious marriage. It destroys heaps of sins. When he received the auspicious *patrika*, what did Mahadeva do? Make me hear about the divine account of Shankara, the *paramatman*.'"

'"Brahma replied, 'O child! O immensely wise one! Hear about Shankara's great glory and about what Mahadeva did when he received the auspicious *patrika*. Shambhu happily accepted the auspicious *patrika*. Pleased in his mind, the lord smiled and honoured them. Following the norms, he read it and accepted the proposal. Showing a great deal of respect, he also informed other people. He said, "O sages! You have carried out the auspicious task properly. I have accepted the proposal of marriage and you must come to my wedding." Hearing Shambhu's words, they were delighted and prostrated themselves before him. Having circumambulated him and praising their great good fortune, they returned to their own abodes. O sage! After this, Shambhu, lord of *deva*s, immediately remembered you. The lord engages in great pastimes and was following the customary practices of the world. Praising your great good fortune, you arrived, full of joy. You lowered your shoulders humbly and prostrated yourself, joining your hands in salutation. O sage! You repeatedly praised and worshipped

him with exclamations of "Victory". Praising your good
fortune, you asked for instructions. Pleased in his mind,
Shambhu demonstrated that he was following customary
worldly practices. He used auspicious words of affection to
address you, the noble sage. Shiva said, "O best among sages!
Listen lovingly. I am speaking to you because you are loved by
me. You are like the royal crest jewel among all my devotees.
Following your instructions, Devi Parvati undertook great
austerities. Satisfied by her, I granted her the boon that I would
become her husband. I am subservient to my devotees, and
I will marry her. The *saptarshi*s have determined the perfect
lagna. O Narada! It will occur seven days from now. Following
the practices of the world, I will arrange for great festivities."
O son! Hearing the words of Shankara, the *paramatman*, your
mind was pleased. You bowed before the lord and addressed
him in the following words. Narada said, "It is my view that
you follow the vow of being subservient to your devotees.
You have acted properly by granting Parvati the wish that
was in her mind. O lord! Please tell me about a task that is
fit for me to carry out. Knowing that I am your own servant,
show me your compassion. I prostrate myself before you." O
lord among sages! Addressed by you in this way, Shambhu
Shankara, affectionate towards his devotees, was pleased in his
mind and replied lovingly to you. Shiva said, "O sage! Follow
my words and invited Vishnu and the other *deva*s, the sages,
*siddha*s and everyone else. Full of enthusiasm, let them all
come, full of radiance. Showing respect to my words and out of
love, let them come with their wives, sons and companions. O
sage! Those who do not come to the great festival of marriage,
*deva*s and others, are not my own and can be disregarded."
Dear to Shankara, you accepted Isha's command. O sage!
You left quickly, so as to invite everyone. O supreme sage!
O Narada! You swiftly carried out your duty as a messenger
and returned to Shambhu's presence, waiting for his command.

Shiva remained there, eagerly waiting for everyone to arrive. In every direction, his own *gana*s celebrated the festival with singing and dancing.'"'

"''At this time, attiring himself in excellent garments, Achyuta quickly arrived in Kailasa, along with his own attendants. Along with his wife and followers, he happily prostrated himself before Shiva, full of devotion. Having obtained his permission, pleased in his mind, he remained there, in an excellent residence. With my own companions, I also came to Kailasa quickly, happy. Along with my companions, I joyfully prostrated myself before the lord and remained there. Indra and the other guardians of the world arrived, along with their companions. All of them were ornamented and arrived for the festival, accompanied by their wives. The sages, *naga*s, *siddha*s and minor divinities arrived. Others who had been invited came for the festivities. Rejoicing, Maheshvara separately honoured and welcomed all those who had come, immortals and others. There were extremely great and wonderful festivities in Kailasa. As is appropriate, the celestial women danced. O sage! At this time, Vishnu and the others who had come desired to arrange everything for Shambhu's wedding procession. All of us were like instruments and followed Shiva's command. All of us served Shiva and carried out his tasks. Delighted, the seven Matrikas carried out the appropriate tasks for dressing Shiva. O best among sages! He possesses natural garments and ornaments. Following his wishes, they became extremely radiant. Approaching him, the moon took the place of a crown. His beautiful third eye became the auspicious *tilaka* mark. O sage! Two serpents came to assume the form of his earrings and these earrings were studded with many gems. The serpents that were on his other limbs became ornaments on those limbs. They were extremely beautiful and were studded with many gems. The ash on his limbs turned into sandalwood paste. The hide of the elephant became a beautiful and divine girdle. All of these assumed such handsome forms. It is impossible for words to describe them. Ishvara himself possessed every kind of prosperity. All the gods, *danavas*, *nagas*, birds, *apsaras* and *maharshis* approached Shiva and joyfully proclaimed that the great festivities had started. All of them said, "Go! O Mahadeva! O Maheshvara! Leave for the marriage with Girija Mahadevi. Show us your compassion." Vishnu possessed *vijnana*. Pleased in his mind, he devotedly prostrated himself before Shankara. Using appropriate words, he proposed. Vishnu said, "O lord of *devas*! O Mahadeva! O one who is affectionate towards those who seek refuge! You carry out tasks for your own devotees. O lord! Please listen to what I have to say. O Shambhu! O Shankara! You should carry out your marriage with the daughter of the lord of the mountains in accordance with the norms laid down in the *grihya sutras*. O Hara! You should perform your marriage following those rules. They will then become extremely famous in the worlds. Following the *dharma* of the lineage, construct a pavilion and carry out a *nandimukha* ceremony.[1014] O lord! If you lovingly do this, you will establish your own fame in the world." Shambhu Parameshvara was thus addressed by Vishnu. Devoted to the customary practices of the world, he performed all those rites. Given the right by him, I, lovingly and affectionately, performed all the appropriate rites. I was aided by the sages—Kashyapa, Atri, Vasishtha, Goutama, the *guru* Bhaguri, Kanva, Brihaspati, Shakti, Jamadagni, Parashara, Markandeya, Shilapaka, Arunapala, Akritashrama, Agastya, Chyavana, Garga, the great sage Shilada, Dadhichi, Upamanyu, Bharadvaja, Akritavrana, Pippalada, Kushika, Koutsa and Vyasa, along with his disciples. There were many others who had come to Shiva's presence. Following what I

[1014] *Shraddha* ceremony for ancestors, undertaken before an auspicious rite like a marriage.

said, they performed the appropriate rites. All of them were accomplished in the *Veda*s and the *Vedanga*s and knew about the rites spoken about in the *Veda*s. To protect Mahesha, they performed all the auspicious rites. Many hymns were recited from the *Rig Veda*, *Yajur Veda* and *Sama Veda*. All the *rishi*s happily undertook many other auspicious rites. Instructed by Shambu and me, they lovingly worshipped the planets. The gods were worshipped in the pavilion, so that all impediments might be pacified. Shiva was greatly satisfied that everything had been performed in the proper way, following customary rites and the rites of the *Veda*s. Happy, he bowed down to the *brahmana*s.""

""Sarveshvara then placed the *brahmana*s and *deva*s at the front. Rejoicing, he left Kailasa, the excellent mountain. Once outside Mount Kailasa, along with *deva*s and *brahmana*s, the lord happily stopped, accepting many kinds of offerings. *Deva*s and others undertook great festivities there. To satisfy Mahesha, there was singing and dancing and the playing of musical instruments.""

Chapter 135-3.3(40) (The Marriage Procession)

" "Brahma said, 'Shambhu summoned Nandi and all the other *gana*s. He happily told them to go with him. Shiva said, "With me, you will go to the mountain's city. Let a few *gana*s remain here and undertake great festivities here." Thus instructed, the leaders of *gana*s cheerfully emerged, taking their forces with them. I will tell you a little bit about this. Along with Shiva, Shankhakarna, leader of *gana*s, left for Himachala's city with one crore *gana*s. In those great festivities, Kekaraksha took ten crore *gana*s. Vikrita, leader of *gana*s, took eight crore *gana*s. Vishakha, leader of *gana*s, took four crore *gana*s. Parijata, bull among *gana*s, took nine crores. The handsome Sarvantaka and Vikritanana took sixty crores each. Dundubha, leader of *gana*s, had eight crore *gana*s. The lord of *gana*s, known as Kapala, had five crores. O sage! The brave Sandaraka had six crore *gana*s. Kanduka and Kundaka had one crore each. Vishtambha, leader of *gana*s, had eight crore *gana*s. Pippala, leader of *gana*s, happily advanced with one thousand crores. O supreme sage! The brave Sandanaka, leader of *gana*s, had the same number. Aveshana, leader of *gana*s, had eight crores. Mahakesha, leader of *gana*s, advanced with one thousand crores. O sage! Kunda had twelve crores and so did Parvataka. The brave Chandratapana advanced with eight crores. Kala, Kalaka and Mahakala, leaders of *gana*s, had one hundred crores each. The one named Agnika had one crore. Agnimukha, leader of *gana*s, advanced with one crore *gana*s. Adityamurdha and Ghanavaha had one crore each. Sannaha and Kumuda, leaders of *gana*s, had one hundred crores each. Amogha and Kokila, leader of *gana*s, had one hundred crores each. Sumantra, leader of *gana*s, advanced with one crore *gana*s. Kakapadodara and Santanaka[1015] had six crores each. Mahabala, Madhupinga and Kokila each had nine crores. Nila had ninety crores and so did Purnabhadra. Chaturvakra had seven crores and Karana had twenty crores. Ahiromaka, leader of *gana*s, advanced with ninety crores. O Narada! Yajvasha, Shatamanyu and Meghamanyu, all leaders of *gana*s, separately advanced with one crore each. Kashthangushtha, leader of *gana*s, had sixty-four crores. Virupaksha, Sukesha, Vrishabha and Sanatana had the same number. There were Talaketu, Shadasya, Chanchasya, Sanatana, Samvartaka, Chaitra and the lord Lakulisha. O sage! There were also Lokantaka, Diptatma and Daityantaka. The divinity Bhringiriti, the handsome

---

[1015] There is no inconsistency since there was more than one leader with the same name.

Devadevapriya, Ashani and Bhanuka had sixty-four crores each. Along with Shiva, observing festivities, they went for Shiva's marriage. There were one thousand crore *bhuta*s and three crore *pramatha*s. Virabhadra had sixty-four crores and Romajana had three crores. In the great festivities connected with Shankara, Nandi and the other leaders of *gana*s advanced, surrounded by crores and crores, thousands, hundreds and twenties. Kshetrapala and Bhairava were surrounded by crores and crores of *gana*s. They happily advanced for the great festivities connected with Shankara's marriage. There were other innumerable leaders of *gana*s, immensely strong. Greatly rejoicing and full of enthusiasm, they joined the great festivities connected with Shankara. All of them had thousands of arms and wore matted hair and crowns. They were marked with the lines of the moon. They were blue in the throat and three-eyed. All of them wore *rudraksha* beads as ornaments and smeared their bodies with *bhasma*. They were ornamented with necklaces, earrings, bracelets and crowns. They resembled Brahma, Vishnu and Indra and possessed *anima* and the other qualities. Those lords of *gana*s shone like crores of suns. Some roamed around on earth. Others roamed around in the nether regions. O sage! Some roamed around in the sky. Others roamed around in the seven heavens. O *devarshi*! What is the need to speak a lot? They resided in all the worlds. Rejoicing, all Shambhu's *gana*s joined the festivities connected with Shankara.'"'

'"'In this way, with *deva*s, *gana*s and others, the lord Shankara advanced towards Himalaya's city for his marriage. Along with the gods and others, Sarvesha advanced for the sake of the marriage. At that time, something extraordinary occurred. O lord among sages! Hear about it. Rudra's sister, Chandi, arrived there. She was extremely happy but caused terror to others. She was astride a seat made out of a *preta* and she wore snakes as ornaments. She was extremely radiant and

there was a golden pot[1016] on her head. She was with her own
attendants. Her face blazed and her eyes blazed. The extremely
strong one generated delight and excited curiosity. O sage!
There were crores and crores of *bhutas* and *ganas* there, divine
and malformed. Along with these innumerable ones of different
types, she was radiant. The fierce Chandi, malformed in face,
advanced in front. She generated curiosity and joy. She could
cause happiness and calamities. Chandi placed all Rudra's
ganas behind her. They numbered eleven crores. They were
fierce and loved by Rudra. There was the sound of *damaru*s
being played and this pervaded the three worlds. There was
the tumultuous sound of kettledrums and the blaring of conch
shells. Drums were sounded and there was a tumultuous noise.
This brought everything auspicious to the world and destroyed
anything that was inauspicious. O sage! All the eager *deva*s,
all the *siddha*s and the guardians of the world were behind
the *ganas*. Ramesha advanced in the middle, astride his seat
on Garuda. O sage! A great and sparkling umbrella was held
aloft his head. He was surrounded by his own companions,
who fanned him with whisks. All his attendants were with him,
attired properly in their respective garments. As I advanced, I
was radiant along the route. With me, the *Veda*s, the sacred
texts, the Puranas and the *agama* texts assumed personified
form. Sanaka and the other great *siddha*s, my sons, the
Prajapatis and my family was with me, intent on serving Shiva.
Shakra was astride the elephant, Airavata, amidst his own
soldiers. There were *shakinis*, *yatudhanas*, *vetalas*, *brahma-
rakshasas*, *bhutas*, *pretas* and other *pramathas*.[1017] There were
the supreme *gandharvas*, Tumburu, Narada,[1018] Haha, Huhu
and others. *Kinnaras* advanced, delightedly playing on musical

---

[1016] Full of water.
[1017] Various types of demons, male and female.
[1018] Also the name of a *gandharva*.

instruments. There were all the mothers of the world and all the divine maidens. There were Gayatri, Savitri, Lakshmi and all the divine women. There were other wives of *deva*s and mothers of the world. Full of joy, all of them advanced for Shankara's marriage. Mahadeva is devoted to *dharma*, and he was astride a bull. This bull was as pure as crystal and was beautiful all over. In the *Veda*s and the sacred texts, *siddha*s and *maharshi*s speak of this bull as Dharma. As he[1019] was served by *deva*s and *rishi*s and advanced, he was resplendent. Mahesha was ornamented in many kinds of ways and was radiant, along with all these successful *maharshi*s. Accepting Mount Himalaya's invitation, he was going to his residence to accept Shivaa's hand. Such was Shambhu's conduct as he advanced for the supreme festivities. O Narada! Now hear about the virtuous incident that occurred in Himalaya's city.'"'

Chapter 136-3.3(41) (Description of the Pavilion)

' "Brahma said, 'Hari consulted with Shankara and obtained his instructions. O sage! He first sent you to the mountain's residence. Urged by Hari, you, Narada, lovingly prostrated yourself before Sarvesha and then went on ahead, to Himachala's house. O sage! Having gone there, you saw your own artificial image, created by Vishvakarma. You were ashamed and surprised. O great sage! Tired of looking at your own artificial image, you started to look at the other things created by Vishvakarma. You entered Himachala's pavilion, studded with jewels. It was adorned with golden pots and many

---

[1019] Shiva.

plantain trees. It has one thousand pillars and was wonderful and extremely amazing. O sage! On seeing the altar, you were filled with surprise. So amazed were you that your intelligence was confused and the *jnana* in your mind was destroyed. O sage Narada! You spoke to the lord of mountains. "O lord of mountains! Please tell me. Has Mahadeva, astride the bull, surrounded by the *gana*s and with the divinity Vishnu leading the way, already arrived? Have all the *maharshi*s, *siddha*s and minor divinities also arrived for the marriage?" Full of surprise in your mind, you spoke these words. O sage! Hearing them, Mount Himalaya told you the truth. Himalaya replied, "O Narada! O immensely wise one! Shiva has still not arrived for the marriage with Parvati. Nor have the companions who will come with the groom. O Narada! Use your intelligence to understand that these are images created by Vishvakarma. O *devarshi*! Give up your wonder and get a grip on yourself. Remember Shiva. Show me your compassion and happily eat and rest. Along with Mainaka and the other mountains, then go to Shankara's presence. O immensely intelligent one! Along with these mountains, go and entreat Shiva. His lotus feet are worshipped by large numbers of *maharshi*s, gods and *asura*s. Along with the *deva*s, bring him here quickly." You agreed and swiftly did what he said. You ate and did everything else that needed to be done. Then, with the sons of the mountain, you went to the great-minded Shiva's presence.'"'

'"'You saw Mahadeva, surrounded by *deva*s and others. You prostrated yourself and so did the devoted and blazing mountains. O sage! I, Vishnu, all the devas, along with Vasava and all of Rudra's followers questioned you. Seeing the mountains, our minds were filled with suspicion. Mainaka, Sahya, Meru and the others were adorned in many kinds of ornaments. The *deva*s said, "O Narada! O immensely wise one! We are surprised to see you. Did Himalaya treat you well? Tell us in detail. Why have these excellent mountains come here? Mainaka, Sahya, Meru and the others are extremely powerful and are bedecked with ornaments. O Narada! Does the mountain wish to really bestow his daughter on Bhava? O son! Please tell us what is happening now in Himalaya's residence. We, the residents of heaven, have doubts in our minds. O one excellent in vows! That is the reason we are asking you. Please tell us and remove our doubts." You heard the words spoken by Vishnu and the other residents of heaven. O sage! You had been amazed by Tvashtri's[1020] *maya* and you now spoke to them. O sage! You took me and Vishnu aside and spoke to us in these words. There was also Shachi's consort, the lord of all the gods. Earlier, he had severed the wings of the mountains. Narada said, "To confuse the residents of heaven, Tvashtri has created distorted and artificial images. Though created with love, he desires to bemuse all the gods. O Shachi's consort! Have you forgotten everything? Earlier, you confused them and acted like a destroyer.[1021] There is no doubt that the great-souled mountain wishes to defeat you in his house in this way. I was confused by my radiant image. In that way, Vishnu, Brahma and Shakra have also been created. O lord of *deva*s! What is the need to speak a lot? All the large number of *deva*s have been artificially sketched out. Not a single one has been left out. This has especially been done to bemuse all *deva*s. These artificial images have been constructed using *maya* and are meant to laugh at us." Hearing these words, Indra of the *deva*s was filled with fear and trembled from head to foot. He immediately spoke to Vishnu Hari. Indra of the *deva*s said, "O lord of *deva*s! O Rama's consort! Using this deception, Tvashtri will kill me. He is tormented by grief on account of his

---

[1020] Vishvakarma's.

[1021] With wings, mountains flew around, causing a disturbance. Indra used his *vajra* to sever their wings. Henceforth, they became stationary. Only Mainaka escaped this fate.

son."[1022] Hearing his words, Janardana, lord of *deva*s, laughed.
He comforted Shakra with the following words. Vishnu said,
"O Shachi's consort! You have earlier been confused by your
former enemies, the *nivatakavacha*s.[1023] They possessed the
strength of their great knowledge. O Vasava! Following my
command, you sliced off the wings of Mount Himalaya and
all the other mountains. Remembering that, let the mountains
now show us their *maya*. Those foolish ones wish to vanquish
us. But the immortals should not be afraid. Shankara is
affectionate towards his devotees, and he is Ishvara for all of
us. O Shakra! There is no doubt that he will ensure all is well."
He spoke in this way to Shakra, whose mind was agitated.
Girisha was following the customary practices of the world.
Thus, at the time, he spoke to Hari. Ishvara said, "O Hari! O
lord of gods! What is this that you are conversing with each
other about?" O sage! Having said this, Mahesha replied to
you. "O Narada! Please state what the great mountain really
said. You should tell us everything that happened, not hiding
anything. Does he want to bestow the daughter of the mountain
or does he not? Answer that quickly. Having gone there,
what did you see and do? O son! Tell us everything." O sage!
Seeing the divinity and addressed in this way by Shambhu, you
revealed all the mysterious things you had seen in the pavilion.
Narada replied, "O lord of *deva*s! O Mahadeva! Listen to my
auspicious words. O lord! There is no impediment of any kind
to the marriage. The lord of mountains will certainly bestow
his daughter on you. There is no doubt that these mountains
have come here to take you there. However, to bemuse the
immortals, a wonderful *maya* has been created. O omniscient
one! It excites curiosity but does not lead to any impediment.

[1022] Indra killed Vritra, Tvashtri's son.

[1023] They were descended from Prahlada's lineage and possessed
powers of *maya*. Eventually, they were destroyed by Arjuna.

O lord! Following his command, Vishvakarma, who possesses great *maya*, has constructed a wonderful pavilion in his house. It is full of marvellous things. To cause confusion, all the *deva*s have been created there. On seeing that, I was amazed and confused by the *maya*." O son! The lord was intent on following the customary practices of the world. Hearing these words, Shambhu was filled with delight. He laughed and spoke to all the gods. Ishvara said, "Mount Himachala wishes to bestow his daughter on me. Therefore, what do I have to do with this *maya*? O Vishnu! Please tell me the truth about this. O Brahma! O Shakra! O sages! O gods! Tell me the truth. Since the mountain is going to bestow his daughter, what do I have to do with this *maya*? Those who are learned and know about good policy say that the objective must be accomplished through whatever means. Therefore, with Vishnu leading the way, we must proceed swiftly and accomplish the task." In this way, Shambhu, lord of gods, conversed. He was overcome by Smara and behaved like an ordinary man who has succumbed. At Shambhu's command, Vishnu and the other gods and the great-souled *rishi*s overcame their confusion and delusion. O sage! Placing you and the mountains at the front, they proceeded. They were amazed to see the extremely wonderful residence of Mount Himalaya. Vishnu and the others happily arrived, along with their own companions. Having arrived in Himachala's city, Hara rejoiced.'"'

Chapter 137-3.3(42) (Meeting between the Divinity and the Mountain)

❛ ❛❛ B rahma said, 'The lord of mountains heard that Girisha, who can go everywhere, had arrived on the outskirts of his city. Himalaya was delighted at Isha's arrival. To welcome

Ishvara, he collected various objects. The mountain sent all the *brahmana*s with these. Full of devotion, he himself went to see Ishvara, whom he loved more than his own life. The mountain's mind was full of faith, and he happily praised his own good fortune. Seeing the army of *deva*s, Himalaya was amazed. He advanced in front of him, thinking himself to be blessed. Seeing his great army, *deva*s were also filled with great wonder. *Deva*s and mountains were both delighted with each other. O sage! There was a great army of mountains and another of *deva*s. When they met, they were as radiant as the western and eastern ocean. When *deva*s and mountains met each other, both sides thought that they had accomplished their objective and were filled with great joy. Seeing Ishvara in front of him, Himalaya prostrated himself. All the mountains and *brahmana*s prostrated themselves before Sadashiva. Astride his bull, he was pleased. He was adorned with many kinds of ornaments. The radiance of his divine form illuminated the directions. In an extremely delicate silken garment, his body was radiant. His bejewelled crown shone. His smile spread pure radiance. The serpents had become radiant ornaments on his limbs. His divine form was resplendent and the immortals and lords among gods fanned him with whisks. Achyuta stood on the lord's left and Daksha's father stood on the lord's right. Indra stood behind him and the various gods were along his sides. The gods praised the one who brought welfare to the worlds in various ways. He was Sarvesha, the one who bestows boons. He was the *brahman* but had himself assumed a body. He was *saguna* and *nirguna*. Showing compassion, he was subservient to his devotees. He was beyond Purusha and Prakriti. He was existence, consciousness and bliss.'"'

'"'The mountain saw Hari Achyuta to the right of the lord.[1024] He was astride Vinata's son[1025] and was bedecked in

[1024] Vishnu was to Shiva's left. But since Himalaya was facing Shiva, Vishnu appeared on the right. This applies to Brahma too.
[1025] Garuda was Vinata's son.

many ornaments. O sage! He saw me to the left of the lord. I was four-faced and surrounded by my own companions, was radiant. He saw these two lords among gods, always dear to Shiva. The lord of mountains and his companions lovingly prostrated themselves. The supreme lord of mountains also saw the extremely radiant *devas* and others behind Shiva and along the sides. He prostrated himself. Following Shiva's command, the mountain returned to his own city. Hari and all the sages and immortals followed him. Along with the lord, all the sages and gods went to the mountain's city. O Narada! They rejoiced and praised it in many kinds of ways. Himalaya instated *devas* and others on the beautiful summit that had been created. He then went to the place where the altar had been erected, following the norms. He had special quadrangles constructed, with gates. He bathed, donated gifts and checked that everything was in order. Himalaya, king of mountains sent his own sons to Shiva, along with Vishnu and everyone else. With great festivities, he wished to ensure that the rites for receiving the groom were performed. Along with all his relatives, the king of mountains was extremely happy. The sons of the mountain and their relatives went and prostrated themselves, informing him about the request of the lord of the mountains. Obtaining his permission, the sons of the mountain returned to their own residence. They happily informed the king of mountains that the marriage party was coming. O sage! On hearing about the mountain's request, Vishnu and the others, along with Ishvara, were filled with joy and rejoiced greatly. The large number of gods and sages attired themselves properly. Along with the lord, they got ready to leave for the residence of the king of mountains. Meanwhile, Mena desired to see Shiva. O sage! She used you, supreme among sages, to invite the lord. O sage! Dispatched by the lord, you went there. You desired to fulfil the desire that was in Shiva's mind. O sage! Mena was amazed in her mind. She prostrated herself before you and spoke. She said that she wished to see the lord Shankara's form, the one that destroys pride.'"'

Chapter 138-3.3(43) (Shiva's Wonderful Pastimes)

'"'Mena said, "O sage! I will first see Girija's husband. What is Shiva's form, for which, she performed those excellent austerities?"'"'

'"Brahma said, 'O sage! She lacked *jnana*. Therefore, along with you, she immediately went to the terrace.[1026] Shiva got to know that there was *ahamkara* in her mind. The lord engages in wonderful pastimes. O son! Therefore, he spoke to Vishnu and me. Shiva said, "O sons! Taking *deva*s with you, each of you go separately to the mountain's gate. Follow my instruction. I will follow later." Hearing this, Hari, along with me, summoned all the gods and told them about this. Full of enthusiasm, they immediately departed. O sage! Vishveshvara made Mena remain on the top of the house, accompanied by you, so that she could see this and be bewildered in her mind. O sage! At the time, Mena saw the extremely auspicious army. Having seen it, she was generally delighted. The handsome and extremely fortunate *gandharva*s arrived first. They were attired in excellent and sparkling garments and wore many kinds of ornaments. They had many mounts and played on many kinds of musical instruments. There were colourful flags, and they were accompanied by large numbers of *apsara*s. She saw the supreme lord of the Vasus there. Mena was delighted and exclaimed, "This must be Shiva." O supreme among

---

[1026] *Chandrashala*, a room on the top of the house, from which, the moon can be seen.

*rishi*s! You told her, "These are Shiva's attendants. This is
not Shiva, Shivaa's husband." Hearing this, Mena began to
think, "Someone superior to this! What will such a superior
person look like?" Meanwhile, she saw Manigriva[1027] and the
other *yaksha*s. Their radiance was double that of the Vasus.
She saw their radiant lord, Manigriva. Delighted, Mena said,
"This must be Rudra, Shivaa's husband." You replied to
the mountain's wife, "This is not Rudra, Shivaa's husband.
He is Shiva's servant." Meanwhile, Vahni arrived, with a
radiance that was twice that of the *yaksha*s. Seeing him, she
said, "This must be Rudra, Girija's husband." But you told
her that this wasn't he. Meanwhile, Yama arrived, with twice
the radiance. Seeing him, Mena was delighted and said, "This
must be Rudra." You told her this wasn't he. Nirriti, the
auspicious lord of the *punyajana*s, arrived, with double the
radiance. Seeing him, the delighted Mena said, "This must
be Rudra." You told her that this wasn't he. Varuna arrived,
with double the radiance. Seeing him, she said, "This must be
Rudra, Girija's husband." But you told her that this wasn't he.
At that time, Vayu arrived, with double the radiance. Seeing
him, the delighted Mena said, "This must be Rudra." But you
told her that this wasn't he. Dhanada, the resplendent lord of
*guhyaka*s, arrived, with double the radiance. Seeing him, the
delighted Mena said, "This must be Rudra." You told her that
this wasn't he. Ishana arrived, with double the radiance. Seeing
him, she said, "This must be Rudra, Girija's husband." You
told her that this wasn't he. At that time, Indra arrived, with
double the radiance. He was the lord of all the immortals. The
lord of *deva*s had many divine aspects. Seeing him, Menaka
said, "This must be Shankara." You told her, "This is Shakra,
lord of gods. This isn't he." At that time, Chandra arrived,
with double the radiance. Seeing him, she said, "This must be

[1027] Kubera's son.

Rudra." But you told her that this wasn't he. At that time, Surya arrived, with double the radiance. Seeing him, she said, "This must be he." But you told her that this wasn't he. Then Bhrigu and the other lords among sages arrived. All of them were masses of energy and were with large numbers of disciples. On seeing Vagisha[1028] in their midst, Menaka said, "This must be Rudra, Girija's husband." But you told her that this wasn't he. At that time, the splendid Brahma arrived, with a mass of energy. He was being praised by the *rishi*s and by his noble sons and was like *dharma* personified. O sage! On seeing him, Mena was filled with great joy and said, "This must be Shivaa's husband." But you told her that this wasn't he. At that time, the divinity Vishnu arrived there. He was splendid all over. He was handsome and four-armed and possessed a dark blue complexion, resembling clouds. His charm was like that of one crore Kandarpas gathered together. He was attired in yellow garments. He was his own ruler, and his eyes were like the petals of lotuses. He was serene and his mount was the supreme Indra among birds. He possessed a conch shell and the other signs. He was adorned with a crown and other ornaments. The *srivatsa* mark was on his chest. Lakshmi's lord possessed a splendour that could not be measured. On seeing him, her eyes were dazzled. Filled with great joy, she said, "This must be Shivaa's husband. There can be no doubt that this is Shiva." Hearing Menaka's words, you toyed with her and replied, "This isn't Shivaa's husband. This is Keshava Hari. Shankara is the lord of every task. This one is loved by him and obtains his rights because of that. Know that Shiva, Parvati's husband, is a groom who is superior. O Mena! I am incapable of describing his radiance. He is the lord of the entire universe. He is Sarveshvara and rules himself." Hearing these words, Mena thought that her extremely auspicious daughter

---

[1028] The lord of speech, Brihaspati.

was extremely fortunate and would bring great prosperity and happiness to three lineages.[1029] Her mind was filled with joy and when she spoke, her face was full of pleasure. She repeatedly described herself as greatly fortunate. Mena said, "As a result of Parvati's birth, I have now become blessed in every possible way. The lord of mountains has been blessed now. Everything connected with me is blessed. I have seen *devas* and leaders who are exceedingly radiant. The person who will be her husband is a lord over all of them. Even if I try for one hundred years, how can I have the capacity to describe her good fortune? Though I have not seen him yet, he is the lord over all these." With her mind full of love and assurance, Mena spoke in this way.'"

'"'At that time, the lord Rudra, who does extraordinary things, arrived. O son! His own *ganas* were extraordinary and robbed Mena of her pride. He showed himself in his own form, without any *maya*. He was devoid of attachment and indifferent. O sage! O Narada! On seeing him arrive, you showed Mena Shivaa's husband and spoke to her with a great deal of affection. Narada said, "O beautiful one! Look. This is Shankara himself. He is the one for whose sake Shivaa tormented herself through austerities in the great and desolate forest." Thus addressed, full of joy, Mena happily looked at the lord. Ishana's form was extraordinary and those who followed him were even more extraordinary. Rudra's greatly extraordinary army arrived at the same time. There were *bhutas*, *pretas* and others and many kinds of *ganas*. Some were in the form of winds. Others had harsh tones and held flags. Some had crooked mouths, others were disfigured. Some were cruel, with beards. Some were lame, others did not have eyes. Some held staffs and nooses. Others held clubs in their hands. Some rode backwards on their mounts. Others blew on horns. Some played on *damarus*,

---

[1029] Father's lineage, mother's lineage and father-in-law's lineage.

others played on *gomukha*s.[1030] Some had no faces, others had malformed faces. Some *gana*s had many faces. Some had no hands, others had malformed hands. Some *gana*s had many hands. Some had no eyes, others had many eyes. Some had no heads, others had malformed heads. Some had no ears, others had many ears. The *gana*s were attired in many kinds of garb. In this way, there were many powerful *gana*s, with malformed figures. O son! Their number was innumerable, and they were extremely valiant and awful. O sage! You used your finger to point out Rudra's *gana*s to her. "O one with a beautiful face! Look at Hara's servants and at Hara." O sage! On seeing the innumerable *gana*s, *bhuta*s, *preta*s and others, Menaka was immediately filled with great fear. Shankara was in their midst. He was *nirguna*, but superior to those who possessed *guna*s. He was astride a bull. He possessed five faces and three eyes, and his body was smeared with ashes. He had matted hair and the crescent moon was on his forehead. He possessed ten hands and held a skull. His upper garment was the hide of a tiger. The supreme Pinaka was in one hand. He wielded a trident, and his eyes were malformed. His figure was malformed. His garment was an elephant's hide. On seeing him, Shivaa's mother was terrified. She was stunned and started to tremble. She was confused and agitated. You used your finger to point him out and told her, "This is Shiva." As soon as she heard your words, she became like a creeper struck down by the wind. Full of grief, the virtuous Mena immediately fell down on the ground. "What is this disfigured form that I have seen? I have been deceived by a wicked planet." Having said this, Menaka immediately lost her senses. Her friends tended to her and made many kinds of attempts to revive her. Gradually, Mena, loved by the lord of mountains, regained her senses.'"

[1030] A kind of musical instrument.

Chapter 139-3.3(44) (Mena Gains Her Senses)

'' Brahma said, 'Mena, the virtuous lady loved by the mountain, got her senses back. Agitated, she lamented and reprimanded everyone. Initially, she repeatedly reprimanded her sons. Then she addressed her daughter in harsh words. Mena said, "O sage! Earlier, you said that Shivaa would marry Shiva. After that, you engaged Himalaya in performing rites of worship. The fruits can truly be seen now. But they are perverse and harmful. O sage! O evil-minded one! Since I have been deceived by you in every possible way, I am an inferior person. She then tormented herself through austerities that are difficult for even sages to follow. The fruits obtained as a result of that can be seen here and they bring misery. What will I do? Where will I go? Who will dispel my misery? My lineage has been destroyed. My life is harmful. Where are those divine *rishi*s? I will tear out their beards. Where is that cunning woman who came here on her own, pretending to be an ascetic wife? Whose crime has led to everything being destroyed for me?" Saying this, she looked at her daughter and addressed her in bitter words. "O daughter! What have you done? This is a wicked act that has brought grief to me. You have yourself wickedly given away gold and brought a piece of glass instead. Having given up sandalwood paste, you have smeared yourself in mud. You have made the swan fly away and have clutched a crow in your hands. You have flung sanctified water far away and drunk water from a well. You have cast aside the sun and have carefully collected a firefly. You have thrown the rice away and are eating the husk. Throwing away *ghee*, you are lovingly eating oil from a duck.[1031] You have freed yourself from

---

[1031] The text has the word *karanda*, which we have taken as *karandava*, duck. It is likely this is a typo for *eranda*, in which case, she is having castor oil.

serving a lion and are serving a jackal instead. You have freed
yourself from learning about the *brahman* and are listening
to wicked songs instead. There were extremely auspicious
ashes from sacrifices at home. O daughter! But you have flung
them far away and have instead accepted inauspicious ashes
from funeral pyres. You have given up supreme *deva*s, Vishnu
and other supreme lords. Instead, wicked in intelligence, you
have performed austerities for such a Shiva. Shame on your
intelligence. Shame on your beauty and conduct. Shame on
the person who has instructed you. Shame on your friends. O
daughter! Shame on us, those who have given you birth. Shame
on Narada's intelligence. Shame on the *saptarshi*s, who gave us
wicked intelligence. Shame on the lineage! Shame on the skill in
performing sacrifices. Shame on everything that you have done.
You have burnt down the house and that is like death to me.
Let this king of mountains not come near me. Let the *saptarshi*s
not show me their faces. What have all of you accomplished
together? You have destroyed the lineage. Why was I not born
barren? Why did my foetus not miscarry? Why did I not die?
Why did the daughter not die? Why did *rakshasa*s from the
sky not descend and devour her? I will slice off your head now.
What will I do with the bodies?[1032] If I give you up, where will
I go? Alas! My life has been destroyed." Saying this, Mena fell
down on the ground and lost her senses. Agitated and suffering
from grief and anger, she did not go to her husband. O lord
among sages! At that time, there were great lamentations.'"

'"'One by one, all the gods approached her. O sage! I
myself arrived first. O supreme among *rishi*s! On seeing me,
you spoke to her. Narada said, "You do not know about
Shiva's true handsome form. This is a form he has assumed in
his pastimes. This is not the real Shiva. O one devoted to your
husband! Therefore, give up your anger and gather yourself

[1032] In the plural, implying that Mena would also die.

together. Give up this stubbornness and do what must be done. Bestow Shivaa on Shiva." Hearing your words, Mena addressed you in the following words. "O wicked one! Get up and go far away. You are worst among those who are wicked." When she said this, Indra and all the other *deva*s and guardians of the world arrived and addressed her in these words. The *deva*s said, "O Mena! O daughter of the ancestors! Listen cheerfully to our words. He is the supreme Shiva himself and brings supreme happiness. As a result of your daughter's extremely intolerable austerities and because of his compassion, Shambhu showed himself and bestowed a boon on her. He is affectionate towards his devotees." Addressed by the gods in this way, Mena lamented repeatedly. She said, "My daughter will not be bestowed on Girisha, who possesses a fierce form. Why are all of you *deva*s engaging in this deception, so as to render her supreme beauty futile?" O lord among sages! When she said this, the seven *rishi*s, Vasishtha and others, arrived there and spoke to her. The *saptarshi*s said, "O daughter of the ancestors! O one loved by the mountain! We have come here to accomplish a task. In this connection, how can we possibly have a contrary view? The sight of Shankara is the greatest gain. He has come to your house with a vessel for receiving alms." Though they addressed her in this way, Mena paid no heed to the words of the sages. Weak in *jnana*, she angrily replied to the *rishi*s. Mena said, "I will slay her with weapons, but I will not bestow her on Shankara. All of you should go far away and should not come near me." Saying this, she immediately stopped. But she was agitated and lamented. O sage! Great sounds of lamentation could be heard there.'"

""'At this, the agitated Himalaya arrived there. He lovingly tried to kindle her understanding, speaking to her about true insight. Himalaya said, "O Mena! Listen to my words now. O beloved! Why are you dejected? So many people have come to our house, and you are reprimanding them. You do not know

Shankara. You have seen this disfigured form and are agitated. Shambhu has many forms. I know about Shankara. He is the one who protects everyone. He is worshipped by those who are themselves worshipped. He is the one who shows compassion. He is also the one who chastises. O one whom I love more than my own life! O unblemished one! Do not be stubborn. Get rid of your misery. O one excellent in vows! Get up and do the tasks that must be undertaken. Earlier, Shambhu arrived at our door, assuming a disfigured form. Let me remind you. He indulged in many pastimes. On seeing his supreme greatness, you and I agreed to bestow our daughter on him. O queen! O beloved! We have given our pledge and must fulfil it." O sage! Her husband, the mountain, said this and stopped. Hearing these words, Shivaa's mother, Mena, replied to Himalaya. Mena said, "O lord! You should listen to my words and act accordingly. Seize our daughter Parvati and bind her by the throat. Without any hesitation, fling her down. She will not be given to Hara. O husband! Alternatively, go with our daughter to the ocean. O lord of mountains! Submerge her there, abandon her and be happy. O husband! If you give our daughter to the malformed Rudra, I will certainly give up my own body." Hearing Mena's stubborn words, Parvati herself arrived and addressed her in these charming words. Parvati said, "O mother! Your intelligence has turned perverse, and it brings what is inauspicious. You should seek support in *dharma*. Why are you giving up *dharma*? This Rudra has no one else who is superior. He is himself Ishvara and everything flows from him. Shambhu is beautiful in form. He bestows happiness. He is described in all the *shruti* texts. Mahesha Shankara rules himself and is the lord of all *deva*s. O mother! He has many forms and is addressed through many names. Hari, Brahma and the others serve him. The lord is the foundation for everything. He is the creator and the destroyer. He has no transformations. He is lord of the three divinities.

He is indestructible and eternal. It is for him that all the *devas* have come here, as servants. They are engaged in festivities at your gate. What can be greater happiness than that? Get up and make efforts to make your life successful. Bestow me on Shiva and make your own *ashrama*[1033] successful. O mother! Bestow me on Paramesha Shankara. O mother! Please accept him. I am humbly requesting you. If you do not bestow me on him, I will not accept another groom. How can a jackal, which deceives others, receive a share meant for a lion? O mother! In thoughts, words and deeds and through what I have heard, I have myself chosen Hara. That being the case, you can do what you wish." Hearing Shivaa's words, Mena, loved by the lord of mountains, lamented a lot. Extremely angry, she gnashed her teeth and seized her body, beating her with her fists and knees. Agitated and full of rage, she struck her daughter. O son! O sage! The *rishis* and others who were there rescued her from her hands and took her far away.'"'

'"'She repeatedly censured them and her own destiny. She spoke and made them hear all the wicked words once again. Mena said, "See what I, Mena, will do to the wicked Parvati, who has been seized by an evil planet. I will give her virulent poison. I will certainly throw her into a well. Alternatively, I will use *shastras* and *astras* to slice Kali into bits. I will indeed submerge my own daughter, Parvati in the ocean. Otherwise, I will cast aside my own body. It will not be otherwise. I will not bestow my daughter, Durga, on Shambhu, who has a malformed figure. What kind of a terrible groom has the wicked one obtained? Everyone is laughing at me, the mountain and the lineage. He has no mother, father or brother. He has no relatives, or anyone from the same *gotra*. He possesses neither beauty, nor cleverness. He does not have a house or anything else. He doesn't possess garments or ornaments. There is no

---

[1033] As a householder.

one who is his aide. He doesn't possess an auspicious mount. He is not young, nor does he have riches. He has no purity or learning. What kind of a body does he possess? It causes affliction. What do I see that I should bestow my extremely auspicious daughter on him?" In this way, Menaka lamented a lot, in many kinds of ways. O sage! Overwhelmed by grief and sorrow, she wept.""

""'After this, I came there and spoke to Menaka, telling her about Shiva's excellent *tattva*, so that her great ignorance might be dispelled. Brahma said, "O Mena! Listen cheerfully to my auspicious words. If you listen to this lovingly, your wicked intelligence will be destroyed. Shankara is the creator, preserver and destroyer of the world. Since you do not know about his form, why are you suffering from this sorrow? The lord has many names and forms and engages in many kinds of pastimes. He rules himself and is the lord over everything. He is the lord of *maya* and there is no alternative to him. O Mena! Understand this and bestow Shivaa on Shiva. Give up this wicked stubbornness and evil ignorance. It destroys all tasks." Thus addressed by me, Mena lamented repeatedly. O sage! Without the least bit of shame, she addressed me in these words. Mena said, "O Brahma! Why do you wish to render her great and supreme beauty futile? Why don't you kill this Shivaa yourself? You should not speak to me about bestowing her on Shiva. I will not bestow my own daughter, whom I love more than my own life, on Shiva." O great sage! When she said this, Sanaka and the other *siddha*s arrived there. Extremely affectionately, they addressed her in the following words. The *siddha*s said, "He is the supreme Shiva himself, the one who bestows supreme happiness. Out of compassion towards your daughter, the lord showed himself to her." Lamenting repeatedly, Mena replied, "I will not bestow her on Girisha, who is fierce in form. Why are all of you *siddha*s trying to deceive, seeking to render her supreme beauty futile?"

O sage! When I heard her words, I was amazed. All the *deva*s, *siddha*s, *rishi*s and humans were surprised. At that time, hearing about her great and firm stubbornness, Vishnu, loved by Shiva, arrived there and spoke to her. Vishnu said, "You are the beloved daughter of the ancestors, born through their mental powers. You possess all the qualities. You are the wife of Himalaya, directly born in Brahma's excellent lineage. Your aides are like him.[1034] In this world, you are blessed. What more can I say? You are the foundation of *dharma*. How is it that you are giving up *dharma*? Can *deva*s, *rishi*s, Brahma or I say anything that is contrary? You should reflect on this. You do not know about Shiva, who is both *nirguna* and *saguna*. He is both disfigured and handsome. He is served by everyone and is the objective of the virtuous. He is the one who has created Devi Prakriti Ishvari, the foundation. On her side, he has also created Purushottama. Along with them, Brahma and I have forms that are based on *guna*s. To ensure the welfare of the worlds, Rudra has himself take an *avatara*. The *Veda*s, *deva*s and everything that is seen in the universe, mobile and immobile, originated from him. Everything was created from Shankara. Who can describe his form? Who knows it? Brahma and I cannot reach him. Everything that can be seen in the universe, from a blade of grass to Brahma, know that all this is Shiva. There is no need to reflect on this. In his own pastimes, he has descended in this form that can be seen. He has come to your door because of the power of Shivaa's austerities. O Himalaya's wife! Therefore, cast aside your grief and serve Shiva. You will obtain great bliss and all your hardships will be destroyed." O sage! In this way, understanding was formed in Menaka's mind. Instructed by Vishnu, her mind turned softer. But she did not give up her stubborn view that she would not bestow her daughter on Hara. Mena did not accept the idea because she was confounded by

[1034] Brahma.

Shiva's *maya*. Having understood a little, Mena, loved by the mountain, spoke to Hari. Hearing Vishnu's beautiful words, Girija's mother said, "I will bestow my daughter if his form is beautiful. Otherwise, even if one crore of different attempts are made, it will not happen. I have told you about my firm and true words." Firm in her vows, Mena spoke these words and was silent. The blessed one was goaded by Shiva's wishes, which confound everyone.'"'

Chapter 140-3.3(45) (Shiva's Beautiful Form)

‘ ‘‘ Brahma said, 'O sage! At this time, urged by Vishnu, you quickly went to Shambhu's presence, so as to make his inclinations favourable. Having gone there, to make Rudra understand and wishing to accomplish the task of *deva*s, you praised him with many kinds of hymns. Hearing those words, Shambhu was pleased. Displaying his compassion, he assumed a divine, excellent, wonderful and handsome form. Shambhu's beautiful form surpassed that of Manmatha's and was full of great charm. O sage! On seeing this, you were greatly delighted. Full of great joy, you praised him with many kinds of hymns. O sage! You then returned to the place where Mena and all the others were. O sage! You were full of great joy and overwhelmed with supreme love. Having gone there, you delighted Mena, the mountain's wife, with the following words. Narada said, "O Mena! O large-eyed one! Behold Shiva's excellent form. Full of compassion and out of pity for you, Shiva has created this." Hearing those words, Mena, loved by the mountain, was astounded. She saw Shiva's supreme form, one that bestowed bliss. It was beautiful in all the limbs and resembled one crore suns. There were colourful garments, and he was adorned in many kinds of ornaments. He was greatly pleased and possessed an excellent smile. He was agreeable and enchanting. He was fair in complexion and resplendent. He was adorned with the lines of the moon. All the large number of *deva*s, Vishnu and others cheerfully served him. The sun held an umbrella over his head and the moon made him radiant. He was handsome in every possible way. He was adorned with ornaments. It was impossible to describe the great radiance of his mount. Ganga and Yamuna fanned him with whisks. In front of him, the eight *siddhi*s performed an excellent dance. Vishnu, I, Indra and the other immortals attired ourselves in our respective excellent garments and followed Girisha. *Gana*s, with many different forms, exclaimed "Victory". They were ornamented and rejoicing greatly, walked in front of Girisha. Extremely happy, *siddha*s, minor gods, the extremely delighted sages and all the others, walked with Shiva. *Deva*s and all the others were full of wonder. Along with their own ornamented wives, they sang about the supreme *brahman*. In front of him, Vishvavasu and others, along with large numbers of *apsara*s, sang about Shankara's supreme fame. O supreme among sages! In this way, there were many great festivities there and Mahesha reached the gate of the mountain's house.'"'

'"'O lord among sages! Who is capable of describing the special radiance of the *paramatman* then? Seeing him in that form, for a while, Mena became as still as a picture. O sage! Full of joy, she then spoke these words. Mena said, "My daughter is blessed. She has tormented herself through great austerities. Through the powers of those, Mahesha has reached my house. Earlier, I used intolerable words to criticize Shiva. O Shivaa's husband! Please pardon those and be pleased with me now." In this way, Mena spoke to and praised the one who wears the moon on his forehead. The mountain's beloved joined her hands in salutation and prostrated herself. She was full of shame. Giving up whatever they wished to be engaged in, a large number of women gathered there. These residents of the city emerged outside their homes, wishing to see Shiva. A lady was bathing and emerged, still holding the powder used for the bath. She was extremely eager to see Shankara, Girija's groom. Another was engaged in serving her husband and, along with her friend, abandoned that task. Full of affection and eager to see Shambhu, she arrived, still holding the whisk in her hand. Another was lovingly engaged in feeding a child milk from her breast. Though the child was still not content, eager to see Shankara, she abandoned it and came. Another was still tying the cord around her girdle and came holding it. Yet another came, wearing her garment back to front. A beloved had sat down to eat his food, but the wife left him and came. She was full of eagerness and curiosity to see Shiva, the groom. Another wife held the stick she had used to apply collyrium in her hand. Though she had applied it to only one eye, she left, to see the groom of the mountain's daughter. Another beautiful lady was applying lac dye to her feet. Hearing the sound, she gave that up and came, eager to see. In this way, the women abandoned various tasks and their houses and arrived. Beholding Shankara's beauty, they were confounded. They were agitated and full of love, delighted at having seen Shiva. They fixed his image in their hearts and spoke these words. The women who resided in the city said, "The eyes of the residents of the city have been rendered successful. Since we have seen this form, our births have been rendered successful. A person's birth and a person's rites are successful only if he directly sees Shiva, the one who destroys every sin. Having undertaken austerities for Shiva, Parvati has accomplished everything. She is blessed and has accomplished every objective. Shivaa has obtained Shiva as a husband. If Brahma had not happily united this couple of Shiva and Shivaa, all his efforts would have been in vain. Since he has united this excellent couple, he has done well. All the various tasks have all been rendered successful. Without austerities, it is impossible for men to see Shambhu. Having seen Shankara, all of us have accomplished our objectives. In ancient times, Lakshmi obtained Narayana as her husband. In that way, by obtaining Hara, Devi Parvati has now been adorned. Sarasvati obtained Brahma as her husband. In that way, by obtaining Hara, Devi Parvati has now been adorned. All of us, men and women, are supreme and blessed. We have seen Sarvesha Shankara, Girija's husband." Uttering these words, they used sandalwood paste and *akshata* to worship Shiva. They lovingly showered him with puffed rice. All the women who were eagerly waiting with Mena described the fortunes of Mena and the mountain as exceedingly great. O sage! Hearing such auspicious words used by the women in their descriptions, the lord, Vishnu and everyone else rejoiced.'"

Chapter 141-3.3(46) (Arrival of the Groom)

' "Brahma said, 'Shambhu was pleased in his mind. Along with the *bhuta*s, his *gana*s and the gods, he eagerly went to the mountain's residence. Mena, loved by the supreme among mountains, went inside the house, along with the large number of women. To perform *nirajana*[1035] to Shambhu, the virtuous lady prepared vessels with lights. Along with all the wives of the *rishi*s, she affectionately arrived at the gate. Mahesha Shankara, Girija's groom, arrived there, served by all the gods. On seeing him, Mena was happy. His complexion was as beautiful as that of a *champaka* flower. He only had one face, with three eyes. His face was pleased, and he seemed to be smiling a little. He was adorned in gold and jewels. He wore a garland of *malati* flowers and a blazing bejewelled crown. He was ornamented with an excellent

---

[1035] Waving of lights, the same as *niranjana*.

necklace and beautiful bracelets and bangles. He was attired in
two beautiful and delicate garments, purified in the fire. They
were wonderful, priceless and radiant. Because of sandalwood
paste, *aguru*, *kasturi* and *kumkuma*, his body was charming.
He held a bejewelled mirror in his hand and his eyes shone with
collyrium. He was extremely enchanting, spreading his own
radiance everywhere. He was exceedingly young and beautiful,
his limbs adorned with ornaments. He was best among all those
loved by women. His lotus face resembled one crore moons.
He was handsome in all his limbs and his image surpassed that
of one crore Smaras. Mena saw this excellent divinity standing
in front of her residence. Seeing her son-in-law, she forgot her
grief and was filled with joy. She praised her own good fortune,
that of Girija's and the mountain's lineage. Mena regarded
herself to have been successful and rejoiced repeatedly. With a
delighted face, the virtuous lady performed the *nirajana*. After
this, Mena happily gazed at her son-in-law. Remembering what
Girija had said, Mena was filled with wonder. Her delighted
face resembling a blossoming lotus, she remembered those
words in her mind. "I can see the beauty of Paramesha as he
stands in front of me, and it is far more than what Parvati told
me then. Mahesha's present great charm cannot be described
in words." Surprised in this way, Mena entered her own house
again. Some other maidens proclaimed that he was blessed,
some that the mountain's daughter was blessed. Some said
that Durga had now become Bhagavati. "As far as we know,
such a groom has never been seen." Other maidens said, "Devi
Girija is blessed." The best among *gandharva*s sang and large
numbers of *apsara*s danced. Beholding Shankara's form, all
the *deva*s were delighted. Many kinds of musical instruments,
with melodious notes, were sounded. Many kinds of artistes
lovingly played on these. Himachala rejoiced and performed all
the rites that must be undertaken at the door. Mena and all the
women engaged in great festivities. Asking about the welfare of

the others, she cheerfully went inside her own residence. With the ganas and immortals, Shiva went to the place earmarked for him.'"'

'"'Meanwhile, the women in the mountain's inner quarters took Durga outside the house, so that she might worship the divinity of the lineage.[1036] Without blinking, devas happily gazed at her. Her complexion was like that of blue collyrium, and all her limbs were adorned with ornaments. Ignoring the steadfast glances of others, her eyes were fixed on the three-eyed one. As the beautiful one cast a sidelong glance, there was a faint smile on her happy face. Her beautiful hair was gathered up in a heavy bun that was decorated with flowers. Along with a dot made out of kasturi, she was decorated with a dot made out of sindura. There was a radiant and bejewelled necklace that hung over her breasts. She wore armlets made out of jewels and also bangles made out of jewels. The shine from her bejewelled earrings made her beautiful cheeks even more lustrous. She possessed beautiful teeth and there was the radiance of gems and jewels on her hands. There was red lac on her lips and her lower lip was like a sweet bimba fruit. There was a bejewelled mirror in her hand, and she playfully held a lotus. Her body was smeared with sandalwood paste, aguru, kasturi and kumkuma. Her feet had the sounds of anklets, and the soles of her feet were red. On seeing Devi, the origin of the universe and the one from whom the universe originated, all the gods and others were filled with devotion and lowered their heads before her and Menaka. The three-eyed one saw her through the corners of his eye and was delighted. Having seen Sati's form, Shiva gave up the anxiety that resulted from separation. With his eyes fixed on Shivaa, Shiva forgot everything else. As he glanced joyously at Gouri, all his body hair stood up in joy. Kali went outside the city and

[1036] Kuladevata.

worshipped Ambika, the divinity of the lineage. Along with the *brahmana* women, she then entered her father's beautiful residence. Along with the gods, Hari and *brahmana*s, Shankara also happily went to the place indicated by Himachala. There, everyone happily served Shankara. The lord of the mountains honoured them with many kinds of riches.'"'

Chapter 142-3.3(47) (Festivities Inside Himalaya's House)

' '' **B**rahma said, 'Rejoicing, the supreme mountain used *mantra*s from the *Veda*s to enthusiastically have sacred threads prepared for Durga and Shiva. Requested by Himachala, Vishnu and other *deva*s and sages eagerly entered the mountain's residence. They properly performed the rites mentioned in the *shruti* texts and the rites followed on earth. Shivaa was ornamented with ornaments given by Shiva. She was first bathed and then bedecked with all the ornaments. Her friends and the wives of *brahmana*s performed *nirajana* rites. The one with the beautiful complexion was radiant in a pair of new garments. The great mountain's daughter, loved by Shankara, was resplendent. Her *kanchuki*[1037] was wonderful, supreme and divine, with many jewels. O sage! When Devi wore that, she became even more radiant. She wore a divine necklace, studded with gems. Her extremely expensive bangles were made out of pure gold. The extremely fortunate one stood there, meditating on Shiva in her mind. The daughter of the great mountain, the mother of the three worlds, was resplendent. Both the sides happily engaged in great festivities.

[1037] A woman's upper garment, a bodice.

Many kinds of pure objects were donated to *brahmana*s. Others were given many kinds of great articles. There were many kinds of festivities and amusement, with singing and the playing of musical instruments. Vishnu, I, Vidhatri, Shakra and the immortals and the sages were filled with joy and immensely happy, participated in all the festivities. Remembering Shiva's lotus feet, they devotedly prostrated themselves before Shivaa. Having taken leave from Mount Himalaya, they returned to their own respective places.'"'

'"'Meanwhile, Garga, skilled in the sacred texts of *jyotisha*, addressed Himalaya, Indra among mountains, in these words. Garga said, "O Himachala! O lord of the earth! O lord! For the sake of accepting the hand, please bring Shambhu, Kali's lord and husband, to your own home." The mountain thus got to know that the right time for bestowing his daughter had arrived. When Garga told him this, his mind was exceedingly happy. Rejoicing greatly and desiring to bring Shiva there, the mountain sent mountains, *brahmana*s and others. The mountains and *brahmana*s held auspicious objects in their hands. In the midst of the festivities, they went to the spot where the divinity Maheshvara was. At that time, many musical instruments were played and there were repeated chants of the *brahman*. With great enthusiasm, there was singing and dancing. Hearing the sounds of the musical instruments, all Shankara's servants, along with *deva*s and *rishi*s, happily stood up simultaneously. Full of joy in their minds, they spoke to each other. "Desiring to take Shiva, the mountains have arrived here. There is no doubt that the time for accepting the hand has arrived. We think that the time for our great good fortune is imminent. In particular, we are blessed that we will certainly witness the marriage of Shiva and Shivaa. This will bring great enjoy and ensure everything auspicious for the world." In these ways, those affectionate conversations took place. The ministers of the Indra among mountains arrived. They went and requested Shiva, Vishnu and the others, since the right time for bestowing the daughter had arrived and it was time to go. O sage! Hearing this, all the gods, Vishnu and all the others, were extremely happy in their minds. Addressed to the mountain, they uttered words of "Victory". Desiring to obtain Kali, Shiva was also extremely happy. However, he kept these wonderful signs hidden in his mind. The wielder of the trident was extremely delighted. He used all the auspicious articles to bathe himself, so as to show compassion to the worlds. He bathed and attired himself in excellent garments. He was surrounded by all the others. He mounted himself on the shoulders of the bull and was served by the guardians of the worlds. With the lord in front, all of them left for the residence of Mount Himalaya. Many musical instruments were enthusiastically played. *Brahmana*s sent by Himalaya and those excellent mountains proceeded ahead of Shambhu, full of joy. A great umbrella was held aloft his head. Maheshvara was fanned with whisks and a canopy was held above his head. I, Vishnu, Indra and the guardians of the world went on ahead, extremely radiant, handsome and brilliant. Conch shells, kettledrums, *pataha*s, *anaka*s and *gomukha*s were repeatedly played.[1038] In the great festivities, many musical instruments were played. All the singers sang supremely auspicious chants. Following many kinds of *tala*, all the dancers danced. The radiant Paramesha is the only friend the universe possesses. He proceeded with them and was served by all the lords among gods, who happily showered down flowers over him. Worshipped in this way, Shambhu entered the sacrificial pavilion. While he was still outside, Parameshvara was praised. The supreme mountains made Mahesha descend from the bull. Extremely happy, amidst those great festivities, they took him inside the house. When Ishvara arrived, along

---

[1038] *Pataha* and *anaka* are different types of drums.

with *devas* and *ganas*, Himalaya devotedly prostrated himself before him. He followed the norms and performed *nirajana*. Amidst the great festivities, he prostrated himself before all the gods and sages. He joyfully praised his own good fortune and honoured them. He offered *padya* and *arghya* to Achyuta and Ishana and took the foremost among *devas* inside his own residence. In the middle of the arena, he made all of them, especially Vishnu, me and Isha, sit on bejeweled thrones. Along with her friends, Mena, the *brahmana* women and other women from the city happily performed *nirajana*. The learned priest offered *madhuparka* and other things to the great-souled Shankara and happily did everything else that was necessary. O sage! Proposed and urged by me, the priest carried out all the auspicious rites and extremely delighted, made him enter inside the altar prepared by Himalaya. The bride, Parvati, was already there, adorned in every kind of ornament. The slender-limbed one was extremely radiant, seated on the altar. Along with me and Vishnu, Mahadeva was taken there. Noticing that the auspicious *lagna* for bestowing the bride was arriving, Brihaspati and the other priests were extremely delighted. Garga was seated at the place where the clock[1039] was kept. Until the exact time arrived, Pranava *mantra* was chanted. Garga announced that the auspicious moment had arrived. Filling his cupped hands with *akshata*, he showered these on Parvati and Shiva. With a beautiful face, Parvati worshipped Rudra with excellent curds, *akshata*, *kusha* and water. She glanced intently at Shambhu, for whom, she had earlier performed supreme austerities. Shivaa was extremely happy and radiant. Shambhu was devoted to following worldly practices. O sage! Therefore, urged by me, Garga and the sages, he worshipped Shivaa. In this way, Parvati and Parameshvara, who pervade the universe, worshipped each other and were resplendent.

[1039] *Ghatika*, some instrument for measuring time.

With all the prosperity of the three worlds in them, they looked at each other. Lakshmi and the other women performed special *nirajana*. After this, the *brahmana* women and the women from the city performed *nirajana*. They looked at Shivaa and Shambhu and were delighted. There were great festivities.'"

Chapter 143-3.3(48) (Bestowing the Bride)

' '' Brahma said, 'At this time, urged by the *acharya* Garga, Himalaya, along with Mena, started the arrangements for bestowing the bride. The immensely fortunate Mount Himalaya was attired in excellent garments and ornaments. He and Mena held a golden pot, each on one side. Along with his own priest, the delighted mountain offered *padya* and other things to the groom, accepting him with garments, sandalwood and ornaments. Himalaya asked the *brahmana*s to mention the *tithi*, pronouncing that the time for bestowal had arrived. Agreeing to this, the excellent *brahmana*s, all of whom knew about time, announced the *tithi* and said that the excellent moment had arrived.'"

'"In his heart, Himachala was full of affection towards Shambhu. Goaded by this, he smiled and spoke to Paresha Shambhu. "O Shambhu! Please state your own *gotra*, *pravara*,[1040] lineage, name and the branch of the *Veda*s you are associated with it. Please do not delay." Hearing Himachala's words, Shankara immediately turned his face away. Though he never suffers from sorrow, he was immersed in grief. The best among gods, sages, noble *gandharva*s, *yaksha*s and large numbers of *siddha*s saw that no reply issued from his mouth.

[1040] Within a *gotra*, *pravara* is the line of descent from a particular *rishi*. A *gotra* will have several such *pravara*s.

O Narada! At the time, you did something that should be
laughed at. O Narada! You know about the *brahman*. Your
mind is fixed on Shambhu. But Shiva must have goaded your
mind. You picked up your *veena* and started to play. The
intelligent Indra among mountains, Vishnu, I and all the *deva*s
and sages tried to restrain you. But you were stubborn. Since
this was Shankara's will, you did not desist. The mountain
said, "Please do not play the *veena* now." O *devarshi*! O
learned one! Though you were restrained in this way, you
were stubborn. Remembering Maheshvara, you replied to
the lord of mountains. Narada said, "You are foolish and do
not know anything. Your face is turned excessively outwards,
and you have spoken about Mahesha. You have asked Hara
himself to state his *gotra*. On this occasion, such words should
be laughed at a lot. O mountain! Vishnu, Brahma and others
do not know about his *gotra*, lineage and name. What need
be said about others? O mountain! During one of his days,
one crore Brahmas are destroyed. Through the strength of her
austerities, Kali saw this Shankara. He is the supreme *brahman*
and has no form. He is *nirguna* and is superior to Prakriti.
He has no form and has no transformations. He is the lord
of *maya*. He is greater than the greatest. He has no *gotra*,
lineage or name. He rules himself and is affectionate towards
his devotees. When he wishes to be *saguna*, he assumes many
bodies and names. He has an excellent *gotra*, but he possesses
no *gotra*. He comes from a noble lineage, but he possesses no
lineage. There is no doubt that he has become your son-in-
law now because of Parvati's austerities. Through his pleasures
and pastimes, all mobile and immobile objects are deluded. O
supreme among mountains! Even a wise person does not know
Shiva. When Mahesha assumed the form of a *lingam*, Brahma
could not see the head. Vishnu went to the nether regions and
was astounded when he could not see the feet. O best among
mountains! What is the need to speak a lot? Shiva's *maya* is

impossible to understand. The three worlds, Hari, Brahma
and the others, are subject to it. O Shivaa's father! Therefore,
you must make efforts to reflect on this properly. You should
not have the least bit of doubt about the groom who has been
chosen." O sage! You possess *jnana* and carry out Shiva's
wishes. Having said this, you spoke again to the Indra among
mountains, delighting the mountain. Narada said, "O son!
O great mountain! O Shivaa's father! Listen to my words.
Hearing them, bestow your daughter, Devi, on Shankara. In
his pastimes, Mahesha assumes a *saguna* form. Know that
nada is his *gotra* and lineage. It is true that Shiva is full of
nada and *nada* is full of Shiva. There is no difference between
nada and Shiva. O Indra among mountains! At the beginning
of creation, *nada* emerged first. In his pastimes, he assumed
the *saguna* form later. Hence, *nada* is superior to that form
of Shiva. O Himalaya! Sarveshvara Shankara urged my mind.
Goaded by him, I played on the *veena* then." O sage! Hearing
your words, Himalaya, the lord of mountains, was content.
Bewilderment vanished from his mind.'"'

'"'Vishnu and other gods and the sages also lost their
sense of wonder. All of them praised those words. All those
discriminating ones comprehended Maheshvara's depth.
Amazed and rejoicing greatly, they spoke to each other. "This
entire extensive universe has been created as a result of his
will. He is greater than the greatest. He can alone understand
his form. Sharva rules over his own progress. He can only be
approached through supreme sentiments. He is the lord of the
three worlds. We have seen that now." Meru and the other
excellent mountains were filled with fear. In one voice, they
spoke to Himalaya, lord of the mountains. The mountains said,
"O lord of mountains! Do not budge from the decision you
announced, of bestowing your daughter. Do not destroy your
deeds. We are speaking the truth. There is no need to hesitate
about this. Bestow your daughter on Ishvara." Himalaya heard

the words spoken by his well-wishers. Urged by Vidhatri, he
decided to bestow his daughter on Shiva. "O Parameshvara! I
am bestowing this maiden on you. O lord over everything! Be
pleased and accept her as your wife." Using the *mantra 'tasmai
Rudraya mahate'*,[1041] Himalaya bestowed his daughter Parvati,
the origin of the three worlds. The mountain placed Shivaa's
hand on Shiva's hand. His mind was delighted, like the wish
of crossing over a great ocean being fulfilled. Parameshvara
was pleased. Reciting *mantra*s from the *Veda*s, Girisha quickly
accepted Girija's hand, which was like a lotus, in his own
hand. O sage! He touched the ground and chanted, "*kamasya
kodat*".[1042] Shankara happily read this and showed the world
the path to follow. There were great festivities everywhere,
conducive to happiness. Sounds of "Victory" arose on ground,
the firmament and heaven. Delighted, everyone uttered words
of applause and obeisance. The *gandharva*s happily sang. Large
numbers of *apsara*s danced. The minds of Himachala's citizens
were delighted. There were great and exceedingly auspicious
festivities. I, Vishnu, Shakra, the immortals and all the sages
were delighted, and our happy faces resembled lotuses in bloom.
Extremely happy, Himachala, supreme among mountains,
bestowed not only his daughter, but appropriate gifts on Shiva.
His relatives devotedly worshipped Shivaa and following the
rules, gave Shiva and Shivaa many kinds of objects. O lord
among sages! Himalaya's mind was content. For the pleasure
of Parvati and Shiva, he gave them many kinds of objects. He
gave him objects for amusement and many kinds of jewels.
There were wonderful jewels and many kinds of vessels. There

[1041] To the great Rudra.
[1042] This is a *mantra* from Vajasaneyi Samhita. 7.48 states '*ko
adat kosma adat kamo yadat*'. Loosely translated, 'Who bestowed
it? Who was it bestowed on? Kama bestowed it, it was bestowed on
Kama. Kama is the giver and the receiver.'

were one hundred thousand cows and one hundred harnessed horses. There were one hundred thousand devoted servant maids and articles and ornaments. O sage! He gave one hundred thousand each of elephants and chariots that were inlaid with gold and decorated with jewels. In this way, Himalaya bestowed his daughter, Girija Shivaa on Shiva Paramesha, in accordance with the rules. He was successful in his objective. The best among mountains joined his hands in salutation and using excellent words, used the *madhyandina* hymns[1043] to happily praise Paramesha. Instructed by him, the large number of sages, knowledgeable about the *Veda*s, cheerfully sprinkled Shivaa's head with water. Uttering the names of the divinity, they performed the *paryukshana* rites.[1044] O sage! There were great festivities and they brought great joy.'"

Chapter 144-3.3(49) (Vidhatri's Delusion)

' "Brahma said, 'Following my command, the *brahmana*s kindled a fire, offered oblations and placed Parvati on Ishvara's lap. To the sound of hymns from *Rig Veda*, *Yajur Veda* and *Sama Veda*, Shiva offered oblations into the fire. Kali's brother, known as Mainaka, poured parched grain into her cupped hands.[1045] O son! After this, following the customary practices of the world, Kali and Shiva happily performed *pradakshina* of the fire.'"

[1043] *Madhyandina* is a branch of *Shukla Yajur Veda*. More specifically, Himalaya probably chanted from the Vajasaneyi Samhita.

[1044] In *paryukshana*, water is sprinkled all around the spot, but silently, without uttering any *mantra*s.

[1045] The bride offers these into the fire, while the groom recites hymns.

""'At the time, Girija's husband performed a wonderful
act. O *devarshi*! Hear about it. Out of affection, I will tell you
about it. At the time, I was confounded by Shiva's *maya*. I
glanced at Devi's feet and saw her beautiful toenails, shaped
like the crescent moon. O divine sage! As soon as I saw them,
my mind was extremely agitated, and I was overwhelmed by
desire. Deluded by Smara, I repeatedly stared at her limbs. As
soon as I looked, my semen oozed out and fell down on the
ground. When the semen oozed out, I, the grandfather, was
ashamed. O sage! I pressed my penis with my feet and tried
to keep this a secret. O Narada! However, Mahadeva got to
know and became exceedingly angry. He instantly wanted
to kill Vidhatri, who had been deluded by Kama. O Narada!
There were great lamentations everywhere. Everyone trembled.
The one who preserves the universe was also filled with fear.
O sage! Vishnu and the other immortals sought to pacify
Shambhu. As he got ready to kill, he blazed in rage and energy.
The *deva*s said, "O lord of *deva*s! O one who pervades the
universe! O Paramesha! O Sadashiva! O lord of the universe!
O Jagannatha! O one who is everywhere in the universe! Please
be pacified. Your *atman* is behind all sentiments. You, Ishvara,
are the cause. You are without transformations. You do not
decay. You are eternal. You are without a second. You are
without destruction. You are supreme. You are the beginning,
the middle and the end. I, and everything else, has flowed from
you. You are without decay. You are eternal. You are truth. You
are the *brahman*. You are consciousness. Those who are firm
in their vows and desire emancipation, serve your lotus feet.
Sages worship you and rid themselves of fear and attachment.
You are the *brahman*. You are complete. You are *amrita*. You
are devoid of sorrow. You are *nirguna* and supreme. You are
only bliss, without any anxiety. There is no transformation in
your *atman*. You are the cause behind the universe, leading to
its creation, preservation and destruction. You are beyond it.

You are the lord of *atman*s. O lord! You are always impartial.
You are one. You are existence and non-existence. You have no
duality. Whether it is gold, or an object fashioned out of gold,
there is no difference in the essential object. In their ignorance,
people think that there is an alternative to you. Therefore, the
best counter to this is to meditate on you, without a form. O
Mahesha! As soon as we have seen you, we have been blessed.
O Shambhu! You bestow bliss on people who are firm in their
devotion. Please show us your compassion. You are the original
atman, without an origin. You are beyond Prakriti. You are
Purusha. You are Vishveshvara Jagannatha. You are without
transformation. You are greater than the greatest. O one
whose form is the universe! This Brahma, the grandfather, is
your *rajas* form. O lord! Through your favours, Purushottama
Vishnu is your *sattva* form. Rudra, the fire of destruction, is
your *tamas* form. You are the *paramatman*, beyond the *guna*s.
You are Sadashiva Mahesha. You are the Maheshvara who
pervades everything. You are manifest. You are Mahat. You
are the elements and other things. You are the *tanmatra*s. You
are the senses. O Maheshvara! Your form is established in the
universe. O Mahadeva! O Paresha! O ocean of compassion!
O Shankara! O lord of *deva*s! O divinity! Please show us
your favours. O Purushottama! Please show us your favours.
The seven oceans are your garments. The directions are your
mighty arms. O lord! The firmament is your head. The sky
is your navel. The wind is your nose. O lord! The sun, the
moon and the fire are your eyes. The clouds are your hair. The
*nakshatra*s, stars and planets are your ornaments. O lord of
*deva*s! How can I praise you? O lord! You are Parameshvara.
O Shankara! You cannot be approached through words or
thoughts. You possess five faces. O Rudra! You possess fifty
crore forms. You are the lord of the three. You are the greatest.
You are the truth in learning. I prostrate myself before you.
You cannot be indicated. You are eternal. Your form blazes

like lightning. Your complexion is like the fire. O divinity! O Shankara! I prostrate myself before you. I bow down before you. Your radiance resembles that of one crore lightning flashes. You are extremely beautiful, with eight forms in eight corners. You have assumed a form and are established in this world. I prostrate myself before you. I bow down before you." Hearing their words, Parameshvara was pleased.'"'

'"'Affectionate towards his devotees, he immediately granted Brahma freedom from fear. O son! At this, all the gods present there, Vishnu and the others, and the sages smiled and engaged in great festivities. O son! I had repeatedly pressed down on my semen. This transformed into many drops that were extremely radiant. Thousands of *rishi*s were born from these and they were the *valakhilyas*.[1046] They were born from those drops of semen and blazed in their own energy. O sage! All those *rishi*s presented themselves there. Full of great joy, they presented themselves before me and exclaimed, "O father! Father!" O Narada! Goaded by Ishvara's will, you spoke angrily to the *valakhilyas* and firmly rebuked them. Narada said, "All of you go to Mount Gandhamadana. You should not remain here. There is no need for you here. O lords among sages! Go there and torment yourselves through austerities. Become Surya's disciples. Following Shiva's command, I have told you this." Thus addressed, all the *valakhilyas* instantly bent down before Shankara and went to Mount Gandhamadana. O lord among sages! Because of Vishnu and others and because of what Paramesha urged the great-souled ones to do, I was able to breathe again and lost my fear. Sarvesha Shankara is affectionate towards his devotees and gets every task done. He destroys false pride. Knowing this, I praised him. "O lord of *deva*s! O Mahadeva! O ocean of compassion! O lord! You

[1046] 60,000 sages who are the sizes of thumbs. They precede the sun's chariot.

alone are the creator, preserver and destroyer. All mobile and immobile objects are established because of your will and are like tethered bulls. I have especially understood this." Saying this, I joined my hands in salutation and prostrated myself. Vishnu and the others also praised Maheshvara. On seeing that I was miserable, purified and bent down, and hearing Vishnu and the others, Maheshvara was pleased. Pleased in his mind, he bestowed on me the great boon of freedom from fear. O sage! Everyone was greatly happy, and I rejoiced.'"'

Chapter 145-3.3(50) (Amusements)

' "Brahma said, 'O Narada! Following Shiva's command, I and the sages happily carried out the remaining rites that needed to be carried out for Shiva and Shivaa's marriage. Their heads were affectionately sprinkled. The *brahmanas* affectionately had Dhruva shown.[1047] After this, the *hridayalambhanam* rite[1048] was conducted. O Indra among *brahmanas*! With great enthusiasm, benedictions were read. Following the instructions of *brahmanas*, Shambhu applied *sindura* on Shivaa's forehead. At that time, Girija's complexion was such that it is impossible to describe it. Following the instructions of *brahmanas*, both of them sat down on the same seat. They looked extremely radiant and brought joy in the minds of devotees. O sage! They were engaged in their wonderful pastimes. Therefore, when they returned to their own places, they followed the instructions and happily observed

---

[1047] Dhruva (the Pole Star) is shown by the groom to the bride in the night, indicative of stability in marriage.

[1048] A marriage rite—touching (*alambhanam*) the heart (*hridaya*). The groom symbolically touches the bride's heart.

samsrava-prashanam.[1049] In this way, Shiva's marriage was completed, following all the rules. The lord gave me, Brahma, the creator of the worlds, a full vessel.[1050] Following the norms, Shambhu donated a cow to the *acharya*. He happily made great and auspicious donations. He separately gave each *brahmana* hundreds of gold pieces. There were crores of different kinds of jewels and many other objects. All the immortals, other living beings and mobile and immobile entities were extremely happy and uttered words of "Victory". In every direction, there were the sounds of auspicious songs. The playing of musical instruments enhanced everyone's delight. Hari, I, *deva*s, the sages and all the others happily took their leave from the mountain and returned swiftly to their own respective abodes.'"

""'In the city of the mountain, the women happily conveyed Shiva and Shivaa to the excellent chamber where various amusements are carried out. The women affectionately carried out the various customary practices. There was great enthusiasm everywhere and it brought joy. The couple, who brought welfare to people, was taken to the excellent residence. Amidst the rejoicing, the customary practices were carried out there. When the couple reached the residence, the women from the city of the Indra among mountains carried out all the auspicious rites. Uttering sounds of "Victory", they untied the knot[1051] and carried out the other rites. Their minds and bodies were delighted, and they smiled and cast sidelong glances. The excellent women entered the residence and as they gazed at Parameshvara, they were enchanted and

[1049] *Samsrava* is what is left of oblations and *prashanam* is the act of licking them up.
[1050] As *dakshina*.
[1051] At the time of the marriage ceremony, the ends of the garments of the groom and bride are tied.

praised their own good fortunes. He was extremely handsome and charming all over. He was in the prime of youth and charmed the minds of the ladies. Pleased, he smiled a little and cast enchanting glances. His garments were fine, and he was radiant, decorated with many jewels. At the time, sixteen divine women arrived and with a great deal of respect, saw the couple. They were Sarasvati, Lakshmi, Savitri, Jahnavi, Aditi, Shachi, Lopamudra, Arundhati, Ahalya, Tulasi, Svaha, Rohini, Vasundhara, Shatarupa, Samjna and Rati. These were the divine women. There were several beautiful daughters of *devas*, *nagas* and sages. Who is capable of enumerating the ones who assembled there? A bejewelled throne was offered to Shiva, and he happily sat on it. One by one, the goddesses smiled and addressed him in sweet words. Sarasvati said, "O Mahadeva! You loved Sati more than your own life. You are delighted that you have got her back now. Look at your beloved's face, which has the complexion of the moon. O one who desires! Give up your torment. O lord of time! Spend your time in Sati's embrace. Because of my wish, there will never be any separation in your embrace." Lakshmi said, "O lord of *devas*! Forget your shame and clasp Sati to your bosom. Keep her there. What is the reason for this shame? You lose your breath of life without her." Savitri said, "O Shambhu! Quickly feed Sati and eat yourself. Do not be dejected. Rinse her mouth lovingly and offer her camphor wrapped in betel leaves." Jahnavi said, "Your wife's hand has the complexion of gold. Take it. Brush her hair. For a woman, there is no happiness greater than the good fortune she receives from her husband." Aditi said, "O Shiva! O Shambhu! After she has eaten, so that she can rinse her mouth, lovingly give her water. A love like that of this couple is extremely rare." Shachi said, "You lamented because of her. Now clasp Shivaa to your bosom. Day and night, you wandered around in your confusion. Why are you now ashamed of your beloved?" Lopamudra said, "O Shiva!

After eating, in the bedchamber, a requisite duty must be
performed for women. Before sleeping, you should give betel
leaves to Shivaa." Arundhati said, "It is I who persuaded Mena
to give Sati to you, since that wasn't the wish in her mind.
Using many techniques, I made her understand. You must
therefore pleasure yourself with her." Ahalya said, "Give up
your old age and became exceedingly young. Mena is extremely
tormented in her mind. Let her approve of you." Tulasi said,
"Earlier, you abandoned Sati and burnt Kama down. O lord!
How did you then send Vasishtha as a messenger now?" Svaha
said, "O Mahadeva! Be steady. These present words are those
of women. At that time of marriage, it is the practice of women
from the inner quarters to prattle." Rohini said, "You are
accomplished in *kama shastra*. Satisfy Parvati's desire. You are
yourself a lover. Make the woman who loves you cross over
the ocean of desire." Vasundhara said, "O one who knows
about sentiments! You know the sentiments of a woman who
is full of desire. O Shambhu! She not only desires you as a
husband, she also constantly desires Ishvara." Shatarupa said,
"A person afflicted by hunger is not satisfied until he eats and
enjoys divine food. O Shambhu! Do everything, so that the
mind of a woman is satisfied." Samjna said, "Lovingly and
quickly, send Parvati and Shankara away. Give them betel
leaves and a bejewelled lamp. Prepare the bed and let them
be alone." Hearing the words of the women, Shiva himself
replied. Bhagavan is without transformations. He is the *guru*
of all the *guru*s who are Indras among *yogi*s. Shankara replied,
"O goddesses! Do not speak such words in my presence. You
are the virtuous mothers of the worlds. How can you utter such
frivolous words in front of your son?" Hearing Shankara's
words, the divine women were ashamed. They were silent and
nervous, like puppets that have been drawn back. Pleased in his
mind, Mahesha ate sweetmeats and rinsed his mouth. Along
with his wife, he chewed betel leaves with camphor.'"

Chapter 146-3.3(51) (Kama Comes Back to Life)

" " Brahma said, 'Meanwhile, Rati discerned that the time was right. Shankara is affectionate towards those who are distressed. Therefore, she spoke to him pleasantly. Rati said, "You have got back and accepted Parvati. This is an extremely rare good fortune. I loved my husband more than my own life and he did not act out of any selfish motive. Why did you reduce him to ashes? O *paramatman*! In my journey of life, I desire my husband. Please remove my torment, caused by separation from him. In these marriage festivities, all the people are happy. O Mahesha! Without my own husband, I alone am miserable. O divinity! O Shankara! Be pleased and give me my husband back. O supreme lord! You are the friend of the distressed. Make what you yourself said come true. Other than you, who in the three worlds, mobile or immobile, is capable of dispelling my grief? Knowing this, please show me your compassion. These festivities, in connection with your own marriage, have brought joy to everyone. Please show compassion towards the distressed. O lord! Give me a reason to celebrate. When my husband comes back to life, your amusements with your beloved Parvati will be complete. There is no doubt about this. You are Parameshvara and you are capable of doing everything. O Sarvesha! What is the need to speak a lot? Let my husband quickly come back to life." Having said this, she offered him Kama's ashes, tied up in a piece of cloth with rope. She wept in front of Shambhu, lamenting, "O lord! O lord!" Hearing Rati's cries, Sarasvati and the other women, all the goddesses, also wept and spoke these miserable words. The goddesses said, "You are known as a person who is affectionate towards devotees. You are the friend of the distressed. You are an ocean of compassion. Please revive

Kama and infuse Rati with vigour. We bow down before you."
Hearing these words, Maheshvara was pleased. The lord who
is an ocean of compassion quickly cast a favourable glance.
The wielder of the trident's glance was like nectar and Smara
emerged from the ashes. His beautiful form and attire made
him distinctive, and he appeared in embodied form. He was
smiling and held his bow and arrow.'"'

'"'Seeing her husband in that form and figure, Rati
prostrated herself before Maheshvara. Successful in her
objective, she joined her hands in salutation and repeatedly
praised the divinity Shiva. He is the one who had brought her
beloved husband back to life. Shankara heard the praise of
Kama and his wife. He was pleased and with his heart full of
compassion, he spoke to them. Shankara said, "O one who
conquers the mind! I am pleased with the praise uttered by you
and your wife. O one who has created himself! Ask for your
desired boon and I will grant it to you." Hearing Shambhu's
words, Smara was filled with great joy. He joined his hands
in salutation, prostrated himself and spoke in faltering
words. Kama said, "O lord of *deva*s! O Mahadeva! O ocean
of compassion! O lord! O Sarvesha! If you are pleased with
me, be the one who will bring great pleasure to me. O lord!
Please pardon that crime that I had committed earlier. Let
me be greatly affectionate towards my own people. Let me
have devotion towards your feet." Hearing Smara's words,
Parameshvara was pleased. The ocean of compassion smiled.
He uttered "AUM" and spoke.[1052] Ishvara said, "O Kama! I
am pleased with you. O immensely intelligent one! Give up
your fear. Go near Vishnu and wait outside." Hearing this, he
bowed his head down, circumambulating and praising the lord.
He went out and prostrated himself before Hari and the *deva*s.
*Deva*s pronounced benedictions over Kama and addressed him.

[1052] AUM is uttered before making any pledge.

Remembering Shiva in their hearts, Vishnu and the others were happy and spoke to him. The *deva*s said, "O Smara! You are blessed. You were burnt, but Shiva has shown you his favours. He is the lord of everything. A portion of his *sattva* has cast a favourable glance towards you and has brought you back to life. No one else causes happiness or misery. A man enjoys the consequences of what he has himself done. Who is capable of countering destined protection, marriage and conception?" Having said this, the immortals happily honoured him. Having obtained their wishes, Vishnu and all the others remained there. Following Shiva's instruction, he too remained there happily. There were sounds of "Victory" in the firmament and words of applause.'"'

'"'In the bedchamber, Shambhu placed Parvati on his left and fed her sweetmeats. Rejoicing, she also fed him sweetmeats. Shambhu followed all the customary practices of the world. Taking leave from Mena and the mountain, he went to the place where all the people were residing. O sage! There were great festivities and the sounds of chanting from the *Veda*s. People played on the four kinds of musical instruments.[1053] When Shambhu arrived at the spot, he worshipped the sages, Hari and me. He was following the customary practices of the world. The immortals honoured him back. There were sound of "Victory" and sounds of "I bow down". There were the auspicious sounds of chanting from the *Veda*s, removing all impediments. Vishnu, I, Shakra and all the *deva*s, the *rishi*s, the *siddha*s, the minor gods and *naga*s praised him separately. Devas said, "Victory to Shambhu. O universal support! Victory to the one known as Maheshvara. Victory to Rudra. Victory to Mahadeva. Victory to the lord Vishvambhara.[1054] Victory

---

[1053] Stringed, covered (like drums), hollow (wind) and solid (like bells).

[1054] One who sustains the universe.

to Kali's husband. You are the lord who enhances victory and bliss. Victory to the three-eyed Sarvesha. O lord! Victory to the lord of *maya*. Victory to the one who is *nirguna* and without desire. You are beyond causes and you go everywhere. Victory to the reservoir of all kinds of pastimes. We prostrate ourselves before the one who assumes forms. O ocean of compassion! Victory to the one who grants the wishes of his devotees. Victory to the one whose form is bliss. Victory to the one who causes *maya* and *gunas*. Victory to the fierce lord. You are in all *atmans*. You are a friend to the distressed. You are an ocean of compassion. Victory to the one who has no transformations. O lord of *maya*! Your form cannot be reached through words or thoughts." In this way, the lord Mahesha, Girija's husband, was praised. With great love, Vishnu and the others served him in the proper way. Shambhu Mahesha is the lord of many kinds of pastimes and had assumed a body. O Narada! He honoured them and granted boons to everyone. O son! Vishnu and all the others took their leave of Paramesha and extremely happy, returned to their own respective abodes, their faces beaming with pleasure.'"[1055]

Chapter 147-3.3(52) (Feeding the Groom's Party)

'"Brahma said, 'O son! The best among mountains was excellent in his fortune and discriminating. After this, he made arrangements in the arena for feeding people. He made arrangements for the sweeping and scrubbing. Many kinds of fragrant objects were lovingly used. Through the mountain's

---

[1055] As will be clear, this only means they returned to residences Himalaya had constructed for them.

sons and others, the mountains invited all the gods and Ishvara to eat. O sage! Hearing about the mountain's invitation, the lord, Achyuta and all the gods cheerfully left, to eat. The mountain honoured the lord and everyone else in the proper way. Rejoicing, he made all of them sit on excellent seats inside the house. Many kinds of excellent food were served. Joining his hands in salutation, he respectfully invited them to eat. *Devas*, with Vishnu leading the way, were honoured in this way. Placing Sadashiva at the forefront, all of them ate. They sat down in separate rows, smiling and eating. The immensely fortunate Nandi, Bhringi, Virabhadra and the *gana*s were in a separate row and ate with enthusiasm. *Deva*s, Indra and the guardians of the world were resplendent. Those immensely fortunate ones joked while they ate. All the sages, *brahmana*s, Bhrigu and the other *rishi*s happily ate, seated in a separate row. All of Chandi's companions also ate with enthusiasm, happily joking in different ways. Having happily eaten in this way, all of them rinsed their mouths and left to rest. Rejoicing, Vishnu and the others also went to their respective residences.'"'

""'Following Mena's instruction, the virtuous ladies devotedly requested Shiva to go the excellent bedchamber, where all kinds of great festivities were going on. Mena gave Shambhu a handsome and bejewelled throne. Seated on that, he happily looked at the bedchamber. There were hundreds of radiant and bejewelled lamps, creating illumination. There were bejewelled vessels and pots. Gems and pearls were strewn around. There were radiant and bejewelled mirrors and white whisks, studded with jewels. There were expensive necklaces made out of gems and pearls everywhere. It was great and divine, without a parallel. It was wonderful and extremely beautiful. The place had been constructed in wonderful ways and brought pleasure to the mind. The power of the boon granted by Shiva had led to this unmatched prosperity. Since it resembled Shiva's world, he saw it and was pleased. It was

fragrant with many kinds of scents and was illuminated well.
There was sandalwood and aloe. The bed was covered with
flowers. Using many kinds of excellent colours, Vishvakarma
had constructed it. He had used the essence of the best of jewels
and excellent necklaces. In some places, the divinity had created
the beautiful Vaikuntha. In others, he had created Brahma's
world. In others, he had created the cities of the guardians of
the worlds. In some places, he had created the beautiful Kailasa.
In another, he had created Shakra's residence. Above all these,
there was the resplendent Shivaloka. Maheshvara saw this
bedchamber, wonderful in every possible way. He was content
and praised Himachala, lord of mountains. There was an
excellent bejewelled bed there. In his pastimes, Parameshvara
happily lay down there.'"'

'"'Himachala fed all his brothers and others. Extremely
happy, he completed the remaining rites. While Ishvara slept,
this is what the lord of mountains did. The night passed and
it was morning. Full of enthusiasm, the people started to play
on all kinds of musical instruments. Vishnu and all the other
gods woke up happily. They remembered the lord of *devas* and
respectfully got ready. Following Vishnu's command, Dharma
approached the bedchamber. The *yogi* addressed Shankara,
lord of *yogi*s, in words that were appropriate for the occasion.
Dharma said, "O Bhava! Arise. O lord of *pramatha*s! Arise.
Please come to the place where the people are residing and
gratify them." Hearing Dharma's words, Maheshvara laughed.
He cast a glance of compassion and got up from his bed. He
smiled and told Dharma, "You proceed in front. There is no
doubt that I will quickly follow." Addressed by Shankara in
this way, he went to the place where the people were residing.
The lord Shambhu also desired to follow him. Getting to
know about this, all the women arrived enthusiastically.
Glancing towards Shambhu's feet, they sang auspicious songs.
Following the customs of the world, Shambhu performed the

morning ablutions. Taking Mena's permission, he and the mountain went to the place where the people were residing. O sage! There were great festivities there, with chanting from the *Vedas*. The people played on the four kinds of musical instruments. Following the customs of the world, Shambhu arrived at the spot and worshipped the sages, Hari and me. He was worshipped by the gods and others. There were sounds of "Victory" and sounds of "I bow down". There were the auspicious sounds of chanting from the *Vedas*. There was a great tumult.'"'

Chapter 148-3.3(53) (Preparations for Shiva's Return)

' " Brahma said, 'Vishnu and the other *devas* and the sages, stores of austerities, completed the remaining rites. They told the mountain that they wished to return. The supreme mountain bathed and attentively worshipped his *Ishta devata*. He summoned his relatives from the city and happily went to the place where the people were residing. He happily worshipped the lord and requested him, "Along with the others, please remain in my house for a few more days. O Shambhu! Since you have glanced at me, there is no doubt that I have become successful in my objective. Since you have come to my house with the gods, I am blessed." Joining his hands in salutation and prostrating himself, the lord of mountains said many such things. He requested the lord and Vishnu and the other gods. The sages and *devas*, Vishnu and the other gods, lovingly remembered Shiva in their minds and replied cheerfully. The *devas* said, "O tiger among mountains! You are blessed. Your deeds are great. In the three worlds, there is no one with such a store of good merits as you. Mahesha is

the supreme *brahman*. He is the destination of the virtuous.
He is affectionate towards his devotees. Out of compassion
towards you, such a person arrived at your door, along with
his servants. The residences you have created for people are
beautiful. You have shown us many kinds of honours. O lord
of mountains! It is impossible to describe in detail the various
types of food you have offered. But this is not surprising in a
place where Devi Shivaa Ambika resides. We are complete in
every possible way, and we are blessed that we came." In this
way, those excellent ones praised each other. There were many
kinds of festivities, accompanied by sounds of "Victory" and
chanting from the *Vedas*. Auspicious songs were sung and large
numbers of *apsara*s danced. The *magadha*s sang words of praise
and many kinds of objects were donated. The mountain took
his leave from the lord of *deva*s and returned to his own house.
Following the different kinds of rules, he made arrangements
for different kinds of food to be prepared. In the proper way,
he lovingly and enthusiastically invited the lord Ishvara to
come and eat, along with his companions. With a great deal
of respect, he washed Shambhu's feet and Vishnu's and mine.
The lord of mountains, helped by his relatives, happily invited
all the immortals, the sages and all the others to enter the
pavilion and be seated, in due order. The mountain satisfied
the gods with diverse kinds of food. Along with Shambhu,
Vishnu and I, all of them ate. Cheerfully, the women from the
city abused them.[1056] Then they used gentle words to laugh at
them, carefully observing what they did. O Narada! Invited
by the mountain in this way, they ate and rinsed their mouths.
Happy and content, they returned to their own respective
residences. O sage! Similarly, the lord of mountains honoured
them on the third day too, lovingly honouring them with many

[1056] Done in jest.

kinds of gifts. On the fourth day, the *chaturthi karma*[1057] rites
of purification were observed. Without this being performed,
the separation could not have taken place. There were many
festivities, sounds of "Victory" and words of praise. There
were many gifts, excellent sons and many kinds of dancing.'"'

""'On the fifth day, full of great love, the delighted *deva*s
informed the mountain that they wished to leave. Hearing this,
the lord of mountains joined his hands in salutation and told
the *deva*s, "O gods! Please show me your compassion and stay
for a few more days." Addressed in this affectionate way, the
lord, Vishnu and the others resided there for a few more days.
Every day, they were respectfully honoured. In this way, many
days passed, and we resided there. After this, the gods sent the
*saptarshi*s to the lord of mountains. They made him and Mena
understand what was right for the occasion. With praise, they
happily told them everything about Shiva's supreme *tattva*.
O sage! They made them understand the pledge Paresha had
made. Along with the immortals, Shambhu told the lord of
mountains that he wished to leave. Along with Shivaa and the
immortals, the lord of *deva*s had pledged to leave for his own
mountain. Hearing this, Mena lamented loudly and spoke to
the ocean of compassion. Mena said, "O ocean of compassion!
Show compassion towards Shivaa and make the pledge you
have made come true. You are quick to be satisfied and you
must pardon one thousand of Parvati's faults. From one birth
to another birth, my child has been devoted to your lotus feet.
In her sleep, in her *jnana* and in her memory, there is no one
other than the lord Mahadeva. As soon as she hears about
devotion towards you, her body hair stands up in delight. O
Mrityunjaya! As soon as she hears you being criticized, she
is silent, as if she is dead." Saying this, Menaka bestowed her

---

[1057] Performed on the fourth day after marriage and indicative of
the bride being separated from her parental home.

daughter on him. She wept loudly. In front of him, she lost her
senses. He made Mena understand and took leave from her and
the mountain. Along with *devas* and amidst great festivities, he
made arrangements to leave. With the lord and his *ganas*, all
the immortals started to leave silently, wishing auspiciousness
for the mountain. In a grove outside Himachala's city, along
with Ishvara, the delighted gods waited for Shivaa to arrive,
amidst those festivities. O lord among sages! I have thus told
you about Shiva's departure with the *devas*. Now hear about
Shivaa's journey and amidst the festivities, about her separation
from her parents.'"

Chapter 149-3.3(54) (*Dharma* of a Virtuous Wife)

'"Brahma said, 'The *saptarshis* spoke to Himalaya,
the lord of mountains. "O mountain! Please make
arrangements for your daughter, Devi, to leave today."
Hearing this, the lord of mountains understood about the great
separation. O lord of sages! Because of his great love, he was
depressed for some time. In a short while, the king of mountains
regained his senses. The mountain agreed and told Mena about
the message. O sage! Learning about the mountain's message,
she was overwhelmed by both joy and grief. However, Mena
made arrangements for the journey. O sage! Following the
norms of the *shruti* texts and her own lineage, she had all the
rites performed. Mena, the mountain's beloved, carried out the
various festivities. Girija was ornamented with many jewels
and excellent silk garments. She was adorned with the twelve
ornaments of *shringara*, revered by royalty. Understanding
Mena's mind, a virtuous *brahmana* lady instructed Girija
about the supreme tasks of a devoted wife.'"

"'The *brahmana*'s wife said, "O Girija! Hear my words with great affection. They enhance *dharma*. They bring joy in this world and in the next one. Hear about what brings happiness. A woman devoted to her husband is blessed. There is no one else who is specially worshipped. She purifies all the worlds and destroys floods of every kind of sin. If a woman lovingly worships her husband, as if he is Parameshvara Shiva, she enjoys all the objects of pleasure in this world. When she dies, along with her husband, she obtains an auspicious end. There are ladies who are devoted to their husbands—Savitri, Lopamudra, Arundhati, Shandilya, Shatarupa, Anasuya, Lakshmi, Svadha, Sati, Samjna, Sumati, Shraddha, Mena, Svaha and many other virtuous ladies who have not been mentioned. That would be too much of detail. They have purified through their vows of *dharma* and have been worshipped by everyone. They have been revered by Brahma, Vishnu, Hara and lords among sages. Therefore, you must always serve your husband, the lord Shankara. He is the one who shows compassion towards the distressed. He is the destination of the virtuous and must always be served. The great *dharma* and vow of serving the husband has been spoken about in the *shruti* and *smriti* texts. It has been determined and described that there is nothing as supreme as this. A beloved wife who is devoted to her husband will eat only after the husband has eaten. O Shivaa! If he stands, the woman must always stand. When he sleeps, she sleeps. But an intelligent woman will always wake up before her husband. With single-minded attention, she will always do what he likes and what is beneficial. O Shivaa! Without being ornamented, you must never show yourself to him. When he goes elsewhere on work, she must avoid ornamenting herself. Under no circumstances must a woman who is devoted to her husband utter her husband's name. Even if the husband abuses her, she must not abuse back. Even when he strikes her, she will remain pleased and will say, 'You are my lord and can kill me. But please show me your compassion.' When summoned, she must abandon the household tasks and go to him quickly. She must lovingly join her hands in salutation, prostrate herself and say, 'O lord! Why have you summoned me? Be pleased and let me know.' With a happy mind, she must perform whatever task he asks her to do. She will not stand near the gate for a long period of time. Nor will she go to another person's house. She will not take anything from him, however trifling, and give it to someone else. Even if she is not asked, she will herself arrange for all the objects of worship. She will wait for an opportunity and the right time to do something beneficial for him. Without her husband's permission, she will never undertake a visit to a *tirtha*. From a distance, she will shun the desire to witness a festival where there is an assembly. A woman desiring to visit a *tirtha* will drink the water obtained after washing the husband's feet. There is no doubt that all the *tirtha*s and *kshetra*s are present in it. She will eat her husband's leftovers and any other food that is given by him. She will not eat without first offering food to *deva*s, ancestors, guests, groups of servants, cows and noble mendicants. O Devi! A lady devoted to her husband must always be accomplished in running the household with limited means and must not be prone to excessive expenditure. Without her husband's permission, she must not fast or observe vows. Otherwise, there are no fruits in this world and in the world hereafter, she will go to hell. After happily amusing himself, when the husband is lying down, or when he is amusing himself as he wills, she must not wake him up, or go inside the house on some task. Even if he is impotent, distressed, diseased or old and regardless of whether he is happy or miserable, a husband must never be contradicted. For the three days of the feminine *dharma*,[1058] she must not show her face or make him hear her

---

[1058] The monthly period.

words, not unless she has purified herself through a bath. After bathing, she must first see her husband's face, not that of someone else. Or, after thinking about her husband in her mind, she can look at the sun. If a woman devoted to her husband desires her husband's long life, she will not discard turmeric, *kumkuma*, *sindura*, collyrium, a bodice, betel leaf, auspicious ornaments, cleaning and braiding the hair and earrings and other ornaments. She must never become friends with a washerwoman, a harlot, a female ascetic[1059] or an unfortunate woman. She must not converse with a woman who hates her husband. She must never stand alone. She must never bathe naked. A virtuous lady must not sit on a mortar, a pestle, a broom, a stone, a mechanical contrivance or the threshold. Except at the time of sexual intercourse, she must not talk excessively. She must love whatever her husband is interested in. When he is happy, she will be happy. When he is miserable, she will be miserable. She will love whatever he loves. O Devi! A woman devoted to her husband will always desire her husband's welfare. A virtuous lady will have the same nature, irrespective of prosperity or adversity. She will always resort to her fortitude and never deviate. When *ghee*, salt, oil and other articles are exhausted, a woman devoted to her husband will not directly tell him this and cause exertion to him. O Deveshi! For a woman devoted to her husband, it is held that the husband is superior to Vidhatri, Vishnu and Hara. Her own husband is like Shiva to her. If a woman transgresses her husband in matters concerning vows, fasting and *niyama*s, she reduces her husband's lifespan. She desires hell for herself, after death. When spoken to, if a woman replies in rage, she is reborn as a female dog in a village or a vixen in the desolate forest. She must not sit on a lofty seat or walk near a wicked

[1059] The word used is *shravanaa* and cannot be translated any other way. But it is possible that this is a typo.

person. A woman must never address her husband in agitated words. She must not utter words of slander and must avoid quarrels. In the presence of seniors, she must not speak or laugh loudly. When she sees that her husband has returned from outside, she must quickly bring him food, water, betel leaves and garments. She must massage his feet. After this, she must use skilled words to get rid of his exhaustion. When the beloved is pleased, the three worlds are pleased. What the father gives is limited. What the brother gives is limited. What the son gives is limited. However, what the husband gives is unlimited. Therefore, he must always be worshipped. O Devi! The husband is the *guru*. The husband is *dharma*, *tirtha* and vows. Therefore, ignoring everyone else, it is the husband alone who must be worshipped. If an evil-minded woman abandons her husband and engages in secret dalliances, she is reborn as a cruel female owl that lives in the hollow of a tree. When struck, if she strikes back, she is reborn as a tigress or female cat.[1060] If she casts sidelong glances at another man, she is reborn with a squint in her eyes. If she ignores her husband and eats sweetmeats alone, she is reborn as a female pig in a village or as a wild goat that eats its own excrement. If a woman addresses her husband as '*tvam*', she is reborn dumb.[1061] If she hates her co-wife, she is repeatedly reborn as unfortunate. Hiding it from her husband, if a woman glances at another man, she is reborn one-eyed, malformed in face or ugly. When life leaves the body, in an instant, the body heads for the funeral pyre. Like that, even if she bathes properly, a woman without a husband is impure. O Devi! In this world, if a woman devoted to her husband is present in the house, the mother's lineage, the

---

[1060] *Vrishadamshika.*

[1061] *Tvam* and *bhavan* both mean 'you'. The latter is used to show respect and is the form that must be used for the husband. The former is used for close friends and juniors.

father's lineage and the husband's lineage are blessed. Because of the good merits of the woman who is devoted to her husband, the mother's lineage, the father's lineage and the husband's lineage go to heaven and enjoy happiness there. If a woman is evil in conduct and violates good norms, she makes three lineages—the mother's, the father's and the husband's—miserable in this world and in the next world and makes them fall down. Wherever a faithful lady's feet touch the ground, those spots are purified and sins are destroyed. The lord Bhanu, Soma and the bearer of fragrances[1062] touch the limbs of a woman who is devoted to her husband to purify themselves, not someone else. Water always wishes to touch a woman who is devoted to her husband, saying, 'Our sluggishness has been destroyed today and we can purify others.' For a householder, the wife is the foundation. The wife is the foundation for happiness. It is the wife who yields the fruits of *dharma*. The wife ensures that the offspring flourish. In every house, there are women who are proud of their beauty and charm. However, it is only through devotion to Shiva that a woman becomes a faithful wife. Such a wife wins over both this world and the next one. A man without a wife is not worthy of performing rites for *deva*s, ancestors or guests. A true householder is a person in whose home there is a woman devoted to her husband. Every day, others are devoured by *rakshasa*s in the form of old age. The body is purified by immersing oneself in the Ganga. Like that, on seeing a woman who is devoted to her husband, everyone is purified. A woman who regards her husband as a divinity is no different from Ganga. Such a couple is like Uma and Shiva themselves. Therefore, a learned person worships them. The husband is the high tone, and the wife is the low tone.[1063] The husband represents austerities, and the

[1062] Vayu.
[1063] In music.

wife represents fortitude. The wife represents the rites, and the
husband represents the fruits. O Shivaa! When a couple is like
that, they are blessed. O daughter of the Indra among
mountains! I have thus described to you the *dharma* of a
woman who is devoted to her husband. Now, lovingly and
attentively, hear from me about different types. O Devi! There
are said to be four types of women who are devoted to their
husbands—superior, middling, inferior and very inferior. These
are the differences, superior and so on. Even if one remembers
these, sins are destroyed. I will describe their characteristics to
you. Listen attentively. O fortunate one! If a woman constantly
sees her own husband in her mind, even in her dreams, and
does not look at anyone other than her husband, she is described
as superior. O daughter of a mountain! If a woman devoted to
her husband possesses intelligence such that she looks at other
men as a father, a brother or a son, she is said to be middling.
O Parvati! If a woman thinks about her own *dharma* in her
mind and does not transgress, she possesses good conduct and
is described as inferior. If a woman devoted to her husband is
scared of her husband or the lineage and does not transgress,
she is said to be very inferior. Earlier, learned persons have said
this. O Shiva! But all these four types of faithful wives destroy
sin. They purify all the worlds and enjoy happiness in this
world and in the next one. There was a *brahmana* who died
because of the *varaha*'s curse. Atri's wife was devoted to her
husband. Because of her powers and for the sake of the three
divinities, he came back to life.[1064] O Shivaa! Knowing this,

---

[1064] Atri's wife, Anasuya, was devoted to her husband. Brahma,
Vishnu and Shiva went to Anasuya, in the form of sages, to test her.
They desired that she give them alms while she was naked. Anasuya
used her powers to convert them into infants, whom she fed as
babies, after taking off her clothes. In a separate story, the *brahmana*
Koushika had been cursed that we would die. But Anasuya used her
powers to bring him back to life. Koushika had been cursed by the
sage Mandavya. The allusion to *varaha* is unclear.

your task is to always serve your husband. O daughter of the mountain! If you always do this lovingly, you will obtain everything that is desired. O Maheshi! O Jagadamba! Shiva himself is your husband. As soon as they remember you, women become devoted to their husbands. O Devi! What is the need to mention all this in front of you? O Shivaa! But, since you are following the customary practices of the world, I have told you about it now.""""

"'Brahma concluded, 'The *brahmana*'s wife said this and stopped, prostrating herself. Shivaa Parvati, loved by Shankara, was greatly delighted.'"'

Chapter 150-3.3(55) (Shiva's Return to Kailasa)

❝ ❝ B rahma said, 'The *brahmana* lady taught Devi about the vow. She[1065] then asked for Mena's permission to start the journey. Though overwhelmed by love, she spoke words of assent. Suffering from the imminent separation, she resorted to her fortitude. Assuring herself, she summoned Kali and embraced her. She embraced her repeatedly and wept loudly. Parvati also uttered piteous words and wept loudly. Suffering from the grief, the mountain's beloved and Shivaa lost their senses. As a result of Parvati's weeping, the wives of *deva*s also lost their senses. All the women cried and lost their senses. At the time of departure, the supreme lord, the lord of *yoga*, himself cried. Meanwhile, Himalaya quickly arrived there. All his sons and advisers and other *brahmana*s were with him. As a result of his confusion, he too wept, clasping his daughter to his breast. He repeatedly exclaimed, "Where are you going,

---

[1065] Parvati.

leaving the house empty?" The priest and other *brahmana*s
knew about *adhyatma*. Full of compassion and resorting to
jnana, they made everyone understand. Parvati devotedly
bowed down to her mother, her father and the *guru*. Following
the customary practices of the world, Mahamaya repeatedly
wept. When Parvati wept, all the other women also wept. This
was especially true of her mother, Mena, her sisters and her
brothers. Out of their love and their firm bonds of affection,
Shivaa's mother, her sisters, other women, her brothers and her
father repeatedly cried. The *brahmana*s arrived and lovingly
made them understand. They informed them that the *lagna* had
arrived for the journey to be a happy one. At this, Himalaya
and Mena resorted to their fortitude. They had the palanquin
fetched, so that Shivaa might ascend onto it. The *brahmana*
women helped Shivaa mount. Her mother, her father, the
*brahmana*s and all the others pronounced benedictions. Mena
and the mountain gave her royal objects. There was a collection
of auspicious articles, extremely difficult for others to obtain.
Shivaa prostrated herself before all the *guru*s, her mother, her
father, the *brahmana*s, the priest, her sisters and the other
women who were present. After this, she started. As a result
of his affection, Himachala followed her, along with his sons.
They reached the spot where the lord was happily waiting,
along with the immortals. Everyone was delighted and there
were great festivities. Prostrating themselves devotedly before
the lord and praising him, they returned to the city.'"'

""""You always remember your past life.[1066] But I am
reminding you. If you remember, please speak. O Deveshi!
In my pastimes, I always love you more than my own life."
Parvati heard the words spoken by Mahesha, her husband.
The virtuous lady is always Shankara's beloved. She smiled
and replied. Parvati replied, "O lord of my life! I remember

[1066] This is Shiva speaking to Parvati.

everything and also that you became silent. I prostrate myself before you. Please propose that every requisite task is now carried out." His beloved's words were like hundreds of flows of nectar. Hearing them, Vishvesha was extremely happy. However, he was devoted to observing customary worldly practices. Therefore, he had arrangements made for the collection of many agreeable objects. Devas, with Narayana leading the way, were fed. The lord lovingly fed all the others who had come for his marriage, using many kinds of succulent food. Having eaten, devas were bedecked in many kinds of ornaments. With their wives, all the ganas prostrated themselves before Chandrashekhara. They praised him with eloquent words and happily circumambulated him. They praised the marriage and left for their own respective abodes. O sage! Shiva prostrated himself before Narayana and me. He resorted to customary worldly practices, just as Vishnu had done to Kashyapa.[1067] Shiva was in front of me, and I embraced him and pronounced my benedictions. However, knowing that he was the supreme brahman, I also used supreme hymns to extol him. Then Vishnu and I joined our hands in salutation and happily took our leave from Shiva and Shivaa. Praising the marriage, we left for our own excellent abodes.'"

""'On his own mountain, Shiva happily sported with Parvati. All the ganas were extremely delighted and worshipped Shiva and Shivaa. O son! I have thus described to you Shiva's extremely auspicious marriage. This destroys grief and generates happiness. It bestows a long lifespan and extends wealth. If a man purifies himself, is devoted in his mind and following the niyamas, constantly hears it or makes it heard, he obtains Shiva's world. This narrative is described as wonderful and brings everything that is auspicious. It destroys all impediments and destroys all ailments. It bestows fame, heaven, a long

---

[1067] Vishnu was born as the sage Kashyapa's son.

lifespan, sons, grandsons and everything that is desired in this world. It always bestows objects of pleasure and emancipation. It dispels accidental death. It is auspicious and brings great serenity. It destroys all bad dreams. It is a means for obtaining intelligence and wisdom. People who desire the auspicious must make efforts to read it whenever there are festivals for Shiva. This brings pleasure and satisfaction to Shiva. In particular, it must be read when *deva*s and others are instated. One must lovingly read it before any rite for Shiva is undertaken. Having purified oneself, if one hears about the conduct of Shiva and Shivaa, one is successful in all one's endeavours. This is the truth. There is no doubt that this is the truth.'"'

This ends Parvati Khanda.

This ends Volume I.

Rudra Samhita and Shiva Purana will continue in Volume II.

Acknowledgements

The corpus of the Puranas is huge—in scope and size. The Mahabharata is believed to contain 100,000 *shlokas*. The Critical Edition of the Mahabharata, edited and published by the Bhandarkar Oriental Research Institute (Pune), doesn't contain quite that many *shlokas*. But this still gives us some idea of the size of the epic. To comprehend what 100,000 *shlokas* mean in a standard word count, I'd like to point out that the 10-volume unabridged translation I did of the Mahabharata amounts to a staggering 2.5 million words. After composing the Mahabharata, Krishna Dvaipayana Vedavyasa composed the eighteen *mahapuranas*, or major Puranas. Or so it is believed. Collectively, these eighteen Puranas amount to 400,000 *shlokas*, meaning a disconcerting and daunting number of 10 million words.

After translating the Bhagavat Gita, the Mahabharata, the *Harivamsha* (160,000 words) and the Valmiki Ramayana (500,000 words), it was but natural to turn one's attention towards translating the Puranas. This is the daunting Purana Project, so to speak. (All these translations have been, and will be, published by Penguin India.) As the most popular and most read Purana, the Bhagavata Purana was the first to be translated (3 volumes, 500,000 words). The Markandeya Purana, another popular Purana (1 volume, 175,000 words), came next. This

709

was followed by the Brahma Purana (2 volumes, 390,000 words) and the Vishnu Purana (1 volume, 175,000 words). That these translations were well-received was encouragement along the intimidating journey of translating the remaining Puranas and I am indebted to the reviewers of these various translations. There was some dislocation because of the Covid pandemic, but translation and publication has now resumed.

Which Purana should one choose to translate next? I have earlier remarked on coincidences that seemed to indicate the choice and guide the path. Most people have heard of Maha Shiva Ratri. Loosely, this translates as Shiva's great night. In determining auspicious days for worship, we follow the lunar calendar and lunar days (*tithi*s). A lunar *tithi* does not exactly correspond to a solar day, which is why a *tithi* may change in the course of a single solar day. The lunar cycle is divided into *shukla paksha* (the bright lunar fortnight, when the moon waxes) and *krishna paksha* (the dark lunar fortnight, when the moon wanes). The former culminates in *purnima* or *pournamasi*, the night of the full moon. The latter culminates in *amavasya*, the night of the new moon. *Chaturdashi* (the fourteenth lunar *tithi*) in *krishna paksha*, the night preceding *amavasya*, is the night for worshipping Shiva, every month. Thus, there is a *masika* (monthly) Shiva Ratri, once every month. Of these twelve Shiva Ratris, one is special and is known as Maha Shiva Ratri. This falls in February or March of the Gregorian calendar. Depending on whether the lunar month is calculated as ending in *amavasya* or *purnima*, the month will be Magha or Phalguna. In 2019, the date happened to be 4 March. Covid had started its onslaught, but its virulence and vehemence had not been fully fathomed, in India or in the rest of the world. Sadguru (Jaggi Vasudev) invited us (me and my wife) to the Isha Foundation for the Maha Shiva Ratri celebrations. As the celebrations went on throughout the night, before Adiyogi, it was an amazing, ethereal and mystical experience. When we returned, it was as if we had been permeated by Shiva. I was still completing the translation of the Vishnu Purana. Covid's impact was still relatively muted and wherever we travelled, we seemed to be drawn to places with Shiva *lingam*s, including the *jyotirlingam*s.

'Which Purana are you going to do next?' asked my wife. 'Probably Matsya Purana', I remarked. She responded, 'Why don't you do one on Shiva? You have already done several associated with Vishnu and there is Devi in Markandeya Purana. Time for Shiva.' I was reluctant. Among the Puranas associated with Shiva, the Shiva Purana is the most important. It is also a difficult Purana to translate, as the reader will discover while reading the translation. Contrary to popular impression, generally fewer people are familiar with Shaivite philosophy, Shiva's *tattva*s being a case in point, than with Vaishnava philosophy. The liturgy of worship, in this text, had several *mantra*s that needed to be tracked down. Stated briefly, this is the most difficult Purana I have translated so far. With almost 25,000 *shloka*s (3 volumes, 675,000 words), this is also a relatively long Purana, as the reader will also discover.

As I have traversed the route of the Purana Project, my wife, Suparna Banerjee Debroy, has been a constant source of support and encouragement, providing the conducive environment required for the translation work to continue unimpeded. तया विना स्म नो याति नास्थितो न स्म चेष्टते। तया विना क्षममपि शर्म लेभे ना (3.2(21).27). Shiva Purana says this about Shiva's behaviour, vis-à-vis Sati. 'He didn't go anywhere without her. Without her, he didn't do anything. Without her, he did not obtain the least bit of peace.' भार्या मूलं गृहस्थास्य भार्या मूलं सुखस्य च। भार्या धर्मफलावाप्त्यै भार्या सन्तानवृद्धये। (3.3(54).64). Many texts have highlighted the role of a wife and the Shiva Purana also has a chapter on the *dharma* of a virtuous wife. 'For a householder, the wife is the foundation. The wife is the foundation for happiness. It is the wife who yields the fruits of *dharma*. The wife ensures that the offspring flourish.' Suparna has been that and much more.

As I translated the Shiva Purana, through the second half of 2020 and 2021, Covid raged around us. We lost friends and acquaintances, near and dear ones. The entire family was affected by Covid, during the second phase. But it was as if Shiva's unseen hand guided and protected us. It was as if Shiva's unseen hand ensured the translation was completed.

The journey of translation hasn't been an intimidating one only for me. Penguin India must also have thought about it several times, before going ahead with the Purana translations. Most people have some idea about the Ramayana and the Mahabharata. But the Puranas are typically rendered in such dumbed down versions that the readership has to be created. However, Penguin India also believed in the Purana Project, which still stretches into some interminable horizon in the future, almost two decades down the line. For both author and publisher, this is a long-term commitment. But the Bhagavata Purana, Markandeya Purana, Brahma Purana, Vishnu Purana and Shiva Purana have been completed. Brahmanda Purana, in 2 volumes, comes next. I am indebted to Penguin India. In particular, Meru Gokhale, Moutushi Mukherjee and Binita Roy have been exceptionally patient, persevering and encouraging. The exceptional editing has ensured the final product is superior to what I delivered. These Purana translations have been brought alive by the wonderful cover designs and illustrations and I thank the illustrators and the designers.

Who should these three volumes of Shiva Purana be dedicated to? Who else but Sadguru, Jaggi Vasudev, who has brought all of us closer to Shiva.

Bibek Debroy
October 2022